The Adventures of Elizabeth Stanton
Series   Volume 4

Chaos in the Aftermath

Vic Broquard

The Adventures of Elizabeth Stanton Series   Volume 4:

Chaos in the Aftermath

Vic Broquard

Published by:
Broquard eBooks
http://Broquard-eBooks.com
author@Broquard-eBooks.com
103 Timberlane
East Peoria, IL 61611

Artwork by Crooked Willow Studios

For Morgan and L. Ron Hubbard

Table of Contents

Chapter 1 Consequences

There are consequences, there always are. At least that is how I see events in the physical world. You drop a rock, it falls. You lean too far over the side of a fishing boat, it tips over. You drink too much ale, you feel badly the next day. Life is like that. There are always consequences. I am learning this unyielding fact of this universe the hard way.

Who am I? I'd tell you, but even my name is currently a confusion. My body, this body, was born some sixteen years ago; my parents named me Ket of Cuch Glen, which is a small fishing village on the southwestern coast of the island called West Reach or Cymry as we locals call our island. Cuch Glen is, or used to be anyway, the southernmost village of that section of West Reach called Tewdwr. Folks in Tewdwr seldom have sir names.

However, this male body is now my third since I came to Tarra. The first two were female, and yes, I am still having a very hard time adjusting to being the opposite sex. I have two petty vanities: I love very long hair and I love the name Bethany. Though a male now, I have extremely long, flaming red hair — red hair is quite common in Twedwr — and I have adopted the name Ket Bethany, my friends call me Bethany.

It's midnight and my wife of two weeks, Caitlyn Amir, lies fast asleep in our new bed. She's home once more and safe. So that makes me now Ket Bethany Amir. However, sleep has not come to me, though it should have. I'm sitting here staring out of our bedroom window onto the snow-covered town, pondering my situation. Perhaps, I should explain my situation and that of Tarra first.

My name is-was Elizabeth Stanton, originally, and as I said, my dearest friends still call me Bethany. When that body died, my next lifetime I was called Bethany Madelyn Adid, until I married and became the wife of Jes Amir, who was the Great Messiah. I was then known as Bethany Madelyn Amir and also, I discovered much later, the Blessed Holy Mother. I've had two lifetimes of female bodies and have gotten that role down pat. Now I find I am in a male body. Although sixteen years have passed, I am still struggling with my identity. Hum, I suspect this is not helping much! Okay, perhaps I should begin at the very beginning.

You see, I, like you, am a being — an immortal spirit. I've lived in many bodies and will have as many more as I desire, assuming the world, Tarra, our playground, is not destroyed. It began some seventy-five years ago. I was part of a group of like-minded people, the druwids. In my group, I was revered as the Wid Bethany — the title, which I took nearly nine hundred years ago now, as I sit here and look back upon my past. I am Truth and Knowledge. Yes, you may call me a witch, a demon, or a heretic, but, in doing so, you mark yourself as just another Blind One. I chose this road — this path I follow — knowingly and willingly. I do it for all mankind, even you. Rats, this still isn't working out right. Please give me another chance; I'm more than a little confused right now.

For me, it all began in 550 AH (After Hodhekansis, the legendary twins and founders of Megalos) in a small village called Uru in the northern part of the rolling green hills of the Greenway here on Tarra. Uru at that period in history was one of the first farming settlements on Tarra as far as anyone knows. No written records date from before 558 AH. We know that writing was invented by the great artist and philosopher Niccolo Helios in the land called Megalos. Geography plays a vital role in understanding what has happened to me and to so many others. Let me begin properly with a description of the planet we all call home, Tarra.

Tarra is a blue-green world about eight thousand miles in diameter consisting of vast oceans and one enormous continent shaped much like a dog bone — that is, the two huge continents we call Eastern Tarra and Western Tarra are physically joined by one long, narrow, nearly impassable desert region that is some two hundred miles wide and three hundred miles long. Where this narrows joins the roughly circular lobes of the two continents, two towering mountain ranges block any passage into this desert region that goes by the name of the Desert of Desolation. On our side, Western Tarra, the blocking eighteen thousand foot range is called Kathas, while on the Eastern side the similar range is named Helios Grande after the great Sun God himself. None of us really knows what lies in Eastern Tarra because no one has been there and returned, though through the centuries, I have heard tales of some who have tried.

Straddling the southern side of the Desert of Desolation is a huge, rocky island, Megalos, which is four hundred miles long but only one hundred miles at its greatest width. Here on the Western Tarra side, Megalos nearly touches the continent. The Sallow Firth, as it is called, is two miles wide yet only three feet deep at low tide! Yes, horses and people often walk across the Firth, but there are ferries for those with money and passes from the Emperor of Megalos. The eastern side of Megalos is some twenty miles from the rocky coast of Eastern Tarra, but there treacherous tides thunder against many hidden rocks in that wide channel. From the dawn of time, Megalos and Western Tarra share the annals of history, both good and bad.

Now Western Tarra is roughly divided into halves by the great Med Sea, which opens onto the ocean at the western most part of the continent. This pale blue sea is nearly eight hundred miles long; its width varies between fifty and a hundred miles. Along the northern shores of Med Sea lie the principalities of the Seven Sea Princes. On the eastern shore of the Med Sea, abutting the Sea Princes, is the arid land called Juda Arad which stretches all the way to the Kathas mountain range. My early years last lifetime were spent living in various towns in Juda Arad, but more on that in a moment. All across the southern shore of Med Sea lies the giant Red Desert uninhabited and proven unpassable, at least seventy-five years ago. South of the Red Desert lay the Southlands with rich, rolling green savannahs and forests, rich in animal life but with few, dark-skinned inhabitants. The Southlands and Megalos share a close relationship as far back as anyone can remember, though not necessarily a good one.

North of the principalities of the Seven Sea Princes is a mountain range known as the Appian Way. These spectacular eight thousand foot tall, granite peaks stretch nearly across all of Western Tarra dividing the continent in half. The lands above the Appian Way are divided by nature into three roughly equal sized areas. At the far north lies the cold but timbered lands called Volksholm, whose people are called the Axemen. To the east is the Northern Steppes, an arid land home to nomadic horsemen called the Galts, while to the west lies the Greenway, a land of contrasts. Greenway consists of heavily forested, rugged hills interspersed with lush green valleys. My original village of Uru lies in the north central portion of the Greenway.

Many islands both large and small dot the lengthy coastline. However, of note is the large island called West Reach or Cymry as we locals call it. It lies some ten miles off the coast of the Greenway and is a large island kingdom unto itself. Though largely unpopulated, it plays a role in this story, obviously — it's where our kingdom lies or rather Caitlyn's kingdom.

The world at this time is roughly divisible into three political camps. Megalos, rumored to be the cradle of civilization, has great marble-stone cities, is very hot during summers, and has produced the first great thinkers, including the great artist and inventor Niccolo Helios, whom I met years ago. The principalities of the Seven Sea Princes are the feudal city-states of wealthy men, who sail the Med Sea trading there, as well as up and down the coastline of Western Tarra. Finally, all the lands above the Appian Way are inhabited warring hunter-gatherer groups or primitive farming communities. However, everywhere, rule is by the strongest sword and the mightiest forces, of which the Megalos Centurions are reputed to be the best at this time in history.

Megalos is an old civilization dating back well over five hundred years and currently has the highest level of civilization of any land, though of technology might be a better statement. Currently, they are ruled by Emperor Titus, a young man recently placed into power by the Church of Sol. Originally, these people worshiped the Sun God. Their Senate made the laws of the land, while the Emperor carried them out. However, over the centuries, the Senate became an ineffective ruling institution and the Emperor became all-powerful. Their previous Emperor Hiro turned the entire empire into a promiscuous brothel. When the Emperor drugged me and tried to rape me, I killed him, forcing a change of power. The Church of Sol took on more power and placed Titus on the throne.

However, for many years, Megalos attempted to bring their version of civilization to the barbarian lands. Definition of barbarian lands: any land not theirs. Long ago in the depths of history, they conquered the Southland, at least the eastern sections. Their soldiers are called Centurions and are bronzed-skinned, carry enormous shields, and fight often with spears and short swords. Some even ride war chariots into battle. They fight in tight formations and have been largely unstoppable in their forward march across all the lands.

In the Southlands, they operate wealthy gold and gem mines and have taken many dark skinned natives back to Megalos as slaves. Today, there are many second-generation slaves on Megalos, who know only of life as a slave and nothing of their original homeland or people.

Around 520, the Centurions conquered the land adjoining the Southlands, Juda Arad, taking its vital port on the eastern edge of the Med sea, Al Barq. Next, they proceeded to attack each of the Seven Sea Prince cities or sectors or principalities, one by one, beginning with Zargarb and ending with Velona. Their style of assault was interesting because they built a straight, level, paved stone roadway from where they currently were located right up to the next city to be attacked. Once that city fell, they resumed their road construction toward the next target. Thus, they were assured of rapid supply and movement of soldiers.

My original land was the Greenway, north of the Appian Way, a land of farmers and hunter-trappers, and sparsely populated. In contrast to the cities of a hundred thousand or more in the Lands of the Sea Princes, our largest city, the port of Calgary, only boasts some thirty thousand people. Only one other town in the middle of the Greenway, Brownsville has a population over ten thousand. Most of the towns and villages have only a few thousand, while we do have numerous hamlets of fifty to a hundred inhabitants.

Yes, all this does tie together. In the Greenway, several hundred years ago, one man, Alabaster Benjamin Crowley, founded a special group of people, called the druwids. We are usually trained from about the age of six to become a part of this group, because it takes ten full years of study to learn what was required. The druwids are organized into Circles of seven members, each with their own specialties.

The Protector is a highly skilled fighter whose task is to defend the others. The Loremaster is wise about Nature, plants and animals. The Planner is skilled at design and construction of buildings and such. The Judger is both a conjurer and an arbitrator of justice. The Communicator is skilled with telepathy and acts as the communicator between members of the group and other Communicators in other groups. Thus, distance plays no part in holding us together. The Healer is highly skilled in all aspects of healing the sick and injured. Finally, the Wid is the wisest and the leader of the Circle because the Wid is always seeking to know all about everything in the world. Wids are the rarest of all the druwids and hardest to become. I was a Wid in my Circle, the Lightning Circle, before my untimely death.

Now every druwid is skilled in healing, it's just that the Healer has far more skill than the rest of us. The entire purpose of Alabaster's druwids is to protect and serve all the people of the Greenway. To that end, most of the druwids used to live out among the small towns and villages, protecting, healing, arbitrating disputes, and helping with new constructions. We lived to help our people and our lives are dedicated to helping them. As an aside, every druwid is a being, just like all the others on Tarra, but a druwid is not located in their body's head, but rather some distance from it. Most of the people on Tarra are stuck solidly in their heads. Druwids derogatorily call them the Headers, a disgusting word rarely spoken.

Further, because of our intense study and total love and devotion to Nature, yes, you may say that we worship Nature; we have developed powers that many find remarkable. We can bring into existence fire, ice, and lightning. My specialty is lightning. Given a cloud in the sky, I can cause a bolt to strike where I desire. However, the druwids only use these intense powers to protect our people from the raiders. In the past, the raiders came from the Galts of the Northern Steppes or from Axemen of Volksholm.

In the past in Greenway, men and women are treated as equals in all things, save the men do the heavy chores and the women bear the children. However, in the Sea Princes, this Holy Balance of Nature went awry long ago. Back in 550, women were less than second-class citizens! They could not speak unless a man gave them permission. They were abused both physically and mentally. Speaking without permission resulted in one's tongue being cut out. Fathers routinely raped their daughters!

Into this mess, the defiled women banded together into the Sisterhood. Under their guidance, these battered, tortured women were taught how to fight and fight well, among many other things. Each sector, that is, each city-state, has its own band of the Sisterhood. Among the population of the Sea Princes, these amazon women were derogatorily called the Abominations. They were highly respected for their fighting skills, for none of the guards of the Sea Princes could ever best a Sisterhood warrior! Thus, these women survived on the edge of civilization.

First with the Centurion invasion and then later the invasion of the Galts, the Sisterhood ended up providing assistance to the survivors and gained enormous respect. Originally, the Sea Princes and the Church of Tur ruled each of the seven city-states. After the last invasion, power was usurped and is now shared among the nobles, the prince, the church, and the Sisterhood, via High Councils. So yes, things have changed for the better. However, behind the scenes, the druwids or guardians played a major role bringing about some of these changes.

During that earlier time of Centurion invasion, the problem we in the Greenway faced was the simple fact that we were next on the Centurion's assault list! Our people are farmers and hunters, not fighters. At that time, there was no central government as such. Hence, Alabaster had sent my Lightning Circle to visit the Sea Princes, Juda Arad, the Southlands, and even Megalos in an attempt to find out their strategies and tactics and find some way that we might defeat them. Yes, we managed to find ways to delay their immediate plans on the Greenway by several years.

With Alabaster's death, my Lightning Circle became the leader of all the druwids! We did find an acceptable alternative to war and slaughter by creating a mutual treaty in which the Centurions came and built their paved road system across the heart of the Greenway, provided security and guidance, along with iron farming implements. Shortly after that, my young body was killed while I was attempting to quell an uprising by King Randolf, who was building his own empire by bringing in a thousand of Galt raiders to help him. With Alabaster's help and that of a renegade druwid Erline Herbiscus, we eliminated that threat.

Alabaster then assigned me to find out about the Great Messiah of Juda Arad, who was supposed to be freeing his people from the infidels, the Centurions of Megalos. Thus, I picked up my second body in Juda Arad and grew up with Jes Amir, the Great Messiah and the Son of God, eventually becoming his wife and mother of his children. These people had both prophets and messiahs. The prophets continuously spread the word of God, helping the people keep their faith. The messiahs, though deeply religious, were more like religious zealots and attempted to carry their fight for freedom from the Infidels, their word for the Centurions. They attacked Centurion supply trains, humiliated city guards. In short, they did everything in their power to convince the Centurions to leave their land. My goal originally was to find out his methods of handling the Centurion problem in Juda Arad so we could use that to help remove them from the Greenway.

Yes, I would have to say that Jes was the Son of God, for I saw him perform many miracles. True, he would heal the sick and infirm, but also he had the ability to help a person move out of his body and discover their true state, that of an immortal spiritual being. To free his people, his plan was to educate them so that they could become free, powerful beings as they once were, and thus, the Infidels or Centurions would have no impact over them any longer. His goal of freedom was misinterpreted by the prophets of Juda Arad to mean that he was going to lead a rebellion, a war against the Centurions.

When the Arads realized that he was not going to war, they took it upon themselves to attack their overlords. After three days, the entire rebellion was completely squashed with a large loss of life among those that rebelled. Meanwhile, Jes pretended to be crucified upon the cross and then be resurrected from the dead as the most powerful way he could imagine in a last attempt to communicate and reach his people. He left it to his disciples to spread the word everywhere. Then, in secret, Jes, our family, and his brother's family left Juda Arad and ended up in West Reach, or Cymry. Here there was no Centurion presence.

Above all, Jes wanted to nurture his bloodline, who, he claimed, were the rightful heirs to be the Kings of Tarra. Hence, we needed a safe place to raise our three children and those three of his brother, Josh. West Reach was the only place on Tarra where we could be completely safe.

In time, the religion known as Jehosanity took on three versions. Obviously here in Cymry, Jes and I, after he left, preached the message that we were all spiritual beings. I added in harmony with Nature, which also happened to align with the local religion practiced by the original inhabitants of the island. When my body passed away, the followers began calling me the

Blessed Holy Mother.

One group of his disciples founded the Church of Jehosanity in the Sea Princes, calling it the Bandar-Hamah version or simply the Northern Orthodoxy. Finally, another disciple traveled all the way to Megalos and there he founded his Church of Jehosanity. All three sprang from Jes's teachings.

At this time, a pair of orphaned Galt twins, Mikhailovich and Zdlenka Strokova, accomplished a feat that had never been done before. After having a magical sword built to their specifications, they managed to unite all the clans of the Northern Steppes into a single fighting unit. Their cavalry, or wild barbarians as they were known by their victims, swooped down from the steppes and conquered all the Arad, driving the Centurions out of that land. Brutal and harsh were their methods, nothing could stand in the way of Mikhailovich and his magical blade. The survivors retained nothing of monetary value after the barbarians passed through a town. Over a period of three years, these twins next conquered all the Sea Princes as well, except for a tiny northerly portion, which was not easily accessible and didn't offer any reward for being conquered. Thus, Fortress d'Grange became the Eight Sea Prince Sector. Great were the Galt caravans of booty heading homeward at the end of each year of the war.

Next, they moved southward, driving towards Megalos itself, driving all the way south to within a hundred miles of Sud and Megalos itself before the Galt army was annihilated. At this time, the disciple of Jes, Yazi Rigan, who now calls himself Pope Yazi I stepped in. A master of sweet words, he had manipulated the Centurion beliefs, clearly demonstrating that Sol was either not a god or that he had forsaken them. Filling the void, he preached his version of Jehosanity and found an ever-growing audience and followers. Indeed, he made a bargain with the Emperor, who gave him some land, which was entirely controlled by this new church, and proclaimed that Jehosanity was now the official religion of all Megalos. In return, Pope Yazi I promised a miracle: the Hand of Jehosa would intervene and destroy these barbarians from the north. On the battlefield, the promised miracle did occur in that the Hand of God shattered the magical blade of Mikhailovich as the General battled him. Footnote: I now firmly believe that this was not the intervention of a deity, but the evil creatures that I will describe shortly. The Galts then routed. Hundreds were slain and the rest driven relentlessly back toward their own far northern lands.

His sister, Zdlenka, who has played a vital role, being the eyes in the back of his head as well as the consummate planner of all their battles, watched in horror as her brother died. Zdlenka buried herself in the mud and slithered through the rain and deep mud of the battlefield to escape. She found herself totally alone by the ocean just above the island that they had sought to conquer. Slowly she attempted to make her way on foot back north during the dead of winter. Nearly frozen in a winter storm, she was rescued by a remote family of Centurions, and she survived, but forever after kept her identity a secret. The ordeal profoundly changed her.

All right, that is the history as it is known at this time by the parties involved. However, and this is a big however, I discovered a vastly more sinister and evil undercurrent at play here on Tarra, one that may even account for why the vast majority of spiritual beings are so thoroughly convinced that they are a fleshly body and not a spiritual being. During my travels, I encountered two secret groups of strange creatures, one located in the inaccessible, high peaks of the Appian Way. The other is located in the impassable Red Desert near three tall pyramids.

The ones in the Appian Way are giants of grey skin, with three toes. They have some machine in the shape of a pole. When a being's fleshly body dies, they have been ordered to report in to this machine. Personally, I have watched numerous spiritual beings, whose bodies have just perished, follow this implanted order slavishly. Once they arrive, the pole is activated, and the beings are literally sucked into the pole, where all their memories, their mental pictures, are completely scrambled! Once they are completely dazed and confused, they are given the order to go get a new baby body and, when it dies, to report back here once more. They then take off like a bolt of lightning to carry out that order.

The group in the Red Desert operates similarly, though their bodies are even stranger. I liken them to that of a fifty-foot tall praying mantis! The mantises seem to collect spiritual beings from the southern portions of Tarra, while the Grey Creatures collect those from the northern half. At first, only my Lightning Circle and Alabaster knew about these creatures. When Alabaster's body finally died of very old age, he took on the task of spying on the Grey Creatures to gain more information. Jes, my late husband and the Son of Jehosa, also found out about these creatures.

For years, Jes brooded over the impact that they were having on his people. We both speculated that these two sets of creatures were somehow interfering with the humans on Tarra, though we could not prove it. Our hypothesis was that they could be acting as a hidden influence, perhaps causing all the wars and conflicts between the different peoples on Tarra. At the very least, they could be responsible for convincing immortal spiritual beings that they were a fleshly body. In the end, Jes had to do something about these Grey Creatures. He left us safely in West Reach and traveled to their location, high in the Appian Way. After spending some time spying on them, he found one of these creatures alone and attempted to kill its body.

Alabaster was also in the vicinity, and he did a Mind Join with me, so that I could watch what happened. I pleaded with Alabaster to help save Jes, because I knew these creatures had immense powers, far beyond anything that I could muster. In the end, the creature, though wounded in both legs by Jes, smashed his fist into Jes's face, killing him instantly. I watched in horror as Jes was then sucked into the machine and his memories scrambled. In vain, Alabaster tried to free him from the diabolical trap, but he too became trapped. Alabaster's last message to me was that if he did not contact me within the next thirty years, I was to come and find him, for he would need my help.

Unfortunately, these Grey Creatures detected my presence and attempted to suck me into their contraption. However, the secret to their machine is simply not to resist its effect and then it cannot pull a being into it. I escaped. Back in my house in West Reach, I continued preaching the truth of our spiritual nature. Additionally, I began a special ceremony. Whenever anyone in our town died, that is their fleshly body died, I would Mind Join them with their relatives and friends. In this way, they could say a final farewell. However, I also effectively blocked their implanted command to return to the Grey Creatures in the Appian Way.

In hindsight, I think this is what finally brought me to the attention of these diabolical creatures. One night while my daughter Sarah and I were riding back after delivering Sunday sermons, the Grey Creatures attacked me. They had some kind of flying machine that hovered over our position. While I escaped, they were relentless in coming after me. Not wanting to bring harm to my fellow townsfolk or daughter, I left in secret, intending to hide out in the foggy portion of the island known as Tewdwr. Footnote: my two grown boys had already donned their mantles of Kings and ruled over a pair of towns each. I also did not want to bring this down upon their heads either.

I was found almost at once and attacked by one of these Grey Creatures. While it instantly killed my body with a massive fist blow to my face, I again escaped. Even though they had a portable sucking device and tried to capture me, I eluded them. In frustration, they reversed their tactics, which took me by surprise. A massive energy bolt smashed into me, blacking me out, as I dove deep under the ocean just off the coast.

I waited for a time until I thought it was safe to emerge from underwater. When I did, to my shock, several years had passed! I had intended to join with the baby that Naessa was soon to have, which would have been my sister, Fianna. Can you imagine my double shock? Years had passed, not days, and I now had a male body, which I've never had before.

By the time that I was fourteen, the Grey Creatures had fomented trouble among the different groups on Cymry. A southern self-proclaimed king of the Layamon region attacked our defenseless village, intending to annex it into his kingdom. My parents were killed in its defense. Naturally, I came to the aid of our village, bringing down lightning strikes, slaying nearly all those who had attacked our village. However, my sister and I were forced to flee for our lives in the aftermath. Since they were looking for a young man, I disguised myself as a young woman, not hard to do with my long hair.

Fianna is three years older than I; together, we began to wander. Nearly penniless, I had to do something to support us. Since I had learned many of our local songs, we two became traveling musicians, troubadours, playing for our supplies.

Two others joined up with us as we traveled the island, Caitlyn Amir and Fergus of Aine. Caitlyn had run away from home, disguised as a young boy. Her father, King Ahmad Amir, had been my eldest son last lifetime.

However, one of the Grey Creatures became his trusted advisor. Yes, he was driven insane, launched an ill-fated attack on a neighboring king, and was slain. Before that, he had forced his eldest daughter to marry a pig of a man. She committed suicide instead. When he tried to force Caitlyn to marry another vile older man, she ran away, joining up with Fianna and myself. As it turned out, when we returned to West Reach a few weeks ago, Caitlyn discovered that she is the only living member of her family and is now the queen of her kingdom, which makes me the king, if I accept it.

Fergus is the eldest son of the King of Aine and Queen Ros. Ros, whose maiden name is Amir, is the daughter of Josh and Milla Amir, Jes's older brother. Both Fergus and Caitlyn worship the Blessed Holy Mother, that is, Bethany Madelyn Amir, me last lifetime. Together, we four began my search for Alabaster. You see, more than thirty years had passed without so much as a word from him. I knew instinctively that he was in perilous trouble indeed. I had to find him, but no one had any idea where on Tarra he might be. Hence, becoming wandering troubadours became the answer. We could travel to all the lands, playing for our keep, and search for him.

Once on the mainland at Fortress d'Grange, just south of the Greenway and Calgary, I ran into the Guardians and was reunited with the druwids. I even got to meet my daughter from last lifetime, Sarah, and all my children and grandchildren from my first life there as Elizabeth Stanton. It seems that Elizabeth Stanton was now almost as famous as Alabaster! I took heart in that so many of my children and grandchildren had also become druwids and Guardians. The Guardians gave us their full support in the quest to find Alabaster, since they very much needed to find him. The Grey Creatures had caught on to the druwids and had been systematically eliminating them, one by one! At that time, our numbers had already been cut by more than one half!

To guarantee our security, a group of Sisterhood Fighters accompanied us on our travels. It proved a very wise move. As we crossed the Sea Prince sectors, we uncovered several diabolical plots by the Grey Creatures to manipulate the sectors into wars of various kinds. All these, we successfully thwarted. However, in the Zargarb Sector, we ran into a different kind of trouble.

The earlier Galt Invasion had materially altered the nomadic lifestyle of these people. Having confiscated so much gold and silver, the clans found themselves no longer mobile, the sheer weight of their accumulated treasures combined with the loss of so many young males in their devastating defeat, left the clans fixed in one location. The northern Axemen took advantage of this and swept down through the eastern Greenway, plundering the Galts. Some might say that it served them right or they got what they dealt out. However, the Axemen did not stop at the Northern Steppes.

A large band of five hundred moved into the northern portion of Zargarb. We met up with Lenkova Pazzio, the daughter of Mikhailovich Strokova, the Galt barbarian conqueror, and Rosalita Pazzio, the Zargarb Sisterhood Fighter Group Leader. Rosalita had saved the entire Sisterhoods of all the sectors from the barbarian sacking by agreeing to bear Mikhailovich two children. Lenkova was his daughter. When Mikhailovich was slain down near Sud, Rosalita had snuck into the steppes and stolen both her children back. She and her husband had raised them as their own. However, Illanovich, the older boy, had a mean streak and had abandoned them, returning to the steppes years ago.

Lenkova followed in her mother's footsteps and was now the Fighter Group Leader for all of Zargarb. When Lenkova heard the news that the Axemen had entered the Zargarb Sector, she gathered her force of fifty Sisterhood fighters and headed to cut them off. Naturally, we went along to help. It was ten to one odds against us, but we druwids intervened, particularly me. I went a little nuts with the lightning bolts once again.

Because of our aid, Lenkova offered to assist us in our quest to find Alabaster. Having searched all the Sea Princes, Juda Arad was next. This arid land was now a vast no-man's land. The locals who remained here had been forced into banditry to eke out the basest survival. After all, they had now been sacked so many times that nothing of value remained in the land. Most of the Arads had already immigrated to the Sea Princes or West Reach. Further, the land was constantly harassed by the Galts and now by the Axemen. Worse still, Pope Yazi I had sent bands of his Holy Paladins into the Arad in search of Holy Relics, anything touched by the Son of God, Jes Amir. These were utterly ruthless men; their title, Holy Paladins, was a grim joke.

Hence, we really did need the assistance of Lenkova and two of her fellow Sisters, who had emigrated from the Arad to Zargarb. They knew their way around these arid lands where water was nearly as precious as salt. On our second encounter with a band of these Holy Paladins, we found Alabaster at last. He had taken a new body and was now a young woman. However, the mind scrambling done by the Grey Creature's device had made him seem totally, helplessly insane. His older sister, the last of their family, had been taking care of her and had been trying to flee the Arad when a band of Holy Paladins trapped them. Dispatching these vile men, we rescued the two young women.

However, Alabaster's body had a horrible infection, to say nothing of his insanity. We needed a safe place to work our healing magic. We learned that his sister had been trying to get to the Grey Havens, a place of sanctuary high in the foothills of the Kathas mountains in the extreme southeastern section of Juda Arad. Rumor spoke of a Lady in Blue who gave sanctuary to any in need. Thus, we decided to try the Grey Havens.

Their official name was the Holy Order of the Blue Servants of Jehosa at Grey Havens. It was run by Prophet Emil Al Amir and his wife, the Lady in Blue. As it turned out, the Lady in Blue was actually Zdlenka herself. She had spent the vast majority of her life atoning for her earlier atrocities against mankind by providing a safe haven for anyone in need. Lenkova gained an aunt, while Zdlenka gained a niece. We gained a much-needed respite to work our healing.

While we stayed at the Grey Havens, I managed to undo the mind scrambling done by the Grey Creatures, but in the end, we were unable to cure her body of its diseased state. She had been raped repeatedly and suffered from an advanced sexually transmitted disease. Yet, Alabaster had recovered enough to resume operations.

He and I came up with a plan to get rid of both the mantises and the Grey Creatures. While we could not physically harm either one, we devised a way for them to kill each other. We already ascertained that these two alien groups were in contest with each other, though we knew not their game plan. By dropping a hint that the other side was planning a sneak raid on their base of operations, both sides launched a counter-raid on the other. I delivered the message to a Grey Creature operating within the Church of Jehosanity in Zargarb, while Alabaster journeyed out into the Red Desert to deliver the same message to the mantises of the pyramids. Alabaster's journey was a one-way trip. Her body was dying, but he managed to deliver the message. The result was better than we hoped: both sides destroyed the other side. Finally, the people of Tarra were no longer being manipulated by either of these alien beings!

Instead of returning to the Greenway and getting a new baby body, Alabaster told us that something had caught his interest in the Southland and that he wanted to explore it fully before taking a new baby body. I've not heard from him since. Until tonight, I've not thought much about it; I've been a bit preoccupied with getting married and returning here to Cymry with Caitlyn.

Wid John Henry wanted me to take over the leadership of the entire druwid movement, but I didn't and convinced him to continue as our leader. However, he did allow me to form up a new Circle of Guardians, the Cymry Circle. Most had been in my original Lightning Circle; their original bodies had passed away, and all had new youthful ones.

Three were the youngest children of Roger Alan and Sue Ellen Wilkins. Benjamin (previously had been Thomas Wilkins, Loremaster) was now fifteen and just finished with his training as a Loremaster once again. The younger twins, I found inseparable. Paul Wilkins (previously had been Simon Donegal, Judger) was barely fourteen. This time he chose the ways of a Protector. His twin sister, Paulette (previously his wife and had been known as Sandy Donegal, Communicator) was very dear to me. She, as expected, was a Communicator this lifetime as well. Because they were siblings, they could not marry this lifetime. Still, they continued to be very close to each other, more so than brother and sister.

Allan Albert Donegal (Raphael Penton, Planner), eldest son of Willow Jane and Tom Albert, was seventeen and already had great plans for more great constructions. Yes, he continued down the path of Planner. Our Healer was Beth Ann Donegal (previously his wife and had been known as Sarah Jane Penton, Healer). Allan and Beth were already married this lifetime and were still inseparable. Beth Ann's identical twin sister, Lilly Ann, was a Judger. Both were sixteen and the twin daughters of Percival and Sarah Penton Amir.

Lilly Ann, however, was the only member who had not been in our original Lightning Circle; she took the place of Roy who had died much earlier than these had and who was, this lifetime, much older than the rest of us. Lilly Ann had a crush on Paul Wilkins; Paulette (Sandy) was actually jealous of her, and it made an interesting triangle.

My dear druwid friends were sleeping in several nearby rooms in this large wooden great hall, which had been my son's former palace here in Nuadilan. Caitlyn was now the ruler, Queen Caitlyn Amir and was by bloodline to rule over the two large towns of Nuadilan and Amathon. When we arrived here today, Caitlyn bubbled a childish enthusiasm as she gaily and proudly pointed out her childhood haunts, rooms, and such. I brooded over our situation, however.

How would she react on the morrow when she officially began her reign as queen? How could I get out of having to be their king? I had no such ambition of being a king, period. I am a musician and a druwid seeker of knowledge. I am more suited to being a priest than a ruler. Besides, this whole thing went against the very principles for which I strove: give the common man some power of choice in those who are to govern them. Here, the citizens of the two towns had no choice: the bloodline claim was backed by her Uncle Emil Amir, my youngest son of last lifetime. Had it been his idea all along that I was to be the actual ruler or had he felt that Caitlyn should?

I just could not get to sleep that long, cold winter night in late January of 623. Unknown to me, others scattered throughout Tarra also could not sleep this same night; they were embroiled in confusions of their own.

Chapter 2 Rox Thraxton, Alias the Rooster or Cock

Rooster sat in the very back rows of pews of the large church, squirming to make himself as invisible to the packed crowd as possible. He had to, if he wished to avoid making a public spectacle out of himself yet once again. Rox Thraxton, alias the Rooster, had the misfortune to look like his nickname. Actually, the children in his distant youth had made up that name during their constant teasing. He couldn't help that he was born with a deformed head, whose width was nearly half as narrow as ordinary people's heads, which, along with his hair that insisted on spiking towards the sky, gave him the appearance of a cock's head. Long ago Rooster, or the Cock as he was called in his circle of criminals, had given up on trying to be ordinary. No matter what he had done, no one ever accepted him as ordinary. At least now, as he approached thirty years of age, the name of the mysterious Cock was widely known around the entire island of Megalos, especially in the capital city of Galantas. The Cock was the most ruthless and feared thief in this century, although only a handful of his closest associates actually knew that the Rooster and the Cock were one in the same.

In hopes of not causing a scene, he had entered the church wearing a rain toga, which, much like a raincoat, covered his head so that only his piercing eyes could be seen by those around him. Indeed, the Rooster desperately wanted to hear this man, this Pope Yazi I, who once a week journeyed from Constanza City up north to Galantas to preach here in this magnificent church. Secretly, he had been coming to every mass that the Pope personally conducted. Rooster was utterly convinced that Pope Yazi I was indeed God's personal messenger walking upon Tarra. Rooster believed without the slightest doubt every word the man preached. One could speculate that finally, the Rooster had gotten religion, but he'd be completely and utterly wrong in that assumption.

Pope Yazi I was nearing the end of the mass, and he'd just finished saying something in the Holy Language (which was the language spoken in Juda Arad) and was now delivering his weekly plea. "The Laws of God tell man that woman tasted the forbidden fruit and thus brought on the entire downfall of man with their total lack of faith in the Lord. Yet even here in Galantas, women still have not learned their lessons. Do we not still have women issuing orders within the Senate? Making men cow-tow to their misguided ideas of righteousness? I caution you once more, do not believe anything those women utter, for they are the cast-outs of Heaven above — wicked women sent here to tempt man and woman yet once again. Remember, proper, holy women know their place in life, tending the home, supporting men, subservient in all ways to the needs of man."

"Now let us pray together for our deliverance from sin. As each of you who seek forgiveness comes by the High Altar, receive the token of the Son of God's fleshly sacrifice and taste the blood of life given unto you by the Lord above, the all-powerful Jehosa." The choir began singing in unison the Communion Prayer and those in the front pews far ahead of the Rooster rose and formed a line to accept the Lord's forgiveness. Actually, the Rooster knew that the wafers were just that; one could buy them at the local bakers. The taste of blood was merely imported wine from the Sea Princes. These he had carefully researched years ago before he became a believer. No, the Rooster was convinced that Pope Yazi I had actually blessed these items, that in accepting them on one's tongue, one did receive a truly Holy Blessing from Jehosa. At least five hundred people were here today accepting Holy Communion before lunch. At the very rear, the Rooster would be nearly the last person in the line, which was also precisely what he desired.

He fidgeted with his robes, wondering if he could do this. For weeks now, he had debated in the dead of night whether to approach this most holiest of men. What would the Pope say? Would he just laugh and condemn him as all others had done all his life? Or would this the holiest of men see into his deepest desires, see his true worth as a servant of the Lord? Rooster mused for the countless time upon whether he actually had the courage to bare his deepest soul to this man opening himself up once more to the ridicule he'd experienced all his life. As always, the debate ended when a voice inside his head said, "Cock, you have to try." Funny, that voice often reminded him of his father who had said similar words to him when he was a young boy. That was, of course, before the Rooster had had enough, slitting his father's throat one night, just to silence that perpetual optimism. Only the Rooster knew what he had to endure each day of his life. Three times before today, he had gotten to just this position, but each time, his courage failed him, and he merely accepted the Holy Communion without a word. Today, today would be different, he swore to himself. The minutes dragged on endlessly; his mind continued its whirlwind avalanche of conflicting thoughts.

Then suddenly, he stood before this holiest of men, who offered him the Holy Wafer. Rooster mechanically opened his mouth to receive it and then sipped the gold and jewel-encrusted wine goblet that pressed to his lips. Swallowing quickly, he whispered, "Holy Father, may I have a very private word with you when you are finished with the Holy Communion?" There, he had finally spoken the first words ever to his idol on Tarra! Pope Yazi I looked at the hooded man and then stared at him. Falteringly, he added, "Yes, it is I, the Rooster."

"Follow me when I leave," Pope Yazi I whispered back, a gleam in his eye. He had indeed recognized the Rooster. Yet, he held no fear of this man. Pope Yazi would never say aloud whom he actually feared, though one might make an educated guess. This was the day for which the Pope had prayed and had suffered these infernal weekly trips from his realm, Constanza City just outside of a northern port town, to the seat of power here in Megalos,

Galantas. Each week he hoped this man, of all the men in Megalos, would reach out to him. The Pope knew it had to be this man who reached. No matter how much the Pope wanted to talk with the man known as the Rooster, he knew instinctively that the Rooster would have to take this first step.

Quickly, the Rooster moved on, following the line of those who had taken their Holy Communion. However, instead of heading on out of this huge church, he sat back down on the front-most pew closest to the outer wall. Bowing his head to look as though he was praying, he kept his eyes on the Pope, scarcely believing his incredible good fortune. The Pope would actually hear him. For an instant, panic seeped into his frame. Was he just setting himself up for yet another round of utter ridicule? No, not from this holiest of men, of that the Rooster was certain. One thing that the Rooster had learned and learned well all these years was how to judge a man's intentions. During that brief encounter with the Pope, the Rooster detected no sign of ridicule. On the contrary, he sensed that the Pope was interested in listening to him.

As the last man filed out, the Pope blessed choir, and they too left for lunch. While several adepts began to clean up the altar, Pope Yazi I quietly walked past the Rooster. Giving him a slight head nod, he moved on down the aisle. The Rooster stealthily rose and followed quietly behind him, trying to make himself invisible to the others present. He followed the magnificent sky blue robes as they moved on down the red carpeted floor of this isle or hallway. Pope Yazi I paused for an instant at a side door, glancing to make sure that the Rooster had followed him. He entered his private robing room with the man right behind him.

"Come my son, take a seat. Tell me, what it is you wish to speak to me about?" Pope Yazi said using his holiest voice tones. Inwardly, Yazi Rigan, he seldom used his last name, could scarcely contain his excitement, his enthusiasm, but he dared not show it just yet. He'd seen the Rooster here at his church many times and always hoped the man would desire to meet with him.

"Holy Father, it is I, the Rooster, the Outcast of Megalos. I am a true believer in Jehosa. I have skills that few others possess and I want to donate them to the Church of Jehosanity. I want to become a Holy General in your army. For years, I have watched so many others join your army of Holy Paladins and go off on great quests for the Holy Relics. All too often, I have seen them return empty handed as well; some, not even returning. In all my life, I have never returned from a quest with nothing to show for it. The fondest desire of my heart, the total goal of my life is to be one of your Holy Generals, to lead forth holy men on holy quests."

These were precisely the words that Pope Yazi I had prayed that he would one day hear. The feats of the Rooster were well known to him, for he had always kept a close ear to the real news about the city and island. Where words were not forthcoming, a small money purse brought forth what Yazi desired to hear. Inwardly, Yazi wanted to yell for joy; his prayers had once more been answered. He knew that he was firmly following the path the Lord

Jehosa had intended for him to travel; he had no doubts in his mind. However, he could not let his enthusiasm show; he could not let the Rooster know just how happy he felt over Rooster's request. Instead, he continued to speak in his most holy manner.

"Jehosa accepts all who would cast aside their fleshly sins and revel in the Holy Spirit. As you might expect in a terribly important matter such as this, Lord Jehosa would prefer to see some actions on your part — you know, a token of your eternal faith in him. As you know, the church is having a bit of a problem with this Devil Woman, Senator Lenora, who has been stirring up trouble in the Senate, suggesting that the Church of Jehosanity is supplanting Emperor Justinian's rule. Jehosa greatly desires that this wickedness should just, shall we say, go away." He carefully chose his words; he could not afford to link the Church directly with this situation.

The Rooster did not disappoint him, "My Holy Pope, consider the problem handled. I accept this test of my faith. I will return when the problem has disappeared. Thank you Your Grace. This means more to me than you can ever know!" With that, he stood to leave, knowing that he had already consumed more than his share of this most Holy Man's time.

"May the Blessing of Jehosa be upon thee," Pope Yazi I spoke, making the holy sign of the cross over the Rooster's head. The Cock could not suppress the tears of joy that streamed uncontrollably down his cheeks. The Holiest of Holy Men had just given him, the Outcast of Megalos, the highest blessing imaginable! He bowed and quickly left before the Pope could change his mind.

It was a hot Monday afternoon, 623 AH, in the Senate Amphitheater. Tempers flared even hotter as Senator Lenora once more brought her motion to the Senate Floor. The Senate was a huge, square marble structure, with ever-rising seats on all sides. Looking down from the public viewing section near the top row, the main stage looked small. However, the acoustics were such that even in these distant rows, a whisper could be heard from the speaker who stood before the senators. (This marvel of construction could no longer be duplicated, because the technology had been lost through the long years since its construction, as had so much of their ancient knowledge.) The senators all wore grey togas and were seated in the front rows closest to the central stage. Senator Lenora was in her mid-fifties and a shrewd politician. As usual, she delivered a highly impassioned plea for passage of her bill.

"Our brave Centurion warriors deserve to die for our country, not on some ridiculous religious icon quest. Have we not heard that half a legion has been wiped out in the Arad by forces unknown? Who would believe the story that women were their attackers? Certainly not I! I cannot even lift one of our Centurion's heavy swords let alone use it. Ridiculous. No, I say again, this imposter Church is covering up something of great magnitude. We must pass my bill giving our illustrious new Emperor Justinian the authority to overrule this snake of a religion and carry out a true and honest investigation. Ill was the day that his predecessor, Titus, allowed them into our lands." She carefully avoided referring directly to Pope Yazi I. There were too many senators already backing him. "Besides, what lands have we brought civilization to since the mighty General Theos Lacerta defeated the Barbarian Horde? Tell me what lands? I'll tell you. None! We do not even control the Arad anymore!"

The catcalls and condemnations flew thick and heavy in the stifling heat. Her supporters, though outnumbered three to one, yelled back all the harder. Finally, the President for this term rose and brought order back to the senators. When near silence finally appeared, he called out, "All in favor of bringing the motion of Senator Lenora to a vote here today signify by raising your hands. Accountant, count the hands, please." An elderly gentleman in grey robes rose and began the short count. Only her supporters held their hands up. Apologetically, the President said, "I'm sorry Senator Lenora, there appears not to be enough votes at this time. Perhaps another day?" It was his gracious way of appeasing her. "I believe that we have some new business that Senator Luxious wishes to bring to our attention."

From his high public viewing perch, the Rooster had watched the diatribe flowing from Lenora's mouth, his hatred for her rising to a fevered pitch. The man had not the slightest doubt that this woman was Evil Incarnate, sent here to undo all the good works of the Church of Jehosanity. Perhaps, she was even one of the Devils sent to condemn good men to the Fires of Hell, which the good Pope Yazi I had so often commented upon in his sermons. He muttered only a single short sentence, "Time for the Cock." He rose and left the Senate building. A short while later, a man covered in the pale yellow robes, which indicated an important man in the Emperor's service, took up a position just outside the Senate building. He waited in the shadows between two other buildings.

Around four in the afternoon, the Senate disbanded for the day once more. As typical of these meetings for the last half century, nothing of substance was done, only a lot of rhetoric. They still had not figured out how to rebuild the dam that had been destroyed so long ago. The dam fed the aqueducts that brought fresh mountain water down to Galantas. The dam had been destroyed shortly after the gods had slain the corrupt Emperor Hiro nearly a half century ago, though some speculated that some visitors from a northern land had a hand in its destruction and perhaps as well as the slaying of the emperor. Their last committee decided that no one now knew how to rebuild the dam, and thus water wagons continued to bring in their fresh water, amid much grumbling, one might add.

"We'll meet at my place tonight around seven," Senator Lenora explained quickly to the small group of her fellow senators on her side as they filed out of the Senate building. One by one, the mass of Megalos leaders thinned out down the various crowed streets, joining the throngs of others heading home after work. No one paid any attention to the various colored togas worn by the crowd. Each color signified the wearer's status within their society. Only the emperor himself was allowed to wear the bright yellow toga, indicating his supposed direct connection to the Sun God himself. Admittedly, worship of the Sun God had largely been supplanted by this new religion, the worship of Jehosa. Still, many hated this newcomer religion and what it represented. Senator Lenora was one of these. She turned onto the side street that led to her villa complex just two blocks ahead. Here, the numbers on the street had thinned to a trickle. She had not noticed the hooded man in pale yellow robes that had been following her discretely all the way from the Senate building.

The man quickened his pace, rapidly closing the gap between him and her. The Cock was now right behind her. He made an insignificant motion with his right arm. A nasty dagger slid out from its concealed location on his inner forearm, arriving with a well-practiced motion into his hand. His arm went out in a circular motion around the head just ahead of him. He pulled back on the dagger and felt the soft resistance of her neck. A quick slicing motion as he pulled it back toward himself and the deed was done. Raising his arm, the dagger slid back up his sleeve, as he pivoted and began walking in the opposite direction, not even glancing back at the woman.

By the time the dying woman collapsed upon the street, blood gushing from her neck, the Cock was more than thirty feet away, disappearing into the distance. He heard the commotion of startled voices coming from the distance behind him and knew that others had discovered the late Senator Lenora, dying in the street close to her own home. A smile creased his lips as he walked on towards his safe house. He, the Rooster, was definitely qualified to become a general in Pope Yazi I's army of Holy Paladins, no doubt about that.

Five minutes after entering his tiny home, the Rooster had washed up, hid the toga, and dressed in his normal street clothes, those of a beggar. His trusty dagger was snugly hidden, its tip in the special holder inside his right boot and its hilt under his loose pant leg. He carefully placed a second dagger into his left boot, making sure its tip was positioned properly in its holder. Yes, the Rooster was very proud of his achievements — no, more like advancements, in the art of concealed weapons. Finally, he placed a tiny stiletto in his unkempt, long, upright hair. This one was more like a darning needle than a knife. It could easily cut ropes and deliver a staggering punch, if thrust into an unsuspecting ear or eye socket. Only once had the Cock had to resort to such a tactic, narrowly escaping capture, but that was years ago while he was still learning his trade.

Finally, he slid a floorboard back to reveal robes and togas of every color save that of the Emperor, of course. There was only one bright yellow toga and no need for him to have one of those. He picked out the one best suited for his ultimate purpose this evening, a brown one worn by tradesman, carefully stuffed it into a bag tying it securely to his belt. Satisfied with his nocturnal preparations, the Rooster, wearing a white commoner's toga left and headed for his local tavern, where he often spent the early evening hours.

At the Ire's Head, a poor tavern in the poorest part of Galantas, the Rooster entered unceremoniously, nodding to the barman, as was his custom. He took his usual seat near the open window, back against the stone wall. Yes, one quick movement and he could be out on the street, if need be. "Usual," he grunted to the barman, who brought him a large quart of stout. The Rooster looked at the others who were already here. All were regulars, he noted. Sipping his strong, dark beer, he listened to the conversations.

"Hey Rooster," called out one man with no front teeth, sitting at a nearby table, "heard the news? Senator Lenora has been killed tonight. On her way home, it's said. Just a few hundred feet from her own house. Guess no one is safe on the streets anymore, eh Rooster?"

"Nah, not heard it. Tonight you say?" he replied sounding incredulous. He sipped at the froth, "They catch her assailant?" He asked the obvious next question.

"Nah, no one saw anything. Broad daylight even. I says, how can that be? Noble Senator killed right out on the street in the daytime and no one saw anything. That'll give the Emperor something to think about, won't it?" Everyone who overheard him, which was just about everyone in the tavern, roared with laughter, images of a frightened Emperor flashing through these dirty minds. In this section of town, the Emperor was not a well-liked man.

When the guffawing ceased, the Rooster asked innocently, "How did she die? Sword stab to her heart?"

"Nah, throat was sliced clean in two! Couldn't even scream if she'd a wanted too. Whoever did it sure knew what he was doing. Maybe it twas the Cock again."

"Well, she sure made a lot of enemies," the Rooster offered.

"I dunno. I kind of liked the old woman. Sometimes she was on our side, you know. She pushed for laws to protect the likes of thee and me from the constant pestering of the City Patrols. Gotta have a reason to stop us now, they do. So I suppose I ought to feel a bit sorry for her." Several others agreed with him and they toasted her memory. The Rooster joined in as well, but then fell silent, enjoying his beer as the time slipped away.

Around eight, the Rooster took his leave, claiming to be drunk and heading home to sleep it off. He was not intoxicated, and as soon as he was clear of the tavern, he ducked down a poorly lighted alleyway. Making sure no one was watching him, he pulled out the robes he'd brought with him. Two minutes later, with a brown hood covering his head, he looked like a presentable down-on-his-luck noble or tradesman. He headed for the Frolic's Tavern, where he knew many of the associates of Senator Lenora often drank. His assumption that many would be here drinking away their memories of Lenora was quite correct. The place was packed, which suited the Rooster perfectly.

He entered, went to the bar and purchased a stout, before quietly slinking, unnoticed, into the darkest corner of the tavern. He pulled up a chair, sipped, keenly listened, and observed. The next few hours were vitally important to the Rooster. There were ten more women Senators with which to deal, though none as vocal and obstinate as Lenora had been. "I tell you the streets are not even safe in the daytime anymore. All heck is going to break loose if the Emperor does not act swiftly," one noble commented to several others at a nearby table.

Another replied, "Aye, you can say that again. I won't let my daughters or wife go anywhere without two body guards accompanying them. Yet after this, perhaps I should double their guards, though it costs me a pretty ducat." (A ducat was the gold coin of the realm. It took ten silvers to make one ducat and ten bronzes to make a silver.)

A companion thumped his fist futilely on the table, "Damn, I sure hope the Emperor catches whoever did this vile deed. She will be sorely missed. How are we going ever to stand up to all those who are on the side of the Pope? Surely, they will elect a replacement who favors the Pope, not us. I say it was the work of that vile Church of Jehosanity, that's what I think. The City Guards ought to just go and arrest that Pope and put an end to all this nonsense."

"Careful, Senator Jax, talk like that can get you into trouble," cautioned another. The Rooster detected the faint, unmistakable trace of fear in these men.

"Things are going better than I planned," thought the Rooster to himself.

"Well, who's going to step in and fill her role on our behalf?" asked another man.

"I'll talk to all the others tomorrow morning," promised Senator Jax. "Don't get your hopes up too high. Probably we will all lie low until they catch the assassin. I'm more than a little concerned about the other ten women in the Senate and how they will take this. I know Senator Athena was right there with her, though not as outspoken about things. Perhaps she will step in and fill Lenora's shoes. We'll know by the weekend I'm sure." Having heard what he needed, the Rooster quietly departed.

The next day, the Rooster once more took up his seat in the highest row at the Senate, wearing his light yellow robe. As expected, the Senate began with a solemn prayer service for one of their own fallen senators. A priest of Sol delivered the eulogy. The Rooster noted that the ten remaining female senators now chose to sit together in a tight bunch, not trusting anyone present. As soon as the prayers finished, a lively discussion about how such an assassination, for assassination it was now being called, could happen in broad daylight, right out in the open, not a hundred feet from her own home. The Rooster sensed emotions, for this he was a master at doing. Using his uncanny skill at empathy, he could sense enthusiasm, mild interest, boredom, antagonism, anger, fear, grief, and even apathy. The overall emotion he felt from the group was that of anger, not sufficiently low for the Rooster to feel comfortable. *I've more to do.*

The President's words resounded in the Rooster's ears, "I've asked the Emperor to come and give us a report. I give you the Emperor himself." A perfunctory round of applause greeted the man in bright yellow robes as he stepped onto the central platform. From this distance, the Rooster could not make out his face, but could hear his words, which was all that mattered to him.

"This is a sad day for the Senate. I grieve along with you. Senator Lenora was a good, kind woman, whose legacy will not die with her. It has been twenty years at least since a senator was killed while in office. I want you to know that I will leave no stone unturned to find the guilty party and have them executed! However, there are few clues. No one actually witnessed the evil deed. In fact, the only clue we have to go on is that a member of my own class, a man wearing light yellow, was the last man to be seen close to her. Of course, none of those in my service would ever do such a thing. However, we are questioning all my employees to see if we can find the one. It is my fondest hope and prayer that he will have seen something and will give us a solid clue to the assassin's identity. Until then, I have ordered a doubling of the City Guards. Actually, I have placed an entire legion of Centurions on patrol. Hopefully, our security will be sufficient to prevent anything like this from happening again. Any questions?"

One of the women rose. "Senator Athena here, your eminence. I would like to request that a trusted City Guard be posted to each one of us women senators. They would follow us wherever we go. None of us feels safe walking the streets anymore. It could happen to one of us next. Notice it was a helpless, defenseless woman who was slain, not one of you men. Surely, you can provide us with one guard." The Rooster detected fear in her voice, just what he had hoped to sense; his plan was working well.

Acting in a grand manner, the Emperor declared, "It shall be done, Senator Athena. Ten guards will be here by lunchtime. Now if you will excuse me, I have to interview all my staff. Wish me luck." He left to the sounds of a much louder applause than his entrance. The Emperor smiled, *I have the female Senators right where I want them.* Ten guards were nothing compared to their reliance upon him, the Emperor of Megalos. He certainly could count on their votes when needed. Unlike his predecessor, he was a follower of Sol, but was helpless to undo what Titus had done before him. He smiled all the way back to his palace.

Senator Athena was not finished yet, "Look, we all know who was ultimately responsible for Lenora's death. Only the Pope has anything to be gained by her sudden demise. We argue and discuss many things among us, but we never desire our opponent's untimely death, now do we? Look it wasn't Senator Flavius or even Senator Lacy who was killed. Both he and she are supporters of the new religion. No, it was the most vocal opponent of the Pope who was slain. We all know the Pope's opinion of women; that man is insane. I respectfully request that we form our own committee to look into the Church of Jehosanity's involvement in the assassination of Senator Lenora. If they have nothing to hide, why, then the committee will find that out, and we can all rest easier. In fact, if the committee does not find that the Church was implicated, I will cease being so vocally against them."

Of course, a great deal of bickering followed. In the end, she had her way. A committee of twelve, six who supported the Pope and six who did not, were chosen and given the full Senate's approval to delve as deeply into the matter as desired. *Damn*, cursed the Rooster, *though not unpredictable.* He left the building during the lunch break.

Around one in the afternoon, while the Senators reassembled for the hot afternoon session, City Guards wearing their red togas also began arriving just outside the white marble building. These were the ones promised by the Emperor. However, when all had arrived, taking up a position outside the main entrance, eleven were present, not ten as expected. One man grumbled, "I get to watch after Senator Thallia; her mansion is half way across the city! Boy, did I not luck out."

"Know what you mean, I got Senator Ria Helios, the mulatto. Of all the rotten luck, I get to escort the outcast. I've already been teased by my whole squad!" griped another.

"I get the loudmouth bitch," said a third, "Senator Athena. My luck never seems to get the good ones. Who's got the pretty blonde senator? Now there's a catch worth walking home!" Everyone laughed and guffawed.

The Rooster broke in, "Well, doesn't that take the cake! Someone really screwed up royally this time! I got the loudmouth one too, Senator Athena. What a waste, two of us to escort her! Wish it were two of us with the blonde Senator. I hear she gives favors. Bet Senator Athena doesn't even thank us. What do you think?" he said to the third guard who was to escort Athena.

"Damn, two of us, ugh. Well, I sure won't go back and query the orders, that's for sure! My captain would read me the riot act for questioning his orders."

"Yeh, me too. Orders' orders. Ours is not to question 'em," the Rooster replied. After more grumbling, some of the men broke out their dice and began a craps game to pass the long afternoon. The Rooster, who had his own loaded dice, did not play, preferring to stay back in the shadows and not bring any undue attention to himself.

Midday was a scorcher with the temperatures reaching nearly a hundred degrees, perfect for what the Rooster had planned. Finally, around four, the senate adjourned for the day. Presently the ten women arrived looking for the escorts promised to them by the Emperor. Several guards winked at the lucky one who got to escort the young and very attractive blonde Senator Lia home.

"I have two? Well, that's a pleasant surprise," exclaimed a very hot and tired Senator Athena.

"I'll watch the rear. You take point. How's that?" the Rooster suggested. Gladly, the other guard led the way. The rear guard often took the initial brunt of street attacks, so he was very willing to lead the way. The streets here near the center of Galantas were now quite crowded with hot, irritable people. Sweat streamed from Senator Athena as well as the two guards.

"One moment, Senator, I took the liberty of bringing along a water gourd. I got it fresh from the wagons when they arrived around noon. Fine, clear mountain water. Here, let's take a short break." He handed her his small goatskin water bag. "Hey, help yourself too when she is finished. I've already had my fill. I'll keep a sharp lookout for trouble."

Senator Athena graciously accepted the offered water skin. Such thoughtfulness, she thought to herself. It was still cool, and she drank deeply before handing it to the lead guard. Meanwhile, the Rooster kept looking about for signs of trouble. However, he kept a covert eye on both of them. Once he saw that the other guard had taken a good drink, he called out, "Hey, you two. Looks like some trouble is coming our way. You both get going, and I'll fall back and deal with these men. I'll keep them away from you two."

Suddenly, Senator Athena looked very worried; her fear crescendoed. The guard eagerly complied, grateful for the Rooster's offer of dealing with the trouble. He led the senator onward at a brisk pace. The Rooster fell back into the crowds, heading away from the two. He reached a side street, ducked down it, and then ducked into a side alley. Hiding behind a pile of refuse that had not yet been collected by the night collectors, he quickly switched togas. Now wearing a dirty white robe of a commoner, the Rooster headed on home; his work was done.

Sometime later, dressed in a brown toga of a tradesman, the Rooster walked along the major street where he had left the senator and guard. Sure enough, he found the way blocked by two dozen red robed City Guards, who were keeping the gawking passersby from interfering with their work. Lying in the street were Senator Athena and one of their own guards. Both faces were blackish looking, and their hands were clasping their throats, a look of utter horror frozen upon their dead faces. As he passed by, someone else uttered, "Poisoned!" Satisfied that his mission was accomplished, the Rooster headed on to the next tavern where he intended to gather additional news.

The next morning session of the Senate found the Rooster again in attendance. Everyone was talking about the latest assassination of Senator Athena and a City Guard as well. Finally, the President took the stage, holding a scroll in one hand. "This meeting is now called to order. First, I must read you this announcement given to me early this morning." He cleared his throat before he began reading aloud.

"Considering that two female senators have been assassinated in just two days, including a City Guard who was supposed to be protecting us, we remaining female senators are hereby withdrawing from the Senate and returning to our homes in other cities. We will return and resume our elected duties only when the culprit or culprits have been apprehended, and our complete safety can be guaranteed. Yes, this is the biggest disgrace on the Senate since its founding five centuries ago. You did not act, and we suffered the horrible consequences, which now you must live with, if your guilty consciences can."

"It is signed, Rea Helios." He paused, letting the full impact of the brief message sink into their minds. "She is right; the disgrace brought upon the Senate is absolutely appalling and unheard of in all these centuries. Two senators assassinated in broad daylight! Unthinkable!" The rest of the morning, nothing else was discussed. However, nothing concrete was actually done about it, and the Emperor carefully did not make an appearance this time. Neither did the High Priest of Sol.

Meanwhile, the Rooster re-read the small parchment, which he'd found slid under his door this morning. It read: "Do not be alarmed at what is said today." Nothing more. For the twentieth time, the Rooster tried to imagine what it meant. He still had no clue. However, shortly before the noon recess, Pope Yazi I, surrounded by two dozen of his Holy Paladin guards arrived ceremoniously at the Senate. The guards respectfully stayed at the entrance while Yazi entered the Senate in a grand, pompous manner, befitting his highly revered status. A hush fell as the President brought him on stage.

"I give you Pope Yazi I," he said with a voice full of surprise. A visit from the Pope was quite unexpected by everyone here, including the Rooster.

In a regal, dignified manner, Pope Yazi I began a vitally important speech, one coldly calculated in its impact. "Mister President, Esteemed Senators, I come before you today full of sorrow and remorse for the recent loss of two of your honored senators. Yes, I know that they were followers of Sol. Yet they were human beings, as are we all God's children. I have prayed for both of their souls, that they may yet reach the Pearly Gates of Heaven where they will be made accountable for their deeds committed while in life. May they have the strength to atone for their transgressions against God, as we all must one day do."

"I wanted to speak to you today to let you know personally that the Church of Jehosanity was in no way responsible for their deaths. Further, Mister President, I wish to make all the resources of the Church available to the Senate, in hopes that such aid as we can give may help you to find these vile culprits. I do not know what that aid might be, as I am not a warrior or diplomat, but a mere Caretaker of Men's Souls. Yet, any assistance that you feel the Church might be able to supply to help in this matter, simply ask and it shall be granted."

"Senators, know then that today all Megalos stands united behind you. The Church of Jehosanity desires nothing more than to make Megalos a safe place to live and work — a place devoid of sin and where the Word of God is in every heart and soul. May the Laws of God help you to remain focused in your tasks of ruling our great empire. Finally, though everyone here is not a member of our church, instead of offering a prayer for the fallen senators, instead, let us take a minute of silence — each praying for the souls of the dearly departed, each in their own way." He bowed his head and an utter silence fell over the entire Senate. Such normally only happened at night when the senators left. After a minute, he raised his head and humbly left the stage.

The President called out, "Thank you Pope Yazi for your generous offer of assistance and for taking the time to meet with us." The Pope bowed graciously, a covert smile upon his lips; his mission was completely accomplished. He just hoped that the Rooster had grasped the meaning of his secret note; he'd dared not say more.

During the start of the Pope's speech, a wave of terror suddenly swept over the Rooster. Could his beloved Priest have just turned against him? Could his very life be in dire danger? His fingers still held the scrap of paper, and he found his eyes re-reading it once again. "Do not be alarmed at what is said today." Suddenly, he grasped its meaning! Now everything fell into place. He could see the brilliant wisdom, the incredible strategy being brought into play right here in the Senate! Pope Yazi I was manipulating the entire Senate! After this speech, no one here would ever suspect that the Church had any connection to these sudden deaths! The Rooster felt humbled, and his awe for his supreme leader rose to even higher heights!

Come Sunday when the Pope himself conducted the High Mass, the Rooster attended, sitting in his usual position at the very rear of the Church. Once more when the service was over and the long lines formed to partake of the Holy Communion, the wafer, and wine, the Rooster found himself the last person in line. He could wait the half hour; he was about to see the Pope himself, and with his first Holy Mission completely accomplished. The Evil Wicked Women were handled. Two were dead, and the rest had fled the Senate, with no intentions of returning anytime in the near future. The Rooster summoned all his own self-will to keep his incredible emotions of joy and happiness restrained. The half hour seemed like an eternity!

Once more, the Pope whispered to him to follow him out, although this time, the Rooster had said nothing at all to the Pope. This, of course, only made his spirits rise even higher! The Pope was reaching out to him! The Rooster! The Cock! The Outcast of Megalos! Only with difficulty could the Rooster keep his breathing under control; he felt elated beyond all elation.

"Have a seat, Mister Rooster," Pope Yazi I said as they entered his private study. Several tables held the books and scrolls that he was personally reworking. "Or should I call you by some other name?"

Rooster took the nearest seat; his legs suddenly felt very weak. "Rooster is fine Your Holiness."

Yazi nodded and pulled on a bell rope. Almost at once, a young adept knocked and entered. "I'll take lunch in here, for two, please," Yazi said offhandedly.

"As you wish, Your Holiness," the adept said and hastily left. Yazi said nothing until the man returned with a large tray of food and drink, at which Yazi thanked the adept, who again made a rapid exit.

"Come let us dine, Rooster. We have much to discuss," Yazi said. Rooster had no choice but to sit beside his idol and eat. The roast duck and wine was perhaps the best that the Rooster had ever had, succulent and moist with traces of herbs that he had never tasted before. A half hour later, sipping their tea, the men faced each other.

Pope Yazi I began the all-important conversation. "Rooster, seldom in my life have I found a man who is as brilliant, cunning, and resourceful, and yet able to respond rapidly and effectively to ever changing situations. I bow to you, Rooster. You have so exceeded my expectations in this recent matter that

I am almost at a loss for words. Yes, you have done magnificently well; the situation is now terminally handled. We will have no further difficulties from the Senate. Thank you very much, Rooster."

Poor Rooster could not speak. Such praise he had never been given in all his life. Thankfully, the Pope did not need a reply. Yazi continued, "Now as I recall your request it was to become a general of my Holy Paladins." Rooster managed to nod his deformed head affirmatively. "I will stand behind our agreement. However, such a position for you would be a tremendous waste of your natural talent and skills. Would you consider a slight change of position? Let me explain." Yazi knew that he had only one chance to make this proposal, and he wanted it to be perfectly done, so much depended utterly upon it.

"As you so wisely pointed out when we last spoke, many of my generals and Holy Paladin warriors are, shall we say, incompetent? True, they are honest, sincere, and holy, but they lack the skill of thinking on their feet. How to be a soldier is all that they know. Yet, we are not at war and they do not adapt too well, I am afraid to say. For years now, I have been looking for someone to provide total Constanza City security. We call our estate here within Megalos, Constanza. As you have probably heard, already, a small city is forming around our huge church complex. I have great plans for the expansion. Constanza will become the ruling church for Tarra, all in good time, however."

Yazi got to his punch line, "I am desperate for someone with your skills and talents to take charge of the total security of Constanza and my own person, especially. As you know, there are many out there in the world who would love to try to put a dagger in my heart. There always will be, I'm afraid. We both know that it is the height of folly to place one's life in the hands of soldier garrisons or City Guards. Look what happened to Senator Athena who did so?" The Pope chuckled and the Rooster smiled, pleased that his master realized how easy it had been for him to take out the senator along with the guard.

"That is why until now I have not formed up any Security Forces in Constanza. You, Rooster, are the first person whom I would trust with my life in a perilous situation." Rooster could scarcely believe his ears. The Pope would actually trust him with his Holy Life! Again, he could not speak; his mouth was dry; he fought the urge to gag, sipping a bit of tea to hide his embarrassment.

"Rooster, I want you to be my General of Constanza Security. Your primary duty would consist of doing whatever, I stress whatever, is necessary to first and foremost protect the life and well-being of your Pope. Second, when the Pope is not immediately threatened, protect and keep secure Constanza City and those who live here. During the coming years, we face many challenges to our autonomy and authority. You will be hard pressed to provide the total security that we need, but I feel confident in your native skills and abilities. Rooster, will you be my General of Security? Of course, you will have to move from here to Constanza City. It is a full time task that I am asking of you."

The shock of the offer finally began to lessen. Rooster hoped that his eyes did not seem to look like they were popping out of his head. He hoped that the Pope would not notice the difficulty he was having keeping his teacup from shaking. Back in the inner depths of his mind, the magnitude of the job he was being offered registered, along with a flood of potential problems — anyone of which could undermine his ability to successfully carry out his master's wish. This side of him took control over his vocal cords.

"Indeed, Your Holiness, this is such a tremendous honor for me. I can see that you are offering me a position potentially higher than that of a mere general in the Holy Army. However, if I am to fulfill this mission of protecting you first and Constanza City second, there are any number of factors, which may prevent me from carrying out your charge. For example, when I handled the recent situation in the Senate, I observed what was occurring, formulated an effective strategy, and then carefully executed it. I had total and complete control over every aspect of the operations. You gave me the goal and I worked out the means of achieving it. More to the point here, I took no orders from anyone on how best to accomplish my task. No one said, 'Rooster, why don't you do it this way.' I was in complete control and in complete charge of the operation, second to none."

"That is as it should be," the Pope responded, sensing what the reservations of the Rooster might be. Yazi was a shrewd judge of people and their ulterior motives. "As the Chief of Security, you take orders from no one except the Pope. You are responsible to no one in Constanza City except the Pope personally. No go-between's, ever. In matters of security, your word is law, again second only to that of the Pope. However, I will lay down a hard and fast rule that the Pope must have a vitally important reason to veto a security measure you have ordered. Do not expect the Pope to be second-guessing your security decisions, ever. We both know that that is tantamount to ruin, especially when in a crisis. This is your province and I trust you implicitly."

Yazi hastened to quell related doubts he felt that the Rooster may be having, "Further, you must be kept informed of all our non-religious plans. Hence, I would expect your attendance at all the Holy Council meetings, except when we are discussing religious matters only. Your security can be only as good as you know what is *really* going on around here. If I kept you in the dark about some clandestine activity, that alone could completely compromise security and cost me my life. No thank you."

"Then you have answered my deepest fears. You are the wisest man I know, Your Holiness. Seldom have I met anyone who grasped matters of security as you sir. You have done me the highest honor imaginable. I solemnly swear that I will die before I let anyone harm a hair on your head."

"Let us change that to any hair on the Pope's head. Rooster, I am getting old and you are still young. Down the road, there will be another Pope. I wish you to provide him with the same service you are giving me."

"I so agree," the Rooster replied without hesitation.

"Thank you. The next question is who will be your troops? Probably we could use some soldiers as mere guards. Yet, guards can be easily bought. I would like you to pick your own key men. Pick men whose loyalty can be counted upon, men with whom we can trust our lives and safety. Choose men who can do this most important, most vital action that is second only to spreading the Holy Word of God Jehosa to Tarra. For starters, tomorrow you may visit with every one of my Holy Paladins that are still here in Constanza City. If you find any worthy, they shall be instantly assigned to your Security Force."

"I am to choose my own men?" the Rooster asked, scarcely believing his ears. Indeed, if he were to assume the responsibility of Constanza City security, he would prefer his own choice in men.

"Absolutely. Now you best head home and pack your things. Tomorrow will be your first day as General of the Constanza Security Force. Perhaps we ought to find a better name for your organization, but that can wait. On your way out, an adept will give you your official robes of office. Oh yes, I nearly forgot. Pay. Would five hundred gold ducats a month be sufficient for your personal needs?"

The Rooster, who was rapidly finishing his tea so he could leave, choked, catching the flying tea on his robes. "Your Holiness! Yes, that is a fabulous sum — more than adequate. Yes."

"We see eye to eye, Rooster. If we do not pay our security forces well, then they are far more prone to accept bribes. The men you choose will be more than adequately paid for their services; you can count on that."

The Rooster grinned, the cunning of his idol shone through. "Yes, Your Holiness, well paid men are far less prone to bribes. When it comes to your security, we will tolerate no bribes ever!" With that, the two shook hands.

As the Rooster reached the door, the Pope quickly added, "Oh yes, one other tiny matter. I have written down, documented fully our arrangements in the past, and will continue to do so in the future. This ongoing document will be kept under my private lock and key. Only the Pope will read it. My successor will definitely need to know all the details, if you are to be able to provide him with the same security you will to me."

"Thank you sir!" the Rooster replied, eager to leave and get his hands on the pale blue robes. The thought that having everything they had agreed to written down — the assassinations of the senators and such — did not in the least concern the Rooster. That such could be used to blackmail him never entered his reality. Yet it most certainly did with the Pope. The ongoing document would be his ultimate weapon over the Rooster, should he ever need it. Further, whoever became the Pope when he was gone would also have this weapon. One never leaves total power in another's hands but your own; that was Yazi's philosophy.

"And one more thing," Yazi added, "about your name. Do you really want to have others here in Constanza City know you as General Rooster of the Constanza Security Forces? I will formally introduce you tomorrow and want to make sure this is your desire."

"Aye, it does sound a bit strange, now that you mention it, doesn't it," the Rooster replied. "How about General R. Thraxton?" The two shook hands on it and finally the Rooster left the room. Outside, an adept handed him his sky blue toga and robes befitting his highly elevated new status. His feet felt light as a feather all the way home to his dwelling.

His home was a tiny stone building with wooden flooring and roof. It appeared as dilapidated as all the other homes here in the poorest section of town. Yet, all these years, it had proven an excellent base for his operations. Once inside, he first made sure the door was securely locked and then he had to try on his new clothes, admiring his powerful new look. Yet, not all was vanity on his part. For the next few hours, he experimented with various techniques for carrying his many concealed weapons and tools, such as lock picks, trying to find the most optimum way to carry them without calling attention to them.

In the end, he retained his old leather harness contraption worn under his new toga. To this, he could fasten numerous items, all of which remained concealed, yet within a quick action reach. Rooster was only satisfied when he stood before his mirror and had the following on his person, invisible to all but the most discerning eyes: two daggers, four throwing daggers, three needlepoint stilettos, two full sets of lock picking tools, and four throwing darts whose tips could be poisoned if need be. To this, he strapped his short sword on the outside so that he looked the part of a Security Man.

Next, he took stock of his possessions, determining which he should bring with him to his new quarters and which to leave back here in Galantas. He already knew that he would keep this home. Who could say when he might be called upon to do some new clandestine operations here in the capital city? Hence, this home with its numerous concealed spaces, housing any number of disguises and equipment, would prove invaluable. He decided to leave most of it here, opting to take with him a heavy crossbow and one set of robes, brown, in case he needed to make a hidden quick trip back here to this home. He easily passed as a tradesman; it was his usual disguise.

He had accumulated a considerable wealth in his many years, considerable for a thief and assassin, at least. Most of it was very well hidden and protected by some cunning, if not diabolical, traps. It was probably safer here than at his new home. Thus, he opted only to take a small pouch with a few gold ducats and a handful of inexpensive gems. Finally, he filled up a small bag with normal living items, razor and hair brush, for example. Satisfied, he finally turned in for the night, falling asleep thinking over all his preparations for the move.

Chapter 3 Of Plans and Counter-plans

Father Jax led the new general to the meeting room in the adjoining building next to the imposing Church of Jehosanity in Constanza City. Rooster was early, a habit he'd had all his life, ever since he was teased as a child for being late to a birthday party. The room was secure enough, he convinced himself as he examined it carefully. No windows and only one door seemed secure, though he immediately nosed around a bit, testing the solidity of the walls. He convinced himself that the stone would make conversations held in here impervious to eavesdropping, his prime concern. Thus, if anyone found out about anything discussed within this room, one of the participants would naturally be the culprit.

His last test was to close the door and then call out using a normal voice to Father Jax who was outside awaiting the arrival of the Holy Council of Bishops. Since Father Jax did not answer, Rooster felt confident and took his choice of seat, one in the far back of the room. If forced to sit at the right of the Pope, Rooster would be so self-conscious that he could not do his job. He hated being the center of attention in any way.

Sounds of conversations drifted into his ears, as the door opened once more and the High Council members, led by the Pope, filed into the room. As they took their seats, several adepts passed out some tea. As expected, the Pope took the larger seat at the end of the table, the other ten sat around the table on either side. Rooster, alone, faced his mentor. As soon as the adepts left and the door closed, Pope Yazi I spoke.

"Officially, our meeting begins. First, I wish to introduce all of you to our new General of the Security Forces, our chief, General R. Thraxton." He moved his right hand toward the Rooster, who nodded humbly. Several murmurs greeted his welcome; Rooster suspected that some of these Bishops might recognize him. After all, he was the only man in Megalos whose head was distorted, resembling a cock's head. If they recognized him, then certainly they would be familiar with some of the wilder rumors that circulated around Galantas concerning his nefarious activities. Hence, the murmurs.

"Some of you recognize our new Chief of Security. Be it known that General R. Thraxton has already proven his excellent worth to our Church. He has accomplished much of which we can be proud. Let us welcome him into our fold." The Bishops all nodded and said greetings, which he acknowledged tersely.

Pope Yazi I put on his most serious mien and said, "Now then just so that everyone here understands, General R. Thraxton has the *highest* security clearance of any of you. He is second only to the Pope in all matters involving our security and that of Constanza City. Let me be perfectly clear on this matter. I trust him with my life and you should as well. If the General gives you an order, you are to follow it immediately and without question, just as I will. Your lives may depend upon his great skills, of which he has already more than adequately demonstrated to me. I will tolerate *no* second-guessing of his actions or decisions. He reports directly and *only* to the Pope in all matters regarding security. Is this perfectly clear?" Although there were some grumbles, all the Bishops agreed; how could they not? He was the Pope and their leader. Yazi now considered the matter entirely settled.

"As Chief of Security, we must bring him up to date on all our plans and our current situation." Thus began a very lengthy meeting that summarized the progress of the Church of Jehosanity in Megalos. Essentially, Constanza City was entirely autonomous from Megalos and Galantas by royal decree from the late Emperor Titus himself. That document was stored in their most heavily guarded vault. The land, approximately fifty acres, consisted of mostly a stony, rolling hillside, just outside the current city limits of a small northern port town of Athos, some twenty-five miles north of Galantas.

"Our Church is finished, at least a small one," Yazi continued. "However, the outer defensive wall is not likely to be finished for another year. General, would you please look over the current outer wall construction for security flaws? There is still time to correct them. I've asked for plans for a barrier wall entirely around our fifty acres, but I'm told that will take several years at best to construct. My idea is to have our city surrounded by a barrier wall with controlled entrances to Constanza. Our actual religious center complex must be totally secure with its own impenetrable wall."

Rooster interrupted him, "No wall is impenetrable — only the degree of difficulty. Real security lies in layers of defenses."

"Ah ha. See, what did I tell you? Our Security General really knows his art!" Pope Yazi I exclaimed, taking this opportunity to help raise the Bishops' opinion of their new Security General. "Please General look it all over carefully."

"Now at this point in time, we are in perilous times. Jehosanity is just now taking hold as a religion of choice here in Megalos. Yet our initial success has, I am afraid, stepped on many toes, the ardent worshipers of Sol. We can expect a backlash not only from their priests but also from some of their more die-hard followers. I would suspect that their priests would be sponsoring no end of activities designed to bring us harm. It is still possible for Emperor Justinian to proclaim his predecessor's land grant to us null and void for any number of made up reasons. Constanza City must be made secure from any outside attacks or threats. I mean that if they try to reclaim our land, we must be so strong, so defensive, that Centurion generals would judge an assault on us to be next to impossible. So far, we have been successful in getting popular opinion on our side, which is why Justinian has thus far not acted against us."

"How long do you estimate that we have?" asked one bishop.

Bishop Reneau replied, "My educated guess on the physical construction side is that if we can hang on for twenty-five years, our defenses will be such that we could not be overthrown by physical forces without the attackers sustaining unacceptable, massive losses in the action. My prognosis is based upon the current rate of construction progress, assuming that we stick to the original plans, that is. If our new General of Security insists on too many changes, you may add on many more years to that."

Pope Yazi I resumed control of his meeting, "Gentlemen that is particularly why I chose General Thraxton here. As long as we maintain our surveillance and vigil, anticipate their next moves, and then smash them to a pulp before they can be executed — just as we have done thus far — we should be able to make it. Remember, we still have not used our diversionary plan. Oh, sorry Thraxton. That plan is to convince the Emperor to hold public gladiator combats in the central arena, giving a high award to that Centurion who can defeat all challengers. Such will keep everyone's attention completely off the Church." Rooster grasped precisely the plan's overall impact at once; he caught on very quickly to plots.

Bishop Solace, a middle aged man, added, "Are we still planning to implement the Confiscation of Vulgar Art Plan? Is it still on hold? Do we have enough popular support yet?"

For the benefit of Rooster, Yazi explained, "When the time is right, we will start a popular rebellion against all the vulgar art pieces scattered around the land. Pieces showing naked bodies, especially those of women, statues, paintings, and tapestries of such are everywhere, probably brought into vogue during Hiro's reign." Looking at Solace, he said, "Yes, we go forth with that plan, but not until we can better guarantee our security here. As soon as we put that one into operations, you can expect an awful lot of backlash against us. We must be prepared for it. Right now, we are not. Whether we can go forth before the outer barrier wall around our fifty acres is built or not is up to General Thraxton's opinion. It's his job to keep us all alive, no matter what comes against us."

An hour later, Bishop Reneau, who oversaw the construction projects, took Rooster on a lengthy tour of the complex and extensive, rugged grounds. He carried with him the many scrolls outlining everything that was being built in this third phase of building. The Church was the first phase, living quarters and the beginnings of a city had been the second. Rooster was not impressed favorably with the wall designs or of the overall security measures that had been sketched out on the drawings. However, his eyes brightened up when they toured the newly finished catacombs beneath the Church. Essentially, one long tunnel with side burial niches had been excavated or carved from the rock beneath the Church itself. Bishop Reneau explained that Pope Yazi I insisted that all Popes be buried here beneath the mother Church.

Rooster saw not a burial chamber, but rather an elaborate maze of interconnecting tunnels, one of which led to some safe, remote location — a last ditch method of survival. Further, in such a maze valuables would be far safer, vaults of sacred items less prone to sacking. He knew that one of his design changes would be to make a maze down here. An hour later, standing on the bare, rough stone hillside overlooking the ocean to the north, he realized another key ingredient was missing: Constanza was landlocked. With no soil suitable for agriculture, the city would be entirely dependent upon the importing of food.

Where their bit of land actually touched the ocean, only great boulders protruded upwards, like fingers of a giant hand rising unexpectedly from the blue, crashing waters. In stark contrast, just a mile to the northeast, the land formed a natural bay with sandy beaches. He could even see the tops of several ship masts rising above the rocky ground. At supper, Rooster made his first report to the Pope; it was not encouraging.

However, Yazi immediately saw the wisdom in his suggestions and so ordered two significant design changes. First, the catacombs would be greatly enlarged with a maze of intersecting tunnels. At one distant location would be their valuables vault and one passage would lead to an opening down close to the ocean. Second, though costly, a small, man-made harbor would be constructed. With luck, two ships could be docked there at one time. Yazi then began to consider having a Holy Yacht constructed. Just now, he knew that he needed it not. However, years down the line, such would allow the Pope to travel to more distant places to conduct the High Mass. That idea appealed to him.

Yazi was planning for the distant future. Always now, he knew his time on Tarra was very limited, and his total goal was to have his Church survive and become the Church of all Tarra. Yazi would then be more famous that the Great Messiah himself! Certainly he, Pope Yazi I, had done far more for Tarra than had Jes Amir, of that he was certain. Jes left behind virtually nothing but a few Holy Relics. Yazi was leaving an entire Church movement behind him! Further, he had gone into the lion's den of the Infidels, as the holy Arads called their oppressors, and converted the Infidels to Jehosanity, something that Jes Amir had never even considered! In many ways, Pope Yazi I considered himself to be vastly superior to the Great Messiah himself.

At night, he often had dreams of being taken personally into Jehosa's realm when his fleshly body died. Usually, a dozen angels appeared to lead him; his royal entrance into Heaven was always accompanied by the sound of a trumpet fanfare. Jes was too cowardly to confront the Infidels, yet Yazi had, and had in effect defeated them, bringing the Infidels into the worship of Jehosa. Such irony, he thought.

That same night, Rooster began to consider whom he could get to assist with the security forces. He knew that he could not just pick any assassin or thief in Megalos. No, they had to be like him, devout in their belief in Jehosanity, willing to suffer intense physical pain and humiliation and still have the presence of mind to function fully and optimally. When in a tight situation, one cannot shrink from fear of pain or humiliation, not when the Pope's life was in jeopardy.

He began to drawn up a list of possibilities. After he filled three scrolls with names, he then went back and began to eliminate those that did not meet his qualifications. An hour later, he stared at the scrolls. Every name had a line drawn through it. None met his high standards! Unable to think clearly any longer, he went to bed.

The next morning when he met with Pope Yazi I, he humbly explained his problem. "Your Holiness, other than myself, there is not another person that I know of on Megalos whom I would trust your safety to, sire. I am doomed!"

Yazi smiled, "Take heart, Rooster. I agree completely with your findings. Long have I waited until you came to me. Only to you would I trust my life, Rooster. You have made me proud, and you've reached the same conclusion that I have reached, my son." Rooster managed a smile; his Holiness had indeed paid him the highest compliment that any living person had ever done.

"I might offer you a suggestion, Rooster." He looked up into the blue eyes of the Pope, rather like a puppy to its master, begging for some tiny morsel of table scrap. "If you cannot find them, why not make them? Find likely candidates and mold them into what we need." Somewhere in the back of his mind, the idea germinated and took hold. Train them, yes, train them to be impervious to pain, to fear, to humiliation! Only one man on Tarra knew how to train someone to be such, he, Rooster! Once more, Rooster knew that he had yet again been touched by God's human representative on Tarra! Such wisdom! Such brilliance!

With more enthusiasm that he ever knew he possessed, Rooster exclaimed, "That's the answer! Oh, thank you, Your Holiness! I will begin at once!" He rushed out of the room, heading for his own small quarters, his mind racing through methods of implementing the plan.

The next day, Rooster returned to Galantas. By lunchtime, he had gathered his three closest associates together for a private lunch in his old home. Cax, Karlos, and Thondakas listened to his proposal. Cax asked, "But where's the profit in all this?"

"What would you say if you were paid four hundred ducats a month for your services?" Rooster replied, knowing that money was the entrance point for these men. Money would entice them, but their service of Jehosa would eventually convince them.

Thondakas pulled his beard and commented, "Aye, tidy sum. More than we make on the best of jobs. You have a point, Rooster."

"Yeh, well, I don't know what you mean about functioning fully in spite of pain. Men fear pain, dog gone it; it hurts, man!" protested Karlos. "I broke my arm once; damn if it didn't hurt like the devil for weeks after that!"

"Fear of pain is a root cause for inaction, Karlos. You know that. How many times have you threatened a noble with a sword, seen them recoil, and give you their purse? In our line of work, entrusted with such burdens of tremendous importance, we simply cannot ever fail to perform the needed action because of pain or even fear of pain. We are being entrusted with something more valuable than our lives themselves! We will be repaid handsomely for it, mind you."

"Ah, but how do we *know* that what we are being entrusted is actually worth our lives?" retorted Karlos, still not entirely convinced. Pain was one thing, but operating over it, another.

"Point taken, Karlos," Rooster rubbed his chin in thought. He had half expected it to come down to this: proof. Somehow, he needed to provide proof to these men that what they were protecting was the most valuable of all valuables on Tarra. They discussed other minor matters before Rooster left to return to Constanza City. His would be the task of obtaining the proof his men would need.

After supper, he held a private meeting with Pope Yazi I. "Your Holiness, I do have one problem: obtaining the proper men to provide the security you deserve. How do I say this? Please take no offense by this, but the men that I require need visible, tangible proof of what they are laying down their lives to protect. I know miracles cannot be asked of Jehosa, but that's really what I need right now to convince the right men to join up. If they can be convinced, I know that I can shape them into just what is needed: men who can act as needed, despite any physical pain or fear that they might be under. You see, to guarantee your survival, the men must be like me, able to act no matter what else is happening to them."

"Yes, that is as it should be," Yazi replied, thinking hard. This was Yazi's first test with the Rooster; he had to rise to the challenge. Everything depended upon his not letting Rooster down. "Let me pray to Jehosa for guidance, Rooster. I'll let you know in the morning." The Rooster nodded, humbled that is idol would actually commune with God personally on his behalf. Quietly, unable to meet the gaze of his idol, Rooster left the room.

Next morning during the morning briefing of Bishops, Yazi had the answer for Rooster. "Gentlemen, the time for more convincing has arrived. We know that there are many non-believers out there, along with even more who are just waiting to see some sign. True, Jehosa worked the Miracle Sword Destruction so many years ago when General Lacerta was facing extinction at the hands of the barbarians. Yet, how quickly so many do forget. The time has come for more convincing, if we are to continue to grow and expand. We must bring miracles close to home."

Thus, it was that the Healing Sunday Masses began. Naturally, the Pope picked Galantas as the first city in which to conduct his "holy miracles of healing." The Rooster and his three chosen men attended, sitting quietly in the rear pew, watching intently as the much-advertised event began. His bishops had spread the word during the week, and this Sunday more than a dozen sick, hurt, or cripples were in attendance, hoping for a miracle cure for their maladies.

In fact, the church was packed to overflowing. Many had come just to see if miracles did occur. Others came to bear witness to the power of their Lord, knowing that Jehosa would heal those worthy of such. Nearly seven hundred were packed into the pews; all eyes were upon the Pope and the dozen seated close to the High Altar behind which Pope Yazi I now stood. "Welcome once more to the House of the Lord Jehosa," he began as regally and solemnly as he could muster. Today just had to go right! He had already given the High Mass, and now the time for his miracles was at hand. "Once more, I urge you to pray daily to the Lord Jehosa, who is always present to hear your prayer. He is everywhere around us, above us in the heavens. He wants to hear from each of you at least on a daily basis."

Raising his hands upwards toward the sky and God, he continued. "Today, we begin a new service to the faithful here in Megalos. Many are deathly ill, physicians give them no hope — no cure. Some I see before me have been crippled by life itself. One young girl has been traumatized, I am told, by some horrors that she's seen. Today, I on behalf of all mankind, I beseech our God, Lord Jehosa, to come down and touch these lives. Heal those you deem worthy. Show us the almighty power of God. Let us pray that we may bear witness to the mighty power of the Lord." Only the coughing of one ill man could be heard, as the hundreds bowed their heads in holy prayer. Many wondered just what they would actually see.

Speaking directly to the dozen, he addressed, "You have come here seeking a miracle. Before a miracle can occur, you must repent and shed all your sins, accept the Lord Jehosa as the One God. Let his immortal spirit flow through your fleshly bodies. Pray to him. Accept him as your savior and your salvation. Cast aside your doubts and fears. Make your heart pure, and accept God's Holy Grace into your soul, your being. From this day forward, dedicate your life, your existence, to doing the work of God."

For ten minutes, Yazi continued in this vein, extolling these dozen to repent their sins and accept the Lord into their hearts and souls. Finally, when he deemed their minds were properly prepared, he began his walk down the line of those that had come looking for a miracle. To the large audience, he commented, "Lord Jehosa works in mysterious ways that a mere man cannot hope to understand. Today some of these very people here will be touched by God, healed of their misery; others will not." To the dozen he added, "Should Lord Jehosa not heal you this day, despair not. There is always next week. Some of you might not have bared your sins fully and completely. Others might not have truly opened their hearts and souls to the breath of God. Some may not have had true faith in our Lord, or perhaps been slack on their prayers. Others, Lord Jehosa may have different plans for their lives. I say unto you, do not question whom Lord Jehosa shall cure this day. Accept his Divine Judgment. Strive for another day."

Turning to his Holy Communion golden platter, he blessed the Holy Wafers and Holy Wine. With an assistant holding the plate, Yazi took the jewel encrusted golden goblet in his hands and walked before the first person waiting to be healed. "Let us pray together as each accepts the judgment of our Lord above." While everyone prayed silently to themselves, the choir began a solemn chant, somewhat hiding from the throng what he was saying to each individual that he came to as he stood before each of the ill.

"Accept this token as the Holy Flesh of God and sip of the Holy Blood given by his Only Son that you may be free." After he placed the wafer in a person's mouth and held the goblet to their lips that they may sip, he added, "Accept Lord Jehosa and arise cured of your malady if that is the wish of Lord Jehosa." This last was spoken softly so that only those nearest them could hear him. It was a private matter between each of these people and Lord Jehosa.

When he had ministered to the dozen, Pope Yazi I received his miracles. The young traumatized girl spoke her first words in four years, and her words were heard throughout the church. "Thank you. Daddy where are you?" she said. Tears of joy and happiness streamed down her father's cheeks. She had witnessed the brutal slaying of her mother four years ago and had not said a word since that time, not until this day.

A man who had a bum leg suddenly was able to walk normally, once more to make his living as a shepherd. A man whose right arm had been paralyzed found the paralysis had vanished. These three were well known to their friends and families. Thus, there could be no claim to fakery with these Holy Miracles. With each, many could, and did, vouch for the conditions that had miraculously vanished right before everyone's eyes this day. Pope Yazi I had worked his miracles.

More to the point, Rooster's friends actually knew the man whose arm had been paralyzed. After examining him when the service was done, all three were convinced that they had indeed witnessed a miracle cure. This was all the ammunition that the Rooster needed. Without reservation, the three agreed to join the Rooster's Security Force and undergo whatever training the Rooster demanded. Yes, the gold ducats also went a long way toward convincing them as well.

For the next year, once a week, these special Healing Masses were held on a routine basis. Each week, nearly one of every five was blessed with a miracle cure. First, all Galantas was talking about them and later on, the rest of Megalos. It seemed true miracle faith healing had finally come to Megalos.

Later that day, Pope Yazi I held a private meeting with the Bishops, explaining in detail just how to conduct this most special ceremony. He ended by saying, "Always have at least ten before you who desire a miracle cure. You may then expect two of them to be cured." His Bishops left the meeting in utter awe; their Pope had their highest respect.

Later that night, Yazi wrote in his diary in the Arad language so that it was unlikely to be easily read by anyone else. "When I was a youth, I observed that one person in five would get well no matter what you said to them, as long as they believed in you and what you were doing. If a man was convinced that by drinking this specially blessed water he would be cured, in fact, one in five would be so cured, though the water was just drawn from the well from which he drank every day. All you have to do is properly sell them that this will cure them. However, as a footnote, I add that I personally did see the Holy Son of God, Jes Amir, cure all that came asking for healing. Of that, there can be no doubt whatsoever. Reluctantly, I do admit before Lord Jehosa that I also saw that abomination of a wife of his also heal where there should not have been healing, but I will never ever publically admit said fact. I set it down here, just between you Lord Jehosa and myself. We must do all that we can to gain followers and support at this, the most delicate time of our ministry."

Across town Emperor Justinian, a young man in his thirties with the typical bronzed skin and blonde hair, paced his throne room for the fiftieth time. His trusted advisor, Theo Kronos, huffed and puffed after him; in his sixties, he definitely did not like all this motion! Both were ardent supporters of the Temple of Sol, which of late was losing worshipers faster the mosquitoes at the first frost. Since the founding of Megalos, the Temple of Sol had the power to appoint the Emperor, as they had Justinian a few years ago. Emperor Justinian knew all this was in jeopardy.

He raked his hands through his hair once more. So much was in jeopardy these days and he had so little power to do anything about it all. So many problems, so few solutions. "Damn, if the world is going to a chamber pot!" he exclaimed in utter frustration. "Where's General Theos Lacerta anyway?"

"Remember, Lord, he is retired now. He was scheduled to be here anytime now." Theo endeavored to keep his Emperor as calm as possible. No need for rash, brash decisions and orders; ill comes to those who rush, he reminded himself of his own saying. Mentally, he made a note to speak to Lacerta about being on time or even earlier for meetings with the Emperor. Thankfully, a crier announced the arrival of the ex-general. Theo was relieved; for a few minutes, he would not be under pressure.

Justinian put on his noblest face, "Ah there you are, General Lacerta. Thank you so much for taking the time to meet with me this morning. I certainly do appreciate your time."

Lacerta detected the familiar covert hostility in his Emperor's voice and knew that probably the opposite was really the case. Theos showed his age; he'd spent his entire life in the army, campaigning across Tarra. Now his elderly body fought back: arthritis pains made walking a chore; his hands barely could grasp a heavy goblet of ale. Worse was the infernal shaking of his arms, which he did his best to hide from everyone. He bowed in the royal fashion when entering the Emperor's presence, which caused him no end of pain in his legs and arms, but such was demanded at times like these, he reminded himself. "Greetings Justinian," he replied. He still could not adjust to this man having been promoted to that of the Emperor. "How may an old war dog be of service?"

Justinian noted the stiffness in Lacerta's walk and remembered that the retired general had joint problems. "Please, General, sit with me." Together they sat down at a small marble table. The throne room was open on all four sides; great columns of marble rose to support the ornate stone roof high overhead. Thin gauze sheeting draped down, undulating in the soft breeze blowing through the room. Perched on the highest point in Galantas, from this vantage point, the view to the north was spectacular. One could even see the ocean some twenty-five miles to the north.

"Let me be frank with you. Please, be just as frank with me, General," Justinian began. "I am surrounded with problems begging for solutions; yet no one seems to have the intelligence to solve them. First, I assume that you have heard the reports that have come in on the state of affairs up north in the Arad?"

"Aye," Lacerta smiled. Although no longer active in the Centurion army and since he was the most famous general ever, all the current generals felt obliged to keep him fully informed. He suspected that one day these very generals would be asking him for advice. Why else would they go out of their way to let an old retired general know the precise situation?

"The shining point is New Barq, Sire; it is thriving and doing well — up to forty thousand, at last counting. Steady commerce, I believe New Barq is supporting the empire rather well with its taxes," Lacerta began with the only bright point.

"Yes, I know that," Justinian interrupted, slightly annoyed. "But what about the rest of the northern lands? Is it really as bad as reports say?"

"In Juda Arad, yes, it's bad. Our few legions have been completely ineffective in re-establishing the rule of law there. For every bandit that is killed, ten more seem to spring up from nowhere. The roaming bands of Holy Paladins hamper our efforts. While I won't say that they are not there on Church business, they certainly are not winning us any friends. The Galts still raid there, and for the last year now, the Axemen from the far north have made their presence felt in the northern parts of the Arad as well. Yes, Juda Arad had become a wild, lawless frontier."

"How many legions do you think that it would take to bring the Arad back under our firm control?" Justinian asked the key question whose answer he'd most desired to know. He trusted not his generals on this issue.

Lacerta thought for a moment. He made allowances for the ineptitude of some of these newer generals. "Sire, fifty legions in addition to the twenty that we have in New Barq and along the southern road."

"Damn, we don't have that many in the entire army!" cursed Justinian.

"I am fully aware of that, and some of the blame lies fully on my head. So many, many men were lost to the barbarians before I finally was able to defeat them. It will take a generation before we can fully recover all that lost manpower." Lacerta's eyes watered — a fact that was not missed by Justinian.

"General, you are not to blame for that loss of life. If it wasn't for you, all Megalos would have been destroyed, and we would not even be here today. No, the blame rests squarely on the foul barbarians of the Northern Steppes. It is a shame that we do not have the forces to march there and wipe that scum off the face of Tarra! Sol knows, if I had the legions, I would not hesitate to do so!" He smashed his fist onto the marble table to drive home his determination to Lacerta.

"Still, they were under my command," Lacerta could not let go of his part in the deaths of so many young men. "However, ten legions are in reserve here in Megalos. Five of the twenty cannot be spared from garrison duties throughout the Southlands. I am not sure how many legions you have in your personal guards, however. Surely not forty-five." He did not want Justinian to know that he knew very well precisely how many men the Emperor had confiscated into his own personal battalions. Every Emperor did so. Justinian had fifteen legions secreted away for his own personal use.

"Ten legions," Justinian replied, unwilling to be completely honest with Lacerta. "You are right then; there is no hope whatsoever of bringing law and order into the Arad at this time. We simply do not have the legions. Ah well, then I will continue efforts to rebuild new legions. And what of the situation in the Sea Princes? Are those lands gone from us forever? It seems such a waste that we had them all conquered and then lost the whole thing. How embarrassing!"

"If we were to re-conquer the Sea Princes, I understand that now there are eight of them, we would need at least one hundred legions. All the key cities are now surrounded with a stone barrier wall. To retake one requires a lengthy siege. We would have to batter down the walls. We cannot even starve them out; they can easily be re-supplied by sea. Moreover, as I understand it, several sectors now have sizeable cavalry units and armed forces. Our losses would be appreciable this time, unlike before."

In anger, the Emperor commented, "We cannot even stop their ships from re-supplying the besieged cities! The Sea Prince ships out-number ours ten to one."

"Besides, Sire, their ships can carry at least three times the cargo as ours do," Lacerta pointed out. "However, you might consider attacking the Sea Princes another way. What if you build a huge navy of fighting ships in secret somewhere down long the southwestern coast of the Southlands? Make sleek, fast ships that can ram. Now supplied with superior fighting ships, we could assault the cities from the Med Sea. Personally, I would rather attempt an attack this way than with a long, drawn-out land siege. Also, it would take far fewer legions."

"Hum, excellent idea, General. My staff never thought of such a plan. I will get to work on it immediately. Yes, no need to raise ten thousand Centurions when we can accomplish the same thing with a thousand men on powerful, ramming ships! Brilliant, General, positively brilliant!"

"There is another matter which I wish to discuss with you, General," the Emperor coyly continued. He had to be very careful in his choice of words. "You are also aware of the crumbling state of homeland security? The recent assassinations of two of our leading women Senators?"

"Yes, my Lord. A sad, sad day for Megalos!" Lacerta replied cautiously.

"You've heard that one was killed along with the body guard I assigned to personally guarantee their safety?" Lacerta nodded. "Now, all the remaining women Senators have deserted the Senate. They have gone back to their own private estates, as I understand it. I cannot say that I blame them, though."

"Yes, it is indeed a black spot on your otherwise illustrious reign," Lacerta replied, stating the obvious, though he was a bit hesitant in speaking so boldly. It would not do to get his Emperor upset. "How are you doing on finding the assassins?"

"I'll be honest with you, General. We have no suspects, no leads. In fact, we know nothing more about the assassinations than we did when they occurred! I am at my wit's end. I don't know what else I can do to flush them out. At first, I thought that the Church of Jehosanity might have done these assassinations. You know, they were the only ones actually to benefit by the sudden demise of their two most outspoken opponents in the Senate. You must know the low opinion your Church has of women in a leadership role. Your Church would seem to be the only ones who benefitted in any way. No one else has any motive that I can see. Still, the Pope has publically denounced the assassinations and has given us the Church's full support in helping find the culprits."

"Perhaps the true motives of the assassins have not yet been seen?" Lacerta tried to be helpful. Political assassinations were entirely out of his sphere of experience. Further, he cared little for the Senate; even less for politicians.

"Some have been calling for me to put several legions of Centurions on patrol throughout Galantas. I have resisted that request so far. What do you think?"

"Wise, my Lord. Centurions are soldiers, not peacekeepers. Besides, they attack first and ask questions later." After a pause, he added, "Seeing numerous Centurions all over the city, one might get the idea that this is a police state. You might foment rebellious attitudes among our citizens. I know of no time in our long and illustrious history when our soldiers had to patrol our capital city, or any city for that matter."

"I agree, it would be folly for me to do that. I'm glad we see eye to eye on this one," Justinian replied, greatly relieved to find support for his decision from the General. For a minute, he pondered whether to ask the General about his problems with the Church of Jehosanity. In the end, he thought better of it. General Lacerta was merely a follower, not a church leader in any way. Thus, he thanked the elderly man for his advice and sent him on his way.

Once General Lacerta had gone, Justinian commented to Theo, "See, what did I tell you? Lacerta provided just the support for my decisions as I had hoped he would. Now I feel more confident that I've made all the right choices. Plus, he has given me a new avenue of thought, building a navy of ramming ships so that I might retake the Sea Princes. Now that would be a prize."

"Yes, the plan does have merit, especially in these hard times, but I noticed you didn't say anything about the problem with his church?" Theo replied, curious about whether Justinian had changed his mind about the Church of Jehosanity.

"Not at all. Lacerta was just used, a popular medium for their so-called miracle, that's all. He has no other importance or say in this religion. No, it is the self-proclaimed Pope Yazi that must be dealt with and soon."

"You are determined to follow your plan with him?" asked Theo, giving his boss one last chance to change his mind. "It is awfully risky. What if it should backfire?"

"It's not going to come back on us. I will have that possibility covered. Send for Kar. It's time we started solving our problems."

That evening, a rough looking man, long beard and hair, who looked as if he had not had a bath in days, though he did not smell, was brought before the Emperor. Unlike the open space where he'd met Lacerta earlier this day, Justinian met Kar in a back storage room. This was one of the few locations where a conversation could not be overheard by anyone. A scented oil lamp dimly illuminated their two faces. "I have a special job for you, Kar. The empire needs a certain individual disposed of in whatever manner suits your fancy, as long as the man is deceased. An *accident* would be perhaps the best way, if you take my meaning."

"Ah, yes, an untimely accident," Kar sneered agreeing. He loved "accidents." "And who is to be the recipient of this accident?" he asked, a note of curiosity in his voice.

Justinian found this tone encouraging and smiled. "Let us say that it would be fortuitous for all the followers of Sol, to say nothing of our empire, if the head of that other religious organization — the one which thinks it is an autonomous state on our northern coast, only twenty-five miles from here — had a very unfortunate accident along the road between here and there. He comes here at least once a week, I am told. You know how dangerous the open road can be, rock slides, and all."

"Ah, the fat Pope, y'er referren' to, I see," Kar drawled. "Been wondered how long it would be 'for I got that job. Just surprised that you waited so long. You've more patience than I have, it seems. However, it's going to cost you. Going to be tricky and expensive for the Pope to have an accident. He always travels in a small caravan — lots of them silly Holy Paladins around him. You don't mind if some of them have an accident as well?"

"I don't give a hoot about how many, only that the one is no longer a problem. Here, is this sufficient to cover your expenses?" Justinian handed Kar a bag of gemstones. The man poured a few out into his palm and examined them carefully.

Sliding them back into the bag, he replied, "Always nice doing business with you and the empire. How soon?"

"As soon as you can manage it," Justinian replied. "Just remember, there cannot be even the slightest hint that the Emperor is involved in this action. If you are caught, I will deny everything and will have no qualms about beheading you, when you are found guilty. This conversation never happened, if you understand me."

Kar chuckled, "'Course, wouldn't want it any other way. I'll get right on it." Justinian motioned for him to depart, and the Emperor waited until the man had time to leave the grounds before he reappeared from the storage room. He whistled a peppy sea tune; his biggest problem was soon to be solved. Now his mind envisioned a great fleet of ships doing battle upon the open sea.

Chapter 4 Now I Am Supposed to. . .

"What's with Caitlyn and all her 'now I am supposed to's?'" whispered Lilly Ann, our Judger. She had finally stopped flirting with Paul Wilkins. Caitlyn's behavior pricked her curiosity more than Paul did.

"Dunno," I replied honestly. Indeed, Caitlyn's behavior on this first day of her reign as Queen was very different. I was as surprised as the others were.

Over breakfast, Caitlyn had become a whirlwind of chatter. "Let's see. As Queen, now I am supposed to wear fancy court dresses. Does this one look queenly enough? I suppose I can have lots more made later on, but I *am* supposed to look regal. Does this look regal to you, Ket?" I thought she looked beautiful; then I am biased and would think she looked magnificent if she were wearing a seed sack. Ignoring my nod, she continued right along, "Well, I don't know if it is good enough, but I suppose it will just have to do. I am supposed to wear a different outfit each day, so I had best see to the seamstress right after breakfast."

"Now, Ket, we are supposed to hold court in the Great Hall in the mornings, but since we only just got here, I don't think we will have to do it today. We are supposed to settle things for others, but I may leave most of the settling things to you, though, Ket, since you are much more experienced than I am. Then, in the afternoons, we are to dine with any visiting guests. I think that we are supposed to walk around Nuadilan in the afternoon; we are supposed to dole out praise to the townsfolk, I think. We should also visit Amathon frequently. I suppose we should do so at least twice a week, don't you think?" I grunted inaudibly.

Later, when we were taking tea in the Great Hall and Caitlyn was seated on the throne that her mother used to use, she launched into it once more. "You know, we are supposed to have a bunch of advisors here. Trumpeters are supposed to announce the arrival of the courtiers. I wonder where the old advisors have gone? I haven't seen any trumpeters, for that matter. Have you?" I shrugged that I hadn't. "Do you suppose that we ought to ask someone?" she asked me. Tired already of this king business and her chatter, I was not paying attention. Hence, she poked me, "You are supposed to be paying attention, Ket. We have to get this king/queen thing right, you know. We don't want to be the laughing stock of Nuadilan, now do we?" I agreed that we didn't.

Caitlyn rolled along, "Now we are supposed to have servants in attendance. I wonder where they've got to? How do we summon them when we need something?"

"Why don't we just get it?" I retorted. "We aren't invalids."

"But that's *not* how it's done!" she said acidly, as if her words could burn out my protest. "Ket, you are supposed to act like a king. I'm doing my best, so you can at least try," she continued.

I was saved when the woman who had prepared our breakfast entered to ask Queen Caitlyn about the evening meal. "What's with her?" Lilly Ann whispered to me again, while Caitlyn was distracted. Lilly Ann's comments spurred my curiosity. The Wid in me, that part of me that wants to know all about everything, kicked in. My annoyance evaporated. I concentrated and moved into her body beside her, as we do when we're making love, and observed what she was seeing in her mind. Okay, so I was eavesdropping, but I needed to know what was going on with her.

I ought to have known what was happening with her. I blame myself for not paying attention. Now it was obvious. Poor Caitlyn was completely overwhelmed by suddenly having to be the queen. She had no advance preparation, no training, and no guidance. Her mind was swimming with all the images she had of her parents when she was just a child of five running around the building. In fact, Caitlyn seemed to be trying to be her mom as her mom appeared to her in her memories! Caitlyn was now thoroughly in her mother's valence!

A valence is an identity, complete with all the details. We all have adopted valences knowingly as children while running and playing. I can recall several times pretending that I was one of the legendary fighters in the Greenway, running around swinging a stick as if it was a mighty sword. I believe in your world, children often adopt the valence of Superman or is it Batman? For that period of time while they are in that valence, they are Superman, acting as they think or believe he would act.

However, Caitlyn was not playing a game. She was really so overwhelmed by suddenly having to be the Queen that she was more or less reactively being her mother. In fact, she was so socked into her mental images, she was not even aware that I was beside her looking at them as well!

Quietly, I explained what was going on to Lilly Ann, who seemed to grasp what I was saying about being in a valence unknowingly, though she gave me a queer look that I could not interpret. We were saved by the arrival of Beth Ann and Allan, who had been out for a walk. Allan said, "Ket, you should really come and take a look at the town. *Now*!"

"Really you should!" insisted Beth Ann. The very serious look on their faces convinced me at once that whatever they wanted to show me was important, of that I was certain.

"Caitlyn, come on. We need to go and see what Beth Ann and Allan have found. Come on; all this will wait." She looked entirely befuddled, but I physically dragged her out of the Great Hall. Only when we drew a breath of cold fresh air did she start to relax a bit.

It was February 1 now. Five inches of snow covered the landscape, though it had been packed down considerably on the dirt streets of the town. Smoke clouds rose from hundreds of chimneys. People were bustling around the streets, though walking carefully to avoid slipping, I noticed. Allan, with his arm around Beth Ann, led the way. With Caitlyn on my arm, we followed right behind them. Lilly Ann took Paul's arm without waiting for him to offer it, while Ben offered Paulette his arm. I must admit that it felt like I had just been released from some kind of prison! Free at last! I breathed the fresh air deeply and then looked about to see what had so upset Allan and Beth Ann. Everything seemed normal, though I had not really seen much of the town.

It had grown considerably since I was last here in my last lifetime as Bethany Madelyn Amir, the Blessed Holy Mother. I had helped with the overall town design. Following my plans, a circular wooden stockade wall surrounded the King's complex at the top of the hill, a moat and bailey design. Then, other sections of the town were built around it, each with ever-increasing stockade walls encircling that section. When I had left, there were seven concentric circles, great for defense, since there were no direct roads from the outside entrance up to the King's complex. I noticed that it had been expanded to nine circles now, more than doubling the total dwellings within the town. "What am I supposed to notice?" I asked Beth Ann.

"We'll give you a clue. Notice the people," she replied. We did so, saying hello to all that we passed. Everyone seemed very friendly indeed, but then one would expect so when their rulers were addressing them. A half hour later, we had arrived at the main southern gate, beyond which a well-worn dirt road headed on south toward Bregia on the coast. The walk did wonders for Caitlyn, who finally was back to her old self once more; for the moment, she had left her Queen problems behind her, along with being her mother. I took notice of the fact that a long walk had really helped Caitlyn and vowed to make good use of this therapy in the future. This valence thing was quite curious, when it was done mostly unknowingly and out of the person's immediate control.

"Well?" asked Beth Ann. Seeing a silly look on my face, she smiled, knowing that this one time, she had outdone me, her Wid! Can I plead that I was pre-occupied or had a lot on my mind? I think not.

"Okay, Beth Ann. You and Allan win. What?"

"You should get some more Observing the Obvious lessons when we visit Mount Blanc later this year," teased Beth Ann. It was common knowledge that I had to sit in a refresher course in this last year. Observing the Obvious is one of the very first lessons taught to raw beginners in our druwid movement. I was the oldest person in that class; most had been children. Word spread to all the Guardians: Bethany had to refresh Observing the Obvious! I took my lumps good-naturedly.

"Alright then," Beth Ann went on rapidly. "It's as plain as the nose on my face. Where are all the young men?"

"All the blacksmiths are at least fifty years old," added Allan. "The teamsters are all young boys or women in their teens. Beth Ann and I walked all over town, but did not see more than two or three men our age. There are almost no men here between the ages of about fifteen and forty!"

"And there are about ten women for each man here," Beth Ann added.

Once they pointed out this obvious fact, we all let out a cry! Yes, it was indeed plainly obvious. We had all just witnessed it. "By golly, you are absolutely right!" I exclaimed.

After many similar exclamations from the others, I did the obvious thing. We were right by the gate, so I asked the gateman, who was about fifty; I detected a twinge of grey protruding from his fur cap. "Excuse me sir, we could not help notice that there are a lot a men missing here. Where are all the young men between our age and yours?"

"Your highness, your ladyship. I'm Tom, the South Gatekeeper. Very pleased to meet you." We shook hands, which impressed the man even more. "Dead, your highness. All died in the great battle down south, along with your father, ma'am." Seeing the shocked looks on all our faces, he went on, "If it weren't for the timely intervention of King Emil Amir, why you'd not even have a town to which to return. He sends a cavalry battalion around here at least once a week as a show of support."

Tom proudly continued his explanation, "Now I says, you do have a lot of mighty fine, brave, stalwart women here in Nuadilan, if I do say so myself. They've all lent a hand in keeping the town operational. Even though most have been recently widowed, they all work hard to keep things a'going. You can be proud of them; I sure am. If I were you, I'd be planning how to get some young men in here fast. Come spring, word of our plight will have spread across Cymry, and you can bet that some king somewhere is going to attack us, if only for our women and easy pick'ens. Not even the Blessed Holy Mother can do anything about this, I'll wager."

I resisted the temptation to retort, "You are talking to the Blessed Holy Mother right now!" Instead, I bit my lip and then said, "Thanks Tom. We do have many problems to put to rights. We'll get on it right away." Hastily, we began walking around this outer section of the town.

Presently Ben commented, "Ket, it is worse than you thought. Look here at this stockade wall." Allan, whose specialty was building things, also looked.

"Rotten! The huge logs are rotting," Allan commented. "These walls are long overdue for replacement. I'll bet a horse could break down the walls."

"I wonder if it is the same in our sister town, Amathon?" asked Paul. "Protecting two towns with no men and rotting walls is an awfully big challenge, Wid Ket." He used my formal title and name, so I knew that he was exceedingly worried about being able to do his job, protecting the other members of our Circle.

"Come on. Let's go see," I ordered. Okay, I was glad of an excuse to go for a ride, if only a five mile one, anything to avoid going back into the Great Hall and sitting on the throne. Besides, the more time Caitlyn had away from her throne, the better she felt.

The winter sun was slowly sinking as we re-entered the western gate. I admit that I was more than a little appalled. Amathon was in just as bad a shape as Nuadilan: few men and rotting stockades. The only redeeming feature was that the most recently constructed outer stockade was still stout, no rot visible yet. However, once the outer wall was breeched, all the inner walls would fall very easily. None of us felt very secure, especially because the two cities were very tempting targets.

Over dinner, Caitlyn was so worried about what we had discovered today, that she forgot completely about all her now I am supposed to's. We were all grateful for that. "Ket, I am so worried," she said. "Both towns are just sitting ducks waiting to be conquered. What can we do? It's all my dad's fault." Tears began swelling up in her pretty eyes.

"No, it is the aftermath of the Grey Creature, my love. Your dad was just under his spell and could do nothing about it, even if he had desired. However, you are asking the right question. What can we do about it?"

The table was cleared, tea served, and all dishes removed, and still my Circle discussed various ideas. All were clearly disturbed about our discoveries today. Ideas flew thick and fast, but all were far-fetched. Suddenly I saw what we were missing, "Wait a minute everyone. We are still mostly ignorant of the *true* situation here. What we need to do is to get a total picture of how everything is in these two towns. What are the actual problems? What strengths do we have? What finances? What supplies? Our people could be starving to death, for all we know. Caitlyn, how many people do you think could fit in here, even if a bit crowded?"

"I know mom once held a party when I was real young. I think she said there were two hundred guests," she replied. "Why?"

"Look, we need a rapid assessment of everything. Who best to give us this data but the townsfolk themselves? I know that we cannot play host to tens of thousands, but we can host say a hundred from each town. Tomorrow morning, let's spread the word throughout both cities that we want one hundred representatives from each town to report to the Great Hall here for a town meeting. Let each town choose whom they want to represent them. Ah, it begins to give the people some power of choice," I added suddenly seeing some additional wisdom in my plan.

Lilly Ann, our Judger, spoke up coyly and at a very rapid pace, "Ket, since we are doing this, why not do it right? Tell them that we need to be briefed on every aspect of life in both towns, everything from what supplies we have, to armaments, the works. Further, why not have each town block elect someone to represent them on this council. Let's call it the Queen's Advisement Council. Purpose: to keep their rulers properly informed on all important matters. They will then have a say in their government."

Never give a Judger their head in such a discussion, for they will extol endlessly. "Whoa, I totally agree!" I finally got her to stop when she needed to catch her breath. I looked at Lilly Ann in a new light. Cleverly she had made it the Queen's Council, not the King's, placing Caitlyn in a far more important role. Besides, with mainly women in the two towns, they would feel far more comfortable advising another woman than a strange, red haired man whom they'd never seen before. Lilly Ann was good at her craft, really good. Later that night, I told her so and she smiled as only a sixteen year old young woman can.

"Caitlyn, I think that we can dispense with all the usual king and queen 'supposed to's now. We have a very serious situation to handle. Time enough for the pleasantries later on, once this very dangerous situation is handled.

Don't you agree?" I deftly prepared her to let go of all her earlier "supposed to" plans.

"Absolutely, I never dreamed things would be this bad. What if we are attacked? How can we defend the towns? What if there is no food or very little? We've been eating like there was no tomorrow," she replied, her voice full of concern and worry.

"Will you need me any more today?" the cook interrupted us. We were still sitting around the great table, teacups and pots scattered about. Dalny was her name; she was fifty and had been the cook for Caitlyn's late father. Her husband, Remy tended the stables.

"Good grief, Dalny!" Caitlyn exclaimed, finally realizing the full domestic situation. "Thank you and Remy ever so much for being here to look after us. I am just realizing how much I don't know about the true situation here at the Great Hall. Are we okay on food supplies? You haven't been feeding us from your own stores have you?"

She smiled, "No, dear child. There used to be a staff of twenty here to run the place. Since the demise of your father, everyone has left to take care of their own lives. Things have been grim around here. When King Emil notified us that you were returning, Remy and I tried to get the place somewhat presentable."

"We don't really know the full situation here at all," I added, "but obviously we need some staff to clean and such. Tomorrow can you ask those who used to work here that did a good job — in your opinion that is — descent folks you would like to have around — ask them if they would like to work here again. If so, have them report in tomorrow sometime. Say, did the late King leave any coffers? Are there any funds with which to run things or pay our staff? We don't even know if there is any left, let alone what food is in the pantry."

"I can show you where the treasure chest is at. King Emil was very keen about that. He said heads would roll if the funds were missing. So it's all there. Food, well, that is a problem, sort of. Since no one was living here most of this past year, nothing much has been stored up. Yes, I've been bringing in stuff from our house. If you will release some funds, I can shop for what we need in the market tomorrow." She added rather shyly, "It will be very different with all you young ones around here. I'm pleased you are back, Queen Caitlyn."

"I'm glad to be back as well. I missed everyone, but not my father," she still had not forgiven him for what he had done to her.

"I'm glad you didn't marry that pig that he tried to force upon you. Just between us, Remy and I cheered when we heard that you had run away from home. We did have many laughs when the men that the King sent out in search of you kept coming back without any clues at all. I just knew that the Blessed Holy Mother was watching over you! I said so to all that would listen to me," she declared.

I stifled a grin. I was the Blessed Holy Mother, and yes, I had been watching over her all last year. Caitlyn gave me a wink; she'd picked up on the irony of Dalny's proclamation as well. We followed her into a back windowless room. While I held a lantern, she fiddled with the lock. Inside the small room were a few weapons and two large chests, both locked. Dalny opened one that contained the coins: gold, silver, and bronze. The second chest contained gemstones, jewelry, broaches, and the like that Caitlyn's mother had worn. While Caitlyn was looking over the jewelry, which brought back childhood memories, Dalny handed me the tally sheets so that I could verify nothing was missing. I thanked her profusely for all that she had done.

Once Dalny and Remy had left for the night, I commented, "Well, we have funds. That's a start. We have a roof over our heads. I want all you to have rooms here in this main building. In the morning, let's look over this whole place and see just how we want to set things up. However, if you want your own house, I am sure you can take any of those here in this complex. I have this feeling that we eight should stick close together, especially at night. I will sleep better, if nothing else."

"Ah, so you *do* expect a nighttime attack," Paul, our Protector pressured me.

Not wanting to alarm the women unduly, I replied, "I'm not sure what I'm edgy about, but I just feel better if we are together nearby, that's all."

The next day was filled with a bustle of activity. My Circle went about the task of visiting folks in both towns, telling them about the new situation. They reported that nearly everyone quickly accepted the idea that they would be now be represented. However, Lilly Ann was precisely correct, calling it the Queen's Council made it readily acceptable to the women. It certainly gave everyone something to talk about during the day.

By noon, Caitlyn had officially hired a dozen women who came at Dalny's request. However, only two men in their fifties came, plainly obvious now the lack of men in both towns. The fitter of these two, Dan, became our doorman and main guard. The other helped the domestic staff with heavier chores as well as assisting Remy in the stables.

By late afternoon, the whole house was filled with the heady aroma of freshly baked breads. We intended to serve tea and bread to our expected two hundred guests, who began arriving shortly after supper. We also fixed up four more bedrooms for my Circle; we had all been sleeping in the master bedroom, which was extremely spacious. Now we all had private rooms. Thanks to the new staff, the rooms were quickly converted into bedrooms, complete with freshly made beds and linens.

Late in the afternoon, we took a tour of the ten buildings that made up the complex here on the hilltop of Nuadilan. Allan, our Planner, carefully inspected each of these wooden buildings. He announced his findings, "Well, Ket, Caitlyn, you have at most five years left in these buildings before they have to be replaced. Obviously, they were all built at the same time and not taken care of at all well, if at all. Wood is beginning to rot in places. I can make some repairs, but honestly, you need to think about replacements. I suspect that is going to be the case with many of the older buildings in both towns. You should consider using stone when you rebuild. A good stone building will last nearly forever. Come spring, I will search the nearby lands to see what kind of stone may be found here. Of course, the real problem is that of manpower and no stone masons. As I remember, that was my biggest problem building Mount Blanc, serious lack of masons. The Centurions solved that one for us way back when." He continued to chat about future constructions, while I wondered what other problems we were about to encounter.

We did not have chairs for two hundred, but we did make do with blankets, logs, and such. Our staff arrayed one long table with teapots, cups, mugs, and anything that could hold tea. In hindsight, we ought to have told them to bring their own cups! Bread was mounded into huge piles. Immediately after supper, our guests, the duly elected, chosen, appointed, or ordered representatives began arriving. Caitlyn had placed eight chairs for us against one wall so we could face everyone. Lilly Ann gave each of us a scroll on which to jot down things that needed to be handled, insisting that we compare notes on the morrow so we could agree on what had to be handled first.

As the folks entered, I realized that for most, this was the first time that they had seen me. I followed Caitlyn's suggestion that we personally greet everyone as they entered the great hall. Lilly Ann was all for making a good first impression, and she lent us a hand, ensuring that everyone got to shake our hands and say hello as they entered. All told, it took an hour before the room was completely packed and we eight took our seats before the gathered crowd. Thirty were older men, while the rest were women ranging in age from twenty to fifty. Lilly Ann hinted to me that these were probably the opinion leaders in the towns as well. Caitlyn pointed out that five of the men were the local priests of the Church of the Blessed Holy Mother. It was an interesting assemblage, no doubt of that.

We took our seats and a hush fell over the great hall. I stood up. "Welcome everyone. Let me begin by telling you a little bit about ourselves. You all know Caitlyn Amir who has accepted the throne vacated by her late father. As you may be thinking, things are going to be utterly different under her reign. First, I am Ket Bethany Amir, well actually just Ket of Cuch Glen. Yes, my body is Tewdwr. I too lost my family to the recent wars here. Cuch Glen was one of the southernmost hamlets along the coast. Last year the king from Layamon attacked it, and my whole family was killed, save my sister and I. While I managed to kill most of the attackers, my sister and I were forced to flee for our lives."

"Fianna and I became troubadours and formed the Cymry Minstrels; Caitlyn here met us and joined up. Later on, Prince Fergus d'Aine also joined. Together, we have spent the past year traveling the length and breadth of the Sea Princes and even into the Greenway and Juda Arad. Now that it is safe, we have returned. My sister has married Fergus and, as you probably suspect, one day they will rule as king and queen too."

"While in the Greenway, I spent a lot of time with Sarah Amir. She's married now and is a queen there. She sends her love and will likely come for a visit this spring. I've brought back with us a group of Guardians from the Greenway. These are my dear friends here." I gestured toward the members of my Circle. "I am well versed in Jehosanity and especially the Blessed Holy Mother, Bethany Madelyn Amir. I will be continuing the Holy Communion ritual that she began so long ago. Whenever one of your family dies let me know right away, and one of us here will conduct the holy ceremony. Yes, it will work just as it did when the Blessed Holy Mother used to hold it." I caught a number of stares of wonderment and even disbelief from the priests. Many others were whispering among themselves, so I knew that I had reached them. I did not continue for a couple of minutes, giving them time to exchange comments.

"Next, I want to notify everyone that officially you now have seven *true* healers here. We," I gestured towards my Circle, "are all competent healers, though Beth Ann is by far superior to the rest of us. Let the word go forth: anyone who is sick or injured, just come and get one of us right away. We will do our very best to help." Now the whispers really began in earnest. Many of those here were mothers, so I knew I touched upon something that meant the world to them.

"Yes, things have changed. Caitlyn is your queen and leader. Personally, I really do not want to be a king. Instead, let's call me your Protector, not king. I will do my very best to ensure the safety of this kingdom and everyone in it, rather as a mother does for her children. So don't look to me to be a ruling king. That is Caitlyn's task, to rule, that is." Of course, now the chatter rose so loud that I was forced to pause once more. I'm sure that they all fully expected that I would be their new king. Instead, they just found out that they have a female ruler, nearly unique in all Cymry.

This was as good a place as any to turn the meeting over to Queen Caitlyn, so I did just that. Accompanied by a loud round of applause, she rose, slightly embarrassed by so much attention. "Thank you all. I, ah, well, I must admit that when I first got here, I tried to be like my mother. I went around with all these 'now I am supposed to do this and that.' Only I discovered that the way it used to be is — well, it just isn't right; it's not going to work. I only have some slight idea of the huge amount of suffering and hardship you have all undergone! I just cannot imagine how bad it has been. I thought my plight was bad, but after being here just a few days, mine pales in comparison to what you have been through. And I do want to know all about it, so in the coming days, please don't hesitate to tell me about what has happened here. It is my home too."

"I've had quite a year, I will say that. I've had the most phenomenal luck in meeting Bethany, er Ket, here. He didn't actually say so, but he is also a Guardian and their leader. When I fled from here, I had no idea what the rest of the world is like. Yes, there are evil men doing evil things nearly everywhere, and I have had to learn to defend myself fairly well with a sword. But also, there are plenty of amazing people, good folks, kind and caring. I learned that there are far more good people out there than bad. Actually, the bad ones are only a tiny minority. In fact, we now have many good friends on the mainland. I'm sure they will lend a hand if we need some help."

"And help we need. I guess I need to explain how this is going to work. You all are my Advisory Council. I hope we can meet every week for a while, until things get better. I need you all to keep me informed about everything. What is broken, what needs mending, what your problems are, how much food we have — literally anything you think I need to know. I, well we all here, will do what we can about fixing them. I want our towns to do really well. I mean, thrive, and be a safe place to raise our families. No more wars, but we will defend ourselves, if need be. So tonight, we all want you to tell us about everything you think is important. We are going to take notes, because I think there are going to be a whole lot of them. We don't want to overlook anything that needs to be done. Also, you can ask us as many questions as you like at any time. I want to be a queen that is there for you when you need her. So much for pomp and courtly niceties."

Next, the folks began to respond with their problems and concerns. True, they began rather hesitatingly, as all this was completely new to them. No ruler before had honestly sought their input; some had to be convinced that Caitlyn meant what she said. However, within an hour, the details were coming fast and furious as the two hundred representatives finally opened up. Good thing we had the scrolls for notes. The list seemed endless!

Before the ill-fated war last year with the king in Layamon, the towns boasted a population of some twenty-two thousand. However, now there were only perhaps fifteen thousand. All the men fit for soldiering had been conscripted into Caitlyn's father's army; none had returned from that southern campaign. The women had to handle the spring plowing, the sewing of seed, crop tending, and then the harvest. Most had little or no experience with any of these actions. Consequently, the harvest was smaller than normal, very haphazardly distributed, and stored. Still, with fewer mouths to feed, food for the winter was not really a problem, except for fresh meat. Only a handful of women could handle a bow and had been pressed into service as the hunting party with marginal success. Only two trappers remained, and they tended their traps endlessly, trying to help with fresh game.

The many flocks of sheep were in complete disarray. What was normally a well-organized venture had turned into complete chaos. No one knew what should be done or when or how or they seemed to disagree upon such. Sheep had turned the nearby pastures into mud lots because they were not moved in time. Sheering for wool had been a complete fiasco, but the women salvaged enough wool to handle the need for yarn and thus clothing.

Currently, finding enough firewood or charcoal for cooking was the biggest single day to day problem nearly everyone faced. Many homes were nearly freezing because of the shortage of wood. In desperation, several abandoned homes were slowly being torn down and used for firewood!

Additionally, we discovered that priests were now in short supply.

Before, the Churches of the Blessed Holy Mother had a dozen priests officiating every Sunday. Now only five remained. As you have probably guessed, I immediately volunteered to don the priestly duties at the church nearest us in Nuadilan. Since each town had six churches, we decided to continue their stopgap measures. On Sundays, I would deliver three services at three of the churches. Between the six of us, we provided at least one weekly service that everyone could attend who chose to, that is.

By nine, the last of the folks had left. The massive pile of bread was now only a massive pile of crumbs. We'd gone through gallons of hot tea. Yet we were all really fired up, so while most of us began the cleanup duties, Caitlyn went off to brew up still more tea. We certainly did not want to leave this mess for our newly hired staff. Besides, we were not helpless.

Sitting around our cozy fire a little while later, Lilly Ann proclaimed, "Boy, do we ever have the problems to solve here! Sure glad we all took notes. Now comes the hard part. We need to prioritize them and find workable solutions. Let's compare notes first." This was her area of expertise, and I was more than willing to let her run our meeting. Poor Caitlyn was completely overwhelmed by the magnitude and sheer number of problems that we faced.

Manpower, so many things came down to that. We agreed that we men would make a day of firewood gathering in the morning, which gave me time to wrestle with the major problem. The girls had to change their plans because of the steady arrival of folks who were sick or injured. By the end of the day, we had fifty makeshift beds occupying our great hall.

Chopping firewood is very physical work, but it left my mind free to ponder where I could find men, at least some. Completely exhausted, at the end of the day I had come up with several plans to remedy our plight. If only it was not the dead of winter. In hindsight, this turned out to be extremely beneficial for us.

"I've got to build us a proper public bath house!" declared Allan, as we ate our supper in the kitchen. Beth Ann had already given us a summary of her patients. None was life threatening, but two badly set broken limbs had to be reset.

"Make sure you wash off, Allan, or I won't let you into our bed tonight," Beth Ann teased him. "You really stink!"

"Sweaty job," he attempted to defend himself, but found that was useless.

The rest of the evening, everyone pitched in to help me make dozens of posters. One of my plans was to put up posters in several nearby larger towns — ones that we knew already were friendly towards us. A large town always had young men, who have found few opportunities where they lived, eager to seek their fortunes; so why not invite them here? We listed out the key occupations for which we were in the greatest need. Plus, I hoped the promise of free food and lodging for a year would also be an enticement. Now if only love could spring this spring, maybe some of the hundreds upon hundreds of widows might begin a new life.

I knew better than to ask for men who could fight and assist in our defense. That would be pulling the soldiers away from the other towns and kingdoms. We stood no chance of that. To compensate, I devised an even bolder plan.

"You're kidding, aren't you?" Caitlyn exclaimed when I announced my plan. Even those in my Circle gasped in shock.

"I'm dead serious, my love. Where else can we get a strong body of fighters on such short notice? Besides, it will be good to make them apart of our culture, not having them as enemies. Perhaps it will bring peace to our island."

"But Bethany, they're Axemen!" Paulette pointed out, as if we didn't know that fact.

"Precisely the point. In Velona, a group of five hundred Axemen, who were dissatisfied with their homeland, has been accepted and welcomed into Velona's population. Why not here as well? I just have to get them to realize the mutual benefits of doing so. I do speak a little of their language now, so I am willing to give it a try."

"You're not going anywhere without me!" insisted Paul.

"I figured our Protector would insist on coming along. However, I want the rest of you to stay here and continue working on solutions to the multitudinous problems we have. I will contact Fergus and see if he can manage to put together a small cavalry group to take us there. Don't worry; it won't be just the two of us heading into the Axeman village." We talked about this plan for another hour before we retired for the night.

The next night, Paul and I rode into the Highlands town where Fergus and Fianna were waiting out the winter. "Aye laddie, tis a strange request yea be making. Donna know if yea canst trust them Axemen, but I'm with yea," Fergus related after we shook hands in a warm greeting.

Fianna had also latched onto me. Although my sister and I had been apart only a few weeks, it seemed like an eternity. She looked radiant and I concluded that married life agreed well with her. Footnote: she too had now become a lengthy list of "now I am supposed to's," as she was being coached on how to be first a princess and then a queen.

The next day, we set out under the guidance and protection of Prince Fergus d'Aine. He had twenty-five seasoned cavalrymen riding with us, and he also provided us with the necessary winter gear and supplies. He calculated that we would need four days on the trail to get there, three if it wasn't the dead of winter. However, we could expect even more days should the weather not cooperate.

During the first day of riding, Fergus did his best to try to dissuade me from doing this. I, of course, could not be budged from my plan. I really stopped listening to his remarks and just enjoyed the pristine winter beauty of the highlands. Snow blanketed the landscape but great stones occasionally poked their grey and brown massed up out of the white. The stone fences marking the outlines of the pastures and fields looked particularly impressive to me, perhaps because nowhere else on Tarra had I ever seen them. The quaint stone buildings of the towns and villages lent color to the white before our eyes, as did the occasional sleighs of young folks out for a good time.

All this changed by mid-afternoon of the third day. We left the last of the highland villages behind, pushing out into the northernmost, uninhabited portion of Cymry, Ruthcroghan, or the Rock Barrens. Here the barren landscape slowly descended to the turbulent ocean. The landscape appeared much like the hand of God had swooped down and removed everything down to the bedrock.

Here, we turned due east. From our previous travels here last year, we knew that the Axemen had established a large village at the northern edge of the Dark Forest, where it meets Ruthcroghan. Here, they had begun logging the virgin timber, exporting it back home to be turned into homes and ships. All attempts by several nearby kings and their armies had utterly failed to dislodge them. By now, they were very well established on our island.

Fergus insisted that our point rider carry a white parley flag. The last thing we wanted was to do battle with these burly men, especially in the dead of winter. Both Paul and I kept our senses alert, hoping not to be caught by surprise. Near the end of the fourth day, we began seeing boot prints in the snow and then a telltale smoke cloud rising into the blue sky some distance ahead. We were riding through a matchstick forest of barren trees and hilly rock outcrops. Paul called out, "We have company ahead on our right."

"We should dismount; less threatening," I suggested. No sooner had we done so than I spied several men moving rapidly away from us. Obviously, their task was to alert the town in advance. "Okay, let's wait here for them. They've obviously seen us, and we, them. I don't want to seem threatening in any way. We ought to act like guests and wait for them to make the first move."

The highlanders were a bit edgy and kept their hands upon their sword hilts, as prepared for trouble as I would let them be. About an hour later, we spied a column of men, two abreast, battleaxes in hand, rushing through the snow. As they drew closer, the column split, one encircling us on their right, the other circling around us on the left. Several highlanders made drawing motions with their swords, so I had to calm their fears and nerves. This had to be a parley not a fight. I had the flagman wave the white flag a bit. I found it difficult to tell which of the fifty men was their leader. I held my hands up non-threateningly and looked about, calling out "Leader? Wish to speak to your leader."

Even though the burly men made occasional threatening or taunting gestures with their bodies and huge battleaxes, we made no move to draw our weapons. Finally, one man wearing a helm, which had a large set of horns adorning it, or should I say protruding out from it, took a small step forward. I squared to face him. "Greetings from southern West Reach. We come in peace. I have a profitable deal for you. I wish to discuss it with whoever is your town leader. My name is Ket Bethany Amir, King of Nuadilan and Amathon down in the Layamon region, four days from here, down south. My Volksholm speech is not good. Do you understand any of what I am saying?"

The tall, heavyset man replied cautiously, "Aye, I understand you sort of — your speech is worse than a child's. I am Lief Elverun. Peace. You don't look threatening; tis folly to attack us with so few men. There was one called Ket Bethany in d'Grange."

"That's me. I returned to West Reach a month ago," I answered, since it sounded very hopeful that my name was known to him. Memories flashed in my mind of when I had sailed out from Fortress d'Grange and erected giant walls of flame to stop a fleet of Axeman supply ships from bringing supplies to their forces who were threatening the Fortress.

"Show me your hair," he ordered. Quickly, I pulled off my fur hat, revealing my extremely long red ponytail.

Lief laughed, "Aye, thee must be the same woman-man. Okay, follow me, but do not try anything. My men will not hesitate to attack you." I nodded and began to follow him, leading my horse. After an hour of trudging through the deep snow, I appreciated the easy ride that we had had getting here. As the sun set, the men lit torches, and we continued marching nearly due east. Another two hours and the sounds of a large town could be heard clearly in the cold clear air.

Soon we were marched down a long, muddy street with huge log cabins lining either side. Long houses, they were called, holding perhaps twenty men each. Everywhere, Axemen came out of their homes to stare at this spectacle trudging through their streets. We gave them something to discuss this evening. We halted before one somewhat larger building. Lief knocked and said something to whoever opened the door. Next, the door opened wide and another large man stood framed in the doorway, illuminated by oil lamps from within. He looked like a mountain of a man, very imposing, though I suspect this was his intention.

"I am known as Red Eric, leader of New Holm, our town here. I understand you speak our language crudely."

"Yes, just don't talk too fast," I replied. "I am Ket Bethany and I would like to talk with you about something that would be profitable to both of us, if I may."

"Take them to the guest lodge and feed them," Red ordered and motioned for me to follow him inside his cabin. Paul desperately wanted to follow me, but decided that he ought to remain with Fergus and the others, just in case they encountered some trouble. It was a tough call for Paul, our Protector, to make, since his primary goal was to protect me, their Wid.

I'd never been inside one of the long houses of the Axemen, and I found this very interesting indeed. In the center, a large blaze provided both heat and cooking facilities. Crude log chairs encircled the fire, and we sat on a pair close to the fire. I quickly took off my winter furs, either that or sweat to death. In one corner were cooking utensils and a pantry, or what I assumed was a pantry. Most of the space within the cabin held the sleeping quarters for a number of people. I spied several women cleaning up dishes from the evening meal. All stared at my long, red hair. Red produced a mug of hot ale for each of us and said, "So what is this deal that has brought you into the bear's den?" I could see why he was called Red; though he boasted typical blonde, long hair and beard, his face was very ruddy in color.

"I have recently become king of a small kingdom in northern Layamon. We have two large towns with about," here I ran into major language troubles. I did not know the word for thousand or hundred. Knowing only their word for ten, I had to sketch out the equivalent of fifteen thousand in tens! After five frustrating minutes, he finally grasped the magnitude and taught me their word for a thousand. Whew! Meanwhile, everyone else in the cabin was guffawing at me, rightly so. I must have sounded like an idiot to them.

"Yes, we have fifteen thousand people. Last year their king led all available younger men off to a war and lost. None returned, thousands of our prime men were killed. Ours is a town of mostly women and old men and children." Now they really laughed, I caught some catcalls of "king of women" coming from their women folk. Then, I got my shock of the night.

"You really need to learn our language better; you speak worse than a four year old!" Red chuckled, using our language! He could see the surprise on my face, and added, "I let you struggle just to see how you did. I've picked up your language better than you have ours. Let's continue in yours." He didn't have to ask twice!

"Thanks! Okay, the way I see it is this. You folks are here to stay. I know that in the past some neighboring kings have tried to force you off our island and failed utterly. I say, why not live together in peace? Our island is large enough for all of us." I watched his face closely for any indications that what I was saying was in anyway appealing to him. I thought I detected a flicker of keen interest. Hence, I continued.

"What I propose is this. We need plenty of good, strong, young men. I think that you probably have got far more men here than women. Perhaps some men with you would like to move inland, find a wife, and settle down. We have plenty of work available. We will guarantee any man a house and food for an entire year in exchange for their work. If any man and woman should fall in love and wish to marry, that is all the better and encouraged — but both the man and woman must desire the marriage. All will be granted citizenship in our kingdom. I see no reason that we could not establish a strong trading arrangement between your town here and ours. We are mostly an agricultural and hunting people, so perhaps such a life may not suit many of your men. We can supply you with grain and wool for example. We need metal farming instruments and woodworking tools, such as axes to chop down trees with which to build houses. Oh yes, I will also see that any man who comes is paid honestly and fairly for his work. However, while in our kingdom, they must obey our rules and decrees."

"Ah but inland. What about all the other kingdoms through which we must pass? Will we not be attacked?"

"Good point. If for the time being we always travel a route through the highlands to get to my kingdom, I believe I can arrange for safe passage, especially if some highland cavalrymen accompany you. That's one reason I brought a small group with me. If this venture is successful and some of your men like our lifestyle, I believe that other kingdoms will join in and cease being warlike to your people. For my money, there has already been far too much bloodshed on both sides."

"Words are all well and good, but you have no army with which to back up your promises you make here," he replied.

"You speak the truth. I do not at this moment in time. Eventually, I will have some forces for our defense only. However, at the moment, I have only my close friends to help me enforce it." I had to relay the truth of the matter.

He laughed once more. "Ket, you are being honest with me. I like that in leader. Perhaps I know more about you than you do me." I wondered what he meant by that. He continued very seriously, "If you are who you say you are, then you and your friends carry a force worth that of an army. So I must ask you to prove who you are. Make the Fire of the Gods for me; show me that you are the Ket Bethany and that your words can be backed up by force."

Now I knew what he meant, he wanted me to bring down fire or conjure it. I knew I would have to do this or he would not trust me at all, and the deal would be rejected. "Right here inside your cabin?" I asked.

"Yes, unless it would burn down my cabin. Perhaps outside would be better. I am partial to my house. I assume that the friends of which you speak can also make the Fire of the Gods?"

"Yes, all of us can, but we only use it in self-defense." That was not completely the truth, however. As we walked outside into the chilly night air, I sensed that this man was a leader who respected other leaders that were both honest and strong. I decided to play another card. "One of my friends is with me, here he comes outside now. I have already asked him to also make the Fire of the Gods for you."

"How can this be? You have not talked with him. You arranged this before hand?"

"No, I just now asked him. We can communicate across any distance with our minds." I thought that detail would give him something further to think about, while we were making fires appear. I noticed that a rather large number of men and women had stepped outside to watch the display. Proof, they wanted proof; we gave it to them. Suddenly two sheets of fire appeared at opposite ends of the street. Slowly we moved them closer together, intertwined their streaking tendrils and formed them into a large circle, stretched them high into the sky, and shrunk them down small before we let the fires die out. After a stunned silence, the watchers began to clap, slowly at first and then a roaring round, filled with cheering. Paul turned around and went back inside the guesthouse, all without me uttering a single word to him, a fact not missed by Red.

As we entered, Red heartily slapped me on the back, nearly knocking me over, but I regained my footing and smiled as broadly as he did. "Thee be the Ket Bethany. I will talk to my people tonight and let you know in the morning. How soon do you want them?"

"I'd like to escort as many as want to try it out when I return. Sooner the better. We need many strong men at the moment." We shook hands, his was more like a vice grip, and I joined the others in the guesthouse.

"Well, laddie? How did it go? We saw the magical fires. That must have impressed them," Fergus spoke up first.

"He knew about the fires and me from when I stopped the ships just off Fortress d'Grange. Evidently, I have made an indelible impression on these Axemen." We chatted for a while, but soon the warm ale took its toll, and we all turned in for the night. Fergus insisted on posting a guard; he still did not trust them and feared our throats might be cut as we slept. He was probably right. However, nothing happened.

The next morning we were served some breakfast, and then Red joined us. "If you can delay your return by one day, I think that a hundred young men will join you. However, I wish to add a stipulation. If some do not like it in your towns, you will return them here safely personally or perhaps with one of your 'friends.' Is that acceptable to you?"

I could not conceal my feelings. "Terrific! May this be the start of a long, rewarding friendship! You have my word that those who wish to return will be brought back here safely by me or my friends."

"Good. It is done then. Come spring when the Sea God permits boats to travel in his domain once more, many more young men may want to join up," Red said the magical words I wanted to hear.

"Good," I replied. "We can take at least a thousand men." I smiled using his word I learned painstakingly last night for "thousand." We laughed. The day passed idly as Red insisted we stay indoors in their guesthouse. He obviously did not want us getting a clear picture of their entire town and its defenses, naturally.

The next day at dawn we set out, one hundred young men formed up into a paired column, their standard marching order. Each man carried a heavy sack with all his possessions as well as food supplies. Once out of their immediate portion of the forest, we all passed the time by learning the other's language. This turned out to be a fun game for everyone, including the highlanders.

That night, Paul commented to Fergus and me, "You know, Ket, your scheme is brilliant. Once everyone knows that we are home to Axemen, others will think twice about attacking us."

Fergus added, "Aye laddie. Everyone knows that one Axeman is better than ten of our fighters are. So you see these hundred are equivalent to a thousand of our footmen."

I smiled and teased, "You both see through me. There is a method in my madness. Yes, I considered this aspect before I made my decision. However, I point out that if they are divided evenly between the two towns, fifty Axemen are not going to be able to withstand an attack by several thousand. No, my friends, this is just a start, but a good one, nevertheless."

Further, as we passed through each of the highlander towns and thus kingdoms, Fergus and I explained to each king that these Axemen were now citizens of Nuadilan and under the jurisdiction of Queen Caitlyn Amir. My reasoning was two-fold. I wanted to lessen any chance that we or they would be attacked en route, and I wanted to begin to spread the word that our kingdom was home to Axeman fighters. I also knew that I was stirring up a hornet's nest of protests, but for the sake of peace and our survival, it had to be done.

By the time that the week's travel was done and we arrived back home, all of us spoke the basics of the other's language. Yes, there were many cultural difficulties as you may well imagine, but in the end, it did indeed work out for the best. At first, the women in our towns looked upon these big men as barbarians, but that attitude changed rapidly as these men began doing the necessary heavy work, such as building up a huge supply of firewood and bringing in fresh meat. By the end of summer, none of these men had left and all ended up finding a loving wife.

We also discovered that the posters were also having an effect. During the two weeks Paul and I were gone over a hundred young men from the nearby towns came by to explore the possibilities offered. They saw an excellent opportunity and stayed on as well. Hence, early February of 623 saw the first of the integration of the Axemen into our population here on Cymry.

When we arrived back in Nuadilan, I was surprised and grateful to see that our Great Hall was nearly empty once more. All the sick and injured had been healed sufficiently and had returned to their own homes. Now it was back to problem solving once again.

The next day, Allan took me aside, "Bethany, there is something that you just *have* to see. I went out on a hunting party while you were gone, helping to bring in some fresh meat. I would not have believed it if I had not seen it with my own eyes."

"Okay, okay," I replied, "what was it?"

"I watched Leane Finn bring down a deer with one arrow shot." He paused, adding emphasis. "She was at least two hundred ten yards away when she let it fly! That's at least a hundred feet beyond the absolute maximum range that any bow I have ever seen could shoot an arrow. Leane claims she can shoot even farther, but not accurately. One shot, Bethany, one shot from six hundred-fifty feet away!"

"Incredible, that must be a super powerful bow, really big or what?"

"Leane says that her late husband, Raghnall Finn, developed a new kind of bow. He called it the longbow, special wood and construction. Unfortunately for us, Raghnall was killed during that war; he never came back. But Leane learned how to make them and has been making some longbows in her spare time. She is quite the archer, though she claims that several other women around here are better marksmen than she. Come, you have got to meet her; she is in Amathon."

An hour later, Paul, Allan, and I rode into Amathon. Allan led me to her home-shop. She and her late husband had a combined home, workshop, and storefront where he used to sell his bows. Leane was gluing feathers onto a pile of arrows when we entered. The smell of the warm glue permeated the shop. "Sire!" a startled Leane exclaimed when she saw us and got up to curtsey to me and nearly knocking the glue pot off her table in her haste to greet her king properly.

Leane was around twenty-five, tall and sinewy. She wore a leather outfit, which nearly matched her shoulder length brown hair. Wide blue eyes greeted me and I could not help noticing her long thin fingers. She reminded me of a willow, supple and graceful, but she was not particularly comely.

Allan broke the silence, "Leane, I've been telling Ket about your bow and its capabilities. One shot brought down that deer. Ket, it was a head shot too. You should have seen it." She flushed, unused to having this much attention on her archery skills.

"Do you usually make such shots?" I asked, suspecting one lucky day for her.

"Aye, My Lord. Meat's better," was her reply. I looked confused and she explained further. "If an animal is scared and in fear when you shoot it, the meat always has a slightly bitter taste. If you take it when it doesn't know death is coming, the meat tastes much better. Hence, I always shoot from extreme distances so that it does not feel threatened and thus not sour the meat."

"Interesting, Leane, I must admit that I did not know this detail, one well worth remembering indeed." Proudly, Leane showed me her bow, which was nearly as tall as she.

"Raghnall made this one for me as a wedding present. Those over there are the ones I have made. I am still learning how to do it right, I am afraid my bows are not quite up to Raghnall's quality yet. Do you want to try one out? I have a range out back." I could not resist trying it, though I am not skilled at all with a bow.

She handed us each a bow and she brought hers along with a quiver of arrows. Behind her store, she had an archery practice range setup. The stockade wall would prevent any stray arrows from harming others beyond her range. "There's the target stuck on that bale of straw way down there close to the wall. If you hit the wall, the arrow will probably shatter, so try not to hit the wall, please." We were some six hundred feet at least from the target, which seemed impossibly small to my eyes. While we all strung our bows, I knew I didn't have the faintest chance of hitting the target from this distance; heck, I could barely see it!

"Like this," Leane said softly. She notched an arrow, drawing back the bow slowly. I could see that she made good use of her back muscles, not just her arms. She had the bow pointed directly at the target. Then in a swift movement, she raised it up in about a forty-five degree angle from the ground and let it fly. Twang! I watched in amazement as the arrow flew true, thudding solidly into the center of the target.

"Wow! Great shot!" I exclaimed and meant it. Impressed I was!

"Not really," she replied. "Raghnall could hit it from seven hundred feet away. I am not accurate beyond about six hundred fifty feet." I could tell she really felt the loss of her husband still. "Go ahead, let one fly."

"Is there any chance that I can miss and send it over the wall? I don't want to accidentally shoot someone."

"None, not from this distance." So I drew the bow back, emulating her motions. Twang. I watched in amazement as my arrow arced high and then came down somewhere close to the straw bale. Paul had to try next as did Allan. Paul, a Protector, was very familiar with short bows and his shot at least hit the bale. Enthused, Paul let fly another six arrows and had two actually hit the target, at least the outer edge of the target.

"You are pretty good with a bow," Leane complimented him.

"This is one incredible bow, Leane! Do you have any for sale?" When we left, Paul had purchased one along with a quiver of arrows.

Just then, her three children came outside. Since we finished shooting, Leane motioned to them, and they ran to retrieve the arrows. Once they gaily returned them to her, they scampered off to play in the snow. We went back inside. An idea was forming in my mind.

"Leane, how many of these long bows are there in both towns? Or do you know?"

"Only twenty remain, the others went off to war and never came back. Six hunters in Nuadilan have them, while twelve here in Amathon use them, including me. I've got twelve in my shop I can sell, but business has been slack, if you know what I mean," she replied.

"Okay, how long does it take to make one and how many longbow makers do we have between the two towns?" I asked, my plan was expanding by the minute. Paul suddenly saw where I was heading with this.

"Oh, I usually spend a week or so on one. Only me," she answered, with a note of curiosity in her voice.

"Could you teach others to make longbows?" I continued.

"Sure, but why? I cannot sell those I have already made," she answered, still perplexed.

"Suppose that the towns are being attacked. What would happen if we had hundreds of these bows and plenty of arrows? Women could stand in groups behind our outer walls and let them fly, beginning at maximum range, firing blindly over the walls. A rain of arrows hits our attackers. Even if they run to the walls, they are going to get dozens of arrows flying about them all the way. Let's say that the archers can get off a dozen arrows a minute, then that will make a murderous run to the walls, eliminating a good number of our attackers before they can really attack us. Accuracy is not an issue, firing speed and range is all that matters in making a rain of arrows."

Her eyes shone brightly as she grasped my plan. "A hundred archers equal over a thousand arrows in that minute. A thousand archers, well, it's mind boggling! I sure would not want to charge the walls with that many arrows filling the air." Hope of her own defense blazed from her eyes and face; hope for the survival of her children was uppermost in her mind.

"Paul, Leane, your assignment is to first find the most likely people to learn bow making from Leane. Next, get all out production going, top priority. As the bows and arrows become available, form up squads of women, say in groups of twenty-five. Train them to loosen as many arrows as possible in the shortest amount of time at the required ranges. It is a rain of death we are after, not shooting at one particular target. Leane, you are going to become very wealthy. I will see to it that you are paid nicely for all the bows and arrows you can make. If there is anything you need or any problems arise, if Paul cannot get them solved at once for you, just come and see me! I don't think that we will be facing an attack until spring has come, so we have some time to get this project going full blast!"

Allan and I returned to Nuadilan, leaving Paul and Leane to begin planning. As a footnote, within one year, Leane Finn became the most famous longbow maker in all Cymry, well respected and wealthy as well. Our meager defenses were beginning to take shape, if only we had enough time before the attacks.

Chapter 5 An Unexpected Visitor

Late February, a singular event occurred, one wholly unexpected. Midmorning, a gate runner, a young lad of twelve, came running breathlessly into our complex, demanding to see me on urgent business at the gate. "It must be important," I stated the obvious when he was brought before me.

"Yes, sir. Gate man Bill told me to rush and fetch you right away. A large cavalry force is at the northern gates asking to see you. You must come at once!" He was quite excited. From our hilltop location, we can see down to all the gates. The lad pointed out the long line of mounted soldiers halted before our northern gate. A quick estimate yielded at least fifty. Quickly, Paul and I headed on down to the gate, while the others began to implement security measures. Surely, this was not an attack, but Caitlyn preferred to be prepared in any case.

A few minutes later, Paul and I reached the gate. The leader of the cavalry dismounted as we walked up to Bill, who stood squarely in the middle of the entrance, as if the presence of his body would somehow stop the advance of these cavalry, should they chose to enter anyway.

"Hello, I am Ket Bethany Amir and my friend Paul. How can we help you?" I broke the silence, amid snorts and puffs of the medium warhorses. Obviously, they had been ridden at a good pace very recently. Definitely, these were fighting men. All wore expensive chain mail over their winter furs, along with metal helms over their hats. So bundled up from the cold were they that I could not really identify who they might be. Sword scabbards hung at their sides, heavy crossbows hung from their pummels, daggers strapped to the outside of each boot. Definitely armed for a conflict I concluded.

The imposing figure who stood before me was nearly indistinguishable from the others, save for a shinier helm and perhaps a better set of mail. This soldier had muscles of which any man would have been proud to display, at least twice the thickness of my own arms! I could not help noticing the ornate talisman hanging from a chain around the soldier's neck. I'd never seen such a talisman before, intertwining snakes, which appeared to be in the process of devouring each other. The alto voice spoke startling me, for a woman's voice I was not expecting. This imposing fighter standing before me was indeed a woman! "Hail King Ket Bethany Amir. I am called King Lachlan Laird of Brea, Highlands of Ruadan."

No doubt about her origin, her thick highlander accent reminded me instantly of Fergus and his father, the King of Aine. "I have come seeking a private audience with you Sire. Grant me several hours of your time. Please," she added this last as an afterthought. I gathered at once that she was not used to having her orders and requests questioned or not instantly followed. "And can my warriors be housed at an inn tonight while we discuss important matters? We have traveled long and swiftly this day." Again, I detected that she added that last to help smooth over her abrupt request.

"Yes, to both," I replied. Turning to Bill, I asked, "Bill, have we got an inn that can accommodate this many at one time?" I know that it did not give a good impression; the king did not even know the state of his own kingdom's inns! Yet, it could not be avoided. I had no idea about our inns.

Stretching himself up to his full height, displaying some importance, Bill replied, "Aye Sire, the Pig's Head ought to satisfy them. I'll have me lad here show them the way." The young lad's face now took on that look of "I am doing something really important!"

I smiled, "Okay, that's settled. King Laird, if you will follow me. You may prefer to ride, however; the streets are a bit messy with the snow and mud." She nodded and remounted, following Paul and myself as we wandered the streets, slowly heading up the hill.

"Good defensive move, having concentric stockades with gates at ninety degree angles from each other. The enemy cannot breach one and charge on up the hill," she complimented me.

I instinctively answered without thinking, "Yes, these gates here saved my life one time long ago." I recalled the time last lifetime when Sarah had come running into our house in a panic, telling me that a Grey Creature had just entered the main gate and was looking for me. I grabbed a few things, mounted my horse, and made a hasty exit. By the time the Grey Creature discovered I had just left, he could not get through the maze of streets and gates fast enough to catch me. Of course as I said this, I instantly regretted it and hoped that this King would not press me on this statement. Thankfully, she did not. I was not facing her and did not see the fleeting, strange look upon her face in reaction. Paul, however, did.

At last, we passed through the last gates and onto the hilltop. "Remy can stable your horse, if you like," I said as our stableman walked over to join us.

She handed him the reins, saying, "Just loosen the cinch, give him some water, but leave him tacked." Sam acknowledged her orders and she followed us to the front door. Just inside, Paul and I took off our muddy boots, sticking them off to one side. She looked at us with a questioning look.

"Oh, we don't want to spread mud all through the house. Just thinking of our staff. No need to make them clean up after us. You don't have to bother. Your boots are not muddy. This way." She gave me another stare, as if to say, "They are just staff. It is their job."

Since she was in full armor and with full winter gear, I suggested, "Here, you may stay in the guest room. I suspect you will want to take off some of your stuff. If you need anything, just give a holler. One of the staff will be nearby. When you are freshened up, I'll meet you in the Great Hall. Someone will show you the way. Acceptable?" She nodded and marched into the small guest room. I was now very glad that Caitlyn had insisted upon us keeping one room available for surprise visitors. Paul and I went to tell the others about our visitor; we found them all gathered in the Great Hall, weapons at hand.

After I explained who our guest was, Caitlyn became flustered. "Oh dear. Visiting king. Now what am I supposed to do? I think I am supposed to greet the king by sitting on the throne. Golly, where has that crown gotten to? Dear me, I am supposed to offer them something to drink. Should it be ale, hot mead, wine? I've forgotten. I don't have my fancy queen dress on, oh dear, what will the king think of us? What are we supposed to do now? Ket, you are supposed to sit on the big throne here, and I sit here. Where will the rest of you sit?" She would have gone on and on; I intervened.

"Caitlyn!" I said sharply and with full attention. Indeed, my communication did pierce through her confusions. She stopped abruptly. "Everything is fine, my dear. This is not a formal state meeting. She has just ridden long and hard to get here, and she just wants a private meeting is all. Now think: if you had just come in from a long, cold ride, what would you want?"

"Oh that's easy," she said, back to her normal self. "I'd want a warm fire and some tea and biscuits. I'll send for them at once. Why don't you all stoke the fire a bit? It's kind of chilly in here." She headed off to the kitchen to order up some refreshments. Dutifully, I added a few more logs to the fire, bemusing the fact that I had just spent so much effort in cutting the wood and it burned up so quickly. It did not seem at all fair. Paulette, our Communicator, who knew my thoughts, just chuckled.

A short while later, King Lachlan Laird entered. Tea was on the table along with biscuits a plenty; the fire crackled. The eight of us were sitting around the giant table close to the fire. She had removed her armor and winter clothes. Lachlan now wore an expensive leather shirt and pants, with matching soft boots. That same talisman was still around her neck, resting upon her full, rather well developed bosom. She had long blonde hair, which she had obviously just brushed out. A small gold crown band with several sparking gems held her hair in place. She had deep blue eyes and a healthy complexion. As tall as me, she weighed significantly more than I did, and it was all muscle. Even her legs were thicker than mine were. Thankfully, she carried no visible weapons on her person.

Quickly I spoke up, "Everyone, this is King Lachlan Laird of Brea in the Highlands of Ruadan. King Laird, this is the real ruler here, Queen Caitlyn Amir. These are my very close friends, inseparable companions. Come; please have a seat with us. Help yourself to some hot tea and biscuits. If you are hungry, we can send for something more substantial."

"Interesting," she commented. "Not the Royal Court that I expected. Tea and biscuits will do fine. Queen Caitlyn," she bowed before her and took a seat near the fire. I detected that Caitlyn was about to have another bout of "Now I am supposed to's." She observed that Laird was wearing a crown, and she had failed to think of finding hers and putting it on, let alone one for me, though she knew she would be hard pressed to get me to don a crown, even in the most formal setting.

After sipping a bit of tea, Lachlan said dryly, "I specifically requested a private meeting with you, King Ket. While your friends might be inseparable, I would formally request they separate at this time."

Chuckling, I replied, "Okay, okay. Not a problem. Gang, carry on." My Circle grinned at me as they got up to leave, and Paulette sent me mentally, *Have fun with this tough cookie!*

When they had left, Lachlan seemed still uneasy. "Perhaps I do not understand the rule here in this kingdom. I was led to believe that Ket was the king."

"Well, actually the throne is really Caitlyn's, as she has the ancient bloodline. Even though we are married, I feel that this is her kingdom to rule. However, to the outside world, I may be King Ket Amir; internally, she has the throne. I really do not want to be a king."

"Ah, I see, she runs things within the kingdom and you handle the external world. Makes sense, I can see that she is not a fighter and could not stand in battle if needed. Okay then, I need to talk to you Ket, privately, about the external world. Would you excuse us for a while, Your Highness?" Though phrased as a question, Caitlyn took it as an order. Although I could tell that she was very curious about our new guest, she was more than willing to leave us alone.

Instead of being an awkward situation, Caitlyn gaily said, "No problem. I have lots to do for the towns. I will leave you two to chat as you want. If you need anything, just give a holler. I'll make sure you are not interrupted." She bowed to our guest and swiftly left the Great Hall, defusing what could have been an iffy situation.

Once we were alone and the doors shut, I poured myself some more tea and sat down across from her. "Well, King Lachlan Laird of Brea in the Highlands of Ruadan, you definitely have my curiosity aroused. I must admit that I have not heard of either you or your town of Brea. I mean no insult; I grew up on the southern coast of Tewdwr and later traveled up the central portion of the highlands with Fergus d'Aine. I've been all over the mainland, and I am very familiar with those lands. So I am all ears, but I will admit that I thought all kings were men. I didn't know that women could also be kings. Shows you how little I know about such matters."

"No apology needed. I did not expect that you would know me or my kingdom, though had you known, perhaps this meeting would be easier. A king is one who rules and governs their lands. For a woman, I have found that it takes fighting strength to command the allegiance and respect of men. Brea is our largest town, located near the Ath mountains, just south of the valley of the standing stones. We are about twenty thousand strong."

"Hold on a minute." Seeing her startled look, I quickly added, "I assume it is all right for me to interrupt you." Seeing no protest on her part, I asked, "Standing stones. Fergus and I camped out one time in a deserted valley that had these ancient stones arranged in a circle. Is this the place you mentioned or is it a different place?"

"Ah, then you have indeed been a stone's throw from Brea. Yes, my kingdom lies just south of that mystic place. My line traces its ancestry back to the makers of the stones in the distant past. It is a holy place, a valley of immense spiritual power, held sacred by those of my line. I am the bearer of the Holy Talisman of the Annwn. The bearer is also the King of Brea, according to our customs. I am its keeper until my death."

From my point of view, things just got a whole lot more interesting. Remember that I am a Wid by nature. That some of my questions about these standing stones might be answered through Lachlan excited me greatly. We druwids use the standing stones for our ceremonies, though we do not know their origin. However, last year, I also discovered that our druwid spells cast while within these standing stones had their power and impact more than doubled. Further, I had detected strange lines of force emanating and flaring out from these circles. I wanted to know more.

Lachlan continued, though she did notice my intense curiosity. "The talisman gives me the ability to foresee the immediate future. Yes, I am well known in Brea as a Seer and highly respected as well, though you will have to take my word for that detail at this point. I am thirty-three years old and the bearer of the sacred talisman for the last twenty. In the twenty years, my visions have never been wrong, though several times I did misinterpret them, mostly when I was a young girl — in my own defense, mind you. I foresaw the devastating battle on the plains of Layamon last year, in which so many young men died. Your wife's father was one of them. Yes, my guards and I were there, observing from a distance. I always want to see if my visions are true. Never have I witness such a brutal, wholesale slaughter of men. And for what? Nothing."

"Then, on New Year's Day, I had the most powerful vision ever. I foresaw things that I could not imagine could happen or were real, unless. . ." Her voice fell to a whisper and failed altogether. I thought that was at least a nice effect, I was utterly spellbound, enchanted, dying to hear the rest.

"Unless. . ." I encouraged her, but she did not finish her thought.

"Since then, I have followed that path as foreseen. Thus far, everything has gone just as the visions have shown, but I am now entering the strangest portion of the visions. I do not have words for some of the things that I have seen." If she had been a salesperson, I was completely sold. I just had to hear her out!

"I will give you the broad vision first and then some of the details, King Ket Bethany Amir, if that is who you really are. In the not so distant future, all the Kings of Cymry will be united together in a Grande Council of Kings. I will be the first Council Leader, who is to preside over the meetings. The purpose of the Grande Council of Kings is to ensure that peace and cooperation exists throughout all Cymry. In short, no more devastating wars. The Council shall settle matters of disagreement between kingdoms peacefully. If we are ever attacked by outsiders, the Council will act as a unified group instead of isolated kingdoms or simply towns with their earls and dukes as it used to be a number of years ago. Is this not indeed a grand purpose, one worthy of all kings?"

How could I not agree? "Absolutely. The problem with having all these independent kingdoms is the continual strife between them. Peer pressure from all the other kings ought to put a solid damper on further aggression, I would think. Yet, mere words may not be enough, the Council ought to be able to back up its rulings as needed, don't you think?" I tossed it back into her court.

She smiled, "Yes, you responded exactly as you did in my vision. Interesting."

That was definitely not what I had expected her to say! Not letting her know my surprise, I rapidly continued my train of thought. "What happens if you only get, say half, of the kings to join this Council?"

"If the visions are true, they all will join, though slowly at first. Yet, in the end, all will agree. Following the course laid out in my visions, I have been contacting my peers. I have tentative agreements from all the Highland kings. They will join if the vision is fulfilled. I have traveled throughout Tewdwr. As you know, they have no set kingdoms or kings. Yet, the ten major towns have agreed to join, sending their town leaders to sit as kings on the Council. I found the folks in Tewdwr very willing to support the idea of the Grande Council. They've suffered greatly from Layamon raids and land confiscations during the last few years. The loss of Cuch Glen was only the first of these." My heart ached at the sudden memories of that ill-fated day; once more, I relived watching my parents dying at the hands of the cavalry from southern Layamon.

She continued, "However, and this is a very big stipulation, initially this Council will only work if it has a powerful, strong Council Leader, one who can back up her decisions with the requisite force as required. The visions show that I am the one to lead, but only if the *magician* stands at my side. Without the magician and his magical powers, the entire vision fades into chaos and nothingness. This magician, then, is the ultimate key to the success or failure of the Grande Council of Kings of Cymry and ultimately to the peace of our island and its people."

After a pause, she stared intensely at me, eye to eye, "In the visions, I know not his name, only what he looks like and what he has done, though the places I see in the visions I know not." Again, she paused, watching my reactions closely. I said nothing and did not react visibly, but I began to have a sneaking suspicion where this was headed.

"Since obtaining this magician is the key to the entire success of the Grande Council, I will do something that I have only done once before. When I was younger, I shared the talisman and vision with my youngest brother. I wanted to prevent his death, you see. I thought that by showing him what would happen if he followed the course he was planning, then he would change and avoid it. Even though he saw what I saw, he declared that he could change the future and avoid it. He did not listen to me and died just as we foresaw in the vision. Will you allow me to show you the visions and the magician who is so utterly pivotal and vital?"

How could I refuse? I had so many questions that needed answering and a lot of them centered on this talisman and her visions. Was she truly seeing the future or just an invented one, one that her mind created which she then believed utterly and carried out actions to bring it about? "Certainly you may," was my brief reply.

"Thank you, Sire. I usually do this lying in bed. It can be utterly disorienting to the senses. Please stand up and put one hand firmly on the table." I did as instructed and she came around to my side, facing me. The talisman was on a long chain. Carefully, she leaned close to me and put the chain around my neck as well as hers. She put her hand firmly on the table as well. "Okay, all you have to do is relax and the visions will come. Do not be alarmed, they are only visions. If you cannot face the visions, you only need to call out and I will cause them to cease at once. Do you understand these orders?"

I felt like a little kid, but I said that I did. "Wait a second before you begin. Can you control what visions we will see?"

"I can cause to be replayed any vision that I have seen. I cannot determine when I will see a new one, if that is what you desire to know." She added with a coy smirk, "You will easily recognize the magician of which I speak when you see him. Now close your eyes and relax."

I did so. Okay, I admit that it took me a minute to let go of the scent of this woman's body so close to mine, the thoughts of her large bosom, the scent of her hair, the slight bulge in my pants. I did relax and let go all mental thoughts. Suddenly my space seemed to swirl and twist; I could not tell up from down, spatial orientation went haywire. Only the firm grip of my hand kept me from falling down. I knew now why she preferred to do this laying down.

Out of the swirling mist a vision of the world appeared. I heard my body intake a gasp of surprise. Heart Break Hill. There I was last year at that incredible battle. Hundreds of Axemen were storming up the steep sides of this heart-shaped hill. Lenkova and some fifty of her Sisterhood fighters were attempting to defend it, along with myself and my Guardian companions, Andre, Alton, Elona, and Waverly. There stood the seven standing stones, nearby was Caitlyn, Waverly, and Fergus readying the bandages for the expected wounded. It was if I was watching a movie recorded from a point high above the standing stones! At least that seemed to be the point of view of this scene. As I watched, slowly the Axemen crushed our defenses. I watched as one by one the Sisters were wounded and forced to retreat slowly back to the stones. Now we were entirely surrounded. My fellow Guardians were wounded. Then, I witnessed my insane lightning bolt attack. No wonder everyone thought I had gone completely insane, a crazy man. My eyes took on an unearthly look as bolt after bolt arced down, destroying the Axemen. The rain of devastation continued long after the last of the enemy was felled. I watched myself as I hit some of the bodies five times, dead five times over! Then, the image faded and the swirling, disorienting energy field flooded over me again.

Once more an image formed. Again, it was Heart Break Hill. There was Elona and myself. Ah, this was the day that we were experimenting. I watched as she and I explored the effect of casting our spells from within the standing stones. I saw again the radiating lines of energy that arced up high into the sky, eventually coming down into the center of another set of very distant standing stones. I heard myself say, "Perhaps this is an unknown force of Nature herself of which we know nothing about." Then the vision faded.

Shortly, another image played out in my mind. This time the perspective was more distant. I seemed to be looking from a vantage point high and behind the small bodies down below. It was that day in Fortress d'Grange when I paddled out onto the ocean and raised sheets of fire to stop the supply ships of the Axemen from sailing past d'Grange. I could see another set of standing stones that I did not know existed. There it was, nevertheless, high on the side of the mountain — further down its side lay the twin towers of d'Grange. Once more, the images faded and from a distance miles off an alto voice said, "You can open your eyes now."

I did so and tried to re-orient myself to the Great Hall and the "now." She carefully removed my head from the long chain, walked back to her seat across from me. I quickly sat down before my legs failed me. She looked me squarely in my eyes and asked, "Who are you, magician?"

My voice sounded distant and ethereal to me. "My god!" My shaking hand reached for some tea. Evidently, my reaction to the visions was not unexpected. She said nothing and allowed me to regain my senses before she repeated her exact question once more. I knew that she had to have an answer.

"That was utterly incredible and awfully humiliating. I really did look insane there didn't I? No wonder I scare my friends out of their wits when I do that! Okay, King Lachlan Laird of Brea, Seer and keeper of the sacred talisman. I am a Guardian, a druwid from the Greenway, originally, though my current body is of Tewdwr birth." I saw no reason to withhold the truth from this seer. "Let me explain more fully. We are all immortal spirits who are for a time inhabiting these fleshly bodies." I gave her my normal spiritual being presentation at this point.

"A very few of us are not pinned down inside of the body's head. As a result, though I do not know why, we seem to be more able. Anyway, a long time ago, a man called Alabaster Benjamin Crowley founded the druwids. To become one, we spend at least ten solid years in intensive study, which often takes the entire day. I want you to understand just how difficult and how hard we must study to become a druwid. Near the end of our studies, we begin to specialize in different areas in which we are most interested." I described the seven categories and their specialties: Protector, Judger, Planner, Loremaster, Healer, Communicator, and Wid. "I have been a Wid for three lifetimes now. I still am an avid seeker of knowledge and wisdom. I have this passion to know all about nearly everything, you see. As Guardians, we are organized into Circles. You have already met a complete Circle, my friends; we are the Cymry

Circle. We are the only Guardians on West Reach at the moment."

"What you saw in your visions actually did happen last year. The first one, that was at Heart Break Hill in northeastern Zargarb. Those were members of the Sisterhood, trying to stop the advance of some five hundred invading Axemen. Had they failed, the invaders would have sacked their safe haven, where all their young mothers and children were being raised in a safe place. Already these men had destroyed a more eastern village and had taken the survivors captive, marching them away into slavery. We rescued them, of course. Yes, we were outnumbered ten to one. You saw what kind of fighters these Sisterhood women actually are. They are the best I have ever seen. Still, fifty could not hope to stop five hundred. So I acted. We druwids command some of the forces of Nature. We can bring down fire, ice, and lightning, though I am ever partial to lightning. We can control the weather, if need be."

"The second one was where Elona and I suspected that these standing stones — which by the way are found all over the Greenway and which we consider as our sacred places, holding our religious ceremonies there — we suspected that at these standing stones our Nature spells were somehow being doubled in strength. That day we were experimenting and we saw those incredible lines of force radiating up and out. That such a force of Nature existed is unknown to us and I swore to learn more about it, though I must admit I have discovered nothing more about them. Evidently, we are the only ones to have discovered it."

"The last one was when we had returned to Fortress d'Grange, just across the waters that way. Some Axemen had invaded the Velona sector and these ships were bringing them the supplies that they needed to survive the winter in Velona. I stopped the ships without harming anyone. Later on, Elona was successful at integrating the Axemen into her sector. Those invaders are now active, productive members of Velona."

"So your visions are of what has happened, no doubt about that. By the way, all that I have told you is to be kept secret. We do not want to advertise our presence. We're here to guard, protect, help with constructions, settle disputes, and heal and comfort those in need. We only resort to using those spells that you have seen as a last resort when all else fails. Also, don't expect other druwids to launch lightning bolts quite like that. Only one other person can launch lightning bolts like I do."

"And yet you do not want to be king?" she replied in disbelief.

"Absolutely not. I am a Wid, a protector, a healer, not a king or ruler of men. I have not the slightest interest in such, a fact that dear Caitlyn has discovered. Unfortunately, since she has become the queen, it is being forced upon me. However, I am only performing such duties toward the outside world. Within this kingdom, Caitlyn alone rules. It is my fondest hope that once she gets the hang of it, she can take that aspect over as well."

Lachlan pulled on her hair while she listened intently to my explanation. Sensing that I had finished, she said determinedly, "I think that I shall still call you magician. It is as in my vision, then. Caitlyn will be sitting in the Council as king, while you will stand at my side as the magician. You will accept that role, will you not?" It was more of an order than a request; King Lachlan was comfortable in her role as supreme leader and not at all at ease in asking for help.

This was tricky; one cannot have two allegiances. Eventually they will collide. Diplomacy was Lilly Ann's specialty, not mine, but I did my best. "Look Lachlan, I am in complete agreement with your Grande Council of Kings. I'm sure that Caitlyn will be thrilled to be a member; you can count on that, though we must speak with her about it first. I'm sure she will agree. I am sure that you are aware that every king will first desire to do what he or she feels is in the best interests of their people. I assume that you have already taken that into consideration." She nodded that she had, so I continued, "Which brings us to my participation. My primary allegiance is to the Guardians, Caitlyn and her people, second. Thus, if I am your magician, you are third in line. Expect that some circumstances may arise where I will not do precisely as you might desire. Will that be a problem?" I put the ball back into her court.

"Are you saying that at the council meeting you might veto my orders before the other kings?" she protested, slightly antagonistically.

"No, that would not be honorable. If I should disagree, I will always discuss it with you beforehand, whenever possible. I do not intend to embarrass you in public. That would undermine your authority as Council Leader, and that would harm our overall goals considerably. Further, that we are actually Guardians, druwids from the Greenway, is to be our secret; just call us the magicians. In addition, my Circle must be told all about this. You see, even if I wanted to keep our discussion here today a secret from them, in all likelihood I would fail. We read each other's minds all the time."

Lachlan laughed in relief. "This I can live with! I half expected that I would have to give you half of my kingdom to get your participation. The fewer that know the true situation the better, especially among the kings. I will make no mention of the Guardians, just magician." She shook my hand solidly, sealing our deal.

"When do we start and what must I do?" I asked, just a little worried that I would suddenly have even more problems to solve.

"In due time. Do I call you Magician Ket Bethany Amir? That seems a little wordy."

"Hum, you realize that my identity is known only to some of the Amir kings and queens around here and in the Highlands? I'm sure that they will not talk openly about it. Best not use Amir."

"Agreed. Also, around here the locals seem to be worshiping one Bethany Madelyn Amir, the Blessed Holy Mother, I'm told. Perhaps it should just be Magician Ket?" she asked. "We don't want to be seen as favoring one religion."

"Magician Ket will do just fine." I still had no answer to when I would be required to begin my new duties as court magician.

"Good. Now the time for the Council is not yet at hand. I still have many other kings to get to agree to come on board. Further, one major vision has not yet occurred. It is that event that will finally bring the last holdouts into the Grande Council, but it will not occur for several months yet, if the vision is true. However, there is yet another matter I wish to discuss with you." She changed her voice tone to a serious mien. You do know that your towns are sitting ducks, ripe for attacks and plundering?"

"Of that I am acutely aware," I jested, making light of our dire plight. "I've brought a number of Axemen into our community and hope that more will join us later in the spring. You have undoubtedly seen my posters in the nearby towns of the Highlands asking for young men to come to our kingdom to seek their fortunes?" She nodded. "I know that the King of Aine will lend his support as will some of Caitlyn's cousins."

"It is a small step, but a sound one," Lachlan replied, adding, "You also know that your stockade walls are rotting and will not withstand an attack?"

"You don't miss anything!" I teased her playfully.

"Not if it has to do with fighting," she grinned back. Her face then got serious once more, "Look, when the battle comes call on me. I will be here in force to aid."

"Thanks, if and when any attack comes, we will be very grateful for all the support that we can get."

"One last thing, Magician Ket. Do you need a good, well-made sword? From all that I have learned about you, you do not have a sword. I can get you a Highland sword; they are of the very best quality to be found anywhere."

"Thanks for the offer. I do not have a sword nor do I want one. I just use my trusty pole." She looked aghast and baffled, so I added, "Look, over three lifetimes, I have spent a great deal of time and effort sewing up and tending sword slashes on my friends and companions. The world would be a far better place if swords did not exist. Besides, one on one, I have not yet met a person whom I could not disarm with my pole."

"You are a strange man, Magician Ket, I will say that. You have more the outlook of a woman than a man." My cheeks flushed slightly, and I hoped that she did not notice.

Hastily, I said, "Shall we bring the others back in here and explain everything to them? Also, will you stay the night with us before you hit the trail once more?"

"Aye, laddie, that we ought," she lapsed into the Highland accent once more. "I'd be honored to accept your hospitality and hope you will accept mine when you are in Brea later on."

Three minutes later, the others filed into the Great Hall, Caitlyn brought along more hot tea and biscuits with her. Everyone was exuding intense curiosity about our secret meeting. I took it upon myself to explain the salient portions of our discussion.

When I finished, Caitlyn gladly volunteered to join the Grande Council as the King of Nuadilan and Amathon. However, as expected, the members of my Circle were fascinated with the standing stones and asked numerous questions about them.

Lachlan explained that her people believed utterly that they were immortal beings, children of God, who were sent here to Cymry and housed in fleshly bodies that they might experience life and triumph over evil and hardship. Only by experiencing true life in totality could they hope to reach complete Purity of Being. These original ones called themselves the Annwn, meaning in part those spirits housed within mortal bodies. They believe that God is housed in every particle that makes up all life and the universe. When they succeed in experiencing life and achieve victory over evil and hardship, they believe that they then leave the fleshly bodies behind and move into the realm called Gwynfyd, a purely spiritual kingdom close to God. This is the primary circle in their ornamental motifs. The other circle, which intertwines in and out, above and below the circle of Gwynfyd, represents their lives, the Annwn, their ups and downs, their constant struggles to triumph over temptation and evil. Their decoration patterns began to make sense to us. These people celebrated their religious beliefs on their clothes and as decorations on virtually all things that they made. Even tables and chairs had similar hand carvings depicting this eternal challenge of life.

Further, I realized that Lachlan probably was optimistic that if she succeeded in her enormous quest with this Grande Council of Kings, she might be worthy of reaching the realm of Gwynfyd. Although I noticed that she, like we Guardians, resided outside of her body's head, she was only barely outside. I suspected that she might be disappointed later on when her body passed away, but I did not say anything.

Their legends told of the original making of the standing stones sometime in the far distant past. Lachlan was unable to quantify the years only that it was very long ago. During our discussions, Lachlan seemed quite surprised to learn that the stones were additionally an astronomical calendar. We promised to demonstrate how they worked at the next solstice or equinox.

Once the formalities were completed, she relaxed and began to enjoy our company. Indeed, she took pride in sharing what she knew about the standing stones. Most folks totally ignored the stones, as Fergus had once told me. Therefore, I knew Lachlan was truly elated to find others who appreciated them. Indeed, we all had a very enjoyable evening with her company.

Later that night when Caitlyn and I crawled playfully into bed, she whispered her exciting news into my ear, "You're going to be a father come harvest time!" We spent a very loving night in each other's arms, proposing various names for our baby. I could not have been happier.

Chapter 6 Interlude

The ruddy sun cast long shadows like grey rocky fingers as King Lachlan Laird of Brea, Seer and Keeper of the Sacred Talisman, rode into her main army's encampment high on a rocky ridge of the southern Highlands. Night chill created rising stream from the lathered horses as she and her small band dismounted before her main tent. Taryn Laird, her younger sister, and General Tiergan Doh stood before the opened flaps, awaiting Lachlan's arrival.

Barking a few orders to her men and giving her reins to her Captain, she followed the two into her battlefield tent. Quickly Lachlan began taking off her heavy outer clothes; then her chain mail armor. Taryn brought her a steaming cup of mead and the three sat down on logs, which served as chairs. Two smoky lanterns provided a dingy light as well as soot.

"Well, how did it go?" Taryn asked eagerly, unable to withstand the suspense any longer. "Did he accept? Is he with us?"

King Lachlan blew on the rising steam from the mug, took a tentative sip before replying. "Perfect, just perfect. In fact, far better than any of us imagined! He and his group are with us. We have our Magician of Power!" Her sister let out a cry of relief and excitement.

Sternly, General Tiergan asked, "Did you show him the images via the talisman?"

"Yes, that clinched it, just as you suggested," she replied.

Even more soberly, he asked, "And did you have to show him all the images?" emphasizing the word 'all.'

"He saw only the images that lead up to the formation of the Grande Council of the Kings of Cymry. He did not see the ultimate outcome of his actions."

"Ah, that is good. Had he seen how it will end for him, he might not have agreed," he commented dryly.

"You mean because it will lead to his death?" asked Taryn.

"Precisely. Would you freely join a group knowing that your involvement meant your eminent murder?" he replied. The young woman's face contorted in pain but only briefly.

"Did he wonder why the towns were not attacked last year right after the army was defeated? Or why the towns are facing an attack this spring?" the general asked.

"He suspects nothing. King Ket is just a young, immature kid," Lachlan explained. She took another sip of the warm mead. "However, he does possess the powers that we need. He is the magician in the visions. I think we will be able to bend him to our will. Any news from our spies? Have they picked a date yet for their attack on the two towns?"

"No Your Highness, no date as yet, but soon. All signs point to an early spring attack," the general replied. "Again, I caution you, take care around this magician. Looks can be deceiving. If he is the magician, he must be powerful."

"Stop worrying, I know how to handle men," Lachlan retorted, displaying a touch of annoyance in her voice. "Just be sure that we have plenty of the right witnesses present when the attack comes."

Chapter 7 Yet Another War

"My guess is that any attack ought to come after the spring planting is finished," Paul explained optimistically. Caitlyn and my Circle were conducting our weekly planning meeting, which always occurred the day after Caitlyn held her weekly Queen's Advisement Council. During her meetings, the elected two hundred representatives, mostly women of course, aired their local problems and concerns. Our task the next day was to find solutions to them. However, here in mid-April, all those that we could handle in short order had been solved, except of course the manpower shortage and the rebuilding of the walls and re-fortifying of the moat and baileys.

By now, five hundred or so men had taken our generous offer for resettlement in the two towns. Fully a hundred fifty more Axemen had come a few weeks ago. Between our two towns, we now boasted a little over two hundred fifty of these young, burly men from the far north. Thus far, they had merged into our communities fairly well, considering the extreme cultural and language difficulties. Indeed, ninety had already married and more than one woman was expecting another child later in the year.

Another two hundred men from nearby towns and villages had also come, bringing with them vital skills we were sorely lacking, particularly in the farming and husbandry trades. The Axemen proved excellent hunters and metalworkers. Overall, we felt that given time, things were looking far better than when we arrived.

With the coming of the spring thaw, Paul and Ben began taking lengthy rides, becoming familiar with all our adjacent lands. They were also taking a crude census. Obviously, should an attack come, there would be nothing that we could do to protect all the outlying settlements. Paul insisted that we have an accurate count. He also instructed each household to flee to the towns should they see the vanguard of any invading army coming their way.

Paul continued, "Look, if they do not get their crops planted, there will be no food for the coming winter. Only a fool would launch an attack before their life's blood is planted. Makes sense."

I could not help but remember my ill-fated attempts to reason with the insane King Randolf so many years ago. I took an arrow in my head and lost everything as a result. I replied, "War is basically insanity. You cannot reason with an insane man, I ought to know. Why should we count upon such a man being sane enough to wait until his crops are planted?"

"I agree with Bethany," Caitlyn added. "We need as much advance warning as we can possibly have. I can just feel it in bones; we are going to be attacked; I just know it. If they come marching into our lands, those in the farming houses out there, why, they might not get the chance to flee and warn us."

"Okay," Paul consented, "how about this idea. Outriders. I am confident the attack will come from the southern areas. North of us are the Highlanders, our friends. West lays Tewdwr, which does not seem to be the slightest threat. Why not send outriders patrolling our southern and eastern borders on a periodical basis? They could leave here heading west by south. Upon reaching our border, circumnavigate the whole southern border, returning from the east. That would be a good day's ride. We could send them out daily."

"What about enemy cavalry?" asked Lilly Ann, pulling her lip. Fighting wars was out of her line of training. She settled disputes peacefully.

"They would most certainly have cavalry with them. However, Lilly Ann, cavalry alone cannot take a fortified town. You need foot soldiers and battering rams to bust down the stockades. We ought to have at least a day's warning of an approaching army," Paul replied confident of his analysis. I was not so sure.

"What I'd like to know is will we be forced to defend both towns simultaneously or will they attack one town first?" broke in Allan.

"Ah, that is a really good question, Allan," Paul acknowledged. "I'd like to say that only one town will be attacked at a time. We could then pull all our defensive forces to one place and be twice as strong. On the other hand, if we did just that, put everyone from both towns here in Nuadilan, then they could choose to bypass us and hit Amathon. That would force us to leave the fortress and meet them out in the fields; that would be suicide for us. So we must opt to equally defend both towns from the onset of any attack; there really is no other valid choice for us."

"Where do you want all of us?" asked Beth Ann. She was worried about all the healing of our wounded. "Are we all going to be here or do half of us go to Amathon? I need to know and get healing supplies setup in both towns."

"That's my call," I broke in. As Wid of our Circle, it was my obligation to make such a call. "We split up, four here, three in Amathon, unless Amathon is more threatened, in which case, reverse the numbers. Ben, Paul, and Paulette, you three will ride to Amathon. The rest stay here with me. You have my full permission to use anything in our training to fight off the attackers, anything. If Amathon appears to be the main attack point, Allan, you will go with Paul."

"Let me go instead," Lilly Ann interrupted. "Beth Ann will have a fit if Allan goes off and leaves her." Beth Ann shot her a glance that said "Thank you!"

"Okay, okay. Lilly Ann, you go. Allan and I will support you as best we can from this distance. This way, neither town will feel left out. I'm not about to sacrifice one town for the other," I pronounced.

Thus, it was that the next day, Paul's Riders, as they became known, began their lengthy daily rides. Leaving at dawn from Amathon, they returned at dusk riding completely around our entire southern and eastern borders. One day they rode west first and the next few days, east. Paul was loathed to have their timing become predictable at any location.

May Day, 623 dawned a magnificent, warm spring day. Not a cloud obscured the deep blue sky. Our crops were half planted now. I watched as hundreds of folks headed out of the town to begin their day's toil in the fields. All spring, Ben and Allan had been working with the farmers, teaching them all that they knew about proper techniques. Allan looked over the fields near Nuadilan, while Ben did the same for Amathon. Already, more acreage had been planted than all last year, better done as well. Another couple of weeks and the planting would be completely done, save for the local garden plots which appeared nearly everywhere possible around town.

We had just finished lunch when the dreaded news came. One of the daily riders came galloping into town, crying continuously to everyone he passed, "They are coming! Invaders! Sound the alarm!" My long rehearsed signal plan momentarily surprised even me. Suddenly, a church bell began clanging; one by one, all the other churches chimed in.

"Are we, are we under attack?" asked a suddenly frightened Caitlyn. The unexpected sounds had taken her off guard as well. I nodded and we both knew what we had to do. Together, we dashed outside the complex to await the rider who would soon appear at a gallop. In the crisp clear air, the bells of Amathon echoed faintly in the distance as well. "I guess Amathon knows about it too," she whispered in my ear. I think that we both were more than a little awed by the sudden attack that must be eminent.

Shortly, we saw people dashing around in the streets near the outer section and caught a glimpse of our rider dashing through the streets heading for another gate. Here at the hilltop, seven wooden, circular walls surrounded us. With each circle's entrance gates offset from each other, any rider would have to take a winding path to reach us. Impatient for the news, I rather wished that we had a straight-line route to follow, but quickly changed my mind; my eyes met those of my loving wife carrying our baby. "Donkey's butt!" I exclaimed, venting my frustrations. "Why do men have to always pick a fight?" No one answered my rhetorical question.

'Sire,' a breathless lad exclaimed as he did a flying dismount. "King Amelon of Waterbysee comes from the east with an army of thousands and King Tiernmas of Penkawe has brought hundreds of cavalry up from the south!"

"Calm down Coffey, how far away are they? How soon will they be upon us?" I put my arm around the teenager's shoulders, hoping to instill some calm in him.

"Tas has gone to tell Amathon. We tried to count their numbers, but as soon as we were spotted, they shot a volley of arrows at us, so we lit out as fast as we could ride. Dunno on the time, maybe tomorrow. How can I tell when they will get here?" he asked. His face reddened as he realized that he could not answer the most important question.

Paul, our Protector, spoke up, "Bethany, how about I take Ben and Coffey here and go scout them a bit — get a tighter handle on what we are facing. Coffey can lead us to them."

"Okay. Just be careful out there," I had to agree; we needed data and fast. "I'll send out a dozen plus riders to notify all the farmsteads. Hopefully there will be time for those folks to seek the safety of the town walls." We nodded and the three went to get their horses. A fresh mount was given to Coffey.

Lilly Ann commented, "Sure is a nice sunny day for a battle. I guess we can only use fire and ice; no lightning today. No clouds."

"Donkey's butt! I need lightning," I replied, knowing very well how much I truly favored and depended upon electrical bolts from the sky when fighting battles. "Okay, let's all work together and see if we can pull in some nice thunder heads."

Nuadilan was a flurry of action, men, women, and children scurrying about setting up defenses and such. An air of fear slowly descended upon our town; we still counted far too few men in our defense. However, the first action I took was with the remaining members of my Circle. The five of us began a concerted effort to pull in a storm. Weather can be controlled, but it takes time. Far out to the western ocean, squalls were in progress. We just gave them a nudge in the right direction. Still, at least a day would pass before the front moved close enough to us to be usable. That took us only an hour of concentration. Then, it was my time to take charge of the city's defense. I sent Paulette over to Amathon to help them prepare. Allan and Ben would join her once they had reconnoitered our enemy's forces.

Lilly Ann and Beth Ann assisted Caitlyn and her staff prepare our buildings for all the wounded. Bandages, herbs, water, fires, food, drink — the list seemed endless as the women made their preparations. We are protectors of life; casualties would be a certainty in this battle, but we wanted to save as many lives as we could. I wondered whether the two kings with their armies advancing upon us felt the same about their soldiers. I doubted it very much.

My task now was to help organize our defensive forces. The women archers outnumbered the men ten to one. All able-bodied men were on the front lines, ready to repel the invaders, should our gates or walls fall. Seeing the several hundred burly Axemen with their heavy battleaxes marching up toward the gates filled me with pride. On Cymry, one Axeman was worth at least three or four of our fighters, they were that good. Yes, the enemy would get a nasty surprise when they breeched our gates! I overheard several Axemen discussing just how bad our barrier walls actually were. The stout timbers had been allowed to rot over the years since they were first planted in the ground. The only redeeming feature was that the city's rapid growth had force the city planners to build an even large wooden palisade around the outer edge of the city. Here the timbers were not as rotten as those around the central hilltop were. I suspected that one Axeman could break through the walls around our hilltop complex, but there was not time to rebuild them. That would take months of work, assuming that we even had the manpower to do it, which as yet we did not.

Note that not all our women folk were on the front lines, so to speak. Paul had organized well. Many began setting about the task of preparing food and drink for those who were on defense. Others worked on the makeshift bedding. From this moment on, all those who would actively defend our city would be at their assigned posts and would need such support. The smaller children scurried about with water buckets, bringing drinks to each group of fighters. Still other larger children and some women began to fill other buckets for fire prevention. Paul had theorized that the attackers might shoot flaming arrows over the walls into the town in the hope of creating fires and confusion behind the lines. Each town had one hundred firefighters on patrol now. I hoped that would be enough, we could not spare the able-bodied men to help fight devastating fires.

Within an hour, families began arriving from the nearby farmsteads, seeking protection of their town. These were our hardy farmers, and they were put up at the various inns around the town. A few would join in the defense, but most would be held in reserve and used to fight fires, carry the wounded up to our hilltop infirmary, and similar actions. I was preoccupied for several hours, moving from one group to another, answering questions, calming fears, and reminding them of their precise duties.

A few hours later, the scouts returned, and we held a conference in our Great Hall, now converted into an infirmary. Paul reported, "I estimate we face something like five hundred cavalry, five hundred foot soldiers, and a similar amount of short bowmen from the south. Probably the cavalry will be used to cut off any escape. The main attack force comes from the east. They have a thousand foot soldiers with nearly the same in archers, again armed with short bows and light crossbows. Based on their rate of progress, which is pitifully slow, they will not be within striking distance for two days. I doubt that they will risk an attack at night."

Caitlyn interrupted; she'd suddenly remembered something vitally important. "Shouldn't we send a messenger to my Uncle Emil? He promised to help defend our towns."

"I'll make a mind contact with him once we are through here, Caitlyn. That will be faster than sending a rider. It looks like he has two days to get here in time for the battle. I'm sure he will send all that he can spare, dear."

Directing my attention to Paul, I asked, "Will they attack both towns simultaneously do you think?"

He thrust his hands through his hair, which he often did when thinking through a tough problem. "Honestly, I cannot say for sure. Certainly, from their direction of arrival, Nuadilan will be hit first. If they find little resistance, I suspect they might send half of their force on to Amathon. Unless these kings are fools, they ought to test Nuadilan's defenses before committing to two battles at the same time. You still want Ben and me down in Amathon? I know Paulette has already been organizing things there."

"Yes, you two head on down there. She's expecting both of you. We will do our very best to give them such resistance here that they will not attack Amathon right away. However, stay alert to their cavalry. They might try something tricky."

"Okay. Paulette will maintain our telepathic communications link. If you need anything, just send word," our Protector still was not comfortable leaving the Circle's Wid. I could tell from his nervous tone of voice. Still, we had two towns to protect; I was unwilling to sacrifice one town to save the other.

For several more hours, chaos reigned. Everywhere, people ran to fetch this or drop off that. Had Paul not spent the last many weeks drilling key personnel on what needed to be done in the event of an attack, it would have been completely unmanageable. As king, every decision filtered up to me to make. I found quickly that by saying, "What has Paul told you about this situation?" completely handled each. They would mutter and stammer a bit, but then remember Paul's instructions. Actually, they just needed reassuring from me.

Late that afternoon, the gate man's messenger came to the hilltop looking for me. "My Lord, a young gypsy lady is at the north gate asking to see you. In these times, it might be a trick, so I've not let her inside. I told her I'd come get you."

"Very well, I'll come to her. Lead on," I replied, wondering who could possibly want to see me just as we were preparing for an attack.

"I'm coming too," Caitlyn announced, undaunted by the strange event. Lilly Ann, Beth Ann, and Allan, refusing to let me out of their sight, followed us. Walking through the bustling streets was a bit of a challenge. So many people had their lives disrupted this afternoon. War, I hate it.

A half hour later, we arrived at the barred north gate of the outermost palisade. Twenty guards were in position, so I had them open the gate. "Take care," commented the captain of the guards. Comforting to know others wished me well. We stepped outside.

A horse was ground-tied, and a cloaked woman was sitting on a stump, smoke rings floating up and away from her. I'd smelled that aroma before. As we stepped out, she hastily removed her pipe and threw back her cloak, facing me. It was indeed Reza, wife of the gypsy leader Bardia Zoreh.

Reza, still a stunning woman, stood well over six feet, with a thin, wiry frame with a full bosom that could not go unnoticed. As always, her hair demanded my attention; she had black hair with a slight curl to it and was at least as long as mine was. She had black eyes and wore long golden earrings, six rings, and several necklaces of varying lengths. Rounding out her appearance, she wore many golden bands on her arms, all of which jingled as she moved. "Reza say we meet again. Reza never wrong. Good see red head and pretty blonde wife." She smiled in her infectious, disarming way, designed to melt anyone's heart.

"Yes, it is good to see you again too, Reza. I wondered when you all would drop by to visit us. Now is not a very good time. We are about to be attacked," I explained.

"Reza knows that. Ah, blonde be mother zoon. Reza knows. Reza told Ket zo."

Caitlyn became a bit annoyed at always being referred to as "the blonde." I could sense her frustration rising, so I added. "Yes, she's Queen Caitlyn Amir now. We are expecting later this fall. Your band is more than welcome to come and visit our towns once this war is finished." I hoped that Reza would take the subtle hint and use Caitlyn's name.

"Reza knows. Dat's why Reza here — come tell Ket Bethany. Reza had vision. Has to warn Ket. Our wagons are now in the ghost town, Cuch Glen." My eyes opened wide of their own accord! My home village was now a ghost town? After that fateful battle in which my parents were slain and after which my sister Fianna and I fled, we knew that the survivors were leaving, but I'd always assumed that they would later return and rebuild the village.

"Reza had vision. Must tell Ket."

I suppressed my curiosity about my home village and said, "Must tell me what?"

"Reza seez Ket at a fork in 'es grand path, right now. Zea be'st at that fork now and a second one comes in few months. Ket no join up with King Lady from Highlands. No join her. If Ket joins her, Ket dies untimely soon. Ket no join; pretty blonde and Ket have many fine children. Later on, Ket no go south on voyage. Ket stay with pretty blonde, have many kids. Ket go south; pretty blonde dies. Ket no go south voyage; Ket no join King Lady, Reza begs."

How could I help not remembering her previous warning nearly a year ago about not going south? Alabaster went south and was killed when we eliminated the aliens from controlling our lives on Tarra. She was very right about that. I was speechless for a moment, not knowing how to reply. Caitlyn turned ashen. My Circle members came to my rescue.

Lilly Ann, our Judger, replied for me. "Ah, joining up with King Lachlan Laird of Brea, Seer and Keeper of the Sacred Talisman, to form a Grande Council of Kings is a wise idea. Such an alliance of kings may well prevent other wars, such as the one we are about to face tomorrow, but I can see how doing so may well make us enemies. That is the risk we must take. However, we have no plans to go on any southerly voyage. We know nothing about that part."

"Reza knowz nothing bout alliances or wars. Just Ket no join with King lady; Ket does; Ket diez young. Reza no want Ket diez."

I muttered, "What is this south voyage thing, Reza? We have heard nothing from anyone about going south."

"Long voyage in beeg boats, not like zee ones brought us 'ere to Cymry. Reza never zees such boats. Ket no go. Ket goes; blonde diez. Reza no want blonde diez either. Reza never wrong. Ket no go." She looked me squarely in my eyes, until I flinched, so strong was her stare and intention.

"Reza go now. Reza toldz Ket. Reza come visit when warz done." We said our goodbyes and thank yous, and watched as she mounted and rode north across the river before heading due east, following nearly the same route that I had taken last lifetime when I fled this city with a Grey Creature hot on my trail.

As we walked back up the hill, I explained, "She is a gypsy fortune teller that we met last year. Her predictions did hold up. Alabaster chose to go south and died; I went north as she said and lived. Spooky."

"Ah just fortune tellers," Lilly Ann commented. "You can't put much faith in them." She was trying to defuse the situation by making less of Reza. "We know that making a Grande Council of Kings will be risky. It's those that do not join or those that are forced to join against their will that we will need to watch. I promise you that we will watch over you very carefully, Ket. I'm sure that Paul will want to be your permanent bodyguard, so to speak."

"Yes, yes, but what is all this about taking a trip to the south on a Sea Prince ship?" I asked. "Do you all know something that I don't?" I was slightly annoyed. For a moment, I wondered if my Circle was withholding something from me.

Lilly Ann surprised me, "No, Ket. Honestly, I have no idea what she was talking about. Our only assignment is to be here with you, but really, I wouldn't put much stock in a gypsy fortune teller. I shouldn't fret over any of it, Caitlyn. Just fortune telling. If you believe them, then you actually work at bringing about what they predict. Rather silly, don't you think?" Caitlyn seemed a bit relieved at her pronouncement. Still, I had an edgy feeling the rest of the day.

After dark, I sent two dozen riders out on patrol. "Remember, just watch from a distance. We need to keep track of their activities; no surprise attacks during the night or such. If they veer away to the east towards Amathon, let me know right away. No heroics. I need you all back here helping with the defense when the battle is joined." The twenty-four young lads, heck they were barely teenagers, acknowledged me with a youthful brush-off, as if I was their parent. I watched them enthusiastically riding out into the dark night.

Ill I slept that night; guess no one really slept well for that matter. Doom hung over the entire town, and rightly so. Men, women, and children would likely die on the morrow. Wars, I hated them even more now. And for what? Crude men attempting to take advantage of a town of mostly women recently bereft of their husbands, brothers, and older children. Rather like the spoils of war.

Around two am, Caitlyn whispered in my ear, "Ket, if, if the town falls and all goes badly for us, promise me that you won't let them take me alive. I don't want to be a slave to some conquering man. I'd rather die first. Promise me."

Shocked, I realized many other women in our towns must be thinking this as well. I tried to console her with a lame, "Love, we will prevail. Don't fret so. If things go that badly, I will try to evacuate you and my friends as well. You'll not become someone's slave over my dead body, that's for sure. Now we ought to try to get some sleep." She snuggled up close, but I could sense that I had not vanquished her gnawing fears.

Over breakfast the next morning, the late night scouting reports came in, giving me a clearer picture of what we were about to face. The initial estimates of the numbers were verified. Additionally, long slow moving ox carts hauling their supplies had been spotted a mile to the rear of the advancing troops. Dozens and dozens of carts lumbered along a safe distance behind the soldiers. These two kings had spent time organizing their campaign, which I surmised was why we were not attacked during the last year when the two towns were most vulnerable.

The only thing that brought the slightest cheer to me were the high clouds trailing in from the southwest, a sure sign that we were being successful at moving a squall closer to us. If the storm continued to move our way, the afternoon might become stormy and I would have plenty of power for lightning strikes. After eating, we four made our rounds, visiting with each squad of defenders throughout the city. I made sure that all had had a good meal, that they had all their needed equipment and gear, and that everyone had the fallback plans down, just in case the outer wall should fall. Repeatedly, I told each woman personally, "Remember, if the walls fall and the town is not surrounded, you have our permission to flee northward for your life. I'd rather you settle in the highlands than become a slave to these cowardly bastards!" More often than not, I sensed a good deal of relief from the women. To the few men, I added, "If the walls fall and we are surrounded, form a wedge, and make a hole through which our women can escape to the north." None of this was what the few fighter trained men expected for a final pep talk just before a battle.

Of course I also heard many commenting, "My Lord, my late husband and I built our home here. I'm raising our children in this home. The Blessed Holy Mother will protect us. I will fight to the death to protect my home!" However, the most frequent comment I heard was simply, "The Blessed Holy Mother will protect us." These people had tremendous faith in their Blessed Holy Mother.

When we were finally alone once more in our hilltop retreat, Caitlyn commented, "Spooky. They are all saying that the Blessed Holy Mother shall protect us. They do not know that you are the Blessed Holy Mother and that you are indeed going to protect us once more. How ironic, don't you think?"

"Yes, but what if all that I've done and will do is not enough and the town falls? What will they think of their Blessed Holy Mother then?" I countered, rather gloomily. How strange I felt. All these people were worshiping me, rather the body I had last lifetime, Bethany Madelyn Amir. I had not asked to be worshiped, I detested it. Yet, I could think of nothing to undo their blind faith in the Blessed Holy Mother.

Waiting. I hate waiting. We all hated waiting. Doom was slowly moving our way. No escaping it, only a matter of when would it arrive. By early afternoon, all our advanced scouts had returned to the safety of the walls. How long would the wooden stockade last?

Around midafternoon, the vanguard of the two armies became clearly visible, marching inexorably towards Nuadilan. From the hilltop, I began to study their formations. That two different armies were coming was clear. From the east, two ranks of soldiers marched in step. The one further south contained their archers, using short bows, if the advanced reports were correct. The one closer to us would lead the close assault with spears, swords, and shields. Two great battering rams formed from the trunk of a pair of enormous oak trees lumbered along in their midst, pulled by teams of six oxen each. Off to the south, long lines of cavalry stretched out into the distance. My guess was that the cavalry would be used to surround the town, while the others did the actual assault.

Via Paulette, our communicator and excellent telepath, Paul sent, *Can we make a mind join so I can see their tactics and offer appropriate countermeasures?* Presently, I felt Paul's mind joining with mine. Ordinarily, this is so intimate an action, but today, it was all business. *Look, already the cavalry is breaking into quarters. Probably they are going to encircle Nuadilan; they'd be fools to get within arrow range. So you can ignore them for the time being, mostly. Keep your eyes on their archers. I predict that they will be marched into long-distance short bow range and then rain projectiles down on you so that their foot soldiers can move in relatively unhindered.*

I replied, *So we should use our long bows at maximum range to eliminate as many of their archers before they get close enough to retaliate?*

Precisely. Pivot in a circle so I can see the placement of your archer groups, please. I did so, strange having another peering out through your eyeballs. *Okay. The key is to deal out as much long-range damage as possible. You have them evenly spaced around the outer wall as I ordered. Let the enemy commit to taking some field position and then move your archer groups. Odds are they will assault either the eastern or the southern gates. You could gamble on such and begin moving some archer groups now.*

Once their archers are within range, then if I move my archer groups, they will be at great risk from the rain of enemy arrows, right?

Yes, that is why I said it is a gamble. Remember, our best hope lies in dealing a crippling blow at long range, a range longer than theirs, seriously damaging their morale — you know, taking casualties without giving out any.

Should I send them all to the southern and eastern sections?

No, leave at least a few behind to harry any cavalry, which might decide to attack the northern and western gates or walls. It's just that once their short bow men are within their range, moving your people will be very risky.

Okay. I'll break the Mind Link for a while and go see to it; certainly looks as if they intend to strike at the eastern or southern gates. Paulette broke the link, and I rushed off to reposition dozens of archer squads. For a half hour, mass pandemonium filled our streets as hundreds of archers and their support groups repositioned themselves. Then we waited once more. I hate waiting, so did nearly everyone else.

Our priests made a last minute visit to each of our defensive groups, whether combatants or support groups. With each, they shared a group prayer to the Blessed Holy Mother. I could restrain myself no longer. I began tagging along with the priests adding my final words to theirs, "Just do your best. That is all that either I or the Blessed Holy Mother asks of you." I think between the prayers of the priests and my simple words that our people were more at ease. I wanted them to know that I did not expect miracles from them.

Finally, the enemy committed their forces. Lines of archers began running nearly due west, just out of short bow range. Their plan was clear, while out of our range, extend great lines of archers all along the entire southern half of the town's outer wall. Then, together, move forward into range, firing rains of deadly arrows into the town. The five hundred from the southern king broke into five lines and moved to our southwestern side. The thousand archers from the east formed into five rows and trotted towards positions stretching from due south of our gate off to the southeastern flanks.

"They are within range," Leane Finn said softly to me. I was standing beside her handpicked group of longbow women. These were the best markswomen in our town. I looked into her green eyes, before giving the command.

"Fire at will, just as you have all practiced. Let's show them what our longbows can do!" I bellowed the orders at the top of my lungs. Quickly, thirty other group leaders barked their orders to their squads of twenty-five archers. The twanging sounds of countless bow strings filled the air. Hundreds upon hundreds of arrows flew in a huge arch high into the cloudy sky.

At this extreme distance well beyond short bow range, men appeared little more than tiny creatures, deer perhaps. I watched but lost sight of individual arrows, so great was the distance. The effect, of course, was impossible not to miss. Tiny creatures dropped to the ground randomly. Surreal might be an appropriate description, had these not been men who were falling wounded or dead.

Ten flights of arrows later, the surviving hundreds of archers had been routed from their position, racing away from the rain of dead. The first three minutes of the attack had cost the enemy nearly half of their archers. At least five hundred bodies lay scattered about their original lines. A great cheer arose spontaneously from those in Nuadilan; I could not help but yell with them, though I knew this was only the very beginning of a bloody day.

Then it was back into the waiting mode once more. The enemy regrouped, but made no further advances toward the town, staying well beyond the clearly marked line of death. Via Paulette, Paul sent me another warning. *They will likely change tactics now. Under cover of shields, they will rush into firing range and then let rain their arrows. Probably the foot soldiers will advance simultaneously, using their shields as protection. Stay alert and get back up to the hilltop!* Reluctantly, I did as he asked. War, I hate it. Fighting, too, ah well. The offer of King Lachlan Laird of Brea and her Grande Council of Kings began to sound even better to me.

Their next tactic became obvious to everyone who could peer out onto the hillside before Nuadilan. At uniform intervals, flaming barrels began to appear, a harbinger of things to come. Still, we waited. As I watched from our hilltop command post, our enemy looked more like colonies of ants, swarming back and forth, just out of our longbow range. Industrious, unswaying, dedicated utterly to the task. Ants, just ants. Ants to be squashed. I could stamp on ants bent upon the destruction of my town, my people, my friends, my wife, and my unborn. A distant peal of thunder woke me to the present.

The enemy likewise took this as a portent. Drums began pounding in the distance, marching cadence; the ants were on the move. In a sea of shields held over heads, long lines all across our eastern and southern approaches began to march towards Nuadilan. I need not give orders. Paul had trained the various squad captains well. He knew that when the battle came, I could not be everywhere issuing orders. Each group had to act independently, but for the greater good. Inwardly, I thanked the heavens that Paul had done this, for I found it hard to speak any words, words that would send some of these brave women and children and volunteer men to their graves. Images of a burning, ransacked Nuadilan tormented my mind.

Twangs of arrows brought me out of my introversion at least momentarily. Even with shields, ants fell, ending their stately march, but now arrows began hitting within the town. Sharp thuds announced the arrival of flights of their short bow rain of death. Shrill cries of pain drowned out the thuds and crackling sounds of flaming arrows igniting thatched roofs. War had begun. So much death.

Paul, via Paulette, issued the order to commence our lightning bolt strikes. I was only vaguely aware of his commands to us. Mechanically, I obeyed, bringing down strikes upon the ants in the distance. At my side, Allan, Beth Ann, and Lilly Ann began their long distance attacks as well, even before I did. However, I knew that Beth Ann would soon cease her attacks and, along with Caitlyn, begin to help our wounded as they were brought up to our hilltop strong hold. She had not the stomach for such wanton destruction. Yet, again, I had placed her in just such a position. Beth Ann was a healer, not a warrior.

Afterwards, Lilly Ann provided the best overall description of the battle. Heavy rains of arrows took their steady toll on both sides for the first five minutes of the assault. Outside, the wounded remained where they fell. In stark contrast, inside Nuadilan, our rescue squads, mostly older men, women, and younger children moved swiftly to help those hit by arrows to get to our hilltop great hall, now the infirmary. Here, Beth Ann and Caitlyn worked as fast as they could, but were swiftly overwhelmed by the sheer number of patients. Beth Ann's strategy was simple. Pull the arrows out; let the wound bleed, and then hold a bandage on the wound. Only those in life threatening need did she spend more than a minute tending.

Outside, our fire brigades were quickly overwhelmed as well. The fire arrows were too many and too scattered around the town, setting far more fires than the bucket brigades could handle. Old Amos, a sixty year old man, was in charge of all these brigades, assisted by all our priests of the Church of the Blessed Holy Mother. Twenty minutes into the assault, Amos gave the orders to abandon all efforts at saving the buildings in the southern half of the outer ring, moving his too few fire fighters back to try to keep the flames from jumping the second inner wall and the two flanks on the east and west halves of the outer circle. In this, they were successful. Only the southern half of the outer ring was ultimately lost to the fires.

Assisted by the cavalry, two great battering rams were moved into position before our southern gates. Shields protected the accompanying foot soldiers from the shower of arrows that our archers sent their way. Admittedly, the shower was drastically smaller; many were wounded and many had been ordered to retreat to the second wall. Our women archers are not front line troops. About two hundred men, mostly the Axemen, swarmed behind the gates, ready for the onslaught, once they were breached. Lilly Ann reported that these Axemen had been terribly difficult to hold in place; as soon as the assault began, they begged to be allowed to rush out onto the field of battle to engage the enemy in glorious combat! Lilly Ann had used every ounce of persuasion she could manage to keep them in position ready to handle the breech she knew would come soon.

I heard Paulette fairly screaming Paul's orders into my mind. *Fire. Fire. Drop walls of fire upon the battering rams now. Now! Fire sheets now!* Dutifully, I complied, creating horizontal walls of fire just above the heads of the ants before our gates. With no effort at all, I just let go of my creation; the wall of flames dropped down like fire from heaven upon the attackers, joining and merging with Lilly Ann's. Screams, cries, panic shouts echoed in the overall din of the assault. Smoke from the many fires brought tears to my eyes and coughing as well. Yet, I persisted.

Wham! I heard the great logs smashing into our gates; the end would come soon now. A sickening splintering sound foretold our doom. I heard an enormous yelling as the Axemen, long held back against their natural will, swarmed out of the gates to attack at last the enemy. Their axes spelled doom to the invaders, heads and limbs began to roll. None in that initial assault party of two hundred lived.

Meanwhile, the instant the gates were breached, the cavalry began to charge. Their intention was clear now. The cavalry would take advantage of the breech to swarm into the town, mopping up all resistance. This was the last straw for me. Smoke blinded my eyes; breathing was difficult. That old, long held anger, surged within me, that same anger I felt so long ago when the king's men attacked my family in our wagon, nearly slaying Ellen, my mentor, to say nothing of my family.

I backed way out of my head. Anger surged. Images of the thousand attacking Galts that rainy day when Alabaster, Erline, and I had fought merged with the scene before me. Images of the swarming Axemen attacking the Sisterhood on Heartbreak Hill added to my confusion. Clear of the body, I saw the field before me and acted, acted as fast as I could. Connect a line from a rider up to the dark storm clouds, move on to the next rider. Down the return line came the inevitable strike of lightning. I had total certainty. Connect a line up from the rider and the strike would come. Bam. Bam. Bam. Faster and faster I worked.

Now I saw new cavalry arriving from the north. Help was coming that I could see. Sunlight glistened off the shiny chain mail of King Lachlan. Ah, Emil and his forces were off to her right. More help was coming. Positioned high overhead of Nuadilan, I saw a group of a hundred cavalry riding out of Amathon, followed by a number of archers on foot, racing towards Nuadilan. Probably Paul's doing. *If King Lachlan wants a magic show, then a magic show she shall get!* I tripled my speed. Bam. Bam. Bam.

Emil's cavalry, according to Lilly Ann's account, swept far to the east, eliminating their supply wagons and cutting off any possibility of retreat. Once done, his forces turned and hit the enemy from their direct rear. In contrast, King Lachlan drove straight into the hastily reformed lines of foot soldiers, heading right towards the eastern King's main command position. Her well-trained, well-equipped, seasoned cavalry cut a path through the men on foot, like a knife cuts through butter. They passed through without breaking stride, driving straight for the eastern king.

King Lachlan was always in the lead, perhaps two horse lengths ahead of her men. She swooped directly down upon the king. With one mighty swing, her sword beheaded the king. King Lachlan called out to the stunned generals, "You will need a new king now!" Of course, the generals had little time to ponder her words, as the remainder of her force rode through their ranks with devastating results. All this action took place on the far southeastern flank.

I concentrated my attention on the southern, close in zone, where the majority of the enemy still fought. Bolt after bolt flew to my command. Yes, I went off the deep end once again; I will admit it now. The universe shrunk down to nothing but the lovely, breathtaking, marvelous, magnificent, beautiful black energy masses in the clouds and the ants far down upon the ground. Bam. Bam. Bam. Over and over and over, bolt after bold after bolt.

The battle was soon over, but not for me. Lilly Ann explained that with the death of the eastern king, all will evaporated. The soldiers tried to flee. Those near Emil and Lachlan's forces were captured, as were the few cavalry to the north and west, who surrendered to Paul's small forces. Our Axemen had eliminated utterly all the enemy who had breached our gates. However, absolutely everyone fell back as the wild Nature light show continued unabated. Some counted at least a hundred lightning strikes per minute. Bolts struck every object upon the southern battlefield, which is why everyone fled that area. I did not distinguish between enemy and friend. If there was a body before me, it was hit. Round and round I went, visiting each ant form upon the ground.

Such power flowed through me. I felt like a god unleashing his terrible wrath upon the ants below me. The energy felt so good, so exciting, so energetic, so fantastic, so sensuous, and so natural that I did not nor could not stop! Lilly Ann later told me that I was out of control for over fifteen minutes! Hundreds of bodies were dead many times over, still I did not relent! I did not want to!

Lilly Ann screamed at me, though I heard her not. "Stop it, Bethany! It's over. Stop!" She hit my body hard. She shook my body to no avail. At last, she slugged it, knocking the body unconscious. She panicked when even that had no effect! *What do I do?* She screamed mentally to Paulette.

I'm working on it! Paulette shot back. She was galloping towards Nuadilan, coming from the north along with Paul and Ben. *Go help Beth Ann.* "I can't reach him galloping like this, Paul. Get me to his body as fast as you can." They urged their mounts to an all-out canter, Paulette hung on for dear life. Within minutes, the trio entered the north gates and moved as swiftly as they could to get to the hilltop. Paul cursed the twisting path required to get there, this was one time that the natural barrier was hindering rather than helping.

"He's out cold," Paulette said as they dismounted.

"Is that good or bad? Can you get him to stop?" asked Paul, unable to hide the fear in his voice.

"Only Willow could. I don't know if I can. Leave me. Go help Beth Ann, you too Ben," she ordered and began to chant. *Music was the only thing that Willow could do to reach him, as I remember vaguely. I don't even remember what the song was. Damn. Ah well, Paulette, you have to try something.* She closed her eyes and reached upward. Soon she made contact with Ket Bethany, floating several hundred feet above the town.

The problem with telepathic contact with another is that it works both ways. I felt her enter my awareness, my mind, but she then felt, sensed, and saw mine. She instantly faced my madness, my insanity, faced it full on, full force. Tremendously stunned, Paulette couldn't do anything for some time! She was staring insanity squarely in her awareness, her mind. So overwhelming it was that she involuntarily vomited and lost her contact with me. Paulette was forced to call for help.

A few minutes later, surrounded by Paul, Ben, Allan, Beth Ann, and Lilly Ann, Paulette made contact with me once more, mind joined with the five others for support and assistance. Of course, all six now received the full backlash of a telepathic contact. Each had no choice but to view my insanity full force. I make no excuses; it was terrible. I would not wish this upon my enemies, yet they had to do it or lose me, possibly forever.

Six to one is good odds. Their combined strength finally allowed Paulette to reach me. *Stop Ket! Stop Bethany! It is all over. Stop!*

I don't want to stop. This is so beautiful.

Clever Paulette. She knew music was the key, but she was not a musician. She added Caitlyn into the mind link. Dear Caitlyn began humming my favorite flute song, the one that the blind musician from Fortress le'Grange had taught me. *How dare anyone intrude upon my solace; I am one with this black energy mass! I've heard that before. But where? I cannot think. I don't want to think. I must think, recall. So soothing! Donkey's rear! I'm separating from this lovely energy mass. That music. Try not to hear. I can't.*

*I'm slipping away from this sensuous energy field. Ahieee. So peaceful. No, mournful, yes that's what I need, to relax, to flow with the music. Why did I ever leave music behind? I don't want to be king, only to make such music! God, I am **so** tired! I think I shall sleep.*

Chapter 8 Aftermath

"Oh my head!" I exclaimed rubbing the spot where Lilly Ann had slugged me. Faint red sunlight helped illuminate our great hall. I struggled to get to my feet. All around me were hundreds of wounded women, children, and a few men. Moans of those in pain filled the room.

"Ah, you are awake. How are you feeling," Beth Ann spotted my arousal and moved to my side immediately. Her clothes were covered in blood. I glanced about and saw the others of my Circle and Caitlyn tending the wounded as well. They too were drenched in the blood of our people.

"My head hurts. Must have fallen. Don't seem to have any broken bones or holes in me?" I ventured.

"Lilly Ann knocked you out, but that didn't help. You gave us all a scare once again, Bethany. How's your mental state?" Beth Ann replied briskly, masking her fears about my well-being.

"I feel like a horse has fallen on my head, that's what I feel like. My head feels a bit like it might explode or something. Otherwise, I am just exhausted," I replied more than a little ashamed of having lost control once again. Then, I remembered the battle. "How goes the battle?" I asked agitated, fearing that it was still being fought and here I was knocked out in the infirmary.

"Battle's over. We won," Paul quickly interjected, an enthusiasm in his tone, a smile on his face. All his advance preparations had worked miracles. He was rightly proud of his achievement.

"Er, there is an unforeseen complication," Lilly Ann hesitatingly interrupted Paul, before he could launch into a detailed description. "We're playing host to a number of kings now. Some came to our rescue, while others came to observe King Lachlan's Magician in action. All are most impressed, although fear might be a better analysis. However, and this is a big however, you now have at least ten thousand townsfolk — both here and in Amathon — all are swearing they have witnessed a Holy Deliverance Miracle from the Blessed Holy Mother, who has obviously answered their prayers to rescue the two towns! All the churches are packed with prayer givers. The priests are having a field day with this!"

How utterly ironic, I thought. I was their Blessed Holy Mother last lifetime; I had done it, given them their "miracle." Lilly Ann, looking a bit sheepish, added, "Sorry Ket, for knocking you out. I had to get you to stop," she justified.

"I wish that would have worked," I acknowledged her, though I knew that my physical body had nothing to do with my temporary insanity.

"Well, if you are okay, Bethany, how about lending a hand with all the wounded," Beth Ann interrupted us all. "We've still got hundreds that need our mending; they are lined up outside. Come on, all of you, my back is getting sore."

I joined the healing squad, relieving Caitlyn so she could make us all something to eat and drink. It was well past suppertime and I was famished. Quickly, Beth Ann hatted me up on her procedure. Those we could safely patch up, we sent home, with strict orders to report back here tomorrow for a checkup. Those in the worst shape were housed here in our great hall, which was nearly filled to capacity. Thankfully, the hundred or so still waiting in line for healing were not critical, a slice here or an arrow protruding there. Beth Ann had already seen to the worst cases, which numbered close to two hundred.

Dusk had already begun when we finished with the last of the walking wounded. After washing up, all of us dove into Caitlyn's meal. After diner, I thought about taking a walk to survey the damage. I could see the smoldering remains of the fire, but the total darkness and light rain disabused me. It could wait until the morning. The awaiting kings would not; I owed them a visit. Accompanied by Paul, Allan, and Ben, I walked over to our stables where they had set up a base of operations.

"Ah, our Magician comes!" King Lachlan's strong voice announced our arrival. Emil's friendly face was a bit pallid, for he too had been startled by my insane lightning deluge. Quickly, Lachlan introduced me to the gathering of kings. Not counting me, twelve were sitting around a small fire drinking ale. I drew up a log and joined their circle, while my friends followed suit, setting behind me.

"Although as yet I do not know what all assistance you have all provided, I can say that I am truly indebted to your assistance. You saved the day; we were terribly outnumbered. Thank you one and all for your part," I said trying to be as gracious as possible. I must have looked like a wreck, covered in dried blood. Noticing several staring at my clothes, I added, "No, I am not wounded. I've been healing some of our townsfolk. We don't have an accurate count yet, but I am told that we have lost sixty-nine people. Many hundreds have been wounded, and the eight of us have been working hard at healing them. I'll know more in the morning."

One king whom I did not know asked, "What do you mean by this healing? Are you a physician too?"

"Beth Ann, Allan's wife, is probably the best healer in Cymry. The rest of us, though nowhere near as skilled as Beth Ann, are likely far better healers than any of your physicians. I'm sorry, but I'm so tired that I'm not in a mood to play games with you all and be modest. What I hate the most about wars are all the people who are wounded, even the innocent. The least that we who dole out these wars can do for our people and soldiers are to give them the best medical care we possibly can — not just leave them on the battlefield to bleed to death."

King Emil came to my aid, "Aye, I'll vouch for that. One of my cavalrymen took a nasty sword wound to his leg. Ordinarily, the only thing my physicians could do would be to cut it off and hope the soldier somehow survived. He was brought to your great hall, and I watched your Beth Ann at work. Lyle is recovering nicely and is expected to be back in the saddle in a few weeks. Miraculous, I'd say." Several others nodded in agreement; evidently, they had seen our infirmary in action while I was unconscious.

"I think King Lothgar, that we have all seen firsthand superior healing skills by the Magician's friends. What remains is this Grande Council idea. King Lachlan has proposed this council with herself as its leader. She has also said that you are to be her personal Magician. Is this so? You take orders only from her or can we count on your assistance when we are in need?" another king whom I did not know spoke up, asking the key questions I suspected that many here wanted to know firsthand. What was my role to be in this Grande Council of Kings?

"Lords, let me be perfectly clear on this point. I am not nor will I ever be King Lachlan's personal Magician, subject to her orders alone. I am Ket Bethany, nearly unwilling King of Nuadilan and Amathon, by marriage to Queen Caitlyn. If I agree with a council's decision, I will fully support it any way that I can. I will lend my 'magic' to all worthwhile needs, but I make the final decision whether or not it is worthwhile. Magic is not a trifling thing to be flaunted. I am no man or woman's puppet, if you take my meaning. I trust that each of you, likewise, is not a puppet, but will stand up for what you deem right and honorable. It seems to me that this Grande Council of Kings might be a way to put a complete halt to these petty, but devastating, senseless wars. If this council can put a total stop on these silly wars on Cymry, I am all for it."

I noticed that many seemed relieved to hear my defiant words, although King Lachlan did seem slightly ill at ease. King Emil spoke up, "Lachlan, I think that after what we have witnessed here today, you now have your Grande Council of Kings. Although I cannot speak for my peers, you have my support. When do we meet?" Uniformly, all the other kings added their agreement.

Smiling in her supreme moment of accomplishment, the achievement of her long planned action, King Lachlan announced, "Our first meeting will be in Brea on the solstice coming up. I will send word to all the kings of Cymry. May this be the last war fought on the soil of Cymry!" Everyone gave a cheer of support. I felt encouraged that at least in principle, these kings desired peace. Perhaps now our island could thrive and prosper without the constant threat of war and fighting. I sincerely hoped this was not just wishful thinking on our part — a world without war.

Caitlyn had warm tea and biscuits waiting for us when we returned drenched from the warm spring rains that we had pulled into our land to help with the battle. Exhausted, I longed to just fall asleep. However, my Protector insisted on giving me an accurate account of the damage and the slain. Paul added, "In their thirst for battle, four of our burly men rushed too far out from the gates and were caught in your torrent of lightning bolts, I'm sorry to report, Ket. I didn't want to tell you until now," he added unsure of himself. His obligation was to report accurately to his Wid; he feared there might be repercussions. He was right. Suddenly, my face felt excruciatingly hot, burning. It must have been as red as my flaming hair! In my madness, my insanity, I had indiscriminately killed four of my own men!

"Oh my god!" I heard my disembodied voice speak. "I didn't mean to harm our own men," I heard myself justifying.

Lilly Ann, our expert Judger, saw my distress for what it actually was. She was trained to observe such and quickly broke in, "You must not blame yourself, Ket. You did what you had to do to save the town. Had we not stopped them utterly at the outer gate, the enemy would have easily taken the town with wanton loss of life. No one can hold you responsible, Ket." She ended sternly.

Her words were perfectly logical, probably an accurate assessment of the situation. However, inwardly, I felt no comfort. I had gone insane. I had lost complete control over my actions, lightning bolting everything I could see, hitting the same dead bodies many times over. For the first time, my insanity had cost the lives of my own forces. Always before, somehow miraculously my people were not injured. But this time, I had gone too far with it. "I can no longer trust myself to use lightning bolts," I found myself thinking sternly to myself, admonishing myself, as if that somehow made up for my actions. I was too embarrassed to look my dear friends and wife in the face, so I stared downward at my cup.

In the back of my seething mind, I knew that Lilly Ann would be watching me carefully, noting every word I now uttered. Such was her job as a Judger, an arbitrator of disputes. She would be looking for the "I am so sorry; I am to blame; I wish I could take back my insane actions." I felt enormous pressure just to scream those works out, but I knew it would not help. "Nothing can help me now," I thought to myself, "nothing!" I said nothing.

Uneasy with my sudden silence, uttered, "Honestly, Ket, it isn't your fault. Those men let battle lust overcome their good sense. They were ordered not to go after the retreating soldiers. They disobeyed orders." Paul's voice trailed off. An uncomfortable silence fell upon our table, broken only by the occasional moans from ill resting wounded in our Great Hall.

"I am so tired. I need sleep," I finally uttered and got up to head to bed, dirty clothes and all. I heard the others talking under their breaths as I left the room, Caitlyn trailing silently behind me. I didn't even try to hear what they were saying. I vaguely remember Caitlyn doing her best to wash me off before we collapsed onto our bed. She snuggled up close, mechanically, I put my arms around her, but my mind was still absorbing the magnitude of what I had done, killed my own men.

The next day, found me in an ill humor, as Paul, Allan, and I toured the damaged sections of the town. Indeed, the entire southern gates and surrounding walls were now gone, smoldering ruins remained. Half of this outer circle of buildings were either completely destroyed or badly damaged and would need to be rebuilt from the ground up.

"Our casualty count has risen, seventy-one have died. Two didn't make it through the night," Paul went on with his summarization. We have three hundred sixty-one wounded. Ninety-six are still in critical condition, according to Beth Ann, but she expects those will survive. Those long bows really helped save the day. Already, I have been hounded by four kings asking about them and where they can purchase long bows."

I heard myself acknowledge, "Yes, we should thank her in some grand manner befitting her assistance. Also we should probably get in a large order for more for Mount Blanc as well."

"Enough of the war talk," Allan broke in, "Ket, I have some grand ideas on how we can rebuild the town and its walls. The outer walls ought to be made of stone, not heavy timbers which rot in time, even with the best tarring." Enthusiastically, Allan rattled off his grand ideas and I nodded my agreement periodically, admittedly not really listening to him.

I just could not get the haunting of having killed four of my own men out of my mind! How could I face my Circle or even the townsfolk after this? At last, we stood where the southern gate once opened onto the green rolling grasslands. Corpses and carrion birds dotted the torn up, muddy ground. Here and there, some of our men were going from body to body, searching them, and piling them like logs onto carts. Paul had issued orders to bury them all in mass graves far away from the city, out of sight over the next southern hill. Already, a great pile of weapons and tack formed a small hill near the remnants of our outer wall.

I spied a half dozen kings, with their numerous attendants grouped around an archer. We moved to join them. Ah, they had already found the longbow maker, Leane Finn. "If you want a good bow, it takes a good week to craft one," she explained as we joined the small crowd. Leane was giving them a demonstration, expertly hitting the tiny target far beyond normal bowshot range. To her credit, her target was a life-sized wooden deer, though deer was not what these men were envisioning.

"Ah, I see you have already found our master bow maker, Leane Finn," I declared as we joined them. "Honestly, gentlemen, hers are the finest bows on all Tarra."

Paul enthusiastically added, "Leane's bows made a huge difference in the outcome of the great battle. Our bow crews, though outnumbered, were able to nearly halt the opposing archers before they could get close enough to fire back." This the kings had witnessed for themselves yesterday.

However, Leane squirmed uncomfortably. I knew that she hated wars and the use that her magnificent longbows had been put. She was a huntress, not a soldier. Her goal was to help put meat on the family table more easily, not the slaying of men. I quickly interrupted with, "However, Gentlemen, their main use is for hunting. We can send out far fewer hunting parties when they are equipped with her longbows. They are more accurate and deliver meat more readily. If you haven't already noticed, women can easily use them as well." Leane blushed, and I could tell she was very grateful for my turning the conversation onto a better path.

An aside, Leane Finn became the wealthiest person in Nuadilan within five years' time. With our help, she opened an entire factory devoted solely to making the finest longbows in the land. Hundreds of orders came almost at once. In fact, it took her nearly two years to make all the bows that were ordered that day. Ten years later, a longbow personally made by Leane fetched over hundred gold coins! Over the next few years, I shipped three hundred longbows to Mont Blanc, an action that would prove vital in later years.

Three days later, the assisting armies had gone, and the fields before our town had been cleaned up, and those that could be spared returned to the farming duties, having to replant many of the fields, which had been trampled by the enemy. Many from Amathon came over to help the slow process of rebuilding the town, pitching in heartily, though probably most relieved that their town had been spared.

However, I was still moody and sat on a charred stump of what had been the south wall, watching the hundreds of hands working away, clearing out the rubble. Lilly Ann joined me, her steely eyes had been watching me constantly now for days, though I still said nothing, refusing to talk about my doom and gloom. As she sat down beside me, I fully expected a lecture on how it was not my fault that I had killed four of my own men in my madness. She surprised me completely!

"You know, Ket," she began in an offhand manner, as if toying with some idea. "One thing strikes me as rather odd."

Amused with this unexpected remark, I could not help myself from replying, "What's odd?"

"It's the late King Amelon of Waterbysee and King Tiernmas of Penkawe. They marched a long way to get here. Yet, at the very time of their arrival, so many other kings and forces also arrived here to help us out. I can understand Uncle Emil's being here, but all those others? Many of the kings came with just their own bodyguards to witness the battle. I think this battle had more outside witnesses than any battle in history. Quite odd, don't you think?"

"Maybe it was all King Laird's doing," I responded, beginning to see her point. "She probably got the other kings to come to bear witness to what her 'magician' could actually do."

"Perhaps, perhaps. Certainly, it all played according to her plans with the kings and all. However, I still find it a bit odd, especially in the timing of it all," she bit her lip and tossed an errant strand of hair aside. "Would you mind if I did a bit of exploring down in Waterbysee and Penkawe?"

"Not at all, but you must take Paul with you always. Those are the enemy's main towns. Actually, I guess that those towns are expecting us to eventually ride in there and take control of them. To the winner go the spoils and all that. However, I want nothing to do with those towns, save to be allowed free and safe passage of our people through them. We need to have a direct line to the port of Bregia for sure so we can sell our products to the mariners and receive supplies from them as well."

"Okay, I'll take Paul with me and get started on that today. Leave all that to me, Ket. After all, this is my specialty." Lilly Ann fairly bounced off to corral Paul. She was more animated and excited than I had ever seen her.

Days passed into weeks. Crops grew; new homes and shops appeared, along with the beginnings of a rudimentary stone wall to replace the rotted and now destroyed outer wall. Caityln's tummy also grew, rather alarmingly, I thought. The last of the wounded had long been returned to their homes or new quarters, and our Great Hall had been scrubbed and returned to us. Only now, Queen Caitlyn's council met daily, she was a master at organizing the rebuilding efforts, coordinating everyone to the tasks at hand.

Lilly Ann and Paul, along with twenty-five cavalrymen, were gone for almost a month. Late one afternoon, the group rode across the green hills toward Nuadilan. Yes, Paulette, our Communicator, kept in daily touch with them, relaying the minor news of the day. Hence, we knew of their arrival, and all stood at the edge of town, watching them ride in over the hills. I expected to see the cheery, happy face of Lilly Ann.

Instead, she rode in completely solemn, dismounted, and said, "Ket, we must have a private conversation immediately. Cymry Circle and Caitlyn, join in. Where's Allan? He should hear this too." Something was wrong, but none of us had any idea what. She'd not reported anything via the daily mental mind links with Paulette, who immediately sent Allan an order to drop everything and come join us.

Five minutes later the eight of us stood out on the green grasslands, out of earshot of anyone. After glancing in all directions, Lilly Ann was convinced she could not be overheard. "Remember I said this war had odd aspects?" I nodded. "Well, I used my Judger skills. We know that men do not inherently want conflict with each other. That for two people to begin fighting, there has to be a hidden, third person actively fomenting the trouble by telling lies to each side — lies about the other side. Well, I began asking the people I met questions like 'Who told you that the people in Nuadilan were evil? Who told you Nuadilan was easy pickings?' I bet I interviewed close to three hundred men in both towns. Quite remarkably, the same two names kept coming up, repeatedly, and in both towns! You'll never guess who?" she paused teasing us, proud of her accomplishment.

Since she was determined not to go on unless we responded, I replied, "Well, who?"

She accepted my return tease and shocked us all, "The two men are ambassadors for King Laird! There can be no doubt about it. King Lachlan Laird had her hands behind the scenes inciting this war!" While the rest of us gasped in total surprise, Lilly Ann glowed, supremely pleased with her now completed investigation.

"That Bitch!" exclaimed Caitlyn, stamping her foot on the ground in disgust. "She lied to us. She caused this war!"

"Caution, Caitlyn," I urged, fearing she was jumping to the wrong conclusions. "The two dead kings caused the war. They attacked us, not King Laird. Yet if Lilly Ann's observations are correct, King Lachlan incited these people to attack us. All we could hold her for is gossip. Yet, war is the direct result of such loose tongues. Lilly Ann, do we have enough to confront her before her High Council? Let her peers try her?"

"Afraid not," she bit her lip. "Just my analysis and survey. Insufficient to try her or even bring the matter before the Council. However, it is enough for us never to trust her in anything. You were very wise when you made your speech the other day before the kings. You made it clear that you are not her 'magician.' It's almost like you already knew this," she coyly teased, but was unsure whether I had suspected her treachery or whether my actions were simply those of a trained Wid, the Circle's leader.

"I had no idea, Lilly Ann. I was just protecting all of us that day. I can speculate why she did it. She needed something to force all the other kings into her High Council. What better way than to have those undecided kings watch 'her magician' at work."

"Only they got far more than they bargained for," put in Paul. "I sensed a deep shock in those kings and even Laird herself, for that matter. I don't think that they expected quite the devastation they witnessed. They'll think twice before challenging us again, which is what we need just now. We have an awful lot of rebuilding to do."

"Ends justify means, it is said," dryly commented Ben, rather sarcastically.

"I hear you," I replied.

"Well, if there are no more conflicts on Cymry and all the rulers have a vehicle in which to settle their disputes peacefully, then perhaps all this was worth it," Lilly Ann noted, a hopeful tone in her voice.

"Well, I suppose so," Caitlyn's anger finally melted. "Only I don't what that treasonous creature in my towns ever again," she exclaimed flatly and with a tone of finality.

"We can use this on her," Lilly Ann noted. "If Lachlan ever tries anything, we can take her aside, point out what we know of her part in this war, and threaten to expose her. Blackmail might keep her in line."

"Let's hope some good comes from this treacherous evil," I ended the discussion. I was in a dark mood anyway. This revelation only added to my depression.

Chapter 9 Mano del Dio

The sun burst forth its brilliant yellow light in sharp contrast to the deep blue sky, utterly devoid of clouds on June 1, 623 AH. It was Saturday early morning, the Holy Day, but the Rooster had already been up hours before daylight. He had many details to oversee personally. His Holiness, Pope Yazi I was making his weekly trip from Constanza south to Galantas to conduct another of his Sunday Holy Healing Masses at the Great Basilica in the heart of the capital of Megalos. He, General R. Thraxton, was responsible for the Pope's safe passage over the twenty-five miles to the city. Indeed, he was in charge of not only the Pope's security but also all that of their entire city-state, Constanza.

Given carte blanche, the Rooster had handpicked each member of his special forces. Originally, his bland title was General of the Security Forces, however months ago, with the blessing of Pope Yazi himself, Rooster's organization within the Church of Jehosanity was renamed Mano del Dio, the Hand of God. His title was now Supreme Prelate, befitting his magnificent sky blue robes.

Rooster's original three choices, Karlos, Cax, and Thondakas had measured up to his intensely brutal training and were now his lieutenants, called Prelates. Each oversaw or commanded ten other men, known as the Initiates. However, Rooster always handled personally their training. Each man had to undergo intense physical pain and yet still function optimally, for theirs was the most valuable charge on Tarra, the ultimate safety of Pope Yazi I and Constanza City. Rooster was always dreaming up new ways of inflicting low-grade pain for their training use. However, the belt of thorns, now called the Cinghia Canta, proved the most workable. His men, out of all the men on Tarra, could operate highly effectively despite personal pain and injury, just as the Rooster had done all his life, until entering the Pope's service.

However, maintaining focus and a clear head while under pain was only part of the intense training each member of Mano del Dio underwent. Each handpicked member had to be just as focused and intense when under humiliation and emotional distress. Nothing, absolutely nothing could be allowed to interfere with their task of protecting his Holiness, nothing. This, the Rooster drilled into every member of his force on a daily basis. He knew his men were ready for anything now.

Before joining the Church, the Rooster was the most feared assassin and thief in all Megalos. No one had the cunning and skill that this man possessed or all the shady connections. If something was going on in Galantas, the Rooster was certain to get wind of it. At least once a week, he donned his brown tradesman robes and spent time in his old haunts in the seedier pubs of Galantas. His three Prelates did likewise. His wisdom had born fruit. Rumor had it that the assassin Kar was forming up a group of thugs. The Rooster knew that Kar was often in the service of the Emperor Justinian, the archenemy of Pope Yazi I. Justinian was handpicked for Emperor by the Church of Sol, which was rapidly losing it members to the Church of Jehosanity.

"Good morning Supreme Prelate," Pope Yazi I called out, as he and a half dozen priests walked out to the stables. "Fine day for a drive to Galantas, is it not? Are you ready to go?" Suddenly, Yazi noticed an extra carriage. Normally, he rode in his elegant covered carriage, while the others followed in theirs. Today, he saw four carriages, well actually the usual two and two others that had been last used several years ago, before Yazi had commissioned the Royal Carriage befitting his high post. Now that he began looking, Yazi also saw the entire compliment of his security force present as well.

"Your Holiness, today my men will take the carriage that you normally use. I will personally drive you in the older one. We will follow about a mile behind the Royal Coaches to be on the safe side. I fear for your safety this morning."

While the other six priests grumbled soft protests at having to ride in the much less comfortable old coaches, Pope Yazi I commented, "A wise man always trusts his Security General, Supreme Prelate Thraxton. I will be honored to follow your wishes." This was not what his other priests had hoped Yazi would say, and they had no choice but to climb into the old coach. Yazi, with assistance from the Rooster, climbed into the old coach. Definitely, it lacked the comforts built into the new Royal Coach.

Yazi watched ten security men squeeze into each of the Royal Coaches, which were designed to seat only four. Once inside, they rolled the canvas windows down, hiding the occupants from outside view. Karlos and Cax each took a seat beside the Pope's usual two drivers, and with a hand signal from the Rooster, they moved out of the Royal Stables onto the paved road. Only his Prelates caught the extra hand signal, which meant, "Kill them all." Each gave a barely perceptible head nod to the Rooster, acknowledging they fully understood their leader's orders.

Rooster climbed up to the driver's seat. An open window behind his seat allowed him to talk easily with his mentor. "We will give them a few minute's head start, your Holiness," the Rooster explained, as he watched his third Prelate, Thondakas take the driver's seat on the remaining coach. "Today, we take extra precautions," he continued his private conversation with the Pope. "Every Saturday for months now, you have followed the same route at the same time, going to Galantas to conduct our Holy Mass. Your enemies most certainly have your itinerary down pat by this time. So today, we vary it slightly."

"I see," Yazi said scratching his beard. After a pause, he asked, "You suspect an attempt on my life today?"

"I am not sure that it will be today, your Eminence. However, there have been many clandestine activities of late. I wish to err on the side of caution. Sit back, relax, and enjoy the drive. It is a fine day indeed," the

Rooster added, as he gently brought the pair of horses into motion.

Pope Yazi I did his usual actions on this five-hour ride into the capital city. He spent a few minutes reflecting upon the words he would say, his special sermon. Then, he dozed off, something he found himself doing far more than he desired these days. "Ah, body's growing old," he explained to himself. Hours passed slowly.

An hour out of Galantas, Karlos, who was on the lead Royal Coach, commented to his driver, "Caution now, something is not right up ahead."

"Ah, do you really think that something bad is going to happen to us today?" asked the driver for the tenth time. He'd made this trip hundreds of times, and the only mishap was one cracked wheel. His was a boring job indeed.

"It has already happened. Look up ahead there in the distance. See that rock fall. It's blocking the road. The coach will have to stop while we clear a passage. Don't you find that alarming?"

"Not the least. Rock slides happen, you know," the driver replied still bored, but with a slight hint of curiosity that he might get to stop and do something for a couple minutes. Still moving rocks out of the roadway was only slightly less boring than driving the coach.

Karlos stuck his hand through the window opening behind the driver's seat and signaled his men. Turning to the driver, he said dryly, "If something happens, if you want to stay alive, duck down here and stay out of sight. We will handle it." This was more words than Karlos normally spoke to others not in his group. Yet it was his duty to keep the driver alive, to protect him.

Minutes later, the driver reined in the horses close to the apparent rock fall. Karlos dismounted, walked slowly over to the pile, and called out pretending to speak to Pope Yazi, "Your Holiness, it seems some rocks have fallen onto the roadway. One minute while I clear them out of the way. We'll still get to Galantas on time for your High Mass." He slowly walked toward the rocks, but his eyes caught glimpses of men attempting to sneak around the boulder-strewn landscape on either side of the two carriages. These, he left confidently to his hidden men. How many would attack him and when was his prime concern. He pretended not to see the twenty men moving in behind him on either side.

All his senses heightened to full alert. If Kar was behind this, he knew that Kar would leave no one alive here. Would Kar come after him or would Kar be one of those moving in for the supposed assassination of the Pope? He gave a barely perceptible wiggle with each arm and felt the pair of throwing daggers drop from their concealed harness into each hand. He held his arms at his side as though walking as he finally reached the rock pile.

Suddenly, without warning, two thugs jumped up from their hiding places behind the rock pile. Both waved swords and began scrambling over the rocks to attack this unarmed driver. With a simple, highly practiced motion, Karlos swung both arms upwards, flinging the throwing daggers out before him. The thug on his right took the dagger squarely in his forehead and dropped like a rock upon the rocks.

The man on his left took the dagger in his belly, forcing Karlos to pull a spare dagger from his back harness. In one swift motion, he let it fly. The thug took this one in his throat; he too went down onto the rocks. Seeing no others coming after him, Karlos turned to see the action going on behind him. Once all the thugs were down, he could return and make sure none lived.

Five men on each side of each coach rushed towards the side doors. To their utter amazement, all doors were suddenly flown open, and armed men jumped outside to confront them. Four others pointed heavy crossbows out of the windows, ready to shoot needed targets, in case one of their own got into trouble. The fight, if one could call it that, lasted all of sixty seconds. When Karlos turned to watch, he got to see the last thug fall. Dead silence filled their ears.

"Kar, did anyone see Kar?" Karlos called out. Several "No's" broke the silence. "Fan out; search the area, Kar must be here somewhere. Cax and I will make certain all are dead." At once, twenty men fanned out over the boulder-strewn landscape, searching cautiously for the assassin. Meanwhile, the two Prelates visited each of the fallen thugs and slit their throats wide open on the off chance they were not dead. They also gathered up their men's daggers.

"Over there, he's trying to get away on horseback," called out one Initiate. Distinct twangs from four heavy crossbows broke the stillness as the two Prelates looked up from their work to see a man fleeing on horseback. Suddenly, the man's arms rose up in surprise, the quarrels found their mark. He slid off the startled, bolting horse, which had also been hit. Both Prelates rushed as fast as they could to the fallen assassin. Both knew that their Initiates would be in grave danger if Kar were still alive.

Karlos called out, "Stay back, men. Leave him to us!" Cox and he maneuvered as fast as they could over the rocky terrain. If Kar was only wounded, given a bit of time, he could recover and begin to take action against them. As they approached, that was indeed just what Kar was doing. Although his leg was broken and he lay at a weird angle on the ground, the master assassin was in the process of applying poison to several throwing daggers. Another minute and Kar would be ready to face them.

"Drop those daggers, Kar!" commanded Karlos, the first to reach him. Karlos had grabbed a heavy crossbow and now had it pointed straight at Kar's head. "One tiny move, Kar, and I'll fire."

"You will kill me anyway," cursed Kar, who attempted to throw a dagger at Karlos. Due to his pain and awful body position, the dagger missed completely. Karlos did not miss. As soon as he saw an arm muscle twitch, his finger pulled the trigger. The quarrel skewered the assassin's head, coming out its back and shattering on the rocks. Kar never saw his dagger miss.

"Nice shooting," Cax called out as he joined Karlos. "Ah, poison. You alright?"

"Yes, he missed me by a mile. Slit his throat for me, will you, please? Then, we best douse this poison with some water. Don't want our Initiates to get poisoned."

Cax leaned over the assassin and did the deed; however, Kar was already dead. They returned to the coach for a couple water gourds. Next, they assembled their men and gave them an impromptu lesson on assassins and their use of poisons. Meanwhile, the two drivers climbed down to look, and they followed Karlos' orders to remove the rocks. Pope Yazi I would soon arrive, and he didn't want to delay His Eminence.

Indeed, the drivers barely had the rocks moved when the Rooster pulled up behind the two Royal Coaches. A hand signal from Cax told him that all was clear. "Your Eminence, it seems I was right. The Royal Coaches met with some trouble. It is safe for you to get out and inspect now, but do not leave my side." The Rooster climbed down and helped the old man out of the carriage.

"What happened here?" Yazi asked looking about at the bloody mess to either side of the road.

"An attempt upon your life occurred here. They blocked the road with a supposed rock fall, which forced the coaches to stop. Five men charged each side of each coach, expecting to slay you and your other priests."

"It was Kar!" called out Karlos to the Rooster. "He's quite dead now."

"Ah, your Holiness, this was a planned assassination. Their leader was called Kar, a known assassin of Galantas."

"Who would order such a thing as this? Murdering Holy Priests?" asked one of the dumbfounded priests who had joined their spiritual leader.

"Assassins are well paid," the Rooster replied. "Someone paid Kar to kill all of you. It is likely that we will never know who paid Kar. He would never tell his men who had hired them, nor could we have gotten that information out of him. I know Kar. That datum he took to his grave, I am afraid."

"Rotten luck. Someone wants us dead and we don't know who!" another priest cursed angrily.

"Ah, but you have a pretty good idea who hired him don't you?" Pope Yazi I winked at the Rooster.

"It is a well-known fact that Kar often took assignments directly from Emperor Justinian," the Rooster replied. Just then, Karlos joined them, holding a very nicely made bag in his hand.

"Look what we have here?" he displayed the finely made pouch, opening it, and showing the men the handful of valuable gemstones it contained. "A royal payment, if I ever saw one."

"Still, there is nothing here to directly connect Justinian to this attack is there?" Yazi replied.

"Unfortunately not," the Rooster answered truthfully. "However, it is time we continued the journey. We do not want you to arrive late. You may continue your journey in the Royal Coaches now. I will again accompany the driver; my men will finish up here and join us in Galantas."

With that, the priests climbed into their comfortable coaches, thankful now for these new Royal Coaches. They had much to discuss among themselves, praising the foresight of their Pope in hiring these incredible security men. Their opinions of the Rooster and his Mano del Dio grew enormously this day.

Late that night, Pope Yazi I held a private meeting with the Rooster. "I want to thank you personally for your wisdom and actions today. You saved my life." The Rooster bowed his head humbly; he had no words for which to reply. "Were any of your men wounded?" he asked, realizing that in the confusion, he had failed utterly to inquire about their well-being.

"Only two Initiates. They passed their field test, and both brought down their man, even though slightly wounded. No serious wounds, your Holiness. Twenty-one of the enemy dead; two of my men received minor sword cuts. We will do better next time, your Holiness." Indeed, the Rooster felt somewhat discouraged that two of his men took minor wounds; it marred an otherwise perfect field action.

Yazi roared with laughter, "Rooster, twenty-one enemy dead and only a couple minor scratches. I would say that is more than fabulous. You have done tremendously well indeed. He shook the Rooster's hand vigorously. Poor Rooster was dumbfounded with this high praise and could not utter a single word. Later, in the privacy of his own room, he wept tears of joy before falling asleep.

The next day, the Pope held a special advisory meeting of his security forces and his High Priests. "Gentlemen, I believe the time has come for us to implement the next plan, the removal of all obscene, decadent art throughout all Megalos. I intend to issue Papal Order #7: Destruction of Decadent Artwork. All paintings, sculptures, frescoes, any and all artwork that depict lewd sexual scenes, such as naked women, penises on male statues, anything obscene shall be confiscated and properly disposed of by those of our staff. What say you all? Please speak freely."

"Your Holiness, will this not cause a violent backlash among many, especially the followers of Sol?" asked one Priest.

"Indeed it should," Yazi replied. "It is all due mostly to that heathen Emperor Hiro some fifty years ago. He fostered a community that dwelt upon lewd, promiscuous, heathen attitudes, reflected in the art of that era. If our people have any hope of reaching Heaven, they must repent such sins and accept the salvation of our Lord."

A good deal of discussion followed, especially upon how this Papal Order would be carried out. Yazi was shrewd. "Let the people do the Lord's work for us. Let them confiscate the vile artwork and bring it to some central destruction site. A Priest can oversee its destruction. This way, the Church will not be seen as doing the actual dirty work, just the normal citizens of Galantas." This the priests liked, for some were in fear for their lives. The scare from yesterday was still very fresh in their minds.

They discussed their plans for over an hour. The Rooster and his three Prelates sat quietly at the back of the room, their usual positions. Neither said a word during this entire time, listening quietly to the ideas expressed, forming their own opinions as to the potential problems and pitfalls this new plan would bring. At last, Yazi commented, "And what have our Security Forces to say about this Papal Order?" He desperately wanted to get the Rooster's opinion.

"Your Eminence, there will most certainly be a significant backlash, as you say from the followers of Sol. Major trouble will follow as certain as night, the day." He saw a glimmer of doubt appear subtly upon the Pope's face and knew that he had registered the correct impingement. He'd given the Pope a dire warning. "However, you also have another plan that may counter somewhat the expected backlash." The room became intensely quiet; the Rooster could hear himself breathing and tried to control it. He preferred to be invisible.

"Implement public Gladiatorial Combat events," was his answer. The Rooster did not elaborate, but let his words sink into the collective minds present. A slight nod from his three Prelates convinced him that they also thought as he did. Give the public an exciting spectacle to watch will take their minds off matters at hand.

"Excellent point, Supreme Prelate Thraxton, excellent," Pope Yazi I effused praise upon his prized security man. "That will give the people something positive to discuss and to look forward to watching. In order to implement this effectively, we need Emperor Justinian both to propose such and to support it completely. The idea must not be seen as coming from the Church, and I know just how that can be accomplished. Supreme Prelate, I'll need to make a special visit to the Senate two days from now. Arrange my security, for the Emperor will also be addressing the Senate that day. I will meet him beforehand. Scribe, take down this message," Yazi ordered, and began dictating a letter to the Emperor, asking to meet briefly before his address to the Senate. Rooster, on the other hand, began making vast mental preparations; his liege was walking right into the lion's den, so to speak.

Although everyone now thought the meeting finished with the dictation of the letter, Pope Yazi I raised his hand to silence the soft chatter. "There remains one additional matter to discuss, one aspect of these proclamations must be addressed." Everyone straightened up hurriedly, a bit abashed that their assumption that the meeting was over was incorrect. Priest looked at priest; puzzled looks reflected back.

"Being the Pope brings with it an enormous responsibility. The Pope must have great wisdom and above all foresight. Yes, this is a training exercise for you. One day perhaps one of you will step up to fill my shoes when I have gone to join Jehosa in Heaven. Whoever that is must be able to see the ramifications of their decisions and be able to handle those before they actually arise. So what detail has been overlooked, my friends? Who can foresee what else must be done, eh?" Silence filled the room for an interminable time.

The Rooster had an answer, but thought that Pope Yazi I wanted his priests to answer, not him. Hence, using the hand signal system he'd devised, he messaged his three Prelates. All three concurred with his choice. Finally, breaking the complete silence, his voice in a near whisper, the Rooster asked, "Your Eminence, may I put forth an answer?" Hearing the harshness of his voice, the Rooster wished that he had not said anything; perhaps he was totally out of place saying anything just now.

"Absolutely, Supreme Prelate. It seems that my High Priests have no answer, no foresight. I am very curious to know what our Chief of Security would offer," Yazi encouraged the Rooster.

Hoping the priests would not see his imagined reddened face and still speaking in a whisper, the Rooster replied, "Your Eminence, there remains the question of what to do about the artists who have made these unholy works of art. You destroy their products, but what of the makers? Do we send them to the Fires of Hell?"

In sharp contrast to the whispers of the Rooster, Yazi stood up, pounded his fist on the table for added emphasis, and spoke loudly, "Brilliant, positively correct! What of those artists? Gentlemen, our Supreme Prelate of Security has more foresight than all of you combined! Again, you would do well to always listen to him!" Now Rooster's face did turn crimson, and he reactively pulled his cowl up, trying to hide his face.

Now that it had been pointed out to them, the problem of the artists was plainly obvious to all the gathered priests. Many chided themselves silently for not having seen it themselves. The table discussion rapidly turned to what was to be done with the artists. Some were all for sending them to the Fires of Hell, as the Rooster put it — a polite way of saying they would be assassinated. Others opted for maiming so that they could never again paint or sculpt such vileness.

High Priest Silas, who had long coveted Pope Yazi I's position, had a different line of thought. *Yes, I did miss that aspect of the Papal Order, but I see that our Security Man did not. Once again, I learn from Yazi. Do not discount your Chief of Security. Often he can see what you cannot. I promise always to make excellent use of our Security Chief, when I am the Pope. Yes, we could easily kill these wicked artists, but what would Jehosa have us do? Ah, yes.* Now he voiced his opinion aloud.

Silas said, "Why not offer these artists a chance at redemption? Offer them reasonable funds to paint, sculpt, et cetera marvelous works of art for our churches, praising and exulting Jehosa? That way, we may save their souls and adorn our Churches with the best art in all Tarra."

Even the Rooster was humbled by such powerful wisdom. He took note that it did not come from Pope Yazi I; Silas made an indelible impression on the Rooster with this remark, one that would prove vital years from now. A broad grin broke the stern face of Yazi, "Yes, Father Silas, that is precisely what we must do. I thought of that last night, but I wanted to see if any of you could also realize the same. Well done, Silas, well done indeed." Silas smiled, thinking that perhaps Yazi had just given him support for his bid to become the next Pope when Yazi passed away.

Tuesday morning proved to be an unseasonably hot morning in Galantas. The two leaders spied each other, amid the throng of grey togas of the milling Senators. The sole brilliant yellow robe of Justinian and the sky blue robe of Yazi stuck out, causing much whispered conversation among the Senators. All wondered what brought both leaders to the Senate on such a hot day. Even more interesting, Pope Yazi I waved to Emperor Justinian, and the two men, along with their guards, moved towards each other, even shaking hands!

"Ah, there you are, Emperor. Fine morning. Glad that we can meet in person," Pope Yazi I began, presenting a cheerful mien without the slightest hint of the foiled assassination plot just days before. He detected that the Emperor was slightly ill at ease, a sure sign that he had commissioned the botched assassination attempt. Yazi ignored the other man's discomfort, "I asked for this meeting because we both hold the same guiding principles, we want only the best for our people. I've thought about this for some time now, and I wanted to bounce an idea off of you."

Clearly, this meeting was not about what Justinian thought it would be. He came prepared to deny any part in the recent assassination plot. In fact, that twenty-one men lay dead beside the roadway to the northern port was all the information his Centurions had — just the remains of a crime, but nothing by which even to identify the intended victims. Most thought this was a particularly baffling crime. Thus, Justinian came prepared to offer only sketchy information about it. Taken completely by surprise, he felt immense relief coming over him; his vitality returned at once. "Yes, these are indeed trying times. What is this idea you have?" he replied rather cheerily.

"Our people need some kind of entertainment with which they can use to take their attention off of the travails of life. Perhaps something like a gladiatorial fighting match every few days would do it. I'm sure that you could organize it well. Nothing like a good roust-a-bout to get your attention off life's problems, eh? What do you think?"

"Yes, I like it. We could even allow betting on who might win; nothing like friendly wagers to attract attention. The amphitheater is mostly unused these days. It holds several thousand people. Ah, but what would be the Church's position in all this?" he asked, momentarily controlling his enthusiasm over the sparkling idea just presented. He did not trust this Pope.

"We just want our people to be happy. I suppose if you need some financial backing, the Church could assist, but it would be behind the scenes. We do not want any limelight over this. No indeed, such belongs to your men and the stalwart Centurions performing the fighting demonstrations. We can just help with any needed finances, if that is acceptable to you," Pope Yazi I replied, knowing that he had played Justinian perfectly. Instead of confronting him over the foiled assassination plot, he had given him a good solution to some of the ruler's more pressing domestic problems. Justinian bought it completely.

"Great! Consider it done," the Emperor replied. "Say, I am just about to address the Senate. This will make a wonderful opportunity to make the formal announcement. How about standing beside me as a show of our combined unity on this venture? It would be a good gesture, don't you think?"

Inwardly, Yazi roared with laughter. Outwardly, he feigned a serious mien, "Well, it would show our unity. I bow to your political wisdom, but please don't ask for a big speech from me." This was precisely what the Emperor desired to hear. Arm in arm the two archenemies walked onto the central platform to address the full Senate, less of course, the women senators who had stopped attending some time ago. The Senate clapping was deafening.

Beginning June 7, 623 AH, the Imperial Gladiatorial Combats were held weekly, with the Emperor netting nearly one thousand ducats each week in betting profits. He had a new source of income. The fights quickly became an instant success with the citizens of Galantas.

Even the wanton confiscation and destruction of all types of lewd artwork from all quarters of Galantas was overshadowed by the weekly fights. Statues, paintings, ceramics — piles upon piles were brought to the official Destruction Station by ardent followers of Jehosanity. Many, however, protested this wanton destruction of magnificent artwork, but they could take no effective action. The Senate hotly debated this topic for months. As usual, the Senate took no real action to stop it.

However, both by word of mouth and by posters prominently displayed around the city, artists were encouraged to visit the Church of Jehosanity. The Church was commissioning quite a lot of new artwork with which to adorn their ever-growing number of churches. The fact that they also paid well did much to dissuade many artists from launching into violent protests. On the other hand, this large influx of artists wishing for commissions led to an additional problem for the church.

"Gentlemen, gentlemen, let's all calm down a bit," Pope Yazi I brought his large assemblage of Priests and High Priest back into some semblance of order. He had called this special meeting to address the artist challenge: what do you want us to paint or sculpt? The ideas were as numerous as the priests in attendance were. However, Pope Yazi I took this opportunity to issue Papal Order #10, which had been years in the making. Over the past several years, his special scribes had been busy rewriting all the sacred texts, the accounts written by the Son of God's Ten Disciples. Yazi had personally overseen this vitally important project; the entire future of the Church depended upon his actions.

"First, allow me to present you each with a first edition of our most sacred liturgy: The Holy Gospels of Jehosanity. Years in the making, we have just finished combining all the ancient records into a coherent account of the life of the Son of God, Jes Amir. I have made some slight changes that are crucial. We all want the salvation of all our people, do we not?" None could disagree with him on this point. "So Jes Amir must be viewed as not a mere man but as the one and only Son of God. His birth must be seen as a Divine Miracle. Henceforth, Josephus and Mary Amir had one son, Josh, the older brother of Jes. Unable to conceive and bear more children, Jehosa appeared unto Mary, saying 'Thy barren womb shall give birth to my Only Son.' Thus it was that Mary and Josephus beheld the Immaculate Conception. This removes all taint of the Initial Fall from Grace initiated by the women of Tarra. It places the Son of God into the godhood that people can accept." Only a few priests voiced any objections to Pope Yazi. On the contrary, many saw this as a terrific way to improve their ministry. They would now have the Son of God being immortal and above the common man, as befitting his station.

Yet, Yazi was not done, "Further, since the Son of God is immortal, we cannot ever let it be known that he took a fleshly woman of sin as wife. That will never do, as it lends credence to the common man's sins. Oh no. All mention of that vile heretic of a wife, that prostitute Bethany Madelyn Amir, has been stricken from all records. It is as though she never existed." He paused while the assembled priests digested this doctrine change. Considering the times, even fewer raised complaints about this.

"Now these changes provide us with all the direction we need to inspire and direct all the artists. Depict scenes of the Divine Miracle, the Immaculate Conception, the Holy Crucifixion, and the Holy Resurrection. Adorn all our churches with artwork depicting the life of the Son of God." Now the priests chatted openly, and ideas flowed like water, precisely what Pope Yazi I had intended. These several hundred would now go forth and commission art such as had never been seen on Tarra before. In a decade, the population would become so familiar with the art and the images and stories they told, that history would have been completely rewritten. All would forget the fact that Jes was merely a man, had married a prostitute wife, and fathered children by that unholy womb! However, he did not anticipate Rooster's visit later that night.

All that afternoon, the Rooster pondered the significance of the two new Papal Orders. True, since these were ministerial and not security matters, he had not been asked to attend. Indeed, he would have felt so utterly out of place had he been asked that he would not have uttered one word, attempting to become completely invisible in the deepest corner of the room. However, the impact of these two new orders did not escape him, nor did their overall ramifications. Thus it was that the Rooster had requested a private meeting with the Pope that evening after evening Mass.

"Rooster, you look most troubled, my son. Come on in, tell me about it," Yazi spoke reassuringly to his Chief of Security. The Pope was not expecting what the Rooster had to say. For once, he had not foreseen as well as his Security Chief! He felt rather humbled by it and made a long entry later on in his private journal, to be read only by his successor.

"It's about your two new Papal Orders, your Eminence," the Rooster began, choosing his words carefully. "It is one thing to claim that the Son of God was Immaculately Conceived and quite another to say that he remained a virgin, that he did not marry and father children. I foresee this aspect causing the downfall of the entire Church." Seeing the startled look upon the Pope's face, Rooster knew that he had better explain it more fully and quickly.

"You see, up in Juda Arad, it is common knowledge that he took a wife and of the role she played during his life here on Tarra. It is known that she bore him at least two children before he was crucified on the cross. Rumors have it that she then fled the Arad for the Sea Princes, seeking sanctuary. So many years have now passed that their children ought to have grown up and born families of their own. What I am saying is that by this time, there must be quite a lot of direct descendants of the Son of God. What will be their reaction and the reaction of those that may be following them when our Church denies their entire existence?"

For the first time ever, the Rooster saw his mentor, Pope Yazi I, pale; lines of worry crossed his face. "My gods, Rooster, you are so utterly right, so keen in your observations! I missed this detail entirely. I was so caught up in the rewriting and getting it implemented that I failed to see the broader ramifications of it. Yes, I personally know that the prostitute fled with her children right after the Holy Resurrection. She fled toward the Sea Princes, that I am certain, but where she may have ended up, who can say. If we do nothing, once these people get wind of what we have done, undoubtedly open rebellion will follow, perhaps dooming our entire Church! Thank you, Rooster, most sincerely! Your observations have saved the Holy Church!" Again, such praise caused the poor man to stare at the floor, embarrassed. No one other than this Holy Pope had ever bestowed such praise upon this deformed man.

The Pope paced the floor for a time. "Correct me if I am wrong," he said at last. "There appears to be only one avenue that we can follow, if the Church is to be saved. We must make a pre-emptive strike and slay all living relatives of that entire bloodline, wipe them all out. If even one direct descendant of Jes Amir remains alive, that person could bring down the whole Church! Do you concur?"

"Yes, your Eminence. Really, there is no other way. It is as you say; one person of his line could spark an entire revolution against the Church. All must be hunted down and slain. I will do this task for you, if you ask it of me."

"Thank you Rooster," the Pope replied with a sigh. "You are the most qualified person to undertake such a Holy Mission. However, I cannot spare you from here; I need you too much here in Constanza City. I cannot entrust this to my Holy Paladins; they are mostly incompetent. Good soldiers, yes, but they lack the ability to see through deceptions and disguises. No, pick out your best Prelate for this Holy Mission. He will be in complete charge of the mission, and only he will know the true nature of the mission. I will send along fifty Holy Paladins to support him. Intelligence, cunning, wisdom, we need a man who will stop at nothing to accomplish this incredibly vital mission."

On June 10, 623 AH, Karlos set out on horseback accompanied by fifty Holy Paladins. He knew his orders well. Still the magnitude of his mission weighed heavily upon his mind. Pope Yazi I had entrusted the future of the entire Church on his shoulders. He swore that he would not let them down. Swiftly, they rode northward up the long road toward Juda Arad. Karlos knew that he would have to be swift, stealthy, and crafty, if his mission were to be successful. Blood from his Cinghia Canta oozed slightly onto his sky blue robes as he rode, the pain, a constant reminder of his Holy Mission. He would not fail.

Chapter 10 The Benevolent Monarchy

Elona Woodgrove Po, the last of the Po line in Velona, paced her makeshift office. Although five months pregnant with her first child, she still put in very long days. She was twenty-six now with blonde hair and brown eyes. Her ancestors forged the city-state of Velona from the wilderness ages ago. Now she was the sole ruler of the Velona Sector, Sea Princes — its benevolent monarch. Elona was also a Protector, having apprenticed to her husband, Alton Woodgrove Po, also a Protector.

Alton Woodgrove Po was twenty-nine. Many years before, he was the Protector for the now defunct Oak Circle. Well built, with medium black hair and eyes of the kind that seemed to penetrate you when he looked at you, Alton cut a striking figure. His first wife, their Circle's healer, had been killed, leaving him to raise their three children. Now that they were fully trained at our Mont Blanc fortress, they had begun dating and contemplating beginning their own families. Thus, Alton's absence was actually desired.

Their new Circle, the Velona Circle, was definitely a very strange one indeed. Both Thomas Algrove and Benjamin Thrush were Protectors of Circles that had been nearly wiped out by the Grey Creatures. They were also in their late twenties and itching for a fight. Hence, they jumped at the opportunity last winter to assist Elona and Alton with the Axemen. Afterwards, they decided to remain in Velona. Thus, the Velona Circle had four Protectors in it instead of one. This was a very judicious choice because of the numerous attempts on Elona's life during that first winter and early spring.

However, three others arrived midwinter to complete the Velona Circle. Again, these were older druwids, whose Circles had been severely broken by the Grey Creatures. Albert Jonstone, the Planner, was thirty-one. His entire family had been killed during a Grey Creature attack. Moving to Velona actually allowed him closure on his former life and a chance to begin anew, which finally brought him out of his melancholy. Mary Dietz, the Healer, was thirty-five. Her story was similar to Albert's; she was the sole survivor of her original Circle. Sally Longton became their Communicator. She was twenty-five and had never been married; she was homely. Yet she spoke five languages fluently.

Elona and her Circle faced disaster in its teeth that first winter. Velona had been betrayed numerous times in its past. Perhaps the biggest impact was the former ruler unleashing the plague upon the land. True, the plague wiped out the invading Centurions, but it also killed half of the entire population of the sector. Even the Sisterhood abandoned that sector for good, just before the plague struck. Later on, after sacking by the Centurions and then later by the Galts, most of the wealthy nobles moved to safer sectors, abandoning Velona to its ruin. Banditry sprang up nearly everywhere. Making matters even worse, the Axemen invaded last fall, easily conquering all resistance. Into this mess,

Elona had plunged, the sole rightful heir to the throne of Velona. Backed by the Guardians, the Sisterhood of Fortress d'Grange, and the Count of d'Grange, she took back the sector.

That had been the easy part, the integrating of the Axemen into their sector. The four Protectors made an indelible impression on the hearty fighters from Volksholm, the Axemen, with their Holy Fires from the Sky, the Holy Flames. Their leader, Eric the Bold, called her the mighty War Maiden Po, High Priestess of Tur. The real reason the Axemen invaded Velona last fall was overpopulation at home. With massive under-population in Velona now, it made good sense for Elona to allow many Axemen to immigrate to Velona. Indeed, once the ice floes melted this spring, several thousand more came, many with their complete families to settle in this new land.

During the winter, she visited every town and village in the sector, delivering the same speech to all her people. It's illustrious to see how she explained her rule to her subjects.

"My role as supreme leader is going to be one of simply bringing in order, just order. I want to make the environment here very conducive toward allowing every person to be just as productive as they desire. Rulers should not be enforcing their will on everyone, no heavy-handed laws to be obeyed. I will, when needed, make judicial rulings to settle disputes and such. Every citizen of this sector ought to be free to make their own choices in life. I will step in only when those choices harm others here more broadly than they help. It is my duty and obligation as ruler to bring in as much order as I possibly can."

"If we have to heavily police our people, forcing them under duress and threat of immediate punishment to do my bidding, then they have already lost their power of choice, have they not? I do not want a slave society here, no need for rebellious populations. Besides, heavy-handed policing actions are highly detrimental to a person's production. It's by having every person in Velona actually producing what they can to their fullest extent that will turn this mess around, making Velona a thriving place to live once more. I want to end up with a Velona in which a naive virgin with a large money pouch can walk the entire breadth of our land without encountering the slightest problem!"

"It will be hard at first, I know. Expect much confusion to foment and boil off as I put in order here. For a while, it will seem like more chaos is resulting than order, but that always happens when one puts in order."

"Anyone can immigrate here as long as they agree to the few conditions I set down. They must agree to support the local government, which is me, with a small fee. I am asking for one percent of everyone's production. Said fees will go toward projects that help everyone in the sector out in some way. For example, a stone wall should be built to protect the city. A reserve of food and supplies should be established in case of emergencies. Wagons travel much faster on the Centurion paved roads, so we must extend the paved roads out to other towns. Vastly more ships are needed to expand our merchant trading."

"To live in Velona means that you support the sector's ruler, me, or if you prefer to call it the local government, you may. Citizens of Velona ought to be supporting their government, whose job it is to bring the order they need, so that they can put their undivided attention onto producing their products, whatever they may be. In times of crisis when Velona is being attacked from some outside invader, each will do their part to support the defense of Velona."

"I am and will always be a Priestess of Tur. The key is a person's power of choice over matters. If you take away a person's power of choice, they will fight back or succumb to apathy, doing nothing. If I go around issuing Laws that everyone must obey or else I have them forcibly arrested, confined to a dungeon, beaten, or whatever, at once they lose their power of choice. People in apathy produce little and of poor quality. Rebellious people turn out products with defects, getting even, so to speak. I want people here to act because they believe what they are doing is for the best for everyone, including themselves, their families, and the sector. I think if I can bring in enough order, the vast majority of you will come around; it is, after all, in your best interests to do so. Still, I am not a dreamer. There will be a few that will not, no matter how much order I bring to the sector. They will be dealt with on an individual basis."

"When I returned victorious to Velona, I met with the old High Council. I told them flatly: You've had your chance and you blew it! I am now the sole ruler of Velona. Besides being my birthright, I am the last living Po, and I have earned the right to rule. I have ended the Axemen invasion amicably by bringing them into our folds. In time, you will see a highly productive group and reap large profits from their trade goods. All these years and you have still not begun to use our mineral resources to make metal goods, now have you? I suspect that within a year or so, these immigrants will be producing vast quantities of infinitely tradable goods. What wife of yours would not love to have new metal cooking pans? Shipwrights, new quality woodworking tools, even quality swords to trade. Gentlemen, I am giving you the opportunity to put Velona back on the map, expanding into a thriving economy that vastly exceeds all the other sectors! Need I add that you will have more wealth than you can possibly spend?"

"I told the old High Council: I want the High Council expanded to thirteen members at least. The four noble houses are already on it. I will appoint a Priest of Tur to be on it, that's five. We no longer have the Sisterhood present in our sector; otherwise, I would place one of them on it as well. I reserve the right to do so, if they ever make their presence felt here in our sector again. A seat goes to the Shipwright's Guild and one goes to the Mariner's Guild. Where will we be without those two? Nowhere. They must have a vital say in the running of Velona. That makes seven. What of the other six? I want these filled with a representative of six other guilds that you all here deem the most vital to the recovery and expansion of Velona. So your first action is to decide what other six guilds will be represented on the High

Council. I expect to have your decision within twenty-four hours."

"As you may have heard, I did not get their answer; they could not agree on the guilds. So I decided for them. Our new High Council consists of a representative from each of the four noble houses, the Shipwright, Mariner, Warehouse, and Teamster guilds, a Priest of Tur, an Axeman representative, two representatives from the outlying towns. These town representatives serve a year before another pair of towns get their turn. That way, even the remote villages have a say in the ruling of our sector. I also added a new position, the Defense Guild, a new group dedicated to the protection of our sector. Thus, it is now a High Council of Thirteen."

"Please understand this, if nothing else. All that I am doing and am ever going to do is put in more and more order. This is precisely why I am conducting this meeting today. No, it was not to tell you that I am now the sole ruler and you must follow my laws or face death. That has not ever worked, nor will it ever work. I am truly ashamed that so many of my deceased family chose to go that route. No gentlemen, I am only going to establish lots of order in Velona. I already have begun that by ousting those nutty, so-called priests of Jehosanity. From my vast travels, I can say honestly and truthfully, there is much good in that religion, the worship of Jehosa. However, those priests who came to Velona have perverted that Arad religion almost beyond recognition. I assure you that the Priests of Zargarb would be flabbergasted to hear the perversions done here in Velona in the guise of their religion. They might even arrest those priests if they could find them. I will allow proper Priest of Jehosanity to enter Velona and re-establish their church, but only proper ones. No more of these insane ones."

"Now what exactly is the High Council to do under my rule? Help bring more order into our sector. Look, isn't there some part of your lives that you think you could bring a little better order into?" At this point in her speech, Elona would pick out a likely candidate from the audience and address them: "How about you. Isn't there something in your own life, which could do with a little more order? Surely there is something in your life you are not totally satisfied with and which could stand a little more order being brought into it." Invariably, the person would answer up with something.

Elona uniformly replied to the person, "Good. Can you think of some ways that you could bring more order into that situation?" She worked the person until they vocalized some action that they could take to do so. She would add, "Well said. Let me know how it works out; send me a message about the results." Nearly everyone had at least one, sometimes many, areas, which they thought could use better order. One by one, those who listened to her began to grasp what their High Priestess was asking.

She would end her speech with a challenge: "What I want you to do is just this: work out what areas of life here in our sector need more order brought into them. If possible, prioritize them. You know, what needs order brought to it the most. Write the findings down on an official document and bring it or send it to me. If I concur with your analysis, together we will find ways and means of bringing more order to those. Let's begin with the areas that need it the most. Over time, all of us working together bringing more and more order to life here will make Velona prosper beyond our wildest imaginations."

"Additionally, I will provide the security. It will be my responsibility to prevent Velona from being attacked and sacked again. So if I fail and let some army despoil our land, you have every right to dethrone me. I'll deserve it, and I'll not stop you from removing me from my position. In fact, I will probably beat you to it!"

When she sensed general agreement, she continued, "Finally, you ought to know how I will be evaluating your documents. I will be looking for two key data. One: the actions we take must be for the greater good for all individuals directly involved, for our families, and for the good of all of us in the sector. Secondly, I am partial to always giving a person some power of choice over how matters are handled or resolved. Know then, that if a request meets both of these as I see it, then I will back you completely with all my resources. If a request fails to meet both of these as I see it, I will unilaterally reject it in writing and state precisely why I reject it. Said rejection will specifically be because it would do more harm than good and/or eliminate people's power of choice. We have a lot of work to do, but we are all up to the challenge. A few years from now, we can all look back on this day and mark it as the turning point in the history of Velona. I fully expect Velona to be the most prosperous city in the Sea Princes and the safest in which to live and raise a family."

It was early June 623 AH. Elona and their Circle still were living in their makeshift quarters, a confiscated church abandoned last winter by the fleeing priests of Jehosanity. Located in the heart of the warehouse district down by the docks, Elona found this location to be ideal for her office, but not for a home. Alton had construction of their new home going well, and both had high hopes that they would be able to move into it before she gave birth. Albert, their Planner, did the design work. A city block was walled in enclosing four stone homes in each corner with an open garden in the center, ideal for raising a family. All members of their Circle would be housed here.

She paced the floor of her office once more, before Alton arrived, answering her summons. "What's up dear?" he asked, out of breath from running here.

"This," she thrust a parchment into his hand. "Came this morning from Eric's Camp. Here we go again."

Quickly Alton read the crude handwritten note. "War maiden Po, I regret to inform you that Felio Atwan has run off. He refused to adapt or reform. He swore to get revenge on you. Eric."

"Wasn't he the brigand we caught last week stealing food and intimidating the folks in that village up north?"

"Yes, that's the one. I had such hopes that our scheme would salvage these thieves," Elona sighed.

"Well dear, it has worked in some cases. What is the tally now? About fifty-fifty?" She nodded agreement with his figures. "Your plan is sound. There are always going to be those who refuse to work and insist on thievery and banditry as a way of life. Your idea that they become criminal because they have lost their self-respect and can no longer trust themselves is sound. Shipping them off to live with the Axemen is also wise. Either they work cutting trees or they don't eat. The Axemen have shown us that at least half that we've sent them did recover their self-respect and have returned as viable citizens once more. Work is good therapy. Eric calls it his Boot Camp for Lost Souls."

"I know, but I always feel so let down when the process fails. I know I cannot redeem every soul, but that doesn't keep me from trying," she admitted. "Anyway, this one left on foot. If he is intent upon revenge and heads straight here, we had best be on guard from now on."

"Right, you don't go anywhere without Tom and Ben at your side. Promise me, my love," he insisted. She consented went to find Sally, their Communicator. She would mentally alert the other two Protectors, who were working elsewhere in Velona. Alton did not leave until they arrived. "Take good care of her," he jested as they arrived and he left.

"Another ruffian threat?" Ben inquired. Elona filled them in on the details.

"I remember him. I had to capture him last week," Tom explained. "Honestly, I didn't think he'd be salvageable. He's a hardened criminal, Elona, so stop your fretting. Your plan works at least half of the time."

Just then, a courier arrived with the High Council's Weekly Summary Report. This document absorbed her attention for some time, sharing it with her Circle. Albert, Sally, and Mary soon joined them to go over the figures and make suggestions. "Look at these tallies," Elona exclaimed. "We've got more crops planted than needed by at least fifty percent!"

"Ah, if this holds up, we should have a great deal of produce to market," Mary replied. "No one will want for lack of food this winter."

"Now that we have the figures, I'll send out a pair of inspectors to verify them," Albert commented. Just then, they were interrupted by a knock on their front door, and Sally went to answer it.

She found a poorly dressed young boy on their doorstep. "Please ma'am. I've come to see the High Priestess."

Sally replied, "She is very busy right now. The latest High Council's report has just arrived. What is it that you want of her?"

"I've just got to see her. It is very important. It won't take long, I promise," he pleaded with Sally.

Elona could not help hearing the boy's voice and called out, "It's okay, Sally; let him in." To the others she said, "What good is a High Priestess if she cannot take a minute to hear one of her parishioners?" The boy entered sheepishly, as if he was entering some holy shrine. He had a small sack slung over his shoulder.

"I'm Elona. What is your name, son?" she asked, ignoring the other adults grins.

"Pietro, ma'am, Pietro Alvarez," he said.

"Well, then, Pietro, what is it that you came to see me about?"

"Well, I heard you say several times that we all need to do what we can to make things better here. So I did. I know that the shipwrights are building lots of new ships. But I have a better design than the one they are using. Can I show you?"

"Shouldn't you be talking to the Shipwrights about this? I know very little about the building of ships," Elona replied, hoping to direct him to the proper people.

"I've tried, honest I have. I've been there twenty times. And the last time, they threw me out into the street and told me never to come back again." He was near tears.

Quickly, Elona changed the topic, "Say, how old are you anyway, Pietro?"

"Thirteen, ma'am," he replied, regaining his composure. "May I show you?"

"Sure, let's see what you have," Elona could think of nothing else to do but at least look at the boy's design.

Lovingly, he pulled two wooden ship models from his sack. "Do you have a tub of water I can put these in? I can show you better than I can explain it." Two minutes later, the group stood outside at the rain barrel beside the church, in which rain runoff from the roof was gathered. "Here is a model of the ships they have always been making." He placed a small replica into the barrel. It was an accurate scaled down model of the ships in use in Velona and elsewhere in the Sea Princes. It was the same design handed down by the shipwrights from the time of the original founding of the Sea Princes, well tested and sturdy.

"Here is my new design. I call it a caravel. It is larger, can carry nearly twice the load, has better quarters for the crew, and should withstand storms far better. Let me show you." He began placing pebbles equally into each model, representing potential cargo. "This is as much as our current ships can hold. Watch how both handle waves." He gently rocked the tub. We watched as the current model swayed and nearly sunk, while his caravel merely bobbed. "I'll add more to mine." He doubled the number of stones. Only then did the caravel appear in danger of sinking. Still it handled the waves better than our current ship design.

"Albert, go fetch the Master Shipwright here at once. I am ordering him here immediately. Do not take no for an answer," Elona said sternly.

"Yes, ma'am," Albert replied in mock jest. He rushed off to find the man. Since they were close to the docks, he would be close by. Within ten minutes, both men return, slightly out of breath from the haste that Albert forced upon the shipwright.

"Ah Carlos, glad you could come on such short notice," Elona began. "I understand that Pietro here has been trying to show you his new ship design and you have been refusing to see him."

"Aye, your Holiness. He is but a boy. What does a boy know about ship building?" Carlos replied, obviously very annoyed to find this was what all the fuss was about.

"Carlos, look and watch. Okay, Pietro, do your demonstration once more, from the beginning. This is his new design called a caravel. Watch closely, Carlos," she admonished him sternly. Pietro dutifully went through his little demonstration once more.

Slowly Carlos grasped what he was seeing. Then, he pushed the boy out of the way and experimented with both models further, growing more and more excited by the minute. "I do believe the boy has something here!"

"Glad that you see it as we do," she replied. "Look, if his design proves out, our ships will be vastly superior to all other ships on Tarra. Since we are rebuilding our fleet right now, why not give his design a try?"

"Yes, but," he began the usual protests she so often heard.

"Potentially, one of his caravels would be worth two of ours," Elona nudged him. "If this design proves itself, what is the good of wasting all our time and efforts on inferior ships, eh?"

"Yes, but we've been making them our way since the beginning," he began to retort, but stopped mid-sentence, feeling rather foolish.

"I want you to take this boy on as an apprentice shipwright. Drop all other work; put every resource we have onto making one single caravel and then test it. If it proves itself, we will make a whole fleet of them, abandoning the old models as fast as we can get the caravels on line. Now how soon can we see an experimental caravel model to test?"

"Well, let's see. You mean stop all the construction crews?" he looked startled.

"Yes, put everyone to work on making one of Pietro's design. Work day and night shifts, but get a test ship just as fast as you possibly can. How long?"

"Well, let's see," he repeated himself. "Can we cannibalize existing constructions?"

"Anything, just get us a test ship as fast as possible. If the test ship works as well as this model, all our new ships should be caravels, don't you think?" He could not disagree.

"Well, let's see," he said once more. "You mean stop all the crews and put them all on making one of these?"

"Yes," she said sternly, beginning to lose patience with the shipwright. "And follow Pietro's design precisely. No deviations, unless Pietro okay's them."

"Two weeks, Your Holiness. Give us two weeks. Of course there will be hell to pay if this does not work and we end up losing all this time, effort, and materials."

"I accept full responsibility if the project fails, but not if it fails because of shoddy construction or because you did not follow Pietro's design." She made this perfectly clear and wrote out her orders on a parchment.

Just as she handed the paper to the shipwright, Ben, who had been standing to her right, dived over the intervening barrel, deflecting an arrow aimed at Elona's head. About fifty feet further down toward the docks, a rough looking man hastily notched a second arrow. Before anyone could react, a second arrow flew towards her head. Ben was still in the process of falling over the barrel and could do nothing. Tom, who was on the other side of her, was too distant to take action. Elona watched as the shaft came straight at her. At the last instant, her right hand snapped into action, catching the arrow just as its point was about to impact her forehead.

A dozen dockworkers witnessed the attack. Without waiting for any orders, they all dropped their loads and charged toward the man, preventing him from making a third attempt. The first worker hit him with a full body tackle, knocking him to the ground. Others swarmed on top of the two, fists pounding, feet kicking.

"You okay," Tom called out to Elona.

"Yes, get him," she replied angrily. The shipwright and Pietro stood transfixed, staring at Elona with their mouths open. Neither could believe what they had just seen; their High Priestess had just snatched an arrow mid-flight!

The noise of the fight pulled everyone's attention to the attempted assassin. Rushing to them, Tom yelled, "Okay, thanks guys. That's enough. We have him now." One by one, the angry dockworkers backed away.

One yelled, "Slime! Filth! How dare you try to harm our High Priestess?"

"You said it Bill!" exclaimed another. Grunts and other agreements came from the men as they back off slightly, allowing Tom to reach the man.

"Thanks, guys," Elona called out to the men, most of who flushed and seemed somewhat ill at ease with their High Priestess talking directly to them.

One called out, "Any time, Priestess, any time." Several slapped him on the back for being so bold and saying what they had not the courage to speak in so public a place. By now, a rather large crowd gathered to see what was going on.

Turning to the still stunned pair, she said, "Okay, you have your orders. Pietro, you make sure they build the caravel the way you want it designed. I'll follow up in a couple days to see how it is going. If you need anything or run into problems, dispatch me at once." They agreed and the Master Shipwright led Pietro off to the shipyards, while Ben escorted Elona and the others over to her attacker.

Tom, examining the body, looked up, "Dead. Dockhands handled it for us. It's Felio all right. Case closed."

"Damn, this makes the sixth attempt on your life," Ben exclaimed.

"Predictable, not everyone can tolerate order being brought into an area, especially an area that was as lawless as Velona was. But we are making progress." Ben escorted the women back to the church-office-home, while Tom saw to the burial of the corpse.

Two weeks later, High Priestess Elona, surrounded by her Circle, stood on the docks as their newest ship, Pietro's Folly, was christened. True, much grumbling accompanied her building, especially when all other construction had been halted and scarce materials commissioned for its construction. Yet, as her new crew moved about onboard readying last minute rigging for her maiden voyage, the overall comments were favorable. She looked sleek yet aesthetic, a very modern design.

For the last week, bets had been placed on whether she would sail, would sink, would capsize, would move slowly, or would handle like a cow. Elona had secretly inquired about the odds. No ship had ever had so many coins wagered upon her maiden voyage. However, the odds were running pretty much five to one against that it would be successful; ten to one that it would flounder.

In the tradition of Tur, Elona formally blessed the ship and its new crew, pouring a golden goblet of wine down its side as an offering to Tur. Once the wine hit the water, the crowd cheered. The new captain saluted Elona and began barking orders to set sail. Dockhands undid the mooring lines, and Pietro's Folly bobbed freely in the water. More cheers, but a few didn't for they had just lost their wager that she would sink when free of the docks.

Broad bow with high stern, Pietro's Folly definitely look very different from all other Sea Prince ships. Indeed, she sported two main masts, each with two large square sails. Current ships only had one main mast. Similar to the current ships, the caravel also had a shorter rear mizzenmast sporting a large spanker sail. The crew only used the spanker to navigate away from the dock and out into the large open bay of Velona. Once clear, the main square sail dropped, followed by the foremast's square sail. The large crowd watched as the crew tightened the various lines, and the sails billowed into power pull mode. Again, several groans were heard as other men just lost their bets.

In a few minutes, the Salty Dog pulled alongside of Pietro's Folly, ready for the speed test. "You made it this far," yelled its captain to Felix, the young, new captain, "I'll give you credit for that. Ready for the race?"

"Give us a minute and you are on," the grinning Felix yelled back. "Okay men, let's see what she can do!" The race, or speed test, was on in earnest. Flying with their backs to the wind, both ships were ideally suited to make their fastest run. Neither ship carried any cargo, so this would represent their best possible speeds.

In less than a minute, the race was over. Clearly, it was no race at all! Pietro's Folly left the Salty Dog in its wake. She pulled away from the Salty Dog so quickly the crowd on shore began laughing heartily. Never had they witnessed such speed! Pietro, standing beside Elona, commented, "Look at her go. I didn't know how fast she would be. Is the Salty Dog holding back or something? Are they teasing me?"

"No son," commented the Port Master, who was also beside Elona supervising the launch. "Salty Dog's pushing it as hard as he can go. Yours is at least twice as fast. I would not have believed it if I had not seen it with my own two eyes! Amazing indeed." Pietro smiled, his last concern had just been put to rest. Models could not tell him how fast the real ship could sail.

A half hour later, Pietro's Folly returned to dock, her crew cheering wildly. Everyone could hear their accolades, their intense praise. No ship was as easy to dock as this one, nor as fast, nor as easy to sail, though she did require three additional crew members because of the additional sails. "Now for the tough test," spoke the Port Master loudly. "We will now load Pietro's Folly and see how she does under working conditions. Master Eric, you may begin."

Eric, the Axeman leader, motioned to his burly crew. For cargo, heavy logs were used. No one wanted to risk real cargo, in case the ship sank. Using heavy timbers, if she sank, why, the logs could be salvaged and may well keep the boat from sinking in the harbor, creating even more salvage problems. The dockhands took the logs from the Axemen and carefully stowed them in the cargo hold. This took a good deal of time. The Port Master had carefully measured the cargo weight. Halfway through the loading process, he called out to the crowd, "Okay, now she is carrying a normal maximum load for our ships. You may continue loading." Still more logs were stowed, and she was now visibly lower in the water.

Finally, the Port Master called out, "Okay, Pietro's Folly is now carrying double the cargo weight of any of our existing ships. Captain Felix, take her out for the test run. Ladies and Gentlemen, High Priestess, here comes the crucial test: Can the caravel actually sail and perform satisfactorily under working loads?"

As everyone watched and many held their breaths, the sleek caravel very slowly maneuvered away from the docks, again under the spanker sail only. Gone was the light bobbing, that carefree motion. Slowly Pietro's Folly lumbered its way across the bay. Once the two main sails were dropped, it stabilized and picked up speed, naturally. Felix called out to the Salty Dog, "Hey, give us a race now. Let's see how she does loaded down!"

Laughing, the captain replied, "Okay you're on, but be prepared to lose gracefully. I'll beat you this time for sure!" The Salty Dog drew alongside and the impromptu race began once more.

"What's this?" the Port Master called out. "They aren't supposed to be racing this trip. I've got to stop them."

"Ah leave them be. Let's see what happens," Ben suggested, knowing that Felix was not foolhardy and would not risk sinking the new ship.

This time, the Salty Dog won the race, but only by a ship's length. The crowd went wild with enthusiasm, even the elderly nobles broke from their conservatism and laughed and cheered with abandon. Loaded down with double the cargo of any existing ship, this new caravel could still nearly beat an empty ship! They saw large dollar signs written plainly on Pietro's Folly.

An hour later, the new caravel docked once more, edging its way to the dock extremely slowly. Felix knew the massive weight the ship bore and knew instinctively that if they came in too fast, the ship would smash the dock to splinters! His final comment was, "Man, do you every have to exercise care when docking with such a load!"

Alonza Moreno, the senior member of the Moreno House, leader of the High Council, and the wealthiest man in Velona, commented to Elona, "High Priestess, who would have thought that a mere lad who's just turned thirteen could have come up with such a design? I just cannot believe it. I admit that I lost heavily in the betting today," he grinned, but he could afford it. "I publically admit to you, High Priestess, that I had my doubts about you from the beginning. Now, I will be your strongest backer. Anything you want, any time, you just let me know, and it's yours! Can you even imagine what a whole fleet of these caravels will do for us?"

She smiled, "Yes I most certainly do know what they will do for us. That is why I had to take this gamble. Every person in the Velona Sector depends upon this, from the lowliest farmer up north, to the cask makers, to the dockhands, to the shipwrights, even to you, Alonza. These ships represent our future survival in abundance. Now, the task is to build a whole fleet of these caravels as fast as possible."

"You can say that again. We have six ships of the older design under construction, as you well know. Immediately, they should be converted to this new caravel design, but honestly, we need four times that many," he lamented.

"I'd rather see ten times that many, maybe even more. Let's call a special meeting tomorrow. Right now, I am going to have to conduct the ceremony," Elona replied, a twinkle of success in her bright eyes. She and her entourage of Protectors moved to the center of the docks, the wildly waving crew on her right, the shipwrights on her left, and as many of the townsfolk as could jam the docks before her.

She raised her hands to quell the cheering. "To one and all, I say this day marks the rebirth of Velona as the greatest sea power on Tarra!" Wild cheering, yelling, and shrill whistling halted any further words for several minutes. Poor Pietro. Several shipwrights had lifted him high into the air, and folks went wild with their enthusiasm.

"Let today be a lesson for us all. In Velona everyone gets a chance to contribute as they can, even our children!" She waved to Pietro; once more the crowd yelled at a fevered pitch.

"Finally, let us all take a silent moment of prayer to give thanks for this miracle we've witnessed here today. Some of you I know worship Jehosa, others, Tur, others, the Gods of the North. I say unto you, whom you worship does not matter, only that you worship the higher powers. Let us all pray and give our thanks." She bowed her head, and the jubilant crowd fell silent, as each person proclaimed their thanks. After a minute, she spoke in a normal tone, for her voice could now easily be heard. "Let our celebrations begin. To each and every one of you, enjoy the rest of this magnificent day!" The crowd again yelled and cheered, as they began heading for the local pubs.

As she watched her people disburse, Pietro finally got the chance to regain her side. "Thank you very much, High Priestess Po. This is all your doing to make my ship real."

"No, Pietro, it is we who owe you our eternal thanks. It is one thing to come up with a new and better way of making something and quite another to have faith in your creation, enough confidence to see it done, no matter the obstacles. Very well done, Pietro. Very few men have the ability to push something through, despite such obstacles. If you ever need anything, just come to me." She could not help giving the boy a loving hug, which, of course, both embarrassed him and pleased him — hugged by the High Priestess herself!

The next day, the meeting room, converted from the old church's chapel, was packed. Normally, only the High Council members met here, but today, representatives of many guilds were here as well, including the Axemen. Elona opened the meeting by announcing, "Ladies and gentlemen, the topic today is caravels. After yesterday, I would like to see Velona sport a fleet of sixty of these new ships, though Senior Alonza would be more than happy with two dozen of them. The reason I have brought us all together here is to work out how we can best build such a fleet, two dozen, four dozen, six dozen, whatever, as many as possible as soon as possible."

Thus began a lengthy discussion about shipbuilding. After a time, Elona discerned that the two biggest obstacles to rapid construction of a goodly number of caravels were lack of skilled wood workers and lack of heavy timbers. An idea formed in her mind to bring more order. "Eric," she addressed the Axeman leader, "your people build long boats all the time. I know that the design is different, but is the wood working skills so different?"

After some discussion, everyone concluded that the new immigrants from the North could help fill the manpower shortage. "Now about the timber. As I understand it, Eric, isn't there a lot of virgin timber up in the Dark Forest of West Reach, where an Axeman village is located?"

"Aye, Holy War Maiden Po, there certainly is," he replied. He still considered her a direct servant of his God.

"Good. Also, you mentioned to me last winter that there are a lot of your fellow countrymen and their families that might like to immigrate here, correct?"

"Ah, I see where you are headed," he replied with a broad grin. "Yes, many hard working young men and their wives and children desire a better chance in life. I can send word, if you like."

"I do like," she teased him. "Tell them that as many can come as want to, only please bring with them as many heavy timber logs as they can manage with their long boats. That's the price of admission; bring some logs that we need at this critical juncture. We have work for all that may come! Our crops this year are nearly double what we now need, so food should not be a problem."

True to his word, Eric sent word that very day. Working together, but not without numerous arguments about how best to do an action, the Axemen and the Shipwrights managed to construct six caravels by June. During the summer months, over two thousand men, women, and children arrived from the North, bringing with them vast flotillas of logs and varied skills needed in Velona. By the end of the summer, a dozen more caravels had been added, but by year's end, two dozen more were built, bringing the year's total to forty-three. In terms of cargo carrying capacity, her fleet by year-end was equivalent to nearly ninety older ships, greater than most all the other Sea Prince Sectors!

The week following that meeting, Albert approached Elona with his port plans. He had been studying, designing, and experimenting on the defenses of the port and city for nearly half a year now. He'd constructed a scale model of the city and port, and then added in his new ideas. Following the concept of Pietro — make a scale model to show — he now could easily present his plans. First, he needed to convince Elona.

"Safety, security, expansion. Those are the three key, guiding principles upon which this design rests," Albert explained to his attentive Circle. "Already, the shipwrights have begun using the bay just east of us, while the Axemen are using the one to the west. On these two outcrops that separate the three bays, we build these stone watch towers and another set on shore, here and here. Now we lay two enormously long, heavy iron chains between these watch towers, like so. They sink to the bay floor. Now pretend that this model represent an invading force coming from the Med Sea. We raise the chains like so, one about ten feet above the water, the other right at water level. Look what happens to the invaders." He demonstrated. The higher chain snapped the masts off the models, while the lower chain literally stopped all forward progress.

"Now we can send out fleets of long boats to board and attack our attackers. Problem solved, don't you think?" he asked. His visual display was totally convincing to everyone who saw it. "Now for the city defense. The problem with most walled cities, besides keeping people in and invaders out, is that the city get built right up to or close to the wall itself. This is no good, because the attackers can lob rocks and fire over the walls and destroy from a distance. Here's my plan. We build three sets of walls around this whole area, each about a quarter mile from the other, way out here, miles from the city. These boxes here are the periodic guardhouses from which guards are always watching. Now should invaders come overland, we can defend the outer wall. Should it fall, we back up one wall. Attrition of the enemy should win the day for us and it keeps the battle far from the population."

"But isn't that an enormous amount of construction of stone walls? Won't that take a very long time to build?" asked Elona.

"Yes, but the walls do not have to be built all at once. You see, invaders are not likely to come overland from the west, only from the east. So we begin by making the wall on the eastern hemisphere. At the same time, we build up our cavalry forces, taking a clue from history and the Galts. Station a sizeable cavalry garrison here where the wall ends allows them to respond early to invaders. The partially completed walls force the enemy around to here, where the wall is unfinished. Here is where we position our ground forces to stop them, until the wall is completely finished. It may take ten years to get the walls completed. Until then, we can make do with the nearly finished walls our predecessors have built. No, I am more worried about attacks from the Med Sea at this time."

Elona approved his plans, and he then presented them in detail to the Security Guild, who in turn adopted them. By June, construction on the four towers began, along with the construction of the enormous iron chains. By the end of the year, the bay defenses were fully operational. At night the chains were raised; no ship could get in or out of the bays. However, when a ship did need to enter or leave, the Port Master had them lowered.

In 623 AH, Velona had become a curious religious mixture. Some worshiped Tur, the Sea God; others, the combination of druwid and Tur principles as taught by Elona Po; others, worshiped Jehosa, particularly those who had earlier immigrated from Juda Arad; and others, the gods of the Volksholm. It was a curious blend of religious tolerance that was practiced in Velona.

Chapter 11 Mounting Tensions in Zargarb

Andre le'Goeur, previously the Protector of Waynesville Circle, was twenty-two, tall, and blonde with blue eyes. He was in many ways a woman's man, a dandy; yet, his skill with the sword was something to behold. Having met many women and dated almost as many, Andre met his match with one unusual looking, middle aged woman whose skin was a shade more yellowish than her companions were: Fighter Group Leader Lenkova Pazzio. She was thirty-four, but looked twenty-one, slim at the waist with strong arms and legs. Her skin had a slightly yellowish hue making her remarkably attractive. She had shoulder length, straight black hair that shone in the sunlight, making her one of the few Sisterhood fighters who did not cut their hair short. Yet it was her eyes that caught people's attention; they were sky blue — so unusual they commanded your attention, one could not help but notice them.

Andre and Lenkova fell madly in love with each other and married just before my group had left the Zargarb Sector last year. They now called two places "home." Because her duties as the Zargarb Sisterhood's Fighter Group Leader took her all over the sector, when they were near the sprawling city, they stayed in the magnificent Sisterhood Inn, where they permanently had a large suite. When they were up north, they stayed at North Point, where her parents lived at the secret safe house, a cavern complex. Rosita Armino Pazzio, the previous Fighter Group Leader for Zargarb, and her husband Antonio stayed there.

Actually, Antonio was not her real father — that had been the infamous barbarian Galt Mikhailovich Strokova. By agreeing to bear his children, Rosita had prevented the Sisterhoods of all the Sea Prince Sectors from being attacked by the invading Galts. She had Lenkova and a son, Illanovich, who had long ago abandoned her, returning to the Northern Steppes. Antonio raised Lenkova as if she was his daughter. Lenkova and her parents were very close, but she knew they both were getting very old indeed. She and Andre treasured the time that they could spend with them, listening to their tales of history.

During the first half of 623 AH, they had very little time to spend with them. Troubles seemed to continue to grow. You must understand geography in order to grasp their precarious position. The easternmost sector, Zargarb lay at a vital crossing point. Just to the east lay Juda Arad, once home to the Great Messiah and his deeply religious people, the original followers of Jehosa. Adjoining the Arad in the north was the vast Northern Steppes, home to the wild barbaric horsemen known as the Galts. It was these barbarians that nearly conquered all Tarra some years ago, before being defeated at the doorstep to Megalos.

Just south of the Arad lay the vast Southlands, controlled by the Centurions of Megalos. Now, the Arad had become a vast desert wasteland.

Many of its inhabitants, weary of so many invasions, had immigrated westward into the Sea Princes or even on to West Reach. Those that remained had become increasingly war-like; banditry, a way of life.

Worse still, a clandestine group known only as the Old Man of the Mountain, an extortion-assassination group also operated out of eastern Arad. These men would hold a town for ransom. If they failed to make payment, one of their own people would be kidnaped, drugged, convinced he was in heaven, taken back to his original town, told to assassinate the leader, and then he would return to heaven for all time. Crude, but highly effective, this group had its tendrils all over the Arad and into the Steppes. However, the Sisterhood had, for a time now, defeated their attempts at extortion within Zargarb. From all the extortion attempts, the brilliant Sister Calli had deduced their location to within some twenty miles. Andre wanted desperately to take a group of Protectors across the Arad to the assassins' strong hold and bring it down upon their heads.

It seemed at least once a month, a new attempt at extortion would appear somewhere with the Zargarb sector. The Sisterhood would move in and take action to prevent the assassination. Most of the time, they had been successful, though it was not without cost. Twice, the Sister who had prevented the assassination had herself been killed from the vile poisons used on their weapons.

Further, the Axemen from the far north had been traveling down a river through the Greenway into the steppes. They were after the accumulated gold and jewels that the Galts had stolen during their attempt to conquer the world. Some had continued down into the Arad. Finding the arid desert not to their liking, some had ventured on into Zargarb, where the Sisterhood was forced to meet them and drive them back. Lenkova was now forced to keep fifty Sisterhood fighters on constant patrol throughout the eastern edge of the sector. Twice during the first half of the year, she had to mobilize a large fighter group to dislodge invading Axemen.

The next problem was with the Churches of Jehosanity. Here in Zargarb, the Church of Jehosanity Northern Orthodoxy reigned supreme. Actually, this religion held true to the original teachings of Jes Amir and the original religion of Jehosa. Within this sector, it had become the primary religion, and many of the sisters freely joined the church. One of the original disciples of the Great Messiah, Bandar Dero, had founded the church, but he recently passed away. The main idea to grasp is that the people of this sector and several other sectors were now very devout followers of this version of Jehosanity.

In contrast, down in Megalos, Yazi, another of the ten disciples of the Great Messiah, had formed his own version of the religion. Here in Zargarb, everyone felt very strongly that his was a completely bastardized and perverted version. However, Pope Yazi I had formed up his group of Holy Paladins, young, ill-trained fighters and ex-Centurions, and had sent them to pillage the Arad, looking for Holy Relics of the Great Messiah. Traveling in groups of twenty-five men, wearing blue tunics with a white cross, these men were ruthless, taking what they wanted where they desired. The Arad inhabitants as well as those in Zargarb hated these Holy Paladins.

The two versions of the church definitely did not get along. In fact, for years now, the southern church has sent what were called Holy Paladins of Jehosa up into Juda Arad. Supposedly, they were searching for Holy Relics of Jehosa, items touched and blessed by the Great Messiah, the Son of God. Whether or not they have ever found any, none here can say. Except that if some were found, they would have been taken at once back to the church in Megalos.

Not to be outdone, the Zargarb church sent several expeditions into the Arad as well. One group returned with the actual cross upon which the Great Messiah was crucified! It is the church's most prized possession. In fact, they brought back three of them. I think that they are still trying to ascertain upon which of the three our savior was placed.

Pope Yazi I somehow heard of the Zargarb discovery and had demanded that the crosses be turned over to his Holy Paladins and brought to the True Church of Jehosanity. Archdeacon Bandar Dero, of course, flatly refused all such demands. Since there were a relatively large number of Holy Paladins scattered around the Arad, everyone presumed that at some point they'd try to take them back by force, starting a religious war. The High Council sent a good deal of its defensive cavalry to Florintine Junction, where the mother church is located, just in case of trouble. The Sisterhood was also asked to send forces and to provide scouts. More than a few are widely scattered throughout that area, looking for advance signs of a congregation of these Holy Paladins. To date, the Holy Paladins have only continued to press their demands and not tried to take them by force. Yet a fight could come at any time. Often Lenkova has been heard to retort, "Now if I were Bandar Dero, I'd move the Holy Relics, if they are truly valuable, down into one of the many churches within the walls of Zargarb."

What of the Centurions who were the first to conquer Zargarb so many years ago? Just south of the sector, they had rebuilt New Barq as their staging city for trade goods. At this time, Megalos merely is a good trading partner. However, many older citizens still remember the Centurion invasion and predict that sooner or later they will be back, claiming Zargarb as their possession.

"God, I hope nothing happens for the next week!" exclaimed Lenkova to Andre, as they rode southward down the spoke road from North Point. In two days, six druwids were due to arrive in Zargarb, Andre's new Circle, to be called the Zargarb Circle. He was ecstatic over finally having other Guardians with him. Perhaps, he just missed me: Bethany — I couldn't resist that tease; he's such a dandy.

The layout of all the roads in the Sea Prince sectors was similar, except of course for Fortress d'Grange located mostly in mountainous terrain. Imagine a large city on the coast of the Med Sea. This is the hub of a great wagon wheel. Spoke roads fan out from the city heading north, east, west, and angles in between. Periodically, rim roads arc from the Med Sea northward and then back down to the sea on the other side of the main city. The rim roads are about five miles apart. The duo were riding hard down the main north-south spoke road that led from North Point to Zargarb, some hundred twenty-five miles due south.

"Do you think that they will like me? Will I fit in?" she asked.

"Hey, silly. Did you fit in with Ket, with Alton, with Waverly?" he replied.

"Sure, but," her voice trailed off. She had very fond memories of us and the power we displayed. In truth, she owed us druwids much. It is just that she was a little nervous; six new druwids were coming and she knew nothing about them.

She changed the topic. "When they get here, are we going to go after the assassins in eastern Arad?"

"Dunno, to be truthful, dear. I don't know these new recruits or what their skills actually are. If they were all highly trained Protectors, such as me, then I know that we could do it. I'm afraid none of these is supposed to be a Protector. I keep putting in requests for John Henry to send me a half dozen Protectors so we can put an end to the assassins. I've heard nothing back. This was a sore point with Andre. However, he was not trained in telepathy; hence, John Henry was hard pressed to communicate back to him, not trusting sending anything written.

Andre continued, "Unless I'm mistaken, my new group will need some time to adjust. I suspect their command of the Sea Prince dialect will be rudimentary. Certainly, their knowledge of the geography and people will be marginal at best. I know mine was when I first came here."

"Glad you came?" she could not resist a loving tease.

"The best thing I ever did in my life, Lenkova. I love you more than anything!" She smiled, and would have kissed him, except that they were galloping along the road.

Dusk was falling on the fourth day of hard riding when they halted above the last hill before Zargarb. From here, they had a magnificent view of the city. Spectacular and impressive was the walled city of Zargarb! Boasting a population of nearly two hundred thousand, its numbers were enlarged considerably by those fleeing Juda Arad, looking for a better life. The docks could handle three dozen ships at one time. Stretching in nearly a perfect semicircle centered upon the docks lay the imposing barrier wall, fifteen feet tall and twenty thick. Six enormous gates allowed entrance to the city. The two-storied guard towers on either side of the six gates provided a solid defense should someone attempt to assault the gates in a time of siege. Of the six gates, only one was operated and controlled by the Sisterhood and manned with their fighters. This allowed them to enter the city with no fuss or entrance fee.

As usual, the streets that ran east-west were curved, paralleling the walls, while those running north-south were straight like the spokes of a wheel. The curve of the arcs was small over the space of a city block, which was about three hundred feet long and sixty deep. Since the shape was semicircular with spoke roads heading outward from the docks, to avoid a sector being longer than three hundred feet near the outer wall, many of these spoke roads were not through streets, that is, they did not run the entire depth of the city from the docks to the wall. Rather they often dead-ended in an arc street.

There were three residential areas of the city, each containing some hundred blocks of homes, nearly two thousand. The wealthy nobles and their families lived in the western area; the merchants and trades folk, the middle area; those from the Arad, the eastern area. Further, the warehouse district surrounded the docks for easy access to ships. Further, three additional areas had been established, these lay close to the northern arc of the wall. To the east were housed the City Guards; to the west, the Sisterhood complex stood; in the central area, a vast wide open space devoted to grass provided a place to house others during an emergency siege as well as room for future growth and expansion.

Most all the buildings were constructed from stone with red tile roofs. A consistency of design and color was clearly visible, as were the numerous Churches of Jehosanity, whose white steeple crosses often stood taller than any other building in the city. All told, there were twenty-five of them.

The explanation given for the segregation into sections within the city was this was what the people desired. The many immigrants from Juda Arad desired to live close to each other, likewise with the nobles and their families. Tradesmen also found living close to the business district more conducive to their needs. Hence, the city was built around these guidelines. Nearly every building in Zargarb was new or nearly completely refurbished. The Galt sacking had the side benefit of urban renewal on a citywide scale.

They entered the Sisterhood gate and went directly to the Sisterhood inn. One benefit that Andre enjoyed was that they could just leave their horses at the stables, and one of the Sisters would unsaddle and take good care of them. Lenkova had privileges. Once inside, they quickly headed for the public bath. As usual, they found a number of others there as well.

Tonight, both Sister Cecilia Amal, the leader of our Sisterhood in Zargarb, and Sister Alicia Madriosa, their High Council Representative, were relaxing in the warm waters. "Come on in and join us," Alicia called out to them, adding to Andre, "Hope you don't mind smelling like lilacs." It was her usual tease. Men rarely bathed here in a Sisterhood inn.

He grinned, "She'll then at least let me into our bed!" He gave Lenkova a loving pat on her rump. Cecilia was matronly in outlook and age, at least forty. Streaks of grey had begun appearing in her otherwise brown hair. She was a short woman but not overweight. Her voice was steady, commanding, and almost motherly in tone.

Alicia, her right arm, was fifty-four years old, her hair was definitely greying. Lines of age creased her face, but gave her an elegant look to accompany her keen eyes and sensibility. Her greatest talents lay in both being able to detect when someone was not telling the whole truth and in being a negotiator par excellence. Her reputation, impeccable; her record for bringing sense and balance, for bringing the High Council to formulate optimum solutions to Zargarb's many problems, was legendary in the city. No other woman was as well respected by the common man as Alicia. Every tradesman trusted her judgment implicitly; she'd proven herself to them repeatedly.

Alicia asked, "We've heard that six Guardians are to arrive tomorrow. Is this true? Will they be staying long?"

"Yes, we are forming up the Zargarb Circle," Andre replied. "You'll now have a full Circle with all our talents, especially a Healer. I'll be very glad to hand those duties over. I'm just not very good at it." He was being modest, thought Alicia; she had seen him work wonders on those wounded in combat.

Inwardly, Andre had only one reservation: he would now be part of a complete Circle once more. The Wid was their leader. Therein lay his reservation; he had grown very accustomed to doing what he wanted to do. He was not sure that he could follow orders, especially if they conflicted with Lenkova. However, he voiced none of this to her.

The next morning Andre and Lenkova stood on the docks watching as the Spirit of the Med slowly tacked into the sprawling port. Quite a number of other Sisters were there too, curious about the arrival of six Guardians from the Greenway. As the ship finally slowly slid alongside the dock and mooring lines flew, Andre spotted the six passengers excitedly watching the action on the port side. He waved to them, caught their attention, and they waved back. He knew what it felt like to be suddenly arriving in a foreign country, barely able to speak the language, knowing almost no one, exciting, but just a bit daunting, nevertheless.

Within a few minutes, the six scrambled down the gangplank, toting heavy bags containing their gear. Both Andre and Lenkova grabbed some of the women's heavier bags. "Hi, I'm Andre, if you didn't already guess. And this is my beautiful bride, Zargarb Sisterhood's Fighter Group Leader Lenkova Pazzio."

"Whoa, you are going to have to talk slower or else speak Greenway," the older woman replied, a sheepish grin upon her face. "I'm Leann Weatherby, Wid, and this is my husband, Art, Judger. Tom and Mary Bridgeport, Planner and Communicator. Fred and Ann Waterton, Loremaster and Healer. Am I ever glad to have good solid earth beneath my feet!"

"Let's get you all to the Sisterhood inn where you can bathe, and we can talk freely," Andre replied.

As they walked along, the six newcomers repeated two comments many times. Fred kept saying, "Look at all these exotic flowers! Flower stalls everywhere. Incredible." Ann, his wife, kept teasing, "Okay, then you have no excuse for not bringing me some." The others kept repeating, "The city is so huge! We've never seen a city anywhere near this size. Two hundred thousand, unimaginably huge!"

When they arrived at the inn, the sheer size of the establishment put all six in complete awe. However, when they entered and saw how plush the place was and the magnificent artwork, they were speechless. Andre had arranged for them permanently to have three rooms next to his and Lenkova's. The women were flabbergasted at the luxury of their rooms; nothing they ever seen compared to these quarters. "Are all the rooms like these?" Leann asked.

"Well, these are the larger ones, usually two stay in them," Lenkova replied. "Of course, Andre and I have the Bridal Suite permanently assigned to us. Perks of being Fighter Group Leader," she added. "Bring some clean clothes and follow us to the bath. You can get lost in this complex pretty easily; I did the first time I came here."

Even the immense size of the bath impressed them. While relaxing in the warm waters, Andre studied his new Circle members. Fred and Ann were both twenty-eight, somewhat older than he was. Inwardly, he was glad that all were married. It made things much easier. Fred kept asking about all the plants; not being a plant person, Andre let Lenkova chat with him. Ann, he noticed had very delicate hands and was very soft-spoken, a shy person. All the men had short cut, brown hair, and blue eyes. The women were also similar, brown hair with blue eyes, not much variety here. Ann's hair was curly and shoulder length.

Tom and Mary were older, thirty-nine. Typical of a Planner, Tom continually commented about the architecture of the building and the construction of the bath. Andre had no idea how the water was warmed or where it went. However, their attendant Sister cheerily explained its workings, talking so fast that I expect Tom only grasped one word in three. In contrast, his wife, Mary, relaxed and expanded her mind; Andre felt her gentle touch as she reached him; she was getting a feel for him, he assumed. Tom sported a close-cropped beard and moustache, while Mary had limp, straight hair that hung to her shoulders like damp string. She was not much to look at, Andre thought.

Art and Leann were older still, he was forty-one while she a year younger. Thus, Andre had a much older Wid than he expected. Art had a moustache and still looked rather handsome; his well-built frame commanded respect. Andre wondered why he had not taken up the role of Protector, for he was built for it. Leann, Andre noted, was one of those women who always bore that stern look, as if to say, "don't mess with me." He wondered if she ever smiled at all. No nonsense, he figured, was her personality and wondered if he could get along with her at all.

While they were bathing, a Sister in leather armor walked in, saw the newcomers, looked at Lenkova, and flashed some hand signals with her fingers. Lenkova became very serious and commented, "Got to go, Andre. I'll leave you all to get to know one another. Catch you all at supper, if I can." She gave Andre a kiss and climbed out hastily.

"What's that all about?" asked Leann, curiously. "The messenger didn't say anything, except for those funny finger wiggles."

"The Sisters have a secret signal system. She didn't know who you were and needed to communicate with Lenkova — something about Holy Paladins and killing No Eyes. I don't get it really, but if it is important, Lenkova will let me know," Andre explained.

"Let's get something to eat," Leann replied abruptly. "Is there someplace we can talk over things? We really do need to talk soon."

Fifteen minutes later, the new Zargarb Circle was served a late lunch in the spacious dining hall, now mostly deserted. Andre noted that all six were very impressed with not only the quality service and food, but also the grand atmosphere the Sisters had created here.

"Okay, down to business," Leann said, after everyone finished their meal and had sat back to sip their tea. "Andre, I've had the luxury of discussing things with the others on the infernally long voyage here. I'll bring you up to speed. This Circle is really just an experiment. We all know that Circles are formed when we are in our teens; we bond for life. Here, we are of widely differing ages and backgrounds. We've never met before and know not the others, except our husbands and wives. John Henry suggested that this reforming of a Circle might not work out at all, but we six are willing to give it a try." Andre added quickly that he would as well.

"Art and I are grandparents, believe it or not, but all our children turned out to be headers and showed no interest in druwid learning. Our Circle was stationed in the Uru valley, living in four villages. One day last fall, Art and I were off buying seed in Karka, when the King's thugs in the dead of night visited the homes of our Circle members and killed them. Our children got word to us, and we fled to Mont Blanc. So if I look a little bitter, I still am. Art and I have not really gotten over the wanton slaying of our dear companions."

"Tom and Mary hail from Brownsville, where their Circle was stationed. The Grey Creatures swooped down one night. They seemed to know precisely where each member of their Circle lived and methodically began killing them. Because Mary was in communication with the others and saw what was happening, she and Tom managed to escape by a hair's breath. Only recently has Mary begun to use her telepathic skills once more. Whatever you do, don't press her too hard or she will break down in grief again."

"Fred and Ann lost their Circle to a conflict with the self-appointed king near the eastern border with the steppes. They were back of the battle line tending the wounded when the king's cavalry charge wiped out the front lines and killed their other members. Since they were amid numerous dead and wounded bodies and covered in blood anyway from their work, they laid down and pretended to be among the fallen, when the charging horsemen rode their way. Later, they snuck away from the carnage and made for Mont Blanc as well."

"All of us are still trying to recover from devastating losses. John Henry said that you have recovered remarkably well, and he has hopes that sending us down here will do the same for all of us," Leann reported. "However, I just don't know how we are all going to get along and bond together as a group. We've so many obstacles to overcome."

Hearing their tales, Andre could not help recalling how he lost his own Circle so many years ago. An uncharacteristic flood of sympathy came over him. "Well, as you know, I've been where you all are. Lost my Circle too. I'm not a Wid, but I got over it by coming down here and making myself useful. It's a completely different world with different language, customs, people, and places. Zargarb is rather at the crossroads of troubles right now. If you don't keep your attention on the present here and now, you can get killed awfully easy."

For a moment, he hesitated, and then decided for the truth, "For my part, I freely admit that I have enjoyed the freedom of not having a Wid from which to take orders. I help those that need it. Now my allegiance is to Lenkova and the Sisterhood." There he had said it, he hoped that the others, especially Leann, would understand. He added, "If anything is going on in these parts, the Sisterhood knows about it first. They have the most remarkable organization I have seen, excepting of course, ours. In many ways, the Sisterhood has evolved into a position not unlike us Guardians used to have with the folks of the Greenway."

"Don't get me wrong, I'll do my very best to protect you, especially our Wid. Just please, please, do not put me into a position where I cannot help or have to go against the Sisterhood," he pleaded his case.

"John Henry assumed as much of you, Andre. I've been forewarned. I will not attempt to come between you and the Sisterhood, not at least knowingly. If I should ever do, will you please directly point it out to me? I know that I have much to learn, and one day I hope to command everyone's respect and trust in our Circle. I know that I will have to earn it, just like everyone else here. For a time, Andre, we all will be leaning rather heavily upon you."

Andre was about to reply, when Lenkova rushed into the room. "Sorry to interrupt. Andre, you have to come with me now. You all can come too. Now. Fast. Get moving."

As we all rushed to grab our things, Andre quickly tried his best to tell the others what to wear and bring with them. Leann asked, "Is she always this bossy?"

He laughed, "She is their Fighter Group Leader and does command all the Sisterhood fighters in Zargarb, something like six hundred or more of them. She's only this abrupt when something is terribly wrong or very important. Whatever it is, it must be vital. Come on."

When they reached the stables, they found that six horses had been prepared for the newcomers. Twenty-five other Sisterhood fighters were already mounted and waiting for them. Lenkova remarked, "I trust you can ride and ride hard."

"Absolutely," Leann sternly replied for her group. They mounted and rode swiftly to the Sisterhood gate and passed out into the open spaces beyond the walls. Lenkova kicked her horse into a gallop and all were off. Circling the city wall, they soon found themselves riding hard down the Centurion made paved road heading south. Once they were beyond all the normal traffic going into and out of Zargarb, Lenkova slowed the pace and drew back to join Andre's group.

"We're heading to a village in the south of the sector, Amal's Point, it's called. It's very near the border of the Cedar Forest and is a melting pot of travelers. Centurions, Holy Paladins, Galts, Arad mercenaries — they all pass through Amal's Point. We had a blind Sister who kept us informed of things she overheard. Sister Ami worked at the inn. She fed us lots of valuable information over the years. A day ago, we heard that she had something very important to tell us. However, when Sister Daria arrived, she found Ami had been brutally murdered. Who would do such to a blind woman, the pig!" She spat on the moving ground. Lenkova continued, "I got word that I needed to see the mess, just outside the village. Daria is keeping the site untouched until we get there. She says we really need to see it. Probably gruesome, so be prepared."

It was very late afternoon as they rounded a bend, approaching the outskirts of Amal's Point. To their right and down a steep cliff the blue Med Sea rolled on shore, its sound echoing in their ears. To their left, the dense, dark Cedar Forest loomed, the air filled with its marvelous fragrance. Andre knew his Loremaster would have loved to stop and spend days exploring this strange woods. However, up ahead, a lone Sisterhood fighter stood, sword drawn, feet spread apart, a defiant stance, Sister Daria, Andre presumed.

As they dismounted, Daria lowered her weapon and moved to Lenkova. "Back there, incredible mess. No one has disturbed a thing. I felt you needed to see this."

"Thanks, Daria," Lenkova sternly replied. "Andre, come with me." She added to the Circle members, "You can come too; just do not mess up any of the signs until we have read them." She just remembered that Andre was a druwid and could read signs as well as she, perhaps these newcomers could as well.

The site was indeed gruesome to behold. Located about a thousand yards from the edge of the village, but hidden from it, lay the murder site. Lenkova and Andre stepped to the edge, bent low to the ground, and began analyzing what they saw. The others in Andre's Circle fanned out doing likewise, though none moved into the tracks.

"Rope around her neck, they dragged her forcibly here," Lenkova commented to Andre.

"Looks like they kept hacking at her with swords, but so many wounds. They were playing with her," Andre noted.

"Torturing her. She was standing for a time; look at the blood patterns. She finally staggered here; see her foot prints," Lenkova added.

"Seems to be quite a lot of different horses," Andre commented.

"Someone see if you can determine how many different riders were here." Fred began counting.

"It appears that they wanted something from her and were torturing her to get her to reveal or give it to them. God she must have suffered; she couldn't even see what was happening to her!" Lenkova spat on the ground once more.

"Love, look at these markings in the dirt here by her fingers," Andre pointed out, they had moved close to the mutilated body, which had dozens of slash marks on the arms and legs.

"She bled to death. The barbarians didn't even kill her, just left her to bleed to death! She couldn't even see to bind her own wounds. Damn them to the Pits of Hell!" she cursed. "Hey, that's our markings, our signs. She was trying to leave us a message, probably after they had gone, and she was dying. That's the sign for 'I' and that means 'no' or 'not' and that is a mouth. She's saying she didn't tell them. But what didn't she tell them? No more message. Damn. What news did she have that she gave up her life to protect?" Lenkova was infuriated.

Twenty-four horses, give or take a couple," Fred announced. "Does that mean anything?"

"Holy Paladins travel in packs of two dozen," Lenkova replied.

Now the eight were stared at the bloody, lifeless form of the young Sister. Lenkova sighed, "Guess we should give her a proper burial now. Nothing more to be learned here."

The meek, shy voice of Mary broke the stillness, "She's still here." We all turned to Mary. "She's still here," she repeated, "Sister Ami, I mean."

Leann explained, "Lenkova, I don't know how much you know about Guardian skills, but we can communicate telepathically with each other and with other spiritual beings. Mary is saying that Sister Ami is still around here. She has not yet left to go find a new baby body and begin life anew."

"Oh, yes, I'd nearly forgotten about that. Waverly used to do that when she and Ket Bethany were here. Can you talk with her? I must know what she wanted to tell us. It must have been terribly vital for these barbarians to murder her so brutally. I figured out her dying message that she did not tell them, but what did she not tell them?"

Mary faltered, "I, I'm sorry. I don't know your language at all well. I'm afraid that I will miss most of the message or get it wrong. Can I, er, can I, ah, sort of join you up to her and let you do the talking? It won't hurt a bit."

"Mind Link, Lenkova, remember Ket and Waverly used to do that?" Andre explained.

"Sure, go ahead, but I don't know what to do," she replied, feeling very ill at ease about this.

"Just think your thoughts to her as if you were talking with her. You can say the words aloud if you feel more comfortable that way. Here goes," Mary answered.

Lenkova felt the presence of another in her mind, a soft, loving warmth.

Now here comes Ami. Wham, Lenkova was ill prepared for the flood of blind horror, grief, and emotional distress coming from Ami. Andre suspected this might be so and had Lenkova in a full body hug to support her.

"Ami, it's me, Lenkova. I'm here," she said aloud, though she need not have.

Oh Leni, I didn't tell them, I didn't, I didn't!

"I know, I know, I saw your message, Ami. You did very well. But I need to know what it was that you didn't tell them, Ami. What news did you hear?"

They are going to destroy the Church of Jehosanity in Zargarb and steal the Holy Crosses. I heard men talking about it at the inn. Oh please, don't let them do that, please, please.

"I won't Ami. I promise you I won't let that happen as long as I can fight!"

I can see again, you know. I see the cedars and the blue sea, and I see you too, Leni. You are crying.

"I know. I loved you. I'll miss you. You can see?"

Yes, I can. It's lovely here, very beautiful.

I'm Mary, friend of Leni. You should go find a new baby body now. Pick out nice parents.

Hi Mary. I can see you too. Oh, I will, but I'm going to stay here a while. It's so pretty.

Lenkova said her last farewell to her friend, and the link was broken. "That, that, that was unbelievable," Lenkova finally explained to Andre.

"I know," was all he said. They then buried the fallen Sister and said a prayer over her grave, which was positioned such that it could see the Med Sea.

"Look what else I've found," Fred got their attention. "Funny looking button, and then there is this coin."

Lenkova recognized both immediately. "Holy Paladins! Pope Yazi's thugs in uniform. That's a Centurion ducat. Now we know who did this atrocity!" She then explained what she had heard from Ami and about the Holy Paladins.

"Sister Daria, go into the village and collect her things. Bring them to the inn," Lenkova ordered.

"Are we going after the butchers?" asked Daria, vengeance in her eyes.

"I can track them," Fred offered, trying to be helpful, though he didn't realize that Lenkova and Andre we also highly skilled in tracking.

"We didn't come prepared for overnight stay, no food, but from the tracks, they are heading north. We could follow them a ways and see. I'd like to be back at Zargarb by full dark, however." They mounted up, and Lenkova led them unerringly on the unmistakable trail left by the Holy Paladins. They cut into the Cedar Forest, so Fred got his first look at these unique woods.

After a time, the trail arrived at the north-south track there at the very western edge of Juda Arad. The arid, mesa land stretched out before them. "Here is the start of the Arad desert," she announced for her visitors. "Looks like they rode on due north from here. We'll head back to Zargarb now. Tomorrow, I will send out our special trackers who are very familiar with the Arad. We don't have the supplies to continue tonight. Besides, this may be the start of something larger. I need to get back and make some plans."

It was after full dark when the group arrived back at the inn. The group ate quickly, and then Lenkova said, "To the maps, Andre." Turning to the Circle members, she said, "You are welcome to come and listen in if you like." Leann's curiosity roused, and they followed the Sisters and Andre.

One room in the inn was devoted to maps. On the walls, the entire Zargarb sector was displayed, complete with all the details the Sisters had accumulated over the years. "Sister Cali made these for us," Lenkova explained. "Now here is the track that the Holy Devils were following. Up here is the seat of power of our Church, Florintine Junction, right at the border of the Arad. Good guess is they are to deliver their message to other groups, which are probably not too far from the Junction. I've already sent a messenger to the Junction warning our people, the cavalry, and the Church of what we've learned. They will be warned by mid-afternoon tomorrow."

"Say, that is a long way. How can a message get there that fast?" asked Leann.

"The rider travels day and night at a full gallop. We have way stations periodically along the way where she stops, eats, and gets a fresh mount. The real question is where and when will they strike and with what force? I dare not commit our forces until we know. Sure hope the Axemen stay away for a while; we don't need them to wander into northern Zargarb right now."

Thinking aloud, Lenkova analyzed, "Take out the Church and steal the crosses. It's common knowledge that we have been unable to convince the Church to move their Holy Relics into the more secure Zargarb. Everyone knows the Council has deployed nearly a thousand cavalrymen into the Junction area. We've never seen any signs of Centurion legions of foot soldiers, only the small groups of Holy Devils. Only an idiot would attack a much larger mounted force. What can their plan be? Fool hardy? Andre?"

"How about a quick end run around our forces?" he suggested. "They feint an attack in one place, while their raiders ride into the Junction and assault the Church directly. They've no defenses there, just priests. I just can't see any other way they could do it."

"I think you are on to something. Look, the cavalry is unseasoned. The devils make a pretend attack, and I guarantee you our foolish cavalry will charge headlong into it, leaving the Junction and Church wide open, save for our few Sisterhood scouts. We have to get there ahead of the attack. Carla, get Alicia here at once. Kasha, roust every available fighter; we ride yet tonight. Misha, go to the staging area and get every available fighter to the Junction at their fastest possible speed. Then, get on up to North Point and have the reserves filter down and take up temporary watch duty, just in case something else arises. I want five hundred Sisters swarming on the Junction by tomorrow afternoon. Tell everyone: under no circumstances are they to leave the immediate area of the main Church." Her three messengers scampered off to begin delivery of her orders. "You coming, Andre?"

"You bet. Leann, you all should come as well. It may amount to nothing, but then we may have some healing to do."

"Right, we ought to get some of our things together. Is it all right to leave stuff we don't need in our rooms here?" she asked.

"Yes, those are permanently assigned to you as long as you are in the sector. The Sisters will be bringing a load of bandages, so just bring what you need, ignoring them. Someone will stow enough rations in your horse saddlebag when they saddle them up for you. These women are a marvel of efficiency."

Just then, Alicia, their High Council representative, came rushing into the room, "What is up? She said it was an emergency." Alicia looked rather worried.

"Sister Ami was killed so that she could not warn us that the Holy Paladins have orders to destroy the Church and steal the Holy Relics. They are headed for the Junction. Andre and I are convinced that they plan to make a fake attack, probably south of the Junction, in order to draw the Council's cavalry away from the Church. I'm mobilizing all available fighters. We ought to be in place by tomorrow afternoon. You can do two things for us. Get a message to the cavalry general and tell him not to react to any attack not directed at the Junction itself, not to get pulled out of position. Second, send another plea to the Church to send their Holy Relics to Zargarb. That would make protecting them infinitely easier."

"The blind woman? I'm sorry. I know she was a friend of yours, Lenkova. Yes, I'll send them right away, but you know the army as well as I do; they seldom listen to a woman. Lord knows how many times we've begged the Church to take advantage of the walls and security here in Zargarb, but I'll try once more." Lenkova thanked her and she left to carry out the requests.

The group headed to their rooms to pack up. As they were walking, Lenkova commented, "We probably have time to get there. The Holy Devils are likely scattered all over the Arad, and it'll take them days to get organized. Let's hope so, anyway."

A band of one hundred-fifty Sisterhood fighters rode out of Zargarb that evening, heading for the Junction. Riding all night and into the next day, they pressed their horses as much as was safe to do so. Indeed, Andre's Circle marveled at the efficiency of these fighters. Well trained, able to think for themselves, and yet caring for each other's needs — these aspects Leann observed during the long ride, before weariness overcame her good senses.

Around 3 p.m. the next day, Andre called out to his sleepy Circle, "Florintine Junction, the largest, easternmost town in the sector; some ten thousand now live here. Look, no smoke. Maybe we are in time," he added optimistically for Lenkova's benefit.

The Junction was a border community, with a huge population of Arad immigrants, who had brought their original version of Jehosa worship with them. The sprawling town had grown without any logical design. When a new bunch of houses needed to be built, the makers went to one edge of town and built there. Likewise, the streets ran in all directions — chaos personified, Planner Tom declared. Homes usually were mostly adobe brick with thatched roofs, because it rarely rained this close to the arid Arad. However, standing tall and prominent were the seven Churches of Jehosanity, their white crosses towering over the town. Lenkova made for the tallest one, the Mother Church.

"How does anyone find their way in this jumble of streets?" asked Tom. The city designers must have been drunk!"

"They don't have any such person," a Sister near him replied. He shook his head in disbelief.

Shortly, they reined in near the Mother Church complex. A white picket fence surrounded nearly an entire city block, enclosing the rectory building, kitchen building, and storage warehouses, as well as the imposing Church. As they approached, some fifty Sisterhood fighters moved out from their semi-concealed positions to greet their leader. One called out, "We got your message. Fifty on duty. No signs of anything unusual. Should I send the scouts out now that you are here?"

This was a big decision. If she sent her fifty scouts out, they could get valuable information. On the other hand, if battle were joined, she would need them here. She used her intuition to decide. "Yes, gather them and come here for orders. Let me get the scouts out first," she explained to the others behind her. Other Sisters relayed what was going on to those in the rear.

Soon, the fifty women lined up before their leader. "All present and ready for action, Fighter Group Leader," one barked.

"Okay, we know that the Holy Devils, yes, I'm now calling them that after they butchered Sister Ami, my blind friend down in Amal's Point. I guess that they are going to feint an attack, probably south of here to draw off the cavalry. Once the cavalry is gone, their remaining forces will try to sack the Churches and steal their Holy Relics. I need advance warning." She began sketching in the dirt of the street. "Here we are. I want you to fan out into three arcs centered on the Junction, like this. The nearest arc should be about two miles out. The next five miles. The third, ten. Keep the ten-mile arc a bit thin. If you spy any grouping of the Holy Devils larger than their normal group of some two dozen, ride back to the next arc and report, then keep tabs on the movement of that mass. Give us as much advance notice as possible. Stay alert out there. I have no idea when the attack will come; it might be days away yet, or come this afternoon even. We just don't know. Okay, off you go. Do your best, but take no risks. That's an order! We won't be able to send assistance if you get into trouble." Several of the scouts grinned at that last.

Andre explained to his Circle, "Her scouts are masters of tracking and moving silently. That's why they are scouts. I swear they can sneak up on you, and you won't even know that they are there!" He knew that the six of them would be very curious to see if this were true.

Lenkova looked at the bustling, wide-open streets full of people, some

146

staring at the fighters, some stopping to watch her arrival. "Lord knows how we can possible defend this position! Okay, horses tethered in the churchyard. Take up defensive positions around the complex. Andre, Guardians, you're with me. We are off to try to persuade the Deacon to abandon this folly."

By the time that they reached the rectory's main door, Deacon Philas was there awaiting them. "Lenkova, it is always good to see your face in here and Andre too. Come on in. I've got tea prepared. Tell me about this strange message that just arrived from Zargarb."

He led the way into his relatively simple rectory. Nothing fancy about these quarters, Leann noted, fitting for a real church, she thought. Andre introduced his Circle. "Deacon Philas assumed leadership of the Church of Jehosanity when Deacon Bandar Dero passed away last winter," he explained.

Sipping tea seemed rather out of place, considering the gravity of the situation, but Andre's Circle went along with it, trying hard to understand what was being said. Andre felt a bit sorry for their plight. Lenkova outlined what she had learned. Deacon Philas became enthralled with the alleged conversation with Sister Ami's ghost, as he put it. "You see, Bandar was right. Lord Jehosa always looks after us. Place your faith in the Lord, he always said."

Lenkova became agitated with him, "Look, I'm saying that Pope Yazi has given his Holy Paladins orders to destroy your church here and steal the Holy Relics."

"Yes, so you've said three times now, dear child. Lord Jehosa will provide, have faith in our Lord," was his reply. Seeing that only made her more frustrated, he added, "Besides, the High Council has got over a thousand cavalrymen in and around the Junction. We are perfectly safe, child. Now sip your tea; it is getting cold. Oh yes, as usual, your Sisters may camp on the Church grounds."

"Well, at least we have a place to sleep," growled Lenkova, once they were back outside and tending to our horses. "I swear those deacons are blind fools!" Leann chuckled. She knew just how Lenkova felt.

Andre's Circle got to see just how efficient these women were that afternoon. Some went off to acquire charcoal for cooking fire. Others set up sleeping bags for everyone, while others handled the cooking duties. Every so often, another small group of fighters arrived and reported in to Lenkova, who tried to keep an accurate count of her forces at the moment. Andre took his Circle for a tour of the town and helped them work on their language skills. The day dragged on slowly, but nothing happened.

Late the next day, everyone noticed that the cavalrymen were being rounded up. "So it begins," Lenkova commented to Andre, as they headed for the cavalry garrison headquarters.

As they arrived, they saw numerous squads of men preparing to go on duty. "Ah there you are, Fighter Group Leader Lenkova, I was just about to message you. It seems that we are finally under attack. The Holy Paladins have committed themselves and have sacked Espresso, a village twenty miles south of here. Reports just in have their numbers in the hundreds and are riding the spoke road towards Zargarb. Our orders are to come at them from the rear, while the Zargarb cavalry rides at them from the city. Together, we will smash them and put an end to them. You and your fighters are welcome to come with us, if you like."

"We are charged with the defense of the Church," she retorted. "We stay. You know that this is just a feint and that the real attack will be here on the Mother Church?"

"Oh be reasonable, Lenkova," the general protested. "If high command thought this was a feint, as you say, they would not order our entire forces to smash these infidels. This time, all glory will go to the High Council's cavalry. We are about to show everyone just what we can do! Talk to you when I get back." He saluted and grabbed his reins, signaling the several hundred men to move out. Andre and Lenkova watched as they galloped south out of town.

"Fools," Lenkova spat on the ground. She and Andre walked back to the Mother Church. "How can we defend this place with four hundred sixty-nine defensive fighters?" she asked rhetorically.

An hour later, a Sister rode up to the complex at a full gallop, her horse throwing lather in all directions, panting from its heavy exertion. "Lenkova, you were right. There is a very large number of the blue coats ten miles due east of here heading this way."

"Donkey's ass!" Lenkova cursed. "You've done well. Get a fresh mount and have the scouts on the northern portions of the arc filter down towards the center. Keep the southern arc still alert. I don't trust these vile men."

"Yes, ma'am!" she replied and rushed off to get another horse, which an alert Sister had waiting for her. She galloped back out of the town a top speed.

"Andre, how the heck are we to defend this complex? This is only a losing proposition," she said completely exasperated.

"Let's try reasoning with the Deacon one more time," suggested Leann. "Let me try something."

A couple minutes later, the Deacon led us into his study once more. This time, Lenkova was terse and to the point. "Deacon, the time has come for decisions. All the thousand or so cavalrymen have gone off on a folly attack to the south. You only have us to defend your Church. I just got word that a large body of Holy Paladins is on its way here to sack your church. They are less than ten miles from here as we speak. Their numbers greatly exceed ours. I cannot possibly defend your Church; all my forces have not been able to get here fast enough."

"But this is not possible," the Deacon faltered, the stark reality suddenly hitting him.

Leann spoke softly, "Is it not in your scriptures that the Lord helps those who help themselves?"

The Deacon noticed her for the first time, "Why, now that you mentioned it, I do believe there is. Oh my. Everything will be lost! It will all be on my head!"

"Act! You have maybe ten minutes to save whatever is of value," Leann replied, shaking him out of his woe.

"Can you evacuate the relics and our priests? Is there still time?" he asked, nearly in tears.

"Yes, but move fast. How many wagons do we need?" Lenkova barked.

"Three, no four. They are in the stables over there."

"Okay. I'll send helpers to you at once; get your staff and get moving. We have to get you out of here in less than ten minutes!"

Lenkova ran outside and yelled her orders. All the Sisters began swiftly breaking camp, saddling horses. A dozen ran to fetch the wagons. Lenkova was suddenly in action, moving from place to place working out her strategic withdraw plans. She left the priest mess to Andre and his Circle, since they seemed to reach him. "I want all our archers, here, form a defensive line as usual, horses behind them. If they come before we get moving, let them have all you have, then mount up and retreat. No heroics!"

Just then, another scout rode up from the south. "Lenkova, the ones who attacked to the south are doubling back and headed this way too. Damn, looks like they are already here!" Suddenly the thundering hooves of incoming cavalry echoed through the town, coming from the east. A fair number of scouts were just ahead of them. "Archers, pick your targets. Let's have every other sword form up a line behind me. We'll give them a show of force. Buy the rescuers some time. Someone go tell them that the enemy is upon us and to get those wagons rolling!"

The locals dove off the street, taking cover in any building they could, in a mad dash to get out of harm's way. Andre, Tom, Fred, and Art came running outside toward Lenkova just as her archers began to launch volleys of arrows at the oncoming Holy Paladins. Many hit their targets; horses and bodies fell, adding to the confusion. The fifty Sisters let every single arrow they carried fly as fast as they could. The result was just what Lenkova had desired; it broke their charge. Horses were rearing, dodging this way and that, creating confusion amongst their ranks. Mount up everyone, orderly retreat!" she barked.

"We'll attempt to stop the next charge and give you more time to exit," Andre called out. The four men began their chanting. Lenkova looked at the clear blue sky, remembering suddenly the lightning bolts of Ket Bethany. No lightning today, she concluded. Her riders headed down the rim road after the wagons; it was like a wave of horses moving across the land. Now regrouped, the Holy Paladins once more kicked their horses into a gallop. Suddenly, four walls of fire appeared in the street, blocking their passage. The lead riders tried to ignore them and rode through the flames, but fell screaming to the ground, their tunics ablaze! Again, their charge was broken. Looking back over her shoulder, Lenkova thought, "Impressive!" The four men hastily mounted and galloped after Lenkova.

As they rode along, several more scouts joined them, riding in from various directions. Their report made her skin crawl, the enemy numbered close to a thousand! "What's the plan?" Andre called out, as he caught up to his wife.

"Rim road to the staging area. Pick up supplies. No arrows left," she called out. "Damn, the wagons are slow!"

"We have some time before they come after us, if at all," Andre suggested. "Undoubtedly they will ransack the Mother Church, looking for the relics. They do not know that we have the priests and relics with us. If they were smart, they ought to make that assumption and come after us. Who knows, though?"

"We ought to pick up several hundred more fighters the closer we get to the staging area," she yelled back. "Okay, scouts, fan out to our rear. Let me know if and when we are being followed and by how many." Dutifully, a dozen riders peeled off, heading back the way they had come.

Several nerve-wracking hours passed before a rider caught back up with the retreating group. "They've burned the Church! Some have gone into the other churches, but hundreds are now heading after us."

"Donkey's ass!" Lenkova spat once again. "At least we've made the staging area. I've added two hundred more fighters and re-supplied our archers, but these slow wagons will be the end of us yet. We need subterfuge," she declared.

One thing Andre knew, his wife was a master at handling crisis situations. "Andre, are you willing to have your Circle split up?"

"What do you have in mind?" Leann asked; it was her duty as Wid, Andre realized.

"I aim to send these wagons up north on the spoke rode here, while I take the major force and egg the enemy to follow us on down toward Zargarb, draw them away from the wagons. I know it is a gamble, if they don't take the bait, the wagons are sitting ducks."

"Worthy plan. We women will accompany the wagons; our men can help you, good luck," Leann replied. She was impressed with the clear thinking and resourcefulness of Lenkova.

"I'm going with the wagons," Fred announced. "I am a master at hiding tracks. I'll trail along behind them, erasing signs of their passage."

"Great, let's get the priests out of that wagon and into one of ours," Lenkova ordered. While the frightened priests scrambled to obey, she explained, "Your wagons are unique. We'll take this one with us and let the enemy see it occasionally; egg them on by trickery."

Ten minutes after arriving at the road junction and staging area, the four wagons with fifty fighters headed due north toward distant North Point. Dutifully, Fred prepared several branches and began following them, wiping out most signs of their passage. Lenkova had the wagon and the bulk of her forces begin heading south toward Zargarb. Now she had nearly a hundred archers and thus prepared her surprise welcome for the Holy Paladins. They moved off the track, taking cover behind boulders, trees, and ridge lines. Lenkova made sure all the archers knew their assignment: fire as many arrows as possible and then retreat in all directions, but quickly rejoin the wagon and others who were heading south. She, the men, and another seventy-five stayed mounted; they were going to charge into the front lines of the enemy just at the height of their confusion, trying to do as much damage as possible before fleeing. She looked back at the dirt of the south track. The wagon ruts were very clearly visible. Not even an idiot could miss them, she thought. Now they all waited.

"Damn, I hate waiting," she said.

"So do I," Andre replied.

An hour later, they heard the thunder of a large number of horses coming down the rim road from the Junction. "Okay, get ready, swords at the ready," she ordered. Now they could see the distant dust clouds swirling skyward. Here at the crossroads, the terrain was hilly and rocky, with a few trees, mainly clumped at the crossroads proper. Soon, the front vanguard of the enemy could be seen riding hard toward them. Lenkova watched the unsuspecting enemy as they continued to drive straight toward her small group, who waved their swords defiantly in the air. "Fools!" was all that she said.

When the lead bunch was perhaps a hundred feet from Lenkova, her archers suddenly appeared on both sided of the rim road, and arrows flew thick and fast. It was very hard to miss; they were bunched together so tightly. Men and horses fell in a mad chaotic jumble of screams and cries. Those in the rear trampled upon the fallen ones in front of them before they could rein in their horses. After several arrow volleys had done their job, Lenkova gave a war cry and her small group charged into their midst, hacking and chopping at any who offered any resistance. This tactic gave her hundred archers time to evacuate their position.

Just as soon as the enemy regained some sense of what was happening, Lenkova ordered her retreat, and they galloped back to the crossroad and on down south after the wagon and others. Shortly, the archers began merging back into the formation, coming in from either side of the track. Lenkova ordered a casualty check and was glad to find out that only four had taken relatively minor cuts. "Okay, I want twenty scouts out, ten on each side, fan out and back. Becka and Carli, you two arc wide to the west and then head down to the crossroad. I want to know if any of them went north after the wagons. If any did, get back to me as fast as possible. Use extreme caution; the enemy must not see you. Now, arrow count, please."

The scouts peeled off on their assignments, while the archers appraised Lenkova on the number of arrows remaining. "Andre, we ought to be able to use that surprise attack a few more times. We've enough arrows remaining. Reinforcements are on their way by wagon, probably a day's travel on south of us. I think Boccacio's Point will work for the next surprise attack," she thought aloud.

"That's where the rocky ledge abuts the track, right?" he replied, pretty sure where she meant. The location was still about four hours ahead of them.

"Excuse me, Lenkova," Art pulled alongside of Andre and her. "One of your fighters has a nasty slice on her leg. Her makeshift bandage is not working well. I need to tend to her, if I may, but I know we cannot stop here."

"You can mend wounds like Andre?" she asked, knowing how good her husband was at healing. Art confirmed that he could. "Okay, then up ahead there is a rocky patch on our right. Take all four who are wounded and peel off there so that you'll leave no tracks. Best go at least a mile west before you stop. I'll send six others to watch over you and serve as lookouts. Don't want you getting surprised by any enemy scouts."

She issued the orders, but the four protested in vain; they did not want to miss any of the action. Lenkova won, however. As the rocky out-thrust appeared, eleven riders swerved onto the stony ground, hooves making distinctive hollow sounding noises as they moved westward from the main group.

"Andre, how many do you reckon we took out with our little surprise attack?" she asked.

"Happened too fast, but a hundred would be my guess, probably some are only wounded, though," he replied.

"'Bout what I thought," she answered. "I sure wish there was some way we could take them all out and be rid of them for good!"

"If the silly cavalry were not running all around over the eastern border, if they could be concentrated on a flank attack, we might have the numbers to do just that," Andre mused. "No way to get them here in time, however."

"Say, how far from Zargarb are we? When will we be able to stop and be safe?" asked Tom, rather unused to such field actions. "You know there are an amazing number of cool rock formations around here I'd love to inspect up close. Looks like good stone to work."

Lenkova laughed, not at his stumbling Sea Prince speech, but that he was more interested in rocks at a time like this! "We cannot push the horses like before, Tom. We're three days from the walls, though I expect to meet up with my reserves any time now, some two hundred more that are bringing supplies and more arrows. I'm afraid you'll have to do your rock looking from horseback," she grinned.

In an hour, Tom saw the solid rocky out-thrust appear on their right, as they approached Boccacio's Point. Judging that Lenkova ought to be here by this time, several scouts rode in to report. "They are about a half hour behind us. They've got outriders now, two dozen on either side." Lenkova thanked the women for their timely report, while Tom and Art marveled that the scouts, who had been out behind the party somewhere had somehow known just when to report back.

"These women really know what they are doing!" Art commented to Tom. Lenkova overheard them and smiled.

Andre and Lenkova dismounted and began sketching the site in the dirt. The rough stone intrusion to the west made traversal on horseback difficult. "Their outriders will be forced back down to the track here," she said.

"Trouble is that it's wide open to the east. If we charge their front like last time, their main body can just peal out to the east and come at our flank or rear," Andre pointed out. "We're going to have to be cleverer this time."

While they were discussing tactics, Tom took the opportunity to dismount and scramble onto the rocky intrusion, studying this interesting stone. It rose ever upwards for some distance before its backside, heavily eroded, fell into a valley to the west. Standing at the ridge crest, he called down, "Hey, Andre. Look here!" Many looked up to see what he was doing. Most of the Sisterhood fighters just smiled at him.

"What?" called out Andre, a bit peeved at being interrupted. He was having a difficult time trying to flesh out a way to make a successful surprise attack without taking undo casualties.

"Lots of loose rocks. How about a rockslide? Would that help?" yelled Tom. "This ridge line is full of loose boulders!"

"Brilliant!" exclaimed Lenkova and Andre simultaneously. Both had gotten the same idea at the same time. They looked at each other and grinned. A hundred fighters scrambled up to assist Tom. "Look, we position enough archers there to take out the outriders as they get forced back toward the road. As the others try to pass by, the rocks will come down along with the arrows. Because of the formation, our people can evacuate long before any enemy can circle around to get at them," Lenkova outlined. Andre concurred; this time they could not afford to rush the front enemy troops; they would quickly find themselves outflanked from the east. However, this delaying tactic was just as good.

A half hour later, sweat pouring from bodies, Tom had all the rocks arranged and ready. The hundred archers were in place, well hidden from view. Other Sisters held all the horses at the ready on the backside of the outthrust. Lenkova, Andre, and Tom, along with another twenty hid behind the rocks, ready to unleash them as the main enemy lines rode by. She had sent the remainder of her force on down the road. Now they waited as the sun baked them on the hot rocks.

"Well, that eliminated another fifty or so," Lenkova commented, as her group rode hard across country. Their surprise attack lasted all of a minute. The two dozen western outriders were cut down in a hail of arrows. More arrows struck the leading edge of the enemy column, followed by a big landslide. A ton of boulders rolled down the escarpment into the frenzied midst of the enemy columns. Immediately, the attackers slide down the backside to their waiting horses and galloped away, eventually catching up to the rear of the Sisterhood column.

"Eventually, they are going to attempt to overtake us. They've got to know the wagons are slowing us down," Lenkova commented to Andre.

"Hey, I have an idea about that," Tom broke in on their conversation. "They think we are carrying crosses right?" She nodded. "I don't know what they looked like, but I could dismantle parts of the wagon as it rolls along and make some crosses which could be carried on horseback. If they try to overtake us, we could abandon the wagon, and it would appear that we are carrying the crosses with us."

"Hey, that is a great idea, Tom! Do it," Lenkova replied. "If you need anything, let me know." Tom caught up to the wagon and jumped aboard, while another Sister took care of his horse.

"Anything in here we need to save?" Tom asked the driver. He had to repeat it twice more before she grasped his broken Sea Prince speech. She pointed out a few sacks, which Tom handed off to other nearby Sisters. Then, he began pitching other things, such as food sacks, over the side. To the trailing enemy, it would appear that they were doing all they could to lighten the load to be able to go faster. Finally, since no one had ever seen these crosses, Tom had to improvise. One Sister, a devout follower of Jehosanity, hopped into the wagon to help him with the design, offering ideas that she had heard. Using the few tools he found in the wagon, Tom ripped the siding off the wagon and constructed three crosses.

Lenkova had three Sisters fasten them to their saddles, dragging the long end on the ground. "We'll need you three to stay at the rear so that the enemy can see that we are carrying the crosses. Once they've seen you, get as far out in front as you possibly can." The three acknowledged their orders.

Just then, two rear scouts cantered up, "They've recovered from the last ambush and are pressing forward at top speed. I think they are trying to catch up with us."

"Thanks for the warning. Okay, everyone, rein in a minute. Quickly, destroy what's left of the wagon. We don't want them to see that we have made fake crosses from it." Quickly, the wagon's remains were smashed, and the horses freed. "Alright, let's get going, rest horses as much as we can. When they get closer, we kick into high gear. We are counting on their horses tiring before ours. They outnumber us two to one, so we are not going to make a stand. If they get too close, I want everyone to peel off in all directions, scatter like wheat in the wind. If we have to scatter, drop the crosses. Rendezvous when you can in Zargarb. Am I clear?"

Many of the Sisters would have preferred to make a stand, but all acknowledged her orders. Her column rode on, resting their horses, before the hectic dash that they knew would soon be upon them. Just then, the final reserves met them, coming up the track from the south, Lenkova now had her full complement of some six hundred fighters. Unfortunately, they also had with them a dozen wagons full of supplies. Only her quick thinking saved the day. The reserves had just passed through a small hamlet; Lenkova ordered the wagons back into the small village, had the drivers hide their weapons, and appear as normal villagers driving wagons. The wagons were parked at inconspicuous locations around the hamlet. Many of the drivers then scattered about the village, warning the residents to get inside. Meanwhile, their main force continued down the road.

"I hope they will be okay," she said to Andre as they rode onwards.

"Mostly food, bandages, cooking gear, and blankets," Andre

commented. "Looks harmless, besides these guys are in a hurry to catch up with us. I doubt that they will take more than a cursory glance at the wagons. They look perfectly normal in the village." He certainly hoped so.

Fifteen minutes later, a scout cantered up with the news that the enemy was less than a mile behind them. This time, the dust clouds and distant noise made the notification unnecessary. "Okay, everyone, get ready. Lead columns take off, maximum speed. Groups of fifty. Now!" Andre watched the precision of these women. Fifty kicked their horses into top speed, pulling rapidly away from the front line. Once they were on their way, the next fifty followed suit. A couple minutes later, Andre could make out the faces of the lead riders coming their way. Lenkova made sure that they could see the three crosses before she ordered maximum speed. The race for survival was on.

It was close; they had to see the crosses for the plan to work. Unfortunately, that allowed the enemy to get within crossbow range. Tom and Art were at the front of these final fifty riders, while Andre and Lenkova stayed at the rear, riding beside the three with the makeshift crosses. Quarrels began flying wildly around them. Shot from cantering horses, the enemy could only shoot in their general direction, hoping for a lucky hit.

One of the Sisters bearing a cross lurched backwards; a quarrel found its mark, she faltered. Without thinking, Andre moved over and pulled the wounded Sister onto his horse, no small feat while cantering at top speed. Another Sister, seeing what he was doing, pulled along the other side, and took the reins, leading the horse bearing the cross. Lenkova came along side Andre, "That was a foolish thing to do!" she called out.

"Pull out the quarrel!" he yelled back; the Sister had already passed out. She maneuvered close to his galloping horse and stretched out her left arm to reach the shaft. It took ten tries before she finally latched onto the shaft. She pulled and jerked, dislodging the shaft. "Thanks," he called out.

The quarrels stopped coming; they had pulled barely out of range, besides, it was impossible for the shooters to reload a heavy crossbow while cantering. Each had but a single shot. "We're pulling away," Lenkova encouraged everyone.

A while later, the land changed abruptly; they'd entered the cork-olive-grape district, famous for its wine, olives, and casks. Cover was aplenty in all directions and well-manicured plantations dotted the landscape. Suddenly they were forced to rein in their tired, lathered horses. The leading group had stopped to rest their horses. Like falling dominos, the remaining groups had to do so as well. Immediately, scouts were sent out to the rear. Walking the horses, everyone took this opportunity to grab what food and drink they could. Dusk was falling, would the enemy stop for the night? That was the most critical piece of information Lenkova greatly desired to know. She could take no effective action with the enemy hot on her trail.

Finally, a scout returned with the best news all day. The enemy had made camp for the night. While Lenkova and Andre discussed their options, Tom and Art looked after the wounded Sister. The quarrel had punctured her lung, and she was barely breathing. Neither man really knew how to treat her, but thankfully, Mary, their Communicator, chose this point in time to contact them to find out the news. They had successfully reached North Point without mishap. Via a Mind Link with Ann, Tom and Art began to deal with the Sister. Strangely, they began by holding her upside down; blood trapped within her lung trickled out of her mouth.

"Andre, as much as I would love to take these vile men on and send them to the Fires of Hell, I dare not," Lenkova commented.

"Subterfuge, my dear, more subterfuge is called for, I do believe. What if our force split off into a dozen groups of fifty, all going different ways? Travel slowly throughout the night as well. At daylight, have each split into five smaller groups, and then around noon, split again. They will never figure that one out. Meanwhile we make a show of entering Zargarb carrying these crosses. Everyone will think they are the Holy Relics. If there are any spies in the city, word will get out that the relics are now in Zargarb. Subterfuge, my dear."

"Andre, sometimes you have a devious mind, I like it." Lenkova then spread word of their new plans to each group leader and watched as the first of the dozen groups peeled off to the west. Shortly afterwards, another headed east by south. Over the next hour, eleven such groups left, leaving only Lenkova's small party of some fifty remaining on the south road. Around midnight, they too left the track, veering to the west.

A small scouting party spread themselves out over the area. Their task was simple, observe what the enemy did, but not be seen. Days later, they would report to Lenkova. When they were finally able to report, their message was simple. In the early morning, the enemy began seeing where the different groups had left the road. Finally, they gave up their chase when they found the last group had left the main route to Zargarb. They then began to head eastward toward the Arad, making great haste.

Late the next day as the sun set, Lenkova and her small band rode prominently through the Sisterhood manned gates into Zargarb. The three crosses were highly visible and noted by many people. That night, the talk around the city was the rescue of the Holy Crosses.

Lenkova did not have time to rest. Just as soon as they arrived, Alicia, their High Council representative, summoned her. "What a fine mess this has turned out to be, Lenkova! You were right, as usual. The cavalry general has been fired. Andisso is now their leader. Seems the cavalry were led on a lengthy wild goose chase, while the Junction was sacked. All seven Churches of Jehosanity were burned to the ground; all the priests have disappeared. Holy Relics gone."

"Not true," Lenkova too tired to waste time, interrupted Alicia. "We got the relics and other valuables along with the priests out of there just as they entered the town. We've been just ahead of their horde all the way here. For the moment, we do not want the location of the relics or the priests known. Just say that the Sisterhood is looking after them for the present."

"Oh that is good news. Yes, I heard strange rumors about crosses being brought through the gate on horseback. Any casualties?" she asked very concerned about Sisters being lost.

"Handful of minor wounds; one serious, no deaths. We did eliminate possibly a hundred-fifty of them, but we were continually outnumbered, by two to one mostly. What's the cavalry's plans now? Are they going to cut the invaders off as they head to the Arad?"

"Don't know. We are getting many conflicting reports back here. I don't think anyone in Zargarb really knows what is going on. I'll report to the council that the priests and relics are safe, and that ought to appease them. You heading to North Point soon?"

"Yes, probably in the morning. We are all beat; we rode all night. Need food, sleep, bath, not necessarily in that order," she jested, her sense of humor returning.

Three days later, Lenkova, along with three hundred fighters arrived at North Point. She had sent another three hundred in groups of fifty out to scour the entire sector, looking for damage caused by the Holy Paladins and to see if they were still hiding out somewhere near. She wanted an accurate assessment of the situation, before she attempted to move the priests or their valuables. Why someone would relish an old cross escaped her.

"As I have been telling your mother, Lenkova, I just cannot thank you enough. Will you accept the apology of a foolish old man?" Deacon Philas Al Mare asked humbly.

"Accepted. Have you heard the bad news about your churches?" she ventured, hoping that he had and that she would not be the bearer of such ill news.

"Yes, a Sister came with the bad news, but as we say, a church is just a building. They say that the stone walls still stand, mostly. It can be rebuilt. I am so glad that we escaped. Were any of your fighters killed trying to help us?" He showed his real concern, people, and not material things.

"No, some minor wounds. We did manage to eliminate a hundred or so of their numbers. Wish we could have been able to get them all," she vented her disdain and anger. "Oh yes, we pretended to carry the crosses on horseback into Zargarb. Everyone there believes that the Sisterhood is holding on to your Holy Relics for you. No one outside a few of us knows that they are here. I have three hundred scouts out now making sure that the enemy has indeed fled the sector. At the moment, it is too risky to try to move them."

"Leann and I have been talking about just that," he replied. "Your mother promised that it would not be any burden on the Sisterhood if we stored them safely here. Now that people believe the relics are in Zargarb, perhaps this is a very prudent action. We need to concentrate fully on rebuilding the churches. At a later date, we can come and retrieve them."

"Now that is the smartest thing I've hear you say yet! Very good indeed. Still, I am more than a little concerned for your church. According to the message, the Pope wants your entire church destroyed. Perhaps it would be wise to stay within the safety of the walls of Zargarb until this all blows over." She really did not want a repeat of the last few days.

"We've discussed it, but we must minister to the people. That is what we do; that is what it means to be a priest, serve the people. If we are to be killed by Infidels, then it must be Lord Jehosa's will. We will not compromise our Holy Principles. You see, child, your integrity is worth more than your mortal life." She left it at that; what life is there, except this mortal life; that was her point of view. "But then I'm not a priest," she thought.

After a week, all her scouts had reported. The Holy Paladins had left the sector and were in the eastern Arad once more, probably hiding out and making more plans. All told, twenty rural churches had been burned and thirty priests slain. Most of the small towns and villages on the route traveled lost their churches and priests. Only half of the priests of the Junction had been saved; these, including the Deacon, were the leaders of the church in the sector. Dutifully, now that it was safe to travel once more, the Junction priests were escorted home to Florintine Junction.

A week later, Lenkova and the Zargarb Circle were back in Zargarb. Once cleaned and fed, Leann took Lenkova aside for a little chat. "Art and I have now had a lot of time to ponder that message Sister Ami overheard. To us, it makes sense that this southern Pope fellow needs to destroy all the northern churches, if his is to become the sole doctrine. Yet, it would take a huge army to assail these walls here. Strong as this Pope might be, we do not feel he can muster that large a force. What we are getting to is this: there are other ways to achieve that goal. Look, anyone can enter the walled city if they have a few coppers, right?"

She nodded. "Art and I suspect what you will see next is a few of them entering the city disguised. They find the churches, assassinate the priests there, set fire to the church, and then meld into the crowd, heading for the next church. We don't wish to sound pessimistic, but we both feel that may well be their next move."

"Donkey's ass!" declared Lenkova. "I never thought of that, but now that you've explained it, it makes very logical sense. How do I guard against this threat? Thousands pass through the gates every day!"

"You can't, that's the point. We must find some other methods. Can you arrange for us to meet with Alicia?" Later that day, Alicia visited them and Leann explained her fears. She also expressed a desire to learn more about the political aspects of the sector. Thus, Alicia began taking Leann and Art to the open High Council meetings. There in the open forum time slot, Art began to put the seeds of what these Holy Paladins might try next into the minds of the council members. He and his wife only hoped that they would have enough time to find a political solution.

Chapter 12 New Orders

The black coach carrying Pope Yazi I's Prelate of Security rolled into the huge encampment south and east of the Junction, the only watering hole for twenty or more miles. The thousand Holy Paladins had received a message that the Pope was sending his second-highest ranking Prelate of Security to straighten out the mess they'd made. All the men were very ill at ease. Never had their Pope ever intervened in their activities here in the Arad. However, their failure to destroy the leaders of the Church and letting the Holy Crosses slip through their fingers by a rag tag band of women no less had infuriated their Pope, at least that was the general opinion in the camp.

Already the Security Forces known as the Mano del Dio, the hand of God, had become the most powerful subgroup within the Church. Rumors suggested that these men were trained assassins, though few actually believed this was accurate. Nevertheless, when anyone from the Mano del Dio appeared, men shrank back in fear. None more so than General Theos Cox, who had led the ill-fated raid on Florintine Junction.

As the coach came to a halt, General Theos stared at the entirely black coach, whose black shades hid all occupants from view. Even the driver was dressed in black. However, the familiar white cross was the sole adornment upon the door, which opened. Half expecting to see a man dressed in black, General Theos was startled to see the familiar sky blue robes with the white cross emblazoned across its front appear. Karlos stepped slowly down to the ground. Theos thought he saw a trace of red near the man's waist, but kept his eyes upon Karlos.

Karlos stepped forward toward Theos, his hands folded together as if praying, his countenance told Theos he ought to be afraid of this man. Stern, ruthless eyes pierced his own. When Karlos spoke, it was soft, yet carried the force of a war hammer behind it. "Pope Yazi I has been disgraced; he gave you a simple order, yet you could not follow it." Now General Theos began to squirm, the blow would come any minute. He said his last prayer to Jehsoa, expecting a sword cut to his neck at any moment.

"I have come to see that you get it done right this time," Karlos continued, a cold threat in his voice.

"Yes, Prelate, yes. Tell me what to do. We will do it, I promise," General Theos began begging, relieved to hear he wasn't dead yet. Disgraced, yes. New orders, yes. Not killed.

"Where are the Holy Relics now and where is the Arch-deacon now?"

"Your Grace, we have spies in Zargarb who witnessed those women entering the city bearing three crosses. We know that the Arch-deacon has returned to Florintine Junction, rebuilding the churches that we burned to the ground," Theos replied quickly, hoping that this information would somehow create some slight favor with the Prelate, showing him that he was not entirely incompetent.

"You have botched the easy situation when they were unguarded and readily available to be retrieved. Within the walled city, retrieving them will be many times more difficult. You realize the magnitude of your blunder? If the Pope sent his entire army of Holy Paladins against the walls, they would not be enough to breech them!" He paused to let his admonition sink into this man.

"If you fail this time, the Pope has ordered me to send you to the Fires of Hell for high treason against Jehosanity. Now listen clearly, here is what you are to do. Discard your tunics; disguise yourselves as local travelers. Enter all the towns and villages in singles and pairs, so as not to draw any undue attention to yourselves. Fan out and spy out the churches and their priests. Discover their daily habits and whereabouts. Then, on July 15, during the night, your men will strike. In every town and village, we strike at the same time, slaying all the priests and setting fire to all their churches."

"Brilliant plan. Brilliant. Nothing can go wrong with it this time," General Theos effused. "What about the Holy Crosses?"

"Leave them to me. I will handle the Holy Relics personally, along with my other Holy Business. Now show me to the water; my men and I are parched."

Chapter 13 The Grande Council of Kings

King Lachlan Laird, dressed in her finest chain mail, a thin golden crown upon her head, stood triumphantly before the Standing Stones not too far from Brea. Dawn was rising; thirty-three Kings, Queens, or Representatives (in the case of Tewdwr) — all the leaders of Cymry — stood in silence. "We, the sons and daughters of the Ancients who settled Cymry, stand here united together for the first time since the dawn of time. Here where our forefathers erected this eternal calendar that we may always know when the seasons are upon us, we stand as one in honor of them. Behold, the first rays of the summer dawn strike the keystone!" As we all watched, the sun's image appeared as a small dagger piercing the center of the marking stone. I had taught her about the astronomical use of the standing stones, and she dramatically used her newfound knowledge.

"The Council of Kings thus now exists. Our purpose: bring peace, uniform justice, and a means to settle disputes to all Cymry. So say one, so say us all." On cue, as we were instructed, all the gathered representatives called out, "So say us all." One by one, we climbed into the waiting coaches and rode back into Brea to Lachlan's Great Hall, where a huge breakfast was served.

My Circle accompanied Caitlyn and me to this first meeting of the kings. Caitlyn still glared at Lachlan; she would never forgive her for having instigated the southern kings to attack our town. Only the prospects of total peace throughout the island kept her barely civil toward King Laird. When breakfast was finished, King Lachlan led the representatives into a special chamber that she had long been preparing for this day. Rich tapestries hung on the walls. In the center was a huge oblong table, capable of seating all of us. She took a position at one end. The other kings, queens, and representatives, took seats around the table. I was supposed to sit at the opposite end of the table from her. However, I chose to sit at the side of the room, along with the rest of my Circle. Caitlyn sat by her Uncle Emil.

Thus, the lengthy discussions began. The first order of business the kings insisted upon settling was how long would King Laird be the Council Leader and what would be her duties and authority. Many also wanted to know how I, her "magician," fit into the scheme and when another took over as Council Leader, would I be supporting them.

The discussion went nowhere until I intervened. "Excuse me, but first decide what the duties and obligations of the Council Leader are to be." I sat down; you could hear a pin drop. Thus, I learned that whenever I spoke, everyone paid very close attention to what I said. I found that very unnerving. Everyone present now knew in great detail, probably exaggerated as well, what happened with the lightning storm during the battle a few months ago.

After focusing them on the first topic, they soon came to agreement that the Council Leader would manage the meetings, send out notifications, and do the "dirty work" of the administration. Emil made it very clear that the Council Leader's vote carried the same weight as any other member. With that decided, I told them to agree on the length of the Council Leader's term. After an hour's discussion, they finally agreed upon five years, after which the council would elect another Council Leader, who could not be the same person that had just been the leader. None of these representatives wanted to see King Lachlan always running the show.

"As for your third question, I will support decisions made by the whole council. However, I reserve the right to disagree with the council if I see fit to do so. If I agree, I will support you with my 'magic' as needed. Does that set the record straight?"

"So you are not Lachlan's lackey?" asked one king, whom I did not know. He was from the far south of the island.

"Be civil, Dori," someone nudged him.

"I am not anyone's lackey, except perhaps my wife's when in bed," I turned it into a bit of levity. Everyone roared with laughter, defusing a tense scene. Caitlyn flushed, however; if I were close, she would have punched me in my ribs.

Next, I had them decide what topics could be brought before the council and when. In the end, they decided that anything was fair game if it involved others on the island. What happened after that, I don't really recall. I rather doped off, nearly asleep; this was utterly boring to me. Lilly Ann nudged me awake, "They are talking to you," she whispered.

"Ah, please summarize it again for me, please," I fumbled for something courteous.

"Recompense. What recompense doth yea seeketh from the two kingdoms that assailed thee towns?" the Highland accent of Fergus d'Aine came through my ears.

"None, sires, save only perpetual rights for our merchants and travelers to pass safely to Bregia and the docks there. No recompense. Enough blood and money on both sides have already been spent." A murmur went through a number of kings. I found out later that I could have asked for a fortune and received it.

Thank heavens for suppertime! I don't think I could have stayed awake any longer. "Actually, Ket, I find it rather interesting. I have a say and all that," Caitlyn gaily admonished me while eating a leg of duck.

"So do I," added Lilly Ann.

"I'm not a Judger!" I tried to defend myself, though I knew that the proceedings were vitally important to the ultimate peace of the entire island. I am not of a political bent.

I was even gladder when the first meeting was over and we were headed home. Caitlyn and Lilly Ann chatted endlessly about how the meeting went. I preferred to watch the enthralling Highland countryside pass by our coach. However, Lilly Ann's comment was acid, "I wonder how the Council will operate when Ket Bethany is no longer around. I mean, after you are dead and buried and they have no 'magician' with which to enforce their rulings. It's one thing to be holding an ultimate weapon over their heads and quite another if such is not present."

"I hope I just never have to 'be' that ultimate weapon ever again!" I declared.

"Oh cheer up, Sarah and Percival are arriving next week," Caitlyn cheerily reminded me. Sarah was my daughter, last lifetime.

"Yes, mom and dad are both coming. They promised to bring our brothers with them," Lilly Ann added. Lilly Ann and Beth Ann were their twins. Arthur, eighteen, was their older brother; Justus, their younger brother was only fourteen. The women had been away from home now for a half a year. Both were excited to be reunited, if only for a short time. They had much to tell their parents.

Sarah, I was so proud of her. She had carried on our ministry here in Nuadilan until the Grey Creatures forced her to flee to the Greenway. She now had a good marriage to a fine man. Okay, I was even more content that those two had taken my advice and had opened communication lines to each person in their kingdom and had the consent of all to be their king and queen. Of all the kingdoms of the Greenway, theirs was the most thriving and happiest to live in, I might add, but then, I am being overly motherish. Yes, it would be good to see Sarah and Percival again. Perhaps, they would pull me out of my doldrums. I still was melancholic over my temporary insanity, killing my own men with lightning strikes.

The week passed excruciatingly slowly. Caitlyn was very pregnant by now and having some difficulty. She seemed excessively large for her time and could not make the long journey down to Bregia to meet the boat. No way would I leave her here alone in Nuadilan, so I stayed behind, sending the rest of my Circle to bring our visitors back. They all had left four days ago.

They finally arrived mid-July. Yes, it was a joyous reunion all around, and full of surprises. John Henry had come with them! He was the leader of the All Greenway Circle, and the lead Wid of our entire movement. Although the others of my Circle had been chatting away with Sarah, Percival, and John Henry for the last couple of days, I got my turn as well. Long we chatted about normal affairs, how things were going in their kingdom. I thoroughly enjoyed their company. John Henry wisely allowed me this personal time with Sarah.

The second day, he finally caught me at breakfast, "Ket, you are probably wondering why I came along."

"Well, now that you mention it, why did you? Need a break?" I jested. Curious, I was slipping. Why would our leader hazard such a journey? Something very critical must be going on that I was not aware of as yet! My joviality vanished in an instant.

"Can we talk privately? Just you and me?" he said sternly.

We went into my bedroom and closed the door. "I'm sorry; it didn't click with me that for you to come here, then something very important must be going on. Sorry. I have been a little off of late."

"Understandable. Ket, I came for two reasons. One is, as you say, critical. The other, just my plain curiosity. First to business. Ket, our druwid movement is in very dire trouble. I don't want too many to know about this just yet. Please, keep this in strictest confidence." I promised and looked very worried. What was going on?

"We are dying as a group. There is no other way to put it, Ket. Our number of active Guardians is now down to three hundred-fifty! Old age has taken its toll, true and expected. However, the real problem is with the breakup of the Greenway into all these isolated kingdoms and with the druwids being kicked out of most of them, we have very little ways to recruit new people. We are having a devil of a time finding any young child who is not firmly stuck in their heads! I have experimented with using "headers," but they progress only so far. Not one has yet been able to master any of our power spells. It's becoming grimmer by the month. I've already gotten another dozen requests from some of the older folks wanting to retire later this year."

"Making matters worse are all the fractured Circles that the Grey Creatures decimated. I keep trying to put the remnants back into new Circles, but the success rate is appalling. They are having a terrible time bonding and trusting one another. I've sent the worst cases as a group down to the Zargarb sector, hoping against all hope that somehow those six can bond with Andre. Where's Alabaster when you need him? Jesting aside, I have tried to contact him, but once more, I can't find him any longer. Have you had any contact with him?"

"Now that you mention it, no I haven't," I replied, concern filled me. "I'll try later tonight and see if I can reach him."

"Thanks, I'm at my wit's end. I can't think of anything else to try. We've only found five new children to apprentice this entire year, outside of our own children, mind you. All those came from Sarah and Percival's kingdom. Unless something drastic happens, we may drop below three hundred of us by this time next year! So Ket, I'm here to beg you to lend me a hand. We've got to do something fast!"

"I knew we lost many to the Grey Creatures, but I had no idea things were this bad! I'll give it my complete attention. I've got to reach Alabaster tonight," I said as encouragingly as I could.

"Thanks, Ket. Okay, the second matter. A few weeks ago, this box arrived at Mont Blanc. It was addressed to Bethany Stanton and comes from Megalos. I took the liberty of opening it in your absence, figuring it may well be vitally important. Someone spent a good deal of money sending you this, but the sender didn't know that Elizabeth Stanton was long dead. Go ahead, open it." I did as he asked.

Inside was a sealed parchment also addressed to Bethany Stanton. John Henry had broken the seal to read the letter. I opened it. Scrawled in a beautiful handwriting were letters, which appeared to be random gibberish. I stared at it. "That's what I thought. Gibberish. Who would spend all that money to send this? And to a long dead person? Makes no sense at all," John

Henry concluded.

I looked it all over — no suggestion of the "sender" of this mysterious letter. I looked again at the letters. Then, I remembered! It was Niccolo Helios, the artist and inventor of Megalos, whom I had befriended so long ago! We used to correspond over the years by sending coded messages back and forth. Could this be another one? Niccolo would be exceedingly aged by this time, well over a hundred years old. I got pen and ink from the drawer and began to decipher it. It was precisely the same code that he and I used! Five minutes later, I had the complete message rewritten. Together, John Henry and I read.

15 June 623

Bethany Stanton,

My father used to correspond with you. I am his daughter. He taught me that you were an extremely powerful and capable person, one that he could trust with his life. Dad told me how he helped you escape from Emperor Hiro. I regret to say that Niccolo passed away a number of years ago.

I am writing you because I am in dire peril, as are all his huge works of art and inventions. I was a senator and against this new Church of Jehosanity. Recently, several of us have been assassinated. I have retired to our estate where you met dad originally. I'm a virtual prisoner here. If I leave, I will be assassinated. Armed Centurions have been stationed just outside the estate to kill me if I stray from the estate.

Worse than my own life and why I am writing you is the latest edict from this unholy church. All works of art that are in any way lewd or display any naked figures are to be destroyed. Word has come to me of the massive destruction of hundreds of marble statues, merely because they showed the human form. Now, they are busily at work destroying all our historical artwork in Galantas. It is only a matter of time before the come here and destroy all dad's paintings, artwork, sculptures, ceramics, and so on.

If you are still alive, I beg of you, please come, and rescue all dad's art and me. I will give you all the money that dad has left me. Come swiftly, or it may be too late to save these treasures for the world.

Rea Helios

"I didn't know he had a daughter," I commented.

"You've got to go," John Henry said solemnly. "We can't let art treasures of the world be destroyed by this Pope Yazi fellow. He was one of your husband's disciples, right?"

"Yes he was. You're right. I have to go for any number of reasons, if only to repay the debt I owe Niccolo for getting us out of Galantas after I killed their Emperor. I've got no other ethical choice, I have to go." Suddenly, the gypsy woman's warning echoed in my mind. "Ket no go south on voyage. Ket stay with pretty blonde, have many kids. Ket go south, pretty blonde dies." I told

John Henry about what Reza had foretold.

John Henry wrung his hands, full of concern. "She's never been wrong with her predictions about you, has she?" He'd remembered hearing about her predictions when I was going after the Grey Creatures.

"No, but." I could not finish my sentence; I felt ill. I wanted to vomit — anything to dispel this horrible feeling in my stomach. I had to go. I owed it to Niccolo, but my dearest Caitlyn — I could not lose her!

When we came out of the bedroom and into the Great Hall where the others had gathered curious about our secret meeting, Lilly Ann said I looked white as a sheet! That didn't help matters for me. Mechanically, I let the others read the letter from Rea that I held limply in my hand.

"I remember this code," exclaimed Beth Ann. "You guys remember the secret code from way back?" The others who had been with me in Megalos so many years ago in our former lives began remembering as well.

"So Niccolo had a daughter. I wonder whom he married? He did not have any girl friends when we were there, as I recall, but my memory way back then is awfully fuzzy," Beth Ann commented.

"He saved our hides, if my poor memory is right," Paul added.

"Yes, I think so," Paulette supported her brother.

"We've got to go, Ket," declared Beth Ann. "All of us. We have an outstanding debt to that man."

In tears, I mumbled, "I know, but Caitlyn. Remember Reza's warning. What's going to happen to Caitlyn? How can I go, if by going I know she is going to die? How can I?" I'm afraid that I completely lost it. Crying, I buried my head in Caitlyn's lap; she stroked my head, like a baby. I couldn't lose her, not when we were finally getting a family.

Everyone sat as still as a mouse staring at a piece of cheese. What can you say at a time like this anyway? After a moment of biting his lip, John Henry spoke, breaking the somber mood. "I believe that there just might be a way around this problem, Ket."

Everyone looked at him; even with tears dripping down my cheeks, I too stared at our leader. "I've just learned some incredible news, verified by the Velona Circle themselves. It seems a young lad has just revolutionized shipbuilding. He calls it a caravel. Alton reported on the trials, and unloaded, the caravel sails over twice as fast as any other Sea Prince ship! If we can hire that ship, you can cut the travel time in half, perhaps. With luck and good sailing, why, you probably can get back before Caitlyn is due this fall."

"You're kidding," Allan, our Planner, exclaimed in complete disbelief, "twice as fast?"

"A child did this?" put in Beth Ann.

"Yes to both. Pietro is his name. He just turned thirteen. He designed it and got Elona to make them build it. Thus far, it has exceeded all expectations. It carries twice the cargo load of any existing ship. Fully loaded, it still sails as fast as an empty current ship! Alton and his Circle actually witnessed the entire test. It's true," John Henry elaborated.

"Second, I will send for some Circle replacements to watch over Caitlyn and things here until you get back. I'll send Mary Rodriguez; she is the best healer we have. I'll make sure there is also a Protector and a Communicator here at all times as well. We'll do everything in our power to protect Caitlyn. Off chance, do you have any idea who might want to kill her or why?"

"Would you? That would ease my mind considerable," I replied, genuinely thankful for John Henry's support. "No, no ideas at all. Complete blank. She is loved by everyone in our towns, as far as I know. Say, we have a huge amount of construction going on. Could you possibly spare a Planner as well?"

"Absolutely, I'll get the three of them on the next boat over here. Better, I'll see if I can hire that fast boat and if so, have the ship pick up the three and drop them off at Bregia when they pick up your Circle. How's that?"

"Terrific idea, I'll pay whatever it costs," I added.

"Then it is settled. You all settle your debt to Niccolo, and we'll make sure nothing happens to Cailyn or your towns while you are gone," John Henry concluded. "If you'll excuse me, I had better start making these connections." He returned to his room, opened his mind, and made contact with Sally Longton, Velona's Communicator. Soon, he had a Mind Link with Alton and Elona."

It felt like a heavy burden had lifted from my shoulders. "Honestly, Ket, I will be all right here, especially with three Guardians looking after me, really I shall," Caitlyn did her best to cheer me up. Honestly, I can say now that she did indeed feel completely at ease with our going on this rescue mission. With some spirit, we eight set about trying to organize what we would take on our trip.

That night, after Caitlyn was asleep peacefully beside me, I expanded my mind southward, looking for Alabaster Benjamin Crowley, the founder of our druwid movement. I now owed it not only to John Henry, but also to all of us. After a half hour of searching, I located the mind I wanted and made a slight contact. *Alabaster? Ket Bethany here. May I have a word with you?* I hoped that he was not asleep.

Alabaster? Strange, I have not heard that name in some time. Yes, yes, I was called Alabaster. Bethany, Elizabeth Stanton? Is this you? Ah, yes it is. My name is Ramithalion now. The befuddled answer I received, like one awakening to some forgotten past, was not at all what I was expecting.

Yes, it's me. I need to talk to you about us druwids. Seems we have yet another serious problem.

When you pass by the Moon People village on the coast where the mountains rise from the sea, seek the narrow inlet. Climb the Steps of Wisdom. I will be waiting. Must go now. The contact was broken.

Huh? What was he talking about? Nevertheless, I memorized his directions and jotted them down on a parchment the next morning so the others could read them as well. Did he know that I was going on a long voyage? That I would pass by the Red Desert and the new Moon People's coastal village? I shrugged it off; no predicting Alabaster. His mind dwarfed mine, and I had long since given up trying to know what he was thinking.

John Henry was ecstatic that Alabaster would meet with me personally. He gave me a list of questions for which I was to attempt to get answers. Primarily, they centered around what do we do now?

Five days later, we packed up and headed for Bregia. Caitlyn, Sarah, Percival, and I rode in the open coach, because Caitlyn was too uncomfortable on horseback now. The two days to Bregia passed altogether too swiftly for me. I found that I really missed Sarah's company. I vowed to try to stay closer to my extended family in the future.

"Wow, what an intriguing ship!" declared Allan, as we all watched Pietro's Folly slowly gliding toward the lone dock. "Two main masts. Look how high the stern decks, or whatever they are called, actually are. What a view the captain must have from up there. Look, there is a tiny little deck thing at the top of the first mast. Incredible." He spoke for us all. Here was a very different kind of ship indeed.

The replacement druwids waved from the foredeck, and we all waved back. "What a ship you are getting," one of them yelled our way. Seems the four passengers were just as excited about this new ship as we were. After the mooring lines were set, the four, carrying their sacks, walked down the gangplank onto the dock. Two ships could dock at once, one on either side, here in Bregia.

John Henry did the introductions, "Mary Rodriguez, Healer; Pete Hedgewick, Protector; Jo Ann Hamilton, Communicator, Ernest Galls, Planner. Here is Queen Caitlyn." As the introductions continued, we all shook hands.

Pete declared, "I rather wish I was going with you, Ket. I give you my word that I will protect Caitlyn with my life. Besides, she now has the services of the best healer on Tarra." Mary blushed slightly.

"Thank you all. I'm sorry to have to pull you away from your other duties and families," I apologized.

"Glad to be able to help out — too routine back at Mont Blanc, if you get my drift," Ernest joked.

"Hey, time's a'waisting; you all coming 'board?" called out the young captain. I waved, gave Caitlyn a farewell hug and kiss, hugged Sarah, and them shook John Henry and Percival's hands. Lugging our large sacks, we seven walked up the gangplank, waving all the way. Sarah, Percival, and John Henry were catching the next boat to Calgary, due in later this very day.

Waiting for us as we stepped on the main deck was a wiry young man. "Mio Amato, your steward and cook, at your service. Captain's asked me to show you around and get you settled. First, yea gets to learn the names 'round 'ere. This is the main deck we're standin' on, see. Yonder," he pointed to the stern, "is the poop deck. The top one there where the captain be, that's the poop royal. Gotta have his permission to go up there, mind you. Your cabins are below the poop deck, quite large, compared to all other ships. Back yonder, is the foredeck; we crew stays in the foredeck cabins, bumpier ride there, you see. There's another set of cabins below deck, both fore and aft, not as comfee, so we's putting you up long side the captain in the poop deck."

He saw Allan staring at the small angular sail flying off the short stern mast, which was being used to turn the ship around. "Spanker sail, sir. Nice for gentle navigation, big ship, small space." Allan grinned and we followed Mio across the main deck. To my surprise, a pair of watertight doors opened into a narrow hallway beneath the poop deck; cabin doors lined each side. All told, there were four separate cabins, two on each side. The stern port cabin belonged to the captain; we were to share the other three and any others we wanted below deck.'

Who was sleeping where became our first decision. Since Allan and Beth Ann were married, we gave them the stern starboard cabin opposite the captain's. Paul quickly stated that he and his sister would share a cabin, so Paulette and Paul took the aft port cabin, much to the chagrin of Lilly Ann, who still had a crush on Paul. Unfortunately for her, he did not reciprocate. That left Ben, Lilly Ann, and me with one cabin.

"Look, it's not safe for Lilly Ann to be below decks all by herself," Ben said emphatically, adding, "and we can't have our Wid staying below deck, so I volunteer to take a cabin below. You are married, so Lilly Ann ought to be safe enough with you," he grinned. Since I had no intention of being by myself below deck, I let Ben's request stand. Lilly Ann and I went into our aft starboard cabin, while Mio ushered Ben down a set of steps to the main cabins.

Later, we discovered that the cabins below deck were far more spacious, but they had little fresh airflow. In the heat of the day, they were quite stuffy, smelling of fresh tar and oils. Lilly Ann and I looked over our cabin. Two hammocks, one above the other, took up the outer side; a porthole half way between them let fresh air in. On the side with the door, two wooden sea chests were secured to the floor. We put our sacks into these. Above the chests were a tiny table and a mirror. Not much space, but it would do nicely.

Paulette stuck her head in our door, announcing, "Lilly Ann, when we girls need some privacy, Paul said he can join Ket, here, and you can join me. How's that?" They both grinned. Our gear stowed, we all went back onto the main deck to watch. Normally, the ship would sail with the outgoing tide, but the captain knew we were in a hurry, and slowly had gotten the large caravel turned around. Now we listened as he barked orders and the five crew members scrambled to carry them out.

Past memories of sailing on previous Sea Prince ships came into my mind. I could not help noticing that this crew was not as seasoned as the other's I'd seen. Occasionally, they got confused with all the rigging lines. I soon forgot about the men working, as the shore and my wife were still waving, but grew steadily smaller. I waved back and marveled once more at the joy of silently moving across the surface of the harbor.

Chapter 14 The Maiden Voyage of Pietro's Folly

Once clear of the bay, both huge, square mainsails were dropped and their many lines tightened and adjusted. With three sails billowing, Pietro's Folly gradually picked up speed rapidly. Soon, we were flying along at an incredible speed. Foam sliced across either side of the bow. Cymry receded at a rapid rate.

"I'm Captain Felix Aroya. Glad to have you all aboard. This is the official maiden voyage of Pietro's Folly. So expect minor glitches as we learn how to sail her best. We are all new with this boat, only been completed a few weeks." He was tall, thin, and rather young for a ship's captain, perhaps twenty-one. "Since you've paid a royal fee for our services, anything you want, just name it."

"Pardon my asking, what did we pay for this trip? John Henry made the arrangements for us," I asked.

"Triple the going rates, five hundred gold coins. So you must be on very important business, no cargo even. Just bear with us as we learn the intricacies of this new caravel. You know that a kid designed it? Barely thirteen years old. A genius, I'd say. He got our High Priestess to back his design. She moved heaven and earth to get it built. She's the fastest ship on the seas. Back in Velona, shipwrights are now making a whole fleet of these caravels. In a few years, Velona will be the shipping capital of the world! However, we might not have all the kinks worked out of the ship yet. So if things go slightly wrong, don't panic; we'll right them as we go. Got extra crew members, but if things go amiss, can we count on you folks lending a hand if need be?"

"Sure, glad to help. Just let us know," I replied.

"Okay, I guess we best take care of the formalities. If you will join me in my cabin, we can discuss our route and destination. They were a bit vague on that."

I followed Captain Felix into the poop cabins. Inside his, he had a large table covered with maps. In the base of the table was a honeycomb of scroll slots, also filled with maps. "All I know is that we are heading toward Megalos."

"I'll fill you in, sir," I began, knowing that I had to level with the captain. "We are on a complex rescue mission. You see a friend of ours in Megalos has a huge collection of magnificent artwork and inventions. However, the insane Church of Jehosanity down there has ordered that all it be destroyed, and the owner assassinated. We are trying to get there fast, and rescue the art and the artist, if we can. I've seen some of the artwork and can vouch for the fact that there is none finer on all Tarra. It would be a disaster for all it to be destroyed by religious fanatics. So in a large measure, our voyage down there is top secret. We don't want to alert them that we are coming. Our precise destination is the southern tip of Megalos by the Shallow Firth and Sud."

"Ah, we are in for a wee bit of excitement this voyage! I like that!" he exclaimed, a broad smile on his face, and a twinkle in his eyes.

"Further, we need to make one stop. I have kind of strange directions and do not quite know what to make of them. Should be just a short stop, few hours at most. I read him the unusual directions that Alabaster had told me. He scratched his head and then dug through his maps.

"Ah, here we are. Latest map just south of the Red Desert." He spread it out on his table. I saw a roughly drawn coastline of the eastern side of the desert. "This is the Moon People port that your directions talk about. It is the only one that we know about. Ships stop there several times each year. Ah, here are the mountains. They are spectacular and tall. No ports, no cities there. Not on the map. I guess we will have to do a wee bit of exploring. I like that. Say, this is going to turn out to be a fun trip for us all."

Next, I showed him precisely where the Helios estate lay on the island of Megalos. This way he would know where we really needed to go, and he could do his job of getting us there better. "We are at top speed now," he announced. "Let's go on deck and watch."

I knew something was happening; the boat was bobbing rapidly and more or less randomly. We sailed up a big swell, tilted to one side or the other, and then more or less fell down the other side of the swell. Foam flew past the bow on either side, sending a spray upon the deck. I found my entire Circle, except Lilly Ann, white with nausea, clinging dearly to the side rail, heaving over the side. She was watching over them.

"They'll get their sea legs soon enough, don't worry miss," Captain Felix commented as he passed them to get to the fore. His crew was still adjusting mainsail lines. "Takes some getten' used to, men. Try tightening the bow line, see if that does it." Indeed, they were still trying to figure out how best to sail her, I thought.

"Glad you are not sick too," Lilly Ann said, as I joined her side. "You can help me nurse these five. I think it would be fun to captain one of these ships, don't you?"

"Absolutely. I've always been fascinated with ships. When I was a boy, I learned how to make a small dingy. It came out good for that matter. Maybe we can buy one of these caravels for the group to use when needed."

"Maybe we could even be her crew," she added wistfully. "Don't you just love the wind blowing through your hair and across your face? Such a feeling of freedom!"

"I know. I used to sail my dingy out to the edge of our little bay. Now that you've mentioned this, I really do miss it. We are definitely going to have to get us a ship one day."

Just then Felix came by, "Say you two want to come with me? I've got to make a complete tour of the boat, checking for leaks and such. Standard practice with a new ship, mind you. You can see all her."

Leaving our moaning companions, we followed Felix all over the inside of the ship. It was at least twice as large in the cargo hold. I now saw how it

171

could carry double the load; it was spacious! No leaks in the cargo hold. Fore, below decks, held the pantry, kitchen, and makeshift dining room. Since there was no cargo this trip, the crew had confiscated part of the aft cargo hold as the permanent dining room and recreation room. A dartboard was nailed to one beam. The aft crew quarters were more spacious than the poop cabins and had portholes for air. Since no one knew the ideal number of crew members the caravel ought to have for optimum sailing, space was available for nine crew members. Felix didn't think he needed nine, and opted for five plus cook, who could be pressed into crew duties if need be. Besides, he also had us to help. Less crew meant more gold for each of them.

"Boy it sure is bumpy in here," Lilly Ann commented while we were looking for leaks here in the fore crew cabins.

"Aye, miss," Felix replied, "fore breaks the sea; always the roughest ride here. Way up and way down, more so on this ship, probably because we are going twice as fast." Now Lilly Ann appreciated more fully the stern poop cabins!

"Incredible! That was fast!" exclaimed Felix. "Only two days out and we are off the Red Desert! Incredible. Ought to have been four days." Off to the port side, we could see the reddish sands and low hills that reached down to touch the ocean. My Circle members had recovered mostly, thanks to the herbs that Beth Ann had thoughtfully brought and which Lilly Ann and I had prepared for them.

"It sure is red," commented our Loremaster, Ben. "Someday I'd like to visit that land. I hear it is not deadly to walk anymore."

"Well, nobody lives there, pretty desolate," Captain Felix replied.

"Huh, then what is that?" Ben pointed out. Sure enough, we saw three people walking with a camel heading down to the coast. The desert was reclaiming people, what a good sign, I thought.

During the daytime, the girls did quite a lot of sunbathing, while Allan and I studied the caravel. Compared to my dingy building this was a monster. Allan was intrigued by its construction — how it was kept watertight by the oakum and tar pounded into the cracks in the boards. We even got our hands messy helping some of the crew with sealing a few leaks that appeared that afternoon. Also, Felix said that we'd make the Moon People's port by tomorrow afternoon. That meant I was soon to meet up with Alabaster.

Centuries ago, the Red Desert was a paradise filled with people, who some claim were the ancestors to both the Centurions and the Arads. Some calamity befell the land, turning it into a desert. Their savior led his people into a maze of underground chambers, filled with some kind of eternal lights. There they dwelled in secrecy for centuries, for even walking on the desert sands was fatal. The rotting disease it was called. Long ago when we discovered these people and aided them, we, the druwids, helped them move from these underground chambers back into the world. They were called the Moon People by the dark skinned inhabitants south of the Red Desert. It was fortuitous that we did so, for when the Grey Creatures and the Mantises fought, the chambers collapsed. With the help of the Moon Circle, the Moon People now were thriving once more, living just south of the desert. For commerce, they had built a single port, a small one, albeit.

As we passed by the next day, one ship was leaving, while another was docked. Another time, I would have enjoyed stopping and visiting with these people, if only to see how they had made the transition from centuries of living underground to normal life on Tarra. However, Alabaster was near and that took all my attention.

My Circle and I reviewed his brief message to me: "When you pass by the Moon People village on the coast where the mountains rise from the sea, seek the narrow inlet. Climb the Steps of Wisdom. I will be waiting." All of us gathered on the poop deck, port side, watching the land slip by, looking for said mountains. By sunset, we saw a large grey mass looming on the distant horizon. Felix said those ought to be the mountains. He slowed our speed down so we wouldn't pass by during the night. Admittedly, I didn't get much sleep that night.

Next morning, we'd arrived at the northern edge of these tall, unnamed mountains. According to Felix, they were not only unnamed, but also uninhabited. No ports or even watering holes were marked on the maps. The only markings were warnings about hidden rocky masses, which could tear the bottom out of a ship. That we wanted to go here made Felix more than a little concerned about the safety of his new ship. He kept two crew members dropping sounding lines every five minutes, but this far out, the water was deep. All our eyes strained to see the narrow inlet.

"Why don't one of you try the crow's nest?" suggested Felix, pointing to the tiny circle platform at the top of the main mast.

"I'm game," I replied, and began climbing the rigging rope ladder Felix indicated. It was a long climb! Ah, but the view was spectacular! Later on, everyone in my Circle climbed up to see for themselves. Each was a long time in descending; such was the view. Around noon, I saw what might be described as a narrow inlet and yelled news of it down to Felix. Now sailing with only the spanker, Felix moved us closer toward that spot, his crew sounding every few feet.

"Twenty-five feet. Twenty-three feet. Twenty-four feet." So it went for a half hour as we ever so slowly closed the distance to that inlet. When we were a mile out, the bottom distance was sixteen feet, and Felix would risk going no further. This large ship required some space in which to maneuver. He had no desire to crash us upon the rocks.

"Take the dingy," Felix requested. Three crew hoisted the dingy up from below decks. I noticed it had a small sail as well.

"Great, I can tack her in, and we won't have to row all the way," I commented.

"You know how to tack?" asked Felix, impressed.

"Yes, I made a sailing dingy when I was a boy, sailed all over our bay in Tewdwr," I explained. The dingy would only hold three people, and I chose

Paul and Ben to accompany me — Paul, because our Protector would never have let me go without him, and Ben, because he was a strong swimmer.

The crew used a block and tackle made from wood to lower the dingy from this high-sided caravel down to the water. We three then scampered down the lines into the small craft. It took me a few minutes to rig the mast and set the sail. Finally, we were off. I was somewhat rusty with my sailing skills, however, not having done it for years. A skill once learned comes back quickly, and shortly I had the hang of it down once more. Tacking this way and that, we slowly drew close to the inlet. I noticed a small waterfall trickling fresh water down the side of a very steep cliff, then flowing a short distance into the ocean. There was a small, grey sandy beach nearby, and I made for that spot. The waves coming in crashed thunderously upon the huge rocks that lined the ocean's edge, making talking difficult. As soon as the dingy hit the beach, Ben hopped out and held her while Paul and I climbed out. Together, we three pulled the dingy securely onto the sands.

Now for the stairs. We gazed upwards at the huge mountain — solid rock faces probably a thousand feet high where we stood. "Hey, over here," called out Paul. He found the stairs, if stairs they were. Each step was about three feet wide, carved out of the granite. Definitely man-made, I noted, but they were incredibly steep!

"I'm not going up there," declared Ben flatly. "No way!"

"You have to stay with the boat anyway, Ben. It doesn't look inhabited, but I don't want anything to happen to our dingy or we are stranded here!" I consoled him. In truth, I was also a bit squeamish about this steep climb! "Paul, you don't have to come. I am just going to chat with Alabaster."

Paul grit his teeth, "Where a Wid goes, so goes his Protector." I knew this would be a challenge for both of us, comforting to know he was right there with me. We began our ascent. The first few steps were mostly like climbing a stairs. However, usually after a dozen or so steps you arrive. Here, we had only barely begun! Soon, we both were breathing heavily. My legs began to ache, and we were forced to stop and rest more than once. Then, I made the awful mistake of looking down the way we had come! Vertigo spun my head. Only Paul's sturdy hand forcing my body up against the cliff side kept me from falling. "Thanks."

"Don't look down," he said with a squeak in his voice. I knew he was having trouble as well. How were we ever to get back down, I wondered! On we went, going slower and slower. The stairs had not changed; they were still the same size and shape. Only now we were hundreds of feet from the bottom — exposure, climbers call it. Standing on the bottom step of a ladder is one thing, standing on that same step hundreds of feet up, quite another.

I wondered if the others on the caravel could see us. Lilly Ann told me later on that we looked rather like little ants crawling up the side of the mountain. On we went, slower and slower, using more and more caution. How long we took, I cannot afterwards say. This was the challenge of a lifetime to climb; I will say that. Finally, the stairs flattened out, and we reached a gentle slope and no more stairs. We arrived in small clearing whose ground sloped gently down toward the cliff side and stairs.

Even more surprising, a stone temple built with pillars supporting a stone roof and open on all four sides sat near yet another cliff and set of stairs. Stone benches sat beneath this temple, which was painted or stained reddish. An ivy type of vine grew up the four supporting pillars. A gentle, warm sea breeze blew inland. A man was sitting on one of the benches watching us. A brown skinned man. His black hair was cut uniquely, as if one had laid a bowl over his head and shaved off everything that was visible. He wore a thin orange robe that fluttered in the gentle breeze.

"I am Ramithalion Thunderkans, whom you once knew as Alabaster. Welcome to the Temple of the Four Winds. I won't give you its official name; you could not pronounce it." He looked young. I'd only known Alabaster as a two hundred fifty year old, bearded man. He made a motion with his arm, and another similarly clad person stepped out of the shadows, bearing cups and a pitcher. She was a woman, I noted. "May I present my wife, Misalthia? Martha used to be her name ages ago. Yes, I finally found her, and we are together once more." She smiled.

"I'm Ket Bethany, used to be Elizabeth Stanton, and this is Paul Wilkins, used to be Simon Donegal. Very pleased to meet you both." I began, a little unsure how to begin; he looked so utterly different, yet his dress, his manner, it reminded me of my old fighter trainer last lifetime, the roaming monk Brother Jackal.

As if reading my mind, which he probably could, he said, "Yes, Bethany, you have indeed found the actual home of the fighting monks as you used to call them Brother Jackal, I believe it was, who was your trainer for a time and even lived on your island with you until his body failed him. You two are the first outsiders ever to reach this point. However, I am not permitted to allow you to go any further. Yes, we monks live in these mountains. We find that the very high altitude removes many mental barriers, spiritual freedom is easier to achieve this way. We brothers are all on the path to spiritual enlightenment. Here, partake of our special juice; it will help you on your return journey down the stairs. Mind you, it is far more difficult going down than going up."

"Thanks and why did you have to tell us that?" my sense of humor returning. It had been an awful climb up, I dreaded going back down. Sipping the delicious juice, I began, "Alabaster, your druwid movement is in dire trouble. With the breakup of the Greenway into some dozen kingdoms, we have been driven out of most of the land. John Henry has found it nearly impossible to find new recruits, young children not stuck in their body's heads. Our numbers have become perilously small. Without new trainees soon, the druwids may be extinct with this generation. John Henry and I beg you to give us some guidance, please. It was the group you founded so long ago." I added that last, hoping to evoke some sense of responsibility for his previous work.

He sighed, "I saw all this shortly after you rescued me in the Arad, Bethany, though I chose not to tell you about it, rather let you discover it for yourself. That is one of the two reasons I chose to have my body killed out there in the desert when we eliminated the alien creatures. The other reason you see before you today, Martha. I found her again, and now we are together once more." I could sense the enormous love each had for the other; part of me wanted to cheer loudly.

He continued, so I did not interrupt. "Yes, I saw that my Guardians were slowly dying and that there was little that I or anyone could do about it. Your Jes Amir was right. Our salvation lies in attaining spiritual freedom, not in fleshly bodies. Together, Martha and I are working on this line, making small successes I might add."

"Don't look so sad, so crestfallen, Bethany. The primary purpose of the Guardians is no longer. We existed to protect the people of the Greenway when they had no form of government or leadership. Now they have chosen their own path; whether we agree with their choice, it is, after all, their choice. How can it not be so? Your prime purpose for existing is gone."

"However, you have come asking for my advice and successfully climbed the stairs to the Temple of the Four Winds. That alone is worthy of an honest answer to your quest. When your current youth are gone, so will the last druwid be gone. Lament not the past. Find new purpose for your existence; remember spiritual freedom is the quest, as Jes Amir knew only so well. One could do much worse than to continue what Jes was attempting to do. That is the best advice I can give you that you will understand. The world is Chaos; only we spiritual beings bring order. I foresee that in years soon to come, much order must be brought, for Chaos is rapidly growing over Tarra, even as we speak. Go now and start to bring that much needed order, before Chaos reigns supreme."

"Rami," his wife spoke softly, "you forgot to tell them about the monks."

"Yes, my dear, so I have. Bethany, know also this; we monks are still here. We will be there when we are needed. You will not have to ask, but it is time for you to go now. If you linger, the winds will soon pick up, and you will be blown down the stairs. Go now." He waved his hands.

"Not without a hug," I declared, and I gave him a farewell hug. Paul chose just to shake his hand.

"I'm very glad to have met you, Martha. Take care of him please," I added as we moved back towards the stairs. I looked back and saw the two of them holding hands watching us go, neither moving, the gentle breeze fluttering their robes.

"Now to get down," declared Paul. "I sure am not going down normally. Here, let's go down like we came up, backwards, so to speak." With our backs to the world and chests facing the stairs, we began our descent. Gravity pulled us down; eventually my knees ached and nearly gave way. Halfway down, the winds picked up, adding to the challenge. It took twice as long to get down as it did going up!

Never was I so glad to set foot on solid ground! Swiftly, Ben had the dingy back in the water, and once more, I used my sailing skills to good use. A half hour later, we were back onboard. Felix timed it right; as soon as the dingy was on the deck, Pietro's Folly was tacking its way back out into the open sea. I stared back at the mountains, but could not even see the area where the temple was. This was indeed an incredible place, unknown to the rest of the world.

"Well, my little ants, out with it," declared Lilly Ann, more than a little impatient with us.

"We did it!" Paul bubbled with joy. "We climbed the impossible stairs! I will admit I was more than a trifle scared, particularly coming down. We could have gotten blown right off the cliff; the winds got that strong, honest. Just ask Ben, he felt the winds come up, didn't you Ben?"

"Yes they did, but that is Nature out here, where sea meets land," Ben replied, with far less enthusiasm. Although he really did not want to miss the meeting with Alabaster nor the incredible climb, he knew that we would not have made it. Even standing on some of the small cliffs around Mont Blanc as a boy, he felt very queasy staring down at the ground below. He'd never have made it. I think that was what bothered him more than anything did.

Adrenaline rush gone, my legs felt like butter! "Whoa," I grabbed onto the closest person, Lilly Ann, for support. "My legs are giving out. Help me get below, please."

"Sure no problem," Paul continued to feel on top of the situation, until he tried to walk over to me and lend a hand. "Donkey's ass!" He collapsed. His legs too gave out, but he still had his sense of humor. Lying in a heap on the deck, he spouted, "Er, perhaps yea all best drag me below." The others laughed and assisted us down into the galley, where Lilly Ann had already warmed up some hot cider and biscuits. She calculated that we would be in need when we returned.

"I think I shall sit here for the rest of the voyage," Paul declared, as his sister served his needs. "Must be what it feels like to be one of those kings back in the Greenway. More cider, sis." We all roared with laughter once more, especially when Paulette intentionally slipped and poured some of the cider down his pants.

"Okay, time to contact John Henry," I broke up the playing. "When I report to him, you all can hear too. All this concerns you as well." I relaxed and reached out to the north and soon found John Henry; we created the Mind Link. Then, speaking aloud, which John Henry could also hear in his mind, I related our conversation with Alabaster. I attempted to duplicate his words, but found that somewhat difficult to do.

When I finished, I continued, "Let me put this in simpler terms. His answer was awfully philosophical and tied to what I already knew. When he and I brought about the self-destruction of the Grey Creatures and the Mantises, at that time, Alabaster saw completely what was happening and the consequences we now face. Our movement is, as John Henry has pointed out, dying. Our numbers have shrunk horribly. His estimates are that we will number less than three hundred by year end. We cannot find enough new recruits, children who are outside their heads; we only really have the kingdom of Sarah and Percival to search now. They've only found five so far this year. Grim. Worse, all those broken Circle are finding it very difficult to re-bond into new Circles. Alabaster predicts that the druwids will be gone when our children pass away, so we've about one and a half generations left."

"He points out that the Cycle of Life is birth, growth, conserve, decay, and death. Even our group is subject to that eternal cycle. Obviously, the druwids are now on the steep decay portion of the Cycle of Life. Yet, he pointed out what we needed to do, find a new purpose. Our original purpose is now fulfilled. He began the Guardians in order to protect and aid the people of the Greenway at a time when they had no leadership, no organization, just folks trying hard to survive in the wilderness. Now, our people have evolved, for good or ill who can say, but they have evolved and chosen to create their own leadership and organizations. Alabaster declares our purpose has been fulfilled and that we need to move on to other things, hence, find new purpose."

"He has suggested that avenue of purpose: to achieve spiritual freedom as separate from these fleshly bodies. My late husband, Jes Amir, the Great Messiah, attempted to do just that. He tried to get people to realize that they are an immortal spiritual being, for a time inhabiting these bodies, that there was more to life than bodies. It is Alabaster's suggestion that we somehow set our new goal and purpose in this direction."

John Henry was crying, but Ket did not relay that information. "John Henry asks, 'What of our beliefs? Are we to abandon what we believe in favor of this Jehosanity religion?' My answer is simply this. Is what we believe in so terribly different from what Jes preached? I was with him. I heard nearly every sermon he ever gave. I witnessed the miracles when he would help a being move out of his head and recover who and what he or she really was, an immortal spiritual being. No, our beliefs are not so very different at all. Perhaps Nature and God and the Supreme Being are one and the same."

"However, since I am the only one with a direct connection to Jes Amir and since Alabaster suggested this as an area to explore for our future goal and purpose, John Henry has ordered us back to Mont Blanc for a time, once our rescue mission is completed." John Henry relayed that the time had come to inform all our members of the situation. I debated with him over whether now was indeed the right time.

If we told them the obvious, that our movement was dying and then did not give them a new purpose, they may indeed fall away from us sooner, finding their own alternatives instead. For once, John Henry took my advice, promising to say nothing until I returned to Mont Blanc.

With the Mind Link broken, my Circle sat there speechless, stunned by the news. At last, Lilly Ann said, "Well, gang, we have all seen numerous signs of the Guardian's demise all our lives. It is only this stark verbalization of it, which is upsetting us. Hey, we have a rescue mission to perform; let's get our minds back on the here and now. Tell us about the climb up the stairs."

The days passed slowly now. We made great speed tacking toward and away from the coastline. At least once a day, sometimes more, we would either pass another Sea Prince ship or meet one heading back towards the Sea Princes. Several times, the other ship would sail close to us to get a look at this caravel, the new ship marvel. Twice, another ship came along side to ask about Pietro's Folly, and left more than impressed.

By the next day, the tall mountain range gave way to a tropical jungle. Here and there along the coast were small villages in which the Sea Princes had built docks sufficient to handle one or two ships at a time. Felix explained that from the jungles came some of the best hardwoods on Tarra. Ebony and mahogany were highly prized, and shiploads of logs proved very profitable. Metal tools, cloth bolts, and beads were the usual price paid by these merchants. "Here comes the village of Molo," Felix announced as we rounded a peninsula. "Lolo is not too much further. Strange local names, aren't they. We've got twenty-five trading villages along this stretch of coast line, something like a couple hundred miles or so."

Steadily, day by day, the heat of the day grew hotter, and nights, warmer. Now we slept with as little clothing on as possible, portholes wide open. During the afternoons, local squalls often appeared. As the ship moved toward one, the crew would stretch out a large cone shaped canvas over the main deck. Rainwater provided fresh drinking water; a hole in the center allowed the rain to flow into large casks in the hold. Felix explained that on these long voyages, fresh water was problematical. Either you trapped rainfall or you would have to put into shore and fetch fresh water from one of the many streams. The mariners found it simpler and faster to catch rainfall, especially here down south where squalls occurred almost daily.

After a week of travel, we were approaching the southwestern section of the continent. Here the dense jungles gave way to vast savannahs. The handful of coastal villages here traded in meat and wild animals. "Next, up are the uninhabited foothills. We call this area the Ragged Forest, both because the terrain is very rugged, but also because the trees grow tall and patchy here. No one lives here, but we've been contemplating opening up some settlements to logging."

An hour later, as we tacked closer to the jagged, rocky shore and were about to tack the opposite way, the lookout in the crow's nest shouted, "Smoke!" Sure enough, a smoke tendril curled its way up into the blue sky. It was coming from a secluded cove just out of sight.

"I thought you said this land was uninhabited," Ben said to Felix.

"It is. No one has ever reported seeing people, villages, or even signs of inhabitation along this stretch. Curious, very curious," Felix commented.

"Captain sir, ought we investigate a little, you know, just a swing by? That's the rules of the sea. Any new sightings are to be reported to the Port Master," a crew member reminded Felix.

"Aye, aye. Drop the mainsails. We go in by spanker. Easy does it boys.

We don't know how deep the waters are. Could be any number of submerged rocks that'll tear our bottom out," Felix ordered.

Slowly the ship lost speed, and we navigated around a peninsular outcropping. Ahead was some kind of concealed, but small bay. Trees and hills still blocked the origin of the smoke. Suddenly, the smoke tendrils ceased; the winds slowly dissipated the last traces of the greyish smoke. "Now ain't that just curious," Felix commented. "If I didn't know better, someone has seen us and doused their fires. Most curious. Take her in slowly boys."

In a few minutes, we found ourselves sailing slowly into a narrow bay, steep rocky walls met the sea on either side, leaving us about a thousand feet of maneuvering room; the bay slanted back to the northeast. Even more slowly, Pietro's Folly slipped into these narrows. Finally, when we were about a mile from shore, we could see someone had built a concealed dock here. A strange vessel was tied up. More significantly, we saw at least four more ships under construction like the one that was docked! Someone had turned this into a shipyard, out here in the middle of nowhere!

That ship was strange indeed. It did have a mast, but it also had dozens of poles propped vertically along each side. It was a very narrow ship, only a third the width of the caravel. However, the bow was long and pointed. Sunlight glistened and reflected brightly off its bow. Only iron could be responsible for what we saw. "Blazes, who would put all that iron on the pointy bow of a ship?" Felix commented.

Suddenly, a horn began blowing off in the distance. We saw dozens of men rushing to the single boat at the dock. Centurions, I recognized their gear at once. "Let's get out of here fast," I suggested to Felix.

"Damn, that is a ramming boat!" Felix screamed. "A trireme, that's what that is! I've heard of them. Got three banks of rowers, designed to ram and sink other ships. Never thought I would see one, though. I don't like the looks of this one little bit! Hard turn to port! Host all sails! Step lively lads or we're fish bait! Lads, can you lend a hand? We have got to get going fast!" All of us pitched in to frantically get the sails up and the ship doing an about face. It was a mad scramble indeed.

Now we heard a rhythmic drumming. A man was pounding out an oaring rhythm. The trireme was rapidly pulling out from shore towards us, gaining speed rapidly. The drumbeats slowly grew faster and faster. They were gaining on us! I turned to look at them. What I saw gave me a fright! In the center of the boat was a roaring fire; I saw six archers lighting bulbous arrows afire! I screamed, "Fire, they are going to flame us!" My Circle dropped what they were doing and rushed to the stern where I was at, standing on the poop royal. We watched as the six took aim.

"Double damn," cursed Felix. We all knew what just one of those flaming arrows would do if it hit one of the sails. Without our mainsails, we would be dead in the water, a sitting duck. A volley of six flaming arrows arched their way towards us. I leaped high into the air off the poop royal and grabbed one mid-flight, preventing it from hitting the spanker. Paul was smarter; he threw up a wall of ice at the very last minute. Five arrows thudded into the ice sheet shattering it; bits of ice fell down into the ocean at our rear. "What the?" Felix yelled. "Get those sails rigged now!" Even Felix frantically began pulling various lines taught.

"Here comes another volley," Paul called out. "Gang we need more ice sheets. One there, one there, one there," he pointed out three areas most vulnerable. The fast trireme was steadily closing the gap. Ice sheets materialized high in the air above the caravel as well as at its stern. Wham, the arrow hit the sheets, shattering the thin ice once more; only this time, the whole deck was pelted with ice bits as they fell.

Now the drumming became furiously fast. "They are going to ram us! Can't we go any faster?" Paul screamed out to Felix.

"Damn them to the Fires of Hell," I cursed. Simultaneously, Paul and I conjured walls of flames just above the trireme and let them drop. Neither the Centurions nor Felix nor the rest of the crew believed the fires were real, not until the fires landed upon them. Suddenly, screams of terror and pain filled the air. Drumbeat ceased; men, their hair and loincloths in flames, dove overboard.

"What the?" shouted Felix.

"Get us out of here, Felix," I commanded with full intention behind my words. He stopped mid-sentence and continued to work the rigging. Now Pietro's Folly began to surge through the ocean, mainsails having picked up the wind. Heedless of direction, we began to fly out of the narrows. Paul and I kept watch on the trireme crew. They were climbing back aboard. Again, we heard the rhythmic drumming, albeit now it was very slow.

"They are still coming after us!" I declared. "Don't they know when to quit?"

"Won't catch us now," Felix sounded optimistic, "we got the wind."

We began to pull away from the enemy ship, altogether too slowly for my liking. Yet, the Centurions did not give up, steadily picking up the oaring pace. They still intended to ram us, if they could. "We've cleared their bay and are heading out into the ocean. They'll stop now," Felix cheerily reported. We all watched.

On the contrary, they unfurled a large square sail, combining wind and manpower. Still, Pietro's Folly continued to pull away from the trireme. At last, Paul judged that we were out of bow range, and everyone relaxed somewhat. "What course Captain?" the helmsman called out.

"Resume our prior course," Felix replied, while watching along with us from the poop royal. From here, we had an ideal view. We had put at least a mile between us now. "Damn, they are not giving up the chase!"

We sailed on for an hour; still our pursuers showed no sign of giving up the chase. Miles back, they appeared as a small dot on the horizon. Felix asked, "What the heck just happened? Where did all that ice come from? It saved our sails. A miracle, I would say. Tur must be looking after us."

"Our doing, I'm afraid," I answered truthfully. "Perhaps you have heard rumors of the Guardians of the Greenway?"

"Fairy stories, yes, we've heard them. Most know them as just that, children's stories," he replied.

"I'm afraid they are not fairy stories, Felix. You are carrying seven Guardian passengers."

His mouth waggled; his crew stared at us as if they had never seen us before. "Did I not see you catch that first arrow in your hand?" Felix finally managed to say. He could more readily deal with that than conjured sheets of ice.

"Yes, I often catch the enemy's arrows. Rather frustrates them," I teased. "I could have just as easily deflected it, but it was on fire, and I didn't want anything on this ship catching fire, so I just caught it. Glad Paul thought faster than I did. His sheets and those of my friends did the trick."

"Are yea gods or such?" he asked, his eyes still could not believe what they had seen or his ears, heard.

"Nope, just ordinary people who try to protect others as we can. Normally, we are not so open with our actions, but the ship was in dire peril, and we had no other viable choices. Sorry to give you all a scare there."

"Well, I'll give you that, Ket Bethany. You sure did save us all. They were out to destroy us. Guess that proves the old saying that curiosity killed the cat." We all chuckled at his attempt at brevity. He asked, "What bothers me is why? Why do they want to sink this ship? All we did was sail into that narrows. We were not going to attack them. It makes no sense."

Lilly Ann replied for me, "In a way, it just may make sense, Felix. I get the distinct impression that no one is supposed to be anywhere around here. You, yourself, said this land was uninhabited. Yet, we find that not only is someone here, but also they have an entire shipwright enterprise going on. I saw at least three other triremes under construction back there. Suppose that they wanted the construction of this fleet of trireme kept strictly a secret. Along we come; wouldn't that explain their actions?"

"My lady, you may just have something there. Yes, that would make sense. But why would Centurions be making a bunch of trireme ramming ships? All they are good for is the destruction of other ships?"

"Destruction of whose ships?" Lilly Ann asked pointedly.

"Damn! Sea Prince ships! Other than the dingys of the Centurions, we are the only ones with ships that are worth anything." He was being very sarcastic about the normal Centurion ocean ships, which were very slow and carried about one-third the cargo the normal Sea Prince ships carried. They really were not a dingy.

Lilly Ann continued, "I think that we have accidentally stumbled upon a Centurion plot to destroy Sea Prince ships or maybe even destroy enough of them so that they could then invade the Sea Princes by sea. With all the walled cities, they cannot easily be assailed overland anymore."

"I think you are right, my lady. Remember, only this ship can outrun a trireme. All the other Sea Prince ships are going to be sitting ducks! We have to warn everyone about this. We'll see to it just as soon as we return."

"They are still following us," a crew member called out from the crow's nest. 'Bout seven miles back now."

"Damn, well as long as we can keep up our speed, we ought to leave them behind. Please Tur, keep the winds blowing!" Felix begged his Sea God.

At suppertime, it appeared that Tur was not listening too well to Felix. The winds calmed down significantly. While not becalmed, our forward speed diminished considerably. Thankfully, the enemy was still a dot on the distant horizon behind us. When darkness fell, Felix put two lookouts on duty each duty period, instead of one. Each of us took a two-hour shift to relieve the crew members. Otherwise, they would end up with two hours on and two off all through the night.

For three more days, we played cat and mouse with the Centurions and their trireme. During periods of good winds, we would pull far ahead of them. During periods of relative calm, they again closed the distance, several times perilously close, for my money. Still, we continued our southward journey.

"We'll lose them for sure when we hit the Spice Islands." Felix got out his maps to show us better. At the southwestern edge of the Southlands, a race of funny brown skinned people lived — Felix's description. They had long, unpronounceable names, but they had something that the rest of Tarra greatly desired: spices of all types and kinds! Indeed, just off the southwestern tip of the Southlands lay a series of perhaps a hundred islands. Some were big, others small. Here many spices grew as grasses do in the Greenway. Hence, the Spice Islands were one of the main destinations for Sea Prince ships. The brown skins, as Felix called them, established nearly fifty ports of call, either on the main land or among the larger islands. Trade was brisk and profitable for both parties. Indeed this was very likely true, for we began seeing far more Sea Prince ships plying these waters than anywhere else thus far.

We were a week out from the near destruction of our ship, and still the enemy ship dogged our trail. Their captain was relentless! Felix and his crew cast more curses at him than a cat has hairs! Of course, that did no good, but they felt better afterwards. Seeing all the islands ahead, Paul had an idea. "Perhaps if we sail among all these islands, we can lose the trireme." Felix thought this was a grand plan, and thus we spent another three days, darting this way and that among the hundreds of islands that make up this archipelago, but always attempting to get closer to Megalos.

It did not work. On the contrary, late the third afternoon, we came becalmed. For a sailing vessel, this was disaster, especially, if you are being pursued. With all our sails up, we were just barely moving in the water. From the crow's nest, we received continual reports. The trireme continued to close the gap. It was now but five miles off our stern. We had to do something, but what?

"Four miles. Three miles." Our luck was rapidly running out. Ben, who was looking forward out to sea, called out, "Hey gang, look at that fog bank rolling in. I've never seen such a dense fog, except once at Calgary in the early spring."

"Make for that fog!" ordered Paul, using his command intention. Felix ordered his helmsman; slowly we turned due south heading towards the fog.

"Good plan, if we can make the fog. We might lose them," Felix finally acknowledged.

"Two miles. One mile." We could see the Centurion oarsmen straining their well-developed muscles. That telltale drumming once more picked up speed; they were moving up to ramming speed, just as we slipped silently into the fog bank. Pea soup. Suddenly, I couldn't see the bow from the stern, where I was at! Felix called out, "Absolute silence from now on. If I hear any noise, I'll cut your throat, laddies!" He didn't mean it, but we all knew that noise might make the difference between life and death. "Ten clicks to port," he ordered, just enough to put us out of the straight line path on which we entered. The drumbeats grew louder and louder. We could almost reach out and touch that trireme, only we could not see it. Yet, it had to be very close to us indeed! We heard their men straining and groaning under the exertion; we heard their curses and swearing. Then, their noise began drifting off to our starboard side. They had missed us. The only sounds we heard now were the occasional creaks and groans from the boat along with the lapping of the ocean against our sides. I feared that alone might give us away.

No one slept that night. Tense, we stood like statues in the night, frozen to our observational spots, listening to everything but nothing, scarcely daring to breathe. Gradually, night turned into day, at least a dense gray day. However, by ten, the fog began to break up. Now it was decision making time.

"Felix, we have lost them for now," I began.

"Good, we can sail south until we spot the coast and then continue on our way," he replied cheerily, glad the whole thing was over at last. "Tur be praised."

"I rather think we haven't seen the last of that trireme, Felix. Think about it. Suppose you were her captain charged with sinking the ship that discovered their secret war ship construction site and were under orders to sink that ship no matter what."

"So?" he replied, not getting my point.

"Suppose that you just lost them in a fog bank. Where would you go to try to pick them back up?"

"Curses! I'd go looking along the coastline. Everyone knows that you have to keep the coastline in sight. You can get totally lost when you lose sight of land. That is our greatest fear, our greatest nightmare, getting lost at sea. Some say if you go too far from land, you'll fall off the edge of the world! Others say that deep-sea monsters reside far out from land, so big they can devour a ship in one bite. Every mariner knows you have to keep land in sight at all times. We are doomed!"

Ben commented, "Boy, I'd love to see one of these sea monsters!" As soon as he said that, he wished he had kept his mouth shut.

"Let's have a look at your maps," I suggested. He and I went to his poop cabin and he laid out more maps.

"I think that we are somewhere here, just east and south of the Spice Islands. We've left the last of them behind before we entered the fog. I had us going in this direction, but our speed was slow. We must be out here somewhere," he indicated a rather large patch of open sea.

"Trust me, Felix. I do know a little about navigation. My dad was a fisherman in Cuch Glen. I made my own sailing dingy, and did nighttime sailing as well. Suppose that we sail along out here, heading east. We must keep careful records of our speed and direction of travel. We pretend that we are paralleling the coastline, see. Where you would normally head north a few miles, we do so out here, even though land is not in sight. Keep a sharp look out for unknown perils, mind you. Normally, how long would it take us to cross the bottom of the Southlands here and near Megalos?"

"Well, no one's ever tried it in a caravel before. Usual ships take two to three more weeks. Us, maybe half of that," he replied. "I see what you are attempting. It's called dead reckoning. Keep an accurate record — that's the key. Still, this is awfully risky."

"I am not minimizing the risks, Felix. It is darn scary even to contemplate sailing out of sight of land. We both know that Centurion captain has thus far been relentless. He will be trolling the coastline looking for us. Are there any other major ports along the way?"

"Nope, only a couple Centurion mining operations. We are seldom allowed into those ports."

"Maybe if we can sail along here undetected for a week or so, then that captain will finally give up the chase, figuring we got lost at sea in the fog," I sounded hopeful, but I was not entirely honest. I suspected that captain would travel all the way to Megalos looking for us. After all, what other ports could be our final destination way down here, if not Megalos proper? I hoped and prayed that that captain would become discouraged after a week or so and give up the chase.

"If we do this, we will help at all times. My people are good with figures and record keeping. Each of us will do our own dead reckoning, and you can use an average of them. We'll, run double watches every night, perhaps going more slowly." Felix agreed; he knew he had very little choice but to try this wild, hair-raising attempt to lose our pursuer.

Next, we held a joint meeting between his crew and my Circle, outlining what we intended to do and why. Everyone could see that returning back to the coastline undoubtedly mean doom. Still, sailing along out of sight of land was nearly as deadly in everyone's mind. Felix and I explained what we needed to do. Each hour, we measured the speed of the caravel, by dropping a weight at the bow and walking along with it as the ship passed by it, until we reached the stern. By carefully counting the seconds, we could calculate our speed. On parchments, we logged the speed and hour. Assuming the ship maintained that speed for the hour, we could calculate how far we'd traveled. Felix and I would average them and plot them on the maps as best we could. Felix finally

185

admitted that he had never sailed these waters; this was also his first trip so far south.

For over a week, we carefully followed a set routine. Eight of us dutifully made our hourly speed observations, noted the direction of sailing, the hour, and the speed. At night, we lowered one sail to reduce speed. Always two were on watch duty, besides the helmsman, of course. One watched from the crow's nest, the other from the bow top deck. By the end of the eight day, both Felix and I felt that our location was somewhere near where the coast began curving northward toward the Narrow Firth, which separated the Southlands from the island of Megalos. Together, we decided that on the morrow, we would sail due north until we found land. After that, we would follow the coastline until we found our bearings and location once more.

Around one in the afternoon the next day, from the crow's nest came the magic words everyone wanted to hear, "Land ho! Dead ahead." I think that everyone of us was extremely happy to see good old land once more! Now came the hard part. We were off the southern coast of the Southlands, but where? How far away was Megalos and the Shallow Firth, our destination? Further, though no one spoke of it, where was that trireme?

We spied a fair number of Centurion made ships, which were only about a quarter of our size, sailing much closer to the shore. Some rode low in the water, indicating a heavy cargo. Others bobbed on the wave, much as we did. All that afternoon we sailed along, seeing more and more ships going in either direction. Late in the afternoon, we spied a rather large amount of smoke clouds rising into the sky, from where we could not tell yet.

Then, just as night was falling, we rounded a coastline bend. There before us was Sud, the Shallow Firth, and opposite it, the island of Megalos. We'd made it perfectly! Now we needed a complete change of plans. High on the rocky ridge above the uninhabited shoreline just opposite Sud across the Shallow Firth lay the estate of Niccolo Helios, or now his daughter, Rea. We'd come this far, but had not made any plans beyond getting here.

Paul came to our rescue, "Why not sail in close to the shoreline there and pretend that we are sailing on east around to the other side. When you get in as close as you dare, we can scout out the coast and determine how to get up there to that hilltop. After passing, turn south and head out of sight of the land. When it is full dark, sail back to this spot, and let some of us off to make contact with Rea. Then, we'll just have to improvise."

"Easily done," Felix replied. Soon under spanker sail, we floated about a quarter mile off from the shore of Megalos. Memories of our previous visit here so many years and lifetimes ago floated into my mind — same with my friends.

"I count six Centurions on guard duty along the coastline just below her estate. Guess she is right; no way for her to even leave!" Paul observed. Now the ship slipped on past our ultimate destination and then turned hard to starboard, heading south away from Megalos. We did not go far before it was full dark. While Felix reversed course and inched his way back to our desired location about a quarter mile off the coast, we raised the dingy up from the hold and lowered it over the side.

Paulette had to stay with the caravel. She was our Communicator. If something happened and Felix had to make a fast get away, she could keep us and him in communication. Otherwise, it could be a disaster, and Felix would have no way to contact us. We six slipped into the dingy as silently as possible. Paul and I began rowing us to shore. The others kept a sharp eye out for the guards we had seen at dusk. Fortunately, the nighttime guards were just three in number. As we gently touched land, Lilly Ann cast her spell, and the guards dozed soundly. As quietly as we could, we pulled the dingy on shore and into the underbrush. Then, we went in search of that path we had used to get to the hilltop. It was right where we had left it. A couple minutes later, we scrambled onto the grassy hilltop of the Helios estate.

Now to find Rea. We remembered that there were a number of buildings, mostly made of marble. The living quarters used to be an open sided building with gauze curtains providing a semblance of privacy. We tried that spot first. I kept whispering, "Rea. Rea. Rea Helios. Guardians have come. Where are you?" We heard no answer, so we kept rummaging around and calling out.

Suddenly, someone appeared swinging an iron fireplace poker at my head. I ducked just in time. "Rea. We've come to rescue you," I whispered.

"Oh," exclaimed a rather startled voice. "How do I know?" I detected a note of fear and distrust in her voice.

"In your message, a 'C' was written as an 'E'. Your father made a painting of Sarah Jane and gave it to her when we left. He had a long distance viewing device mounted near the hillside back there, but it is not there anymore." I hope that I gave her enough clues that we were who we said we were.

"How did you get past the guards down there?" she asked determinedly.

"Helped him do what he wanted to do anyway, go to sleep," I answered truthfully. "Is there anywhere where we can go and talk without fear of being seen or overheard?"

"Well, okay, then. Who was my mother?" she asked.

"I have no idea. When we were here, Niccolo was not married nor had any girlfriends that we met. He only had his house staff. He trusted Kaytlyn to run his estate when he was off in Galantas at the Senate. So I cannot answer that one." Surely, he didn't have an affair with his staff, I thought.

"Okay. It was Kaytlyn. She was my mom. Niccolo caused a big scandal by marrying her. Follow me," she replied and led us through the many hanging gauze draperies. In the center of the building, she paused and pulled open a trap door. A dim light illuminated a stairways going down underground. "Watch your step." Carefully, we followed her; it was a challenge in the dim light. "Last one down, pull the lever down so the door shuts."

Once she heard the trap door close, she adjusted one lantern so we could see well. "This way, she said, before we could get a good look at her.

Single file, we followed her down this narrow hall. She veered right into a large room, with a table and a number of chairs. Methodically, she set about lighting all the lanterns in the room. "Have a seat." She then sat down across from us. "I know. I am a mulato. Probably not what you expected," she said with a note of sadness and degradation in her voice.

"Sorry, Rea. We don't know what a mulato is, but it sounds like a nasty word. I'm Ket Bethany. I used to be Elizabeth Stanton. Your father and I sent quite a lot of letters back and forth, until I went and got that body killed." I then introduced the others in my Circle. All them, except Lilly Ann had been here before as part of the Lightning Circle. However, Paulette was still back on the ship.

"Means half-breed, mixed blood, black and bronze," she explained. "Yes, it is the common term for me around here, derogatory at best."

"Sorry, where we come from, no one makes such distinctions. We only see one strikingly beautiful woman sitting here!" I meant it as a compliment; she was gorgeous.

Paul added, "Where we come from, you'd have guys fawning over you just to get you out on a date!" This touched her and she finally smiled.

"I did not really think that you would come. I figured that you were probably dead and buried, but I had used up every other possibility I could think of, so I had to try. They are threatening me daily now. We have got to get away soon, I think."

"Okay, we have a fast ship standing too just off shore waiting to be loaded. I have no idea what all is to be saved or how we can do it. Perhaps, the best thing to do is show us what and where it all is and then we can make some plans to get it onto the ship. Once we sail, we can then spend lots of time getting acquainted. Right now, time is precious."

"Yes, yes it is! Okay, I don't know how much we can save. So I guess I'll just show you all it. Over these last few months when I became isolated here, I began to sneak everything down here. This was dad's secret storage chamber. Lately, it has been my home at night. I fear for my life at night, though I have already paid the guards handsomely to leave me alone. They took all my servants away last week. Follow me." She handed each of us a lantern, and we followed her.

Old Niccolo surprised even me. This underground hideaway was huge, with ten rooms all told, each about twenty feet square. In every room, Rea had packed away Niccolo's things along with hers. One room held nothing but paintings. Another, Rea had stored all the sculptures that she and her servants could lift. The two large statues weighed too much and would have to be sacrificed. Another room contained his ceramics. Another room held his writings. Another room was packed with his inventions. And so it went — a treasury of art and invention that exceeded imagination.

How we were going to carry all this stuff back up the stairs, down the hillside, let alone how we'd get it all out to the caravel completely eluded me. I hoped that my companions would come up with some bright ideas. "Hey, here is another side door," Paul noted. "Where does it go?"

"I don't know. Dad always kept it locked, and I can't find the key anymore. I have no idea," Rea explained.

"Hah, a locked door! Let your Planner have at it," Allan teased us all. He walked over to the door, pulled something from his pocket, and fiddled with the lock. We all heard a loud click. "Shall we have a look see?" he said. "Don't all thank me at once," he teased us some more.

"Well done, Allan," I replied, refusing to play along with his joviality.

Paul, of course, insisted on going first, sweeping massive spider webs out of his way. "Long unused. Steps. Watch your step. Lots of steps. Going down. Everyone bring your lanterns. Please don't fall on me," now Paul was getting into Allan's humor. Argh. Slowly we seven began descending. It was cool in this stairway. Paul only got the worst of the webs out of the way. My hair got quite a few more. I hoped that I would not now have spiders crawling all over me!

Quite a few minutes later and a long way down, Paul stopped. "Another doorway. Allan, will you do the honors? I wonder what we will find behind this locked door? Mountains of gold? Jewels, perhaps." I was about to scream, when Allan pushed me aside to reach the door. A minute later, we heard the loud click. Carefully, Paul opened the door. In spite of long years of non-use, the hinges made remarkably little noise.

Fresh sea air flooded into our noses. We were outside and not too far from where we'd stashed the dingy! Good old Niccolo had a plan for everything. My respect for him soared to new heights! I whispered for Paul to shut the door so we could talk.

"Here's the plan. There are three dingys on the caravel and three of us guys. Ladies, you start carting stuff down here. Once we have all that we can carry on the first load, I'll row it and we guys back to the boat. After unloading, we'll come back with three dingys. By then, hopefully, you all will have carted enough down the steps so we can just load and row. Lilly Ann, monitor your sleeping guards. Others might come by later on."

Lilly Ann replied, "I don't know who is going to be more tired, the step climbers or the rowers!" We all chuckled; all of us were going to get a work out tonight! Ten minutes later, with a partial load and Ben and Allan, I rowed us back out to the caravel. Paul stayed behind as Protector and hauler of heavier things.

Once we reached the ship and explained what we were planning, Felix and his crew began to help out. Besides lowering the other two dingys, they also handled loading the cargo up the tall side from the dingy. They had a large rope net, which went under the load. Using a boom and block and tackle, they could lift the entire load up at one time. Hence, each of us put one of the rope nets across the floor of the dingy. We would load all cargo onto it, greatly simplifying the unloading alongside the caravel. We then rowed the three dingys back to the secret entrance. Paul was there waiting for us.

Twenty-five trips later, just as the sun was rising, we rowed back with the last few items and our crew. Rea had Allan relocked both doors as we left. Even better, I went topside to where the trap door was located and made sure it was well hidden with rugs and a cabinet. Undoubtedly, one day someone would locate the trap door, but hopefully not anytime soon. As we rowed this final time out to the caravel, the twilight before dawn gave Rea her last view of the only home she had known. In a way, I felt compassion for this woman; the perverted church had literally driven her from her home.

Once we got the dingys on board, we got another unexpected surprise. From the crow's nest, we heard the words we hoped that we would never hear again: "Trireme coming our way!"

Instantly, the crew sprang into action. Only this time we seven knew best how to help them get the ship underway fast. "What's happening?" Rea cried out in a panic.

"We ran into some Centurions who are hell bent on sinking this ship. We thought that we had eluded them. Guess not," I replied.

Our predicament was thus. Coming from the direction that we needed to sail was the trireme. We could not sail to the east, for that would only take us further around Megalos, a total dead end. We could veer back south far out to sea and gamble as we did before, but now we were loaded with cargo. It was anybody's guess whether we could out run the trireme chasing us. If we sailed west, we would be going straight at the oncoming trireme, just what it most desired: an easy ram.

Paul ran to the bow and climbed to the top deck. He yelled, "Trust me. I have one more trick I can pull. Head due west towards them. Trust me!"

Poor Felix. He had only two choices, both equally terrible. Sail south far away from land and all known locations or sail right at the trireme and pray it somehow missed destroying his ship. "Do it! Trust me! Ket, get up here and anchor me down. Fast. Move!"

Felix barked the order, but his voice barely squeaked it out. The helmsman obeyed, as the crew frantically unfurled the three sails, which fluttered in the warm morning breeze. I raced to the bow. "Here tie me securely to the ship." I did as Paul asked. "Now how does that spell go?" Gods, this was not the time to forget a spell, but I dared not break his thought train!

Boom. Boom. Boom. The trireme was drawing closer now, we could hear its telltale beating. Faster and faster came the drum beats as the war ship rapidly got up to ramming speed. I watched it now less than a mile distant, heading straight for us. "One degree to starboard!" Paul yelled.

Felix yelled to the helmsman, "Just do what he says!" And he began a lengthy prayer to Tur. His curiosity did bring him to the top foredeck, if only to see his ultimate doom.

"One degree to port. Steady," yelled Paul, and he began chanting something I'd never heard before. Now the drumbeats came very fast and steady, deafeningly loud! From our high vantage point, I looked down and saw the large number of bronze-skinned Centurions, working up a sweat, rowing in time to the beat, in unison, like a well-oiled machine. Damn, they are good at what they do, I noted to myself. They were bearing straight down on us, intending to ram straight into our bow. "Hard to port now!" yelled Paul. The two vessels were but feet apart. Suddenly Pietro's Folly lunged hard to the left, tilting at a steep angle. At that instant, Paul's spell triggered. With both his hands facing forward, palms vertical, he made an enormous pushing motion, as if he was pushing the very air toward the oncoming trireme.

However, it wasn't air that moved, rather a giant sea swell surged up from the side of our caravel and smashed sidelong into the trireme, veering it off of its collision course and very nearly swamping it. Instead of ramming us, the trireme suddenly took on an enormous volume of water and floundered. Men went flying in all directions. I saw the drummer hit the ocean as Pietro's Folly scooted on by the floundering trireme. Paul had done it!

"That, my Wid, is a Push spell. Never actually used it before. Worked rather well, I'd say," Paul commented. Everyone on the caravel yelled and cheered Paul with wild abandon; he'd turned sudden death into life in one short instant!

"Way to go brother," yelled Paulette at the top of her voice!

"Felix, may we get the heck out of here just as fast as you can?" Paul yelled over the cheering.

Quickly the sails were fully adjusted; lines tightened. The caravel surged through the ocean once more on her way. However, we didn't bob like before. Later, Felix decided that we were carrying about half the maximum weight the caravel could handle. Paul had bought us desperately needed time to get a head start on the trireme. Finally, the rush of the excitement wore off. We were all dead tired, even Rea. All headed to our cabins, and we gave Rea one of the unused cabins below deck, where Ben was staying. Felix agreed to wake us if anything arose. I was asleep before I hit the hammock.

Chapter 15 Of Rea, Typhoon, and Calamities

Rea Niccolo was twenty-five, tall, just over six feet, and well proportioned. Her skin was an enchanting light brown. She wore her curly black hair shoulder length, and her green, piercing eyes commanded your attention. Yes, her body symbolized beauty and grace. I was not wrong about her when I first met her yesterday. Everywhere she walked about the ship, male eyes followed her! She was simply stunning.

At first, she thought that the crew and even the men in my Circle were staring at her because she was a mulato. Such was always the case on Megalos. However, a few choice words from Beth Ann brought a flush to her face and a whole new way of thinking. I'd swear Felix and half his crew were drooling over her! For Rea, becoming a highly sought after woman would take a great deal of getting used to, a complete reversal of her fortunes in life.

However, it was not her body's great beauty that intrigued me, rather she did. Rea, like her father, was also an artist, a painter. One might have predicted that; isolated in that society, Rea had precious other outlets. Even friends were denied her. Considering that her father was both a genius and a social non-conformist, an unwillingly elected senator, I suspected that the two spent long hours together. When she showed me some of her paintings, I could see at once the powerful influence Niccolo had on her artistic development.

Exhausted from the night's heavy work, we awoke at suppertime. Sitting around the table illuminated by several lanterns, Rea told us about her life. I found it amusing that when her father passed away, the locals at this extreme southwestern sector of Megalos, who were even more disenchanted with the way things were going in Galantas, elected her as their senator, if only to spite the Emperor, this new Church of Jehosanity, and even the Senate itself. Never before in the history of Megalos had a mulato, a cross breed, been elected to any post, let alone the Senate. Considering her outcast role in their society, she had taken the senator job seriously, attempting to demonstrate that she was just as good or better than many pure bloods.

All that had changed in recent times. As Yazi's Church of Jehosanity took an ever-stronger control over Megalos, things began to change, subtly at first. Now, however, embolden by their successes, the Church was becoming more blatant. Rea explained how they managed to remove all women from the Senate by an unproven series of assassinations. While there was no evidence to lay the blame for these killings on the Church, no one else had any motive for their slayings. The latest edict, the destruction of most of the historical artwork of Megalos was the final straw for her. She shed tears as she related the works of art that were destroyed, as told to her by those whom she paid to bring her supplies past the Emperor's ever-present guards who had orders to kill or arrest her if she left her estate. "Five hundred years of the best artwork of our people gone in less than a month!"

She explained that the artists were now being coerced into creating "holy works of art" following the dictates of the Church. As more and more facts about how Yazi's Church of Jehosanity operated came out, it became very clear to me just what Yazi was really up to here in Megalos.

I recalled the disciple Yazi that I had known years ago. Back then, he hated women and me in particular. Always, Yazi was covetous of my special relationship with Jes, even envious I thought. If he could have killed me then and gotten away with it, he would have, such was his hatred of me. Yet, his hatred of the Infidels, the Centurions of Megalos, was even greater! An insight began forming in my mind. The ingrained, utter hatred of the Centurions had led Yazi here to Megalos. I knew that he had to have some ulterior motive in mind, not the holy religious piety of Jes Amir. Yazi would want to destroy Megalos. Now the gross perversions that Yazi preached began to make sense to me. Setting back women's rights to the dark ages before civilization came, destroying all the historical artwork, manipulating the Senate, and weakening the Emperor's power to rule, Yazi was well on his way to achieving what must be his goal, the destruction of the civilization of Megalos! All under the guise of religion.

I felt I had to set the record straight with Rea. Long we talked, as I explained my life with Jes Amir, the Great Messiah. Slowly Rea too began to see Yazi's gross perversions of the truth. We both began to see the enormous magnitude of what we had just done in saving an entire boatload of some of the greatest works of art of Megalos! Just then, I had no idea of the extreme importance of Niccolo's inventions; rather that realization would come sometime later.

Finally, our conversation centered on her question, "So now what is to become of me and this art? Where will I go? Where will I stay? I don't understand a word these Sea Prince sailors are saying?"

"Not a problem," Beth Ann replied. "We all speak lots of languages. We'll begin teaching you the Sea Prince dialect and that of the Greenway today. By the time we get back, why you should be able to speak a little of each."

She beamed with thanks but then frowned. "Where are we getting back to?" she asked.

"We are currently living on the island of West Reach," I explained. "However, Rea, we just do not have the facilities there to preserve this volume of art or even to guarantee its safety. Instead, there is only one place that is safe enough on all Tarra, our Guardian fortress complex at Mont Blanc. There this precious collection will be not only safe, but greatly appreciated. You will be free to create as much art as you desire. I can tell you right now that your greatest problem will be fending off suitors!"

She laughed, "I've never had even one. So many?"

Beth Ann smiled, "You can say that again, but you've got me to back you up. I know men. I can help you do just the right thing at the right time, trust me."

Oh brother, Beth Ann, our old Sarah Jane, certainly knew what she was talking about, because she definitely had her role as flirting controller of men down pat! I wondered how she might fare if her next body turned out to be male. Would her skills with men translate into that of a ladies' man? Curious line of thought, I mused.

Finally, I wandered up on deck to inspect the night. Ben was pulling night duty and was standing on the poop royal, watching our wake. His crew member companion was up in the crow's nest. "Still back there, long way though," Ben said as I climbed the short steps to join him. "Nice night, not too hot. Moon looks weird through all those clouds though. Probably means a storm is coming, at least back home that's what it means. Out here, I'm not positive of anything. How's Rea?"

"She's fine, adapting like a trooper. Rea's a brilliant painter in her own right. I found that out. Sometime have a look at some of her oils, super realistic. How far back is the trireme?"

"Oh a good ten miles. I can't see it from here. Winnoa claims he can from the nest. Gonna spell me now?"

"Yes, why not? I am wide awake. Go get some sleep, Ben." I had much to ponder after my long talk with Rea. What had Yazi gotten us all into anyway? How could this perverted religion be so darn powerful and why? How would anyone in their right mind believe all these lies? My incredulity only rose that night.

I listened to the comforting creaking of the ship, its rising and falling as we smoothly passed through the night. Peaceful, yes, that's how I would describe it. Sure, we had to be alert for troubles; still my cares and worries and fears rather melted away, flowing behind us joining our wake. One day, I told myself, I too would have to be a sea captain of one of these new caravels. In fact, I decided that somehow I would save up and buy one from the makers in Velona, just as soon as I could.

Days passed, but the sun refused to pierce the ever-darkening clouds. The consensus among the crew of Pietro's Folly was typhoon. None of us landlubbers, as they jokingly called us, had any idea of what this word meant. Since the weather continued to look ominous, Felix took us all aside for a conference. His dead serious look spelled trouble, though little did I know how much.

"These south seas are prone to great storms that locals 'round here call typhoons. Immense storms, powerful winds. Stories are told of whole houses being blown away, to say nothing of great trees. Seven Sea Prince ships have been lost utterly in these typhoons. Rule is: typhoon comes — you put into port and ride it out. Even so, usually those caught in a port during one of these typhoons sustains significant damage. Why, the Pestle was snapped in two; mighty unlucky for that Pieta crew. Mind you, none 'o us 'ere seen one. Just that we have all heard horrible stories and have standing orders to ride one out in some port," Felix explained.

"Considering our situation, put'in into port with that trireme on our tail is not wise either. It's still on our trail, though fifteen miles back, just barely see it from the nest. If we can even find a port, putting in is just asking them to come ram us. So's I just don't see how we can follow the rule and put into port."

"Makes sense, your analysis does," I replied.

"Gets worse," Felix continued. "We're now approaching the Spice Islands, where we should begin to be very careful, moving among all those islands as we turn to the north. If the typhoon hits us now, we'll likely end up smashed to bits on one of those small islands! According to reports we've heard, we'll have almost no control over the boat. Some say swells will be taller than the crow's nest!"

"So what I'm a saying is we have a real problem. We dare not put into port, even if we can find one. We dare not ride it out or we'll be smashed to bits on the rocky shoals of the Spice Islands. Well, Mister Ket, what do we do?"

Leaders make decisions; for good or ill, they make them. Since the Captain could not find any solution, he was placing the decision on me. Well, that's one way of handling leadership. Ah well, I made the decision; in later years, I wondered if I'd made the right one, because this one cost us time, which ended up costing me dearly. "Well, there is only one real choice left to us, and that is to circumnavigate the Spice Islands, go around them in the typhoon. My Circle and I will concentrate our powers to keep the storm from badly affecting us. You'll just have to trust us that we can."

"But we'll be smashed into kindling wood; we'll fall off the world; we'll get lost; we'll get devoured by sea monsters," Felix protested until he ran out of "but we'll's."

Ben calmly spoke up, "Captain Felix," he began formally, "a long time ago we were sailing from Calgary down to Velona. Our ship was caught in a terrible storm just as it was trying to pass through the Narrows. We joined forces, kept a calm area about a mile in diameter around the ship, and made it through without smashing on those rocks. Ket is right. This is really the only option remaining to us, unless you are willing to lose this ship on its maiden voyage."

"Well," he calmed down somewhat, "the other two choices mean certain death. If anything goes wrong, I want it known that Mister Ket here is responsible for ordering me to sail into the typhoon."

"Agreed," I commented dryly. I gave him a fall guy. "We should study your charts to make sure where we are."

"Better hurry up," the helmsman called out, "rain's a start'n."

Ben and I crammed into the Captain's cabin, one on either side of Felix, who had already had the charts laid out. He'd been studying them, before he came to us. "We're about here," he pointed to a spot about fifty miles from the start of the Spice Islands at the southwest corner of the Southlands. "All these islands — these are the bigger ones. Smaller ones are not on the map."

"We should give them a wide berth," I commented.

"Aye, that yea should, especially in a typhoon. We could get blown right into the middle of them," Felix replied. "Now let's get everything battened down securely. We are in for a very, very rough ride. From now on, nobody goes on deck without being tied to a rope. Come on. I'll show you all how to do it."

The boat was lurching so that even walking to the deck was challenging. The crew members had already fastened a number of rope lines, so we only had to bowline ourselves to one end. I saw that the helmsman was literally tied to his post at the wheel. Satisfied that we knew what to do, Felix joined his helmsman on deck. We went below to help the other crew. Fortunately, the crew had long before secured the artworks and inventions. In fact, they had a clever way of protecting them. The whole lot was tied up in giant rope rigging, and was hanging from the deck beams above. Hence, even if we took on some water, the art would remain high and dry. However, the rest of the gear needed to be thoroughly lashed down tight. With the violent lurching of the caravel, this proved challenging indeed. An hour later, the crew was satisfied that they had done all they could to make the ship secure. Now came the waiting; each member had assigned locations below deck. Watch for leaks or other problems and handle was their task, until it was time to relieve the Captain and the helmsman.

We staggered back to our poop cabins and struggled into the hammocks. Paulette calmed down and slowly Mind Joined us all together. Once we were secure in our connections, Ben and I headed out onto the deck. Ben lashed himself to the poop royal, while I did likewise on the foredeck. Ben would be the focal point for our attempt to ease the weather around us, while I acted as look out for the unexpected ahead. As far as I could tell, the strong winds were throwing the caravel south by west, which was a good direction to avoid the Spice Islands.

In a few minutes, the rains picked up again. Sheets of rain falling nearly horizontal pelted us, stinging any exposed skin. I could not see ten feet in front of us; some look out I'd be. Felix screamed so I could hear, "Some blow!"

Yelling back, I asked, "How long does it last?" I had to repeat it twice more before he could get my question.

"Days," came the reply. I certainly didn't want to hear that answer. Unless Ben with our help could calm things down, we were in for a very wild ride indeed. My respect for a typhoon grew stronger by the minute. After an hour, which seemed like an eternity, Ben managed to calm the winds significantly, but not the torrential rain. Rain, we could handle, not the winds. He had established a small area around the boat, which the winds managed to bypass slightly, rather like an invisible, but not solid bubble. The ocean swells, he could do nothing about, so we resigned ourselves to the violent rising, falling, and lurching. At least the rains were not horizontal any more.

Eventually, fatigue set in; all four of us had to be physically helped to get below deck as two crew members along with Alan and Paul tried to relieve us. None of us had any idea of time. Were we manning our stations for minutes, hours, or days? Even our replacements had no idea. If day came, the dark skies hid it from us. I stumbled into my room, bouncing off the walls. With great difficulty, Lilly Ann managed to get me out of my soaking clothes, dried off somewhat, and into fresh clothes. Getting into a swinging hammock in this storm took ages. Then, I slept.

I awoke to the continuing nightmare; how long I slept no one could say. Lilly Ann kept saying I had to go relieve Allan and Paul. Somehow, I managed to get back to my station, but I also had to help get Allan back down. He was as fatigued as I had been. "Some storm," he finally managed to yell to me.

Partway into my watch, the seas finally calmed, the wind stopped, stars appeared overhead. It was as if Nature had suddenly and dramatically ended the storm. The caravel stopped pitching in all directions, settling down to a standstill. The silence was eerie. "Is it over?" I found myself yelling and had to force myself to talk normally.

"Dunno," Ben called back. "It seems to be."

"No, they call this the eye of the storm. I've heard tales of such, but I did not believe them," Felix called back from his position at the helm. "We are at the exact center of the storm, I think."

"This is truly amazing!" I replied, staring at the starry sky above. Only a couple wispy clouds marred the view. "How long does it last?"

"Dunno. Sure is beautiful though."

"That must mean we have to endure all that again, if we are in the center," Ben reasoned. "Guess I need to keep working on the spell."

"Look over there! It seems we are heading right back into it!" I called out. All of us re-fastened our tether lines once more and braced for yet another round. It was most intriguing. Here the sea was fairly calm, but just over there, it became quite turbulent again. Wham, Pietro's Folly was back into the thick of it once more. I did note that now the winds pushed us in a different direction, back toward the Spice Islands! I yelled, "Heading toward those islands, keep a sharp look out." Afterwards, I wondered just what we could actually do if we found ourselves heading for a rocky island. We had no sails; they'd be torn to shreds; we were really at Nature's mercy.

Night? Day? Who knows? Like mechanical zombies, we took turns on deck, turns sleeping. Hunger, no, the violent lurching, the incredible upswing of the ship followed by the sickening stall mid-air followed by the crashing down fall made any thoughts of food vanish without a trace!

"It's over, wake up, wake up," Lilly Ann was shaking me.

No motion. I felt no motion from the ship. Then, I did feel a slight rocking motion. "Come on; let's go take a look see where we are!" she exclaimed. I followed her out of our cabin, joining the others who were staggering out of theirs. On deck, we saw partly cloudy skies and lots of ocean all around us. "I've never been so glad of no motion in my life!" she declared.

Felix was dancing a jig on deck, "We made it! We made it! We're alive! Ship's still in tack! Yes!" For a few minutes, we all shared his sentiments! Rea, I noticed was not among us. I raced to her cabin fearing that she'd somehow gone overboard, but no, there she was, ghastly white, vomit covering her, her walls, her clothes, her floor. She'd had a very bad time of it all. I sent for Beth Ann and quietly went back on deck.

Felix was issuing orders once more. "She's a mess. Every line is loose. Some ropes have snapped. Boys, let's get cracking!"

"But Captain, cain't we eat something first, maybe take a restful nap 'fore we does all this work?"

"Aye, lads, my stomach's growling too. Okay, let's rustle up food! We aren't going anywhere soon." We all smiled, joyous at still being alive and in one piece. Thank you Pietro's Folly! A mad rush ensued as we all charged the galley, each helping themselves; no one would wait on the cook this day.

Next, refreshed, we all headed back on deck. Felix wanted a complete inspection of every nook and cranny of this ship. Like rats, we scampered about the caravel. We'd lost part of the main deck's railing, but no one had seen it fly off. All the rigging needed attention; six lines had actually snapped. However, that was all the damage any of us could find. Amazingly, our ship had weathered the storm in good shape. Now everyone pitched in to make the repairs. I assisted Allan with the carpentry; together, from the spare wood stored below for emergency repairs such as this, we fashioned a new section of railing that matched fairly well the original. It took us all day, however to finish this project.

I took a break mid-day to assist Felix with estimating where we were at, which was very, very simple: we were somewhere out in the ocean, no sight of land in any direction. Worse still, Ben commented, there were no birds in the sky. He explained that meant we were a good distance from the Southlands.

"Should we unfurl the sails, Captain," asked one crew member, after all the lines had been repaired.

"Heck no. Which way should we sail, eh? Bet you didn't think of that. That's why I am the captain," Felix replied. He'd brought his maps out on deck, partially to dry off. He and I looked them over. "Figure we were blown south to begin with, but how far?"

"Dunno," I replied.

"Then, we were blown north by west some too," he added ignoring me. "Land ought to be that a way," he pointed to the northeast. "Somewhere there any way. Okay lads, set sail now, north by east. Keep a sharp lookout in the nest, fellows." Smiling, I went back to Allan and the sawing, carving, and sanding.

We sailed north by east for nearly a week. Rea recovered from her nightmare and spent hours checking on her precious artwork. There was some slight water damage, but nothing major, thank the gods for that.

However, with each day, the crew became more and more edgy; I think that we did too. No sight of land gave us a sinking feeling that grew on us daily. How far had we been blown off course? How long would it be before we hit land once more? Logic told us that we were sailing in the right direction, but the absence of land was most discouraging. I even tried to cheer them up by showing everyone what we thought had happened to us during the storm.

Making matters worse, food and fresh water were running low. Felix now had us all fishing half the day for our lunch and suppers, trying to stretch our meager supplies further. He kept saying that we'd be okay once we found land again. That was an understatement or is it an obvious statement?

One week after the storm, we heard the sound that we had all been praying for, "Land ho!" coming from the crow's nest. Everyone, I do mean everyone, dashed to the foredeck and stared ahead of us, straining to see good old land once more. Slowly, it came into view, and every one of us began yelling, cheering, clapping, and hugging one another.

Of course, the next question was where were we? That took a little observation. Between all of us watching the coastline slide by as we cruised along northward, we decided we must be just north of the Moon People's port. This had to be the Red Desert! That also meant we were close to home!

Although I haven't mentioned it, at least once a day I checked in with Jo Ann to see how Caitlyn was doing. I also kept John Henry posted on our progress. However, during the storm, we lost contact for those days. I let my mind expand north now in earnest, eager to relay the news that we knew where we were and would be home soon. *Not now, Ket, she's going into labor. It's August 31, silly. I'll contact you when we know more.*

"Eureka! I'm going to be a father! Caitlyn's giving birth!" I yelled to everyone. I felt so elated! I was going to be a father at last. It didn't matter that I had never been a father before and had no idea what that meant. I just was. One by one, my Circle gave me a handshake and their congratulations. I felt so light, so happy. This was going to be a beautiful day indeed.

Two days later, we were sailing beside the Med Sea, halfway between the Red Desert and the Velona sector. That's when Jo Ann contacted me. The instant she made contact, I knew something was very wrong. She'd never contacted me during the day before; I sensed huge grief in her.

Ket, I've terrible news for you and good news. Which should I tell you first? I could tell she was purposely holding back.

Give me the good news first. I just dreaded what that bad news would be.

You are the father of twin boys. Both are healthy and doing fine. Pete and Ernest have secretly taken them away; they are going to try to get the boys to Mont Blanc. The bad news, Caitlyn is dead. She paused, knowing I would likely go into shock over the news. In hindsight, there really is no more horrible task than to be the one that has to tell someone that their most loved one has died unexpectedly. I staggered; grief swelled up in me; I could not help but begin bawling like a baby. Jo Ann compassionately gave me time to grieve before continuing.

How did she die? During childbirth? I was only a day away from her! I finally managed something coherent to send to her.

We don't know yet. She had a tough birth, lost blood, but when we all went to bed last night she was recovering and doing well. No complications at all. Then, this morning, we went to check on her first thing and found her dead. Mary's been examining her; she feels very bad; her patient died on her unexpectedly. That's when she discovered something. She suspects that someone poisoned her! That's when Pete decided to get the babies away to safety. Mary says she will know more in a little while. I'll get back to you in a bit, something is happening here. She broke the connection.

My Circle could not help notice me, and I looked up, tears streaming down my face. "We're too late. Caitlyn's dead, one damn day too late to save her!" I wailed and completely broke down. Lilly Ann put her arms around me, and I clung tightly to her, not knowing what else to do. I just cried.

The joyous mood on the ship changed utterly in those few moments. Even the crew became somber. Finally, I recovered enough to relay what Jo Ann had told me.

"Poisoned? How can that be?" Paul uttered with a note of disbelief in his voice. "That doesn't make any sense. Who would want to poison Caitlyn? She was loved and respected by everyone in the town!"

Jo Ann reached me once more. *More news, Mary has discovered something else. She now believes that Caitlyn was assassinated! Someone stuck a tiny, poisoned needle in her ears while she slept. The assassin also put her pillow over her face so she could not cry out. Bits of down are in her throat. Mary also reports that Caitlyn has left us a clue. In her final struggle with her assassin, she managed to tear part of their clothes off. Locked in her right hand is a piece of black cloth and a fastener, both foreign to this land and to the Greenway. Mary cannot identify them either. We are contacting John Henry next to find out what we should do next. More later.*

Once again, I related what Jo Ann had told me. Paul, confined to the ship when action was demanded, felt horribly frustrated. He longed to be there and assist. "An assassin? Who would want Caitlyn killed? I don't even think that King Laird wanted her dead. This is making absolutely no sense whatsoever! God, I wish I was there!"

"Calm down, Paul," his sister begged him, and managed to get him to unclench his fists.

A few minutes later, Jo Ann contacted me once more. *John Henry asked that I try to contact Caitlyn and help her acquire a new body, something about the ceremony that you all do here when someone passes away. So I tried to do that, Ket. Alas, Caitlyn is not here. I don't know where she has gone either. Any ideas, Ket?*

I'll do it from here. I broke the connection and tried to expand my mind. Unfortunately, I was so much in grief that I could not make even the slightest connection with Paulette, who was standing beside me! "I've got to go lie down. We are trying to find Caitlyn. I've got to find her," and I began wailing once more.

"He's in no condition to use telepathy!" Paulette declared. "Lilly Ann, get him below. I'll do it. I know Caitlyn. If she is on Tarra, I'll find her," she said more determined than I've ever seen her. I let Lilly Ann guide my morose body into the poop cabin and up into the hammock. Paulette quietly came into the room. She sat down on the floor, Lilly Ann sat beside her. I did my best to suppress my crying, but couldn't. I continued to whimper as quietly as I could.

Paulette concentrated and probed for nearly a half hour, before she succeeded in locating Caitlyn. As soon as she made contact with her, she Mind Joined Caitlyn with me. *I'm so sorry I wasn't there. I love you so!* I fairly screamed at her before I calmed down.

I am so happy that you weren't here! You'd have been killed too! At least one of us has to live to raise our twins. I had twins, Ket. Identical twins!

Where are you anyway? We've been trying to contact you. I promise you I will raise them well.

If a spiritual being can blush, Caitlyn blushed. *I have a new body already. I've taken one of the twins. Hope you don't mind.* After a pause, she sent, *That makes me my own mother, doesn't it? How confusing. I'm with Pete and Ernest. We are somewhere in the woods of Moyrath, close to the Lir River. I think they are taking us to Mont Blanc. I love you too. See you soon. Hope you don't mind.*

No, actually it's terrific, my love. Great thinking on your part! Say, can you tell us what happened during the night?

Not really. I was sleeping, really exhausted. I had the first one and thought we were done. Then Mary said to keep on pushing. Out came the other one. That's why I was so big! Twins. Anyway, I was sleeping. Someone put a pillow over my head and stuck something like a needle into my left ear and then my right ear. I tried to fight back but couldn't breathe. I grabbed the person, held on, and never let go! Then, the body went all heavy and cold, and I floated up and out. It was dark; only a candle was burning. I saw a man dressed in black with two needles in his hand leaving on tiptoe. I heard him walking quietly away. That's all I know. Hope it helps you figure out who did this. If you find them, please kill them for me.

I swear to you that I will find who did this to you and kill them, I swear!

Gotta go now, they are trying to feed me. The Mind Link dropped.

"Thank you Paulette! Thank you sincerely. Now I know just how valuable it is for those that live to be able to contact their loved ones like this. Thank you."

"You're welcome. It is the very least I can do. I will report all this to Jo Ann and to John Henry. Why don't you just lie there for a while?" It was more of an order than a question. Lilly Ann stayed with me the whole time. I'd only begun to sense the deep compassion Lilly Ann had.

I'd just relaxed totally, when Jo Ann made contact with me once more. *Ket, more alarming news just in. It seems that several days ago Emil Amir's eldest son, Justice, and his young son died. His wife reported that a man in black knocked out several guards, snuck into their Master Bedroom, knocked her out, and killed their baby and Justice. King Emil Amir, Carmine, and their youngest children, Jamal and Cathleen, were up visiting the King of Aine. A messenger arrived today with the news. King Emil's orders. He is rushing home and on down to Triwaters, where his son ruled over that town.*

What the heck is going on? I asked, rhetorically, since Jo Ann could not possibly know.

I don't know. This is getting weirder by the hour. Beth Ann asked me to relay a message for her. Since she feels this was her fault for not sleeping in the room with Caitlyn, she's taken it upon herself to do some inquiries about funeral arrangements at her Church of the Blessed Holy Mother. In talking with the priest, she discovered something queer. Evidently, days ago, a man in black claiming to be a representative of the Church of Jehosanity on the mainland came by asking many questions about Bethany Madelyn Amir and her children. How many she had, their names, where they lived, and so on. Mary found this disturbing, but it is probably nothing more than church business.

Suddenly a horrible notion swept over me. I'd been all over the Sea Princes and seen their various Churches of Jehosanity. None wore robes of black; none held any animosity for the family of Jes Amir, the Great Messiah. On the contrary, they held them sacred. This man in black could not be their minion. Only Yazi hated Bethany Madelyn Amir with enough passion to want her dead, but their children and children's children?

I heard Rea's voice in my head; it was something she said a while back about this new Church of Jehosanity in Megalos. I heard her voice saying, "Now the Church claims that the Son of God was Immaculately Conceived from a barren womb and that he was celibate his entire life. Artworks are being commissioned now to illustrate such."

Jo Ann, you and Mary drop everything. Get the captain of the cavalry with a small escort to take you to King Emil's town. Get there as fast as you possibly can. King Emil, Jamal, and Cathleen are very likely the next targets! I'll warn them now. I'll get Fergus and the King of Aine to help protect them as well. Fly, Jo Ann fly! She acknowledged and left to carry out my orders. Now I had to contact my son from last lifetime, Emil Amir.

"Why are you shaking so?" Lilly Ann asked, concerned about my sudden behavior change.

"Something is very wrong. No time to talk; got to contact Emil immediately, if it is not too late." I relaxed, or tried to as best I could. Expanding my awareness was most difficult; my mind was racing, and just the opposite of what I needed to use telepathy. It took me five minutes to regain control over my mind. Outward went my awareness at last. Shortly I found my target, Emil.

Grief flooded my mind as I made the contact. *Emil, Emil, Bethany, Ket here. I heard about Justice and your grandson.*

Woe be to both of us, you especially. We just heard about poor, dear Caitlyn. Tragedy has struck both our families at the same time.

Where are you now? Are Cathleen and Jamal with you?

Yes, we are in our coach heading back home at the greatest possible speed. How can something like this happen to both of us? I feel so sick. He was my eldest. You can't imagine how horrible it feels to lose your oldest child like this. His grief again overwhelmed him. I sensed he was crying again. I gave him some time.

Son, Emil, I want you to listen to me very, very carefully. Are you listening? I tried to put my strongest possible intention behind my thoughts. *Emil, my son, I have reason to believe that Caitlyn's assassination and that of Justice and his son are part of a larger plot. I am almost positive that you, Cathleen, and Jamal are their next targets. You have been spared thus far because you were away on vacation. If you had been home, I am almost certain that all three of you would be dead by now. Do you understand me?*

Mom, I feel so utterly lost without you. Can you be here soon? My son, now forty-one, was balling, in desperate need for me, his mother, whose body was long dead. Oh, how I wanted to reach out and put a consoling, loving arm around him! Yet, I could not. I did the only thing I could do.

I'm here Emil. I will be with you as soon as I possibly can, few days at most. Now listen to me, Emil. I am sending two Guardians to you, Mary and Jo Ann, along with some cavalry from Nuadilan. Fergus and the King of Aine will be coming along soon as well. I want you to halt your coach. Stop right where you are. Tell me where you are and then just wait until the Guardians get to you. Do you understand me, son? If you do as I say, we can save you and your remaining two children.

I heard him order his driver to stop at once. That was a good sign. The assassin is dressed in black robes and is probably a foreigner. I then relayed all that I knew thus far. He, in turn, explained where they were. Thankfully, he did have an escort of some twenty cavalry with him. I broke the connection and next tried for Fergus.

Fergus was very willing to go to aid Emil; for him, I detected that it was something that he could actually do. He would be glad to get active for a time. I gave him the directions. Finally, I re-contacted Jo Ann and relayed their location. Already, she had the cavalry ready to ride; she and Mary were just packing some gear when I made contact. Good timing. I estimated that Emil was now about equidistant from both parties and that it would take them a day and half to reach him. I prayed that Emil had that day and a half left!

Next, I gathered my Circle and relayed to them what had transpired, along with my suspicions. "Oh no!" exclaimed Lilly Ann. She and Beth Ann, the twins, looked at each other in horror. "Mom's in danger. Sarah is Emil's sister, Jes and Bethany's other child! If you are right, she's next after Emil."

"Gosh, then we are too, Lilly Ann," exclaimed Beth Ann. "And Arthur and Justus too. We have to warn them! Paulette!" Fear shone from the twin's eyes.

"We are working on it," I tried to calm them down a bit. "Paulette, you contact John Henry. I'll get Sarah. Explain everything to him. I think it prudent to get Sarah, Arthur, and Justice safely to Mont Blanc."

"Don't forget Arthur's baby," Beth Ann added. I grinned sheepishly, for I had completely forgotten about it. "He's in Waynesville, a blacksmith," she added.

Paulette and I once more concentrated and made our telepathic links. *Sarah, it's me, Bethany.*

We've heard the news about Cailyn. I so sorry for both of you. What a way to begin fatherhood. At least your twins are safe. We heard that John Henry sent a boat over to the island to pick them all up.

Sarah, listen to me very carefully. Your life is in grave danger. Caitlyn was assassinated. A couple days earlier, Emil's son and grandson, Justice, were assassinated. Emil, Cathleen, and Jamal are in grave peril as we speak. I've sent them all the help I can, if only they can hold out for a day and a half! I explained my theory about the killings.

Honey, I want you to round up Arthur and his family and Justus and get to Mont Blanc as fast as you can. You'll be safe there. I should be there in two days.

But I'm the queen here. How will that look? Percival can protect me.

Sarah, these are professional assassins. They will kill Percival if he gets in the way. If you are not there, they won't harm him. They left Justice's wife knocked out, but otherwise unharmed. Promise me you will get to Mont Blanc soon! At last, she promised, and I told her I'd stay in touch. This was one day I was sure glad that we druwids had telepathic abilities, so arduously learned.

"John Henry has sent a boat to pick up your sons, Pete, and Ernest. They should be safely inside the fortress at Mont Blanc by tomorrow," Paulette reported. Finally, I thought I could relax. I did, but then my grief returned. I retired to my cabin, laid in my hammock and let my tears flow.

Much later, Lilly Ann brought me in a plate of supper and sat with me, insisting that I eat. "Paulette has heard from Jo Ann. Mary and Jo Ann have met up with Fergus. She says that they have a hundred cavalrymen with them and should catch up to Emil by tomorrow morning. They are riding all through the night. So everything will work out fine, you'll see. Now get some sleep." Lilly Ann took the mostly empty plate away. I tried to do as she asked.

I slept ill, tossing and turning, I kept seeing a faceless man dressed in black going around killing off all my friends and loved ones. I awoke in a sweat. "What's wrong?" asked a sleepy Lilly Ann.

"Nightmares," I shrugged it off. "Go back to sleep." I got up to go get some fresh air. Tomorrow we would make Calgary and I could get off this ship!

Chapter 16 Confusions

I awoke with a start! I remembered going on deck for fresh air after the horrible nightmares of last night. I'd gone back to bed late. Now the sun was up, streaming through the sole porthole in our room. Why did I wake up? I wondered. Lilly Ann was still asleep above me. *Ket! Ket! You there?*

Ah, a Mind Link. Jo Ann was trying to contact me. I sensed her massive confusion, fear, grief, and failure all rolled into one. Amazing that she could even reach me in the state she was in. I firmed up her wobbling contact and told her I was awake.

Ket, oh Ket! You were right. We were too late. Emil's dead! We were a couple hours too late getting to him!

"Oh God no!" I screamed, startling Lilly Ann, who sprang out of bed, falling off her hammock and nearly landing on top of me, terrified. Instinctively, I just joined her confused mind with ours.

We are on the scene now. Fergus and I are examining the tracks. Appears a large bunch of riders came upon Emil's group. Signs of a large battle are everywhere. Emil took five arrows before he fell. From the signs, Jamal killed several of his attackers before they hacked him to death. Fergus wants to report that three of Emil's cavalrymen are still alive, barely, and that twelve of their attackers are dead. No signs of their horses yet. Fergus adds that a lone carriage came up to the battle and later turned around and went back the way they came. Wait a second! Mary is yelling something. Cathleen is still alive, says she has been poisoned. Mary says she thinks that she may be able to save Cathleen! God, Ket, we have failed you utterly! I am ashamed to call myself a Guardian anymore.

Tears streaming down my face, I yelled back at her, *It's my fault again. I should have told Emil to return to Fergus, not just stop! I'm to blame. I made yet another wrong decision. You are not at fault; it is all mine!* I just could not go on and dropped the connection. Lilly Ann, curled up into a ball on the floor, was covering her ears with her hands in a useless attempt to dampen my telepathic screaming. By now, the rest of my Circle sensed something was terribly wrong and came bursting into our cabin. What a sight we must have looked like, she curled into a ball, holding hands to her ears, and me sitting on the floor bawling once more.

"Ket, Ket, it is not your fault, really, it isn't. You did your very best. Look on the positive side; you got Mary there in time to save Cathleen! If you had not acted, she would have died too," Lilly Ann pushed me. Quickly, she related the bad news to the others.

"Oh no!" exclaimed Beth Ann. "Mom and our brothers, are they safe yet? Does John Henry know about all this yet?" I shook my head morosely no.

"I'll take care of it," Paulette offered.

"Make sure mom is safe," Beth Ann pleaded.

Ben thoughtfully brought me a cup of hot tea, I calmed down. Something about me and tea. Shortly, Paulette reported, "Sarah and the boys are under heavy escort and on their way to Mont Blanc. John Henry has already escorted Pete, Ernest, and my twins to Mont Blanc; the babies are doing well. He will be meeting us personally at the docks. I told him we would need about six wagons for all Rea's stuff. So gang, let's get packing. I think we dock around noon. We've only got hours to get all our stuff ready."

Okay, it was something to do, gather up our things and stow them into our sacks. It took me all ten minutes to do, however. Lacking anything else to do, I decided to check on Rea and how she was doing.

I found her standing beside the hanging cargo sacks. Like me, she already had her things in a sack. She looked nervous. "We'll be in Calgary, Greenway shortly, Rea. All set?" I asked the plainly obvious.

"Yes, just a bit overwhelmed by all this. Oh, I am so terribly sorry for what happened to your wife. In way, it is my fault, because I made you come all this way to rescue me. If you hadn't, she might still be alive."

"No, it is not your fault either. You needed rescuing, and Caitlyn insisted that we come. She would not have wanted it any other way, Rea. You nervous?" I decided to ask bluntly.

"Yes, a little. I've never really be away from home before, I mean other than the Senate. I'm not sure what to expect. Do I speak well enough? Will people be able to understand me? How am I going to live? What if they don't like me here? I am from Megalos, after all. How am I going to care for all this art of dad's? I am just a little overwhelmed by it all, actually."

"Well, Rea, you will manage just fine. Give yourself time to adjust. Get to know us here. I think you will find us very understanding and appreciative of both you and your father's art. Initially, John Henry wants to take all it to our fortress at Mont Blanc. This is the safest place on Tarra right now. Just now, things are a bit confused around this neck of the woods. Another dear friend of mine and his son and others were murdered last night. We suspect that Pope Yazi had a hand in it, although we have no proof yet. So do expect a little confusion for the next few days anyway. I wonder what my twins look like?"

"Will they have red hair like yours?" she asked, relieved to have a different topic.

"Dunno. Never thought about that. Shows you what I know about being a father," I replied.

"You'll do fine, I'm sure," Rea encouraged me. She sighed, "I guess we ought to go on deck and see if there is anything but ocean to see. Once I'm all settled in, I'd love to do portraits of you and your twins too. Maybe if you could describe in detail how Caitlyn looked, I could do one of her for your boys. That way they would at least know what she looked like."

I'd not thought about this aspect; the twins would never know their mother's face. "Would you? That would be fantastic!" Together, we walked up the steps to see what could be seen. Actually, a lot could be seen, the forests of

Cymry were clearly visible on our left, while the rocky, rolling hills of that bit of land that separated Fortress d'Grange, Sea Princes from the Greenway, passed by on our right. "Coming up on Calgary real soon now; it's the largest town in the Greenway. I'm afraid it will look awfully small, compared to the cities you are used to seeing in Megalos."

Rounding a bend, there was Calgary. It had been quite some time since I last laid eyes on it from the ocean. The harbor was bustling with traffic. Five Sea Prince ships either coming or going, but only one caravel. Absolutely everyone was staring at this unique ship. Crew members on those ships that were passing us on their way out lined the sides, craning their necks to catch a good look at Pietro's Folly. "Why are they all looking at us?" asked Rea.

"This is a brand new boat design, invented by a thirteen year old boy. This has been its maiden voyage. I guess we thoroughly tested it," I answered.

"A boy designed all this?" she asked in disbelief.

"There's John Henry, our leader, that older man there waving at us," I pointed out and waved back.

Rea watched fascinated by all the strange sights, sounds, and the intricacies of docking such a large ship. I merely reflected on my memories from over fifty years ago when I had first sailed out of Calgary with my Lightning Circle. Soon the mooring lines were cast and the gangplank positioned. Time for action. Carrying our sacks, we eight walked down to the planks of the docks. I noticed that John Henry had two dozen Guardians surrounding us all.

"Well met indeed," he exclaimed and gave me a hearty handshake. He showed no emotional signs, which was perfect. It was all I could do to keep my huge grief at bay just now.

Perhaps a hundred people were here at the docks. Rea walked down alongside of Beth Ann. As Rea stepped of onto the docks, a number of younger men began whistling in admiration of her good looks. A bit embarrassed, Rea whispered to Beth Ann, "Why are they whistling?"

"Because they think that you are a knock out, super good looking. See I told you, around here, your problem will be that too many guys will want to date you! Just smile at them, you know, lead them on a trifle. Yes, like that. Soon you will have every man in the Greenway begging to meet you!" Beth Ann meant it. She had a way with flirting, she always had.

"And this must be our esteemed guest from Megalos," John Henry said, sincerely. "Ket Bethany did not say you were this good looking." She smiled, while I introduced her.

"Rea, this is John Henry Penton, our leader. John Henry, this is Rea Helios, daughter of Niccolo Helios. Both are famous artists from Megalos. Wait until you see their art work and Niccolo's many inventions!" He bowed and kissed her hand.

This was followed by numerous other introductions, in large part to stall while the crew of Pietro's Folly began to unload the valuable cargo. When the first load came off the ship, Rea went to supervise the loading. She had almost too much help from the men. I excused myself and went back on board to find Captain Felix.

Shaking his hand in farewell, I said, "Thanks for an eventful, but safe voyage. You and your crew did an admirable job. Here is a little extra on the side for you and your men." I put a small money pouch into his hand. He thanked me, of course, and we shook hands once more. Only after everything was unloaded and the crowd was tired of looking at the new caravel did he open it. His eye popped out; I'd given him gems worth double what our fare had been. He smiled and called out to his men to come have a peek at their "little extra." I know that it meant a lot to these hard working men.

When he had an opportunity, John Henry whispered to me, "Say nothing about the situation until we get safely to Mont Blanc." I nodded, and again was thankful, since the mere mention of it brought my grief to the surface once more.

Finally, we climbed onboard the ten wagons, all heavily laden; I was glad that he had brought more than the six for which I'd asked. We eight sat on one, which was made to carry people. Two dozen Guardians rode on ahead of us; nothing would interfere with this journey — too much was at stake to take the slightest risks. Mont Blanc was a four-hour ride at the speed we managed, which was slow in order not to jostle the cargo too much. None of it was packed securely in shipping crates, as it ought to have been. We passed the time telling Rea about our land, its customs, and its scenery. Soon, we could see the Langdoc region ahead.

The Langdoc region, which stretches here from the ocean all across the southern edge of the Greenway to the Northern Steppes, is a land of nearly barren limestone hills with many water-worn caverns. Here was a barren land of rough rock, sparse grasses, few trees, and little water. About the only trees that grow here are gnarly oaks. The Langdoc certainly is not good farming land or timberland either. Uninhabited for the most part, here is where the Guardians made their fortress. However, there are miles of underground caverns directly attached to the fortress, providing a safe haven and avenues of escape. The Langdoc was perhaps thirty to fifty miles wide, varying as it moved inland. At seeming random locations, a mountain would thrust itself up above the surrounding landscape. I say mountain, but their elevations were merely one to two thousand feet taller than the rest of the land about them. Mont Blanc was the first of a lengthy series of these mountains.

Our fortress at Mont Blanc is covered with numerous overlapping conjuring spells. When a non-druwid approaches the general area of our complex, they see simply the barren countryside. It has turned out to be very effective at keeping unauthorized people from discovering the fortress, now more so than ever!

"There is Mont Blanc," I pointed out to Rea; it was the tallest mountain around here. I explained about our hiding spells. "There is the fortress itself." Rea looked where I was pointing, but saw simply more barren rocky hillside. Subtly, I altered the conjuration spell to allow Rea access to visibility. "Now how's that?"

"I can see it! Wow, look at those walls!" Yes, the ten-foot tall outer walls gave us much needed protection. "And all those stone buildings. She could not help noticing the wildly varying architectural styles, building to building. "Well, that one looks like a Megalos design!"

I explained that Raphal, the Lightning Circle Planner, had been with me when we went to Megalos so many years ago.

Allan could not help but butt in, "Hey, I am still here. That was me. I designed most all these buildings. I have great plans for more, but perhaps we should heighten the outer walls." Rea stared at him, trying to grasp the significance of his proud outburst.

I changed the topic, "Rea, wait until winter comes. All this land will be covered in snow, and we can go for sleigh rides! You'll love it." I knew that she probably had never seen snow before. Either she would like it or she would detest the cold, time would tell.

In the far distance, I also spied several flocks of sheep, but still no farming fields. We still depended upon some trade for grain, the bread of life. As we rolled up to the ten-foot tall outer walls that surrounded the complex, I saw hundreds of people standing and watching our arrival. "Rea, about fifteen hundred people now live within these walls," John Henry explained.

She grinned, "Fifteen hundred and one, I'm here now." We all chuckled.

Once safely inside, the wagons were moved into a separate section of the dry caverns that were a part of our complex. Here, Rea could sort out her art, make displays, and store them, all with complete safety. Then, John Henry personally took Rea on a grand tour, ending up with showing her where she would be staying for the time being. She had a roommate, Alice, who gaily began chatting with her and took over for John Henry. The last I saw of Rea, she was being shown to the kitchen, pantry, and restrooms, not necessarily in that order.

"Now you seven come with me," he said seriously. "We have much to discuss and plan. On our way, Ket, I'll we'll stop by the nursery where your twins are at for now. I've two midwives handling their nursing. I presume that you will want them with you as soon as you get settled."

My twins. It sure did sound different. I was expecting to be a father, just not twins. One of them was Caitlyn. Would I recognize which was her? When we entered the nursery, John Henry's stern mien melted away. "Here they are — identical twins. Here's your father at long last." In spite of all the cares and woes of the world, John Henry still loved children, our future, he always preached.

Picking up one as gently as I could brought back memories of being a mother. However, I found it awkward to get the second one, so Lilly Ann helped me out. "They are adorable, Ket. Beautiful babies!" The one in my right arm looked at me with his small eyes and laid his head on my arm, rather as if he was hugging me. It was Caitlyn, no doubt about that. I gave her a loving kiss, then my other son too. Finally, the mid-wives took them from me, saying it was time to feed the boys. I should come back later to be with them. We took our leave and headed up to the Grand Meeting Room in the tallest tower.

Sarah and Percival were here along with Lilly Ann and Beth Ann's two brothers. The place was packed with Guardians. Maps littered the tables. "Latest report please," John Henry asked. Quickly, my Circle and I were brought up to speed on what was known and what was happening. Mary had successfully neutralized the poison; Cathleen would live. Three of Emil's cavalrymen would also recover from their wounds. Fergus was leading their small armada to the coast where a boat would be waiting to bring them to Mont Blanc. Cathleen was in a wagon and doing fine. Fergus sent a couple men to bear the remains of the family and guards on into their town. Two dozen Guardians were already riding toward Fergus and would join up with them in a couple days at most. From there, their orders were to fan out and look carefully for clues that might have been overlooked. At the same time, everyone was on the lookout for these strangers in black from the mainland.

"Our biggest and immediate problem will be the funeral arrangements. Ket, you are going to have to deal with Caitlyn's funeral. Someone must take Caitlyn's place and rule. With Cathleen, we dare not let her return to her home and take part in the burial process. It is too dangerous. Besides, the assassins believe that she is dead. None of us are quite sure how the king succession is handled, so we leave that aspect up to you, Ket. Take your Circle with you; you leave for Cymry tomorrow morning. If any other news happens before then, I'll let you know. That's enough for one day. I'm sure that Sarah and Percival want to talk to their children, so let the rest of the day be a reunion." I thanked him for this respite, though he purposely gave me a lot to ponder. I will have to make some heavy decisions and make them within a couple days. In the meantime, I just hugged Sarah tightly. Beth Ann and Lilly Ann joined us.

The next day, I took a stroll just to see how this beautiful stronghold looked, now that I suspected I would be spending considerable time here. On my walk, a woman in her forties whom I did not know approached me. "Ket Bethany, right?" I assumed that everyone here probably knew me on sight. I said that I was.

"My name is Jane Wellington. I used to be a Judger for Karka, until our Circle was driven out of that area. Half were actually killed. I've been sitting around this place with nothing to do really for over a year now." I jumped to the conclusion that she wanted my help in getting a new Circle going — to give her something to do that was purposeful.

"However, I just heard about your tragedy. While this probably sounds impolite and insincere, I assure you that at least half of us here at Mont Blanc do understand what you are going through; we've gone through similar tragedies recently as well. Please accept my sympathies." Ah, I thought, she just wants to let me know that I can survive this. She and others have, though I don't know how they did it. I graciously accepted her condolences.

"Now I bring all this up at such an inopportune time for a reason. I've been studying extensively this idea of kingships. Correct me if I misjudge your particular circumstances," she continued courteously, "your twins are the rightful heirs to Queen Caitlyn's throne, both by blood and by their bloodline heritage." Hum, all a sudden, this was fascinating. She did indeed have a solid grasp of my peculiar circumstances, but where was all this leading?

"I know that John Henry wants you back here at Mont Blanc in the worst way. You probably also want the twins raised here for their safety. So I asked myself, who will take stewardship of Caitlyn's throne? And what of Cathleen's throne? Ket, I don't want to be or seem presumptuous, but I would love to be your steward, running Caitlyn's kingdom and also perhaps Cathleen's as well. I am particularly well suited to be a steward. I am a Judger by nature. My family, though not Guardians, are here with me and find themselves rather out of place here. He is a blacksmith; we've three teenagers who have been forced to leave their world behind and all their friends. My whole family would benefit greatly by such a move. At least, please consider my offer." She ended very unsure of herself, and I detected some doubt about whether or not she should have even mentioned all this.

"Jane Wellington, I accept your offer! I haven't even begun to try to think all the ramifications of her death through, but this is an ideal handling of it! I have to go back and see to her funeral, later on today I think John Henry said. I figured I'd try to begin to think about these details on the way there. This is prefect! How soon can your family be ready to move there?"

Her eyes lit up as if they were on fire! My immediate acceptance took her by complete surprise. Her basic purposes in life, I realized, had just been rekindled, she would be Judging once more, helping the common folks. "Would you have room on the boat to take us with you? Don't you have to clear it with John Henry first?"

"I'm pretty sure we can take on a few more passengers, but I will double check to be sure. I'll just tell John Henry that I am borrowing you for an extended period of time, like years," I grinned, smug with my little tease, which bordered upon a lie. She caught my meaning and smiled as well. By the time my twins were ready to assume their throne, she would be more than ready to retire of old age. In effect, I was "borrowing her" for most of the rest of her life.

She rushed off to make her hasty preparations; I continued my walk. Shortly, John Henry came rushing up, "Ah there you are. Boat sails this afternoon. I think that you should consider keeping Lilly Ann and Beth Ann behind, just in case the assassins come after them next. I know that Sarah is quite worried about their safety over in Cymry. What say you?"

"Actually, I agree. I hate breaking a Circle, even for a short time. Until we have more proof of the motives behind these killings, it is prudent for them to stay here. By the way, I'm confiscating Jane Wellington; she will be the steward for Nuadilan and perhaps even Emil's kingdom. I'll have to talk with Cathleen about that first, since it is now her realm. Hope you don't mind."

"Actually, no, I'm pleased. She was one of those who found re-adapting most difficult. She trusts no one anymore, I'm afraid. Jane was an excellent

Judger in Karka, I might add. Good choice. I'll see to it that she and her family get passage to Cymry as soon as they can be ready."

"Er, no problem. They can sail back with me later today," I explained, watching the surprise fill his face.

"Ket, you sure do act fast," he chuckled.

"No, she came to me with the offer," I had to be honest with him. "Really, I haven't given any thought to what comes next."

I finished my walk and went to the nursery. Time to confront my twins. I knew that I needed to give them their names. I regretted that Caitlyn and I had not spent more time picking out suitable names before I had left. I did know that she wanted to have Cymry first names, symbolic of the union of her ancient bloodline and that of her people in the towns. We had mentioned the possibility of Tegid. "I'd better ask her," I thought, as I entered the nursery. To my surprise, I found Lilly Ann there, helping to change dirty bottoms.

"Hi, they are adorable, aren't they? Just couldn't stay away from them," she added sheepishly.

"Yes, fine looking twins. I have to decide on names before I leave. Caitlyn wanted them to have Cymry first names. Let me think," I replied. Actually, I touched Caitlyn's mind instead. *Hi Love. Need to pick out a pair of names. You still like Tegid?*

Yes, but my new body ought to be called Taliesin, after the famous bard. Kind of fits, ties in my love of music and our people, don't you think?

Perfect, only we have to make sure we call Taliesin the one you are occupying now, I teased.

You can't tell? She teased back. One of the twins was wiggling his hands and looking at me, the other was sleeping peacefully.

"Okay, this wide awake son is going to be called Taliesin Amir and the sleeping son shall be Tegid Amir. There are your new names my sons. Hope you like them," I pronounced. The midwives came in, and I had to point out which was which. One wrote the two names down on separate pieces of parchment and stuck them beside each boy.

"We'll embroider their names on some blankets so we don't get mixed up," she replied. "How are you going to keep them straight? They look identical."

"I've a nice problem ahead don't I," I teased.

Next, I explained to Lilly Ann that we had decided that she and her twin sister ought to stay here, while the rest of my Circle made a quick trip back to Nuadilan. She took the news surprisingly well, I thought. "I rather surmised that we'd end up having to stay behind this time. After all, who's going to keep these twin's names straight, eh?" She lowered her voice to a whisper, and asked, "This one is Caitlyn, isn't it?" I nodded and Lilly Ann smiled that smile of supreme confidence. I didn't ask her how she knew that, however. I just noted that Lilly Ann was a very astute observer indeed. My opinion of her rose considerably.

I found Beth Ann with her mom and Rea. She was very glad to be staying behind, not only to chat endlessly with Sarah about her exciting trip to Megalos, but also she was really helping Rea to adjust to her new life here and didn't want to leave so soon. Hence, without my doing much, things here in Mont Blanc were working out well. I headed to my room to pack my few things.

An hour later, the rest of my Circle and I headed for the wagon to begin the long ride into Calgary. I was somewhat surprised that Jane and her whole family were already at the wagon, awaiting us! I began to suspect that she had planned this for days and had her family all set to go the second she was given permission to become the steward of Nuadilan. Just as we were leaving, John Henry came running up to me. "Quick word, Ket. I just got word that the boat carrying Cathleen will be docking around the time you are to sail. I've given orders for yours to delay sailing so that you can talk to Cathleen. Mary has given you permission, as long as you don't overly task her. Mary says that Cathleen will need a few weeks bed rest to recover fully."

I thanked him and off we went. On the long ride, Jane introduced her family to us. Her husband, Jake, did indeed have the build of a blacksmith, strong, large arms and a stout body. Jennifer, her eldest, was close to being married when the calamity struck; she was moody over the loss of her love. James, their middle child, took after his father and was an apprentice blacksmith already. Janine, their youngest, simply asked if there were any boys her age in Nuadilan. Her eyes brightened and cheeks flushed when I told her that there were quite a few about her age.

At the docks, the boat carrying Cathleen and the others had already arrived, so I went onboard to see her. She was still very weak and lying in a cabin bed, Mary hovering over her. As soon as I came in, tears formed in her eyes, "I'm so sorry about Caitlyn. She was my best friend."

"I know. She talked often about you as well, Cathleen."

"Is she alright? I mean, did anyone perform the Ceremony for her?" She was referring to the Blessed Holy Mother's special ceremony, which allowed the newly departed to have a final conversation with their loved ones.

"Yes, she did. She has a new baby body now and is quite pleased with it and herself. She sends her love and condolences on your loss," I replied honestly.

Cathleen sighed, a small weight lifted from her mind. "She found one so quick," she mused. Then, she suddenly brightened up and asked, "She didn't, did she?" I knew immediately what Cathleen meant.

"Yes, she did, and you can see her when you get to Mont Blanc. Lilly Ann knows which one. However, Cathleen, I must have a solemn word with you about your kingdom. You are now the rightful heir to your father's throne. The question that must be answered soon is what are we to do about it? You see, the assassins believe that you have also been killed. In a way, if we keep it secret, your life would be secure, most likely. On the other hand, if we let it be known that you will one day reclaim your throne, then the assassins will know that they failed and will likely try again to kill you. I am placing a steward to rule Nuadilan and Amathon until the twins are old enough to assume their thrones. I could place a steward over your towns as well, until you are ready to return. It is your choice. I wish you could have more time to decide, but when I return, I am going to have to help bury your family and their towns must know their fate."

"I might as well be dead. Everyone else is dead. Augar proposed to me, but now how can I return and get married?" she said apathetically, emotionally morose.

"If Augar really loves you, he will wait patiently until you recover and have your strength back. Did Emil approve of Augar? If you marry, then he would become the king. If you like, I can have my steward take him under her wing and get him educated and trained so that he would be able to be a fine king for you. If you use your married name, then perhaps that will confuse the assassins, and they might not realize that you are still alive. What say you?"

"I think daddy liked him. Could he get knowledgeable so he would be able to be king? Cathleen Agar sounds very nice doesn't it?" her eyes brightened up bit by bit.

"Okay, I'll have my steward see what she can do with him. It may take a while, but your body does need a while to mend itself as well. Perhaps, I can arrange a visit here for Augar Agar. Would you like that?"

While it was devastating to have her family slain, for a young girl madly in love and close to marrying, being separated from her lover was every bit as bad for her emotionally. Such destroyed her choice of a future. Now, Cathleen broke into a smile, life surging back into her. "Could he? Oh, that would be fabulous! But not right away. I look frightfully pale and cannot even stand up!"

Grinning, I replied, "You just send word when you are up to having Augar come and I'll see to it." Cathleen's smile broadened.

I said farewell and left her in Mary's care, thanking her for all she had done helping while I was gone. I know that Mary felt badly, what with Caitlyn being killed while in her care. Neither of us mentioned it, and I left it at that for now. Time enough for recriminations once matters were settled. We got on board our ship and were off for Bregia.

I chose Bregia way down south because it provided the fastest route to Nuadilan. On the way, I explained to Jane that she would be looking after two kingdoms, an even bigger challenge. However, since Emil looked after Caitlyn's towns after her father was killed, it was merely turnabout. This was the very least I could do for my son from last lifetime.

"You see Jane, when Jes and I settled here, we formed four nearby towns, each about five miles from the others. When Jes was killed, I gave rulership of the southern pair, Bedwyn and Brea, Layamon, to our youngest son, Emil. Ahmad, our eldest, I gave control to Nuadilan and Amathon, Layamon, the two northern towns. The Grey Creature infiltrated Ahmad's towns and fomented a war with a southern Layamon king in 622, both Ahmad and his oldest son, Ashley, were slain, along with most of the younger men of Nuadilan and Amathon. Caitlyn's older sister, Jenny, took her own life to avoid being married off to a pig of a man that Ahmad was forcing her to marry. With Caitlyn's death, Ahmad's line should have ended, except for her twins, an unexpected development. With the deaths of Emil and his children, only Cathleen remains of his line."

"Now Jes could trace his lineage all the way back to the original Arad founder. In fact, Jes was the closest living relative and thus destined to be King of Arad, which he forsook. Thus, his bloodline remains key to the Arad lineage and kingship of his people. Yet, with this new religion of Jehosanity, Jes being the Son of Jehosa, God in other words, his Tarra bloodline becomes even more important, for religious reasons. Following all this?" I asked.

"I believe so. The confusing part is which religion is which," she replied.

"There are three different versions, not counting the original Arad religion from which the other three have sprung. Perhaps the closest to what Jes envisioned is the Church of Jehosanity, Northern Orthodoxy, founded by one of the ten disciples of Jes, Bandar Dero. Not of my doing, the Church of the Blessed Holy Mother has sprung up here in Layamon, especially within these four towns. Believe it or not, they are worshiping Bethany Madelyn Amir, the wife of Jes Amir and mother of his children, the Holy Line. Okay, I did interject much druwid wisdom into their beliefs, I will admit. Finally, the worst of the disciples, Yazi, has taken our religion down into Megalos and totally perverted it, probably for his own gain and reasons. According to Rea, Yazi is claiming that I either did not exist or was a whore and that Jes was never married and never had any children. Further, he has concocted some strange story that Jes's mother was barren and that Jes was immaculately conceived, which makes no sense to me at this time."

"What has appeared to have happened here is that Yazi has learned that Bethany Madelyn Amir was here, along with the children of Jes. It would seem that he is attempting to wipe the entire line out. Only Cathleen, the twins, and Sarah along with her children remain of that lineage."

"I see, motive enough for assassinations, I believe," she acknowledged.

"Now Josh Amir, the brother of Jes, also settled here with his family. As far as I can tell, no harm has come to any of them. If the theory is correct, nothing is gained by eliminating Josh's line. God, I hope so! When I can, I will alert all his line, probably at the funerals. Oh yes, you are also going to have to periodically sit on the Grande Council of Kings, representing for now both kingdoms."

"Ah, yet another political challenge for me. Ket, I like this assignment more by the minute!" I stared at Jane; she was quite serious. Staring back, she gave a little laugh, "Well, I am a Judger." We both grinned.

Naturally, it was raining the day we held Caitlyn's funeral. I suspected that most of the people in both towns would like the opportunity to attend. Between the two towns, that meant over ten thousand folks. Perhaps the children would stay home, reducing the number considerably. To handle the expected crowd, I decided to hold two identical ceremonies, one for those in Nuadilan and one for those in Amathon. Our cemetery was just north of

Nuadilan. Standing on a buckboard and nearly shouting so that the thousands who came could hear, I conducted the usual Blessed Holy Mother Funeral Ceremony. Part way through, I noticed that King Lachlan Laird and another ten kings were also in attendance.

While I appreciated Fergus and Fianna being here with me to share my sorrow, I suspected the kings had ulterior motives. While each of the three highest-ranking priests added their words to mine, I had a chance to survey our people. Uniformly, I felt fear and uncertainty, so I knew I would have to speak once more. Since I really did not want a lengthy confrontation with the kings, I decided perhaps to answer their questions as well.

"Finally, dear citizens, friends, and even kings, I want to address Caitlyn's last wishes. What is to become of her kingdom? To kill rumors, an assassin poisoned her while she was sleeping after giving birth to our twin sons. Queen Caitlyn Amir's desire is that her sons shall reign over Nuadilan and Amathon just as soon as they are old enough and educated to this important task. I have only been your king because of the grace of Queen Caitlyn Amir. I will not assume her throne, which belongs rightfully to Tegid and Taliesin Amir, the twin boys. Hence, since I must now see to their safety and raising, while going after her assassin, I have decided to place a Guardian steward here in the twin's place. Jane Wellington is more than competent to run the affairs of the towns in our absence. She will even take my place at the Grande Council of Kings. Of course," I looked at King Lachlan, "if any situation arises where I am needed here, Jane will let me know, and I promise you all that I will come and handle the situation. I have no intention of abandoning Nuadilan and Amathon."

Relief was the general emotion I felt from the folks. A great weight was lifted from their day-to-day concerns. I continued, "Additionally, you've heard the King Emil Amir and his family were also assassinated a couple days after Caitlyn. I am very pleased to announce that the Guardian Healer Mary was able to save Cathleen Amir. At this moment, she is in a very safe place recovering from her near death experience. She has asked Jane temporarily to be the steward for her kingdom just east of us. When she has recovered, Queen Cathleen will return to her beloved towns and people. Until she does, Jane is also representing her kingdom on the Grande Council of Kings. During this brief time period, Jane will have two votes, one for this kingdom and one for Emil's."

"Finally, Jane has asked me to spread the word that she wishes to resume the weekly Queen's Advisory Council, starting tomorrow. So please let all the representatives know, show up at the Great Hall at one tomorrow. In closing, I wish to thank all you who have helped us at this horrible time of loss. I'm told that many of you have prepared a feast to honor Queen Caitlyn. Lunch is being served now by the remnants of the South Gate. May we observe a minute of silence to honor Queen Caitlyn Amir, whose reign may have been short, but it was honest and true." Utter silence fell for a minute, after which, folks walked passed me, said their condolences, and headed across town for the feast. Actually, for me this was the second hardest part. Fianna held onto my hand, I just let my tears of grief flow. Piffle on formality.

During the brief break, while Nuadilan's folks left and those of Amathon arrived, King Lachlan came close. She said rather awkwardly, "I'm very sorry for her death. She was a great queen. I had thought that we would need to discuss matters, but you cleverly gave us all that we need to know. Thank you. Until we meet again," she held out her hand and gave me a hearty shake. She also shook Jane's hand, sizing her up. Because of the rain, it was hard to tell tears from the warm rain, so Lachlan wisely took her leave.

An hour later, I went through the same speech with similar results. The only difference was the prepared feast was in Amathon, some five miles away. I promised that I would drop in on the feast later on once the actual burial was finished.

The actual burial, a very private affair, was the hardest for me to endure. Yes, it helped a lot to know that Caitlyn was all right and would be with me as my son in the days to come. However, seeing her lifeless body dressed in her finest, royal dress brought uncontrollable tears to my eyes. Putting her body into the ground had a finality to it, dispelling any wild imaginations that she would recover and be well.

The High Priest of the Church of the Blessed Holy Mother spoke briefly to me when this final act was finished. "King Ket, it is the wishes of all the churches in both towns that once we have built our new stone cathedral, her remains shall be moved into a Holy Vault especially prepared for her." I nodded agreement, for my grief was overwhelming me at the time.

Thank god for the feasts! I found that eating, drinking, and introducing Jane and her family to the power leaders of each town allow me to get my mind extroverted from its heavy introversion upon so failing Caitlyn. That night, we packed up and began heading for Emil's towns. Fergus, Fianna, and his escort rode with us until we were safely within the town walls.

The next day, we went through the same routine for each of his two towns, Bedwyn and Brea, Layamon. However, this time, I was not so overwhelmed by personal grief, even though Emil was my son, last lifetime. Enough time and space had separated us so the grief was nowhere near as bad as it was for my wife, Caitlyn. I discovered that rumors were running rampant throughout both towns, some saying several escaped the assassination plot, and others saying all were dead but that not all bodies had been found. Hence, hearty cheering resulted when I told them about Cathleen and her wishes.

When the services were finished, I asked one of Emil's staff to fetch me Cathleen's boyfriend, Augar Agar. An hour later, a bashful lad of seventeen was ushered into Emil's Great Hall. He was tall, but very nervous, probably expecting some drastic punishment was about to be doled out to him. "Come Augar, sit with us. We won't bite." He hesitatingly sat at a chair at the opposite end of the huge table, as far from us as he could get. I chuckled, "This won't do at all, Jane." Together, we moved down and sat on either side of him, making him all the more nervous.

"Augar, I have a very special message from Cathleen for you." Suddenly, his eyes brightened up, his cheeks flushed; life began to flow within him. We were not about to punish him, he'd decided. "Cathleen is now on the mainland in a very safe, but hidden place where she is recovering. She is very weak, but the Healer Mary has assured me that she will make a full recovery. I spoke to Cathleen just before I left to come to Cymry, just a couple days ago. She still wants to go ahead with your marriage, if you will still have her. As her closest relative, I give my blessing on this marriage, as long as you will honestly prepare yourself for the role you will have to assume once you two are wed."

"Honest? We can? How soon? When can I see her? I'm been in utter agony for days now, worrying about her. I kept hoping she was not killed. I've said hundreds of prayers to the Blessed Holy Mother each and every day."

"When she has recovered enough, we will see that you are taken to her. Just now, she is very, very weak. If you marry her, you have to assume the duties and role of king, you know. Jane, here, will help you learn how to be a good ruler. However, marrying Cathleen presents an even greater challenge for you. Once those who attempted to kill Emil and his family learn that they failed to kill Cathleen, undoubtedly, they will make another attempt. So, my young lad, if you marry her, you are going to have to be able to protect her from these evil assassins."

"I know how to handle a sword a little. I promise to work out and practice every day. I will defend Cathleen with my life!" Augar exclaimed with enthusiasm.

"Ah, I knew you would. However, listen to Jane's teachings; you can learn a lot from her. We Guardians will never be too far from you, and you can count on our support when needed." I suspected none of this really made much sense. Augar was just a love-struck boy, soon to be forced into manhood rather abruptly. I left Jane chatting with Augar and headed back to Nuadilan that night. Two days later, the ship which brought us to Bregia and was paid to wait for me to return, sailed back to Calgary with me and the others of my Circle as the only passengers, a rather expensive trip.

For two days, I played with my twins, changed their diapers, and tried to fulfill my duties as a father. Interestingly, Lilly Ann had moved her living quarters here into the nursery. I learned from a midwife, that ever since I left, Lilly Ann had been doting upon the twins. "Aren't they just adorable?" Lilly Ann cheerily said when I walked in after their morning naps, intending to hold and play with them. "They are really alert for a while after their naps. Here, you want to hold Tegid and Taliesin?" Like a mother, she carefully handed me each boy, hovering over me as if I might drop them.

For two relaxing days, I did nothing but chat with Lilly Ann and play with my babies. Good therapy, I thought. Late that second day, John Henry interrupted us. From the severe look upon his face, bordering upon an outright grimace, I knew that something was up. "Excuse me, Ket. I must have a word with you now. My spies have just reported seeing the black assassins in Calgary. Further, they have been making inquiries about Sarah Amir Penton!

Last report had them on the road to their town, Middleton, which is on the Centurion roadway that runs across the Greenway. Percival has already been notified."

Suddenly angry, I burst out, "Let's ride! I have a debt to settle right now!"

"Yes, yes," John Henry said rather boringly, a clever way to calm me down. "There is even more news."

Okay, anger gave way to curiosity, "Well, out with it man!" I said rather antagonistically.

"We've intercepted a message. It seems before this assassin left Calgary, he sent a letter via a Sea Prince ship. Arthur intercepted it, but could not read it. He made an exact copy and then let the captain sail with the original letter. Considering the urgency, I made a Mind Link between Arthur and our best linguist. Unfortunately, the best guess we have is that it is written in the ancient Arad language. Arthur is already on his way here with his copy. I had hoped that you could look at it and see if it can be deciphered. It may well give us vital knowledge on what action we should optimally take with these assassins. Rushing in and killing them might not be the best route to follow."

His Wid was showing. He was trying to deftly appeal to my position as Wid of the Cymry Circle. He did not want to take brash actions just yet without knowing the full picture, if such could be learned from this letter. I had not even noticed, but Lilly Ann had already carefully taken each twin from my arms. I suddenly realized their absence. I looked at her and she grinned back at me, curious, I thought, and considerate.

"Okay, let's get an army ready to ride and then wait for this letter. I want to get these vile men while we have the chance!" I declared. Together, we headed for the stables, where John Henry had already issued orders for an assemblage. I found one hundred Guardians already there, saddling up, armed to the teeth.

A tense, anxious hour passed before Arthur came galloping at top speed into our fortress, his horse nearly spent, poor thing. He handed me the copy he had made. "Well done, Arthur. Very well done indeed!" I exclaimed, and genuinely meant it.

"Thanks, sir. I figured this might be vitally important," Arthur replied and then went to see about getting a fresh mount; no way was he going to miss this battle! He was a Protector.

I opened the parchment and spread it out. What a mess. Imagine that you have a letter written in a foreign language with foreign letters and must make a copy of it. All the subtleties of the written word are easily overlooked. It was a mess. I had not seen this writing for a long time. Memories came back to me from last lifetime, when as a young girl I had been allowed to help the Holy Prophets write down all their teachings for Jes. I was essentially just a scribe then, but I quickly became adept at writing in their ancient Arad language.

Pope Yazi I

Supreme Prelate Thraxton

I humbly report that our problem is rapidly disappearing. As I reported in the last message, three Houses remain. I can report that the House of Ahmad has ended at last. Likewise, the House of Emil has also been terminated. The House of Sarah, I have just found out, is on the mainland in a land called the Greenway, a place of a dozen petty kingdoms. This house has five living members. Arthur, Beth Ann, Lilly Ann, and Justus have been added to our search list accordingly. I am on my way to terminate these last remnants of that Unholiness that besmears God. I shall not fail. As is the Mano del Dio way, once finished, I will backtrack to verify this Holy Task that God has ordered is complete.

Prelate Karlos
3 Oct 523

"You were right, Ket! The arm of this Pope has grown long indeed, reaching way up here to the Greenway, nearly in secret!" John Henry commented. "Now we must think, Ket; what is the optimum course of action to take."

"We cannot let him backtrack. That will put Cathleen and the twins in dire peril," I replied.

"No, we can't allow that. Let me think a moment, you too Ket." John Henry began contemplating, as I should; after all I am a Wid too. I relaxed as best I could and began to examine possible avenues of approaching this problem.

"You know, we should make some use of the fact that this Karlos fellow sends back reports on his work in progress," I mused.

"I've got an idea, Ket. You know that Mont Blanc has a Judger spell upon it so that it is not visible to outsiders. How about this idea? We let Percival and others tell Karlos that Sarah and the children have all gone to Mont Blanc. Let this data be readily known, as it currently is in Southway. Let Karlos have general directions to this place. When he gets here, he sees nothing but the mountainside. A likely conclusion he may come to is that saying that they have gone to Mont Blanc may be the local's way of saying that they have perished. He may decide they are dead and then begin to backtrack, picking up a boat to Cymry."

"We would need to aid his thinking along that path," I added grasping the wisdom of such a deceit. "Perhaps one of us could be out there herding sheep when the black carriage arrives. We could create an illusionary graveyard to add to the myth," I added.

"Excellent. If they think that Sarah and the children are dead, they will leave them alone. Now, I can arrange to have only one ship in Calgary when they arrive seeking passage to Cymry. That will be our special ship with us onboard. Hopefully, he will dash off another report and give us, pretending to be Sea Prince sailors, the charge of delivering it. We take the letter, and the ship mysteriously disappears at sea, but the letter gets delivered," John Henry explained.

"Can we really afford to sink a Sea Prince ship?" I asked. I liked the plan, but the cost could be prohibitive.

"There is an old abandoned ship on the coast that we can salvage and sink. We can either kill them outright or stage an accident. Of course, we will have another boat standing by to rescue us. How many crew does a Sea Prince ship normally have?" he asked.

"Six, counting the captain," I replied. "I should be the captain. I've had the most experience on Sea Prince ships."

"Hey, I get to be the Shipper," Arthur butted in, "Remember, I was the one who intercepted the first letter. I know how this letter sending is done." I grinned. Arthur, like me, did not want to be left out of the action.

"Okay, Ket, pick your crew, but one must be a Judger to help with the illusion. The rest must be Protectors. I'm not sending out unprotected our most valuable Wid to deal with an assassin group!"

While I went about choosing Protectors, John Henry went to see about the other details. Percival was informed to tell somberly any that asked that his wife and children had gone to Mont Blanc some weeks ago, which was the truth. Next, we fielded our best Judger, highly skilled in illusions, to be the shepherd, one Samuel Farmington. I watched him dress for the part and then ride out to gather up some sheep to pretend to be herding.

When I told my Circle what the grand plan was going to be, Paul insisted that he be one of the Protectors with me. I couldn't turn him down. Pete, who had been with Caitlyn during my absence, begged to be given an opportunity to regain his honor. I picked three others, including Henry Alabaster Donegal, the Moon Circle's Judger. He would be our helmsman, because from that position, he could keep an eye on the entire ship. Robert Roy Randell, my son from my first lifetime, also begged to come along; he was also from the Moon Circle. Thus, I had two very experienced men along with the mostly youthful crew. As soon as I had my crew, we raced off to Calgary to find this ship and see if we could get it ready to sail.

I found a rotting hulk of a ship. Yes, the Molly had been abandoned on our shores last year. However, I found that John Henry had not been idle. Fifteen shipwrights soon appeared, and together, we got the Molly ready for her last voyage. Soon, I was barking orders to my crew as we sailed her up and around into the docks. That was a fiasco, since only I knew how to sail. Thankfully, Paul had been observant on our voyage, and he had a good idea what needed to be done, giving instructions to the other crew. As we came in to dock, I noticed that all the other ships were just setting sail; most rode high in the water, unloaded, highly unusual for Sea Prince ships. Later I learned that John Henry paid each captain fifty gold coins to sail out from Calgary this night and back tomorrow night. Easy money for these enterprising captains and their crew. We spent the idle waiting hours practicing our sailing skills. I wanted to put on a believable show; it wouldn't do for these men to become suspicious immediately.

Samuel looked at the morning sky. "Another beautiful fall day, sheep," he said to his flock. He was standing at the junction, where the road from Southway, which ran on down into the d'Grange Sector, was joined with the road from Calgary. Actually, the road from Calgary continued on eastward straight to our complex. However, the protective illusions cast so long ago made the road appear to be just more of the barren, rocky hillside of Mont Blanc. He walked a little this way and then that way, keeping the sheep more or less near the junction. They, of course, wanted to head on out to find the sparse grasses which grew between the rocks. "Time enough for all that once your job is done, my wooly creatures. Get back in line."

Around ten, a dozen riders and one black carriage came speeding up the road from the Southway. "Time for you to do your job, little sheeps," Samuel teased them. As expected, here at the crossroads, the riders reined in. "G'day to you, strangers," Samuel drawled as if he were a shepherd who had not had human company for some time. "Head'n for Calgary? It's that way," he said pointing to the side branch that led to the largest city in the Greenway.

The carriage door opened and out stepped a man dressed in black robes with a white blockish cross emblazoned on its front and back. The man stared off toward where Mont Blanc was located, but saw only the uninhabited, rough countryside and the small cemetery illusion. "Greeting, sir," Samuel drawled towards this man. "Looking for something? Calgary is that way. Of course, there is always d'Grange, a long way that away."

In a broken Greenway filled with a heavy Centurion accent, the man's cold voice spoke to Samuel, "I was told that some people from Middleton, Southway, had gone to Mont Blanc. I am trying to find them, a religious matter."

"Aye, where they are, they not be needing a priest such as yourself any longer. Only thing that is out here is yonder cemetery. It's what we locals mean when we say that someone's gone off to Mont Blanc, ya see." The man took a few steps toward the cemetery, stared long at it, and returned to his coach.

Just as he stepped inside the coach, he barked orders, "Our business here is finished. Back to Calgary. Make haste, soon we head for home." He slammed the coach door shut. Without another word, the small party turned left onto the road to Calgary. They would reach it within a couple hours. Once the men were out of sight, John Henry contacted Samuel to find out if the ruse worked. He then relayed the news to Ket.

"Ship to Cymry? Aye sir, only one in dock is the Molly. She has no shipping orders yet; those be in next week. Only ship in dock and available right now," Arthur, disguised as the Port Master replied to the man in black robes. "Cost the same as your last trip," he added, not knowing what that might be, and cleverly bypassing it.

"Here's your ten coins. I've another letter to post to Megalos, same as the last one?" the cold voice said in very crude Greenway dialect.

"Aye sir. Put it on the next ship to Megalos, which ought to be docking here to load grain in the next couple of days. You're lucky to find any ship available right now, harvest time, grain being shipped everywhere. Busy season." Arthur accepted the twenty additional coins, the cost of sending a letter all the way to Megalos, via Sea Prince ship. Arthur turned and yelled to Ket, "Captain Jack. Got a small job for you."

I walked down the gangplank to Arthur and Karlos. I resisted the urge to kill this murder on the spot. "Aye, sir. Where'll it be?" Arthur removed one gold coin from the pouch, handing me the remainder.

"Take these gentlemen over to Cymry. Bregia is the best port to unload a carriage, that be all right with you sir?" he asked Karlos.

"Yes, when do we sail?" Karlos asked coldly.

"As soon as we get you on board. Want to be back to take a load of grain south soonest," I replied.

Slowly, we got their carriage onto the ship and the horses lowered into the cargo hold and secured. Now came the trickiest part: could we actually sail this thing well enough not to rouse their suspicions? The mooring lines were thrown off; two crew members rapidly coiled them up. I began barking out the orders that I had often heard Felix use. Admittedly, we were a little slow on getting all the proper actions done. However, Karlos and his men quickly accepted the offer of free wine in the cabin area. Hence, they didn't get to see us rather crudely set sail.

I was pleased that we actually did get the heavily patched and rotting mainsail raised, the lines trimmed, and began tacking out into the open ocean. Of course, most of this was totally Paul's and my doing. Once we had the ship properly sailing and a good distance at sea, I went to see our passengers. "Afraid a storm is coming; might get a little rough," I warned them. In fact, with over two hundred druwids pulling in a storm, how could it not occur and soon? Probably it was the fastest appearing squall ever.

Now the Protector's plan was very simple. Get the men on deck to watch the approaching squall and the land slowly receding. Then, they would use their push spells to force each man overboard. In the water, they would bring down lightning bolts to eliminate them. None wanted to risk any kind of close quarters combat with an assassin and his poisons. It was my job to get them back on deck. "Nice view of the distant squall, rainbow even. Nice sight." That did the trick. Several men, having drunk a good deal of wine, staggered onto the deck. I pointed out the incoming squall line.

The three protectors lined up behind the six men and combined their push spells. Honestly, those six never knew what happened. One minute they were looking over the side at the incoming squall line; the next minute they were flying out over the water. Now I yelled, "Man overboard! Man overboard! Drop the mainsail. Right starboard full." Quickly, the Protectors untied the main lines holding the mainsail taught, the sail now began billowing and flapping in the increasing wind. Slowly the ship lost speed and began a hard right turn.

As expected the remaining four men plus Karlos scampered up the rotting stairs. "They fell overboard back yonder. We are turning around to pick them up. No problem. Too much wine, no sea legs. See if you can throw them a mooring line in the meantime," I acted the part of a concerned sea captain. Once more, as the five scrambled to the side to see, the combined push spells detonated. Karlos went to join his companions. Paul kept a steady eye on the bobbing, flailing men, especially Karlos. Meanwhile, I issued the orders that brought us around so that we could get a bit closer to them. Slowly we came to a dead stop.

"I can see all eleven of them," Paul commented. "Are we ready for the next step?" All five of them lined up along the starboard side, waiting for me to join them. As I walked up beside them, he said, "Ket, I leave Karlos to you. Give him his due. Okay, lightning bolt time, everyone. Fire at will." Five lightning bolts arced down from the sky; five men bounced, jerked up and somewhat out of the water, and then slowly sank lifeless to the bottom of the sea. Once more, five arced and the remainder joined them.

I stared at this vile assassin. I wanted him dead, no doubt about that. Something was wrong. No matter what I did, I could not make the connection to the black energy clouds above. It was as if I had never known how to bring down lightning! Paul turned and looked at me, waiting for me to blast Karlos. The others were waiting for me to finish off the assassin. Paul had to act. He knew something was wrong with his Wid. He later confessed he thought I was still in grief over Caitlyn and Emil's death. With a quick spell, Paul brought the final bolt down, ending the life of this assassin from the Pope. Paul, pretending that nothing was wrong, said, "Okay, now it's time to scuttle Molly here. Have we a plan for sinking her?"

With a flushed face, I came to my senses. "Yes, let's use your push spells to bust a gaping hole in the rotting sides down below the water line. Bit risky, got to get up and off the ship fast once she starts taking water. Henry, you lend me a hand getting the dingy launched." Quickly, we six set to work. Henry and I had the dingy in the water and ready to go when we heard a loud noise, and the whole ship lurched. Shortly four Protectors came running as fast as they could.

"I think we over did it," yelled Paul, as the Molly began rolling over in the water. All four Protectors had to jump for it. As fast as possible, Henry and I fished each one out and into the crowded dingy. By the time that all were safely onboard, the Molly was gone. She had sunk very rapidly indeed. I unfurled the small sail and set a course for the docks. By now, four Sea Prince ships were sailing back to dock, their one day excursion finished, and they wanted to dock before the squall hit. One pulled alongside and offered us a ride.

"Molly went down fast," I explained to the captain.

"You fools, Molly was not even seaworthy anymore! Whatever possessed you to take her out?" the captain bellowed.

"Stupid men from Megalos insisted that we get them to Cymry immediately. Would not take no for an answer," I lied convincingly. Now the

224

talk centered on the fools from Megalos.

Arthur entrusted the final report to Yazi to the next ship sailing for Megalos, along with the report of the loss of the Molly and all on board. Yazi would have something to ponder. Of course, Arthur had made a copy of that final report. Riding in a covered coach back to Mont Blanc, I took the time to read it.

Pope Yazi I
Supreme Prelate Thraxton

I humbly report that our problem has been handled fully. The House of Sarah has already passed beyond Tarra. A few weeks ago all five went to Mont Blanc. I went there to discover only a rocky, barren, mountain cemetery. I did not search for a cause of death. Thus, the whore-begotten are no more. Yet, as is the Mano del Dio way, I am backtracking to West Reach to verify. Expect final confirmation within two weeks.

Prelate Karlos
8 Oct 523

What was this Mano del Dio thing? Roughly translated, it meant Hand of God. Was there a church within a church? I had no answer and no way to find that out at present. It was consoling to all that it would be January at the earliest before this report along with the report of the sinking of the Molly reached Yazi. No matter what he did next, the heirs had a period of complete safety until at least next spring. A half year without fear was better than nothing.

Later that night, I briefed my Circle on what had happened. Naturally, everyone wondered why I had not slain the assassin and had let Paul finish him off. Red faced, I had no choice but to level with my Circle; after all I was their Wid, and we all depended upon one another. "I honestly tried to bring down lightning, but nothing happened, nothing at all." My face was burning hot. "It is almost as if I have completely forgotten how to do this."

Cheerily, Beth Ann said, "No problem, Ket. I'm sure that we all can help you relearn it. Besides, you are at Mont Blanc, the center for learning stuff. You have hundreds around you now that can teach you again. See, no problem."

The next day, Paul tried to work with me on it. Later, each of my Circle lent their hands at it. Two days later, the "news" was all over Mont Blanc, "Ket cannot use lightning anymore!" I admit that this was a first for us druwids. Never in our history had an active member suddenly lost their ability to bring down lightning, once learned. Since I was also the lightning king, this was all the more newsworthy. Daily, I began to become more and more self-conscious, more and more moody.

One day, while I was playing with my twins, Lilly Ann asked me straight out, "Ket, does this lightning thing have anything to do with your killing those four Axemen during the attack on Nuadilan?" Her sudden question took me by complete surprise!

My instant answer was, "Yes." I looked at her, and she, me. I believe that she understood me better than I did at that moment.

She said, "I understand. Let me work on it and get back to you later on." At least someone had some idea what was wrong with me. Strange that it was Lilly Ann.

Chapter 17 Counter-plans

It was August 21, 623 when Pope Yazi I called a special meeting of his Bishops and the Rooster. He was more somber than the Rooster had ever seen him, a sure sign that there was severe trouble somewhere. Quickly, the Rooster mentally reviewed all the actions and data of which he was aware. The only item that seemed potentially troublesome was the sudden elimination of all the priests of the vulgar Church of Jehosanity up in Zargarb last July. The Rooster decided that he needed more data and quietly sat in his usual corner of the room, as inconspicuously as possible.

"Gentlemen, I have called this meeting because I have made a terrible mistake that must be rectified at once. I know what you all think; Yazi never makes mistakes. Unfortunately, in my haste, I have made a grave miscalculation, one that I ought to have foreseen. As a test, can anyone here venture a guess what my mistake was?" Complete silence. "Anyone care to hazard a guess where this mistake occurred? Come on gentlemen, don't be shy; surely one of you has also seen this mistake in the making." More silence.

"May I humbly query if this mistake occurred in Zargarb?" the creaking voice of the Rooster filled the room, even though he was trying desperately to whisper it, scarcely daring to speak openly before all these Holy Men.

A broad grin instantly lined the aged face of Yazi. Once more, his prized pupil was keenly correct, whereas his many Bishops were not. "Precisely, Supreme Prelate Thraxton. Precisely. Bishops, observe yet again, that our esteemed Chief of Security can see what you have not. Zargarb, indeed. I admit that when I heard that the Holy Paladins completely botched their assignment and lost the Holy Crosses along with the Archdeacons, I acted in anger and haste, without thinking it through. Recall that I issued orders for Karlos to have them infiltrate all the towns, disguised as visitors. There, they sought out the churches and priests, learning their habits. On July 4, all would then slay these vulgar butchers of our religion. As you know, that mission was carried out with complete success. On the 5th, the entire Church of Jehosanity Northern Orthodoxy was eliminated from Zargarb."

One Bishop offered, "Yes, we all thought that was a brilliant plan, Pope Yazi. Brilliant."

"However, that plan had and has a fatal flaw. We left a total vacuum. We know they had a large following in Zargarb. Reports coming in now indicate that new lay have stepped up to fill that vacuum, preaching what they have heard in the past. Still the Holy Relics lie beyond our reach. Burned churches are simply being rebuilt. What then was my mistake? Anyone care to guess?"

"Ah ha! I see," said Bishop Silas, who had his eye on taking Yazi's place as Pope after Yazi went to join Jehosa. "We ought to have sent in a flock of our own priests to take over and fill that vacuum!"

Finally, someone can think! Thought Yazi to himself. "Precisely so. Now we must struggle to regain our lost momentum. Any ideas as to how we can correct my blunder?" he asked, certain he already knew what they would say. He was not disappointed. No one had any real ideas.

Instead of squirming, one bright Bishop asked, "What news from Karlos? Has he located any of the whore-children?"

"His last report was that he was already two-thirds across the Sea Princes and still no sign of them. Evidently and not unexpectedly, the prostitute got as far from the Arad as possible. I would not be surprised if she went all the way to West Reach. Anyway, think about our problem today. Let's meet tomorrow morning and see if we can find a way out of this mess I have created with my blunder." The Bishops were very willing to break up. The Rooster, on the other hand, sat in the room long after the last man had left. If the crosses were stored in some secret place here in Megalos, the Rooster would not hesitate to retrieve them, such was his skill. However, deformed as he was, not speaking Sea Prince, and not knowing the city and its customs and people, the Rooster had to think more than twice about such a venture.

He knew that the last reported sightings of these Holy Relics was when the Sisterhood riders brought them through the city gates shortly after the Holy Paladins completely bungled their job. Chances were good that this Sisterhood was hiding them in secret for the Church. That this was a likely conclusion was demonstrated by the fact that no trace of the Holy Relics had been found when the Holy Paladins searched the churches after killing the priests who lived in the nearby rectories. The Rooster knew nothing about this Sisterhood group, save history told that, when the original invasion of the Sea Princes began half a century ago, five hundred of these women warriors nearly defeated the Centurion army, inflicting heavy casualties upon them. That no other serious losses were subsequently sustained throughout the rest of the lengthy campaign made an impression on his calculating mind. There was something powerful about this Sisterhood, a force to be reckoned with.

He reasoned that sheer force alone would not accomplish Pope Yazi I's objectives. Zargarb was now a walled city, which dictated a lengthy and costly siege. Besides, supplies could very easily be brought in by sea. No, there ought to be some other way of retrieving these Holy Relics. If only this were not a women-only organization, he thought. "Think, Rooster, the Holy Father is depending upon you!" he chastised himself.

He reasoned thusly. If pressure were somehow brought to bear to have the guardians of the Holy Relics put them on display to show them off, then perhaps an opportunity to seize them would present itself. On the other hand, if he, the Rooster, had these relics, he would not be so bold to allow himself to be coerced into a public showing. Oh no, he would be far more devious. "I'd make copies of them and show them, never the actual Holy Relics!" he said aloud. So if the Sisterhood were forced to present these relics for a public display, certainly what they displayed would be copies, not the originals. Then, another idea struck him. Not unless the relics that the Sisterhood had were themselves fakes! What if the Archdeacon used trickery upon the attacking Holy Paladins? What if they allowed all to see the copies of the relics being safely escorted into Zargarb, while they secretly moved the relics to some other safe location? "Ah, this bit of deviousness would be what I might do," he commented aloud to himself.

At the next morning's meeting, silence filled the room after Yazi asked for suggestions. At last, the Rooster spoke up. "History tells us that this Sisterhood is both intelligent and powerful. I suggest that there are two distinct possibilities. One, the Sisterhood actually does have our Holy Relics secreted away under their protection. If forced to present these relics for public display, they would either present the real relics, which we could then have the opportunity to seize, or they would present fake copies, hoping that no one could tell the difference. I contend that they would not take the risk of being exposed by displaying fakes; they would lose too much face if discovered. Two, the Sisterhood never did have our Holy Relics. Rather, a clever ruse was perpetrated on everyone. While the Sisterhood brought fake relics into Zargarb, the Arch-deacon secretly took them elsewhere and cleverly hid them."

"Brilliant! Positively brilliant, Supreme Prelate Thraxton," exclaimed Pope Yazi I with enthusiasm he seldom displayed. "Now here is what we are going to do," and he launched into a lengthy, detailed discussion.

Chapter 18 Jahdi of Arad

Qa Jahdi was now twenty-one, strong and virile. If the ancient Messiahs still existed, Jahdi may well have been one of them, but the Messiahs and the Holy Prophets of ancient Arad were just as long gone, forgotten, and forsaken, as was the Great Messiah. The messiahs were all killed during the three day uprising against the Infidels, their Centurion overlords. After the devastating invasions of the barbarians from the Northern Steppes, gone too were the prophets, as well as the majority of the faithful Arads. They left behind the poor, the weak, and the helpless, or so Jahdi believed. These pitiful few prayed to Jehosa for deliverance, but saw none, only more invasions, more looting, more pillaging, more raping, and more devastation. Life became that of the barest survival possible out here in the arid desert mesa land known as Juda Arad.

Even now in 623, the Arad was continually subjected to attacks from the horsemen from the steppes, the newest arrivals, the Axemen from the far north, the Centurions, who controlled the southern edge of the Arad in an iron glove, the religious warriors from Megalos calling themselves Holy Paladins, but really just Relic Hunters, and the Old Man of the Mountain, a secret assassin sect. All semblance of town life evaporated like the sands in a dust storm. To stay in a known town was tantamount to a death sentence these days. Out of sheer necessity, the last inhabitants of the Arad moved in secret out into the desert mesa lands, where no roads ran and water was scarce.

Ten of these new communities existed as far as Jahdi knew, and he should know, for he alone had covered the length and breadth of the Arad these past few years. Among his people, Qa Jahdi was known as the freedom fighter. Beginning with nothing but pitchforks, Jahdi and his friends ambushed the unwary, leaving none living when they departed, having confiscated precious food, clothing, horses, and especially prized, weapons. Each new victory, however small, brought greater and greater survival potential to Jahdi's ever-growing band of fighters. As his supply of weapons grew, so Jahdi grew even bolder, now taking on both the Holy Paladins and the barbarians from the steppes, gaining an even better supply of horses.

Qa Jahdi ruled the mesa fortress known as Al Tarn, located southeast of ancient Jerilum, the central city long abandoned to the desert and the continuous searching of the Relic Hunters. Mesa land had a unique geography. Coming from the east, the rough desert land rose sharply to a mesa peak. Abruptly, the edge gave way to a sheer drop of sometimes nearly five hundred feet to the valley below. A select few of these mesa cliffs had natural caverns at their base. Here is where the desolate, desperate people of the Arad chose to make their new homes. Nestled within these caverns, they built adobe and stone buildings, shielded largely from the outside. Around the outer valley perimeter, over the years, they built adobe and stone walls twelve feet high, with tiered steps on the inside, from which they could defend their small habitations.

Al Tarn now held three thousand inhabitants and an equal number of horses. A Council of Ten ruled the town in domestic matters only. Qa Jahdi alone ruled in all other matters, for he was the Jaifur or Supreme Ruler. He counted some eight hundred men and women in his fighter group, another two hundred men, both young and old, serving as the garrison force for the town, along with another three hundred women fighters. The remainder, mostly women and children, handled all the domestic duties. Yes, many Arad women had now taken up the sword in order to survive.

In fact, Qa Jahdi's wife, Zeta, was perhaps one of the best female fighters in all the Arad! Her blood lust against all invaders was second only to Qa's. They rode into battle side by side, each trusting the other with their life. Many times now, this duo had proved themselves mighty in courage and skill.

Qa stood tall and wiry, with long black hair, beard, and moustache. His powerful arm muscles bulging, his black piercing eyes took in everything. Others who gazed upon this fighter shrank back in fear, so strong was his blood lust intentions. Zeta, though a few inches shorter than her husband, displayed an equally formidable appearance with her waist length black hair tied into a ponytail, fair face with jet black eyes and full lips and bosom. Yes, she was fair to look upon, until your eyes met hers. Only then did the fierceness of her hatred and anger against invaders cast all other thoughts from your mind, replaced by a cold fear only slightly less than Qa's!

Qa and Zeta had just returned from a meeting with the fighters in Tal Mazda, another of these mesa towns about twenty-five miles to the north and west of Al Tarn. Dismounting, he and Zeta strutted up to the ten robed, council members. All raised their right hand to the sky, their formal welcome greeting. "It's done," Jahdi barked crisply. "Masai has agreed to join forces under my command. This brings the last town into our fold!"

Zeta added solemnly, "Now the combined strength of all ten shall strike terror and fear to all invaders!" She spat on the ground. "Break out the wine, for tonight we celebrate! As of now, no one can withstand Jaifur Jahdi! Tonight marks a new era for the Arad!"

The council members clapped, greatly relieved that all had gone well. Some had feared that the fiercely independent Masai would not agree to Qa's terms. Yet, Qa and Zeta had been persuasive and done the impossible. Jaifur Jahdi would now have another five hundred under his command, making his the strongest force in all the Arad at this time, indeed a great cause for jubilant celebration.

Nasal sounding reeds accompanied by pounding dumbecks opened the celebration. Women danced about the enormous courtyard located between the wall and the cliff. Young girls and many men joined them. Every soul here knew what this meant: they would indeed survive far better; the promise of more food, more wine, more clothes, more weapons — all this would come to them, perhaps now in very short order.

Carrying a bottle of wine and some leftover chicken legs, Qa followed Zeta into their cavern home. A twinkle in her eye and a sultry curl of her lip, Qa knew what that meant! Their home, as all the others here, was adobe/stone construction, small in size, just two rooms. One room served as kitchen and pantry; the other, their bedroom and living room. Seldom did either spend much time inside, however. The walls were mud plastered smooth, and the floor was the stone floor of the mesa. Hides and furs covered their bedroom floor and a large cache of various weapons lay neatly stacked near the doorway, which consisted of a loose wool rug covering the entrance. While Zeta lit several oil lamps, Qa finished off his chicken, washing the grease away with several slurps of the red wine from Zargarb.

"Give me that," Zeta grabbed the bottle. After taking a long drink herself, she pulled Qa down upon the furs. They embraced passionately. The hour was indeed late before these two finally went to sleep that night.

The next morning, Zeta woke her husband, saying, "Welcome Jaifur Qa Jahdi to the first day of the new year!"

"What are you babbling about, Zeta?" he growled. He'd drunk too much wine last night and his head throbbed.

"First day of your reign, that's what," she explained.

"Oh," he said, rubbing his head with both hands. "We best see to it that the new year starts out right then, hadn't we?" He gave her a slap on her butt; she, a kick on his rear. They both stumbled outside to meet the new day.

Middle August was the exceptionally hot time of year here in the Arad. Already his eight hundred or so fighters were rousing and preparing for the coming battle. Each rider carried a number of water skins, for this time, there would be few chances to stop at water holes. The campaign was about to commence. By ten, the fighters from the four more southerly towns had arrived, and Jahdi ordered his to mount up. As they rode north, fighters from the remaining five other towns would join up with this swarm. By the end of the day, Jaifur Jahdi received the official count: his army was fully eight thousand strong, all mounted, all provisioned, and all expectant of great rewards for this joint effort.

Once the last group had merged with this large armada, Jahdi called for a brief halt. While Zeta held his reins, Jahdi stood on his saddle and yelled to the encircled mass of fighters. "Today, we become the single-most power in the Arad." The men and women yelled and cheered. "We ride north. First stop is the encampment of the Blue Coats, the Relic Hunters. Decimate them!" More yelling and cheering. "We ride through them and then on to our true destination: Florintine Junction. In four days' time, we take that town and all its supplies." Now they cheered with wild abandon. They rode north for the next three days, heading for the main encampment of the Holy Paladins from Megalos.

For several months, the Holy Paladins had been using a large watering hole south and east of the Junction as their base of operations. The July 4 infiltration had been entirely successful, well except for the recovery of the

Holy Relics. Although they had slain every priest, looted, and burned every church, no trace of the priceless relics was found. On the morning of the 18, nearly two hundred of these religious fighters of Pope Yazi I were milling around the encampment; the others were away on other duties.

Without warning, the holy warriors heard the thundering hooves of a large group of cavalry. At first, they half expected to hear their friends were returning. However, their lookouts began screaming something about wild men. Pandemonium broke out in their camp, and men ran for weapons and horses, although not a single horse was saddled before the attack reached them. Within minutes, wild, insane yelling, like thousands of voices, high pitched, filled their ears. It was a sound unlike any these men had ever heard. The army of Jadhi was indeed shrieking in high falsetto cries, designed to strike fear in their opponents, which it did in this case.

Eight thousand screaming riders swarmed like locusts across the entire southern side of their encampment, swords reflecting the hot morning sun. Realizing there was no time for mounting, the general ordered his terror-stricken men to form up a battle line, but it was too late. Galloping, frenzied riders smashed into their midst, swords swinging this way and that. Right on through their encampment, they continued to ride, without turning back. No need to, wave after wave followed right behind Jahdi's initial sweep. In less than two minutes, the Blue Coats oozed red, none alive. As ordered, fifty fighters wheeled around to ransack the encampment, seizing the much needed horses, supplies, and weapons. These raiders even stripped the buttons off clothing! Anything of value was confiscated; leaving the dead bodies for the desert scavengers, the fifty headed back to Al Tarn to await the return of the army and obtain their share of the well-deserved spoils, supplies that would see them through another long winter.

Early the next morning, Sister Nicki, on long-range scouting for the Sisterhood forces in Florintine Junction, spotted the rapidly moving army of Jaifur Jahdi. The path they were following could only make the Junction their target. Leaping into her saddle while her horse began moving, she hit a canter before her feet finally found the stirrups. Rapidly, she spied other scouts and frantically gave the immediate danger signs as she dashed past their positions. Minutes later, she came into the Junction at top speed, nearly mowing down a half dozen pedestrians. Only when she reached the command post of Lenkova, did she make any effort to slow down. Nearly screaming, she advised, "Huge army of Arad rebel cavalry is galloping here. Be upon us within a few minutes. Seven miles out when I returned!"

Lenkova jumped up, knocking over the outdoor table, its contents flying onto the ground. "How many Nicki?" she asked the vital question.

"Thousands upon thousands. They swarmed over the desert like ants. Lenkova we cannot fight this many!" she shrieked, as the reality of the oncoming attack at last overwhelmed her.

"Fighter Group A, gallop through the town and scream out a warning:

massive attack within five minutes; flee for your lives. Then, get out of town as fast as you can; head eastward two miles and stop. Everyone, saddle up, and let's have an orderly retreat! Leave anything that is not vital! Now, ladies!"

Andre ordered his Circle to mount up and assisted several in cinching up their horses rapidly. Speed, he knew, was of the essence. Barely had his Circle climbed aboard their mounts when a very large dust cloud became visible on the eastern hills approaching the Junction. Mass pandemonium broke out; people thronged the streets running wildly in all directions in a mad, desperate attempt to flee the city. Leann exclaimed, "Andre, we need more time!"

Andre called out, "Lenkova, get your fighters out of here now; we'll divert them for perhaps a minute and join you!" She did not question her husband, concentrating on getting her some eight hundred fighters safely through the crowds and out of town. She did look back over her shoulder to see what he had in mind for a stall. She might have guessed, knowing Andre as she did.

"Okay, each one of you launch a sheet of fire no more than ten feet high. One of you hook yours on to mine and stretch it as far as you can. Next one, join his and stretch. Let's lay out a long sheet of flames blocking the eastern edge of the town. Hold it in place for at least a minute; see if it causes them to break their all-out charge into the Junction. Yes, that's it. Here they come, hurry up!"

Now the charging army moved into sight, eight thousand, all yelling in a high, shrieking voice, terrifying to hear. "Good god! What are they?" shrieked Leann, their Wid. None of Andre's Circle had ever seen anything like this ever before. Yes, it unnerved them considerably and their sheets of flames wavered.

"Steady, steady," called out Andre. "Just a bit longer."

"Damn what witchcraft is this?" yelled Jahdi, as he was forced to signal his charging army to slow down. A huge wall of flames crackled just before the outer buildings of the Junction. Jahdi had never seen anything remotely like this before.

Zeta, at his side, yelled, "Some devilry or illusion. Just go around it!"

Yelling his new orders, Jahdi kicked his horse and pulled around to the right of the flames. At least two of his men, perhaps too inquisitive, tested the flames with their hands and were severely burned for their curiosity.

"Now, ride for your lives!" Andre commanded and took the lead, his Circle right behind him as he darted this way and that, avoiding fleeing townsfolk. In minutes, they reached the western edge of the town and spied the distant dust clouds of the Sisterhood fighters. Andre pointed and they followed at a gallop. Two miles out, they stopped to join Lenkova, who had also halted her to get a view of what was happening in the Junction, far off to the east. "Mary, contact the cavalry general who has his two thousand cavalry just to the south. Tell him do not under any circumstances try to ride north to cut this army off. They'll be slaughtered!"

She promptly closed her eyes, made contact with the young general, delivering the news and Andre's stern warning. Meanwhile, Lenkova ordered her scouts out once more, before turning to Andre. "We should know in a couple minutes what their intentions actually are," she said sternly. "I hope and pray that they do not continue further into the sector! Do you see the sheer size of their numbers? And that awful shrieking — it sent chills down my spine. Nothing has ever done that before!"

"That was its purpose, dear, to frighten the willies out of everyone. I agree, it's huge. Where did they all come from? I never dreamed that there was anywhere near this number of Arad fighters! Look, they are still swarming in over the eastern hills! Thousands of them!"

Leann commented to Lenkova, "Let me see if I understand the situation here. If they decide to pursue us or ride deeper into the sector, does this mean we are at war? Does Zargarb have the forces to stop this many invaders in one bunch?"

"War or skirmish or raid. Cannot tell which yet. I hope and pray that this is only a raid on the Junction and not an invasion. No, Zargarb does not have anywhere this many cavalry. My estimate is three thousand at most, with a third back in Zargarb or patrolling the western borders. In the city, there are another three thousand foot soldiers whose task is manning the walls. If they enter the sector, we must send word to all towns in their path and order all the people to flee at once to the safety of the walls of Zargarb. Only there can we hope to defend against something like this." She watched several of her scouts, as they took up concealed positions about a mile closer to the Junction. "Now, we wait; that is really all that we can do, wait and see. I feel badly that the poor folks in the town did not get more of a warning."

"Hey, at least they had some warning, thanks to your scouts," Andre corrected her. "We both know that it is far too risky to send your scouts deeper than seven miles out into that desert!"

Tom, the Planner, commented, "It sure is eventful out here on the frontier."

"Scary is more like it," his wife, Mary retorted. "Message delivered, Andre. He needed a bit of convincing, so I sent him my images of the charging horde as they swarmed into the town. That did the trick. He is circling wide to the west and north, forming an arc to cut them off if they try to drive deeper into the sector. Lot of good that will do if they do, in my humble opinion. Men! Generals! Such piffle!"

Lenkova looked at her blankly, "Such silliness," she repeated and Lenkova chuckled.

"You can say that again," Lenkova smiled. "Well, it's been a couple minutes now, and they are still in the Junction. I take that as a positive sign." About now, townsfolk on foot began moving in and through the Sisterhood position, here two miles out. Grim were their faces, some filled with terror.

One man, carrying his youngest child, his wife leading the two older ones, walked past Lenkova and Andre. He said, "Thank you Sister for the timely warning. We made it safely out. Our lives are more valuable to us than our home." She smiled as graciously as she could, which was hard for her. Lenkova did not accept validation from others outside the Sisterhood at all well.

Eyes peering at the distant town, Andre commented, "I don't see any flames. Perhaps they are not going to burn down the town. That's hopeful anyway. Maybe we are going to be very lucky and only have a raid. We know that the local Arads, wherever they are, are living at the lowest poverty level imaginable. Maybe this is a food raid. Sure hope so."

"If all they want is food," Ann replied, "then why don't they just ask? I'm sure that Zargarb would lend a hand, wouldn't they?"

Zeta commented, "Now this is more like it. Those devil flames had me worried for a minute. I swear the entire town is fleeing before us, Jahdi!" Their fighters had now swarmed all over the rather large town, second in size only to Zargarb itself. More than half had already fled or were on foot trying to flee when the invaders encircled the town and thus those still attempting to flee. Vainly, men, their arms around their wives and children in a mostly symbolic attempt to protect their loved ones, were forced to stop their flight, forced this way and that by the yelling fighters of Jahdi.

Those that did not or could not flee hid in their homes, under beds and in closets, wherever they could hide, hoping against hope that they would not be dragged out into the streets and slaughtered. Most covered their ears to dampen the bone-chilling shrieks from the eight thousand galloping fighters from the Arad. After what seemed to be an eternity, the horrid shrieking slowly died out.

Jahdi issued orders right and left to the messengers of the other nine town representatives. He was amazed that so few townsfolk had been killed, only a handful offered any token of resistance. Thus, his orders were to begin the looting phase. Each of the ten towns sent out fighters in search of wagons with which to haul the precious supplies back into the Arad and their towns. While this was going on, others began looting the warehouses and stores, carting out piles of the basic essentials of life, primarily food, wine, oil for lanterns, and so on. Random chaos ensued as soon fighters from one town skirmished with fighters from another over the stuff being piled high on the dusty streets of the Junction. It took all Jahdi's strength of command to keep some semblance of order during the long afternoon.

By sunset, over fifty wagons began rolling out of the Junction, heading east along the main track that led out of the Junction into the Arad. Many of the fighters had already begun to help themselves to the many wine bottles they had confiscated. Wine and the desert do not mix, as Jahdi well knew. Those that drank to excess would pay a steep price during the heat of the next few days. Water was far more precious. Zeta made very sure that their wagons had several water barrels full of the life giving liquid.

The army still followed his orders, which was a good sign, Jahdi thought. With such a hugely successful raid as this had been, he half expected that the other towns would split off and go their own way. However, they did just the opposite, recognizing that at long last, they had a true leader they could follow, one who would lead them to riches beyond belief. His first order was to continue traveling throughout the cool night, staying on the main track, which the heavily laden wagons could traverse.

His reasoning was thus. Zargarb did have many cavalry, which they had not seen yet. Very likely, the cavalry would be summoned and set out after him. If they camped a few miles from the Junction out in the desert, they could well be surprised and attacked during the night. By traveling all night, that eventuality was ruled out. He had fifty riders patrolling their rear and another twenty-five out in front. For the next two days, they would follow the track as it lead steadily for the ruins of Jerilum and the great north-south paved roadway built decades ago by the Infidel Centurions. There, they would head south on the road. All ten of the mesa towns lay in the central southwest portion of the Arad. Once they had gone some twenty miles south of the ruined city, the second phase would begin. All the cargo would be loaded onto their horses. Wood was scarce out here in the open desert, so even the wagons would be dismantled and the wood used. Nothing would go to waste.

Once the wagons had been salvaged, each of the ten town's fighters would split off from the main group, following down side valleys. Later, each of these large groups would split off yet again, each taking slightly different routes back to their towns. The idea of keeping the exact location of their towns a secret had long been the rule among these fighters. This was an unpleasant fact of life out here in the Arad. Jahdi knew that if they were not followed up to the time they stopped to dismantle the wagons, they would all make it safely home.

All that afternoon, Lenkova and Andre watched as the Junction was being looted. Yet, there was nothing that either could do about it. They were outnumbered by ten to one. Lenkova had scouts sneak up close to the town and perform a crude head count to get an estimate of their numbers. The tally, once figured, suggested that the Arad raiders numbered somewhere between seven and nine thousand strong. Surprisingly, a large percentage was women fighters, her scouts reported.

During that afternoon, the Sisterhood found that they had domestic duties to handle. The evacuees numbered in the thousands and needed at least water. Thus, many went in search of water supplies, while others gathered up the fleeing people, calmed them down, and organized smaller groups, digging latrines, and helping lost ones find their families once more. Each Sister did what she could to ease the suffering of those who had fled.

By dusk, Lenkova saw the huge caravan of wagons rolling out of the Junction, following the main east-west track. She sent a hundred into the town to survey the damage, while the others escorted the townsfolk safely back into the Junction. "Lenkova, we have been mighty lucky today. Only ten dead is the report! Incredible. Looks as if the Arad raiders were merely looking for supplies and not a war."

"They did show restraint," she commented, "I'll give them that, but most of the townsfolk are immigrants from the Arad anyway. It's as if they were robbing their own people. Maybe that is the reason for their restraint."

"What an incredible mess!" Leann commented, looking at the littered streets, torn up shops. The Sisterhood encampment had been thoroughly looted. Even the cooking pots were mostly gone! "Whatever will the thousands that live here eat? Whatever will we all eat? I see a disaster in the making!"

"I had not thought that far ahead," Andre replied.

"Maybe and maybe not," Lenkova commented. "Andre, Leann, come with me." She led them to the burned out ruins of the mother Church of Jehosanity. In the dusk, signs of the rebuilding were quite prominent. "Here, help me move this pile of wood and rubble." The three began moving stone blocks and boards off a storage pile. Once the pile was moved, Andre could see definite signs of an iron door.

"It leads to the Church's underground storage chambers. Remember, that this Church was always coming to the aid of disaster victims. They have a huge tunnel system under here. Last time I was here, it was darn near full. Hope it still is." Andre and Lenkova lifted the heavy iron door. Darkness and a chill greeted them. She retrieved an oil lantern from her saddlebags, lit it, and together the three descended the steps into the tunnel.

After ten feet, the tunnel stopped descending and led straight to a huge, man-made cavern. Their eyes could scarcely believe their eyes. Supplies were neatly stacked on shelves, a mountain of supplies, from blankets, to oil kegs, to dried foods, yes, even wine bottles and tools. "Impressive!" Leann commented. "The Zargarb Church of Jehosanity really does try to help those who need assistance. I am impressed indeed. Shame that all their priests were slain last month."

"The priests' aid their own town as if from the grave," Lenkova commented, waxing slightly philosophical, uncharacteristically of her. "You two keep an eye on things here. I'll fetch my Sisters to come and to spread the word that assistance is here." Later that night, many thousand voices lifted up their prayers to Jehosa for their deliverance.

A week later, Joshua Anson, the Florintine Junction representative, stood before the High Council of Zargarb, demanding the protection of his town. He requested a defensive wall be constructed and that a garrison force of some eight thousand men be stationed at the walls. Of course, there were not that many soldiers in the entire Zargarb army. Other council members took up the mantle, demanding that the army be quadrupled in size. Others protested the exorbitant cost of such, from where the funds would come, where they could acquire so many weapons and horses, and so on. Sister Alicia later commented that this was the worst day she had ever had sitting on the High Council. However, in the back of the mind of everyone present was the certainty that these Arad raiders could invade and steal anything at any time anywhere with the sector, except the walled city of Zargarb.

The General of the Cavalry, Simon La Conte, personally asked that his forces be enlarged ten-fold. He passionately pleaded, "Look, I am outnumbered four to one! All that I can do is to retreat from these Arad raiders! Think of the morale of our cavalry, please." Sister Alicia thought instead of Simon saving his own face, but wisely said nothing. In the end, the High Council had little choice but to begin enlarging their army as rapidly as feasible. Orders for men, horses, weapons, and tack began pouring out of Zargarb in all directions.

Two weeks later, time enough for the towns to celebrate their fantastic victory at the Junction, Jaifur Jahdi called for another massive ten-town raid. This time, he was going for blood and weapons, the Infidel Centurions' southern command post at Al Mari, where the long Centurion paved road coming up from the south crossed the river into Juda Arad. At this command post, the road branched, one heading northwest to their port city of New Barq, while the main road continued up straight through the center of the Arad.

For weeks now, Jahdi had two spies constantly watching the command post. Four legions defended the outpost, some four hundred men. Al Mari was a small town of adobe buildings with a low, defensive wall surrounding it. Inside, a natural aquifer bubbled up to form an oasis. Date and fig trees were abundant here. However, Al Mari was a key location for the Centurions. Merchants using their overland road to New Barq, their primary port into the Med Sea, of necessity had to stop and take on water before heading on up the road to the port city, well over a hundred miles away. This road ran straight and true from Al Mari to New Barq, typical of Centurion construction. However, in doing so, they unintentionally bypassed all the scattered watering holes, known to the Arads who lived out here in the desert. If Al Mari were taken, the Centurion merchants and army would feel the impact severely, particularly their coin pouches.

Actually, as Zeta pointed out to him, this assault upon Al Mari would be the first true test of Jahdi's leadership skills. This was a walled town, heavily defended by expert soldiers. Perhaps less than a hundred non-fighters lived here, serving the needs of the garrison. Zeta insisted that Jahdi must take the town without losing many men in the process. What she feared most was the breakup of their fragile alliance with the other nine Arad secret towns. She kept repeating, "Together, we are strong; separate, weak." In the end, it was her constant insistence on this datum that had convinced the other town leaders to join Jahdi.

Although the walls were neither thick nor tall, just over six feet, they could not be jumped by horses. True, crude ladders could be brought up and the men could then swarm up and into the town, but the losses would be staggering. Four hundred archers would extract a heavy toll, far too heavy for this fragile alliance. Further, Jahdi had no ideas about how one could build a machine with which to batter down the three main gates of the town. However, he knew wood burned and that formed the basis of his strategy.

On September 1, some eight thousand Arad warriors stealthily moved into position. Five miles from the stronghold, the vast army had halted for their final orders. Jahdi sketched a crude map in the desert sand to show the assembled leaders. "When the snake zeniths, send out your men. It should be pitch black, no moon. Remember, stealth will win the battle. Do not allow your men to attract the attention of their sentries!" The nine group leaders grumbled that they understood, and Jahdi broke up the meeting.

Quietly, he watched as nine large groups veered either left of right off of the north-south road. He would lead his force straight down from the north of Al Mari. "Now we wait, Zeta, and now we wait."

"Do you think they will obey and not raise the alarm?" she whispered back. Still she did not trust the skill level of those from the other nine towns.

"We are doomed if they alert the lookouts. Have faith, Zeta; we are all excellent desert survivors. You cannot live in the Arad without becoming stealthy; you should know that, love. Worry rather that the oil will be enough. Come, it is time we began to move into our position." He called out, "Ten scouts, out you go. Do not let any of their scouts detect our coming!" Immediately the handpicked men moved off on down the road and fanned out on either side, the sands covering the hoof beats of their horses. After a few minutes, Jahdi gave a hand signal. He and Zeta veered to the right of the road along with four hundred others, while the remainder went off to the left. It was dark, but the stars shone brightly above, which was all that these desert dwellers required. Jahdi halted his men at the last ridge that overlooked Al Mari, about a half mile ahead. His men spread out wide on either side, tethered their horses, and relaxed on the warm desert sands.

All eyes stared down at their prey, none more so than Zeta and Qa. Their keen eyes spotted five of the small raiding party, sneaking slowly, but surely up to the three gates. These men knew their craft. Taking advantage of the terrain features, slight gullies, small underbrush, they crept on their hands and knees toward their objective. Six sentries paced inside the walls, the tops of their heads clearly visible against the pale illumination from the stars. Evidently, on the inside of the wall, there was a raised section that allowed them to rise over the walls, probably to shoot arrows and otherwise defend the walls. The town was roughly circular about a mile across.

Long minutes passed, while the duo watched intently. Now several had made the gates undetected thus far. Longer minutes passed while the men did their work at the gates. Jahdi found himself holding his breath several times, as if he were actually there alongside of these men, so intense was his concentration. This just had to go right! Everything depended upon these men succeeding. Finally, one by one the men began their slow retreat, going just as stealthily as they had come. Only when the last man had disappeared from view did Jahdi and Zeta finally relax and lay down to rest.

As twilight broke and coyotes howled, Jahdi gave the attack signal. Seemingly out of nowhere, eight thousand cavalry came yelling and screaming in their high pitched voices, thundering down from all sides of Al Mari. The four hundred soldiers and hundred civilians awoke to this terrifying sound. Brass horns sounded the general alarm, although it did not need to be done. Men, half dressed, rushed outside the barracks, weapons in hand or grabbing them from the racks nearby. As the riders closed, many sent flaming arrows at the doors, which, having been soaked well with oil, began blazing. Continuously screaming, the Arad warriors let fly volleys of arrows, aiming just over the walls, hoping to catch some heads looking.

Jahdi did not expect his arrows effectively to do much damage; rather the volleys' purpose was to keep those inside occupied while the oil burned. Everything depended upon the gates burning so that they could easily bust through and charge inside the town. Wildly, the Centurions fired arrows at the circling riders, taking no aim, just shooting. Indeed some did find their marks so dense were the riders. By the time that the garrison commander discovered that the three gates were burning profusely, it was too late. Water buckets began to be thrown from the walls down toward the recessed gates, but did little good. Water thrown on the insides of the gates steamed up into the dim morning sky, adding to the confusion.

During all this confusion, several riders closed to the doors carrying a heavy log held between them. They rode hard and fast straight at the flaming gates. Just as they got to the gates, each rider suddenly veered either left or right, simultaneously releasing the carrying ropes. The momentum of the log carried it smashing into the flaming gates. On the second try, one gate shattered. Soon the other two likewise gave way. In dashed thousands of Arad cavalrymen, Zeta and Jahdi in the forefront.

Spears poked up at them, swords swung at their legs, but the mounted fighters dashed about, their own swords finding easy marks, their horses trampling anything in the way. The attack lasted only five minutes. Jahdi effectively ended it when he disarmed the commander and then lopped off his head. All fight evaporated from the Centurions, who hoped for leniency, but found none. Even the civilians within Al Mari were slain. A single dog remained the sole survivor of this attack.

Amid cheering of thousands, the victorious set to work. Weapons were gathered up, especially the arrows. Each building was thoroughly searched and anything useful confiscated. By noon, the outpost had been ransacked, and the riders were beginning to file out, forming ranks to head north to their secret towns. Jahdi, Zeta, and one other man were the last to leave. "Do it now," he ordered. The two watched as the man emptied a large sealed pottery bowl into the watering hole. The blackish, oily liquid slowly spread out across the water. Jahdi had just poisoned this watering hole. True, the artesian flow would one day disperse the poison making it safe to drink, but not for many months. Jahdi was counting upon the Centurions not having a ready source of water when they reached the Arad. Finally, the three rode out of Al Mari, while the dog still watched.

As the triumphant pair rode slowly homeward, they discussed who should be attacked next. "We are unstoppable," Jahdi exclaimed, filled with the excitement of victory.

"Ah we still lost twenty-five men; don't lose sight of that," Zeta cautioned him, "and don't forget the forty-two wounded. Beside, Qa, we outnumbered them twenty to one. As long as you contemplate attacking small towns, yes, we are unstoppable. However, we would never be able to take on the city of Zargarb. We could go after the barbarians of the steppes, however. What do you think?"

"Yes, yes, you are so pragmatic, Zeta. Can't you allow me to enjoy my victory a little? I know that we could go after the barbarians up north, but what's the point? True, when they were off conquering the world, they acquired vast quantities of gold, silver, and gems. But what good are they my love? You cannot eat them, and they weigh you down. Offer any man in our town his choice between a gold coin and wine bottle, and he'll take the wine any time. We'd have little to no support for attacking the Galts, I'm afraid. Who knows where the Axemen camp? Small bands roam in the Arad from time to time, hardly worth messing with; leave them to individual towns to handle, should they come near."

"No, the only real targets we can tackle next are New Barq and raiding other towns within Zargarb, avoiding, of course, the city. However, at the moment, all them," he waved his arm forward toward his valiant men and women, "all of them have more food, horses, weapons, than they need right now. I think it prudent to sit back and relax for a while. I'll send out double the number of spies, but let's sit back and see what Zargarb and Megalos do."

"Now you are back to the wise man I married," she declared. "New Barq will be a difficult challenge. Raiding Zargarb towns, quite easy, if the Junction was any indication. Yes, let's enjoy our new found wealth. Tonight, we eat heartily my husband."

"Aye, for weeks we can eat heartily," he joked back.

Chapter 19 Illanovich Strokova

Illanovich Strokova had been a wimpy child who whined a lot if he didn't get his way. However, he was Czar Mikhailovich Strokova's son! After his father's sudden death, he was stolen from the Galts and raised by Zargarb's Fighter Group Leader, Rosita, his mother. Illi, as he now called himself, upon discovering that he was not going to be trained to fight, but rather how to herd sheep, packed up his few things and fled North Point, heading for his birthright home, the Northern Steppes.

Those early years in the steppes had been hard on the boy of twelve. Thin and fragile, with no knowledge of life in the steppes, no fighter training, he relied solely on his skill at riding a horse, that and his uncanny way with words and persuasion. While his father had been nearly an unbeatable fighter, Illi lacked the strength, skill, and training to follow that path. However, his keen mind instantly saw what the other person thought and felt, allowing him to say just the right words with just the right tone for Illi to best that other person, achieving what he desired.

For example, when he left North Point, he rode north and east until he found the Centurion paved road, which he knew would lead to the steppes. Days later, he finally rode out onto the rolling green hills of the steppes, a new sense of freedom growing within himself. Knowing nothing about tracking or the ways of the nomadic tribes or even tribal rivalry, he nearly starved to death before he ran into an encampment of Galts. As he slowly rode into their camp, he called out, "I am Czar Illanovich Strokova! I have finally escaped my mother's prison. I have finally come home. I do seem to be in dire need of assistance at the moment." Weak from hunger, he nearly fell off his horse.

He had not arrived at the Strokova Clan, but one of its rivals, the Bear Claw Clan. Mik Radstov, Clan Leader, barely but a boy himself, took charge. Remember that when Mikhailovich was defeated near Sud, Southlands, by the Centurions, nearly all the able-bodied men of the steppes had been slain or wounded along with him. Hence, for a generation, men of fighting age were at a premium within all the clans. While Illi lay unconscious on the ground, Mik stood over him, deciding what to make of this intruder.

"How do we know he is as he claims?" he asked. "Fetch the Augurer." Slowly an old woman walked up to her leader. "Woman, this man claims to be the son of Czar Mikhailovich Strokova, Illanovich. You knew Mikhailovich. Can this stripling be his son?"

She knelt down beside the boy, her grubby, gnarled hands moving his head from side to side, her piercing eyes studying the boy's features. "Aye, to be sure, he is the son of Mikhailovich. He has the same facial bone structure; he's the right age, coming from the right place. Few knew his mother had stolen him from the Strokova Clan, because they didn't want the rest of the clans to know that they let his children slip away from them. Of course, the real question, Mik, is what's to be done wit'im. Want me to slit his throat for you?" She gave a cackle of glee. Considering the destruction that Mikhailovich had brought on her clan and her husband, she would relish this small deed of revenge. She saw Mik hesitating and added, "If he grows up, he'll be Czar over all of us, even you, Mik. Better end it now, right here, unless you fancy him your master." She had her small knife ready to do the deed.

"Stay your hand, hag," Mik barked. To be sure, if Illi grew up, it was his birthright to become Czar over all the clans of the steppes. He was born while Mikhailovich lived, thus his birthright was recognized by all the clans. Yet, while they might recognize such, that did not mean they would support him. Treachery and deceit ran deep within these clans. Instead, a different picture formed in Mik's mind. He saw the future Czar riding tall, once more conquering all the lands, only this time, Mik was right there as his right hand man, his advisor, his closest friend, and his longtime buddy. Mik, the second most powerful man in the steppes, a position he could never accomplish on his own. "Stay your hand! Get him up and into my hut. Someone bring him some food and drink. Tonight we host the Czar. Show him some respect! However, do not mention that he exists or that we even have him here, or I will personally slay you on the spot! Do I make myself perfectly clear? No one outside of our clan is to know about him."

So it was that Illi was fed and given shelter and security in the Bear Claw Clan. The next day, Mik introduced Illi to himself first and then the key members of his clan. He was given a hut of his own and a motherly serving woman to look after his needs, which initially were many. "So Illi," Mik said, "what are your strengths? Your father was immensely strong, eyes in back of his head, or so the legends say." Skinny and lean, Illi looked at this young man, who stood much taller than himself with rippling arm muscles and a powerful physic, and replied, "I am yet too young to answer truthfully, Mik. I've been raised by a bunch of women and not taught the basic skills that any twelve year old here knows by heart. You, on the other hand, Mik, you are strong and able. Yet I detect that you would like to become far more than a mere clan leader. You have what many men do not have, ambition. I say you should be far more, if you want my opinion."

As Illi was talking, Mik found himself becoming embarrassed, and his face grew hot when Illi pointed out his secret ambition to be great. However, Illi's last sentence hooked him completely! Illi said he knew his innermost dreams and that this goal was more than acceptable. It completely disarmed him; his embarrassment vanished as suddenly as it came. This was the first time that Mik experienced the power of his Czar. Although he would personally witness it numerous times in the future, this first one made the most lasting impression on him.

"Well, then, first Illi, we must see to your education — man's work is for you, not women's! You have years of catching up to do. However, let it be at your own pace. If we go too slowly for you, tell us. If too fast, let me know." Mik was sincere and Illi knew it.

"Thanks, Mik. We are going to become very good friends indeed," Illi added, gaining just the precise effect he desired. He knew from the tiny facial movements that this was just what Mik had in mind for the future.

Some months later, while Illi was getting basic sword training with wooden swords, he put his special skills to use once more. Gar, the oldest of the young boys and the toughest, weighing at least twenty pounds more than the other boys, continually bullied the others. Gar especially enjoyed taunting them. Unfortunately, this day he picked on Illi, who was really struggling. "You fight like a sissy. Your mother teach you to do that? Some Czar you'll be. Look, he can't even defend himself from little Rox." Rox was a year younger than Illi, and had the distinction of being the smallest boy getting fighter training.

Illi had had enough. Rox was doing very well and didn't need the put-down. Illi stopped, lowered his sword, and walked straight up to Gar, before he spoke. "Gar, you are nothing but a bully. You have been making less of all the rest of us kids ever since we started days ago." Gar was about to say, "Going to make something out of that?" but did not get the chance, because Illi continued, "Gar, you are bullying us because you completely lack any self confidence in your own skills. You really don't know what you are doing with these swords any better than the rest of us. Hence, you make fun of us, and you hope we don't look too closely at you. Sorry, but I do watch you, and you are better than us only because you are older and bigger. Give us the years to grow up, and you will be bottom dog. Even Rox here has more potential than you have. Now I know that I do not know how to fight, but I am willing to say so, and I am willing to learn. Gar, you know that you don't and are simply too ashamed to face it. You think by bullying us, we will not notice how awful your skills actually are. Sorry, but when the day comes that we need to fight, unless you change your ways now and start learning like the rest of us, we will be burying your dead body. Mark my words, Gar. I speak the truth." Illi turned around, saw the other kids with their mouths open, and motioned for Rox to begin again. He and Rox continued to practice. Mik overheard this conversation, and his respect for Illi's special talent continued to grow.

That night, Illi, alone at last in his small hut, began crying. He knew that he would never be a great swordsman, like his father. "Dad was the best, most powerful, strongest fighter the steppes ever had. And I am the ninety pound weakling son. Woe is me." He cried for some time. Then, a thought filtered into his mind, something he had heard some adults discussing once when they thought he was asleep. His mother was talking with the shepherd whom Illi refused to call father. The man said, "Yes, I know the reasoning behind Mikhailovich Strokova's decision. He was the best fighter in the steppes. You, Rosita, are the best fighter in Zargarb; you even fought Mikhailovich to a draw and disarmed him. Right or wrong, he thought that by mixing his blood with yours, the child would be even more powerful than either of you are. Rosita, you and I both know that is not how life works. The spiritual being animates the body. Thank heavens Illanovich is not growing up with his father. The boy would be devastated, never able to meet any of his father's expectations. He would have grown up considering himself a total failure in his father's eyes."

"But I am a total failure," he sobbed quietly to himself. Again, the memory replayed in his mind. The shepherd added, "Rosita, the boy must find his own path to greatness. He must develop the skills he does have, not the skills his father bred him for; he is not a horse or sheep."

"Develop my skills?" he whispered. "My skills? I dealt with Gar today, didn't I? No one else had the courage or knowledge to stand up to him, except me did they? Maybe my skills lie along quite a different line from my father's." Illanovich began to see that his own worth and talents lay in the handling of men, not the fighting of men.

When Illanovich was fifteen, he asked Mik one day, when news came that the Axemen were raiding the clans, which had settled closer to the western portion of the steppes than the Bear Claw Clan, "The Axemen from the north, they are attacking to steal the gold?" Here in this camp, everyone ate off golden plates, drank from gold and silver goblets. All the women wore numerous gems, rings, broaches, and necklaces. Even Illi had a large golden bowl serving as his chamber pot.

"Aye, lad. That is why the Axemen have ventured so far from their own lands in the far north. They seek our riches," Mik replied.

"And yet we do not pick up and move to greener pastures?"

"Aye, I'm told that is what we used to do — move every six months. As you can see, that is neigh on to impossible, what with all this gold and stuff plundered when your father conquered most of the world. We've so much stuff that it'd take more wagons than we have to move. Too much trouble and work as well."

Illi surprised Mik once again. "So why do we keep it? You can't eat the gold. It keeps us in one spot where the grass is trampled and no longer gives good pasture for our horses. What do we need with all this gold and jewels anyway? Mica is very pretty without wearing all those rings, necklaces, and stuff. I say that all this stuff is detracting us from what is right and what is beautiful about life." Mik sat profoundly moved by the wisdom from the Czar's mouth. Their biggest problem was obtaining enough food to eat and grass for the horses. Staying perpetually in one location deprived them of both game and fodder. Suddenly all this seemed utterly ridiculous to Mik and he began to see how the clans could once more be united when the time was right.

"We should move," Illi declared.

A few days later, the latest hunting party returned with a single hare to show for their mighty hunt. Naturally, hungry stomachs caused quite a vocal growl at these "mighty hunters." Once more, Illi stated flatly, "We should move."

"I totally agree," Mik replied. He called everyone together to explain his newfound wisdom. He ended with, "So look, we cannot eat this gold. We should return to the lifestyle of our forefathers!"

"Aye, but we can't just leave all our wealth," protested several fighters. Many women nodded their agreement.

"What good is that chest of coins over there doing you, Illytch? Can you use it to exchange for food? If so where?" Mik countered in frustration.

Illi saw what was really in the minds of many, and spoke up, "We leave it behind in a safe, secure place. If we ever need it, why, we can return and get it." Mik liked the sound of that, glad that Illi was lending him a much-needed hand convincing the clan.

"All well and good, but where's that safe, secure place? Under yonder tree? We leave it and someone else will come and take it. So says I," the same protester declared argumentatively.

Mik looked very frustrated, but Illi handled everyone, "There is one safe place. Over there. Our cemetery. No one ever dares disturb graves; even your youngest children avoid playing near the tombs. I say we dig a nice tomb alongside the others and leave all that you don't actually need. I assure you that it will be completely safe there. Even if another clan should decide to camp right here, no one will ever dig up a grave tomb, ever."

That convinced everyone. Mik found himself going from person to person, asking repetitively, "Are you sure you really need all that?" Uniformly, the person would decide that they honestly didn't and cart it over to the huge pile. Others began digging the tomb. A day later, another large tomb mound joined the others, only this one contained unimaginable wealth, not the deceased. Illi likened it to the death of the gold, but his humor was lost on everyone.

A week later, they finally settled in the northeastern portion of the steppes. Here the grass was green and lush; creeks, unpolluted; game, plentiful. Several days later, Mik received nothing but the highest praise for his decision. Clan life was renewed. Following their ancient nomadic customs, the Bear Claw Clan now migrated to greener pastures every six months.

Years later, the Axemen problem had grown far worse. Nearly half of the western portion of the steppes had been overrun with these greedy men from Volksholm. One year, the Bear Claw Clan happened to be in the west central portion some fifty miles north of the Strokova Clan permanent encampment. Mic, Illi, and a group of fifty horsemen were out hunting when they spied a large column of a hundred of these burly Axemen marching south.

"Ah, we should follow them without being seen," Illi advised Mik, who by now never doubted pronouncements from his Czar.

"Aye, it'll be good practice for the men," Mik replied. Using hand signals, Mik motioned for silent stalking. The small band spread out and began trailing this raiding party. All that day the Axemen marched southward, making camp at dusk. Likewise, Mik, who also sent out sentries wide on all sides in case they were discovered. Over dinner, Illi explained, "We should learn our enemy and their ways. One day we will have to drive them out of the Northern Steppes forever. We should know their strengths and weaknesses. Hence, the next few days these men observed the ways of their enemy from the north. On the third day, they watched in disgust as the Axemen raided the Strokova clan's encampment. Many of these had been raided previously, some, repeatedly. It was a hit, confiscate, and run battle. On foot, the brave Galts put up a good fight, but were no match for the much heavier set, burly men from the north. These Axemen weighed at least fifty to seventy-five pounds more than their steppes counterparts.

This was carefully noted by Mik, "As long as we are on foot, it is no contest at all. To fight these men, we must be mounted."

"Aye, Mik, that has ever been our strong point. You see, tied down by all that useless gold, they've become crippled. Look, these men are brutal beyond belief."

"War, Illi, there is no honor and glory in war, only death and destruction," Mik philosophized. His pronouncement made an impact upon Illi; for days, he would ponder it.

However, seeing these men torture a Galt who had been futilely trying to defend his wife, who in turn was raped, Illi's anger seethed to the breaking

247

point. "Mik, we must teach that man a lesson!" It was hard to watch from a distance and yet be able to take no action. Finally, when the fighting subsided, the Axemen collected large sacks of loot, rounded up some fifty or so prisoners, women, children, and men, and tied them into a long string. "What are they doing?" Illi asked.

"Taking slaves, Illi. I've heard that sometimes these Axemen take slaves away with them," Mik replied. "Let's watch and see what happens to them." A half hour later, the marching raiders stopped where they had stowed their supply sacks before rushing into battle. Most of the raiders picked up their original sacks, which the two speculated contained their food and other supplies, and then began an orderly march on south. Ten Axemen remained; one of these was the man that Illi saw doing the torture. Next, they forced the tied slaves to pick up the loot bags, while they carried their own supply sacks. Using a whip, they forced the captured Galts to begin marching northward. Mik's band followed discreetly behind them, still unseen.

Several days later, the raiders and their prisoners reached the wide river that separated the steppes from the Greenway, the Elbe River. While they watched, the Axemen uncovered a number of riverboats that they had concealed in some brush beside the river. Now their intent was clear to both men. They had arrived here in the steppes by paddling riverboats up the long Elbe River. Now they would load their loot and slaves onto these same boats and drift back down river, ending up somewhere in the far north.

"Let's take them now," Illi declared.

"You mean attack them?"

"Precisely, we out number them five to one. We are mounted; they, not. However, I want that one alive. I mean to teach him a lesson he will never forget!" Illi's anger and hatred gushed forth.

Mik took charge, for combat was his specialty, not Illi's. Besides, Mik would not risk his precious Czar being hurt or killed; the Czar was his future. Hence, Illi was asked to stay well back of the fight. "Five on each one, two abreast, one on each side of your man, last one gets to finish what the first four miss. Speed, men, ride as fast as you can, veering off just at the edge of the river."

From the Axemen's viewpoint, suddenly out of nowhere came galloping barbarians, swooping down upon them. They turned to face them, forming a line, readying their great battleaxes. While they might be cut down, they steeled themselves to wreak great damage upon these upstart riders. No one had ever attacked their spoils caravans before.

Now the trouble with large battleaxes is that they are slow and unwieldy. Once committed to a great swing, little could be done if the target swerved at the last minute. These men were not horse and rider, but a union of the two. Instinctively, the horse moved out of the path of these great blades, just as the rider knew they would, while they took advantage of the motion and swung their short blades. Only one of the five riders had anything to do, he was under orders to preserve the life of this particular Axeman, Illi's orders.

The suddenness of the rescue brought cheers from the captives, and Mik's men proceeded to cut them free, while Illi rode up to the sole survivor, the one to whom he intended to teach a lesson. Mik spoke strong and loudly so that none of these from the Strokova Clan could possibly not hear him. "Behold, I present to you your rescuer, none other than your Czar! Czar Illanovich Strokova, son of Czar Mikhailovich Strokova. Your Czar has returned." Yes, Mik had decided that this indeed was the time to make the Czar's presence known once more. They gasped, some cried, some looked stunned, but most looked on in disbelief.

One woman called out, "But where is the other one, his sister? Both were stolen from us years ago."

Illi knew he had to answer the older woman, "She has become a traitor and has accepted living with the amazon women in Zargarb. Only I have returned. This man here," he said pointing to the Axeman, "I saw him torture and kill your husband, woman, rape you, and then take you as his slave." Turning now to the burly Axeman, who had taken a sword cut to his right arm and was bleeding, Illi declared, "See now the Czar's Justice to the torturer's from the north!" He ordered them to tie ropes to the man's hands and feet. Next, four riders came up and were given the other ends of the ropes. When they started to ride, they pulled the ropes tight, and the Axeman found himself being pulled four ways at once, lifted into the air above the ground. Illi had the riders gallop about with the now terrified Axeman, and at his signal, all four riders peeled to the right and left, ripping the Axeman's appendages off. His scream was loud and horrible. As he lie helplessly on the ground, his life's blood gushing from the four wounds, Illi rode up, spat on his face, and watched him slowly die. Illi needed to make an impression on the Strokova Clan; he certainly did so this day.

"Now we send them a message," Illi was not yet finished. "Gather up the parts of that one, and drag the other nine down to the river. Place them in their boats. Dump all the gold and loot on top of them and set them lose to drift on down to the Axemen. Let them know that the steppes will tolerate them no longer! I so decree." Hastily, the men fulfilled his wishes, over the protests of the ex-prisoners, who wanted their loot returned to them.

"Foolish old women you have become. You desire gold and gems. Yet what has all that brought you? The sheer weight of it has become your very own prison. When Mikhailovich ruled, you traveled light, moving from green pasture to pasture; food was plenty; water, pure. What have you now? Polluted water, dry dirt, no game to hunt. No, we must return to the ways of our forefathers! Return to your encampment and cast aside the heavy weight of the useless gold. Pack up and return to the freedom of the steppes. If you so do, you may find us at the Bear Claw encampment, north and east of here. Take the Axemen's food sacks, their weapons, and return. Spread the word; to achieve your freedom once again, your Czar says you only have to discard the weight of the deadly gold! Go now. I have spoken." Illi wanted a finality to all this, but for an entirely different reason.

They watched as the survivors grabbed the sacks and picked up the weapons. At least, Illi thought that they would be able to return safely to their encampment. Once they walked off to the southwest, Mik asked, "Why did we not return with them and spread the word of the Czar's return?"

"Because, my good Mik, I want to know what is on the other side of this river and because someone is coming. Look there on yonder hill across the river."

Mik looked where Illi pointed and saw a large covered wagon with two horses pulling it lumbering its way slowly along, heading towards the river's edge. As the wagon neared the water's edge, they saw that this must be a trader merchant. Pots, pans, shovels, and many other tools were tied or dangling from all sides of the wagon. A lone, middle aged man sat on the buckboard reining in the horses and waving to the group of horsemen.

Mik and Illi walked a short distance so they were opposite this man, waving and smiling at him. He certainly was no threat. No sword hung from his side, but he had a knife strapped to his left leg. He spoke first and used the Galt language, albeit rather crudely. "Hail riders of the steppes. I am Vorlag Winchester, merchant and trader supreme. I have in my wagon many useful items that may interest you, but first I must find a shallow ford so that I may cross. It is around here somewhere. By chance do you know where it is at?"

"Sorry, we only just arrived here. We've no idea about the ford," Mik replied, honestly.

"No matter, give me a couple minutes to find it. Been here before, so I know it's here," Vorlag said cheerily. He began walking downstream. Presently, he yelled, "Ah ha. Here it is, I'll be with you in a couple minutes." He went back to his wagon, drove it down to the ford, and then splashed into the river. While the others watched, the water rose halfway up the sides of the wagon, but no more. In a few minutes, Vorlag pulled up beside the fifty fighters, wagon dripping water onto the grass. "There, that's better, we don't have to yell. Now then, what can I offer you? Axes, hammers, shovels?" He began to display his various wares. "Perhaps a sack of wheat?"

As the hour was growing late, Illi, fascinated by this Greenway man and eager to learn about the Greenway, told Mik to make camp here for the night and to show hospitality to Vorlag. Soon campfires burned; shortly after, supper was cooking. Vorlag built his own fire and hauled out all sorts of cooking utensils, which these men had never seen before. Thus, Mik, Illi, and Vorlag struck up a lively conversation, which lasted long after the sky had gone dark.

They learned that Vorlag often came to the western area of the steppes, trading with the encampments he could find. Of course, finding them was his hardest challenge. Sometimes he traveled for a month before finding one. It usually only took one encampment for him to trade off his entire wagon of goods. He accepted gold as payment, but he made it overly clear that he would prefer other trade goods, such as a saddle, harness, or a pouch. These would fetch him a large profit back in the Greenway. Gold only bought him more goods to trade.

Illi sensed the time was right to ask Vorlag about the Greenway. "We've never been across the Elbe River, Vorlag. What is the Greenway like?" That small encouragement was all that the trader needed. For an hour, he filled their ears with life in the Greenway. Great rolling hills, with plentiful timberlands, it was a farming community's dreamland. He talked of the Great West-East paved road built by the Centurions years ago that ran all the way from Melantas, just northwest of here, to the seacoast and Calgary in the far west. He told of the great wagons of grain hauled to markets there in the fall. On and on Vorlag talked.

"Ah, but what about the Evil Witches that live in the Greenway?" Illi asked the vital question. As a child, he had heard marvelous tales of the Witches of the Greenway, who could bring down fires from the sky and lightning and even ice. Mik had told him stories about the Great Raid nearly a century ago. At that time, over a thousand Galts had joined up with a king there to conquer that land. However, the Evil Witches arrived and destroyed them all with massive lightning from the sky. Most now thought that was just a children's story, designed to place a bit of awe in them. Illi knew better.

"Evil Witches? Nah, don't know what you mean. We don't have any spirits or goblins in the Greenway."

"They bring down the Fires of the Sky upon us and Lightning Bolts of the Gods," Illi suggested.

"No, they are all gone now. Long gone. Many say good riddance too. Greenway's broken up into ten kingdoms now. Got lots of kings and queens, though I never met any," Vorlag explained. "I don't have much use for kings, mind you. Just people like yourselves, who need things that I can provide." Vorlag chatted on, but Illi stopped listening to him.

Gone! The Evil Witches are gone! That is the best news that I have ever heard! I heard Rosita talking about them and because of them, dad left the Greenway alone and went south to his death instead. That was the last barrier I needed removed! Now nothing can stop me from taking my rightful place as Ruler of Tarra! I'll do what my father could not! My father was a fool, only a fighter. He had no vision, but I, Illanovich, I can see the future. I can make the future, as I desire it. Illi face broke into a huge smile.

Mistaking its meaning, Vorlag said, "Here, have some more of the bread," and he shoved the remaining iron pot to his new friend. Vorlag had used an iron pot to make bread over the campfire. None of these men had ever tasted bread so delicious.

Illi burst out, "Vorlag, I'll take one of the bread making pots and a large bag of the makings. What do you want for it?"

Sensing his first sale of the trip, Vorlag rubbed his chin and said, "Well, how about a saddle? You all make mighty fine saddles. Illi shook his hand, sealing the deal.

When they retired for the night, Mik asked, "Why did you trade away your saddle?"

"I can always get another one. Now this I am going to give to Mica. I fancy her. Think she'll have me?" Illi asked, his heart momentarily pounding and then stopping, as if waiting for Mik's answer. He did not recognize what these feelings were, but love had long ago struck him. As clan leader, it was Mik's position to grant all marriages.

Mik could scarcely believe his ears! That the Czar of all the Northern Steppes should want to marry into his clan was the highest possible honor. It further sealed his fate, interlocking his with the Czar's. "Absolutely, if she will have you, I give my consent!" Illi's heart resumed its pounding, baffling him somewhat.

Four days later, they arrived at their camp. While the riders began telling and retelling of their great adventures, Illi carried his pot and heavy sack of wheat to Mica's hut. She was standing over the cooking fire when he walked up. "Hi Czar Illi, I hear all went well. The men are more cheerful than I can remember," she said. Illi's heart began pounding once more.

"I've brought you a present from the Greenway. It is a cooking pot that makes the best bread you have ever tasted! Let me show you how it works, if I may," he replied. She gasped for a moment; it was one thing for the Czar to bring her a present, that was special enough, but to be personally showing her and asking her permission was quite another entirely. She blushed, agreed, and watched as the young leader proceeded to show her how it was done. He carefully followed all Vorlag's instructions. Sometime later, the two sat around the campfire, eating their fill of the well-made bread.

Finally, Illi got up the nerve to ask her, "Mica, I've," he faltered. Illi had no training, no experience, and no ideas of lovemaking or courtship. Hence, he just blurted out, "Mica, I've longed for you ever since I first set eyes on you when I came here years ago. I want you for my wife. Mik has already granted us permission, if you'll have me." There, he said it, though he could not figure out why his heart, which had been pounding hard, now suddenly seemed to freeze, waiting her reply.

Mica, four years older than Illi, was pretty, with long brown hair and blue eyes. She had several men courting her, but had not fallen in love with any. Now, however, something completely unexpected just happened; the Czar had asked for her hand! If she married him, she would become the Czarina of all the Northern Steppes, a position of great power and fame. In her mind, this alone was worth far more than love. Illi was nothing to look at, rather homely in fact. However, Czarina appealed to her more than his looks. "If Mik says that I may, I would be honored to wed thee, Illi," she replied daintily.

Illi's heart began beating once more. He quickly added, "If you wed me, that will make you the Czarina. I should ask if you want such a position, I suppose. Not many would. Lots of responsibility and all that." He had no idea what he was babbling about now, but he just didn't know what else to say.

"It's okay with me, Illi," and she move close to him, took his trembling hands, and pressed her lips to his. Illi's arms found their way around her waist.

Mik walked up to the pair, smiled, secure in his future. "Well, Illi, looks like you have your answer. Everyone, may I have your attention! We have a wedding to prepare for: Czar Illanovich Strokova will be marrying Mica, our new Czarina!" Suddenly, everyone began yelling and cheering. Why? Everyone in the Bear Claw Clan knew instantly that their position within the eventual ruling of the entire Northern Steppes was now guaranteed. The Czarina was one of theirs, a truly high honor indeed. Hence, they all cheered. Likewise, Illi knew that this clan would become the most influential clan of the steppes. They deserved it; they were his friends.

A month after they were wed, the entire Strokova Clan appeared one morning. Hundreds upon hundreds showed up at the Bear Claw encampment. All were half-starved and overly thin, but their enthusiasm could not be stopped. It took them a while to grasp the wisdom imparted by their Czar, but at last, they had thrown off the yoke of the deadly gold and traveled in search of Czar Illanovich Strokova. Now normally clans rarely get along; stories of inner-clan rivalry fill their campfire stories. Yet, they were welcomed with open arms. How could they not be, Mik had said. Mik's people had fully recovered their robustness of life, virile and strong. All the newcomers were emaciated, half starved; and Illi was of their clan, whether he liked it or not. It was his father's heritage to him.

Months later, fattened up on the good hunting and pasture for their horses, the Strokova clan renewed its life, just as had the Bear Claws. At this point, Illi embarked on the next phase of his grand plan. He sent out messengers bearing his words of truth and wisdom to all the other clans, which were still under the yoke of the deadly gold. His message also told how to throw off that deadweight and to come to him for renewal of life.

Meanwhile, as the number of fighters available grew, Illi sent them out on raids against the Axemen. Purposefully, he kept all such encounters small, with the chances for victory great. Little by little, he helped the different clans regain their strength and confidence. Mik also pointed out that these skirmishes also battle hardened the fighters. "One small step at a time," Illi cautioned Mik, who took his words to heart.

The winter of 622, Illi called for a massive migration to the northeastern foothills of the Volgost mountains. Once more, they would hold their troka festival. Such had not been held for over a score of years now. In their past, each fall before the snows came and each spring after the snow melt has begun, the troka festival took place. At these two times each year, clans put aside their rivalry and met somewhere out on the vast steppes in a week-long festival. Besides fun, games, and much mead drinking, the trading of goods replenished needed clan supplies. Illi gave his people back their long-standing traditions and self-respect.

During all this time, Czarina Mica had not been idle. Normally, the most powerful position a woman could have within a clan is that of the clan breda, the breeder of horses. The original Czarina Zdlenka was a breda of great renown. Having no other Czarinas to emulate, Mica adopted this as her goal.

She set about learning the art of breeding horses. By the time of the troka, she had several young horses to show the other bredas there. Further, as Czarina, she could order them to share their secrets of breeding quality horses, and this is precisely what she did do. It was the first real test of her true power as the new Czarina. The result of her endeavors repaid her handsomely. Five years down the road, her stock became famous for their speed, endurance, and intelligence. Yes, Mica took well to her new position and used it well.

Illi used the troka as a means to spread the word about his plans. He was still taking but one step at a time. He called for a meeting of all clan heads, some one hundred sat around the campfires of Mik, who sat on the right of the Czar. Illi outlined his plan. "First, I want to thank each and every one of you for having the strength and courage to throw off the killing mantel of the dead gold. I commend each and every one of you for having done so!" This, of course, they relished.

"Next year, it is time for the Great Riders of the Steppes to make themselves known once more to the world. Only this time we will do it properly! Mik and I have personally verified that the Evil Witches of the Greenway are no more. Now the Greenway is divided into ten kingdoms. They are weak; we are strong. Further, we will do it one small kingdom at a time. No longer must we fight all the Greenway at one time! However, we shall take over the Greenway, not as my father did, oh no. We seek not wealth, no gold, no gems. We repeat not the mistakes of our forefathers." Now Illi had their complete attention.

"Yes, we invade and we conquer, but we do not pillage and plunder. No, we colonize!" He gazed out at blank faces; he knew he had to explain in detail. "You cannot eat gold. That was the mistake my father made. No, no gold. Let them keep all they have. We want food and supplies by which we may become even stronger. We conquer and then rule the lands. Each harvest, our colonies send us a tithe of food, clothing, blankets, and tools, whatever we can use to make our lives better. We make them support us!" One by one, the others latched on to this new, novel idea. Make them work for us sounded like heaven to these men, that and the perpetual food supplies. Clothing appealed to the women. In fact, no one could offer any reason why this was not an absolutely brilliant idea.

Illi talked on for hours about how it all would work, and the leaders asked many relevant questions. Each had to be sure of the details, because they, in turn, would have to explain it all to their clan members. Illi had thought it all out carefully; there was something in it for everyone, including the children. No one was left out of the rewards. Cleverly, Illi did not mention anything about himself becoming Ruler of Tarra; only to Mica did he speak of that, and then only in the dead of night.

That they could swap their gold for all the food and supplies that they could ever want or need never crossed Illi's mind! He saw only the golden death. For him, gold was not a means of exchange. Some speculate what might have been had Illi been raised in the city of Zargarb instead of North Point.

Planning began in earnest in the spring after the snow melt. Mik insisted on spending a good deal of time training their fighters. The long years of starvation and sedentary lifestyle needed undoing. Further, supplies had to be gathered or made to support a large army of men. Yet, Illi was in no hurry. One small step at a time, his motto became the common man's words to each other. They were not ready to launch their first attack until the fall of 623, after they had heard about the uprising in the Arad.

When news of the Arad army reached Illi, his mind began to absorb the significance of this singularly unexpected event. In a way, these poor Arads were much like the Galts, conquered, dominated, nearly ruined as a people. Yet among them, a leader had arisen, much like himself. Illi saw numerous parallels between this unknown leader and himself. Mik, on the other hand, saw this news as very troublesome. Here they were about to go to war with the Greenway and a potential new threat had just arisen on their southern border.

"Mik, we need to send an emissary to meet with this leader of the Arad rebels." His words took him by complete surprise. Illi, as usual, took the time to explain his ideas fully. Once Illi explained, Mik also saw the close parallels between the two peoples and agreed with Illi's idea to send someone. Thus, word went out that the Czar needed three men who knew their way around Juda Arad; they had a very special mission to perform.

Illi chose the three well, briefed them fully on what he desired, and sent them on their way. He hoped that they would survive and achieve his objective. Illi greatly desired to meet with the leader of these Arad Raiders and before he began his attack upon the Greenway. "Mic, think of it for a moment. An alliance with the thousands of Arad raiders on our southern border would be incredibly beneficial to us and to them. I do not believe that he and I are so very different, but we shall see, Mik, we shall see. Better find us an interpreter who can speak their language."

Six weeks passed with the only a single message from the three messengers. "All of the villages, towns, and cities are empty ghost towns. Even the Centurion Holy Paladins are not to be seen." Mik moved his clan to the extreme south central portion of the steppes, close to the border with Juda Arad, if only to appease Illi, who fretted and worried about the messengers every day.

Finally, one messenger returned with the news that Illi most desired to hear. The Arad leader would meet with him. As had been suggested, they would meet in the abandoned town of Al Dun, just across the Dragon's Teeth, the razor hills that separated the green steppes from the desert lands to the south. Here is where the ancient Centurion paved roadway ended, at the abandoned Al Dun. Mik insisted on taking eight hundred fighters with him to protect their Czar. However, Illi insisted on the rules he'd proposed for the meeting. Just the two of them, he compromised and went along with this leader's counterproposal, to allow their wives to be with them. Mik, fearing for the safety of his Czar, begged and pleaded, but had to be content with keeping his forces a mile back, per the agreement.

Illi and Mica rode slowly into the long deserted town, accompanied by Rostov, their interpreter. "I'm a little afraid," Mica whispered to Illi, as if there were unseen ghosts that might report on her admission.

"It's natural Mica. We are risking a lot by instigating this meeting. Think about it, if we can get these people as allies, then we do not have to fight them. We don't have to garrison our southern border. Eventually, we may have to deal with them, but by then we may be in a vastly better condition." He did not elaborate what that might be, however. This did little to ease Mica's fears; risking her life was not her idea of being Czarina.

"It's a ghost town, Illi. There is no one here at all!" exclaimed Mica as the three entered Al Dun. Dust and debris lay everywhere. A lone dog barked somewhere in the crumbling town. "I don't like this at all," she declared firmly, hoping Illi would change their meeting place.

"You're right, spooky. Let's wait for them out there on the road. Gosh, the sun sure is hot down here," he observed, wiping the sweat from his brow.

"Maybe we should sit over there in the shade," Mica ventured, spotting what must be a cooler location. Hence, the trio sat near the road beside a dilapidated adobe house. "Perhaps I should lay out our offerings. Here, help me set up these bricks as a table. I don't suppose we should go looking for a real table, should we?" She dallied along, setting up a rich offering of food and mead, the best the steppes had to offer.

Hiding inside the ruined building, an old man listened quietly to the voices outside. Past memories came back to him; he recognized that voice! Thus, he changed his mind and did not go out to greet the visitors, but instead listened quietly to all that was said.

Within a few hours, they heard horses coming up from the south, long before they could see who it was. Mica became even more agitated, but Illi remained calm and expectant. One way or another, history was about to be made, he felt passionately. His interpreter fiddled with his clothing; he was nervous. How good was his Arad language? He hoped it would be sufficient.

Qa and Zeta Jahdi rode slowly up the paved roadway into the southern portion of Al Dun. Eight hundred of his fighters had circled wide around the ruined town about a mile distant. Mik spotted them, and they spotted Mik's forces. However, neither side took any action. "We should be seeing some sign of them," Zeta complained, her trained eyes darting from building rubble to alleyways. She had convinced Qa to bring her along as his protector, just in case this was an elaborate trap, which she had argued it was. From the little that they knew of the barbarians of the steppes, the women there were not fighters. Hence, Qa had the distinct advantage, should this leader attempt anything. Zeta kept her hand on her sword hilt as she rode.

"That has to be them," she whispered to Qa. Near the north edge of town, three people sat in the shade of a ruined adobe building. A table cloth was spread out and food and drinks prepared. Two men and a woman. "Good, she is a domestic, not a fighter. I can tell even from this distance."

They rode up and dismounted, tying their reins nearer the smaller stock from the steppes. Illi said, while his interpreter repeated, "Greetings great leader of Arad. I am Czar Illanovich Strokova, leader of all the clans of the Northern Steppes. This is my wife, Czarina Mica, and our translator." He did not dignify saying the translator's name; he had already forgotten it. "Thank you for coming to meet me."

Qa Fahdi nodded and replied, "I am Qa Fahdi, leader of Arad; my wife, Zeta. Your translator speaks well enough thus far."

"Please have a seat here in the shade," Mica used her hostess mode, "I've brought some bee mead, bread rolls, and honey for a light snack. Is it always this hot here in the Arad?" Sweat was pouring off her, but she noticed that Zeta was not sweating. Of course, she wore the traditional leather of the horsemen, while Zeta appeared to have a flowing robe of some light material.

"Thanks, but it would not be prudent to take food from total strangers out here in the wilds of the Arad. You can understand?" Qa replied.

Mica looked a bit miffed, but sat down and continued sipping the mead. So much for trying to be sociable, she thought.

"Then, let's get right to business, shall we?" Illi replied. "I asked to meet you Qa because I believe that we both have similar goals in mind for our peoples. Food, clothing, blankets, supplies, the things that make life possible. Secondarily, we both wish to drive invaders of our lands out. We have just done so in the steppes, driven the Axemen back north from where they come! No longer will you have these rogue fighters swarming down into your land. We will see to it that no Axeman ever sets foot in the Arad again."

Qa thought to himself, "This Illanovich is a wise leader. He sees what it is that we seek." He replied, "Ah, we have been wondering why the fat men from the northern lands had stopped coming into our desert. My scouts report seeing none of them for the last couple of months. I see now that it is your doing. On behalf of all Arad people, I thank you. We too have been active. The Blue Coats, Holy Paladins, have finally left our desert lands; we've driven them out. Most of the Centurions are also gone now, except for those in New Barq. You are right, what my people most need is food, clothing, blankets — the supplies of life are precious few here in the desert. Perhaps you've heard of our massive raid upon Florintine Junction, Zargarb, a few months back?"

"Aye, we have. That's when I began to see that you and I, our people, are not so different from each other, that we share the same objectives, the same goals, or nearly so," Illi rambled on, a little unsure how best to proceed. This foreign man was much more difficult to read than his own people. "We are soon going to go after the Greenway and obtain much needed food and supplies from them. When we succeed, if your people need more of the basics of life, send word to me. We will bring wagon loads down to you. Just let us know what you need, and if we have it to spare, it's yours. Qa. We should be allies, not enemies." Illi thought that this was about the worst speech he had ever given, but Qa was so hard to estimate. Perhaps it was having to go slow with his words so that the translator could keep up with him.

Qa smiled, which Illi took as a good sign. "We have, at the moment, sufficient basics on which to live: food and clothing. What we need most are good weapons that can be used from horseback. We are not so dissimilar are we not? Both fight from the backs of mighty horses, although yours look substantially smaller than ours. I've never personally seen a horse from the steppes."

"Ah, we've no use for all the Axemen battleaxes or their spears. However, as we acquire more swords from the Greenway, I will send you as many as we can spare. Over time, it should be quite a few," Illi replied, feeling that he had just broken through the ice of this man and that the alliance might be at hand.

However, Mica could not resist his interest in her horses, she was already well on her way to becoming a breda. She spoke up, "I am a breda, a breeder of these fine horses. These are Nikko and Zona, bred for great speed and endurance over long distances. Yes, they are smaller than yours are, but few are swifter than these two. However, we do not have such hot weather up in the steppes, and it snows heavily in the wintertime. Our horses get really furry during the cold of winter." She chatted on about horses, not fully realizing that the poor translator could not keep up with her. Qa and Zeta both had to examine both horses, and Mica, theirs. Poor Illi, this vitally important meeting had suddenly become quite sidetracked on to horses, no less. Nonetheless, he kept on smiling and observing the two, who seem genuinely interested in what Mica was saying about the horses of the steppes.

Qa suddenly surprised Illi. Right in the middle of Mica's explanation of conformation, he took Illi's hand and said, "Illanovich, allies we shall be." Illi returned his hearty handshake, grinning from ear to ear. Afterwards, Illi realized that Mica's genuine interest in horse breeding had turned the tide in favor of the alliance! He complimented her all the way back to their camp; she just beamed with a very satisfied look. She had done well as a Czarina this day.

Qa asked Illi, "Our numbers are small. We fight Megalos. If they come in too great a force, can we send for aid from you?" Illi recognized instantly that this was a critical request, one that would solidify their bond.

"Absolutely. Only keep in mind, our forces may be tied up attacking the Greenway the moment you call. Yet we will do our best to send aid. It is in both our interests to keep the Centurions out of our lands!" Again, the two men shook hands. As the hour was getting late, the meeting promptly ended with both parties riding back the way they came.

The old man stepped out of his hiding place beneath the ruins of that adobe building. "My god! What have I just overheard? I had better send word of this at once!" He was George Wainthrope, the druwid Guardian, who had spent his life spying around the edges of the steppes. Indeed, it was the same man who long ago had helped Rosita and Antonio rescue Rosita's children when Mikhailovich had been killed way down in the Southlands. He knew Illanovich as a boy, but like everyone else, had lost track of him when he ran away from home so long ago. Now he had returned, and the winning, whimpering boy was suddenly a major threat to the peace in the Greenway. He relaxed and made his mental link back home.

Chapter 20   The Old Man of the Mountain's Decision

Mustafa Alwan took another puff on the water pipe, sending the soothing, sweet grey smoke deep into his lungs. He slipped back into his world. The young, beautiful, naked woman rubbed her hands sensuously over his legs and then slipped a juicy, fragrant, delicious date first onto her tongue, licked it, and then slowly placed it into his mouth. Just then, a harsh sounding, demanding voice broke into his universe. What was it saying? He heard it again, "Your Excellency, the reports are here. You must hear them. Your Excellency." Ah, slowly he recognized that voice, the voice of his assistant. What was his name? Ah, doesn't matter really. Mustafa opened his eyes. The world around him was not so different from his other world. He saw the assistant standing beside his couch, reams of papyrus in his hands.

"Your Excellency, what are we to do now? The Arad's have abandoned all their towns and have fled the desert. There is none to serve us here. The barbarians of the steppes have suddenly uprooted from their known settlements. Our Searchers have been unable to find even one of their villages. Speculation has it that they are back to their nomadic ways once more. We have no hope of regaining their service. I know that you said make Zargarb serve us more, but the reports are back. As you know, when we sent but a single Searcher across the desert, he was killed by forces unknown. You ordered the Searcher to be accompanied by two dozen, but here is the report. All but one were slain by Arad bandits, who greatly outnumbered them, appearing suddenly out of nowhere. Jaiffur a'Meda barely escaped with his life to make his report. Then, there is the matter of Al Mari. Your Excellency will remember that you said to use the southern route to get to Zargarb. The report says that way is now blocked. Al Mari is no more; it is gone utterly. Further, the critical watering hole there has been poisoned. There is no hope of reaching New Barq without the water available at Al Mari. We cannot go south to Zargarb. Sire, what shall we do now? Who do we get to service us?"

Mustafa didactically replied, "Evidently they did not leave the Arad or else our Searcher is being attacked by ghosts, eh? Whom shall we get to service us you ask the Old Man? If the desert is blocked and we cannot get around by going to the south, then we go to the north. It's time that we stretch our long hands outward to the Greenway. Send three Searchers into the Greenway, and find likely candidates to serve our needs. Be quick about it. Now leave me."

"Brilliant, Your Excellency, positively brilliant idea. I'll see to it at once," the aide rushed out to relay the terrific news. Long had he argued for hitting the lush lands of the Greenway. Everyone would enjoy this change of pace indeed!

Mustafa signaled for his woman companion, skimpily dressed, to come and light his pipe once more. She gracefully did as he asked. "Come my dear, sit with me, and share my dreams," he beckoned to her. She slid down beside him on the divan and took up the second mouthpiece, inhaled deeply. Both drifted off into their beautiful world.

Chapter 21 Interlude and Decisions

The first snowfall of the season fluttered down large, moist flakes. Lilly Ann and I stood in the doorway holding the twins up to see their first snow. Since we had all gotten back here to Mont Blanc, John Henry just insisted that he had everything well in hand and that I should take a break and spend some time with the newborn twins. I didn't need any further encouragement! For the last couple of months, I forgot about the Guardians, the druwids, Cymry, everything, and just enjoyed my twins. Of course, Lilly Ann could not be parted from them either.

Whenever I arrived at the nursery, there she was ahead of me, doing this and that with them, fussing over their care with the mid-wives. I really did appreciate her help; newborn twins are a handful. "Look how Taliesin has grown," she said today. We could tell them apart, but just barely.

"Here, let's compare them side by side," I teased her, laying Tegid out by his brother. "Look how Tegid has grown," I answered, bringing a smile to her face. It was October 29, 623, the day of the first snowfall.

Just then, John Henry came looking for us; grim was his face and stern his countenance. I knew that something was wrong somewhere. He said, "Can you two come with me now? Got some bad news." We returned the boys to their beds and followed him out of this building and into the tower. Up the circular stairs, we climbed all the way to the top room, the main meeting room. It was empty today. John Henry said not a word until we were inside and the door closed.

"I thought that we were finished with wars, but I guess not. We've just learned that the Galts have invaded and taken Westerfold, the western kingdom of the Greenway. Happened about ten days ago. Of course, because of George's message about two months ago, we knew that this would likely be happening."

"Two months ago?" Instantly, anger surged within me. "We've known about this planned invasion for two months? How come I didn't hear about it?" I was furious. Later Lilly Ann said that she had never seen me quite this angry with anyone before.

Red faced, John Henry defended himself, "With all that you have been through, all the losses you've suffered, I thought that you could use a little time off." It was a very weak, lame excuse, but I accepted it.

"Look, as Wid and Judger here, we need to know everything, I mean everything. I want to hear all the information and messages that we've received here. I don't care what they are about or where they came from. Talk, buster!" I had both hands planted firmly on my waist, staring right at him.

He began by explaining who George was. For several scores of years, he was our spy on the edge of the Northern Steppes. Many years ago, he had assisted Rosita and Antonio on their rescue mission, retrieving her two children when Mikhailovich Strokova, their father, was killed down near Sud, Southlands. Hence, he knew Illanovich as a boy. Although now very old and retired, he still preferred to live out there on the edge of the steppes. From time to time, he would report on their activities and that of the recent Axeman thrusts into the steppes from the Elbe River. Quite by accident, he was in the ghost town of Al Dun the day that Illanovich Strokova reappeared, when he met with the Arad rebel leader, Qa Fahdi. John Henry related all George's report, which was quite interesting and detailed.

Next, he backtracked to fill me in on the reports from the Zargarb Circle and their progress at becoming a unified Circle once more. At last, I found out about the Arad raid upon the Junction, about the Holy Paladin's earlier raids, and even the subterfuge with the Holy Crosses, still being safeguarded at North Point. I was very appalled to learn that all the priests of the Church of Jehosanity Northern Orthodoxy had been slain way back on July 4! Andre's more recent report was very disturbing. It seems that Yazi had sent in about fifty missionaries-priests to begin preaching the proper worship of Jehosanity! Considering that most of Zargarb had long ago adopted this new religion, casting their ancient worship of Tur, the Sea God, aside, many had gone to hear these new priests and what they had to say.

The new priests claimed that Jes was the Son of God, alright, but that his birth had been one of an Immaculate Conception, that he remained a virgin his lifetime and had never married. All trace of his wife, me, had been stricken from their religion. To them, I was a minor prostitute that Jes had managed to save by some divine miracle. Worse still, these priests attempted to arrange the order of the life by having women become submissive, subservient in all ways, to men. This was completely the opposite direction that the women of the Sea Princes were heading. Long ago, they were in just such a position, perhaps worse. Only recently had they gotten a foothold in society as respected, valuable members, obtaining equality with men. This was a total slam in their face, so to speak, the very last thing they wanted to hear or have occur!

Around October 1, the people of Zargarb rallied against this perversion of religion and threw them bodily out of the sector, shipping them back to New Barq. Don't ever come back, was the battle cry. However, I found their last words very ominous and scary, "We will be back with enough force to teach you the errors of your ways. We will cast out your perverted Jehosanity beliefs! You have not seen the last of us!"

When I tied that to what I had seen on our trip to Megalos, the construction of ramming ships, the threat sounded even more ominous. All data to date indicated that the Emperor and the Church were bitter enemies, but what if they joined forces? Visions of yet another Centurion invasion of the Sea Princes filled my head with horror!

Back in Zargarb, the High Council had been slowly increasing the size of its ground forces, already adding another five hundred cavalry and a thousand city defense soldiers. By spring, the numbers would swell even more, according to Andre. On the good side, he reported no further invasions by the Holy Paladins, the Arad raiders, or even the assassins from the Old Man on the Mountain. Still, the Sisterhood there was in turmoil. If the raiders swept through the sector near the northern half, their safe haven at North Point was doomed. Eight hundred to a thousand Sisterhood fighters could not defend long against well over many thousand Arad raiders.

Andre also reported that these same raiders had wiped out the Centurion way station down at Al Mari. Best estimates were five hundred were slain. Worse still, depending upon your viewpoint, the raiders had poisoned the watering hole. This greatly complicated movement across the southern edge of Juda Arad, especially overland travel from New Barq southward.

"If I know these Centurions, they will respond and in strength," I thought aloud.

John Henry had more to tell. According to George, Czar Illanovich had formed an Alliance with the Arad Raiders. From now on, they would help each other out when needed, not only with supplies, but also with fighters. This did not bode well at all for Zargarb, which once again found itself in the middle of potential conflict far greater than it could defend against.

Next, John Henry related what had happened days ago in the easternmost kingdom of the Greenway. Several thousand Galt barbarian cavalry crossed the Elbe River and began systematically attacking every town they encountered. At last, they reached the king's palisade fortress at Avon Hill. The king's cavalry was soundly defeated, and the remnants retreated into the wooden fortress. What I found incredibly interesting was that the Czar sued for peace. Instead of totally conquering the kingdom and ransacking it of valuables, leaving it in total ruins, Czar Illanovich requested terms for peace. In return for not destroying utterly everything in sight, the Czar was given thirty wagon loads of various grains, a large herd of cows, and two flocks of sheep, all this in addition to various other items from the towns, such as chickens, blankets, clothing articles, and even metal tools. At no time did these barbarians take any gold, silver, jewelry, or gemstones! This was a complete reversal from what his father had done! Shocking, but also intriguing. It gave me much to ponder. Calling them barbarians now was very likely a complete misnomer, especially when I heard the rest. The Czar requested another thirty wagons of grain to be delivered next year after the fall harvest. Deliver it to the steppes or they would invade again and take it!

I asked the obvious question, did these men look like they were starving? Answer, no, they were very fit, fighting men, no signs of malnourishment. What was Illanovich up to, I wondered?

Further, that same kingdom had also experienced the assassins of the Old Man of the Mountain for the first time. With the abandonment of the Arad, the inability to cross it because of the raiders and the poisoned well, the assassins had moved north and west into the Greenway. At first, town leaders dismissed their demands, but after two mayors had been assassinated by local bums, crying something about "Take me into Heaven," they had relented and begun meeting their demands for gold, silver, and grain.

The news was not all bad, however. Back in Cymry, Augar and Cathleen had just been married. I had seen Augar here at Mont Blanc a month or so ago, and he took a fully recovered Cathleen home with him. We also sent three Guardians home with them to look after them for a while.

My steward on Cymry had continued the rebuilding and repopulation I had begun, and the people took kindly to her efforts. She blended right in with them superbly. Even the Grande High Council of Kings was apparently working out well. No wars, but in fact, they had peacefully settled five disputes in these intervening months. At least Cymry was finally at peace and could now begin to prosper once more.

Elona's reports from Velona were even more promising! Although they had deflected eight attempts on her life thus far, she had gotten a tremendous amount of order back into this Sea Prince Sector. In fact, her unique combination of Tur, Jehosanity, and druwid Nature religious-meld had now become extremely popular. Velona was now being called the Gnostic Capital of the World. Word of the tremendous successes to be had in her sector had spread throughout the Sea Princes. Daily more and more people were immigrating to Velona, seeking either the prosperity it offered or the religious tolerance it fostered. Over three thousand Axemen and their families had moved there as well. Hers had become a model monarchy indeed. That they also had invented the caravels greatly added to their growing fame.

Instant fame and desire sprang from the caravels. All the other sectors desperately desired to get a hold of one so that their shipwrights could make copies of it for themselves. Elona told each of the sectors that they could purchase one caravel each, but not until Velona had its own fleet completely rebuilt. They could expect to have one probably late next year. However, she knew, just as did anyone else, that once a sector had one of these new caravels, they would simply make duplicates of it. Elona also reasoned that if she did not sell one to each of the other sectors, then they would make all sorts of attempts to hijack one by any means possible. Shrewd Elona doubled the actual price for the single caravel. She then planned to use the funds this generated to establish a ship design school, where new ideas for ship designs could be hashed out and tested, headed of course by Pietro, who had invented the caravel. In her report, she hoped that within a few years that Velona would become the ship design capital of the world.

Elona also reported the final bit of news, that taken by itself meant little. Various ships plying the waters between Megalos and the Sea Princes, having been alerted by what Pietro's Folly had discovered, always were suspicious of new activities along the southern coast of the Southlands. Several ships had reported seeing several new towns spring up in the general area of that boat making bay. I concluded that we were seeing a covert buildup of Centurion forces and that the next attack might well come by sea, not overland from New Barq.

Finally, he gave me the latest figures on us druwids. He had accepted some additional retirements from active duty. By the end of the year, we would have only about two hundred eighty active members, with some additional hundred who were retired but could be called upon if needed. Members like George, for example, could prove invaluable, I thought. Lilly Ann and I had much to ponder now. We were more than surprised to find that three hours had passed and that we all were quite hungry, having missed lunch. John Henry finally finished, and we three went down to a late lunch.

I sat in the meeting room of the tall tower all the rest of the afternoon. Lilly Ann told me she would look after the twins while I was working. I appreciated her thoughtfulness and told her so; she merely smiled. John Henry had many maps built into the floor so that everyone could see them during a meeting. I moved the furniture out of the way so I had complete access to the maps. I added a charcoal sketch of some missing areas, particularly down south. Next, since religion seemed to be holding sway behind much of the actions, I created markers for each. On Velona, I placed a Gnostic marker. Next to it, Barcella got a Jehosanity denotation. After it came Vito with a Tur marker. Bonilla, next in line, received a Tur marker, as did Pieta, which came next. Solamina received a Jehosanity marker, as did Zargarb. Then, I backtracked to the d'Grange sector. Here I placed markers for all three, since this sector was a melting pot of Tur, Jehosanity, and even the Blessed Holy Mother. On Cymry, I placed the Blessed Holy Mother marker.

Next, I placed tokens to represent the Arad Raiders, whose location was unknown but somewhere in Juda Arad. Another token represented the Galts of the Northern Steppes. I placed two different kinds in Megalos, one representing the Emperor's forces, including the new ramming boats, and the other representing Yazi's Church. Exactly where each of their forces was currently located was also a mystery, as were their plans.

Finally, over in the extreme northeastern side of the Arad, I placed a token representing the assassins. We knew where they were located, but had not had the resources to deal with them. This was much better, now I had a good visual, spatial representation of the situation. Ah, but what to do about it all? Further, what possible new goal could I invent that the Guardians would accept? How was I going to tell everyone that our movement was dying? For hours, I stared at the layout, but no real answers came.

That evening, I brought my Circle up to the tower. I showed them my illustrations, brought them all up to date on the situations, and we discussed the situation at length. Paul, our Protector, had the only useful insight. "Look, there is virtually nothing to stop the advance of the Galts here in the Greenway. Each separate kingdom is isolated from the others. They will fall like dominoes against these riders of the steppes. Our most pressing problem, as I see it, is how to keep the Southway kingdom, Calgary, and Mont Blanc from falling to these horsemen. I give it a year possibly two, since they are not likely to attack during the winter season."

He continued, "As I see it, Velona, d'Grange, Calgary, Southway, and Mont Blanc must work together to establish this area as not being conquerable, except at a terrific cost. If d'Grange builds a harbor barricade like the one they have in Velona, they should be the most secure of all of us, virtually impregnable. Their biggest worries will come if we or Velona falls. If Southway falls, they are just north of us, so we are then in big trouble, likewise if Calgary falls. Worse still, our only exit points should we fall here are Calgary and d'Grange." He continued his analysis, but I thought there was one other secret exit point, through the Appian Way mountains just behind us. I recalled how more than a half century ago, we had found a way through the maze of tunnels to get from the Paese di Dio, God's Land to the Langdoc region where we were. I wondered if the passages still existed and had not been destroyed when the God's fought, the Grey Creatures and the Mantises.

When I rejoined the conversation, Allan, our Planner, was talking, "Our walls should be heightened, and we should begin storing food and water for a lengthy siege. Otherwise, I think that we are in relatively good shape here. Southway and Calgary are the weak links. We must fortify them. Percival is one of us, and we should concentrate our efforts on making his kingdom fortified with stone-built fortifications. Calgary is more problematical; still the king is closely allied with us. We should work with him to make Calgary solidly defensible as well."

Beth Ann interrupted, "You know, we ought to have a couple of those new fast caravels. We could keep them maybe in d'Grange or Calgary. If we need a fast get away, we have one."

"What about making our own port somewhere along the coast between d'Grange and Calgary?" put in Lilly Ann.

"We'd have to build it and then staff it," countered Allan. "We might be spread too thin to go quite that far just yet. I'll draw up some plans for it just in case. We'll have to scout out the coastline along there and see if we could find a suitable location. Anyone up for a ride?"

"I think we should make it three caravels," I broke in, "If it came to an evacuation, we need all the room we can muster. We've many folks here. Okay, gang. Allan, pick your crew and go see if there is any feasible location for a port for us. I'll see about ordering some caravels and how much that will cost us." We adjourned for the night.

The next day, Rea came to see me, announcing that the portraits were done and dry. "I've got all dad's inventions sorted out now. Those caves are perfect, lots of room to set things up."

As we walked to her section of the cave complex, she admitted, "This snow is slippery and cold, quite different. Say, I've gotten ten offers to go on a sleigh ride. Exactly what is one?"

I explained and added, "Be sure to bundle up to stay warm."

She nodded and added, "Beth Ann has agreed to accompany me. I've only to ask, she says. I'm not too confident with these men, you see. You were right. I've been deluged with flowers and invitations to dances and now even sleigh rides."

"Hey, if anyone knows guys, it's Beth Ann; she has always had them under her spell," I joked, remembering how she used to flirt with men last lifetime as Sarah Jane. She gave me the oil paintings of Caitlyn and me; they were magnificent, very realistic. It brought tears to my eyes to see Caitlyn so well depicted. I intended to put them in the boy's room so they could see what their mother looked like whenever they desired.

Next, I had a tour of Invention Chamber. There was Niccolo's Far Seeing Eyes, an optical device that brought very distant objects up close. Suddenly the incredible usefulness of this device struck me hard: we could observe the enemy at extreme distances, especially if the device were mounted high up on top of the tower! I had five Planners get to work on making a dozen duplicates of this machine. The next one that caught my attention was an intricate device with a number of inner-meshed gears. Rea said that it would tell the day and time of the year. I had the Planners attempt to make me an experimental copy. I had some vague ideas that the device might help us navigate at sea in our caravels. In fact, there were so many inventions that I decided that I needed to spend several days examining all them. They could prove quite useful, and Rea was very pleased that finally someone was keenly interested in her father's work.

Just then, Beth Ann joined us, "Ah there you are. I heard that you want me to come along on a sleigh ride."

Rea flushed and said, "Well, yes, I do, if you aren't too busy." I left them. This was becoming a girl thing, and I wanted to expedite getting these new devices constructed. Besides, I suddenly missed Caitlyn.

The long winter was occupied primarily by fortifications planning, making defensive arrangements with our neighbors, and helping to train new fighters for both Calgary and Southway. As far as a new plan for our movement was concerned, I had none yet. All my spare time, I spent with the twins and, of course, Lilly Ann, who always seemed to be there with them. They certainly were growing, strong and healthy.

I guess you could say it happened in early spring. Lilly Ann and I were out walking, each carrying one of the twins, enjoying the beauty of the early spring. Crocus flowers dotted the rocky hillside calling forth the promise of new life. Almost without thinking, our hands met, and I found my arm sliding around her shoulders, and hers, mine. I had an irresistible urge to kiss her, but kept fighting the notion. Then, I felt as if someone was pounding on top of my head, and I realized it was Caitlyn. *Go ahead, silly. Kiss her,* she sent to me. For a moment, I flushed. Our eyes met and I did not resist that urge any longer. We kissed long and passionately. Looking back, I suspect that she greatly desired this for some time; yet out of deep respect for both Caitlyn and me, she had said nothing.

Our relationship blossomed rapidly. By late spring, I asked her to marry me. Her reply was, "I will as long as two criteria are met." Her Judger personality insisted upon making sure that we both understood what we were doing. "First, just because we are married and I look after the twins, I don't want to be left out of our Circle activities in any way. No fair playing deference to me because I am your wife. Second, it's me and not my twin sister, Beth Ann, that you are marrying. She's the big sexy flirt, not me. I know Caitlyn really wants me to be her permanent mom; she told me so some time ago, so it is all right with her, if that is a worry of yours, which I can understand fully."

"Agreed, you are our Judger and a darn good one at that. I don't play favorites. It's you that I've fallen in love with, not Beth Ann. You may be twins, but it's you, the spiritual being using this body that I am madly in love with. I guess my only reservation is this. Are you willing to be a mother to my twins? If I had any doubts after all these months, you can kick me in the head or send me back to Observing the Obvious class once more for yet another refresher," I teased.

When we announced it, I thought that it would be a surprise to everyone. Wrong. It seems that nearly everyone fully expected it and wondered why it took me so long to see it and ask her. Ah well. We were married at the Summer Solstice Ceremony by the Standing Stones. However, I suspect that you are not very interested in my personal life, so I'll get back to the situation we were facing.

During the winter, not much that was newsworthy occurred. In the spring through autumn months, the Galts attacked and defeated three more Greenway kingdoms. Again, they did not loot, pillage, or burn. As last year, they demanded food, weapons, and basic supplies. Once more, I began wondering if they had starving people back home in the steppes. Their raids were definitely vastly different from Mikhailovich's; he had stolen all available gold, silver, jewelry, and gemstones.

Down in Zargarb, the Arad raiders once again made a foray into some of the easternmost towns. Just like the Junction, they took only food, supplies, and weapons. By now, we were almost certain that these raiders were obtaining food to live on, since their land had been so badly ransacked over the years. Yet, why didn't they just ask for assistance? However, because of their raids, two things occurred. First, by summer, the expanded cavalry had been put on a continuous patrol along the eastern border of Zargarb. Two large concentrations of their remaining forces were stationed equidistant along the border and about fifty miles from the border. The reasoning was thus. When the patrols detected incoming raiders, then the cavalry could move to intercept them. Andre promised to keep us posted on how this tactic worked. On paper, it looked good.

The second thing that occurred because of the new Arad raider incursions was that the Sisterhood stationed nearly all their fighters up north to protect their safe house at North Point. In addition, they still guarded the Holy Relics that the Archdeacon had given them for safekeeping. Since the entire religious hierarchy in Zargarb was in turmoil with the slaying of all their priests last year, they said little about them and continued to guard them. They did discuss the possibility of moving them secretly into Zargarb proper.

On the Centurion front, things grew steadily more threatening. Five hundred foot soldiers and a hundred cavalry from Zargarb were stationed on the paved roadway at the border of the Arad. Patrols daily rode down into the Arad, but never actually entered New Barq, where the road led. During the late summer months, these advanced scouts reported seeing a buildup of Centurion ground forces. Quite surprisingly, a goodly number of these men were the Holy Paladins of the Church. Somehow, Yazi had made a pact with Emperor Justinian; together they were planning to assault Zargarb. News did reach us late in the summer that the Arad raiders had been causing massive supply problems for these new troops, attacking and destroying most of their supply trains. My assumption was that the superior Centurion fighters from Megalos probably outnumbered the Arad raiders. As a result, they chose to attack where they could be victorious. I also presumed that their constant supply disruption likely caused them not to attack Zargarb at all during 624.

However, problems relating to the Church arose in other sectors during the summer of 624. Barcella and Solamina, the two other Sea Prince sectors in which the Church of Jehosanity Northern Orthodoxy held sway, were visited by a large number of Yazi's priests. As in Zargarb, they attempted to sway both the common parishioners and the clergy to change their beliefs to align with the "official" Church doctrine as set forth by Pope Yazi I, in Megalos. They also made similar veiled threats if the clergy did not reform. Reports indicate that these priests of Yazi did make some small headway in getting their viewpoint accepted, probably because of the fear of yet another invasion from the Centurions. Zargarb's position had not gone unnoticed by the other sectors.

Other priests of Yazi landed in Vito, Bonilla, and Pieta, the last remaining staunch supporters of Tur, the traditional Sea Prince Sea God. Here, they were somewhat more successful and established several churches, though at last report, the number of worshipers was few. Many came once, just to hear what this new religion was all about. However, in Velona, Elona refused to allow them to even land in her sector.

Word spread to all sectors of the Centurion construction of war ramming ships. Now every Sea Prince ship that sailed past that secret bay we discovered last year gave the bay a wide berth, but also were keenly observant as they passed by. As I suspected, the crews continued to report ever-increasing buildup of ground forces there. Worse still, ramming ship construction continued at an even brisker pace. Evidently, we forced their hand, and they decided to ramp up production.

Perhaps all this was part of Justinian's grand plan. By fall, fear and paranoia began to be heard at nearly all High Council meetings in all the sectors, save Velona and d'Grange. As the Sisterhood reported, some council members even suggested giving the priests what they wanted in hopes of staying off the anticipated invasions.

Not all was gloomy however. In Velona, people prospered beyond anyone's expectations, save perhaps Elona's. Orders for caravels poured in, keeping the shipwrights working two shifts and still not meeting the demands. The harbor defenses were completed along with protective walls around most of the sprawling city complex. What began as a hemispherical wall became several arcs, so that the Axemen and new ship construction docks, north and south of the city proper, were included.

By year end, Velona boasted a fleet of sixty caravels! Plus, the Axemen had over thirty of their longboats in their docks, ready to attack any enemy vessel that might threaten the sector. The Axemen had formed up the "Home Guard Unit," consisting of nearly a thousand of these burly fighters, bolstering Velona's defenses enormously.

In fact, immigration statistics were still escalating. Not only Axemen from the north, but also artisans, craftsmen, blacksmiths, and shipwrights flocked to Velona, bring ever increasing skills and much needed manpower. Indeed, Velona's population by year's end was estimated at well over eighty thousand in just the city alone. Many chose to settle in the outlying towns and villages as well.

What I found intensely interesting was construction had begun on a massive stone cathedral right in the heart of Velona. When completed, the Church of the Gnostics would be the most magnificent, largest, and grandest church or building on Tarra, capable of holding nearly two thousand worshipers at one time! Plans called for massive artwork, including exterior stone decorations, interior frescos, giant hanging paintings, and several mammoth tapestries. All this, of course, drew many artists from the neighboring sectors.

Yes, by year's end, we received our three caravels, as did the other seven Sea Prince sectors, which received a single ship each. However, Fortress d'Grange received four of these fast new ships. Being small in comparison to the other sectors, d'Grange could only use four ships. By constraints of the mountainous land, their bay could only support four ships at any one time. Still, they also were able to implement a variation of the chain link harbor defensive system constructed in Velona. Thus, Fortress d'Grange felt a good deal of relief by year's end; they felt secure from the invasions that everyone anticipated.

At Mont Blanc, we were not idle, using the precious time to make our preparations. With all the Planners stationed here, construction projects flourished. First, Percival launched a new construction project. He already had a well-established fortress on a hilltop at Middleton. However, he and the Planners came up with a new and novel idea: construct a giant stone castle, which would be impregnable! Based on the ideas in use in d'Grange, they extended them further to become a full-fledged defensive castle. Percival's idea was to provide food, shelter, and protection for his people in the event of an attack.

Because he expected the Galts to attack within two or three years, he opted to build the fortress in stages. The first stage taking three years to complete was the erection of a stone outer wall surrounding his current hilltop fortress. In subsequent stages, various stone fortress buildings would be built within the walls, replacing the parallel existing structures as they were completed.

Percival and Sarah paid their soldiers well, far better than any other kingdom, except Calgary. Hence, the people of the Southway considered soldiering to be a lucrative profession. At the start of the year, he had five hundred cavalry and five hundred foot soldiers, the latter were trained to provide security of the hilltop fortress. However, as the news spread of continuing Galt invasions, the number of new recruits more than doubled. By the end of 624, Percival had over fifteen hundred of the finest cavalry in the Greenway! His garrison ground forces had also doubled. Because he paid the workers on the new constructions so well, many stonemasons from nearby kingdoms secretly moved their families to Southway. His overall population increased twenty-five percent during this year alone.

Allan had found the perfect place to dock our three new caravels, Point Bleak. This tiny bay was about twenty miles south of Calgary. A promontory of granite arced like a crescent moon out into the ocean, providing a small, easily defended cove where we could dock our ships. It was about a day's hard ride from Mont Blanc, a day's hard ride on south to the start of the d'Grange sector, a day's ride south from Calgary. It was isolated with no other nearby beaches where vessels could beach invading troops.

It took the entire year to build a similar chain across the open bay defensive system, a stone wall around the docks, the docks, and several stone buildings that served as a small warehouse and garrison house for the defenders. Our dock was behind the promontory and could not be seen by passing ships. Thus, it was a very secure location. Next, we needed mariners to operate our ships. Elona offered to train our crews in exchange for our Planners' assistance in helping with the design of her great cathedral. The only problem in our design was wintertime. Ice completely blocked our bay. Thus, in winter, our crews would have to be sailing south for warmer waters. I would have given anything to be the captain of one of those ships! However, as leader, I could not at this time. However, now that we Guardians had three caravels, I knew that one day I would be able to be a captain and sail the seas!

In the summer, my Circle took a brief trip over to Cymry to test sail our new caravel. I had an ulterior motive, however. News had reached me that the priests of Nuadilan were going to construct a new, large, stone cathedral to the Blessed Holy Mother, called Bethany Cathedral. However, that also meant the old one would be torn down, pews and altars reused. Oops. Beneath a certain flagstone near the High Altar was the secret compartment in which Jes had us store the written records outlining the lineage of his line from the beginning at the dawn of their history, proving that his descendants were the rightful kings of old. For years now, we all dutifully kept the records up to date, adding births, deaths, and marriages to the ever-growing pages. Hence, this trip I decided to do two things: make a duplicate copy to be stored on the mainland and find a new location for Josh's descendants and for Cathleen and her descendants to continue to log this tradition.

King Hadir Amir, Josh's eldest son, provided the new safe, hidden location beneath a flagstone of his private church. Together, we let all the others know about this change. Agreement was also reached for me to make a copy and continue the log on the mainland. Sometime in the future, someone could merge the two into one.

I also checked on my towns and brought back with us three hundred longbows and thousands of arrows. Leanne Finn was doing a remarkable business making the finest longbows to be found. She was exceedingly pleased that I would purchase so many for the Guardians of Mont Blanc.

Since all was well and the new constructions going full pace, I took the time to attend the next Grande Council of Kings. I went partly out of respect for King Lachlan, even though she had fomented the attack against my towns. Her council was indeed working as expected, providing a forum in which to settle disputes peacefully. I found the meeting exceedingly boring, while Lilly Ann found it quite the opposite. She also watched my steward, Jane Wellington, in action. Jane was a master Judger, an arbitrator of excellence.

Finally, I spent a week with my sister, Fianna and Fergus. Their son, Angus, was now a year old and quite a handful. Seeing these two so completely happy was very rewarding to me. I hated to leave my sister alone on Cymry. However, seeing her so utterly contented with her new life as Princess Fianna filled me with joy. Both of them were surprised to find out that I had remarried and were pleased with my choice as well. Yes, it was a relaxing, fun week in the Highlands.

Late that summer, word reached us from Andre about an extraordinary event scheduled for early October. For the first time in Sea Prince history, all the sectors were going to meet and plot out some form of combined action against the perceived threat of the Centurions. All eight High Councils, one from each sector, were going to meet in Zargarb. Although d'Grange did not have a High Council as such, they sent several representatives to serve in that capacity. Elona, as ruling monarch, also planned to attend. Further, the Sisterhood decided to hold their Second Grand Council simultaneously, so that the Sisterhood representatives on the High Council could brief the respective Sisterhoods about what was happening. Naturally, the Sisterhood requested that the Guardians be well represented at their meetings.

Because of the monumental potential for unified action this offered, John Henry decided that my Circle should attend, along with Andre's Zargarb Circle and Alton's Velona Circle. For the first time, three complete Circles would attend, something that the Sisterhood thought exceedingly valuable. Besides, it gave us an opportunity to test sail one of our caravels, a shakedown cruise for our new captain and crew of eight. Thus, on September 1, the Flying Pinnacle set sail from Point Bleak. Captain Alan Swallow proved to be an excellent skipper. We stopped briefly in d'Grange to pick up their attendees and then headed around the Narrows to Velona. There we spent a day taking on supplies for the longer voyage to Zargarb.

Naturally, Elona had to show us all the breathtaking new constructions around Velona. It was utterly shocking to see the explosive growth. This was the first time I had been in Velona when the city was really doing well. I enjoyed myself thoroughly. I must admit that the size and scale of her new cathedral was enormous, beyond anything I had ever seen, but it would be years in construction. Only the foundations had so far been laid, still the proportions were staggering.

Normally, two weeks were required to sail from Velona over to Zargarb, but with these new caravels carrying almost no cargo, the time was cut in half. Hence, we took a leisurely sail over to Zargarb, partying all the way! We told stories, traded news and gossip, plans for the future, and just got acquainted with those whom we were not as familiar, such as the Velona High Council members. Still, we arrived almost a week early for the meeting. As expected, we were put up at the Sisterhood inn in Zargarb, as all the other High Council members would be. Why? The Sisterhood inn was simply the finest inn in Zargarb, safest too, with all the Sisterhood fighters present.

During the week as others began arriving, I was delighted to renew my friendship with so many of the Sisterhood leaders and Fighter Group Leaders. Honestly, if the motivation behind these parallel meetings was not so grim, I could have said that these weeks were some of the most enjoyable of my life. As October 1 drew near, we were informed of the scheduling. The High Councils would meet each morning around ten, be served lunch, and continue throughout the afternoon. In the evenings, the Sisterhood representatives would meet with Sisterhood council, relaying what had occurred that day.

The Sisterhood was in the unenviable position of not really being able to decide upon a course of action until the High Councils had made their own decisions. The women would have to determine their course only after the others had decided theirs. Hence, for the most part, we all had the mornings and afternoons off to do as we pleased. Only Elona was allowed to partake of the High Council meetings, as monarch of Velona. While we considered doing a Mind Link with her so that we all could witness firsthand what transpired, Elona thought better of it. "If something becomes vitally important, I will let you know. This is really the business of the sector leaders. Let's leave it that way for now."

One morning I got the opportunity to visit with Rosita and Antonio, who had ridden down from North Point to meet everyone. She took me aside, I could tell that she was emotionally upset, barely able to restrain from crying. "It's all my fault, Illanovich, I mean. He's back, and attacking your lands. I thought he had died after he ran away. I must have done something terribly wrong with him." She was full of remorse. "Perhaps I should have left him behind to be killed by his own people."

Lenkova, Illanovich's sister and Fighter Group Leader for Zargarb, overheard her mother. For months now, ever since word reached them that Illanovich had surfaced and was leading the Galts into wars with the Greenway, Lenkova tried to console her mother, to no avail. "Mom, it's not your fault. He was the one who ran away because he could not get his way. I promise you, mom, if Illanovich ever sets foot in Zargarb, I will teach him a lesson he will never forget!" She stomped her foot hard on the ground, adding as much emphasis as she could, hoping that would somehow reach her mother. It didn't of course.

Antonio tried his approach with Rosita, "Dear, we did try to instill the proper values of life in the boy. It's just that he was not interested in learning them. He never was; this is all his doing, not yours." Rosita continued to hold back her tears, merely nodding that she heard them.

I looked her squarely in her eyes, "Rosita, I've had similar feelings. My son Ahmad I raised to be a king over our towns, yet when I returned much later, I found that he had forsaken everything I had taught him and joined up with the Grey Creatures. My son was responsible for starting a war that killed thousands of good men, and all for nothing, absolutely nothing. In the process, he also caused my grandson to be slain, my granddaughter to commit suicide rather than submit to his capricious orders. Even his own wife died, not being able to stomach his vile deeds. That was my eldest son, Ahmad. Do I ever wish I could take back having that son? Absolutely. But then I think of the whole picture. His youngest daughter, Caitlyn, I married, and we had two fine twin sons. So who can foresee the entire picture?"

"She was his daughter? How did she escape all that treachery?" Rosita asked. I could see that she had similar feelings to mine.

"She ran away from home and ran into me. The rest is history. You see, if I took back having Ahmad, I would not have had Caitlyn nor the twins in my life." She gave a weak smile.

"Well, at least he is only taking food and supplies, I hear, not ransacking, raping, and stealing all their valuables," she admitted. "Perhaps, there is some good in it, although I cannot see the whole picture. Someone must be very hungry, I suppose," she continued to speculate.

"Yes, it could be worse. Still it is a stigma you bear, in part, he's your son, although I suspect that he has disowned you," I answered.

"Yes, I presume he has," she added. Brightening up, she said, "You are right. Look at my daughter, Lenkova. Without her, we all would have been lost so many times. She is the light of my life and the Sisterhood too." Lenkova gave her mom a big hug. Rosita's self-pity evaporated.

That night, the first of the many reports on the High Council meetings were relayed. As one might suspect, all sorts of wild ideas were tossed onto the table. Some suggested that everyone band together and attack Megalos, putting an end to that civilization. Others suggested that perhaps overtures of peace be sent, hoping for a peaceful settlement, such as had happened in the Greenway so many years ago. Some thought that all the forces should be concentrated here in Zargarb to stop their invasion just as it began. Still others wondered if the city walls would be sufficient to keep the invaders at bay. Others countered that with a fleet of ramming ships that could carry troops as well, no ship would be safe, and resupply by sea would be nearly impossible, including last minute evacuations. Only one lone voice thought that everyone was reacting to a non-existent situation and that nothing needed to be done because there was no war.

The Sisterhood representatives uniformly agreed that the main reason for this unparalleled meeting was that the nobles realized that this time they could not simply sail off to their vacation homes in the Med Sea islands and wait it out, holding onto their precious gold and gems. Rightly so, they presumed that those vacation homes might be the first target of attack! Hence, they had to do something, if only to save their own necks.

In fact, the second and third days passed much the same, only tempers rose gradually. These rulers were facing the crisis of their careers; everything depended upon them. The last time the Sea Princes were invaded, the decisions were made by the sole ruling Prince, while the nobles simply sailed off to their island retreats until it was over. Now they too faced what their predecessors had faced, and they were just as frustrated as the Princes had been. Even the Sisterhood representatives had no real solution to offer. It appeared that this meeting of the minds was doomed to failure.

On the fourth day, however, one of the Priests of Tur, Pietro Bonilla, whose distant ancestor helped found the Bonilla Sector, spoke up. His words were repeated later as we listened to the Sisterhood representatives that night. "You know, this is a war not of conquest of lands but of religion. It seems to me that the threats we've all been receiving about accepting the Megalos version of Jehosanity or else face our doom is all about religion. We in the Sea Princes have long prided ourselves on our freedom of religion, of which High Priestess Elona Po is the stellar example. Gnostic, I believe is her word for their unique mixture of beliefs."

After being hounded about where this was leading, he offered his suggestion. "Why not begin a Crusade for Religious Freedom? After all, our people have the ultimate say in this matter of religion. Amass an army of crusaders to go off to fight the Centurions in the name of Religious Freedom. We can still maintain sufficient troops to defend our cities, should they fail. Call upon all people in all lands to come and join the fight for Religious Freedom, create an army of volunteer freedom fighters to march to Zargarb and then down the road to New Barq and then beyond, all the way to Megalos if need be."

Sister Alicia, the Zargarb representative, explained, "Here was an idea that had merit. The council members immediately saw that this would place much of the responsibility onto the common man to defend their rights to their own beliefs and at the same time, ease much of the burden on the council members. Of course, such a massive army would require a good deal of funds to operate, but mostly our esteemed council members are the wealthy nobles, who would rather pay for an army as long as they did not have to actually do the fighting. Yes, this idea really appealed to the vast majority of the members. The tradesmen reps protested saying that they had not such funds; likewise, Sisterhood reps also went on record as not being able to provide a large amount of funding as well. Nevertheless, I think that this will be the route that the council will take." The other Sisterhood representatives concurred with her analysis; they were almost certain that this council would call for a Crusade.

"I believe in the next few days, we will see the details of how this volunteer army will be implemented," Alicia concluded. "So what is our position going to be?" all the Sisterhood representatives definitely needed to have this vital datum so that they could act in consort together, unified in their position on the council.

Andre piped up, "I'm all for it. Assuming that such an army can be recruited and moved into position in time, suddenly two fronts present themselves, something that the Centurions have never faced. While an army is moving toward them in the Arad, they will be trying to move on the cities. Interesting challenge, I would have expected the Centurions to attempt a coordinated action between the growing ground forces in New Barq and the sea fleet. Denied their ground forces, the sea fleet becomes much more vulnerable, far less sure of success in any case. I like the idea, personally." He suddenly discovered that he was now the center of attention here in the large dining room. He flushed and sat down, realizing that he had stood up in his excitement.

"Splitting up our forces? Doesn't that make us weaker everywhere?" Lenkova was the first to respond to her husband's view.

Others began discussing this new concept, but I became thoroughly engrossed in thought. I envisioned the movement of a massive volunteer army across lands. They would need food and other supplies in quantity, to say nothing of weekly pay to spend who knows where. Even their pay was problematical, because a week's pay would be a few silvers or a handful of coppers. Multiply that by thousands and the sheer weight of that becomes a transportation nightmare. Even the weekly food alone would fill many wagons — hence, the lengthy supply trains behind all the armies I had seen or about which I had heard. Add to that the likelihood of a sea blockade by the Centurion ramming ships and you see what I was pondering. Further, the transportation of such large sums of money raised a red flag with me, as I'm sure it would or had with the nobles: an open invitation to bands of robbers.

However, we had the caravels, the fastest ships on the seas, and we had the fighters who could defend such vital cargo without thought of stealing or pilfering. Could this be a new direction for the Guardians to take? Within the Sea Princes, the Sisterhoods were the only people trusted to transport any valuable cargo; they had been so for a century at least. Yet, if we joined forces with them somehow, then we could be the valuable's transporters for all Tarra. As such, we would be traveling everywhere and thus become the most knowledgeable people around. We would know all the news first hand! Thus informed, we might be able to influence events in more positive ways than ever before. In short, we might become the Guardians of the world. Okay, I admit I waxed overly grandiose in my thinking. I was excited about this idea.

As I returned to the conversations going on around me, I heard nothing particularly new, so I took this opportunity to add my coppers to the pot. "Excuse me one and all, might I share some considerations with everyone?" I began very politely and found that everyone yielded the floor to me. I stood up and paced the room as I commenced my lengthy explanations.

"Knowing the nobles as I do and as you do, I will go on record tonight as saying that this idea of a volunteer Crusade army will be adopted and implemented in some manner. I have no doubts about that. The question for both the Sisterhood and we Guardians is how shall we respond? Before I explain my suggestion, let me bring some harsh realities home to us all. What I am about to say will not be pleasant, and if I offend any, you have my apologies at the onset. Yet, you must have my full viewpoint. While it may be true that the Centurions are no longer quite the skilled fighting force that they were a half century ago when they invaded here, they are still a formidable force, and an inventive, resourceful bunch. Look, to counter the sea evacuations and resupply by sea during the Galt barbarian invasion of the Sea Princes, they have developed these new ramming ships. From personal experience, I can tell you that only these new caravels can escape their destructive ramming, but only if the winds cooperate, since these new ships are at least twice as fast as the normal ships of the Sea Princes. What does this tell us? Simply that if war comes, the Sea Prince ships of all sectors, save Velona and d'Grange, are doomed. If used, the risk of their destruction is fairly certain!"

I let this doom and gloom consideration sink in for a minute. "Yes, any attempts to resupply or evacuate using the older ships will likely be intercepted by the Centurions. This has nothing to do with whether there is a volunteer Crusading army around or not. We all think that the nobles have already grasped this eventuality, which is why they are holding this historic conference. They can see the likely future as well as we."

"Has anyone thought of the supply logistics behind supporting a huge army as it moves and fights? It is enormous. The fighters have to be well fed and paid routinely. That means either they carry with them a vast number of supply wagons or they have to be periodically re-supplied. If they want to field an army of say five thousand, then the number of supply wagons following them will be staggering, probably half of all the wagons in the entire Sea Princes! Not likely. So I predict that the council will instead opt for periodic re-supplying by sea. To do it overland would tie up vastly more wagons and personnel than by sea. Yet, if they attempt to re-supply by sea using their current ships, we can predict the outcome, given the ramming ships."

Someone called out in a desperate voice, "Is there no answer?"

"Yes, there is, but let me finish the doom and gloom first. I ask you, what do you all think the likely outcome of another war with the Centurions will be? Your Fighter Group Leaders have always given you a concise, accurate assessment of the fighting capabilities of the Sea Prince guards or cavalry. You have a good idea of how good the enemy is. Some of us have actually witnessed them in action in the distant past. Pit these Centurions against an ill-trained group of volunteers and what do you suppose the outcome may well likely be?" The hushed silence spoke loudly to me.

"Don't get me wrong, I do think this idea of a Crusading Army is perhaps the best counter-move yet, and I am all for giving it a try. However, the pessimist in me wants you not to place false hopes in it. Rather, think about what realistically might be the outcome and particularly the impact that it could have on the Sisterhood and the fate of all women in general in the Sea Princes. This has me, frankly, exceedingly worried and is a primary reason that I came. I want to help if I can."

"The reason that I am so fearful for the women of the Sea Princes is that, unlike the last Centurion invasion, this time their Church of Jehosanity is playing a major role. Their view of women's value and role in society is utterly degrading and inhuman, and I am being polite about it. I knew this Yazi a long time ago. His perversions on women are hideous, and now he has gotten himself into a position of power from which he can spread his poisonous views, yes, even enforcing them upon others."

"Wherever the Centurions gain a foothold here in the Sea Princes, you can expect that women's rights will be set back to the unbelievable state that I found them in when I first came to Velona and saw Horton Po in action. Everything you have fought for and achieved these many years hence will be lost utterly! You will be driven back into a secret society, hiding in the background of the city in disused alleyways. One thing that you can be certain about is that Pope Yazi will not permit the Sisterhood to exist as it now does. You will be eliminated by any means possible, even by assassination, as was my late wife, Caitlyn. The future for any sector taken over by the Centurions this time is utterly grim beyond words."

I know, some women were in tears, quietly sobbing to themselves. I saw horror and sorrow upon the faces of the elderly Sisters who had witnessed much of that of which I spoke. The distinct possibility, that everything these women had spent their whole lives achieving would be gone in an instant, struck home.

"But there is hope yet." I sensed it was time to reverse my course. "Some of you have wondered about how it has gone for us Guardians, since the Greenway has become a fractured group of a dozen isolated kingdoms. The answer quite bluntly is very poorly. We find ourselves in a quandary, perhaps not as bad as yours, but a dilemma we face as well. At this time, all the Guardians are concentrated within but two of the kingdoms, having been driven out of all the others, to their ill fortune, I might add. Our numbers dwindle, it is true."

"However, there remain two undeniable quite important facts about our two groups: first, unquestionably, the Guardians and the Sisterhood have the finest fighters on Tarra." I ignored the monk brothers, because I knew so little of Alabaster's new group. "Secondly, the Sisterhood and the Guardians are perhaps the best organizers on Tarra. Hum, actually, there are two more. We have and can work together well. We also have the only ships that stand any chance of evading the ramming ships. I guess that is four positive considerations."

"No there is yet a fifth. Back at Mont Blanc, our home, we have and are continuing to create a stone fortress that cannot be conquered easily, to stand as a last bastion for the free peoples of Tarra. We have that too. Where is all this leading? I propose that we merge our forces into a single group in a manner I've not yet considered. Here's my overall idea. Between us, we have the only ships that can evade the ramming ships; we have the only trusted fighters and protectors of valuable shipments. Let's build upon that."

"Suppose that we offer our services to the Sea Princes and other lands as providers of supplies and shippers of the most valuable cargos, including coins and gems. We provide the backbone that will support their volunteer crusading army. Eventually, I can see that we alone will be the sole transporters of items of great value for all lands, given that we alone can guarantee the safety of said items. This will put us in the interesting position of traveling everywhere and being fully informed on all key, significant events on Tarra. Having full knowledge, we ought to be able to change things for the better here and there. We would become the most trusted on Tarra and thus be able to wield considerable influence. If the Centurions do get a foothold here in one or more sectors, we may be able to influence them to moderate their treatment of women, for example."

"Are you offering a safe haven if the Sisterhood has need of such? Who would lead such a group? We are used to having our own council. What say would we have," asked Sister Alicia, the Zargarb council representative, after a discrete nod from her boss.

"How about a land army of our own?" Lenkova added. "Some of us would like to fight."

"Yes, the safest haven on Tarra I do offer, when and if it's needed. I firmly believe that Velona, d'Grange, Calgary, Southway, and Mont Blanc will be exceedingly difficult for the Centurions or anyone else to defeat even now. Together, united as one, we may yet swing the day, if not, then the future. As far as who would lead? I'm open to organizational suggestions. Like you, we Guardians are used to our own councils, as is Velona, d'Grange, and Calgary. I'm sure that together we can find an optimum way to make this work for the best interests of all parties. And yes, Lenkova, we ought to also field a powerful ground force, if only to back up the volunteer army. What do you think?"

Lenkova spoke before anyone else could respond, "I for one would feel vastly more comfortable fighting alongside of you folks and not for some volunteer army!" Her face reddened as she realized that she had spoken before her leaders had the opportunity.

The seven leaders of the separate Sisterhoods were seated together. They whispered among themselves briefly. Finally, the eldest rose shakily to her feet. Carmina Bunne, who was seventy-one now, yet had made this long trip from Vito, spoke first. Clearing her throat, she began apologetically, "I'm afraid that the others have opted to go in order of age. Quite why, I do not know. I've lived through it all; I guess that's why. Yes, when I was a young girl, women were treated very badly. All the stories that you've heard are only a tiny bit of what it was like to live under that kind of oppression and suppression. Personally, I was beaten and raped, a mere slave to my father, before I ran away and joined the Sisterhood. When the Centurions invaded long ago, the Prince and his forces were no match for their fighting skill or numbers. We Sea Prince folk are a seafaring bunch of traders; we spend our time on many things other than fighting skills. I wonder if we are any better at fighting today than we were back in the fifties? From what Sister Cecilia Amalio of Zargarb has told me about the effectiveness of the council's cavalry against the recent Arad Raiders, I presume not." She sighed and took a sip of water to clear her throat.

"I will be frank with you. I've never been so worried in all my years as the leader of Vito's Sisterhood. It has scared me nearly to death. That I would live to see women regain their respect and honor among men only to totally lose it all once more makes me shudder with disgust and, well, I don't have words to tell how I am feeling right now." She paused to wipe the tears, which streamed down her face, her voice choked. The room was utterly silent. Recovering, she went on, "To go back to the way of life that I lived and led back in the fifties, I would rather die first! Probably will," she added. "I would not put any woman into that kind of life. So I vote that we give Mister Ket Bethany's idea a try. I would hate dearly to have to move out of Vito, especially at my age, but I would rather move all my dear friends than have them become lower than a dog in Vito's society. We used to be called the Abominations. I swore that never again would I allow that. For what it is worth, I support his proposal as far as it has been discussed. It allows us some possible hope, if the worst happens. I've monopolized the room long enough; besides, I'm now pooped." She sat down, completely out of breath from the stress she was experiencing.

"Guess I am next," Rosita Bellini of Fortress d'Grange said as she stood up. She was in her sixties. "Lucretia, you tell me if I forget anything important," she said to her companion sitting opposite her. Lucretia Botini, also in her sixties, was her Fighter Group Leader, while Rosita was actually the Leader of the Second Tower of d'Grange, the Count leading the First Tower. "I too have lived a long life and have witnessed many miracles. I first began my long career in Velona, at a time when what now we would consider huge atrocities were commonly committed against women. I've known Ket Bethany through two lifetimes now. When we first met, one of our newest members, Thallia, had her tongue cut out. Not only did he and his Guardians show her the utmost kindness, Thomas even fell in love with her and married her. In essence, they gave her a completely new life that was totally fulfilling. These Guardians were primarily responsible for helping us all get to where we are today in our respective societies."

"When the plague came, I took his advice and moved Velona's entire Sisterhood to d'Grange and Mont Blanc. Little did I know that there are men in this world who value women for what we are and for what we can do. Do you realize that I am now considered the equal of Count d'Grange? Seriously, I lead one of the two towers of our fortress! Personally, I can state that he is very correct in saying the assaulting Fortress d'Grange would be incredibly difficult to do with success. We are not large, but we are extremely defensible. Yet, we, all by ourselves, cannot hope to stand alone against the rest of the world. Our docks are small; our volume of trade equally small. No, we must find a way to unite. We have always been allied with the Guardians of Mont Blanc and recently with Elona Po of Velona once more. So no matter what you all decide to do, realize that the d'Grange Sisterhood is completely behind the Guardians of Mont Blanc. There, I've said enough," and she sat down.

The other leaders looked at each other, grinning. They were all about the same age. Cecilia was just slightly older, so she decided to go next. "Cecilia Amal, Zargarb," she began, as if no one knew her. "Here in Zargarb, we've seen plenty of troubles over the years. We, too, have only the highest regards for the Guardians of the Greenway. Yet once again, Zargarb finds itself in the dubious position of being on the very front lines of the initial assault from the Centurions. How about one of you going first next time," she jested and brought several smiles to the women.

"Seriously though, I offer this small bit of wisdom. Assume for the moment that all he says comes true, that the Centurions once more invade and take over Zargarb. Further, assume that they force their perverted religious beliefs onto our society, degrading women into cattle once more. If this happens, how can we best help the women in Zargarb who find themselves once more degraded? Only two choices are possible as I see it. We remain here and go underground again. We haven't forgotten our hand signals have we?" she once again jested, which brought smiles to many faces. I knew these women could carry on complete conversations with only their hands and fingers!

She continued, "We help from an underground position or we try Ket's plan and help from a position of power and force, albeit from the outside. Either way, we must continue to fulfill our mission, our purpose, our goal to aid Zargarb's women. That is not in doubt or what we are even discussing. No matter what choices we make, our goals remain constant. It becomes then simply a matter of the means, the mechanism, and the wherewithal of how we do it. As loathed as I am to have to evacuate my beloved Zargarb, I would rather help our women from a position of power than one of an underground, secret society, where if you are discovered, you would be slain at once. No thank you. I vote we give Ket's plan our full support. I would rather fight back from a position of power this time. Okay, you all figure out who's next," and she sat down.

"Mandi Zoria, Pieta," said the next young woman of thirty-five. "Ket, Rosita Rosario sends her love and affection. I'm afraid her health did not permit her to come to see you again." I nodded. "I know I speak for many here. I will be heart sickened to have to leave my beloved Pieta, should these vile priests turn our society upside down as anticipated. Yet if that does happen, I agree fully with Cecilia. I would rather continue to fight for women's rights from a position of power than from an abomination underground society. See,

I kept it short," she chuckled and sat down.

"Anita Lopez, Barcella," announced the next leader to arise. She was thirty-five with a fair complexion. "I am relatively new to my position as leader. Lucia Lupe has recently passed away. "Loathed am I to abandon Barcella, leaving our women to be treated as dogs once more! Yet, in Barcella, we have seen how this new religion can become perverted, as you say. They began pleasant and nice enough, offering aid, supplies, and assistance in rebuilding. However, when they began to downplay the role of women in our society, that literally drove us out of their religion. Before that, many of our Sisters actually joined their church. Now, all have withdrawn. Barcella is slowly sinking back into that abyss of degradation of women once more."

"While we still retain a council seat as well as our lucrative precious-cargo convoy support, daily our rights are eroding, as dust on the streets in the rain. I have been searching for effective ways to combat this erosion of human rights, but nothing has worked well. Now, I am very angry, although some will say I am violently angry about it all," she added. Several women clapped in support of her position. "Over my dead body will I lead an underground Sisterhood! I say we fight any way we can. Barcella will throw its full support behind Ket's fighter plan." She sat down abruptly.

"Janis Botellio, daughter of Jannisseko, Bonilla Sector," the young woman of thirty began as she stood. "Mom says hi to all you, and especially to all you Guardians. I insisted that she not come on this trip; she's getting rather feebleminded in her old age. Personally, I would find it very hard to abandon my home in Bonilla, very hard. It is not something I take lightly. However, I too would rather fight back and aid our people from a position of power than an underground secret society. We back Ket all the way."

"Mina Lia, Solamina," said the next thirty year old woman to rise and take her turn. "I guess we might be called the last bastion of the true Jehosanity faith here on Tarra. Our priests remain true to the original teachings of the Son of God. We all cried and said prayers for the lost priests of Zargarb. From all of us in Solamina, we send you our deepest sympathy and respect. They were among the greatest religious teachers Tarra has ever seen. All Solamina is ready to fight hard against these vile perverters of our religion in any way that we can. We will also back Ket's grand plan with one stipulation. If Solamina and its religion of Jehosanity should fall to these invaders and the perversion of the religion occur as outlined, we wish that somehow, somewhere as part of this coalition, the true worship and practices of Jehosanity be continued. If you will assist us with this, then Solamina will back you completely."

She raised an issue that I had not yet considered: continuing the proper version of Jehosanity, or at least the Northern Orthodoxy version, which was at least close to what Jes, the Great Messiah, had in mind. I said that we would indeed honor her request, though how I did not know yet.

"May I have a say?" asked Elona Po. The seven leaders gave her their approval. "High Priestess Elona Po, Monarch of Velona, Guardian Protector. I want to speak on behalf of Velona, which at this time does not have a Sisterhood within its borders. Yet, we are part of the Sea Princes, and I feel I owe it to all you to say what Velona's opinion in this matter actually is."

"When I took back my birthright of Velona last year, Velona was the cesspool of the Sea Princes! Only four noble houses remained; thievery was the most common stock in trade; religion was totally perverted beyond belief, and starvation, the rule. Now more than a year later, all that has changed so dramatically that at times I find it hard to believe. Velona is now the Gnostic Center on Tarra, a living illustration of how men and women of various religious faiths can come together and work toward a common purpose. We blend native Velonans with Guardians and even with Axemen. We strive for the highest purposes attainable; we bring order out of chaos."

"Okay, enough sermons. Velona today has invented the fastest ships on the seas, our new caravels, of which we now have around sixty built, fifty in service. We have designed a gate system to prevent an invasion by a sea force carried on ships. Our Axemen have close to fifty of their longboats docked and ready to see naval action, should the ramming ships bother us. As sole monarch of Velona, sole ruler, I say unto you this day that Velona is one hundred percent behind the Sisterhoods. We back you and support you all the way and in every way that we can muster. If a safe haven is ever needed by any of you, you've only got to come to Velona to find it, as well as a new, gratifying life style."

"Further, Velona stands with Ket and the Guardians completely and with no reservations. We will support his grand plan with all our might and in any way that we can. United, we all stand a far better chance against Megalos and their Centurions and their perversion, their so called religion. I felt that you needed to know where Velona and I stand on this. Thank you for allowing me to speak." She sat down. Alton began clapping and soon the whole room gave her a thunderous applause. Elona was a little taken aback by this, however.

Cecilia rose and the noise abated. "Well, Ket, you have your answer. Now, of course, comes the hard work. How do we organize and run this new alliance? We should begin detailed meetings as soon as possible. However, our council reps must keep us informed so that we can coordinate our plans with theirs. Personally, Ket, I would like to thank you for giving us some small measure of hope for the future. I, for one, was very disillusioned, if that is the right word for it. While I would hate like heck to have to pack up and leave Zargarb, I relish that I may still be able to help our women here. Thank you, sir." Now I got the next round of applause. The evening meeting adjourned. Everyone now had so much to discuss that the room became more animated than normal for hours.

For good or ill, I had just set into motion a new set of goals for the Guardians. From the quiet of my room, I contacted John Henry and briefed him fully on what had just occurred. His comment was simply, "Darn good idea, Ket. Positively brilliant, Master Wid!" Time would tell whether this was a good idea or not. I was extremely thankful that I had my Judger with me, Lilly Ann. I would need all her skills at organization at once.

Chapter 22 Formation of the Knights Santi del Dio

As fully expected, the High Councils did indeed adopt the idea of calling for an all-volunteer army, the Crusade for Religious Freedom. Financed by each sector, plans called for the raising of at least ten thousand foot soldiers and five thousand cavalry. Each volunteer needed to bring their own weapons and armor. However, what they might lack would be provided by the Sea Princes, though the cost of which would be appropriated from their basic pay.

Basic pay was established at a silver a day for the foot soldiers, while the cavalry received two. The Sea Princes would provide all food and other basic supplies. Staging areas would be established in each of the eight sectors with the Sea Princes providing the transport to the front at no cost.

Each sector was responsible for the massive advertising campaign to recruit candidates, while a fund was established to broadly promote this campaign in the Greenway, Cymry and other countries. Surprisingly, a task force was setup to attempt to contact the Arad Rebels. The goal was to either bring them on board the Crusade or at least get them to agree not to interfere. Curiously but perhaps not unexpected, considering the situation in Velona, they also sent word to Volksholm, the land of the Axemen, asking for volunteers. However, the pay was tripled for any Axeman who would volunteer.

The High Council's requested treaty documents be drawn up between Velona, Mont Blanc, the Sisterhoods, and the Sea Princes. Specifically, they wished in writing what the positions would be if and when the trireme ramming ships should appear on the scene, as well as what support they could depend upon in the upcoming campaign. Elona promised to use her new caravels and the Axeman long boats to break any embargo and to destroy the Centurion war ships.

However, to address the other two issues, I was allowed to speak to the combined High Councils, as the leader of the Mont Blanc forces. At Sister Alicia's suggestion, I bought some new clothes to look the part of a leader. She insisted that for these people, mostly nobles, first impressions played a heavy role in their acceptance. Looking now like a noble wearing their finery, I entered the large room, which at night was used by the Sisters for their meetings. As I entered, I saw exactly what Alicia had meant. Gathered here were perhaps the richest men on Tarra. True, tradesmen looked more like common folk, but the preponderance of people wore expensive clothing. I was glad that I had followed Alicia's advice this time.

"Greetings from Mont Blanc, Greenway, fellow defenders of freedom," I began, realizing that this speech was perhaps the most important one I had ever delivered. Secretly, I thanked my lucky stars that I was very conversant with their dialect! "Thank you for allowing me to present to you first hand the support that you may expect from us. I am very pleased to announce to you today the formation of a new fighting group to be known as the Knights Santi del Dio, or just the Santi for short. Mont Blanc is home to a large number of perhaps the best fighters on Tarra. The Santi will be composed of these men and women. I have agreed to be their field commander. Additionally, the seven Sisterhoods have agreed to become an integral part of the Knights Santi. Thus, I pledge to you that the Santi will be responsible for all shipments of any vital, critical cargo to the front lines. I give you my personal guarantee that any losses that we might suffer will be replaced from our own pockets. If we lose a shipment of silver wages, we will make up that loss from our own treasury at once."

I paused to let this critical point sink into their consciousness. "You have long trusted only the Sisterhood to guard your most critical shipments. Now you have an even stronger basis for security, backed by the best fighters on Tarra. In this coming war, you can count on us to see that vital supplies reach their intended destinations and relatively on time as well. The Santi will be doing dual duties. One branch will provide security for all critical shipments, while the other, led by myself, will act as an advance strike force. The Santi, acting independently, will do everything in its power to assist the Holy Crusade become a successful one."

"At this time, the Santi is forming up. Thus, I cannot be specific about the total size of our advance ground strike force. However, rest assured that it will be both large enough and powerful enough to handle the situation." I hoped that it would be so, though I was merely speculating here. "On the mundane side, the Greenway will supply as much grain as we possibly can and at no charge to you. We will use our means and funds to acquire said grain and we expect that the Sea Princes will be responsible for its shipping costs. However, Mont Blanc is not as wealthy as the Sea Princes and only a fraction of your size. Hence, the Santi requests a nominal fee for its services of guarding and protecting your valuable shipments, say one percent. I know that the Sisterhood usually gets around ten percent of the shipment's value. The Santi, for the duration of this Crusade, waives that fee in favor of a single percent. Consider it the Sisterhood's and our contribution to the collective efforts to defeat the Centurions."

This part of the speech was entirely Lilly Ann's doing. By having me present our request of one percent of the value of the cargo, both the Sisterhood and Mont Blanc would be making a profit, which in turn would allow us to become even stronger and more able to do our jobs. By making it seem like we had waived nine percent, the nobles immediately considered that they had just made one terrific bargain! Lilly Ann was entirely correct about these men. Several asked nearly simultaneously, if I was kidding, only a single percent? As I replied affirmatively, I knew that I had sold them on this aspect.

"Further, we need to establish solid communication lines between us. Since the focal point initially appears to be Zargarb, any time you need to send a message to the Santi or myself, contact Sister Alicia, who will in turn contact Andre and his band of Santi who will relay the messages from here to wherever the message is destined. You will find that the Santi lines of communication are swift indeed." I did not tell them that Mary Bridgeport, Zargarb Circle's Communicator, would use telepathy to get the message delivered immediately. I was counting upon our having fast, accurate communication lines to offset our smaller numbers.

I had to answer numerous questions for the next hour. Yes, we would provide our own armor, horses, and weapons. Yes, we would need food and the usual supplies. No, we accepted no pay, unlike the volunteer Crusaders. Yes, if we lost a shipment of silver monthly pay, I would make up that loss from the coffers at Mont Blanc. Yes, caravels were twice as fast as the trireme but only if there was wind. No, I had no early estimates on the total size of the strike force. On it went for over an hour.

Our name, Knights Santi del Dio, actually was a compromise with the Sisterhood and the times in which we formed. I wanted the word "knights," while the Sisterhood desired a reference to religious freedom and women's rights. Hence, we compromised on God's Holy Warriors. Many of the devoutly religious Sisters believed that this title gave them more credibility in the eyes of the common man. Now the hard work began during the ensuing nights: organization and planning.

Our planning was to commit to specific numbers by the end of the year. Estimates put fifty caravels needing our protection, between Velona, d'Grange, and our three. Each of these would have one guardian, many of whom came out of retirement to sail on the ships, two Axemen, four fighters from Velona, and ten Sisterhood fighters on board. John Henry made sure that each of the Guardians was able to utilize not only fire spells but also the proven effective push spell.

I insisted that each Sisterhood only donate half of their fighters to the Santi, keeping the remainder for home guard work. By the end of the year, the Santi would consist of one hundred fifty Guardians, five hundred knights who were proven fighters from Mont Blanc and Southway, one hundred fighters from Cymry led by Fergus, who insisted on being in on the action, and another two thousand three hundred Sisterhood fighters. The Sisterhood Santi broke down into three groups. We armed five hundred with Leann Finn's long bows. The second group consisted of one thousand short bow archers. The third group boasted eight hundred mounted fighters.

My rationale behind this arrangement was based on two key factors. One, having seen the devastation that archers caused, especially those with the new long bows, given an enemy closing to battle, this number of archers ought to be able to deliver a deadly blow from a distance. The second factor concerned the fighting style of the Sisterhood, totally defensive. These highly skilled fighters practiced a defensive mode, not an offensive one. It would be folly for us to attempt to circumvent all their years of training to get them to become offensive fighters. Still, once the enemy had finally closed ranks, these archers could instantly revert to their normal fighting skills, holding a line, defending a position very solidly.

The Fighter Group Leaders handpicked the eight hundred Sisters that formed the mounted brigade. These were the very best of the Sisterhood fighters and who had somewhat offensive attacking skills. Thus, from the very beginning, the Santi was organized into two subgroups: an offensive strike force of one thousand fifty cavalry and a defensive line force of fifteen hundred archers. In addition to these numbers, the Sisterhood also provided us with another five hundred non-combatants, cooks, seamstresses, wagon drivers, and others to provide a supporting group for the fighter arm. This arrangement proved very effective indeed.

Equipment was a problem. Normally, the Sisterhood fighters wore only modest leather armor, if any. I wanted the entire strike force to wear chain mail to reduce the number of injuries as much as possible. However, chain mail was costly and time-consuming to produce, around seventy-five gold coins and ten weeks work. I needed thirteen hundred sets and ideally closer to three thousand! This problem I gave to John Henry, who obtained nearly fifty suits on the open market and hired several hundred armorers in Cymry, Velona, d'Grange, and Mont Blanc. By the end of the year, I had all the Guardians in the strike force suitably equipped, along with half of the Mont Blanc knights and half of the eight hundred Sisterhood mounted fighters sporting magnificent chain mail armor. John Henry promised that by next summer the remainder of the mounted strike force would be armored. However, to equip all the archers would require at least another year of hard work. I was pleased with his efforts; it was a herculean task on such short notice.

Another problem was the shortage of quality horses for all our mounted riders. I refused to allow the Sisterhood fighters to bring along their horses since that nearly depleted all their steeds. Then, I remembered Zdlenka Strokova and our Guardian Waverly, who was studying the raising and training of horses under Zdlenka. She had promised a large number of horses in exchange for grains. When I contacted Waverly, she was very pleased to hear from me personally. We had not "spoken" in well over a year, even by telepathy. She did indeed have a herd ready for us, over five hundred head.

Problem solved, except for how to get them. Normally, we sent grain wagons to New Barq and then along the paved roadway to Al Mari and then cross country into the highlands where her settlement was located snuggled up against the mountains. Now, Al Mari's water was poisoned, Arad Raiders were a constant threat, and the Centurions were amassing for a war with us down around New Barq. The normal route was definitely out. Lenkova wanted to see her Aunt Zdlenka, though I suspect she wanted advice about Illanovich really.

Hence, I sent her and the Zargarb Circle along with five hundred Sisterhood fighters across central Arad, leaving from Florintine Junction, via the ghost town of Jerilum, south down the paved road, and then cross country to the Havens. Lenkova and crew arrived back in Zargarb with six hundred horses by the middle of December. They had encountered no one; however, they had been observed many times, probably by Arad Raider scouts. Footnote: during their absence from Zargarb, Sisterhood fighters from Solamina came to take their place, protecting the North Point safe haven.

The council meeting ended on the tenth day; although it was hard parting with so many dear friends, we also left that night at high tide. Sailing at top speed for home, we made the run in an amazing eight days! Wow, were these new caravels fast! Of course, the captain explained that we had perfect winds. When we all arrived back at Mont Blanc the next day, I had a major meeting to hold, one that would change the Guardians forever.

John Henry arranged the massive meeting for the next afternoon, giving me time to relax, visit with the twins, and prepare my speech. He told me often that he was unbelievably thankful that he did not have to give this speech! I had to announce the ending of the druwid movement as such and the formation of a somewhat different group, the Knights Santi del Dio. I had to be convincing and to give them new purpose. Perhaps, this was the most important speech I would ever have to give. I found myself wishing the Alabaster was the one giving it!

Since many Guardians were out on assignment, John Henry arranged for Mind Links with all those who could not be present in our large Great Hall, which at one pm, was now packed with all the druwids and their trainees. Even many of those who had retired recently came to this meeting. While some two dozen here already knew what was going on and the gist of what I would say, but most did not. Slowly I climbed upon the overly tall set of boxes so that I was high above the crowd and so that everyone present could see me directly. I gazed out upon some three hundred plus of the most able, most powerful beings at this time on Tarra; many were very dear friends of mine.

"Druwids one and all, thank you all for coming to hear me. What I have to say is the most important words that I can recall ever having to speak. Let me begin at the beginning. We represent the most powerful, responsible beings on Tarra. Alabaster chose us to become his Guardians of the Greenway. For centuries, we have fulfilled that obligation with honor and dignity. However, as you know or have observed or have guessed or have surmised, now our numbers have been reduced drastically, more than cut in half. How has this come about? By far the attacks by the Grey Creatures accounts for the largest reduction; so many were wantonly killed by those creatures before Alabaster and I put an end to their treachery. Also, the upstart kings who have now divided our beloved Greenway into a dozen or so tiny kingdoms have also played a part, killing many of us, rather than just asking us to leave. Also, old age continues to take many of us as well, but that is part of the Cycle of Life on Tarra."

"In fact, at this point in time, our entire basic purpose, our reason for existence, has ended; we no longer can protect the Greenway as a whole; only Calgary and Southway remain with us. I suspect that many of you have seen this coming for some time now, though not speaking of it openly. Am I right?"

Quite a few gave a serious head nod.

I went on, "There is something that only a few of you know about, but today, all shall know. When I sailed south to Megalos to rescue Rea Helios, I made another stop along the way, one that I had planned all along. Unfortunately, I am under a vow of silence as to its precise location. Prior to leaving and upon fully grasping our dire situation here, I sought out Alabaster, Mind Linked with him, and discussed our plight and asked for his guidance." This revelation brought quite a stir, lots of mumbling and whispering followed. I paused so that they could express their feelings.

"He asked me to come and visit him. Yes, he is now doing well, has a new body, and has even found his wife once more. Both are very happy; in fact, he is happier than I have ever seen him!" This brought a round of cheering, as I expected it might.

"Then, he and I had a discussion about the situation that we now face here. The old man totally surprised me! In fact, when he made the decision to go deal with the Mantises in the Red Desert, allowing me to go north and tackle the Grey Creatures, he had already seen this very situation, our very plight at this time! He said, 'I saw that my druwid movement was dying and that there was no way it could be rectified. Thus, I chose to find a new path.' He explained to me that what we all need to do is simply end the druwid movement as such and for all of us to adopt a new set of goals and purposes in life, ones worthy of our best efforts. What the new goals and organization would do, believe me I begged him for guidance. However, he only said that we should find and make our own new goals, that he could not do that for us."

"Ever since then, I have been searching, seeking, and pondering what that might be. At the unique conference that we were just at in Zargarb, the new goal and purpose literally fell into my lap, so to speak. In the past, we were the guardians and protectors of a single land, the Greenway. I propose that we expand that greatly and become the watchdogs for the Greenway, Cymry, and all the Sea Princes as well. Let me explain fully; there is no one on Tarra at this time who knows as much about it as I do, since I lived it."

"Last lifetime, Alabaster asked me to take an Arad body and seek out this Great Messiah of theirs. Learn from him, for they believe much as we. I did so, even becoming his wife and bearing our children. I do believe that the spiritual being we called Jes Amir was the son of the god Jehosa. I discovered that they believe many of the same things that we do, only they say them differently and without the conviction and certainty that we have. For example, they believe that they are spiritual beings, whereas we *know* that we are."

"Jes chose ten disciples to follow him and record his teachings. One of the ten was this Pope Yazi and another, the late Bandar Dero. When Jes appeared to die upon a cross and then become resurrected from the grave, this was his last ditch attempt to reach his people with his message that they are spiritual beings not bodies. It failed, as I told him it would. At the last supper with all of us, Jes told the disciples to write down his teachings and then to go forth into the world and spread his message. All ten did as he ordered."

"Bandar established the Church of Jehosanity Northern Orthodoxy in Florintine Junction. His great works and humanitarian aid to the people of that sector will never be forgotten. He lived the life by example that Jes Amir would have been proud. Still, Bandar did not fully understand all what Jes taught; hence, his version has twists and variations in it. None are totally ruinous, however."

"Yazi somehow went to Megalos to preach and founded the Church of Jehosanity there. Unfortunately for all Tarra, Yazi has totally perverted all the Great Messiah's teachings! He hates women, all women, but Bethany Madelyn Amir, the wife of Jes and mother of his children, me, most of all. He hates me with a passion seldom seen except in an insane person. Thus, his religion is convincing people that all women are vile, wicked creatures, designed only to bring the downfall of man. Women, he considers, have less rights than that of a dog!"

As I was explaining this to the crowd, I had a sudden flash of insight. In that instant, I fully understood what the real purpose Yazi was attempting to accomplish. "Oh my god!" I exclaimed as I grasped the magnitude of Yazi's true purpose. I then had to explain my inexplicable outburst. "What Yazi is actually attempting to do is bring down the Megalos civilization! He is trying to destroy them from within! The blind old fool! He's not only going to bring down Megalos, but all the rest of Tarra with him! Holy cow!" I then calmed down and explained more about Yazi, who was always pestering Jes to begin a Holy War with Megalos, the land of the Infidels, and destroy them with his God-powers. Jes, of course, refused utterly.

Having explained all this, I then continued, "Now you might think that we are just facing two sides of Jehosanity, but no, there is yet another facet to all this. After Jes was apparently killed by the Centurions on the cross, we immigrated to Cymry to raise our children in safety. You see, Jes Amir's ancestry makes him and his offspring direct descendants of the original King of the Arads, to say nothing of being the children of his Son of God bloodline. He wanted to protect our children from the ravages of the Centurions. Later, as you know, Jes was killed trying to slay one of the Grey Creatures."

"In Cymry, as his wife, I began churches for the Arad immigrants who settled there. After my demise, I discovered that now they have created a completely new religion based upon the works of my life, the Blessed Holy Mother, and I am worshiped. So in fact, there are three branches of religious worship that sprang up from the Great Messiah."

"You have all heard that Yazi's so called Holy Paladins have slain every last one of Zargarb's priests of Jehosanity. Then, they attempted to move in and take over the churches, preaching their perverted religious beliefs. They were summarily expelled. Undaunted, they went into neighboring Solamina and tried to do the same there, with the same result, expulsion and rejection. However, they issued a dire warning that they would be back and force their religion upon all Solamina."

"At the meeting in Zargarb, I learned that indeed this is their plan. Holy Paladins have joined with the Centurion main army, currently down by New Barq. It is obvious that they plan to invade and take over all religions of the Sea Princes."

"Further, Yazi, having discovered that I survived the downfall of the Arad, sent an assassin to seek out my trail. This assassin has killed many of my children and grandchildren from last lifetime, including my dear Caitlyn. However, we outsmarted the assassin, and Sarah and her line along with Cathleen still live. Yes, these are Jes Amir's direct descendants, and the very people of which Yazi absolutely must destroy all traces or his religious teachings would be exposed as the complete fraud that they are. Hence, by whatever means possible, these descendants must be kept alive and allowed to continue the line of Jes Amir."

"What has all this got to do with us you are probably asking right about now? I'm sure if I were in your shoes, I would be. The answer came from the unique meeting of all the leaders of all the Sea Prince sectors down in Zargarb. The High Councils have decided to put out a call for an all-volunteer, Crusaders for Religious Freedom army to come there and fight against the Centurions and Yazi's forces." I explained the details of this Crusade in detail.

"Such a large army is going to need regular pay and supplies, especially critical if the trireme ramming ships appear in the Med Sea, as I suspect they soon will. Here then is our window of opportunity to enlarge our game. In the Sea Princes, the Sisterhoods are the only trusted, reliable protectors of any critical shipment. Thus, by merging the Sisterhood with us, forming a new group, the Knights Santi del Dio, Santi for short, we place ourselves in the unique position of being the trusted carriers of anything considered valuable to many, many different places. I have put us on the most critical communication lines of the northern hemisphere. We will be able to know firsthand all the news from most lands directly. More importantly, as the sole trusted couriers, we will be in a position to influence people and events in many countries, not just the Greenway. Our goals to help the people of Tarra have just moved ahead by a giant step!"

I went on to explain more details and how the merger would work. "Yes, we will continue to seek out young beings that are not firmly stuck in their heads and train them as we can. I see this as an incredibly fortuitous situation."

As expected, some did not like the idea, but most clapped and cheered. The idea that we were taking on a larger sphere of influence struck a nerve with many, who had witnessed the gradual shrinkage of our Greenway support all the way down to just two small kingdoms. Bolstered by the Sisterhood, we were expanding our reach to many, many more people.

"What if this Crusader army fails and the Centurions take over the Sea Princes or part of them?" someone I could not see clearly yelled out.

"If Yazi's forces gain control of the religion of the Sea Princes or even a sector, the rights and humanity of all the women there will be thrown back into the dark ages as it was more than a century ago. The Sisterhood leaders uniformly agreed that they would not revert into being some kind of secret underground order trying to help the oppressed. It is real to them that any such person who is discovered would likely be executed. Rather, they see it as I do, being on the power communication lines is a distinctly better proposition, a position from which they could offer much better assistance to those women in need. If a sector should fall, the Sisters there are prepared to move elsewhere, leaving their homeland behind. Other non-conquered sectors volunteered to take them in as did Velona and as did I. If these women are willing to take such a gamble, we should too." That seemed to satisfy the man, at least he said no more.

"Might I have a word?" asked Allan, our Planner, who in his last lifetime had been responsible for the design and construction of our fortress here at Mont Blanc. I stepped down and Allan stepped up. As we passed, I had a curious look on my face. What was he going to say? I had no idea at all, but I went along with his request.

"Hi everyone, Allan Donegal, Planner, here. I just want to add my own vision of the future to help clarify this Santi thing. Since we will be responsible for the safeguarding and transport of the most valuable shipments around this northern hemisphere, we will need various staging areas in various countries. I would like to propose that all we Planners put our heads together on this matter. In my opinion, I would like to see an impregnable Santi castle-fortress in every key location along our many routes. Not just one Mont Blanc, but dozens of them, places of power for us, providing security for us and our families. How about a fortified stone castle a day's ride from each other, a string of them from here to the Arad and beyond! Anyway, that's my vision of the future." He stepped down and one by one, everyone began clapping. Soon, they yelled as well. His vision was very well received! I liked it too, but wondered how long it would take to build so many of the castles he had in mind. I would find out in due time, however.

The next day, the real work of our total reorganization began in earnest. I found myself attending meeting after meeting for weeks on end. Percival and Sarah were given the task of culling out the very best fighters in the Southway. John Henry and his Circle, intimately familiar with the King of Calgary, did the same in that kingdom. Our standards for new recruits were high, intentionally so, because we would be bringing these "outsiders" into our midst and eventually lives would depend upon their skill and honor.

With a month, the Sea Prince posters advertising for the volunteer Crusader army began appearing, becoming the talk of the towns and villages throughout the Greenway. Close to home, the King of Calgary handled the coordination of the Greenway recruiting for the Sea Princes, housing them where there was space around his city. Whenever he had gotten a group of a hundred volunteers together, he appointed the best man, in his opinion, to be the captain, and gave him four lieutenants to command a group of twenty-five men each. Then, he sent them on their way, down the road toward Fortress d'Grange, who escorted them down to Velona, and so on, eventually arriving in the Zargarb Sector.

One duty I farmed out to my Circle. Their task was to catalogue how many complete Circles we still had, a count of the number of each specialty, such as Protector that were not in a complete Circle, and the number of apprentices we were teaching and their current year of training. Remember, ten years of hard study was normally required to become fully trained. They also made another list of the number and types of the retirees who wanted to lend a hand.

We had full Circles in d'Grange, Velona, and Zargarb. John Henry's Moon Circle and of course my Circle were fully operational. I was shocked to discover that only six other Circles were still complete! There were one hundred sixty-nine other druwids in active service at this time. The breakdown counts were this: Wids-15, Protectors-15, Loremasters-25, Judgers-25, Planners-28, Communicators-30, and Healers-31. It was very clear to me that the Grey Creatures had concentrated upon our leaders, the Wids, and our Protectors. Interestingly enough most all the Healers and Communicators were women, while the Protectors and Judgers tended to be mostly men. The remaining disciplines were about evenly divided.

I was encouraged with the trainees, however. All told, we had one hundred thirty-nine somewhere along their ten years of study. Their breakdown were this: 10th Year-25, 9th Year-23, 8th Year-21, 7th Year-18, 6th Year-17, 5th Year-15, 4th Year-9, 3rd Year-8, 2nd Year-7, 1st Year-5. Over the next three years, we would see a nice increase in our numbers; however, after that it became grim. Now I appreciated the amount of worry and frustration John Henry had been facing for the last three or four years!

Armed with our true numbers, I could then make the necessary decisions. The six southern Sea Prince sectors needed fast communication with Mont Blanc to make organizational communications lightning fast. Hence, I picked six Communicators and six Judgers, all whom were single and who volunteered when asked, and fired them off overland to their assigned sectors. Fortress d'Grange, being close and having a complete Circle, did not need them. Neither did Velona, which had no Sisterhood. Even though Zargarb had a Circle, I wanted the Sisterhood there to have their own dedicated pair. Likewise, each of the seven Sisterhoods sent one of their organizational representatives to Mont Blanc. As the winter came, this proved invaluable with all the myriad details involved.

I had no difficulty finding fifty volunteers to staff each of the caravels, serving as the leader of its defense. All were retirees! They jumped at the chance to be able to travel the world at no expense and to be wintering in the much warmer climates! However, before they were fired off, each one underwent training so that they could effectively cast the highly useful Push spell that Paul had used against the trireme. I wanted each caravel at least to have this option available in their defense. Swamping an oncoming ramming ship could mean all the difference in the outcome of an attack.

In late December, Allan proudly displayed his latest two inventions. He and several planners had been tinkering with ways and means of defending a caravel against a trireme. Just outside our walls in the snow-covered hills, they had setup a demonstration. From memory and measurements of our three caravels, they had created a simulation of the bow and stern decks. At the bow, the Planners had built a huge crossbow. Because of all the rigging lines, the crossbow was about the only thing that could be used here. Off in the distance, they had placed a dummy standing in a mockup of a trireme. Allan demonstrated, firing the huge bolt, which completely took out the dummy, knocking it completely off the ship. "You see, a good shot can eliminate the ship's leader — leader gone, ship falters."

At the stern was an even more impressive engine, one that lobbed a basketball sized object a goodly distance. "I propose that we use burning tar balls for projectiles. Here, I am using a rock. Now watch what happens to that dummy trireme." Another of his Planners fired the mechanism. I watched as the rock arced high into the air and landed on the mocked up trireme, smashing a large hole in it. "Rock or fire, either way, a direct hit spells major trouble for that ship," Allan proudly declared. He admitted that accuracy was going to be a major problem, but with sufficient training and practice, the caravel protection squads, as they had now become known, would have additional means of defending these precious ships. Thus, when the spring thaw came, all fifty caravels had been outfitted with a shooter and a lobber, as they were called by the CPS, Caravel Protection Squads.

Each CPS consisted of a Guardian, two Axemen, four fighters, and ten Sisterhood fighters. During their long voyages that spring, the CPS had something to keep them entertained.

Next, I formed up the Advance Base-Fortifications Developer Squads, the ABFDS, consisting of a Wid, a Planner, a Judger, and a Communicator, wherever possible. These were fired off to all our allies: Southway, Calgary, Cymry, d'Grange, Velona, and the other Sea Prince Sectors. Their task was to find and locate suitable sites on which we could construct a stone castle/fortifications in that sector. All would be along the coast, with the ability possibly to dock a caravel and with good access to the pave roadway system for fast overland travel. Their initial orders were to find one such location and get the building process begun somehow, raising the outer defensive walls were the top priority. While it would take years to finish each one of these sites, with a wall, we would have some protection almost at once. That was my line of reasoning. In hindsight, the entire construction process would have gone far more smoothly had we built the items in a different order, the outer walls last.

The six complete Circles, being composed of the older druwids primarily, I assigned to the defense of Mont Blanc. Many of the younger druwids became my strike force personnel. Now I had the difficult task of attempting to organize the actual mounted strike force. I spent weeks pouring over various schemes. With my Circle's help and suggestions, we came up with our Santi Strike Force organization, making use of the twenty-five 10th Year new graduates. In general, all our squads consisted of around twenty-five members, sometimes with extras.

First, I created two special groups. The Healing Squads were five in number, each consisting of six Healers and two squads of Sisterhood fighters to protect the Healers and to help bring the wounded to them as well as lend helping hands. Next, the five Scout Squads consisted of five Loremasters accompanied by twenty-five Sisterhood scouts, along with one Communicator who would relay news instantly. These proved invaluable in the field!

I placed Fergus in charge of his Cymry Regiment, which consisted of four squads, each of twenty-five fighters. I also added a Healer and a Communicator to his regiment. I needed him alive or my sister would kill me! Four Sisterhood regiments each consisted of four squads of twenty-five fighters and a Communicator. This way, instant communication at the regimental level was assured. The various Greenway fighters made up three regiments, each containing four squads of twenty-five men each. Again, I added a Communicator for each regiment.

Finally, my regiment was a mishmash. Lenkova led her squad of the twenty-five best Zargarb Sisterhood fighters. I had two complete squads of twenty-five Guardians, mostly Wids, Protectors, Planners and Judgers. My fourth squad consisted of the newly graduated twenty-five 10th year apprentices. Plus, add in both my Circle and the Zargarb Circle.

In total, the Santi Strike Force consisted of nine regiments plus five Healer and five Scout squads. Close to eleven hundred of the best fighters made a powerful force indeed. We were backed up with twenty longbow squads and forty short bow squads of Sisterhood fighters, all mounted. I had one Communicator for the bunch.

Five hundred non-combatant Sisterhood women provided support, cooking, sewing, and other needed domestic duties for us. An additional ten squads of Sisterhood fighters would provide depot garrison protection, once we established the drop off point where our supplies would be delivered, most likely somewhere in the Zargarb sector. Yet another five hundred Sisterhood fighters joined the fifty caravel defense squads, the CPS. Our initial total number of fielded fighters was then somewhere around four thousand. Impressive I thought.

Finally, on February 1, 624, Lilly Ann and I kissed our twins goodbye. I hugged John Henry and wished him well defending and coordinating all our activities in the field. We began the long trek overland to Zargarb, adding more forces along the way. Fergus and his regiment joined us in Pieta, because he had to wait until the spring thaw before the caravels could dock and transport him and his men. As we traveled along, more and more of the Sisterhood squads joined up. Each time we added more, I had to pause briefly to get them organized and oriented. However, with the Communicators doing much of the advance communications and organization, this went surprisingly smoothly! I continually praised all them for their terrific efforts, making this a success thus far.

Adding to the overall confusions, the new volunteers for the Crusaders were also traveling much the same route as we. In comparison to us, these units were vastly unorganized, requiring much intervention by the High Council representatives, who were in charge of this volunteer army. Already, our caravel shipments were saving the day by bringing food and supplies to these advancing men, most on foot, walking to the front in the Zargarb sector. Several times, I received a hearty thank you from the sector High Councils, via their messengers, of course.

I should at least present a footnote on my Sisterhood friends who joined us along the way. At Fortress d'Grange, where we picked up the first of the many Sisterhood squads, Adriana Socorro, their Fighter Group Leader, was the leader of the d'Grange Regiment. When we arrived, she came straight up to me and reported in, "Welcome Ket Bethany. We meet again. I just want you to know what a tremendous honor it is for me to be an integral part of our Santi Strike Force. It seems we travel across the sectors together once again." I could not help recalling how much she had helped us a couple years ago as the Cymry Minstrels traversed the Sea Princes searching for Alabaster. Adriana Socorro, a strong willed, middle aged woman, was often trusted with the most difficult missions. She was a proven field commander and a no nonsense leader. I valued her highly!

She continued, "You'll be glad to know that we have our old trail chef, Camilla! She's volunteered to cook for us again. Seems like old times, even more so because Sister Felice Bugatti insisted on coming with me, commanding one of the Scout Squads assigned to our regiment." Felice is the daughter of Florencia Bugatti, the Sister who had accompanied my Lightning Circle across the Sea Princes. Flo knew the land like no one else I had ever known. Felice, now thirty-seven, followed in her mother's footsteps or as the saying goes, like mother, like daughter. Felice or Fel as she preferred, would once more be our guide across the Sea Princes.

"Actually, Adriana, you have it all backwards. It is I who am most thankful and highly pleased that you and Fel are coming with me! I've assigned one of our Communicators to be your personal assistant, so that you can get information to me instantly, and vice versa, of course."

"Wow, a real telepath for me?" Adriana, who knew just how vital this form of communication could be on the trail from our last excursion, was sincerely impressed and honored.

"Hi, Eve Stockbrook," her Communicator introduced herself. Eve was twenty-five years old, but rather homely. Although she loved to talk about men, she seldom dated, feeling far too self-conscious about her appearance. Her double chin did not help. I thought that being with this powerful person, Adriana, might help her own self-esteem. The two took an instant liking to each other.

In Barcella, we added their regiment of Sisterhood fighters, led by their Fighter Group Leader, Ana Fellini, the daughter of Lana, who had been their previous leader. Ann was twenty-five, married with two children. Her husband, a vintner, stayed behind, caring for their children and running his small business. Ann explained that if Barcella fell, her husband would be evacuating with their children. I suspected that many families might just do the same thing.

Later on, we added another regiment from Bonilla, led by their Fighter Group Leader Leda Furstio, thirty-five years old. I had also met her during the minstrel's journey across the sectors. Highly competent, she only added to my growing feeling that we were putting together one incredible force!

In Pieta, I was very pleased to meet again their Fighter Group Leader Alice Augato. Alice had the most marvelous, mellow alto voice and she was a knock-out blonde! Now thirty-two, she was extremely fit. Her muscles were solid, but not overly large, and she was my height, though trim. Once more, I could not help but notice her firm large bosom, pale blue eyes, and flush cheeks. Yes, she was more than an attractive woman indeed. I felt that embarrassing bulge swelling in my pants once more; damn, I hated male bodies.

She smiled her completely disarming smile and said, "It is once more the highest honor to serve with you!" This time I was very glad to introduce her to her personal Communicator. Otherwise, I think Lilly Ann might have given me a punch where it hurts! What a woman Alice was!

Solamina's regimental leader I also knew, Sister Ali Bastia, who was thirty-seven. She had gotten over the impact that the Grey Creature had had on her Sisterhood messenger service. Now she was ready to fight enemies that could be handled, not the superhuman creatures. Likewise, she was highly pleased to have her own Communicator at her side at all times.

By April, our very large army finally arrived at the outskirts of Zargarb. There we found that a temporary staging area had been arranged for our nearly four thousand members, including our non-combatant support Sisters. For the next two weeks, the Guardians worked with everyone, outlining the details of how we all would operate together. Further, we could go no further until the last shipment of chain mail armor and an additional large supply of arrows arrived by ship.

We were encamped on the western side of the city, while the volunteer Crusaders were stationed on the eastern side. During these weeks, the High Council members personally inspected the Santi. Plus, I held numerous strategy meetings with the leaders of the Crusaders. It was important that we keep each other well informed of what we intended to do on the field of battle.

At this time, the Crusaders numbered well over six thousand men. Organizationally, a general led a group of about a thousand men. Two of these were cavalry; the other four, foot soldiers. An additional four thousand foot soldiers were in various states of making their way here to Zargarb. In order to coordinate so many men, another general was in charge of the ten working generals. I found the titles a bit confusing.

The top general was Antonio Prada, a seasoned fighter from Zargarb, who was in his forties. I found him to be a tough man, hard-nosed, and opinionated. Right from the start, this campaign would be run his way. In fact, that was the first words he spoke to me, "Welcome to the front line, Ket Bethany. I'm in charge of the Crusade, which will be done properly, my way. Just so we understand each other. Have a seat."

"How many solders do you have now?" I asked, this seemed to be a benign question that would not get us into an argument the first minute.

"Ah, six thousand good men thus far. Reports have another four thousand on their way. They keep arriving every few days now, have been for the last couple months. We move out in three weeks. Now here is my initial plan." He had a large map of the Arad and the Zargarb sector on his wall and he pointed out his first major movement. "We will move down the paved road to this point here, just beyond the Cedar Woods. History tells us that these Centurions will move down their paved roads, so we ought to be in perfect position to stop them cold. We'll set up flanking regiments of course, but they will likely not be needed."

"The Centurions have begun to move against us then?" I asked.

"Not exactly, I aim to be in position before they begin, nip them in the bud, so to speak. I'm not at all sure that we even need your forces, Santi, is that what you call them?" he asked, a slight trace of a putdown in his voice.

"We are an independent strike force, sir. Yes, the Knights Santi del Dio is the full title, we've around four thousand, mostly Sisterhood defensive fighters," I replied honestly. As the commander, he needed to know our strength.

"Not sure how much 'striking' you can do with defensive fighters. Probably best if you stay here and defend. I'll send word if I should need you. Personally, I wouldn't count on that, however. This time, the Centurions will get a taste of their own medicine."

"Aye, sir. We will probably do some scouting and exploratory probing, just to make sure that the Arad Rebels don't try anything against your flank. You need to be able to concentrate of the real enemy." I laid it on thick, giving myself a way out. It worked well.

"Yes, that's a good idea. Go right ahead. Keep those rebels from interfering, please. That will be all, unless you need something else." I said no, we shook hands, and I left. So much for the meeting of the two army leaders.

When I relayed how the meeting went, my Circle laughed hilariously, until I pointed out that men's lives were at stake on his decisions. "So what and where are we going anyway?" asked Lilly Ann. Paul seconded her question. My reply was a simple I don't know yet.

Chapter 23 The Santi's First Action

That night, I called for a council between my Circle, Elona's Circle, Andre's Circle, Lenkova, Adriana Socorro, Ana Fellini, Leda Furstio, Alice Augato, Ali Bastia, and Fergus d'Aine. First, I explained how the meeting with the Crusade general went. Most chuckled. The Sisterhood did not hold these fighters in contempt, rather just the pomposity of men. They suspected that this general wanted nothing to do with an army of mostly women fighters, especially if they were superior to his men.

"We are off the hook, so to speak. I had feared that he would place our forces in some untenable position. However, we have carte blanche to do as we please. I've asked you here tonight to work out 'what we please.'" More chuckles.

Ali asked, "Seriously, does the High Council really think that this rag-tag band of freedom fighters is going to hold against the might of the seasoned Centurion fighters? I've been watching some of the regiments all day. They might not last the first charge. Are we doomed even before we start? Have the High Councils just found another scape goat for losing yet another war?" She asked what many were thinking and they all deserved an honest answer.

"In truth, I've never held out much hope in an all-volunteer army or this Crusader force. However, the Axemen may make a difference. I just wish there were far more of them. Ali, this is why I have created the Santi organization. If the sectors do fall, I want all you to be in a position to help. I refuse to let you all sink back into some underground organization fighting for basic rights everyone should have. And this really gets to the heart of this meeting, what will be our first objective?"

"Bear with me for a moment; let's speculate on possible futures. Suppose the worst happens and that all the sectors, save Velona and d'Grange fall. Certainly, these priests of Yazi's will return and begin spreading their falsities, destroying and degrading all women in the Sea Princes by spreading all their false sermons about the life and teachings of the Great Messiah. I think that is a certainty. I just don't know if it will be one or six sectors that fall victim to the Centurions this time. I highly doubt that they can take d'Grange, but Velona might be overpowered by forces moving overland from Barcella." Doom and gloom spread on everyone's faces.

"What we need is a way to counter these lies about Jes Amir. We need a way to prove that their perverted version is just that: a total perversion of the truth."

"How can we do that?" asked Lilly Ann, before others had a chance to ask this leading question. Did she read my mind, I wondered?

"Remember, last life I led was that of the Great Messiah's wife. I was his most trusted disciple, more so than the official ten disciples were in fact. Perhaps that is what has set off Yazi so much, for he hated the very air I breathed. Anyway, I know all that went on during those years with Jes. When we had the last meeting with the disciples, the Last Supper it is now called, Jes instructed them to first write down a complete description of everything they had witnessed, all his preaching words, his teachings. Once done, a copy was made and to be sent to the Qaam sect's main vaults. I know from Bandar that this was done. Several copies of these original gospels are still in existence. The few that Bandar had acquired ought to be safe at North Point, along with the Holy Relics. I strongly suspect that part of Yazi's Holy Paladin's many trips to the Arad were in search of other copies. How many Yazi has is anyone's guess, probably hidden away in some underground vault never to see the light of day again, much less be read by someone."

"When the barbarians invaded, just shortly after these copies were taken to the Qaam for safekeeping, their town was attacked and leveled, or so the story goes. Additionally, those vaults hold the originals and copies of all the Arad's prophets' teachings. I know, I wrote them all down, I was one of the three scribes. One time, Jes and I visited there and I know where those secret vaults are located."

Ali could not contain her excitement. "Then, we should go and retrieve them. We would have proof of Yazi's lies and perversions!"

I grinned, "Yes, that is exactly my thinking. We ought to go and see if we can recover them. Also, we ought to take safety precautions and ship the ones at North Point back to Mont Blanc, where they have the greatest chance of safety."

"But where is this place?" asked Adriana.

"It used to be called the Qaam fortress at Al Tarm, situated high atop a tall mesa. Actually, it's the last mesa; its eastern slope blends uniformly into the foothills of the impassable Kathas Mountains. Al Tarm is located somewhat north and way east of the central Arad city of Jerilum, far off any beaten track. There is no destination beyond Al Tarm, just the rocky, sparsely vegetated, steeply rising foothills suitable for the grazing of sheep in the summer months. You see the Qaams believed in the old ways, the simple ways, simple times, believing this path through life led them towards a purification of the spirit, that one might rejoin Jehosa in his Holy Realm. Anyway, Al Tarm is in the extreme northeastern portion of the Arad."

"Wait just a minute, Ket!" broke in Lenkova. "Isn't that really close to where Alicia predicted the assassins' hideout was located, where this evil Old Man of the Mountain resides?"

"Precisely," I replied, curious that she spotted that correlation so quickly.

"Why don't we also go just a bit further and put these assassins to rest," she declared with a passion. She finally saw an opportunity to get rid of these vile men.

"With your consent, I would very much like to add that side trip to our agenda. This is the first opportunity we've had where we have the forces to attempt to cross the desert without being wiped out and cross with the very people I believe we will need to do the job cleanly. We've more than fifteen Protectors among us! What say you to these two being the very first Santi actions we undertake?"

"Yes!" exclaimed Lenkova. Lilly Ann quietly asked for a show of hands. I had one hundred percent agreement. I was not surprised, because I was offering those that followed Jehosanity here in the Sea Princes a chance to acquire the proof that they could use to bring down Yazi.

"Prepare, then. We'll leave a week before the general begins moving his army southward. Water will be our biggest worry. Spread the word to bring along lots of water, and check with everyone to see if any have a good knowledge of the Arad. My data is many years out of date," I explained. If too much had not changed, I ought to be able to get a group this size across the Arad, but the watering holes just could not support four thousand plus an equal number of horses, to say nothing of the supply wagons and personnel.

Later, I took Paul's advice. The thousands of mounted archers would move to Florintine Junction and act as a barricade should the Arad Raiders make another appearance after the main army went south. I did not want our return route cut off. Additionally, that lowered the numbers to eleven hundred plus support personnel. Nevertheless, our water demands would exceed many of the watering oases.

On April 21, astride my new horse from Waverly and Zdlenka, I vigorously arced my right arm from its raised position downward, giving the signal to move out. Thus, the Santi began their first mission. For three days, we rode north up the spoke road toward North Point. Once there, the four gospels that Bandar Dero had gathered along with the three Holy Crosses were carefully packed onto a wagon. Twenty-five Sisterhood fighters who were assigned to protect North Point followed my instructions to the letter. They drove the wagon up onto the Paese di Dio, God's Path, an uninhabited region just below the Appian Way. From there, they traversed the entire width of the Sea Princes, only coming down from this magnificent high country when they reached Velona. After delivering the items to a Protector from Mont Blanc, who met them there, these women then returned home.

Additionally, by having thousands of mounted archers not far from North Point, the security of the Sisterhood safe haven was not compromised.

Three more days later, we paused at the very edge of Juda Arad, the vast desert land. Now would come the tricky part, picking out a pathway across this land that would visit only the largest of the northern watering holes. Consensus among the ten of us who were very familiar with northern Arad was that the usual track had too many watering holes that were too small for our needs. I'm not sure why, but I did not consider veering due north across the Dragon's Teeth into the lush green of the steppes, crossing the long distance up there, and then dropping back down as we neared our destination.

Chapter 24 Moves and Countermoves

Pope Yazi I addressed his staff at their usual weekly meeting. "Well, that attempt in Solamina failed, but I suppose that it was doomed from the start. The biggest challenge of our lifetimes will be to succeed in spreading the proper worship of Jehosanity across Tarra, wiping out these other perverted versions that seem to be springing up like wild flowers after a desert rain." He paused in reflection; none of the other priests dared interrupt him.

"Be that as it may, we still have mighty weapons now. I'm told that the Holy Scriptures are being printed widely now. Soon, we can start handing out the word of Jehosa to those who can read." He was referring to his rewritten gospels; the originals were safely hidden away in his private vault far underground. Although he considered burning them, something always kept him from actually destroying these scrolls. He'd finished his revisions and now had contracted to have books printed. True, only the educated could actually read such a book, but it was a start.

"Our plan to form Scholastic Schools throughout Tarra where the chosen may come to worship Jehosa and learn to read and write is making great strides. We ought to have enough funds donated to this cause to open a dozen monasteries of learning in the Sea Prince sectors just as soon as we conquer them. So that is on track as well."

"Thus it is that I ask you, what is now our biggest problem?" he paused to give them time to answer.

One priest ventured timidly, "We have not the strength to conquer them?" It was phrased more as a question than a statement of fact. Yet, it was the right answer.

"Precisely. How do we achieve that objective? Once more, I have prayed to Jehosa for an answer. Last night, I received the word of God. How do we do it? We join forces with the Emperor! Yes, we make an alliance with him. That the Church and the Emperor can and are working together, side by side, to achieve a common Megalos goal will do wonders for the morale of all Centurions! It is a brilliant solution. No longer will it seem that our Church and the Emperor are antagonists. I've already sent our Supreme Prelate Thraxton to work out meeting details with Justinian."

"Our spies in his court have told us that he is planning to attack the Sea Princes. We know that many legions have slowly been moving northward toward New Barq. What we didn't know until recently that Justinian has been secretly building a fleet of triremes, ships that can ram and destroy the slow Sea Prince merchant ships. Evidently, some Sea Prince ship has discovered their secret construction site, but the trireme actually failed to destroy that ship. Naturally, that crew spread the word about these new ships. What we do not know is how soon Justinian plans to launch his two-pronged attack. If we have enough time, we ought to recruit even more Holy Paladins so that when we join forces, our holy warriors will be very visible and a significant part of the invasion force. Once the invasion is done, our army of Holy Paladins can be used to maintain law and order as well as enforcing Church doctrine. I will make that offer to Justinian, who has probably been worrying about how to control the local population once the sectors are taken. The governor concept always required a large commitment of Centurions, the Home Guards. Our offer requires none, so he should like that idea. It saves him lots of money."

"Are we all in agreement with this?" he asked, looking over all the smiling faces. Of course, this was not really a question. What he decided was what would be, but he made the empty gesture anyway. They all loudly agreed and prayed to Jehosa to thank him for thus enlightening their Pope.

A week later, Pope Yazi I, accompanied by Supreme Prelate Thraxton and ten of his security men, sat down in an open aired restaurant in Galantas. Because of this meeting, all customers were turned away by the Emperor's guards; just the two men would meet here out in the open for all to see. The Rooster picked this location because it was both public and very open; neither side dared any evil acts against the other. The Emperor was late because his guards ordered him to be late. They wanted the opportunity to make sure this was not some kind of trap.

"Ah there you are Pope Yazi I," said a covertly smiling Justinian, as he purposefully strutted into the dining yard, yellow robes flowing in the warm breeze. "Sorry I am late, state business can be so demanding, you understand. I hope I have not kept you waiting overly long." The Pope rose and the two opponents shook hands. Yazi thought that Justinian's hands were overly moist, perhaps sweaty. Could his opponent be so worried about this meeting?

The two men took a seat opposite of each other. Yazi began, "My Emperor Justinian," he felt that appearing to be somewhat condescending might be appropriate here, "I know that we have had our differences. Yet, there is one thing that we both desire, the well-being and thriving of our people." Yazi did not consider the Centurions his people, however. "We both want Megalos to succeed and do well." How could the Emperor disagree? He could not, so he merely nodded and said nothing.

"The Sea Princes is a thorn in both of our sides, albeit for different reasons. Our people would take great pride if you, Sir, could retake that land which we lost so many years ago, would it not?" He did not wait for Justinian to reply. "As you may know, we too, have a problem with the vile, vulgar perversion of Jehosanity that is being preached and taught there. I am very sad to admit this to you, but our meager forces have been wholly unable to alter that, although we have tried." Justinian smiled, he already knew how frustrated this priest must be. Reports of their failures had long ago reached his ears. It was always a good practice to employ spies abroad.

Now came the delicate part. "We've heard rumors that you are planning to invade the Sea Princes at some time, from the sea as well as the land. However, it is common knowledge that at this moment, you lack sufficient legions to make that a certain success. We both know how a failed attempt to reconquer the Sea Princes will make the throne of Megalos look to our people." Yazi was very careful not to mention his name here, hence the word throne. "Often caution is prudent, I always say. Anyway, I also want the Sea Princes brought back under the control of Megalos. Hence, Emperor Justinian, I have come to you today to make you an offer. I will place my entire army of Holy Paladins completely at your disposal to help you in retaking the Sea Princes. Would you be able to make use of another twenty legions?"

Justinian suspected a trap or a catch. He dare not let on just how tempting this offer really was. With twenty more legions, he could move his timetable up considerably. "This is indeed a generous offer, assuming the price is not too great." He attempted to find a polite way to say, what is the catch?

"I'm sorry, Justinian. I did not make myself very clear. I will lend you my army to use as needed. I will pay for their expenses and see to their supplies. Consider it a gift of the Church to a most worthy cause. Yet, I am prepared to go even further. Once you have re-conquered the Sea Princes, then comes the problem of occupying and controlling the population. Here is where I would like to be rewarded. Allow the Church to assume control over all their churches, and allow the Holy Paladins to enforce the laws that you stipulate. Let the Church act as the ill-prepared governors used to do there so many years ago. This way, you would not have to leave behind a large percentage of your legions to handle the domestic matters; they would be freed up to go on to conquer other lands, to help make your reign a most memorable one in history." Yes, Yazi was taking a serious risk with this proposal; nothing would be preventing him from sending Yazi's entire army on a suicide attack, eliminating the Church's entire force. Only the prospect of having those very soldiers later becoming the security forces to govern and run the conquered lands would prevent such a calamity.

This was almost too good to be true, Justinian thought. "You are saying that you will lend your army to me to help conquer the Sea Princes and after we've retaken them, your forces will become the local enforcers of my rule instead of the usual Home Guards? Surely, you are playing with me!"

"Oh no, Emperor Justinian! Our goals have and always will remain the conversion of souls from pagan religions to the one true religion, Jehosanity, along with the abolishment of all perversions of our religion. If we are allowed to control their churches and enforce your laws, why, we will finally be able to do God's Holy Work. That alone is more than ample payment. Besides, consider what our uniting in a common purpose will do for all Megalos."

"Aye, two warring sides joined is a powerful motivator in any case. I provisionally accept your offer, Pope Yazi. Let me consult with my advisors and generals. We need to see what this does to our timetable. I will get back to you soon. Perhaps we should make a public announcement in the Senate?"

"Oh yes. That would be most appropriate, allow all our people to see that you and I are not enemies, and that we can work together for the good of Megalos. Just let me know when and where. My forces are somewhat scattered at the moment, so the longer the lead time I have to get them collected and moved to wherever you wish them to gather, the better. Pray keep me informed so that I may best be of assistance to you."

The two men shook hands and the Emperor left, a bit more spring in his stride. He did not know how he had been able to achieve this tremendous victory over his long-standing opponent Yazi, but somehow he had. The Church was lending him twenty legions and assuming the role of Home Guard, just so they could spread their religion! What silliness, he thought — all that for religion. Justinian thought little of religion, if ever.

When Justinian arrived back at his palace, he summoned his top general, Nikas Theocopolous. "Nikas, what would you say if I suddenly gave you an additional twenty legions of cavalry, fully equipped and supplied by their own means, needing no supplies from us?"

"Surely you jest with me?" the young man of thirty replied, half expecting some punch line delivered at his expense. He hated politicians, but dared not display such before the Emperor, the top politician. Justinian had gotten him his commission, after all.

"I'm deadly serious!" Justinian then explained the bargain he'd just provisionally made with the Pope.

"Well, they are not up to legion standards, granted, but twenty legions of cavalry would help us immensely. All they want is to become the law enforcers afterwards? Doubly good! We both know the difficulty we have been having recruiting for the Home Guard once again. How did you ever pull this coop off?" He was sincere in his awe.

Smugly, Justinian replied, "That's why I am your Emperor." The two began discussing how best to employ these new forces and where.

The following Monday, with full pomp and grandeur, the two men addressed the full Senate, less of course the women Senators. Their cooperation became the talk of Megalos for the next month. Rumors even spread that Justinian had converted to Jehosanity, but those were quelled when Justinian continued to attend the Church of Sol on Sundays. He mostly slept through the sermons, as was his wont.

Considering their invasion plans, the Holy Paladins would best serve their needs if they were stationed in the New Barq area. This was shared with Yazi who issued the orders and began sending routine supplies to that far northern city. Said supplies came, of course, from the generous donations of the followers of Jehosanity.

In late fall of 623, word reached General Nikas of the Zargarb Grand Council and the formation of the Crusaders for Religious Freedom. "This is definitely a setback," he explained to Justinian, "but not wholly unexpected. For some time now, we have been building up our forces in New Barq. It doesn't take any genius to anticipate our intentions. However, I am still annoyed that the Sea Princes discovered our secret weapons, the triremes so soon after we began their construction. At this point, we still have not made enough of them to guarantee any victory from a sea invasion. I still consider the forces at New Barq just the bait; the real assault must come unexpectedly from the Med Sea. So we let them build up their army of rag-tag volunteers in Zargarb, let them have a false sense of security."

"I see your reasoning. I accept the delays then. Have you discovered any means of supporting and supplying our maritime fleet while they are attacking from the Med Sea?" Justinian asked the key question that he had never been able to solve. There was nothing but the Red Desert of death all along the southern shores of the Med Sea.

"We've located three ideal portages along the coast of the Red Desert. Further, rumors of it being a desert of death are false. I've sent out patrols into the desert and they report finding numerous oases, trees, and bird life. One of these days, you might consider constructing a paved roadway across the vastness of the Red Desert; it would prove highly useful at this time, but not enough to delay our attack just to build it."

"Bottom line, General. When is our target date to strike?" Justinian was becoming bored with the conversation and wanted the single piece of information that would end this conversation.

"On June 1, Emperor, we will begin," Nikas replied, confident that all advance preparations would be complete by then. He saluted and left.

"Another three quarters of a year! Ah well, these things cannot be rushed," Justinian commented to himself, once the general had left.

Pope Yazi I met with the Rooster shortly after the joint public Senate presentation. "Rooster, we now have time to prepare for properly taking control of the perverted churches in the Sea Princes. I will get the missionaries fully prepared in time. However, they need additional backing."

"I was wondering when you would see the need for the additional security of Mano del Dio. I will go myself, if you ask," the Rooster volunteered.

"No, you know that I need you here. My life is now in your hands more so than ever before, what with all our Holy Paladins now under the control of Justinian. Neither can we spare your current Mano members. May I suggest that you recruit say an additional one hundred members and get them trained? If there is not sufficient time, we can perhaps substitute the new members for more experienced ones. I cannot sleep nights without knowing that the Mano del Dio is watching over my northerly priests."

"As you request, Your Holiness. It shall be done. By the way, I shall send a Prelate along as well. It will be a good time to recheck the work done by Karlos, who was lost at sea. With something so critical to our Church, I will not rest easy until it has been completely verified. I do not like this Mont Blanc thing. It does not ring true. Doubts are raised in my mind, Your Holiness."

"By all means do so! I agree, we must make doubly sure that all the whore-children have been eliminated. Even one alive threatens our very Church," Yazi re-enforced his conviction.

Chapter 25 The Search

Into the desert we rode. After briefing them, I sent the five scouting squads out on reconnaissance ahead of our main party. I kept all those that knew the Arad well together up front with me, conferring as we slowly moved across the various tracks. Years ago, as the wife of the Great Messiah, I had traveled all the byroads, tracks really, of the Arad, avoiding the main roads, because we were being hunted by the Centurions, who only used the larger roads. However, that was years and a lifetime ago, Nature has a way of changing things, water being the most critical aspect. Although it was late April, still the daytime temperatures rose well into the nineties, while night times were quite chilly.

With this large a force that needed to avoid detection as much as possible, water was our biggest problem. There was a reason that the larger towns and cities of Juda Arad had been located where they were: sources of water. Now, however, only ghost towns remained something I continually found rather difficult to fathom. Where had all the people gone? By all accounts, most had immigrated to the western lands, as far away as West Reach or Cymry. Yet, some had stayed and obviously moved to now secret locations. The ten of us who were most familiar with the Arad spent the first day speculating on where they may have moved. Even for desert dwellers, water was a key commodity, that and salt.

The seemingly inexhaustible salt mines lay far to the southeast. We were certain that the population had not migrated to that locale; the Centurions still operated the mines there. Our consensus was that they probably relocated to the mesas of the west central Arad, where few tracks exist, and even fewer original villages. In the days of the Great Messiah, this was perhaps the driest zone, with few watering holes. We felt that it would be easy to hide among the tall mesas and deep valleys there. On the second day, our scouts did find supporting evidence, signs of large numbers of horses led down one track that led into the heart of the west central Arad.

Our large party had been well briefed on the dangers we would face every day, vipers and scorpions. When on foot, I had stressed the vital importance of paying close attention to the ground just in front of your feet as well as shaking out your boots before you put them on in the morning. Because of this danger, I kept the five Healing Squads spread out uniformly among the Santi regiments. This proved a wise decision, because ten people suffered viper bites during our trip across the northern portion of the Arad.

Spooky was my adjective when we passed through an abandoned hamlet or village. Memories of the people who had lived there so many years ago came back to me. I recalled Jes healing a sick woman here, and a blind man there. Yet, none remained, only crumbling adobe walls marked what once were homes of happy people. I concluded that you could only oppress, suppress, and smash a people so long before they give up entirely and leave. I began to think that may have been a very wise decision on their part, because yet another conflict was building, one that may be fought at the edges of the Arad.

As we camped on the second night, Lilly Ann said, "Ket, did you *really* live out here in this place? It is so utterly desolate, even granting that there once were people in those tiny villages."

"Life was hard, I will admit, but yes, people did live here," I replied. "Actually, there used to be perhaps a hundred thousand or more. Very religious people, the Arads are." My thoughts drifted to times long past.

Slowly the week passed. Our scouts spotted presumably Arad Raider scouts several times the first four days, none the last three. By the seventh day, the foothills of the Kathas Mountains became very prominent on the eastern horizon, growing taller with each passing hour. Snow still lay at the higher elevations, stark white against the deep blue sky. Far off, the lush stretch of green foothills stretched the entire length of the Arad, a narrow zone perhaps five miles deep, where enough moisture fell for grass to grow. Down south lay the Grey Havens where Zdlenka, the Blue Rider, made her home. Still we were a long way from that lush zone, desert stretched out before us.

However, midday of the seventh day out, the track definitely began its slow ascent into the foothills. I knew that we were getting close to our first destination, the ruins of the Qaam fortress at Al Tarm. On the eighth day, we rode into the last valley, the one that led to Al Tarm. Rounding a bend, there stood the remains of that fortress, situated high atop a tall mesa. Its outer defense walls lay crumbing, and we could see where the invaders from the steppes had broken through. There the ground and rubble had been hard packed by the passage of thousands of horses. Al Tarm had been a ghost town ever since the Galt invasion so many years ago.

Here we made camp, once more I cautioned everyone to stay alert for vipers, which now probably were the sole inhabitants of Al Tarm. The first action was a thorough search of the ruins done by the Guardians and the expert Sisterhood trackers. The conclusions of all were that the place had been abandoned many, many years ago, after having been ransacked of everything of any possible use. About all that remained were the crumbling walls, even the timbers of the roofs had long ago been salvaged, removed, or burned as firewood. Further, we were the first to set foot here in a very long time. No hoof prints, no foot prints, nothing disturbed the layers of dust and sand. "What a bleak place this must have been," Lilly Ann commented what most thought to themselves. Yes, stark and bleak Al Tarm was, even when it was occupied; such was the Qaam passion for returning to their historical, religious roots.

"Well," said Paul as the search neared completion, "looks like there is nothing here. Probably the stuff has long ago been stolen, probably by those Holy Paladins."

"Don't count on that," I chuckled. "Bring out the shovels and picks. It's excavation time." I led them to what had been the most sacred temple building near the back of the complex. Its walls had been knocked down, forming a monster pile of rubble. "Dig here, remove all this stuff." I gestured and then marked with small bits of cloth the area to be uncovered. For once, I was grateful for the large amount of manpower we had with us. If I only had my Circle, we would be at least a week just removing this massive pile of adobe bricks and mortar.

Fifty worked in hour shifts, laboring under the intensely hot sun. At dark, a chilling breeze blew down from the distant mountains. At night, we darn near froze, a thin layer of ice formed in our water barrels overnight. Worse, we had no wood to spare to light bonfires, only enough charcoal for cooking purposes. Thus, out of necessity, everyone snuggled as close to each other as possible, just to stay warm.

Two days later, we had moved a massive pile of rubble, revealing a dark gaping tunnel, just where I remembered it had begun. Many lanterns were lit and about fifty of us entered the downward sloping tunnel. About six feet tall but only four feet wide, the tunnel led straight back under the foothills. About a quarter of a mile from the entrance, we found a sealed door. I knew that the treasure lay just on the other side. Unfortunately, it was not only a heavy oaken door, but it was very securely locked.

Allan, claiming, "No problem, let a Planner at it," soon had the lock picked. Still, the door would not budge, not even a hair's breadth! We pushed, pounded, and tried to force it open using our shoulders, but the doors gave not the slightest. This, I had not remembered. It ought to have opened easily. Finally, after an hour's worth of futile attempts, Allan concluded, "It has got to be bolted from the inside. That's the only explanation possible. We haven't wiggled it even slightly when four of us hit it at the same time."

We sent for hatchets and axes. Four hours we spent hacking away at the thick doors until finally we literally cut our way through. Holding lanterns high, we peered inside. "I was right, one moment," Allan called out. He stuck his arm inside and undid a barricading iron bar. Now the remains of the doors opened easily. We went inside.

Lying beside the stone wall just beyond the door was the decaying, mummified remains of a Qaam priest. I could tell that from the robes. His body had literally mummified in this cold, dry sealed room. We paused reliving this man's fate. Seeing Al Tarm being overrun and destroyed by the Galts, this priest had entered this vault and bolted it from the inside, his last protection of the treasures of the Qaam. I wondered if he realized that his action had been completely successful. Probably so, because he had died in here. Once the walls of the temple had come down blocking the tunnel, he was trapped. Whoever this man was, he had saved the single thing that this entire fortress had been built to protect, their sacred scrolls.

We were in a twenty-foot square room, hewn from the solid bedrock of the foothills. Lying in floor to ceiling wooden racks were scrolls upon scrolls, thousands of them. The dozen of us stood in awe, reflecting upon the history that was preserved here. Breaking what seemed a sacred silence, I said, "Okay, bring in five who can read Arad. Let's see what we have here. Oh, and more lights too."

While I awaited four Sisters who were originally from the Arad to arrive, I began inspecting the find. Soon, I discovered the entire collection that I had painstakingly written when I was a young girl, one of the three scribes who had written down what the many prophets said. I mused that here was indeed the find of the century, all the verbal teachings, prophesies of Juda Arad, were here, preserved, written in triplicate.

"All praise to Jehosa!" exclaimed one middle aged Sister when she entered and her eyes fell upon the racks of scrolls.

"It's all here," I replied. "This whole set here, I wrote when I was around twelve. These two batches here are the duplicate copies written by the other two men. We took down every teaching, every prophesy, all the religious theology and history of the Arad people around the time of the Great Messiah. Actually, they were reciting all it to teach him." Oh's and ah's and various other exclamations echoed in the room.

"What we are most interested in finding are sets of ten gospels of the disciples. I have no idea what they look like, since I never saw them. So have at it. One should be by Bandar Dero," and I listed the names of all ten disciples, including Yazi. For an hour, we rummaged through the pile, taking extreme care not to harm these delicate works.

Finally, one Sister, Elan, exclaimed, "Silly us. I just found the master index logbook over here. Come look. It has the location of everything. Gospels, let's see." We crowded around her; sure enough, it was as she described. I hadn't noticed that each shelf had a unique mark on it; they corresponded to marks after the brief description in the index. Near the very end of the logbook, she found what we were after, the gospels. All five of us rushed over to that spot. Sure enough, there were the ten very thick gospels, bound in leather. Success.

Now came the hard part, how to safely package them for the very long trip back to Mont Blanc. Brittle with age, they needed very special care. Considering their value, we spent a day discussing various ways and means. In the end, our Planners used the wooden racks themselves to construct boxes in which to safely store the scrolls for transport. This took us another week to accomplish fully.

Meanwhile, since so many of those with us were devout believers in Jehosa, I decided to give them a taste of what it was that we were fighting for. I began to read some of the disciple's gospels, beginning with that of Bandar Dero. I found the alterations to the Decalogue interesting and dug out my original. I decided that this was critical information, so I carefully went over the Decalogue with them. "Here is the most ancient version of the Decalogue of Jehosa." I read the following to them several times. "The Decalogue of Jehosa, as told by Prophet Emil Tamir, is as follows:"

There is no god but Jehosa.

Do not worship any other god but the One God, Jehosa.

Do not build statues of Jehosa, for Jehosa has no form.

Set aside the Holy Day, Saturday, from your labors and worship the Lord that day.

Respect and serve thy mother and thy father, for they have labored long in your raising.

Do not kill another who worships Jehosa.

Do not steal from another who worships Jehosa.

Do not commit adultery.

Do not lie to another who worships Jehosa.

Do not desire another's house, possessions, or wife, if he worships Jehosa.

"Now here is Bandar Dero's version of the Decalogue. Notice the differences." I read.

There is no god but Jehosa.

Do not worship any other god but the One God, Jehosa.

Do not build statues of Jehosa, for Jehosa has no form.

Set aside the Holy Day, Saturday, from your labors and worship the Lord that day.

Respect and serve thy mother and thy father, for they have labored long in your raising.

Do not kill another.

Do not steal from another.

Do not commit adultery.

Do not lie to another.

Do not desire another's house, possessions, or wife.

Do unto others, as you would have others do unto you.

"The last line is strictly of Bandar's own making. Jes was responsible for all the other changes in the original Decalogue." I launched into a recitation of Jes's lengthy explanation, it had all come back to me after all these years. "Now listen to this one, here is Yazi's total perversion of the Decalogue!" I read.

There is no god but Jehosa.

Do not worship any other god but the One God, Jehosa.

Set aside the Holy Day, Saturday, from your labors and worship the Lord that day.

Respect and serve thy mother and thy father, for they have labored long in your raising.

Do not kill another, excepting your enemies and enemies of Jehosa.

Do not steal from another, excepting your enemies and enemies of Jehosa.

Do not commit adultery.

Do not lie to another, excepting your enemies and enemies of Jehosa.

Do not desire another's house or possessions.

Do unto men as you would have men do unto you."

I watched as these women became enlightened about their Holy Decalogue. How Yazi had altered it became crystal clear to all of us. He had made it perfectly acceptable to steal from, lie to, and kill your enemies and other religions, precisely the opposite of what Jes had preached!

Sister Elan exclaimed, "This is enough to destroy Yazi's entire Church, if only we can get this widely known! Wow! This is the most precious thing imaginable!" The others shared her enthusiasm and conviction. However, she had placed her finger on the crux of the problem, our big difficulty: getting it widely known. I began pondering that one in the back of my mind, no solution was immediately apparent to me.

Transporting this treasure of treasures back to Zargarb and our new Santi secure loading dock was the next challenge. Certainly, the safest approach would be for all of us to return with our cargo. However, that alone would raise all kinds of questions, which we would rather not answer at this time, since we were supposed to be doing a flanking maneuver of the Centurion forces in the extreme southwestern portion of the Arad. Sister Elan had a brilliant idea. "We are now about to send a number of empty wagons back to Zargarb for resupply. They are being escorted by a small garrison force. Why not send them back with these Holy Treasures? Suspicions would not be aroused at all." I gave her a big hug of thanks; she was rather embarrassed by my outflow of affection, however.

Paulette made telepathic contact with the Communicator back at our new Santi location in Zargarb, explaining in detail what we were sending and what was to be done. I realized right here that the entire Santi needed some form of secret code by which we could send messages that others outside of the Santi could not read. We would not always have the luxury of the Communicators. Hence, I also had Paulette send word to John Henry to begin the wide spread propagation of our new secret code. I used the same one I had learned from Niccolo Helios so long ago. This time, throughout the Santi, the code word needed to unravel the message was "Sisterhood." A month later, encoded messages were being sent right and left by everyone in the Santi. Suddenly, even the lowest member could send word of something vitally important on up the line, confident that spies could not read the message. In the end, this precaution on my part proved utterly invaluable, although we soon learned that the code word needed to be changed from time to time.

While we were building the boxes and packing the Holy Treasures, I sent the Arad knowledgeable and the five Scout Squads out to continue to follow Sister Alicia's directions to find the assassins' location, not too far from here. Use extreme caution and go slowly were their orders. About the time that we were finishing up with the packing, they returned.

"Sir, we've located numerous poppy and marijuana fields and what appears to be a giant, inhabited cave complex. It's right where Sister Alicia said it would be. That woman must have been utterly remarkable with her deductions!" The Loremasters gave me a quick rundown on these two crops,

314

which could be harvested to produce the drugs that were being used by the assassins of the Old Man of the Mountain. I concluded that this was very likely our next target. Thus, once the resupply wagons and their garrison force of some two hundred headed back the way we had come, the rest of us mounted up and followed the scouts.

Two days later, we had passed from the desert mesa land and the start of the foothills and nearly through the narrow green grasslands, which ended at the steeply rising sides of the eighteen thousand foot tall Kathas mountains. Here we followed along what appeared to be a well-worn wagon rut trail, paralleling the steep sides of the rock face, which rose sharply on our right. Now the flowering fields began appearing on either side of this narrow path. Accordingly, I slowed the advance, though we had seen not a single person yet, only the fields indicated that humans were somewhere about.

Soon, the scouts pointed out a dark spot about a mile distant. The path veered around a rocky outcropping and then headed towards this location. Cautiously, I signaled the Santi to move forward. Our observant eyes strained to catch any movement that might show signs of defenders. None of us had any idea what to expect in the way of defense of this assassin stronghold. As we in the lead rounded the outcropping, we spotted the faint glint of reflected light and then saw the rush of a large hail of quarrels heading our way following a high arc from the cave entrance area, still a good distance from us.

I deflected two that came close to me, as did several others. Four took hits upon their mail, but they merely stung and bounced off. I glanced at one quarrel lying on the ground close to me. "Poisoned quarrels. Retreat a hundred feet!" Confusion reigned and the entire columns of Santi attempted to relay and follow the order. Paul quickly surveyed all of us in the front to be sure none had gotten the poison either on themselves or under their skin. We were exceedingly lucky; all had missed us. Evidently, this was a long distance warning shot.

While we continued to study the terrain and the enemy's location, more glints reflected in the afternoon sun. Paul commented, "Suspect they have re-enforced their crossbow line, perhaps doubled their numbers."

Adriana cursed, "Damn, we don't dare close to battle; these vile creatures are using poison against us!"

"Ah, but they are well within longbow range. Assemble all longbows here, form up ranks," I ordered, "let's give them a volley or two." Quickly, all those who had longbows dismounted, grabbed their bows and quivers, and hustled to form up a battle line. Since I had mine especially made for me by Leann Finn, I joined them as well. All told, we had just under fifty longbows among us. All the rest were back in Zargarb in the Longbow Regiment.

Paul took command, "Archers, aim for just beyond that rocky ridge line there by the dark tunnel opening. On the count of three. One. Two. Three." Nearly fifty arrows arced high into the blue sky, slowed, and then descended in our rain. From the faint noise and more glints, we knew that some had found their marks. Three more times Paul barked his commands.

"Are we having any effect?" asked Adriana, curious about this extremely long range shooting at targets she could not see. This form of combat was foreign to her, as it was to most of our group.

Paul explained the barely discernable clues that it had some impact, though how much, no one really knew. While we were staring at their position pondering all this, we spied a large amount of tiny reflections in the sun, heading toward the dark opening. "Doggone, I do believe they are retreating! Longbows win out yet again!"

"Guardians who can catch or deflect quarrels, mount up with me. We will test this theory. If they fire, avoid being wounded or having the poison splatter on any skin. Could be very deadly," I advised. Fifteen Guardians mounted up and joined me. Ever so slowly, we walked forward, expecting their rain of poisoned quarrels any second. None came to my complete relief!

Embolden by this, I signaled for the whole Santi to follow us. Still moving cautiously, we closed the gap to the enemy's stronghold. We met no further resistance. In fact, when we drew close to their fortified line, some twenty bodies lay dead on the stony ground. No weapons, quarrels, or poison containers were present. Evidently, in their retreat, they had taken them all with themselves. We stood facing a solid rock wall; no tunnel entrance was visible, as if they had merely vanished into the sheer mountain side!

However, the numerous footprints on the ground all led into a large stone wall. Allan observed the obvious. "Here is the entrance tunnel. However, these guys are clever, I'll give them that much. They've rolled this huge stone to block the entrance. Look, it's perfectly smooth on our side. I doubt very much that we could even move it, assuming that it's not locked somehow from the inside. They've gone underground like ground hogs, probably figuring to just wait us all out."

"I don't think that we should dig them out," Adriana teased with a smile, though I detected a slight note of uncertainty in her voice.

"With all this poisoning going on, not a chance," I explained to everyone. "Okay, Protectors, we will back off as far as you think prudent. Do your thing. Scouts, fan out over this whole area. I don't want them coming up out of some other hole and attacking us from behind with poisoned weapons."

The scouts took off, while the rest of us backed way up, well beyond the original quarrel range. Here, we watched the fifteen Protectors at work. I say watched, but really there was little to see. Lenkova asked, "So what are they doing Ket? They don't seem to be doing much except looking and standing there."

"I'm not entirely sure, but Andre and Alton have been planning this for nearly a year. Guess we all just have to wait and see," was my simple reply. I had some suspicions, but such spells I had never studied nor ever seen in use. Protector arcana, I presumed.

After an hour, Elona walked back from the Protector group, "Ket, it is our opinion that everyone here may be too close. We would like you to back up another three hundred yards. Also, get everyone out of the way downhill from this rocky outcropping. We think you have about ten minutes to get out of harm's way." I acknowledged her and began carrying out her order, while she walked back to the other Protectors.

"It's hard thinking of her as a Protector," Adriana said. Lenkova seconded her. I smiled; she was every inch a Protector at this point and one fine High Priestess, Monarch, and mother. Now we all waited, counting off the minutes.

Suddenly the Protectors swung up upon their horses and came galloping our way as fast as they could ride. Still we saw absolutely nothing amiss or any reason for their near panic ride. The fifteen were about half way to us when the ground began to shake back and forth, violently. I lost my footing and fell hard on my butt. So did many others around me. The horses shied and many broke free, galloping off in their own panic. I watched as the fifteen Protectors valiantly tried to stay atop their frightened horses, like some wild contortionist act; yet all did somehow. I am sure that I would not have been so skillful.

A thunderous noise drowned out all attempts to yell. Turning my head towards the noise, I saw huge chucks of the granite mountain slope crumbling downward, like a stone waterfall. A giant dust cloud arose where falling stone met the ground. Finally, the earth stopped shaking, but my knees barely supported me as I tried to get to my feet. This seemed to be a rather commonplace sensation, as most of the others experienced similar difficulties getting on their feet, while the ones who somehow had kept their balance found their legs acting like putty, and they too ended up on the ground.

Proud as peacocks, the fifteen Protectors rode up to us, while we finally managed to get back onto our feet, brushing off the dirt. Paul said snidely, "Well, that about wraps it up for the assassins." The other Protectors chuckled.

"You — you — you caused the earthquake?" Lenkova tried to speak, her mouth barely operational. Stunned was our uniform reaction, especially from the Mont Blanc and the Sisterhood fighters.

"How? My god! You are Gods!" exclaimed Adriana, wholly out of adjectives. Nothing in their background ever suggested that people were capable of causing the very earth to shake violently.

"Guardians of Nature," Elona proclaimed, raising her clenched fist high into the air in a victory pose. That, of course, didn't help the awestruck men and women gaping at them.

"You see, it's like this," Paul tried to explain. "There is a never-used-before-now spell we Protectors are required to learn but never practice. None of us here has ever cast it before, so we were not even sure if it would work. Guess it really does work after all. All those weeks spent learning it was not wasted as we all presumed."

"The horses," I managed to utter. Finally, here was something the Sisterhood fighters could recognize. Half of our horses were galloping far afield. At once, a large number mounted up and began chasing them down. Luckily, the many scouts that were already far off saw the chaos and also joined in rounding up our steeds.

Once the horses were retrieved, the dust cloud had settled. The entire Santi rode up to where the tunnel entrance had been. Now that entire area was under a massive pile of granite stone slabs and boulders. If we had maybe a thousand workers and a quarter of a year, we might have been able to dig out the tunnel entrance, assuming it still stood. Very probably, it had collapsed.

"Goodbye and good riddance!" exclaimed Lenkova, who had helped prevent more than a dozen attempted assassination and extortions from these men. Since the scouts had reported no other signs of tunnels, entrances, or inhabitants, we concluded that the Old Man of the Mountain's impact upon our world had been brought to an end.

That night the entire Santi celebrated wildly, wine flowed and songs were sung. A great weight lifted from the Sisters, who had been forced to deal with these assassins for so long.

Later that night, while everyone was celebrating, Paul explained a little more to me. "You see we found an irregularity there where the massive granite mountain roots meet the crumbling foothills. All we had to do was exaggerate it a bit, rather give it a little push or shove, actually. I think that the ground had been building up a lot of pressure along here for years. Nature has now relieved herself, bringing herself back into balance." I still didn't grasp this any better, so we left it as is. As a Wid, I merely filed this one for later study when I had leisure time to do so. Right now, I had the orders for the next day to work out. I knew that the rest of the war was not going to be this easy.

The next day, Elona Po and her Velona Circle headed back to Velona. None of them really wanted to go back, but they were needed to help defend and coordinate the defenses of Velona. We all hugged each other and then waved as they rode off.

Secure in his ornate chambers far underground, Mustafa was rudely interrupted. "Sire, an enemy army is approaching our tunnel entrance. What shall we do?" He took another hit on his water pipe, sensing the soothing tendrils of the smoke filling his lungs. He coughed once.

"Call out the bowmen. Bring out the poison pots. Fire at will," he replied, and took another hit from his pipe. Two women caressed his legs and torso; they'd already had their fill of the heavenly smoke. The aide rushed to carry out the orders. A short while later, he returned with more bad news. The enemy had some devilishly log range arrows. "Oh bother. Just close the door, man, and lock it securely. We have all we need in here. We shall just wait them out. Eventually they will go away. So it is written, all things must pass away." Once more, the aide rushed off to see to the security of the underground fortress. Mustafa briefly recalled their preparations. A year's supply of food, wine, and hashish, even opium, would see them through. He took one final hit and laid back on his purple divan.

Visions of ecstasy filled his mind. He felt his women gently caressing his long, thin body. He drifted into a heavenly dream, full of marvelous senses.

Always, he felt his senses were so utterly heightened after he smoked, which is one reason he always smoked as often as possible. Sometime later, he felt a new sensation, as if a very heavy weight was on his entire body. Opening his eyes, he could not see, but he had the strangest sensation that he was floating upwards. Suddenly, the brilliantly bright sunlight nearly blinded him. He was somehow outside the ground. How was this possible? I must be having a bad dream, he thought. Closing what he thought must be his eyes, he returned to his dreams of sensuality, ignoring the fact that he was now floating off into the distance, far from the mountains. He also failed to see hundreds of other spiritual beings doing much the same thing, only their sensations were that of stark terror and utter panic.

Chapter 26 Ali Martek's Decision

The ruddy sun slowly sunk behind the distant dunes of the Red Desert. At the small oasis, sitting on their prayer mats, two hundred men, women, and children chanted their Holy Prayers to Jehosa. The tribal leader, Messiah Ali Martek as usual led them, his tenor voice singing out proudly and loudly to the heavens above. "From ancient Jaleene Amir and Amal Amir came we, down the long ages, cast out of Jehosa's realm by our own sins. Exiled now on Tarra, we have been given these fleshly bodies, from which to learn the errors of our ways, to purify ourselves that we may once more be worthy of entering Jehosa's kingdom. Long ago, we were cast out of the Anuir, but over the long centuries, Jehosa has sent his mercy upon us, rewarding us for our progress in our long journey. He has given us the Anuir back in which to dwell. All around us, we have dates, figs, water, even camels. Hear us Oh Jehosa, only we, thy faithful have heard thy word and have come back into the land you once set our ancestors upon. When so many have sought an easy life elsewhere on Tarra, only we, thy faithful, have heeded your call. We are here, Oh Jehosa!"

"No more do we feel the angry, fiery outburst of Angibus. I, your faithful servant, Messiah Ali Martek, have led the faithful here; we swear unto you that we are here in Anuir to stay. We follow your Holy Decalogue as given unto us by your Prophet Helas Amin. Everyone, join me in our holy prayer." Some two hundred voices chanted, the Decalogue.

> There is no god but Jehosa.
> Do not worship any other god but the One God, Jehosa.
> Do not build statues of Jehosa, for Jehosa has no form.
> Set aside the Holy Day, Saturday, from your labors and worship the Lord that day.
> Respect and serve thy mother and thy father, for they have labored long in your raising.
> Do not kill another who worships Jehosa.
> Do not steal from another who worships Jehosa.
> Do not commit adultery.
> Do not lie to another who worships Jehosa.
> Do not desire another's house, possessions, or wife, if he worships Jehosa.

The sun had set upon this small oasis. Both camels and sheep had bedded down for the night. One by one, the families retired quietly into their hide tents. Only Ali remained seated upon his prayer mat. His scouting party had not yet returned. This was not like them, he mused, worrying that something ill had befallen them.

About an hour after the sun had gone down, three riders finally appeared on the distant dune to the north and west of the oasis. At last, they returned, all three of them; Ali finally relaxed and awaited their report. Once more, Ali thanked his god that he had found Karmanski Zolgoti and his wife and children. Karmanski had become his best and most dependable scout. Yes, Karmanski was a Galt from the Northern Steppes by birth, but had become one of them by marriage to Juli, who had lost her husband in one of the many raids upon the Arad. Karmanski was nearly killed by the Centurions and Juli had nursed him back to health. The two now held a deep love for each other. Having been a warrior in Strokova's army, he was very familiar with scouting, an invaluable skill for their very survival out here in the Red Desert.

Karmanski reined in, dismounted. "Messiah Ali, we have very strange news. Far have we journeyed from the Arad and the Infidels. Yet, again, the Infidels have come into our new land. Northwest of here, down by the Med Sea, we have come across an encampment of the Infidels!" This was indeed the very last thing that Ali expected to hear, very discomforting. The four men sat down by the dying embers of the fire and talked late into the night.

Ali knew that there were now at least two dozen other messiahs, who had led their tribes hither into the Anuir, just as he had done a number of years ago. However, the Anuir was still healing itself and could not support large numbers of the faithful at any one location for long. Nomads they all were; food and basic supplies of life were quite scarce. What Ali found utterly baffling was the report of vast quantities of food and other supplies that were being apparently stored down near the sea. This made no sense to these four. Karmanski commented, "If these are supplies for an invasion against us here, then it is being done completely backwards. First, you bring on the troops. After they have secured the beachhead and expanded outwards, only then do you bring in these kinds of supplies in such volume. From my experience, the Infidels are not that stupid. Ali, I really think that they do not even know that we exist or that the desert is inhabited! That can be the only reason." The other two scouts completely agreed with Karmanski, but Ali paid them little attention, it was Karmanski's opinion that mattered to him.

Ali asked for the third time, "You are sure that only six Infidels are there guarding the supplies?"

"Aye, six. We watched an Infidel ship being unloaded at noon and then it sailed west by north. Just the six. Messiah Ali, all the food we need for a year lies there waiting for us." All four men grinned at that thought.

"If the Infidels desire so greatly to lend us a mighty helping hand, we that they have oppressed for so long, then so be it. Tomorrow, I will go myself and see to acquiring our provisions." With that, Karmanski retired to his hut, where Juli had his late supper waiting for him.

The next day, Ali was led to the site. The four men crawled to the edge of the steep embankment; they were on the top of the last dune, which overlooked the Med Sea far below them, nearly a thousand feet down. Green grass grew from about five hundred feet at the base of the dune on down to the shore. Sitting on the grass were dozens of boxes piled high, tarpaulins secured them, staked into the soil. Four small tents housed the six Centurions. A small flag fluttered in the slight sea breeze. A single campfire curled its plume skyward, grey against the clear blue. Rolling waves of the Med Sea swept periodically onto the sandy beach, in and out rhythmically.

Only two men actually were standing as the posted guards, both were very bored. Everyone knew the Red Desert was completely empty, devoid of all life — had been as long as anyone could remember. Hence, their guard duty was more of an official order than anything useful or practical. Neither carried their traditional spear, only a short sword was strapped to their waists. Their armor lay in a neat pile along with four other sets. The morning was hot; in their minds, there was no need for any armor at all. The other four sat in the shade of a tent, playing cards.

Ali stared at this unbelievable sight for nearly an hour before he too became convinced this was not some kind of diabolical trap. At last, he gave the whispered order. Two scouts crept back to their horses and rode back to their oasis. An hour later, fifty men, well-armed, appeared, hidden behind the dune. Ali gave his orders. One by one, all of them slithered silently down the dune on all fours. At very close range, a dozen arrows flew at the two standing guard duty. The other four didn't know what hit them. Ali ordered their bodies to be buried in the sand.

"What does this flag with the XIII on it mean?" asked one scout.

"Who knows. Bury it with the bodies," Ali replied.

Next, several men climbed back up the long dune, mounted, and rode off a mile to where the rest of the tribe was patiently waiting. An hour later, the entire tribe scrambled down the dune to help gather up their newfound wealth. Sure enough, dozens of crates held various dried foods, enough to feed everyone for a year. One by one, all the boxes were hauled up the steep dune, and loaded onto the few wagons the tribe had. By late afternoon, the last of the crates had been removed; even the tents and shovels were confiscated. The few items not taken were then also buried in the loose sand.

Ali and the four scouts were the last ones to leave. Slowly but surely, using some nearby dead brushwood, they obliterated all the many tracks the tribe had left in the sand. Slowly they worked their way back up the steep dune's side. At the top, they paused to look down upon their handiwork. No visible trace of the encampment remained. It was as if this campsite had never existed, which was precisely what Ali had intended. Topside, the others had already left, heading back to their oasis. Still paranoid, Ali and the three scouts also eradicated those tracks as well, finally ending their labors a mile distant from the dune. The strong night winds would soon remove even those heavy prints.

That evening, every member of the tribe ate until they were completely full, something that had not happened in months. While Juli was eating and basking in the joy that she had more than enough food to feed her growing family, a voice spoke to her inside her head or mind — she could not differentiate. Instinctively, Juli realized the truth of the words spoken to her and she acted upon them. Juli asked, "Ali, shouldn't we share our newfound wealth with our neighbors who have not as we have?"

Ali looked at her and smiled. "Yes, yes we shall!" During the next two weeks, Ali did just that with their four nearest neighbors. Karmanski beamed with pride, because this was Juli's idea and it had been accepted. He dearly loved his wife.

Word soon spread of Ali's lucky find. Within a week, three similar supply depots suddenly vanished without a trace. Interestingly enough, not a single wound or casualty of any kind was suffered by any of these immigrants.

Later that week, Juli was washing the family's laundry near the oasis pool of water. Again, the voice appeared in her mind. *You should call yourselves the Children of Anuir and name this oasis Al Amir.* Startled, Juli stopped and glanced all around. Several other women were also doing their wash, but they were a hundred feet away from her. Juli's three older children were off running and playing nearby. Only their new son, who was one year old, lay near her, nicely wiggling on a blanket. The twenty-seven year old woman, brushed back her long black hair, ignored the voice, and went back to scrubbing the soiled clothing.

Once more, the voice repeated its message, louder and clearer than before. This time, Juli jumped, more than a little frightened, because she was sure that no one was around. "Who said that?" she tentatively spoke, not loud enough so that the other women could hear her. Perhaps she was going slightly mad or crazy, she thought, hearing voices in her head.

I have been sent by Jehosa to prepare the Children of Anuir so that you may regain what you have long ago lost. You, Juli Aldari-Zolgoti, are my first chosen one.

Now, poor Juli was most definitely spooked; frantically she looked in all directions, her hair whirling around. Kari, the baby, began fussing, sensing all was not well with his mother. Other women also saw her distress. Several stopped their work and came over to her, asking what was wrong.

"I keep hearing a voice in my head. I'm going crazy," she blurted out the truth and began crying. One older woman held her close, giving her a shoulder to cry upon and patted her back soothingly. Another ran off to fetch Ali and Karmanski, who came running, thinking something was seriously wrong.

Once more the voice spoke to her, *You are not crazy, Juli Aldari-Zolgoti. I will make all clear tonight around the evening prayers.* Spooked even further, she wailed what was happening to her, as Karmanski took her from the woman and held her tightly. He had no clue what to say to her, such was beyond anything he had ever experienced. Perhaps she did not like living out here in the desert, he thought.

Ali, on the other hand, pulled on his chin thoughtfully. "Juli, have you heard this voice before?"

Sobbing, she said that she had, relaying the very words she had uttered about a week ago, sharing their newly acquired food supplies with others in need. Now, Ali had something to ponder indeed. He had her repeat what the voice had said to her today. "What does it mean?" she wailed after she told him.

"Aye, Messiah Ali, what does this mean?" asked Karmanski, more than a little concerned for his beloved Juli. Only one thing meant the entire world to him now and that was Juli and the children. Yes, he had easily fallen into the role of father for her previous children and now found that he treated them no differently than their newborn. This loving Arad woman had brought him back from the dead, nearly physically that's true, but dead as a spiritual being. She was thus the most precious person in the world to him.

Ali was neither stupid nor foolish; had he been either he would have never succeeded as a messiah. Yet, this was something new and potentially profound. He needed time to think. "Please, Karmanski, take Juli for a long walk around yonder dunes. I'm sure that she is not crazy, not going mad, and will be just fine. Sasha will watch the babe and the kids." He did not hesitate to obey and began walking her off toward the sand dunes just beyond the rim of trees that marked the edge of this oasis.

It was wise indeed to share our captured supplies with the others; they needed them as much as we did, he thought. Perhaps he might have thought to do that on his own, given enough time to realize the good fortune that had come their way. But then, he was honest with himself, perhaps he might not have as well. No, it had been very wise and holy to have done so — to shared their good fortune. Thus, the first statement of the "voice" had been true. Yet, what was the underlying meaning of this new one? It would be a simple task to give their oasis a name, funny that he had not yet thought of doing it. Yet, the "chosen one" perplexed him, what did that mean? Was Juli becoming a prophet, did God Jehosa speak to all the prophets? This arcana he had never been privy to, not as a fighting messiah. In the end, he had no real or satisfactory explanation, deciding to do as the voice asked, wait until the evening prayers.

The walk among the dunes helped calm Juli, who returned to herself, good, practical Juli, capable of doing what was needed when it was needed, as she had done all her life. She apologized for her foolish behavior and returned to her washing task. After all, it was just a voice that she thought that she had heard. However, she could not get the idea of the evening prayers from her mind; she watched that hour slowly approach her all day long.

Finally, as was their custom, as the sun set brilliantly red over the reddish sands of the Red Desert, Ali conducted their evening prayers. He had only just begun when the voice now spoke so that all present could hear. In fact, a bush behind Ali suddenly burst into flames, catching everyone's instant attention. The voice now seemed to becoming from the bush. Juli relaxed, the voice was not in her mind only this time. Now, everyone was hearing it; she was not going mad.

The voice said, "And what name does this place have?"

At once, although more than a little alarmed, Ali yelled, "Al Amir."

"No need to yell, I hear the scorpion's feet upon the sands, the stretching of the roots of the date tree. And what do you call yourselves?"

Ali spoke more softly, "The Children of Anuir."

Ah, that is good. I am now the Guardian of Anuir within the Red Desert. I am of Jehosa. I come from Jehosa. I protect this land for thee and for Jehosa. Long ago, Children of Anuir, you lost your way, seeking to be in and of mortal flesh, hiding even from yourselves who and what you are. I am sent by Jehosa to help you to prepare to re-enter his Holy Realm, to help you recover that that you actually are.

Karmanski's only thought was, "Heavy!"

The bush spoke further. *To the Holy Decalogue, add one more line. Do not wantonly harm either plants or animals within this land, for they are long under my care.* Many voices instantly so promised, although it seemed strange to be talking to a burning bush.

Juli is my chosen one, the first one that I touch. Consider her as prophet, for she shall speak for me and of me. She shall be the first of many. Trust in me as you trust in Lord Jehosa and you shall not want.

With that, the flames ceased just as suddenly as they erupted. Two hundred pairs of eyes stared at the bush, which appeared not to have been harmed in any way by the flames. Mari, the youngest daughter of Juli, asked, "Mommy, was that a miracle?" Two hundred had the same thought, most knew the answer and didn't need Juli's affirmative reply.

After the prayers were finished, Ali cut them short because he could hardly speak. Either everyone complimented Juli or stared at her in awe, as God's Chosen One, whatever that meant. Juli became more and more ill at ease with all this attention, which Karmanski noted. He defused the situation by saying, "We should all give thanks to Messiah Ali for have the wisdom to bring us here to Al Amir!" Immediately, everyone agreed and Ali received a hearty round of appreciation. Although graciously accepting the praise of his people, he wondered how he had come to bring them here to this particular location. Had Lord Jehosa somehow been working through or with him and he did not even notice it? Ali had a troubled sleep that night, pondering too many unponderables.

The next day just as Juli finished washing the breakfast dishes, the voice came unto her once more. *Walk up to the top of yonder dune.* She found her head automatically turning to face the southerly dune. Dutifully, although a bit trepidacious, she obeyed. Once at the top, she had a commanding view of the oasis below and the desert stretching out in all directions. *Sit down; be comfortable.* Again, she obeyed, how could she not? However, nothing could have ever prepared her for what happened next.

The voice spoke softly, *Push against your head and move back out of your body three feet. Yes, like that.* Suddenly, Juli found herself staring at the back of her head, her long hair flowing down her back. In that instant, Juli had a total certainty that she was not a body, that she was something else, something far more than a mortal body. *Look all around,* spoke the voice.

For an instant, Juli felt herself pulling back into her body so that she could "look" with her eyes. However, some gentle force kept her from doing so. She attempted to look around and found that she could see without her eyes.

However, the visions she saw were not clear nor entirely "in focus." *We shall work on that.*

Now a new problem arose for her, she wanted to explain how poor her vision was, but that meant using her body's voice. The Guardian sensed this and said, *Think what you want to say and I will hear it.* So she did. Time passed, the more she looked around, the better her vision became. Suddenly she realized that she was seeing in all directions at one time, which had caused a lot of her initial confusion. *We will continue another day. You do not need to re-enter your body.*

In a state of serenity that Juli had never known, she walked back down the dune to her oasis and family. When Karmanski held her and kissed her that night, she sensed and felt the depths of his love for her as she had never done before. All her senses had been heightened, and she was still a few feet back of her head when she finally laid her body down beside Karmanski's to sleep. Of course, she was right back inside her head the next morning. Although the Guardian did not comment, he took notice of this and spent a great deal of time pondering his next move.

That day, Karminski made an interesting comment to Juli, "You know, I've been thinking. The kids haven't been sick once, not since we came here over a year ago. Can't recollect anyone having been ill all year. Strange, don't you think?" Now that he had pointed this detail out to her, it did seem altogether odd that there hadn't been even a cold or flu anywhere in their group of two hundred, not since they arrived here in the Anuir, the Red Desert.

Chapter 27 Delayed Plans

"What do you mean four of our new supply depots have entirely disappeared?" bellowed Justinian. His Centurion adjunct had just rushed in with the news that Depot 10 through Depot 13 had vanished without a trace. The supply ships arrived at where they were supposed to be only they were not there! Yes, the generals had ordered an all-out search of the coastline, presuming that their ship navigators had somehow gotten themselves lost. "How can you misplace four huge supply depots!" screamed Justinian, venting his anger on the poor adjunct, who could not possibly know the answer to his question.

"Sire, the army has searched that entire coastline; here, let me show you on your map, from here to here. No trace of the four could be found anywhere. They simply vanished! And the six guards at each, they vanished likewise. Gone, no explanation, just gone. The generals desire your orders. I believe that they are completely mystified as well as the ship captains."

Justinian calmed down, he knew that he would have to issue some kind of orders, but what. He stared at the map. His grandiose idea for the assault was now in severe jeopardy. All depended upon supplies being nearby when the ground forces landed. Unlike his predecessors, he was not going to launch an assault on Zargarb from New Barq, and once taken, move on down the line, supplies always in the rear, stretching all the way down the Southlands. That was too risky; the Arad Raiders could easily cut this vital supply link. No, this time, the supplies would be just across the Med Sea, waiting to be ferried across to the soldiers. His was a brilliant plan indeed, only now all the supplies for the Zargarb assault and most of those for Solamina had vanished.

Yet, he was the all-knowing Emperor of the greatest civilization on Tarra. He had to provide an answer. Although he had never been to the Red Desert, or anywhere off the island of Megalos for that matter, he said knowingly, "Ah, it has a simple explanation. You see, the supply depots are still there. They've been covered up by sand storms, which have blown vast amounts of sand over the top of them, apparently making them vanish. Probably they are still precisely where they were, only buried under tons of sand. See, simple explanation." The adjunct beamed with relief, for now he had an explanation to give to the generals. It made sense to him as well.

"Orders. Okay, since that portion of the desert is so prone to sand storms, let's not waste any more time and supplies there. Have them build up Depot 9 to hold five times its planned capacity. We'll supply Zargarb and Solamina from there. Postpone the initial attack until October, which will give them time to make the buildup. Oh yes, have the generals take one legion, divide them by nine or so, and put them on garrison duty at the remaining depots. I don't want others vanishing without a trace. You got all that?" The adjunct nodded and scurried off to relay the message, thankful the Emperor had been utterly kind to him. Perhaps he even liked him!

"Now I've got to tell that darn Pope about yet another delay," cursed Justinian. "Ah, maybe just send him a post. I hate facing him, the old man." With that, the Emperor called for his scribe so that he could dictate the post. The Emperor never wrote anything but his signature.

The next afternoon, Justinian received a return post from Pope Yazi I. He opened it and had his aide read it to him. He disdained even to touch any item that his archenemy had touched.

Emperor Justinian,

I was saddened to hear of our losses due to the sand storms. I warned you that the Red Desert was a very dangerous place. No matter. Delays are inevitable if you intend to launch a successful assault.

I had an idea last night while reading your excellent description of the current situation along the coastline. Mind you, just a suggestion this is. What do you think about you yourself personally going to the front, perhaps actually commanding one of the assault legions? I admit that I am not as knowledgeable about our history as one who was born here on Megalos. Think of the precedent this would set! Think of the tremendous morale boost your very presence would instill upon the front line troops. Consider the political implications as well — our own Emperor has led the highly successful assault upon the Sea Princes. Why, I should think that you would become the most famous Emperor Megalos has ever had! But then, I know that it is a long trip and ruling Megalos takes up so very much of your time that this may be mere fanciful dreaming on my part.

Yours Sincerely,

Pope Yazi I

The Emperor grabbed the post from his aide and re-read it three more times. Damn, that man is clever, he thought to himself. *My throne is secure whether I am actually present or up there. History would rank me the most significant, most important Emperor since our ancient founders. When I return victorious, parading through the streets to the cheers of all my subjects, why, after that, my stature will rise so high that the Pope would never again attempt to cross me. Foolish old man probably never thought of that! I'll have so much support that I might be able to lower that of this upstart of a church! Stupid old man, you have just given me the dagger to plunge into your heart!*

"Summon all my advisors. We ride to join and lead our glorious army to victory!" Justinian exclaimed, unable to conceal his newfound joy.

Chapter 28 Hurry Up and Wait

Mid-September, the entire Santi force was finally fully equipped and in position ready to support the Crusaders. Compliments of the sewing portion of the Santi, each of us sported a black over-tunic with a bold red fleur-de-lis cross emblazoned on it, front and back. The Santi were now easily recognized, even from a distance, which is what we desired, instant recognition wherever one of us went. However, chain mail was still in short supply; I wanted the entire archer group to have this protection.

Earlier as we moved southward, I dispatched a group to take out the Centurion Salt Mines garrison in the extreme southeastern portion of the Arad. However, no real glory came from that excursion. Salt is perhaps the most precious commodity out here in the Arad. Hence, although the Centurions controlled the mines, worked them with their Arad slaves, anyone who wanted salt is allowed to visit and to take what they need. The true purpose of the garrison force was to keep their slaves in line.

Starved and worked until the freedom of death took them, the slaves were found to be in pitiful condition. In a way, I'm glad I delegated this operation to the Zargarb Circle instead of going there myself. Had I seen firsthand how these men were treated by the Centurions, I might have become a slave master myself, putting the Centurions to work as the slaves, starving them to death! Andre and Lenkova merely hunted every one of them down and eliminated them. However, due to the horrid condition of the fifty-five freed Arad slaves, I ordered Lenkova to use wagons to take them all up to the safety of the Lady in Blue, her aunt Zdlenka. Besides, it gave her another opportunity to visit with her aunt. I rightly assumed that she wanted to ask Zdlenka about Illanovich, her brother.

We took up a defensive line along the dry Al Wadi river, just inside the border with the Southlands. Sitting high atop the mesas, we held a commanding view of the red paved Centurion roadway they had constructed nearly a century ago. It wound its way from the north-south road north but mostly west to New Barq, their only port on the Med Sea, here at the extreme eastern edge of the sea.

The ever-growing Crusader army encamped just north of New Barq, forming a solid line from the Med seacoast inland, through the Cedar Forest and out into the mesa lands of the Arad. Here, we took over and our thousands of archery-cavalry stretched further eastward for miles. The nearly thousand strong Santi Attack Force, us, spread out thinly over the rest of the width of the Arad. True, only a few scouts were stationed in the far east, since we did not expect to see any action east of the north-south roadway, which divided Juda Arad roughly in half. The purpose was to guarantee that there could be no surprise flanking attack in force that might hit the Crusaders from the east.

Thanks to our Planners and Rea, we now had six of the Far Seeing

Devices, which were setup on mesa tops at key intervals. Using them, we could watch the marching legions as their columns slowly marched up the long road towards New Barq. Estimates put the Centurion numbers at perhaps five thousand strong, with another thousand of Yazi's Holy Paladins, who were all mounted cavalry. A thousand Centurion cavalry were among the five thousand including three dozen war chariots. Not knowing whether the Crusade generals knew about the use of the war chariots, I sent them a lengthy, detailed dispatch, urging them to eliminate the war chariots as soon as possible. I never heard back from the generals, however.

All that summer, the days were hot and incredibly boring. To help pass the time, we all spent hours practicing our skills. John Henry gave me an excellent suggestion: give first year druwid training to all who desired to learn. By June, we Guardians found that we had some nine hundred apprentices, eagerly learning the basics, beginning with Observing the Obvious. While these trainees, being solidly stuck inside their heads, would never be able to bring down lightning bolts or conjure flames, they still could learn a vast amount of invaluable information and skills. We quickly found that these men and women were eager to learn. Education was sorely lacking everywhere on Tarra, a point that I tucked away for future use.

In this training, High Priestess and Protector Elona Po, who came by for a visit, proved to hold a keen insight on just what ought to be taught and in what order. She had considerable experience with just this in her sector. She was living proof of the ability to merge Jehosanity, Tur, and druwid principles into a gnostic whole. Hence, she became the coordinator of the Santi College of Learning, which we formed up here in the field. One day when we had our permanent castles built, new recruits would undergo this learning and study in better surroundings.

Yet one key aspect that I did not anticipate occurred almost at once. Hundreds upon hundreds of Santi began asking for proper Sunday services, from me, no less. After our success at finding and rescuing the Holy Scrolls at Al Tarm, uniformly I was considered the ultimate authority. Within weeks, I found that I had to conduct Sunday services for the entire Santi field army! An impossible task, to preach to nearly five thousand men and women scattered across miles of the Arad desert mesa land. My Circle quickly pointed out that our new organization was primarily a religious one and that we needed to provide religious teachings and services.

Once more Elona Po came to my rescue. Together, she and I worked out ways and means to accomplish this gigantic task. By June, she and I were the most sought after "priests" for Sunday services. Among our large groups, we found six others who were reasonably knowledgeable about these matters and we eight worked together to plan out how to proceed. Elona and I alternated locations every Sunday, so that everyone had at least one opportunity to hear us every month. Throughout that long hot summer, Sundays were spent traveling around our various encampments, delivering four services at each location. Yes, it helped break the monotony of the long wait. Once more, Elona and her Circle had to leave for home.

In early September, I received the good news that a Santi fortification site had been established in all eight Sea Prince sectors, Cymry, and at our Mont Blanc port. Construction of the outer perimeter walls was well underway, along with temporary housing. Each of these original ten fortifications also contained a dock, which could handle two caravels at one time. While our docking capabilities were small, we were not considered major merchants. These facilities would allow us independent travel by sea.

Further, the Planners at Mont Blanc had already drawn up plans for stone-built castles, complete with a tall tower and manor house. While these would take many years to construct fully, with the exception of Fortress d'Grange, the Santi fortifications would soon be the strongest in the lands of Tarra.

Paul and I, sitting on the mesa top with our Far Seeing Eye covering the far distant bivouacs of the Centurions down around New Barq, were completely bored. He sketched a map of the Med Sea area in the sand and placed a stone marking the major cities. "Here we are, way out over here. Here is the army we are watching down below. Here is the Crusader army. Ket, when war comes, our forces are going to be far out of the way. Have you considered the possibility that we might become cut off from Zargarb?"

"We can always backtrack and take a northerly route back into Zargarb up by North Point. I suppose we could even parallel the edge of the Appian Way through the steppes to the Greenway and head home along the Langdoc region."

"More to the point, Ket, what if all this build up here is a ruse?" Paul added, mostly ignoring my reply.

"What do you mean? They are not going to attack from here?"

"Who knows what happens here. I mean what if they attack somewhere along the long coastline of the Sea Princes? They do not necessarily need to attack the walled cities, just come on land and take over everything else, leaving the cities for later. With their ramming ships, they can pretty much cut off sea re-supply to the besieged cities."

"That wasn't their pattern the last time they attacked the Sea Princes," I replied, becoming slightly interested.

"They didn't have the ramming ships then either. All they need to do is take over the Zargarb sector's outlying lands, leaving the city alone and the entire Crusader army would have its line of supply cut-off," Paul pronounced grimly. "No supplies, no more fighting. How can the Santi possibly bring in enough supplies for that sized army, let alone our own? We don't even have a port nearby in which to bring them. It gets worse. While our caravels can probably go faster than the triremes, given some wind, what happens to us when we dock, say at Zargarb? I'd expect the enemy to attempt to ram us while we are slowing to go in or out of the dock."

"You are forgetting our Santi protectors on board," I added hopefully. "They may be able to stop a few. If they hit one of our ships with a bunch of their rammers, yes, we are doomed."

"Perhaps we ought to rethink our overall strategy," he suggested.

"Look, if we pull our Santi into say the middle sector and the enemy hits here, coming out of New Barq, the net result would be that we'd look awfully stupid and ineffective. Any battle would be over long before we could get here. On the other hand, if their main thrust is here, we may be of use protecting the Crusaders." The prospects all depended upon just what the Centurions finally decided to do.

Paul countered, "Let's look at what we do see. Here, we have estimates of at least five thousand Centurions and perhaps a couple thousand of those Holy Paladins of Yazi. This we do know, it is a sizeable force, slightly surpassed in numbers alone by our Crusaders. You with me?" I agreed.

"So we just cannot ignore the threat here, given the unproven Crusader forces. Still, we continue to get numerous reports of Centurion merchant ships docking along the entire southern Med sea coastline along the Red Desert. From the reported positions, these could be used to supply an invading army in just about any of the Sea Prince sectors, any one, or even all at one time. Of course, what is missing are the troops with which to execute that invasion. No sign of any Centurion troop buildup anywhere, except here. Could they perhaps be planning to use their merchant ships to ferry troops from here to a beachhead in one or more sectors, bypassing our forces entirely?"

"Surely we would be able to spot a large influx of merchant ships needed to move thousands of men and their equipment and supplies," I countered, becoming even more frustrated with the lack of true answers.

"Here's another possibility, suppose the Centurions here marched on down south and west, out onto the coastline of the Red Desert. There, they could be picked up and ferried over to a sector, while our forces are stuck here and have to march overland. By the time the Crusaders got back to, say Solamina, why the battle would be over," Paul theorized. I did not like these theories one bit.

"And here's another one. Suppose that while we sit here watching them, the Centurions march another even larger force across the Red Desert from the Southlands, an army that we know nothing about. They reach the coastline, merchant ships pick them up, ferry them across the Med, and they assault away, nearly unhindered," Paul continued throwing out alternative ideas. I could see why he was a Protector and why I most definitely was not.

"What's the possibility that we could get a small scouting party around the forces here and go check on this unseen army of theirs?" I wondered.

"Well, we might be able to sneak a few by their lines. From what I can tell, they are sticking fairly close to their paved roadway. Nighttime might be the best opportunity to sneak across. It would be easier to do the further away from New Barq the scouts make the attempt. The real problem is that we have no one who has ever been south of the Arad. Any scouts we send will be really on their own and with no idea of what to expect or where the main tracks are located, to say nothing of watering holes. They'd have to take their own food with them, no telling what they will find out in the desert that's edible. I think that is a pretty risky mission," Paul concluded.

"Too risky to try," I decided, unless my Circle would do it, which was out of the question. "What I don't get is the numbers, Paul. At this moment, completely ignoring the Crusaders, the Centurions have barely enough forces to assault one sector's walled city. Throw in the Crusaders, which by now they have to know about, and there just doesn't seem to be enough Centurions to wage this war."

"Precisely, we must not be seeing or have detected the better half of their assault forces. They must be somewhere, but where?" Paul stated flatly.

"Well, they cannot be crossing the Red Desert on foot. I think we can rule that out because of the total unknowingness of the land, lack of water, and lack of game. They cannot be building a road for their supplies to travel upon because the drifting sands would cover it up as fast as they built it, assuming they could even find stone with which to make said road. That's out. Likewise, they cannot be building a roadway all across the Southlands and up the western coastline to the Red Desert coast. That would take them several years and be certainly observable during its lengthy construction. Without a road, overland travel of that distance for a large army would be undoable as well. There is no way to supply a large force on foot over that distance. Besides, it would take a very long time to walk all that way. It was bad enough riding down the paved roadway to Sud, the direct route. It took us months as I remember. So no army is walking up the western coast of Sud," I concluded.

Paul continued my speculations, "Look, their tiny merchant ships could carry maybe twenty-five soldiers. Let's say that they needed an army of say ten thousand strong. That would mean a flotilla of something like four hundred merchant ships! Fanciful indeed."

"Ah, wait a minute, Paul. You may have hit upon it. Not four hundred merchant ships, but rather four hundred trips by merchant ships! We know that there have been many, many merchant ships plying along the southern coast of the Med over this last year. The mariners have told us so. Say, that they have as many as twenty-five merchant ships dedicated to troop transport. Each ship would need to make sixteen trips. Let's be optimistic. Say, that one ship can make the round trip from Megalos in say two months, probably it's more than that, but let's assume that for a minute. Sixteen trips of two months each, which makes three years! They've only been at it about one year. Maybe I'm barking up the wrong bush here, way too long."

"Ah, but suppose they used fifty ships, that would cut it in half, down to eighteen months. In that case, they might not be ready to attack until next spring or thereabouts," Paul speculated.

"And seventy-five ships, they would be about ready to attack now," I pointed out.

"True, true, but suppose this is all nonsense, and they have their ten thousand men stationed on down the north-south roadway, just out of our sight? What then? With that many additional troops, they could sweep on through the Crusaders and on into Zargarb," Paul crushed my hopes. "We'd be in for a fight right here."

"Sometimes I feel like the Centurions are just playing with us," I chortled. "A fine cat and mouse game this is becoming!" I had the last word this day.

In middle October, I received further news that alarmed all of us somewhat. The mariners of Velona spotted what had to be the Emperor's personal ship sailing up off the western coast of the Red Desert, heading north towards the Med Sea! No less than twenty triremes accompanied him. An additional forty merchant ship were in the convoy. The news was indeed stunning. Speculations ran wild throughout our camp, as they did within the Sea Prince cities. Some thought that the Emperor might be coming to make a bid for a friendly takeover. Most, however, believed that he would be taking charge of the attack personally. Yet, where remained a complete mystery.

If he sailed to New Barq, we could conclude that the assault would begin from our location. However, if he landed elsewhere, it was anyone's guess. A few days later, we received reports that his convoy rounded the bend and entered the Med Sea. They sailed awfully close to Velona. Our people there decided that the Emperor was just getting a firsthand look at their new and novel defenses. I certainly hoped that was the case and he would leave Velona alone, at least at first. I was thankful that I had sent Elona back to her city during the summer.

Two days later, I received the report I had been dreading all along. The Emperor's convoy beached at nowhere on the southern coast of the Med Sea, roughly opposite of Barcella, one sector further east from Velona. There was nothing there except a sandy beach, although reports of supplies being dropped off in this vicinity had been coming in all year. My conclusion was that just over the dunes and out of sight lay the main Centurion army. From here, they could attack just about anywhere in the Sea Princes! The only bright spot was the timing. Soon the northern ports would begin icing up; winter was on its way. Within a few more weeks, both Calgary and Cymry would be unreachable by ships until the spring thaw.

As I expected, the High Councils of the sectors began to panic. Their simple war had suddenly become far more complex. The expediency of having the Crusaders fight their war for them evaporated. Bets were rampant upon which sector would be hit first.

Via our Communicators to the Sisterhood High Council representatives, I sent helpful suggestions. We needed an overall strategy, which I negotiated over the next few days. In essence, the High Councils decided that should the Emperor choose to assault one or more sectors, they would be able to hold out for a considerable period behind the protective walls of the city strongholds. Meanwhile, it was imperative that the Crusaders stop the remaining army coming out of New Barq. As long as that force could not come overland in support of the seaborne invasion, the city-forts could hold out. Hence, the

Santi was ordered to remain where it was and to give all needed assistance to the Crusaders, who were still looked upon as the saviors of the Sea Princes.

The High Councils also decided to send out the word to all the sector's outlying towns and villages. Anyone who wanted sanctuary within the city's protective walls was welcomed. Underneath this generous offer lay the simple fact that more people within the walls equaled more people to help defend its walls from attack. Over the next few days, I received reports that some were indeed beginning to make the trek down into their sector's main city. I didn't know whether it was better to be a trapped rat within a walled city or to be a helpless victim at the mercy and whim of the invading army. Neither sounded particularly good to me.

Chapter 29 Justinian Takes Charge

Mid-October, resplendent in his shining golden bronze armor and ornate, bejeweled helm, Emperor Justinian stepped off the Royal Yacht and onto the sandy beach of Depot #1. His seven generals snapped to a rigid attention as their commander appeared. Justinian nodded to them and waited for his chariot to be unloaded and horses harnessed. With his generals leading the way, this Emperor of Tarra rode past the piles of cargo of Depot #1, up and over the dunes, until he was out of sight from any onlookers to the north, all according to plan.

About a mile inland and concealed from prying eyes lay his vast assault army. The generals led him to the Imperial Meeting tent, where food and refreshments awaited this supreme ruler of men. Only when the Emperor had dismounted and sat down on the portable throne did they speak. One asked, "How was your voyage, Supreme Commander Justinian?"

"Long and tiresome," came the terse reply. "What news have you?"

"Permit me to brief you, sir," his Field General Nikas Theocopolous replied. It was his duty as the top commander to brief his Emperor. "Per your orders, the missing depots were located, as you suggested, buried under the sands. However, the six guards at each were all slain, murdered and all the supply boxes and crates carried off by persons as yet unknown. We've sent out scouting parties into the Red Desert, but so far, all reports indicate it remains uninhabited. I wish I had better news for you."

Justinian bit his lip to avoid bursting out with "Then double the searchers!" He realized that he had more important business than searching for some people with his supplies. "Apparently, the Red Desert is not as uninhabited as we all thought. Pray continue."

"Everything is prepared for the assaults. We have fifty legions along with the two thousand Holy Paladins of Pope Yazi just outside New Barq. This Crusader Army probably has more like sixty legions of ill-equipped men, probably a pushover. They are just across the border from New Barq, perhaps five miles distant."

He skillfully paused to clear his throat just in case the Emperor wanted clarification. Seeing no interruption, Nikas continued. "All of the Supply Depots are fully prepared and ready to begin dispensing to our forward units. Here in New Galantas, we have seventy legions ready to invade. You brought the triremes here and an additional twenty merchant ships are due within a week. Hence, all is operational and ready to begin on your orders."

"Excellent, General Nikas, excellent. I looked at Velona's defenses before landing. They are indeed formidable. Can we take that port?"

"We've sent in spies at night to inspect this harbor. They have constructed a barrier of chains around the entrance. If a ship attempts to sail into the bay while the chains are raised, the ship will be stopped and likely highly damaged. Of that, we have no doubts. Worse, we believe that there are at least a hundred Volksholm longboats there as well. If we send in our war ships, the Axemen will send out theirs. While we may ram some, we would be outnumbered. Worse, if we are boarded, we could very easily lose the trireme! Overland? That is the only possibility, but again, reports put several thousand Axemen now living there, so the battle could be very challenging and costly, to say nothing of laying siege to the city walls. I'm afraid that we ought to leave Velona alone, initially. Likewise d'Grange, which can only be assaulted from the south after taking Velona. Even then, that operation will be risky, with little to benefit from taking that rocky sector."

"I concur, General Nikas. We shall leave Velona for the mop up operations, once we have firm control of the other sectors," Justinian agreed.

"There is yet another complication, Emperor, the one I wrote to you about, this Santi organization. Per your orders, our spies in Zargarb have once more provided keen information on them. The vast majority of the Santi members appear to be ex-Sisterhood fighters. We know just how powerful those women can be from the last time we invaded Zargarb. Remember that some five hundred of them nearly defeated many legions of our crack assault troops."

"I remember history, Nikas," Justinian did not appreciate being reminded about the past. "How many are there in this Santi?"

"Our spies have managed to ferret out some fundamental numbers, but they caution us not to place too much confidence in its accuracy. For sure, there appears to be close to thirty legions of archer-fighters, who have moved out into the Arad, presumably over on the eastern side, since they have not appeared near New Barq. Yet, these do not seem to be their main strike force. The Sisterhood has always been known as defensive fighters. Now they have an actual strike force which is unusual."

"How so?"

"Our spies said that the Sisterhood has joined or banded together with these so-called Guardians of the Greenway. We don't know much about this secretive organization, except that they are very likely powerful fighters in their own right. They seem to command the highest respect from even the High Councils of the sectors, so we are probably correct in assuming that they are a respectable foe indeed. This Santi Strike Force contains several legions of these Guardians in addition to a legion or so from West Reach and five legions of seasoned fighters from the Greenway. Our best estimates suggest that this Santi group may well be equal or better than our own average soldiers. Additionally, they all wear chain mail armor, and the whole Santi is mounted. Whether fighting cavalry or just transport — that we do not yet know."

Justinian rubbed his chin. This was not at all good news. "This Santi thing could prove a major problem for us. Is that what you are saying?"

"Aye, sir. We expect to plow through this Crusader army with little resistance. The Santi, though smaller, may pose a very significant problem indeed. They are mobile, armored, and skilled fighters. If we send foot soldiers against them, ours would be cut to pieces, just as the barbarians did so many years ago when they very nearly reached Sud."

"I see. Where is this Strike Force? Are they too with the archers in the east of the Arad?"

"No, sire, they have been seen just east of the Crusaders near New Barq," General Nikas replied.

"You think these Santi are that strong, eh?" Justinian bounced it back to his general, unwilling to make the decision just yet.

"Yes, my Emperor," Nikas replied, emphasizing Justinian's title. He did not want the responsibility for making this call. If it went badly against the Santi, Justinian might lash out at him. "While they are as yet unproven in combat, prudence might suggest caution. Another point, if I may, the Velona problem may be larger than anticipated. We now believe that their ruler-priestess, this Elona Po is also in league with these Guardians and the Santi. Going beyond just support, we believe they are integral parts. Every one of these new caravel ships of hers has a Santi garrison force on them, complete with some new devices designed to attack our triremes."

Justinian looked up; this was the first that he had heard of this. "Santi are protecting the caravels? Well, that does make sense; those are the most valuable ships on the seas. We absolutely must capture one or more of them. What kind of devices can sink our mighty ramming ships?"

"Spies have seen many of these caravels taking target practice at sea. They've some kind of monstrous crossbow and a fireball heaver. At least that is how the spies describe these new diabolical devices."

"Damn these Santi anyway," Justinian cursed. "They are rapidly becoming bothersome to me!" He noticed that Nikas was fidgeting, evidently, there was more. "Is there more about these Santi?" he barked, rapidly becoming agitated.

"Well, yes. It seems that all throughout the sectors, these Santi are in charge of making key deliveries of valuable cargo, such as the Crusader's pay. They have also begun construction of their own fortified positions, usually not far from the walled cities. Spies tell us that the outer walls are nearly finished."

"You are telling me that we not only have to deal with these interminable walled cities, but now to get at the Santi, we have to assault their walled fortifications?" Justinian bellowed, unable to contain his anger any longer. Of course, barking at his top general was not a wise action to take; he regretted his outburst as soon as he had done it, but it could not be taken back.

The general flushed red, but firmly stood his ground. He knew that if he did not make a strong case for these Santi and later the Santi crippled their assaults, the general would find himself working in the salt mines for the remainder of his life. Justinian continued more softly, "Well, I can see that my aides have not kept me up to date. That is why I am here. You cannot run a war from Megalos. Okay, let's make modifications to the Grand Plan of Attack. Bring out the maps." This was precisely what General Nikas wanted to hear. He knew he was off the hook; no matter which way the Santi went, Justinian would take the heat.

A large rug was unrolled, woven into its woof and warp was the entire Med Sea area, at least as much of it as was known. Justinian took the box of tokens from an aide and began placing them. Each represented one fighting group, whether boats or cavalry or foot soldiers. Onto each one, Justinian placed a label identifying what it represented. A few minutes later with the map filled with these tokens, both men stared at the situation, along with the other six generals.

Justinian commented, "The Santi Strike Force is way over here in the Arad. If our legions break through these Crusaders here by the Med Sea, the Santi will be completely out of position. Their supply lines must then stretch all the way back through the Arad to Zargarb, a very long route indeed. Even if they try to follow along behind our advancing army, thinking they are cutting off our supplies coming up from the south, they will be completely mistaken. Another fifteen of my personal legions are marching up the north road as we speak. While it may be a month yet before they arrive, the Santi, who would logically be following our advance toward Zargarb, will find themselves surrounded! We will use our ground attack legions as the Santi bait; let them eliminate these would be crusaders and then use them to draw the Santi down here along the Med seacoast. My legions come up from the south and bam; we have them caught in a pincer action!"

"Brilliant, Emperor Justinian," commented several field generals; all were bucking for the attention of their leader. Nikas, on the other hand, was not so optimistic. Too many things could go wrong. Still, if they did go wrong, it was good to hear that another fifteen legions were on their way to back them up.

"Now I think it best to leave Velona alone at this time; we'll come back to them when we've secured the rest of the sectors," Justinian continued. "We shall hit both Solamina and Zargarb simultaneously with our invasion force, landing on both sides of the walled cities simultaneously. We move quickly to encircle the cities, cut them off from overland resupply, while our triremes make sure none leaves and no supplies come in by sea. Then, we let time starve them all out. First, we need to strike fear into the hearts and minds of the wealthy merchants. Unleash our triremes and sink a few key ships in those two sectors. Once they see we are serious, I think they will come to terms far more rapidly. After all what is a Sea Prince without any ships?" he roared with laughter at his own joke; the generals quickly chuckled as well.

"Okay, back to the next business at hand: what to do with the Holy Paladins. I have an agreement with Pope Yazi. These men will handle completely what we used to have the Home Guards in place to handle, the garrisoning and law enforcement activities. Yes, we will not need to leave a single Centurion in any captured sector. How about that, gentlemen?"

"How did you ever work that one out with the Pope? Positively brilliant," declared General Nikas. "Many of our troops just hate being on civil patrols; we are soldiers not sheriffs. Wait until the men hear about this twist!"

Justinian just smiled and did not answer the rhetorical question.

"Now the problem with these Holy Paladins is simple. We dare not use them in the actual assault; they are just not up to Centurion standards. They will sustain too many casualties and then we will be faced with making up their losses from our ranks, which I do not want to do. Hence, I'll order them all to ride along the southern Med seacoast to Supply Depot #9, where they can then be transported across the sea into Zargarb or Solamina as needed. I suspect that they want in on the fight, so I'll give them the pretext of searching out and destroying whoever has been raiding our four depots along the way to #9. However, under no circumstances are they to leave the coastline and head inland. I cannot afford to have them become lost in the desert, nor can I spare precious cavalry to go and look for them if they do get lost. Is that understood?"

The generals all agreed and nodded. None of them wanted anything to do with these Holy Paladins of Pope Yazi. The generals considered them a nuisance, more trouble than they were worth. Nikas agreed to deliver the orders to the leader of the Holy Paladins.

"The triremes will be in position to attack within five days. I'll give them five days to soften up the shipping before we launch the ground attacks. That puts the assault to begin on October 15, a fine day for it." Everyone agreed with him, but something bothered him, something was slightly out of place in his Grand Plan. Suddenly he remembered. Way back when the Governors controlled the sectors, they had found the Sisterhood the most dependable, secure, and able people, providing secure shipments, bringing law and order to the barbarians, and many other aspects. In fact, history books claimed that the governors actually depended upon this rogue band of amazon fighters. They were incredibly useful way back when. He wondered if they might just be very useful once more.

He spoke up, "One final detail. Let's avoid any direct engagement with this Santi group. If they attack us, go ahead and defend. However, do not openly go after their forces; engage the Crusaders, city garrisons, and the like. Leave the Santi alone if at all possible. They may yet be very useful to us." None dare contradict their Emperor; thus all agreed with him. They left the pavilion to go write up the necessary orders and send out a dispatch ship to New Bark.

The next day, the Emperor sailed out into the Med Sea, along with most of his trireme fleet, heading toward Zargarb and Solamina. He intended to see firsthand just how well these new ramming ships performed. However, he would stay well back of any action, unwilling to risk his own personal ship to some stray shot from these new devices. He also intended to keep his ship surrounded by at least a half dozen of the rammers, just in case some other ship made undue threats upon his ship. He could fight on land, but he felt completely helpless when at sea, a feeling he distinctly hated.

Their flotilla soon entered the normal shipping pattern of the central Med Sea. Ships on the longer hauls would sail in both directions down the middle of the sea, while those going from port to port would hug the coastline. They spotted three ships sailing toward them and four paralleling their course. Since there was no way of determining whether these belonged to either Solamina or Zargarb sectors, they were ignored. One, however, was a caravel flying a black flag with a red cross, signifying this was an official Santi ship. As the Emperor's yacht and the caravel closed, the crew on both ships watched each other curiously, as they passed by each other. One man on the caravel stared long at Justinian; his eyes seemed to pierce the Emperor's soul.

Chapter 30 The First Known Naval Combat on Tarra

The tenth of October, our Communicators were kept very busy relaying messages all over the Sea Princes. The Protector on board the Swallow Tail had spotted what had to be the Emperor of Megalos; the ship flew the royal flag of Megalos. Further, he was headed to the east with a vast flotilla of the triremes. One might have presumed he was on a state visit to the Sea Princes, and one would have been very wrong. Our assumption was simple, he was about to unleash his reign of terror upon the merchant ships. The key question was which ships would he attack? He had bypassed Velona, and rightly so. Via all the Communicators, I sent warning messages to all the High Councils and to all our caravels and those of Elona Po. The waiting game was almost over.

On October 14, the Flying Pinnacle, one of our three caravels, was about ten miles out from Solamina. Empty, she had just unloaded another load of grain for our Santi fortress workers and was heading back to Middleton. Captain Alan Swallow was at the helm, heading westward. A fair number of merchant ships, including one of Elona Po's caravels were in the area, some heading into and out of Solamina, while others were plying to and from the more distant Zargarb. The lookout in the crow's nest, Able, called out, "War ships dead ahead. Looks like trouble!"

Quickly, Alan yelled the words that the crew and protectors had been training for, "Battle stations everyone. Here they come!" A flurry of bodies rushed on to the various decks, untying the equipment, preparing for battle, just as they had practiced it. Protector Tom Johnston and his wife Communicator Aileen, both retired, took up their key positions. He manned the foredeck so he could use his spells upon approaching ships, while she at his side could aid or relay telepathic communications. Sister Kaylee was in charge of the archers and the shooter, the engine that shot the huge quarrel. Karl and Al, the Axemen, took charge of the lobber, which launched flaming balls of fire into the enemy ships. The CPS, Caravel Protection Squad, was ready for action in less than two minutes!

Light in the water, the Flying Pinnacle cruised along westward. Soon it would overtake a heavier laden Solamina ship, the Golden Vineyard. However, just beyond that ship, eight triremes were barreling toward both the two ships. Standing to at a safe distance a mile further off was unmistakably the Emperor's ship. Alan ordered, "Let's see if we can take some of the pressure off of the Vineyard; they are a sitting duck! Eight to one slow moving ship is hardly a fair fight!" He steered ten degrees to port and the caravel gracefully arced out and around the slower moving ship.

As the Flying Pinnacle passed, they saw a very frightened crew trying to muster up as much speed as they could. Alan yelled to her skipper, "We're going to try to cut a path through them for you to follow. Stay on our tail. God speed!" What else could he say or do? The Vineyard was likely to be sunk within the next few minutes. He received cheers from the pale-faced crew; their fear was worn on their faces.

Alan felt the tug of the Mind Link, as Aileen joined him together with Tom, herself, Kaylee, and Karl. She was the coordinator of their key actions. However, wisely, Aileen had Mind Linked me into her group, and I linked my Circle to me. For better or worse, my Circle would have a foredeck view of the first combat at sea.

"You take the one on the right, I, the left. On my signal, push as hard as you can. Our objective is to push them out of the way so that we can slide right through their line," Tom told Aileen. To the others, he explained via the Mind Link, "We will be passing right through their middle. There should be four targets on either side as we pass. Archers and shooter, aim for the leaders. Lobber, see if you can burn one of them! Get ready, steady, about a minute to go." Watching through Tom's eyes, I saw the eight triremes closing the distance rapidly, primarily because our ship was flying through the water at top speed. The two center triremes attempted to take aim on the caravel, while the other six, three on each side, swerved out and away from us and then back in towards us or the slow moving ship behind us, intent on ramming.

Thus, I learned one useful tip, ramming is best done broadside, not head on. Why? Head on, the trireme risks getting an entire side of its numerous oars broken off like match sticks, as it slides along the entire side of the victim ship. Even with the oars raised high, they would get broken in the rigging. I watched intently as the two triremes in the center of the pack had no choice but to attempt the head on collision, aiming for the very bow of the Flying Pinnacle.

At the very last minute, Tom and Aileen let loose their spells. I saw now how it worked, at least from a ship. Our caravel was flying along, its bow cutting the water cleanly. The two druwids merely extended the bow shock wave, rather like an invisible but solid extension of the ship, on out further forward. Both incoming triremes were hit with the full force of our momentum, both careened wildly onto their sides, nearly turning over so strong was the pushing wave. Both floundered and took on a huge amount of water, coming to a dead stop in the sea almost at once. They would not see action for some time, as all hands began frantic bailing to save the ships from sinking.

As the Flying Pinnacle then passed by the other six triremes, which were getting into position to attack the slow Sea Prince vessel lumbering along in our wake, the others began firing from each side of the main deck. Kaylee fired the shooter only once; there was no time to reload before the Flying Pinnacle shot past all the enemy ships. While she aimed for the chest of the captain of one trireme, the undulating motion of both ships threw the aim off slightly. The massive quarrel missed the man's chest, hitting him instead right between the eyes. So powerful was the impact that the quarrel went clean through the man's head, thudding into the curved stern arc that arced down and eventually became the keel. He was pulled off his feet and nailed to the high arcing stern piece — nailed to a cross came to mind.

Two other ships were hit by the normal archers, who were aiming for the beater and captains. Several arrows hit each man and most ended up falling overboard or collapsing onto the ranks of rowers. Three of the six attackers were out of the immediate action at least, while they recovered. However, the last action was the carefully aimed shot from the Axeman lobber. This contraption took considerable skill, particularly in the aiming and timing of its shot, because it was a slow, lobbed ball of fire. I watched fascinated as the flaming ball rose high into the air and then descended. Wham! It hit directly amidship on another trireme, bursting upon impact, a great ball of flaming oil splattering over the wood and nearby rowers. Six men, naked flesh burning, dove over the side in a last ditch attempt to squelch the massive pain of the burning oil. The remaining men began frantic attempts to douse the oil fire before their ship was destroyed.

The score: caravel-6, triremes-0. Our victory was very short lived, however. Two remained, and they continued on their collision course with the slow moving ship. I watched as the poor ship was rammed at about a forty-five degree angle on both its port and starboard sides. The bow of the ramming ships extended a good three feet forward from the normal bow of the trireme and was under water. Thus, the points of impact were these submerged bows, which smashed two huge holes below the waterline of the Sea Prince ship. Her main deck nearly buckled from the massive blows. At once, the rowers began back rowing, pulling the triremes out of the way. The victim vessel began to flounder, as seawater flooded into the already stuffed cargo deck below the waterline. I saw the six crew members abandoning their ship, jumping into the blue waters of the Med. The ship slowed down to almost a dead stop, as it slowly sank lower and lower into the water. It was a sick sight to watch, as the sea flowed over its main deck, sails still fluttering from the masts. Slowly even these disappeared as well. Triremes-1; Sea Princes-0.

From the stern of the Flying Pinnacle, Tom watched as the two victorious ships moved back to join the flotilla, which still headed eastward. The other six slowly made their way back toward the Emperor's ship. It quickly became apparent that the Centurions were going to leave the six crew members to drown in the Med Sea. Our caravel flew into action, making a wide turn to starboard; they intended to risk all by going back to rescue the crew members. While risky, I did not intervene, but watched. Tom and the others kept a continuous watch on the distant enemy ships, while the crew dealt with the sudden shift of direction and got a dingy ready to be lowered.

Five minutes later, the Flying Pinnacle slowed down and lowered the dingy. One man rowed toward the bobbing, floating men. Twenty minutes later, five had been rescued, but their captain had not made it; he had drowned in the sea. Once the men and dingy were safely on board and the Flying Pinnacle once more under full sail, Eileen broke the Mind Link. I looked at my Circle and saw stunned faces.

Clearing his throat, Allan commented, "Well, at least our attack mechanisms functioned properly."

Paulette nearly in tears, cried out, "But that ship didn't have any chance at all! That's out right murder!" For several minutes, we all just stared somberly at one another.

Lilly Ann, ever the Judger, finally pointed out, "Look, gang, they cannot mean to destroy all the Sea Prince ships. If they did that, why, after they conquered the lands, there would be no means of livelihood left. In fact, the Sea Princes might just then depend utterly on supplies coming in from Megalos. I cannot imagine the Emperor wanting to have to support all these people here. The drain on his treasury would be enormous. Rather, I think that he is attempting to sink a few ships as a warning to the High Councils. You know, do not try to resupply from the sea, and do not try to escape by sea, that sort of thing." She sounded both hopeful and very logical.

"Further," she coyly bit her lip as she often did when about to propose some offensive action, "we have now seen this Emperor and, today, roughly where he is located. I think it is high time that we took action directly against him. Let's use our telepathic skills to give him a taste of his own handiwork!"

I suddenly had visions of Lilly Ann and Paulette bombarding the man's mind with ghastly pictures, blasting away at his sanity until he went completely mad. However, mad men often do highly destructive actions in their madness. "You have a good point, Lilly Ann, but let's not get carried away with revenge. Let's put this to use. Rather than driving him mad or crazy, what about giving him nightmares about attacking the Santi, until he is utterly convinced to avoid harming us like the plague?"

"Well, I guess that will do, Ket Bethany," she retorted, "but I still wish him to get a taste of what he is doing to others. I guess nightmares about us will suffice. When do we get started on this project?" She certainly wanted immediate action.

I contacted John Henry and let him arrange the Scaring of Justinian Project, using our best, most able Communicators. Over the course of the next few weeks, every night, one or more Communicators would touch his mind and deliver two things: leave the Santi alone and invented images of horrors befalling him should he attack the Santi. Of course, we had no idea if this campaign would have any effect on his plans or not, time would tell. Further, we did not have long to ponder it; war had finally arrived.

Chapter 31   The First Crusade for Religious Freedom

On October 15, we spied action in and around New Barq. First, the Holy Paladins packed up all their gear, as far as we could see with our Far Seeing Eye, and rode off down the Med seacoast, heading south and west. Evidently, these men were not going to be part of the major assault here in the east. However, more to the point, the many legions of Centurions also began forming up their battle lines. The clash of arms and armor, the test of wills, was about to commence.

"What are they doing now?" I asked agitatedly, Paul was monopolizing the Seeing Eye.

"Foot soldiers are forming lines. Looks like they will be heading down the center. Cavalry are positioned on the eastern flank, closest to us. Wait a minute, the war chariots are moving into position now. Ah, they are moving out in front. Looks like the chariots are planning to blaze a trail through the ranks of the Crusaders; foot soldiers will follow on through mopping up."

"Okay. Time for notifications and actions," I got back into the swing of commanding once more. Communicators were notified, who in turn notified the various leaders, captains, and such. I needed to give them all time to break camp and to prepare for battle. Thus, I avoided giving any actual orders just yet. In addition, I will admit that I had not a clue what would be our best countermove. In this, I was dependent upon the Protectors.

"Get all our Protectors that are nearby here," Paul finally said. "We need a battle conference." This I could handle and headed off to round them up, at least as many as were near enough to our main camp. Naturally, the full Circles insisted on joining the Protector's conference, if only out of curiosity.

The Santi's nine regiments, each with roughly four squads of twenty-five, was positioned in southern Arad along the border with the Southlands. We opted to camp high atop hills or mesas. Theoretically, we needed to patrol and guard the entire southern border, some two hundred fifty miles of it, stretching from nearly the Med Sea in the west to the tall mountains in the east. However, since I expected no real action beyond the halfway point, the north-south paved Centurion made roadway, only one regiment was assigned to cover that easternmost hundred twenty mile stretch. The other eight regiments watched over the remaining one hundred thirty miles. Again, not expecting any real action so far out from the coastal road, I had two regiments each covering some forty miles. The remaining six regiments of Santi covered the last fifty miles, with three regiments, including mine, here at our westernmost position, some fifteen miles from the coast. Using the Far Seeing Eye, we could barely see the Med Sea.

Because of water concerns and not knowing where they would be needed, I kept the fifteen regiments of archer Sisterhood fighters back in Jerilum. Although it was an abandoned town, at least they had shelter and ample water. Jerilum was centrally located, so I could call them down to us or back to Zargarb as needed.

Our vantage point was atop the last mesa to the west and south in Juda Arad. Again, using our Far Seeing instruments, we could discern, barely, activities in the distant New Barq, which lay some twenty miles south and a little west of our position. Had we not been atop the mesa, we would not have been able to see it at all. New Barq was some forty miles from the beginning of the Cedar Forest along the Med seacoast, some ten miles into the Arad. Here near the start of the forest, General Antonio Prada had arrayed his forces, intent upon using the forest as part of his defense.

At the time of the assault, Prada commanded a Crusader army consisting of eighty regiments of foot soldiers; again, each regiment consisted of four squads of twenty-five men. While the High Councils had planned to have one hundred regiments, such did not materialize in time for the war. Also, General Prada had twenty regiments of cavalry at his disposal, not the fifty that had been planned.

His counterpart, General Mikos Dox commanded forty legions of foot soldiers and ten legions of cavalry. A legion contained a hundred men. He also had as his critical offensive weapon fifty war chariots with scything blades affixed to their wheels, designed to cut through anything in its path. These were murderous weapons indeed. His army was well trained, well-disciplined as Centurions are wont to be when in a battle. Armed with a large shield, spear, and sword, they also have various bits of bronze armor protecting their heads, torso, arms, and legs.

General Prada's forces were lightly armored, mostly with leather and similar bits that could be found. Weapons ran the gamut from good quality swords to poor. To stop the cavalry, he had formed up two regiments of pike men, whose long pole arms could be planted in the ground and thus skewer anything that approached it, presumably the chariots and cavalry. He also created five regiments of archers, using short bows and heavy crossbows, whichever he could find; it was a hodgepodge, but would be useful on defense.

He set up his main defense along the paved Centurion road that led ultimately to Zargarb. Three rows of heavy wooden barricades blocked the road, thinning out to two deep a mile beyond the road on either side. Along this line, he placed first his pike men and then the rest of his foot soldiers, ranks upon ranks, with the archer regiments in the rear, because they could shoot over the heads of the men in front of them. The cavalry were positioned in the forest, ready to gallop out into the relatively open spaces when needed.

What none of us knew at the start of the war was that Mikos Dox expected another twenty legions would be arriving within a week or so, marching up from Megalos along the long north-south road. General Dox greatly desired somehow to pull the Santi in behind his main force, apparently cutting him off from his line of supplies in New Barq. Then, the arriving legions could attack the Santi from their rear while he pivoted the rear of his line to attack the Santi from the front, thereby eliminating the Santi. Those were his orders, anyway.

From our vantage point, we could not see the Crusader army; it was behind the hills and forest, some twenty miles as the eagle flies. Unfortunately, in mesa country, one must take a circuitous route to get anywhere, in our case, more like thirty miles. General Prada kept insisting that he didn't need our help, so now that the war started, what were we supposed to do?

That was the question I put forward at our first War Council meeting, which included all the Protectors and all the Regiment commanders. Of note, both my Circle and the Zargarb Circle attended as well, I couldn't keep them away. I began our meeting, "We have alerted everyone that the ground war has commenced. The real question before us right now is what are we to do? Our charge is to provide necessary help where needed. Where is it going to be needed?"

Paul added, "We know the following. The Centurion army here is on the move to clash with the Crusaders, who are sticking to their original prepared position by the Cedar Forest. To date, we've detected no flanking action on their part, which makes keeping some of our regiments to far afield pointless."

To which Andre agreed, "Yes, there is no point in that, we should pull them in to us, but what about our archer regiments? They are still in Jerilum, which is a long way from here."

"But we don't know where they are going to be needed just yet," countered Lenkova.

"We should send out scouts to see just how many legions they've left guarding their base of operations, New Barq," suggested Paul. "It would seem that they have pulled most of their force out of the city, just inviting us to come and take it."

"It would be prudent to capture the enemy's base of supply," Andre pointed out.

"What commander in his right mind would leave his base of supply wide open to an attack?" I asked confused by this turn of events.

Lenkova, who still did not fully trust men, commented, "None would; it must be a trick. I say send out more scouts down into the Southlands. Perhaps there is another huge force there just waiting for us to make a false move." We continued discussing the overall situation. However, it became clear to me that we needed more information before we could act. Thus, I sent two Scout Squads out across the border into the Southlands and one squad headed for New Barq. Meanwhile, I issued the orders for all the regiments to pull in closer, leaving one regiment at the north-south roadway, one between there and our position, all the rest closing upon our location.

A day later, we received the news from those scouting out New Barq. Indeed, only two legions defended the city, relying upon their low adobe walls for defensive protection. It seemed like an open invitation for us to come down from the mesa and take their port city and their major overland line of supply.

At our next council, Paul exclaimed, "Let's do it! We ought to be able to capture their port and supply city. That will cripple their fighting capabilities."

"Men! You are so eager to start a fight," exclaimed Lenkova. "I smell a trap!"

Surprisingly, Lilly Ann pointed out, "Consider this: once you have eliminated the couple hundred soldiers guarding the city, what then do you do with the thousands of civilians? You would then need a garrison force, which we do not have. Besides, the Sisterhood fighters are primarily defensive, not offensive. Should we be taking casualties this soon?"

For an hour, we debated the issue. Luckily, just then a Communicator with one of the Scout Squads reported. I shared the news. "It seems this is a trap. Scout Squad #1 has discovered another twenty legions each with a war chariot on their way up the north-south road! Had we been hasty and charged in to New Barq, these new forces would have caused us severe problems, to say the least. Okay, so now that we know it is a trap, what do we do about it?"

"Well, we cannot let another twenty legions come at the Crusaders from their flank, that is for sure," Paul hastily commented. He loved getting in the first word, I discovered, though not always the optimum word. Yet, this time, we all agreed that we could not let these reinforcements go around and encircle the Crusader positions, nor could we afford to allow them to strengthen the current Centurion attackers.

Lenkova offered an idea, "Since we have to attack these newcomers, we ought to attack them while they are marching and not positioned on a battlefield. We can attack smaller numbers at one time this way. Somehow, we must keep them from forming up a battle line. We can't match their numbers on a normal battlefield. Archers are no match for these soldiers."

"But we do have mobility; all our forces have mobility," Andre broke in, "we should make use of our advantage. Here's an idea. Suppose that we bring in our archers and position them here." He began drawing out the situation map in the sand. "They dismount, hide the horses, and take up concealed positions as close to the paved road as possible, within shooting range. Next, we take the Santi Strike force, cross over the paved road, and take up a position there, also somewhat hidden, but strung out in a long line. Now when the Centurions come marching into the proper position here, the mounted attack force appears. Give them time to form up their battle lines, facing us. That is the key, facing us. Then, we charge toward them. However, at that instant, the archers let lose all the arrows they can until we get too close. These fighters have almost no armor in their rears, and their shields will be facing us. That should give the archers a good chance to wound a fair number before we actually close to attack."

Everyone liked the idea. He elaborated, "Further, it will be up the Guardians to eliminate the war chariots as a very first action, because they can cut our horses up pretty badly, which we cannot afford. The Strike Force ought to charge into them and through them, turn around and repeat, sweeping through what remains of their lines. Under no circumstances are we to dismount and form a parallel battle line." After additional discussion, we agreed upon the plan, and the Communicators contacted their counterparts in Jerilum, where the many regiments of archers were awaiting orders. Theirs would be a long hard ride, however, to get here in time.

Three days later in the early morning, the Santi Strike Force was in position across the road to the south, very close to New Barq, only five miles to our left. Hidden behind the hills of the Arad just north of the road lay all our archers, tired from having such a rushed journey, but itching for some action that mattered. Gleaming in the morning sunlight, the first of the twenty legions came marching up the road, intending upon entering New Barq within a few hours.

Strung out over nearly five miles, we waited until the maximum number of legions could come under our archery fire. On my signal, Paul pulled down a lightning bolt, which then thundered loudly. Although we need not have been so melodramatic, we did have Communicators, the signal also got the attention of the marching men. The Santi Strike Force suddenly appeared on their left side, along a five-mile line, all nine hundred of us. We began charging toward them.

As expected, these seasoned soldiers were not surprised for long. Quickly with well-practiced moves, each legion pivoted, formed up a battle line, shields raised to meet us. Their war chariots moved out in front of their line of foot soldiers, ready to charge into us. Just at that instant and with nearly triple our numbers, our archers began their deadly rain of arrows. Each volley contained nearly fifteen hundred arrows! In the little over a minute that it took us to close, some fifteen thousand arrows hit them, an incredible feat, devastating in its impact and effect upon the Centurions. Initially taken by surprise, but then wildly swinging their huge shields over their heads, over one third of their numbers were down, having taken one or more arrows each.

Worse still, walls of flaming fires descended upon each of the war chariots. The Guardians were quite effective; the men had no choice but to bail out of them and abandon their fighting machines. Most of our people had never seen a druwid wall of fire, and their excited comments were quite numerous indeed. Yes, they were impressed with this coordinated display of spell power. Now, into their confused ranks we galloped, chopping here, thrusting there, and trampling anything in our way. A split second later, we passed through the line and reined in, turning around for the next sweep.

Thank goodness for all the chain mail! It had deflected both spear thrusts and sword chops of the enemy effectively. Only a few of the Strike Force were wounded, more horses than people, actually. Three more times we hit them and then the bloody battle was over.

Perhaps as many as five hundred Centurions dropped their heavy shields and fled the battlefield, running off into the edge of the Red Desert to the southwest. We let them run; they were no longer any threat to us. Without food, water, or salt, in the desert, they were as good as dead.

Now, the archers swarmed in mass onto the battlefield. The standard

Sisterhood action was to guarantee each body was indeed dead. Methodically, these women proceeded down the line, stabbing each in the heart just to be certain. These women had learned the hard way never to trust men, especially fighters.

As the Strike Force regrouped, all our Healers and their assistants appeared from behind the cover of the hills. Quickly, we began assessing the damage inflicted upon people and horses. Squad leaders took count of their two dozen and reported it to their regimental commander, who then brought the tallies to me.

We lost outright five horses and ten people, six women and four men. Twenty-nine horses were badly hurt, and another hundred or so needed tending. Miraculously, we only had one hundred and six people who had wounds, only a few were life threatening. All the regimental leaders repeated Lenkova's enthusiastic report. "This chain mail armor is absolutely fantastic! We ought to have had six times the number of casualties that we actually took. All thanks to this fabulous armor! I know that each suit has cost a small fortune, at least three months wages or more, but it has saved many, many lives! Wow! We cannot thank you enough for insisting on armor for all."

With so many druwids here in the Santi to lend a hand with the healing, our official Healers were left with only the more serious cases. I busily patched up six, including three horses. Yet, it still took time, and we spent well over two hours fixing everyone up as best we could here in the field. Now I realized that we ought to have a field hospital, where the more seriously wounded could go to recover in relative safety and calm. We had none, except our supply wagons, which would arrive by nightfall. Most were coming down from Jerilum.

By suppertime, the battlefield had been cleaned up. The men dug massive pits for the dead, while the women stripped each person and piled them into the holes. In the end, we had this enormous pile of armor bits, spears, swords, helms, and a fair amount of gold and gems as well. The war chariots were pretty well burned, but the forty horses came in handy.

Interestingly enough, just as we were finishing the burial detail, along came the Centurion rear supply wagons! Our scouts reported that they were coming long before they actually appeared on the road, so we were not taken by surprise. However, the Centurions were. They had been riding along in the slow wagons all day long, probably bored to death. They were expecting a nice warm bath in New Barq, wine and ale, and hot food. Their surprise was complete when they appeared and saw their entire army obliterated and thousands of mounted cavalry on the scene.

They had no choice but to surrender, which the drivers did as soon as their minds registered the situation. We confiscated fifty wagons loaded with food, blankets, and tents, primarily. Each wagon had a driver and a cook, and now we had a new problem, we had to take one hundred prisoners of war. I had not thought about this aspect of fighting a war. What do we do with them? Worse, these men were terrified, near a panic. Twenty legions were gone utterly; only they remained; none could speak our language. Many kept waving a white handkerchief, long after we accepted their surrender. Only a few of us druwids could speak their language, and only I did fluently. So I became the universal translator.

Adrianna's suggestion we adopted. We gave them one chariot horse, some food and water, and sent them back the way that they had come. Problem solved.

Over dinner, we again held a war council to determine our next action. Although I was not for it, most wanted to finish off New Barq. Since we were already here, just five miles west of us, and since so few soldiers remained to guard it, the Protectors thought we ought to take advantage of this strategic blunder, cutting off the Centurion overland supply line from the Southlands.

"How could these ultimate fighters fail to send out scouts?" asked Lenkova. "I thought that these Centurions were hardened, seasoned fighters. Are their leaders soft in the head?"

Reflecting upon what I had seen today versus all the other times I had witnessed the Centurions in a fight, I ventured a reply, "You know, I have seen Centurions fighting now over a long time span of at least a half century. I swear that those that we fought today were about the poorest of any I've ever seen. Most were quite young, so perhaps these were newly formed units, reserves not yet fully trained. Either something like that or the overall quality of their soldiers has declined considerably."

"Well maybe it has," ventured Andre. "They nearly lost the entire army during the barbarian invasion a few years back. They probably had to rebuild the army from scratch."

"Then perhaps the Crusaders have a chance against them," I mused.

Next, we began planning how to take New Barq. The city of some forty thousand now held less than thirty thousand, with only some two legions to protect it. The residents were trade smiths, mostly. Armor makers, weapon smiths, blacksmiths, bow makers, plus a host of other trades. The consensus was that we ride up in mass to the walls and allow the defenders to surrender without a fight. Beyond that, no one could agree on how best to assault the city, should they decide to put up a fight.

I spent a restless night, trying to figure out how in the world we would be able to garrison such a large city as this! Our entire force might wind up just patrolling the streets. Heaven help us if they citizens decided upon subtle terrorism to strike back at the occupying force.

The next day, I issued the orders to assault New Barq, following the suggestions by the Protectors. After positioning the Strike Force before the main front gates with the thousands of archers lined up several ranks deep behind us, I rode alone toward the gates. The town had three gates in each of the three sides, none of course to the west where the Med Sea docks were located. I chose the middle gate. Why me? I spoke their language the best.

"I wish to speak to the commander in charge of the defense of the city," I called out sharply. While I awaited any reply, I kept a sharp eye out for trouble, such as someone shooting arrows at me. Paul was beside himself with anxiety — a Protector's job is to guard his Wid, me, his Circle members secondly. For a long time, no one replied. The backup plan was to let the Protectors combine their Push Spells to see if we could smash in the gates. The walls were only adobe bricks and not that high, about six feet. Probably there were two foot raised ledges running along the inner side, so that the defenders could get clear shots at their besiegers, us in this case. The Protectors' line of reasoning went: adobe is not a strong medium in which to secure a gate. A solid powerful push may just crumble the adobe, thereby forcing the gates open.

Just as I was about to return and let them try their spells, one man poked his head just over the wall. "What do you want?" he said. I detected the slight trace of fear in his voice; I knew I had him.

"The Santi Strike Force is going to take over control of New Barq. You have several choices. You can let us bust down the gates and try to defend against an army nearly four thousand strong." Okay, I exaggerated slightly, but I knew they couldn't count us that fast. "In case you didn't see yesterday, we wiped out the twenty legions coming up from Megalos. They should have entered New Bark yesterday afternoon. Or you can surrender, throw down your weapons and become our prisoners of war. Or you can simply walk out the southern gates into the Red Desert, and we will not hinder nor follow you. We are not bloodthirsty savages. It's your choice, what will it be?"

Silence greeted my words, only the chattering of distant chickens somewhere inside the city broke the stillness. At last, the man said, "We need a half hour to get food and water together or we'll die in the desert."

"Agreed. No need slowly to die of thirst. You have your half hour," I said commandingly and urged my horse to back up. Cleverly, I did not turn my horse around, but had him back up instead. I dare not take a chance of getting an arrow in my back. None came, however, much to Paul's great relief.

Since only a handful of our people understood what I said, I quickly related our brief conversation. Then, there was nothing to do but wait. I heard several men making wagers on whether or not they would actually leave; I simply smiled, I knew that they would. Sure enough as the time was nearly up, the southern gates opened and slowly the two legions rode out on horseback, heavily laden with water pouches tied to their saddles. I heard several "Rats, I thought they'd put up a fight!" These were the men who lost their bets; I hope they didn't wager any large sums.

Next, we all rode up toward the three eastern gates, which creaked open. Several townsfolk cautiously opened them for us. Now what? I thought to myself. I had never conquered a city of some thirty thousand before and had no idea of what we ought to do next. Rape and pillage was not in our game plan. Worse still, only ten of us spoke the Megalos language, most not fluently. Thank heavens for Lilly Ann and several other Judgers in the Santi! She quickly took charge.

"Okay, Ket, you are the main interpreter. We'll form up a party of us

Judgers, take along all the Protectors, and go into the city proper. First action, find the city leaders. Second action, talk to them. By the way, do we have any idea what we are to do with this city now that we have it? Other than denying the Centurions resupply from here?"

"Er, no ideas at all. Paulette, you and the other Communicators let John Henry and the others know what we have done. Have someone ask the High Council in Zargarb for advice, please," I asked. I think I sounded rather pitiful.

A few minutes later, thirty-six of us entered New Barq on horseback. The city was well laid out, designed with economy and work ability in mind. Unlike the curved streets of the Sea Princes, here, the streets were broad and straight. In fact, at every corner, street signs denoted the cross streets. All the houses and tradesmen quarters were nearly identical, constructed from adobe bricks. Unlike the usual thatched roofs so common throughout the Arad, here the roofs were grey slate, fireproof, and probably did not leak during heavy rains.

A few scattered people were about, but I spied many peeking out of their windows. For these city dwellers, becoming a conquered city was beyond their wildest imaginings. You could almost smell the fear in the air! These people expected the usual from barbarians, rape, pillaging, and stealing everything of value. Since we were not doing any of that now, finally one man was brave enough to say "Good morning," as he passed by us on the street.

"Excuse me, sir," I stopped my horse, and hence the others with me. "Does New Barq have a mayor, a leader, a governor, someone who is in charge when the army is not here?"

"Aye, that'd be Mayor Romulous Cox," he replied, more than a little curious at my accent and that I could speak his language. I asked for directions, and we headed off to find their mayor.

"If this is like the old days of the governors, look for the fanciest, most expensive mansion," I jested, remembering visits to the governors of the Sea Princes something like a half century ago when the Centurions controlled the sectors. Some things never change! We found the mayoral mansion, which occupied an entire city block with six buildings! An ornate iron fence surrounded the mansion, complete with hitching rail. We took the tip, dismounted, and tied our horses. Thirty-six of us would be a might overwhelming, so I took Paul, Andre, and another Protector along with Lilly Ann and Art Weatherby as the Judgers. Adrianna and Lenkova insisted upon coming as well. We walked up the brick path to what looked like the most promising building.

I spied a servant perhaps peeking out of a window as we approached. Being civilized and not barbarians, I knocked on the door and the door opened rather hastily. "Yes?" asked the middle aged man who had been peeking at our approach.

"We're here to see Mayor Romulous Cox," I replied as politely as I could muster, although seeing eight chain mail clad warriors wearing black tunics with red crosses probably seemed more than a little unnerving to the servant.

He beckoned us to enter and led us into the adjoining large meeting room. Mahogany tables, chairs, desk, and shelves caught our attention at once. I now knew that the wood for these probably came from the southwestern coast of the Southlands. A lush tapestry hung on one wall, depicting scenes from some long ago battle.

Shortly a very nervous mayor entered, dressed in fine silk clothing, sporting a well-tended moustache, and overly oiled hair. "I'm Mayor Cox," he said, voice trembling, his hands twisting within each other. "How may I help you?" he mechanically rattled off, as if we were just another citizen coming to ask for some assistance.

"As you know, New Barq has just been conquered by the Santi del Dio of the Sea Princes," I began.

"Oh just go ahead and steal everything in the house," he conceded, feeling his worst fears had just come true. "Only please do not harm myself or my servants, please. I'll show you where the money is kept," he blurted out rapid fire.

"I'm sorry, Mayor Cox. You must have us confused with the barbarians of the Northern Steppes. We have not come to rob, rape, pillage, and destroy. Rest assured that no one in the city will be robbed or harmed as long as they do not cause any trouble."

"But, but," he fumbled as he finally grasped the meaning and intent of my words. "I thought, we thought, well, you know how rumors go, that you were barbarians. Now, I can see that you are anything but ruffians. Please have a seat," he took the largest one immediately. "I see you have a number of the fairer sex with you." Again, his mechanical reactions were on automatic.

"I hate to disappoint you, but these women with me dispatched any number of your Centurion soldiers yesterday. However, let's talk occupation. New Barq is now belongs to the Sea Princes, Zargarb will be your closest tie. From now on, no one here will supply food, weapons, or anything else that is useful to the Centurion soldiers."

"Or anyone who will in turn give said items to the soldiers," put in Lilly Ann, amending my statement cleverly, she was way ahead of me.

"Anyone caught doing so will be severely punished," I did not elaborate on what that might be; I had no idea. Lilly Ann might, if it ever came to that. "I assume that you have a stockpile of armor and weapons and food here in New Barq?"

"Well, yes, we are the makers of some of the finest weapons on Tarra. Little armor though. We have several warehouses of supplies." He added.

"I'm afraid that we will need to confiscate those supplies, so that they do not accidentally fall into the wrong hands. Consider it the price of going to war. I'm sure that the Emperor will make it right with you."

"That is most acceptable, considering the circumstances," he replied quickly, trying to sound as amiable as possible. Then, he asked the key question, "I suppose that you will want our money?"

Smiling, how could I refuse? "Well, the High Councils have gone to great expense to counter your invasion of their land. It would be proper for the enemy to make some recompense, though the supplies will make a good start in that arena. I am not a barbarian; I don't want to take all the gold, jewelry, and gemstones in New Barq. That would cripple your economy, and we prefer to have your economy continue thriving, however, on our and your behalf, not the Emperor's."

Lilly Ann asked, "Does the city have funds of its own? We do not want to take from individuals by going house to house."

"Well, yes, we do. We could donate say ten thousand ducats to your High Council. That would still leave the city with enough funds to continue daily operations. Would that be acceptable?"

"Very well indeed. Thank you, Mayor Cox," I replied. "One more thing, the Santi will soon be constructing our own garrison towers here and a dock for our caravels. However, this should not be a major concern, as we will construct our new facilities outside your walls, perhaps in the old city ruins of Al Barq. Are there workers here in the city that we could hire to assist with the construction?"

The mayor's smile evaporated and then returned as he heard that our new fortress would be outside his city proper. "Actually, as a matter of fact, now that the Centurions had gone, unemployment has risen. Many could use the extra work. I presume that you will pay them fair wages for fair work?"

"Absolutely, a day's pay for a day's good work. I can see that this is becoming the start of a very nice relationship, Mayor Cox. I believe that you will find the Santi very amicable neighbors and overlords. Now, if you will be so good as to direct us to the warehouses and the supplies, we will be on our way. No need for us to send our thousands of troops galloping through your streets. However, some may want to make use of your public bathing facilities, if not pubs. You will find that we pay for the services that we receive." With that, our first meeting with the mayor ended. He hastily went with us to the Central Money Exchange building and withdrew the funds promised. Meanwhile, he sent word to the warehouses to expect us.

An hour later, we eight began walking through one of the three warehouses along the docks. Rows upon rows of swords were neatly stacked awaiting shipment to the next buyer. More importantly, cases of arrows would restock our supply. There was sufficient dried food to last us at least half a year. The remainder of the day was spent in hauling out the goods. The archer regiments loved the vast number of arrows we brought out. Anyone in need of a new sword or a better one or a spare received one or more. The remainder, which amounted to some two thousand swords, six thousand spears, and less than a hundred bows were hauled out into the desert and hidden away. While we could not use them, under no circumstances did we want them ever to get back into the hands of the Centurions. Later on, we could arrange transport back to the Sea Princes.

The money, we kept, intending to use it to help finance our new construction here in Al Barq, which lay about a half mile north of New Barq.

The next day, I put the Planners in charge of building us a strong Santi fortress here on the coast.

That night, we received numerous communications, some relayed via John Henry. First, the good news. The capturing of New Bark and the elimination of the re-enforcements was the highlight of the year at all the High Council meetings throughout the Sea Princes. He was asked to pass along their thanks and many kudos for a job very well done. I passed the sentiments along to the other commanders and it eventually got down to each member of our party. He thought that having a fortress for the Santi this far down south was a fabulous idea and to use all the funds we'd just acquired to get it built as soon as possible. For the time being, we would have to be the garrison force in New Barq, until a proper force could be found, made ready, and sent. He was not optimistic on said time line, however.

The not so good news was that the Crusaders were actually holding the line, hanging on despite heavy losses. Evidently the clash had turned into a massive slaughter for both sides, thousands were dead already, with the wounded barely getting any care at all. All of us were glad that we had missed this conflict; the horrors would have been too gross to confront for many of us. Still, the Crusaders held on, refusing to give ground. Now that the Centurions would not be receiving more supplies or re-enforcements, the outcome of the battle may well rest with our Crusaders!

The bad news was particularly bad. The Centurions had thus far launched two sea borne invasions, one around Zargarb and the other around Solamina. Thousands of Centurions had come ashore unmolested and unconfronted. Their tactics had now become obvious. This was their main thrust; the overland attack from New Barq was designed to do just what it had, pull all available forces completely out of the way, giving the Centurions an easy assault. Once ashore, they fanned out and took control over all the outer towns and villages. Footnote, North Point had been abandoned; the Sisterhood headed overland, on their way to Velona, along with the vast majority of the remaining Sisters in those two sectors. However, those on the High Councils and a few others were taking refuge with the Santi.

At least the beginnings of the outer barrier walls around the two Santi fortresses had been completed in time. There the remaining Sisters would make their last stand, along with the Santi guarding the two fortresses. The invaders surrounded both cities now. All port activities at the two cities had ended; numerous triremes guaranteed that no ship could go into or out of the two port cities.

On the slightly positive side, both cities still had several thousand garrison troops to help defend the walls. With every available person lending a hand, everyone hoped that the cities could hold out indefinitely, until help arrived. No one could define what that help might be, however. Grim news indeed. I offered to bring our forces back into Zargarb to try to dislodge the Centurions, but the consensus was for us to stay put for the time being. Everything depended upon how the battle with the Crusaders turned out.

Thus, we encamped on the outskirts of New Barq. Many of the Sisters took the opportunity to go "shopping" in the large city, while others took their turns in the public bathhouses. The Planners put most of the men to work on the beginning construction of the Santi fortress. Once the ideal site was located, good ground and a good docking area that could be sealed off with chains similar to Velona, most of the men were put to work on salvaging useful construction materials left in the rubble of the old city of Al Barq.

For our fortifications, plans called for enclosing ten square city blocks adjoining the docks. Interestingly enough, the maze of sewers underneath the old city remained. Allan decided to incorporate them into our design both as a sewer and as secret escape tunnels. As I wandered around the city, I discovered that there were quite a large number of skilled stonemasons who had been put to work on adobe constructions and the like. When I offered them a chance for some real stonework for a fair pay, dozens jumped at the opportunity. They told me of an abandoned stone quarry that lay some twenty miles southeast of New Barq. The quarry had been the source of the paving stones used to build the paved roadways over fifty years ago. We put the quarry was back in operation; Allan's plan called for a rather large amount of heavy stone blocks.

A few days later, I took half of the strike force and rode north to try to find some vantage point to observe how the main battle with the Crusaders was going. The objective was to find some high ground where we could use the Far Seeing Eye to find out for ourselves how the battle fared. Pity that we were unable to have one of our own people in there to report to us telepathically.

As usual, I had several Scouting Squads out ahead of our main body. Their task was twofold, to let us know about trouble ahead and to find some suitable observation post. About twenty miles north of New Barq, we came upon the rear lines of the Centurions, guard posts really. Sitting atop a tall hill some ten miles southeast of the Cedar Forest and the seacoast, we found our ideal location. From here, we had a clear line of sight to the battlefield, at least the part that was not within the forest, and we were sufficiently distant so as not to pose a threat to the Centurions, which might force them to come and attack us.

The fierce fighting had stopped, by mutual action; there had been just too many casualties on both sides. As we watched with our device, we saw men carrying some wounded on board three ships that lay at anchor just off shore. The wounded were placed into smaller boats and rowed out to the large sailing vessels. Return trips brought food and water barrels back to the soldiers. The Centurion camp of pup tents sprawled across five miles from the coast inland.

Thus, I concluded that in all likelihood the Emperor never did count upon evacuation and supply from New Barq. He was taking them elsewhere to some place that was totally secure. However, there seemed to be far fewer men in the camp. Supposedly, the enemy began with some five thousand soldiers, yet the camp below seemed very deserted. I did not know at the time, but their actual numbers were now just over a thousand fit soldiers.

Moving our eye further north, we could barely make out the camp of the Crusaders, with their gaudy, many-colored tents waving in the breeze coming in from the sea. Then, we spied the carrion birds! Both sides had laid their dead comrades in long rows off to one side of the camp, awaiting burials, which had not yet occurred. Actually, the bodies on both sides were mounded in giant stacks, we estimated nearly five feet tall, like kindling wood in the winter! The butchery had been savage. I thank the stars that we were not involved in that foot soldier confrontation.

A troubled, subdued Paul commented, "Ket, what are we to do now? Should we offer healing? Tis probably more than we could handle, though."

"Paul, I just don't know. I hate war, but war has come upon us, and it's a bloody hellhole. I guess we just wait here, keep an eye on things, and wait for orders."

While we were watching the awful scene from this high vantage point, one of the Communicators from Scout Squad One reported a warning to me. *Ket, a vast number of cavalry are coming your way, about a day from you, we estimate. Several thousand, more or less. Plus, there is a party of twenty riders that will be coming your way in a few hours. Our best guess is these are the Arad Raiders that we've heard about — can't tell for sure. We are keeping out of sight.*

After relaying the news, I held a quick war council. With half of the Strike Force still back in New Barq, along with all the Mounted Archer Regiments, we dare not confront this new threat head on. Consensus agreed with my thought, if threatened, retreat back to New Barq. Hastily, we broke camp and prepared for a quick retreat, should that be necessary. However, I continued to ponder the significance of the lead party of twenty riders. Certainly, they were not a scouting party. Why then were they so far, nearly a day, out on front of the main force? Could they desire a parley with someone? That would make sense, but with whom? I had a hunch it was us.

We waited for several hours until our scouts reported they were coming up the back valley to our right. One carried a white flag. Now I was convinced. "Paul, ready a white flag on a pole. Okay, mount up everyone." We formed a double line of riders, two hundred riders side by side. I took the pole from Paul, who very begrudgingly gave it up.

Soon, the unknown riders appeared riding up the flank of the hill, a line of eighteen, with two riders slightly out in front of the line. As soon as they saw our ranks, one raised his hand and the entire force halted. Slowly the pair, one holding the flag, walked their horses on towards us. "They've got two, so looks like you get to go, Paul. Come on," I smiled, knowing that Paul was now very satisfied, the Protector could do his job.

Slowly we rode down to meet the two coming up. As we halted before them, I could see that one was a woman. Interesting, I thought. It reminded me of the fighting messiah bands I knew last lifetime. Speaking in an ancient dialect of Juda Arad, the man spoke first, "I am Jaifur Qa Jahdi, my right arm and wife, Zeta."

Although I had not spoken this dialect for a very long time, I still understood it and hoped my accent would not be too awful. "I am Ket Bethany, leader of the Santi del Dio and its Strike Force. This is my assistant, Paul Wilkins. Please, Jaifur — I am not familiar with that word. What does it mean?"

Both smiled, and he replied, "Your accent is truly horrible, but we understand. I didn't really expect that you would be able to speak with us. I admit I am surprised, though Zeta is not. She predicted that you would. Jaifur is an ancient word meaning Supreme Ruler. I wish to personally thank you for removing the Infidels from New Bark. My scouts reported that your forces eliminated two thousand of them and drove them out of New Barq. Is this true?"

"Yes, New Barq is now in our control. No Centurions are there, only the local inhabitants," I replied. *What scouts? We didn't have any reports of seeing their scouts from our scouts,* I sent to Paulette, who relayed it to the other Communicators of the Scout Squads.

"You and I are not so much unalike, Ket Bethany. Only our armies have many women fighters. Again, I thank you for helping rid the Arad of the Infidels. In return, I grant the Santi the freedom to travel throughout the Arad. My people will not interfere with your passages as long as you stay to the main tracks."

"Thank you. We shall. I presume that you wish us to stay particularly out of the mesa land of the southwest, for that's the only place where your new towns could be located," I replied.

A surprised look on Qa's face greeted my observation, Zeta, however, only smiled, more confident than ever that she had judged me properly. She replied, not him, "You indeed know well the Arad, as if you too were a messiah. Yes, stay out of the southwestern quadrant, please." She was very close to the mark in her observation, but I kept a stone face.

Qa recovered his surprise and said, "We've come to warn you to leave this area. Our army is quickly approaching; our business is with the Infidels, not the Crusaders, unless they choose to fight us. Our scouts have told me of their deadly struggle and their losses, attempting to keep the Infidels from pushing north into Zargarb. Tomorrow, the Arad fighters will finish what they have begun. We shall wipe the last remaining Infidel from our lands. For nearly a century, we have attempted to drive the Infidels from our land, something for which even the Great Messiah failed. Tomorrow, Jaifur Qa Jahdi will finally succeed; all praise to the all-powerful Jehosa."

"Yes, we already know that you have about two thousand cavalry about a half day's ride from here. We've been scouting the Infidels for the last few days. Their numbers are vastly reduced from their initial strength. My guess is that you will outnumber them two to one. Their wounded are being evacuated by sea, but to where, we do not know."

Once again, Qa seemed taken aback by just how much of his movements I already knew. True, his scouts had been observing our scouts for days now. "How is this possible? My men have kept your scouts under observation since they left New Barq a week ago. None have returned, so how can you know this from them?"

I didn't trust Qa sufficiently to tell him the truth, telepathy; neither did I wish to lie outright for that matter. "We are the Santi del Dio," I said, emphasizing the word Dio, while making a smiling grin.

"Ah, Dio, yes, Jehosa works in many ways. Are you not then a messiah among your people?"

"Yes, that might be a good way to state it," I agreed with him. Just then Paulette butted in, *Ket, Lilly Ann says to offer him our Healer services after the battle. An alliance with the Arad Raiders would be in the best interests of the Santi.* I forgot that I had not broken the telepathic link with her and she had been relaying our conversation with the other members of my Circle and Andre's too.

"Jaifur Jahdi, the Santi has the best Healers on Tarra. To bind our alliance with you, I would like to offer our healing services to your wounded after the battle is done. This way, we may learn to trust each other much better." Darn, I am just not a good Judger! Lilly Ann could have done a super job of relaying this; I was just a bit embarrassed about how crude my offer sounded. She would probably be laughing at my incompetence in such matters.

"We would be in your debt," Qa replied, sincerely, though not quite knowing what it meant.

Zeta animatedly added, "It has been told to us that Bethany Amir, the wife of the Great Messiah, was one of such Healers. Ali, now ninety, still tells the children stories of how Bethany Amir healed his wounds after one battle. Also, our scouts reported that in your recent great battle with the Infidels their chariots of war all burst into flames, as if the Fiery Hand of Jehosa touch them. Truly you are 'del Dio!'"

Fascinating how you cannot escape what you do in one lifetime. Here in my next one, I still found echos of what I had done during my life with Jes. Although now, I did not recognize the name Ali, I knew that I had sewn up many physical wounds during those years when Jes and I traveled the length and breadth of the Arad, preaching to all who would listen. I wondered if Jes knew what had happened since then, that most all his people fled the land. Only these few handfuls remained, living their lives in secrecy from the outside world. No, even taking a new physical body does not relieve one from their past acts, good or bad. Ah, but they could pretend to forget all about their previous life!

Strange how flashes of deep insight occur at the most inopportune times. When a person's body dies, they lose all the physical objects they had. After all, we are immortal beings, not made of matter. How easy it is thus to forget the past, when you no longer have it at hand and have a new present to live. In this instant, I knew I had the key to life, but no time to explore it, being in the middle of negotiations. I realized that I had faded from their conversations and made an effort to rejoin it.

Jahdi was mid-sentence, "dawn tomorrow, we will strike. If you wish to aid, be here on this hill by noon. Again, we thank you." He bowed to me, and they turned, mounted their horses, and rode back the way that they had come.

"Tomorrow noon, then," I called after them. Zeta waved and smiled, and then they cantered on down the backside of the hill.

"Let's go inform everyone," Paul commented, and we rejoined the others. I called all the leaders and commanders together and told them of our discussion with Jaifur Qa Jahdi.

"How fortuitous," Lenkova commented, "they will take their revenge on the Centurions, which is exactly what we need about now. Do you suppose that we should help with the combat?"

"I think that this is their fight," Andre explained to his wife, "it is something that they will take immense pride in accomplishing. However, it wouldn't hurt at least to be able to provide some backup in case the enemy is stronger than we think. What say you, Ket?"

"I suppose not. Paulette, send word of all this to the others. Have all the Guardians and Healing Squads report here by noon tomorrow. On second thought, have all that can be spared come, including the archery regiments. I think that all the Santi ought to witness this event. For perhaps a brief time in history, the Arad may be completely free of Centurions, something these people have fought for nearly a century to achieve." A part of me from last lifetime knew the monumental importance this singular event would have upon the Arad people. If only for history's sake, their crowning achievement ought to have witnesses, even though it would be for a bloody slaughter of men.

Later that night in our tent, Lilly Ann prodded me, "Ket, what's going on? You are so moody, so melancholic. Is something wrong, my love? I sense something is, you know. Woman's intuition and all that."

"I know now why I can never use lightning to strike down another. I've figured it out, Lilly Ann," I glumly replied.

"Not that again. I thought that you'd eventually forget about it and be okay. You have seemed to be doing far better these last many months," she replied, putting her arm around me.

"That's the key, forgetting. We are spiritual beings. When we do something in a lifetime, whether for good or ill, it is done. Even in the next lifetime, in our next, new physical body, what we've done follows us. We *know* what we've done."

"It was all that talk of Zeta's, reminding you of Bethany Amir, right? That's what set you off?" she inquired, thinking it was Zeta's doing.

"In a way, yes." I could see I had to attempt to let her see what I had realized. "What happens when your body dies?"

"Well, I hope that doesn't happen for a very long time," she replied, slightly haughtily, refusing to become as morbid as I sounded.

"Think about it for a moment. You lose everything you had: your home, your family, your children, your horse, your money, your clothing, absolutely everything."

"Of course. Your body is dead and gone, no life in it. Never seen a dead man rise up, saddle his horse, and go for a ride, have we?" she replied, not grasping at all where I was headed.

"Precisely, Lilly Ann. It is all gone, all the physical universe stuff we had is gone, lost to us. Now we move into and take over a new baby body to begin life anew, new parents, new home, and a new life."

"I see what you mean, we get a new chance in life, only Paul and Paulette rather messed up, you know, becoming brother and sister instead of husband and wife," she answered.

"So what has your attention in the present? All this new stuff, not what you have lost, follow me? Hence, a person tends to forget that which is not present any longer."

"Yes, but where does this all go?" she asked, more than a bit baffled.

"Forget is the operative word here. We forget, at least the header's do so. We Guardians often recall much of our previous life, don't we? But we are not stuck in our body's head either; we do not think of ourselves as being a body as the headers do. That's the difference between say Lenkova and you, Lilly Ann. She remembers only this life, with a tiny glimpse of the Galt barbarian she used to be before this body. Yet you remember much of what you were and did in your last lifetime."

"Yes, that is all true, but where does this get us?" she asked, still not grasping the monumental significance of this.

"We, all of us, are immortal beings. We cannot really forget where we have been and what we have done. Suppose that one has done something really awful in one lifetime, I don't know, say you were unfaithful to your wife. In the next lifetime that you have, your marital treason is still with you. It follows you forever. While you might attempt to 'forget all about it,' you still know that you were at one time unfaithful to your wife."

"So in the new life, you might feel uneasy around your new wife, maybe not even trust yourself," she added, beginning to see the impact. "Ket, there *must* be some way to undo it, to make recompense, there just has to be. Otherwise, we are all doomed utterly! It's a dwindling spiral effect, you know, as the artists are so fond of drawing. We start out powerful beings, commit some actions we ought not have, lose a bit of our power because we must withhold using it so as not to harm yet again, and down we go until we are all eventually headers, convinced we are just a fleshly body. God, Ket, there has to be a way out of this trap!"

I yawned heavily. That dark grey mass that obstructed all my lives before arriving in Uru here on Tarra some hundred years ago began to lighten slightly. The more I yawned, the lighter it became until it was only a light grey curtain covering my past. I said, "The first requisite must be to realize that one is in a trap. Before you can figure out how to get out of one, you have to know that you are in one. We've now figured out the basic trap that seems to be binding us all here on Tarra. We've taken the first step. That black mass that has always obscured my past has lightened considerably; we must be on the right path now. I don't have the rest of the answers, but we've started. I wish I could talk to Jes Amir about this right now or maybe Alabaster."

"We're in the middle of a dumb war, sorry," she replied. "When the war is finally done, I'd like to help, if I can, Ket."

Grinning, I kissed her and whispered, "You already have, my dear. You already have. I was able to get one other person to see what I discovered today, you. That is a start, but I agree, we must find a way to undo actions or, as you said, we are all doomed for all eternity!"

Dawn came startling us all. Wild, nearly insane sounding yelling pierced the dim light along with the thunderous pounding of thousands of horses galloping at top speed down the valley that separated us from the Centurion camp miles below us. Two thousand Arad Raiders descended upon the unsuspecting Centurions like a plague of wasps, only their stings were most deadly. For a time, we could not see anything further, the dust cloud from their passing rose, blanketing the valley below in a red as pale as the rising sun. All the Santi rushed out of their tents to watch, although we could not see, we could hear. The screaming of the Arads was indeed just a bit scary, even though we were not their targets.

Clank of steel upon steel and wood echoed across the valley, as wave after wave of the Arad cavalry charged through the camp, battling anything that moved. Around nine, the rest of the Santi arrived from the south. They had ridden most of the night to get here early enough. Uniformly everyone dismounted or got out of the wagons to watch, but said little, exchanging only whispered words. The wild, insane yelling continued unabated along with the sounds of the distant battle. While the original dust cloud had long settled, a new one covered the actual field of battle, although we occasionally glimpsed some of the actual fighting.

Around ten, the battlefield became deadly quiet, slowly the dust settled. We could see at last the result of this attack. The Arad Raiders had won, though I never did doubt that they would not succeed. They had dismounted and were tending to after-battle details. "Okay, all healers, with me. Let's ride down there and do our best," I called out. Our five Healing Squads with their wagons, along with some hundred of us mounted Guardians, moved slowly down the hill toward the battlefield.

Less than an hour later, we reached the edge of the combat zone and found many wounded men. Without a word and with usual Guardian precision, we set to work. At first, most of us joined the unwounded Arad men and women who were going from downed wounded to wounded, determining their status: either alive or dead. If alive, we carried them to the wagons if they could not walk or help them there if they could. Although wounded in his arm, Jaifur Jahdi continued to walk among the field, giving his orders. I met him and said, "We came down from the hill a bit earlier than planned. Let's have a look at your arm."

"It can wait. There are some far more injured than I am. I cannot find Zeta. If you want to help me, find her," he replied, though in a good deal of pain. He and I continued looking for his wife. Finally, one of his men called out, "Qa, over here. She's still breathing." Stepping over dead bodies, we came as fast as we could.

Zeta had taken a Centurion spear to her chest, blood oozed from her lips, she was unconscious, but with labored breathing. "Over here, Paul, bring a stretcher fast. Top priority, critical case!" I called out. Immediately he and two others came over, "Spear puncture, probably blood in her right lung," I diagnosed, "critical case, immediate attention."

"Aye, sir," Paul replied and the three carried her off rapidly to a Healer waiting at a wagon for the next critical case.

"Now will you please let us tend to your wound?" I asked Jahdi. Relieved that Zeta was not yet dead, he agreed and I walked him over to the less critical section, where he was quickly examined and treated. Meanwhile, I went back to the search for the living recovery process, made even more difficult by the many horses, which were also wounded. An hour later, we had all the living recovered. The Arad Raiders had taken well over two hundred causalities, but only forty-five dead. Close to a thousand Centurions were most definitely dead. I could not help but see that these raiders had been most thorough, leaving nothing to chance. Each dead Centurion had already had his head chopped off!

While the wounded were lined up being treated, those that were not rounded up the horses, which had fared worse than their riders had. Sixty had been slain, either during the combat or because the raiders felt their wounds were too life threatening. I explained to Qa that we would do what we could for the horses after we had all his personnel patched up. Hence, his men then made a lineup of horses that needed attention, and well over two hundred of them did.

Shortly after noon, the lightest casualties had been patched up and order restored. Jaifur Jahdi then called his men together, leading them in a prayer service. It ended with his pronouncement, "Now it is time. Cast all heads into the Med Sea, followed by the headless bodies. As it was in Al Barq, so it shall be once again. The sea will flow red with the blood of the Infidels, as they did with the babies of Al Barq. Thus, it has come full-circle. Amen." Hundreds of voices echoed his "Amen." With a relish and gusto seldom seen, his men and women began hurling the Centurion remains into the Med Sea.

Me, I just had memories of Al Barq and the night when the Centurions went house-to-house killing all recently born children, thinking one of them was the long expected Great Messiah. Although it has now been over fifty years ago when my Lightning Circle helped rescue hundreds of Arad women with their newborn babies escape through the sewer system of Al Barq, the memory was still vivid in my mind. I noticed that the others in my Circle also were remembering their part in saving several hundred lives during that night of murder. Although none of us said a word, we glanced at each other, and that glance told the entire story. Quietly, I said to Jaifur Jahdi, "That night of infamy has now been redeemed. Six of us here fully understand the full meaning."

He gave me the strangest of looks. "You know of the Night of the Baby Murders? The night of the birth of the Great Messiah?"

"Do you know of the rescue of some three hundred women and their children that night, via the sewer systems?" I asked softly.

"Aye, we teach that to all our children; lessons of how Jehosa works miracles in his own way," Jahdi replied.

I simply said, "Six of us were there, helping out as best we could. You know then of whom I speak."

"But you are barely a man? How can this be?" he replied instinctively, the reaction I hoped he would not have. Then, he realized something and added, "Jehosa works in ways we cannot understand. Our prophets speak of the strangers from the north that came to aid of our people back then. It seems the same strangers from the north have come unto us yet again. May Jehosa always be with you!" And he bowed low to me and then to those of my Circle, who smiled back. Most were still tending the wounded.

"Come, let us see how Zeta fares," I deftly changed the subject. Together, we walked over to the wagon where Beth Ann was feverishly working on Zeta.

"Don't you dare die on me, Zeta!" Beth Ann angrily yelled at the nearly lifeless Zeta. Seeing us arrive, she called out, "Ket, help, fast. Her lung has collapsed; see how her side looks so shallow. She just stopped breathing. Blow in her mouth hard while I hold her nose. We have to get enough back pressure to re-inflate that lung! Breathe, damn it, woman, breathe!" she yelled.

Quickly, I did as she asked, blowing as hard as I could into her lungs via her bloody mouth, while Beth Ann pinched her nose as hard as she could. In and out came the air I blew into her. Repeatedly I blew. Suddenly, Zeta coughed and began to breathe on her own once more. "Great Zeta, keep it up," called out Beth Ann. She did not see Qa's tears flowing down his face; she was oblivious to everything except her patient. "Look, see how her side looks like the other side. I think that's done it, Ket. Now to clean out the wound better." I got up and let her work, within a couple minutes she was sewing up the hole in her chest and applying a healing salve. Finally, she looked up at us. We both were covered in blood, but she smiled, "I think the worst is over now. She needs complete rest for several days, until the internal bleeding stops. Carry her gently over to the critical ward we've setup over there," she pointed to a small cluster of cedar trees. Strong hands did as she asked. Just as soon as Zeta was moved, she called out, "Next critical case."

Someone answered her, "That is the last one. Time to check on the critical ones' recovery process."

"See you guys," Beth Ann commented to us, "gotta go check on our handiwork." She headed over to the cedar trees, along with the other Healers, all whom were covered with their patients' blood. I found a washbasin and cleaned myself up.

By now, Qa had recovered, "Bless you, Ket Bethany, bless you! I thought I had lost Zeta. Through you and your people, Jehosa has worked many more miracles today. Your aid will be taught to all our children throughout all eternity." It was the greatest thanks that he could think of, under the circumstances. I knew what he meant, however.

Just then, our attention was called to the far end of the battlefield closest to the Crusader army. A general commotion complete with a waving white flag caught our attention. Men were yelling for Qa, and we both came running to see what was happening. As we drew near, I saw none other than General Antonio Prada accompanied by two soldiers, one of whom continuously waved the white flag. Men on both sides were talking loudly, but none understood the other's language. Enter me, the universal translator, well, I felt like it this day anyway.

As soon as Prada caught sight of me, he yelled out, "Ket, Ket Bethany. Santi leader. We thought it was you folks." I waved and told Qa who this man was. Qa, in turn smiled and waved his uninjured arm, all which seemed to calm everyone down.

"I'll translate for you," I said in the general direction of both leaders. "We offered our healing skills to the Arad Raiders, General Prada. Looks like the war here is over. The Santi hold New Barq, and now there is not a single Centurion anywhere in Juda Arad." I also translated what I said to Qa, who nodded his agreement.

"Magnificent! Splendid job, Jaifur Jahdi, well done indeed. We have eliminated well over two thirds of their forces before today," Prada explained, greatly desiring the huge contribution of the Crusaders not to go unnoticed.

After translating, Qa replied, "Yes, we have been watching your great battle since it began. Only when you reduced their numbers this far could we dare mount our attack. We are few, compared to the huge army you fielded." By mutual agreement, the two men shook hands, sealing their understanding of the historic battle.

"Ket, I hate to ask this of you, but when you have finished bandaging their wounded, would you please lend our overworked physicians a hand? We've suffered grievous losses in the month long battle." I figured that the situation must be quite desperate for the overly proud General Prada actually to ask for our assistance. I quickly agreed, telling him we would all be along shortly with our wagons. He thanked me and returned to order some barricades across the valley to be removed so that we could pass through their main front lines.

As soon as we got behind the defensive wall of jacks, the stench of rotting, decaying flesh hit our olfactory senses like a hammer! Rows upon rows of tents filled with the wounded were almost more than we could confront. The numbers were staggering. All told, the Crusaders had numbered around ten thousand, though more continued to trickle in even after the battle had begun.

Most were young men and some women, seeking glory or following the convictions of their beliefs or perhaps after the money. Now, some four thousand five hundred, give or take, counts had become totally confused by this time, were actually dead. Corpses were stacked up on the opposite side of the huge encampment; too few remained healthy enough to deal with such a massive burial.

Because of the lack of physicians and medical staff who actually knew anything proper about healing, more were dying from their injuries daily. An epidemic, one young woman called it, as she tried to tend to the suffering within the tents. As we took a brief tour of the first of the huge number of tents, the physician's treatments were simple. Sear the wound with a hot iron and pray. If that was not possible, cut the appendage off and sear that, then pray. Gangrene had set in on the vast majority of these victims; the stench was hideous and nauseating. After looking in on the sixth tent, I left hastily and vomited; it was more than I could bear. Surprisingly, our Healers took it all in stride; how Beth Ann could deal with this I did not know. Yet she and the other Healers did so and well.

"Okay, then, we have a lot of work to do here," Beth Ann spoke on my behalf to the others. "First, get every available pot on fires; we need all the boiling water we can possibly obtain. Second, take all available non-healing staff and get those rotting corpses buried at once. Otherwise, we all will be dead from disease in a few days. I suggest a massive grave, it doesn't have to be deep, just enough to cover them. Prada, your physicians are complete idiots; put them on grave digging detail; it suits them better! All Healers to me, you other Guardians are going to be our support staff, this job exceeds any of your healing training. Get the Archer Regiments to help with the burial task and then set them all to fixing up hot soup by the gallons. Those with weak stomachs, tend the fires, the boiling water, and the soup fixings. Now everyone, get moving!" she barked her commands with such intention that everyone immediately followed her orders without even looking at my messy face for confirmation, thankfully.

Among our entire force, we had thirty-two Healers, including Beth Ann. Those with the most experience, she assigned to the most critical cases. When they had assembled in front of her, she explained, "Okay ladies and gentlemen, we have one fine mess to deal with here. So first, we are going to go from tent to tent and examine all them. Have one of our assistants keep a tally. Sort them into three categories: too far gone to save, critical needing immediate attention before they are too far gone to save, and those who can wait a while before medical attention. We will move those we can do nothing for out of the tent they are in and put them in a special location where others can at least make their last moments as comfortable as possible. Understood?" All agreed and they began their first round, going tent by tent.

Five more died while they were sorting out the injured. Over five hundred men and a few women were moved out into the open and made as comfortable as possible, though many were already comatose. Over eight hundred were in the critical needing immediate attention category, a truly overwhelming number. Close to another twelve hundred would need attention when the others had received theirs. Beth Ann commented when they finished their survey over two hours later, "Well, we are going to lose many before we can even get to them. Let's see if the other Guardians can handle the less serious cases." We agreed; that we could confront and handle, though barely.

Another eight hundred had taken ill from the disease, and these could be easily treated. Only about a thousand men and a few women, most all from the cavalry regiments, were still able bodies. Eagerly they lend their backs to the many Sisters who were digging the graves, fetching firewood, boiling water, and preparing food. I watched these Crusaders go from the depths of apathy up to some enthusiasm, for help had arrived, from their viewpoint.

Thus, the next hour was spent grouping the wounded into three areas. Once that had been accomplished, the Healers began their work, usually two worked on each patient to save time and share expertise and suggestions. The remainder of we Guardians dove into the ill and lighter wounded bunch, again, following Beth Ann's orders of two to a patient. Lilly Ann and I worked together as a team, which made this awful mess more readily confrontable and doable. Far into the night we worked, until we all dropped from exhaustion. I remember loving hands carrying me to the washing station, washing me off, stuffing food into my mouth, and then laying me down on a bedroll beside Lilly Ann. I think it was Lenkova.

For an entire week, we worked what miracles we could. Our basic supplies ran out rapidly, and the Loremasters were sent on an herbal finding mission, accompanied by all the Scout Squads. Short on bandages, we took the deceased's clothing, tore them into strips, boiled them, dried them, and used them as makeshift bandages. By the end of the week, the first round of healing was completely finished, although we lost many more along the way, and they were now being promptly buried.

During that week, I saw little of General Prada, who thought it best to remain in the background, helping where he could, primarily directing the grave digging and firewood searches. Finally, we took a much needed break. Beth Ann ordered all of us to take the entire afternoon off, go for a swim in the Med, sleep, whatever. Lilly Ann and I took a survey stroll around the huge encampment, noticing all the changes. Gone was that horrid stench, replaced by a bustling, energetic group of people, going about their assigned tasks. Order had returned; the Sisters had seen to that detail.

Beth Ann had not forgotten our patients back in the Arad camp. Earlier she sent two Healers to check up on all the patients there. Some forty could not be moved for at least two weeks. Hence, the main force left to return to their towns, leaving a small garrison force behind to look after their injured. Ultimately, they would return with more food for their wounded. Naturally, Qa remained behind with his wife, who I learned was recovering and able to speak now.

General Prada found us on our walk. "I cannot thank you and the rest of the Santi for what you have done here. On behalf of all Crusaders, please accept my eternal thanks."

"I only wish you had contacted us sooner. We could have saved so many lives and limbs. Ah well, hindsight. I stink so bad that I had better do as Beth Ann says, take a swim." He chuckled. I did indeed stink badly. We kept well away from the location where all the Centurion bodies had been dumped, however.

Refreshed and clean, I decided to send much of our force back to New Barq. There was little else for them to do here. Beth Ann observed that we would have to stay here tending the injured for at least the next entire month. Besides, at the moment with the Centurions occupying the Zargarb and Solamina sectors, except for the walled cities, there was nowhere for the Crusaders to go had they been able to move out, or us, for that matter. It promised to be a long month, however.

Finally, when Beth Ann determined that it was finally safe to move the injured, our forces, and those of the Crusaders traveled the short distance into New Barq. There, the Crusaders and our regiments took over the abandoned Centurion garrison quarters. For the first time in nearly a year, the Crusaders had excellent living conditions. They had earned it with their blood. With food and supplies now plentiful, they began to recover quickly. None asked what their next assignment would be.

Chapter 32 Desert Beings

Messiah Ali Martek, conducting the usual dusk prayer service for his tribe out in the Anuir, their name for the Red Desert, was just finishing up with, "We follow your Holy Decalogue as given unto us by your Prophet Helas Amin. Everyone, join me in our holy prayer." Some two hundred voices chanted the Decalogue. However, the sound of a horse arriving at top speed momentarily broke their rhythm as one by one each looked to see who was coming.

Karmanski Zolgoti, their Galt scout, had returned from the east. "Forgive me for interrupting, but I bring most horrible news. The Infidels are back. They are riding into the Anuir even as we speak, up from New Barq is my guess, several hundred of them." Hushed intakes of breath, muffled fearful screams, and moans of disgust marked the reaction of the tribe members. They had fled the Arad to this uninhabited desert land to rid themselves of the Infidels. Now once more the Infidels had come.

One man cried out, "Can we never be free from the Infidels? They follow us like dogs into the desert!" He began wailing and moaning about the hopelessness of life.

"Let us pray once more for Devine Deliverance," Ali quickly called out, attempting to quell the surge of despair running rampant throughout his flock. For a time it did calm them. When he sent them to their huts to sleep, he took Karmanski aside, though his wife, Juli, clung to him, unwilling to be separated from her husband. She had not seen him for several days while he had been out scouting away to the east. She knew a battle was eminent and Karmanski was sure to lead the fight.

Ali had no intention of separating their Chosen One, Prophet Juli Aldari-Zolgoti. No indeed. For months now, Juli was in daily commune with the Guardian of Anuir, a spiritual being of and from Jehosa himself. Often when she would return from her perch upon a dune, she would share great words of wisdom with her people. Further, through Juli was the only way he knew to get a message to the Guardian, which was what he desperately needed to do right now. "Tell me the details, Karmanski," he said in a low, but worried, voice.

"Messiah Ali, Prophet Juli, three days ago, I came near to the borders with the Arad and the Southlands. To my horror, I saw the Infidels coming on foot, sometimes marching, sometimes running, across the sands. Too many to count, several hundred at least. I did note that they are not too well armed. As I remember, they usually carry their huge shields, a spear, and sword. I saw no shields and few spears, but I don't know what to make of this. Undoubtedly, there will be more Infidels coming; certainly some would come on horseback. I chose to make all haste to return with the news, however. We probably have at least three days to prepare for their arrival, though their numbers greatly out do ours." To Karmanski, this was akin to a pronouncement of doom for the whole tribe. How could a hundred stand up to several hundred of the Infidel fighters? He knew they stood no chance of defending this oasis in the desert. Juli and the children were at great risk.

Ali thought for a moment, he hated to make the tribe up and move from this oasis, which they now called home. "Juli, can you pray to our Guardian? Let him know our plight. Ask Jehosa's Guardian if we should flee or stay? For once, Juli, I really do need some guidance."

"I, I will do as you ask, Messiah Ali. Tonight," she said confidently, though she was not sure how to contact the Guardian. He had always contacted her. However, since the Guardian worked with her nearly every day, she figured there would be time enough for contact to be made. With that, they too entered their respective huts for the night.

The next morning after the breakfast dishes were cleaned and the children, done with their chores, were sent playing, Juli walked up to the top of the tall sand dune just south of the oasis. She did this every morning, sitting on the warm sands waiting for the Guardian to come to her. Some days, he did not come, and she would walk back down and carry on her chores. Other days, the Guardian would spend long hours working with her. Today as she sat there pondering the awful situation that was upon them, she felt the warm touch of the Guardian upon her.

Something troubles you, Juli. You are nearly back inside your head once more, the Guardian spoke to her. Quickly, Juli explained their plight. The Infidels had come after them out here in the deserted desert.

I have been aware of them since they first set foot in the Anuir, the desert. They are men of war and cannot be allowed to journey through this land. Come with me, Juli, we shall prepare a feast for the hyenas and beetles of the desert. They too are hungry.

But how can I, she started to say.

Just be five feet above your body. Yes, very good, Juli. Now let's be a hundred feet up. Excellent. Now let's be a mile east of the oasis. Good. Let's be near the Infidels. Thank you, Juli. You are doing very well indeed. She found herself looking down from about a thousand feet above the desert floor below. Swarms of tiny men were slugging their way through the deep sands.

I do see the Infidels, she replied.

All right. Now I want you to make a little puff of air blow one grain of sand around down there. Yes, that's it. Make it move. Good. A particle of sand moved and hopped about on the desert floor, unnoticed by all except a beetle who was nearby.

Now make a bigger puff and blow several around. Very good. Now let's make a big wind blow many grains about. Terrific. Now let's have the wind go around in tight, little circles. Yes, like that. Now let's make it bigger. Much bigger. Yes, even bigger. I'm lending you a hand. A small cyclone appeared near the bedraggled Centurions, who were dying of thirst as well as lost. They had been arguing about which direction to walk when the swirling funnel appeared.

Their cries of dismay turned into fear and then into terror as the cyclone grew to enormous proportions. Blinding dust flew everywhere, abrading their exposed skin. At first, it was more of a stinging sensation. Soon it became painful, but they had nothing with which to protect their bodies from the sudden sand storm. One by one, they laid down in the sand, digging themselves into the soft, slippery grains, if only to find relief from the pain of the windblown sand. Their skin ached from the pain, though relief they found, buried under the sands. However, a breathing problem quickly overshadowed all else. Gasping, their mouths inhaled nothing but sand and more sand. At last, they just let go and knew no more suffering. An hour later, though they could not see it, the sands had shifted. A new large sand dune now rose over where their bodies now lay, both dead and buried, except for the hungry beetles, which had found them at last.

We can stop now, Juli. See the Infidels are gone. We have done it, protected the Anuir once more. Thank you for helping me. Now be just behind your body's head. Yes. I believe that we have had enough lessons for today. You may tell Ali that we have taken care of the Infidel problem and that there is nothing for him to worry about.

Thank you, Guardian, Juli finally managed to find her voice. It had taken her what seemed to be an enormous effort to move just a couple grains of sand. Yet, she had experienced the power of the Guardian's assist with the winds, and she had found that nearly unbelievable; yet she had both experienced it and seen it. She walked down from the dune into the oasis to find Ali and Karmanski.

Chapter 33   The Decisions of Emperor Justinian

From the deck of his royal yacht, Justinian observed the ill-fated attempt by his numerous triremes to attack this lone caravel. True, they had managed to sink the slow, heavily laden Sea Prince ship, but attacking the caravel had been a total calamity. As much as he desired to capture one of these new, super-fast ships, he finally realized that to do so would cost him dearly, a price he could not afford to pay, just yet. Time enough for that later on. During the course of the next few days as he sailed closer to Zargarb, he ordered five more ships sunk. After the initial fiasco with the caravel, he began to pay closer attention to the flags flown by the ships.

Each Sea Prince sector's ships flew a distinctive flag, identifying the sector from which it came or was based. A pair of yellow stars and crescent moon upon a blue background indicated the ship hailed from Zargarb. Solamina flags had one large white star on the blue background. Those of Pieta had red and blue alternating horizontal bands, while Bonilla's flags had a large orange circle centered in the blue flag. Vito flags consisted of alternating orange and blue vertical stripes and the flags of Barcella were sky blue with a large yellow moon in its center. Velona's flags were green with a field of yellow stars, while those from Fortress d'Grange were black with white stars. The caravels of the Santi were black with a large red cross.

Justinian's scribe kept an accurate record of sunken ships. Today the tally was up to five from Zargarb, three from Solamina, and one each from Pieta and Bonilla. As they drew closer to the Zargarb sector, the amount of shipping decreased rapidly. Word of the sinking of the ships was spreading even faster than Justinian had calculated. Although he had no idea why this was so, it served his overall plans admirably. Still an awful lot of Velona caravels were still sailing the Med Sea with near immunity. He had issued stern orders for the triremes to avoid attacking any of the new caravels, and after the calamity, the captains respectfully obeyed that order to the letter!

Finally, his ship was in position, just a few miles off shore from Zargarb. The day of his Operation Invasion was at hand. He watched supremely confident from the quarterdeck as his small, but stout ships carried both men and horses to their assigned landing beaches, far from the actual walled city. Simultaneously, another fleet of merchant ships was doing the same thing this side of Solamina. His plans called for invading both sectors at the same time, cutting off both sectors, giving the Crusader army no more supplies and nowhere to retreat. He smiled as he watched the small forms land and take the beachhead unopposed. "This is going to be easier than I even imagined," he said to his aides, who agreed with their Emperor.

The next day with the beachheads secured, Emperor Justinian was rowed to land, where he proudly set foot on the soil of Zargarb. He was the first Emperor of Megalos ever to have set foot in barbarian lands, as he referred to these uncivilized Sea Prince sectors. On shore, after a formal ceremony denoting the occasion, he climbed onto his waiting war chariot, which he personally drove. Alongside, trotted two of his Royal Guard Legions, some two hundred strong, whose purpose was to protect their supreme leader at all times.

Justinian's first established base camp was in the olive garden of Antonio Muffio, who had no choice but to let the invaders trample his prized garden. Here, the Emperor waited in near boredom, while the remainder of his invasion force was ferried from the northern shores of the Red Desert over to the mainland of the Sea Princes. Meanwhile, once his cavalry were fully assembled along with their supply wagons, he gave them to go ahead to commence operations. The cavalry legions stormed up and down the roads of the sectors, attacking anything that offered even token resistance. As each town fell to the invaders, that is, as the cavalry entered each town, several were stationed there to garrison it until the foot soldiers arrived several weeks later. In less than a month after the initial invasion, Justinian stood on the last hill overlooking the walled city of Zargarb. His foot soldiers controlled every outlying town and village in both of the two sectors. His cavalry was divided, half standing before each of the two namesake city walls.

With his forces fully in charge of all territory except the two walled cities, the Holy Paladins were at last ferried across. To these men of the Pope's fell the task of garrisoning each town and village, thus slowly freeing up the legions of foot soldiers, who a month later finally joined the cavalry surrounding the two cities. Justinian was proud of his grand plan, which was working flawlessly thus far. With the Emperor nearby, this invasion had little looting, pillaging, and raping. In fact, not a single soldier had thus far been injured. The assault was too boring for words.

What the Emperor did not know was that the Holy Paladins also brought with them a large number of handpicked missionaries, whose task was to establish official churches within every conquered sector. Because Justinian left the task of enforcing the laws to the Holy Paladins, these men, under orders from the pope, made sure that every person in the town went to church to hear the holy words of the ministers. Those that did not, were simply executed on the spot. Seldom did these Holy Paladins need to terminate more than one person per town or village to get complete compliance with their law.

Now news of the battle with the Crusaders began reaching Justinian and it was not the news he had hoped to be hearing. Because of the alarmingly large number of casualties, Justinian ordered his ships to begin evacuating the wounded back to one of the depots on the northern shores of the Red Desert, where they could recover in safety and with abundant supplies. As the weekly numbers continued to escalate beyond comprehension, so grew his temper, until at last Emperor Justinian finally realized that even if his legions eventually defeated the Crusaders, they would no longer be a reasonable strike force. Thus, he began to have uninjured legions evacuated and brought here to Zargarb in secret. For each wounded man evacuated, a healthy man came along with him. However, Justinian had not issued this order in time to get them all out. Ten legions remained the morning when the Arad Raiders descended upon the faked camp, stabbing dummies made up to look like soldiers.

When his supply ships returned empty along with the grisly tale of seeing thousands of heads and headless bodies floating where the ships normally were anchored, Justinian became completely enraged. Although he knew that the Santi had eliminated the twenty legions marching on foot up from Megalos and had taken over New Barq, he was convinced that the Crusaders had done this horrendous deed. By all reports, the Santi still were in New Barq.

Blood vessels bulging in his neck, Justinian screamed his new orders. "Barbarians! Sink every one of the Zargarb and Solamina ships. Ram them while they are in their own docks! We'll teach them a lesson they won't ever forget! I'll throw the heads of all the Noble Houses into the sea! I'll have them boiled in oil." He finally calmed down. He dashed off new orders to his trireme captains. Two days later, he watched as twelve triremes turned into the large harbor in Zargarb. From his hilltop vantage point, he could see the tops of nearly twenty ships tied up at the docks. As he watched, he saw the results of the resounding, full speed impacts with the crushing bows of his ships. Tall masts twisted and rolled in different directions and then slowly descended out of view, as the ships with their hulls crushed sank beside the docks. Belatedly a hail of arrows flew out at the triremes as they back oared. The wily captains were prepared for this; each rower raised a shield overhead, preventing heavy casualties. While some men were injured, the hail of death had little overall retaliatory impact. Nineteen ships in Solamina were likewise destroyed this same day.

Justinian calmed down as he watched the destruction of an entire fleet of ships. While this was only a portion of the total number of Zargarb ships, he had sent a very clear message to the High Council of the city.

Justinian had no intentions of bombarding the walls, smashing the gates, or otherwise sieging the city. That would be too slow and costly in lives. No, his was a far better plan: get them to surrender unilaterally. Thus, following his own council and plan, he gave the High Council of Zargarb a few days to digest this new turn of events.

Within the city, the High Council held an emergency meeting just after their entire fleet of docked ships had been destroyed. "Well, Sister Alicia, your advice was indeed more sound than we gave you credit for. At least two thirds of our fleet is still safe in the harbors of Calgary and around West Reach. It will cost us a fortune to rebuild those ships, though we should use the new caravel design instead of our usual one. One ship can cost us upwards of five hundred to a thousand gold coins. That's a twenty thousand loss we just suffered. It will take years to recover from this disaster."

Alicia smiled; she had months ago convinced these men to send at least two thirds of their ships away to the north and west, utilizing every available location around West Reach and the Greenway to dock the ships temporarily. Many of the other sectors had done likewise, placing the ships for now just out of the reach of the Centurions. Up north, the bays would be iced up by now; no ship could go in or out until the spring thaw. Interestingly enough, many of those ship's cargo bays contained boxes of gold and gemstones. The nobles took advantage of the situation to attempt to protect their wealth. It was a gamble that the cargo would not be stolen, but leaving it here was far worse.

"The question now becomes what do we do and how do we respond?" she attempted to get the meeting back on track.

"What is the latest news from the Crusaders? Any help from them in the near future?" asked one nobleman.

"Latest Santi report is that the remnants of the Crusaders have been taken down into New Barq and are being housed in the barracks there. They have one thousand forty-three able fighters, with five hundred supporting cooks and supply masters. Another thousand or so are on the mend, perhaps by spring they will be ready to resume the fight, though I'm told that many of those wounded have lost one or more limbs. Our best guess is that by spring the Crusaders will be ready to field around twelve hundred fighters, certainly no more than that. With the Santi Strike Force also in New Barq, they are guaranteeing that the Centurions cannot use that port nor can they bring up any re-enforcements from the Southlands overland. That is at least a small victory on our side."

Another reported, "We now have almost three thousand garrisoning the walls with plenty of arrows to go around. Fire brigades total another thousand. I think we can withstand a lengthy siege. We've certainly got sufficient food." Thus, the consensus was to continue to hold out until the enemy despaired and left.

Two days later, a strange event occurred. The defenders along the walls reported that a small group of Centurions was approaching the main northern gates bearing a white flag. Hastily, the High Council members were summoned. Alicia, who was staying at the Santi walled compound just east and south of the city, was the last to arrive. It took nearly five minutes to undo all the buttressing of the gate so that it could be opened for the parley. The thirteen High Council members stepped just outside the gates, while hundreds of archers stood at the ready along the adjoining walls.

Facing them was Emperor Justinian, two aides, and ten of his top soldiers. "I am your Emperor, Justinian of Megalos. I have come to dictate the terms of your surrender. Unlike the slaughter with the Crusaders, perhaps you have noted that thus far, we have not taken a single casualty nor have you within the city. I have purposely refrained from bombarding your city into rubble. After all what good is a ruined city to anyone?" He was making a good attempt at being civil to these barbarians. "I must apologize for the destruction of your fleet, at least that portion which was docked here, but I needed to send you the message that I mean business. If you do not accept the terms that I will dictate here, then let me assure you that I will spare no means to totally destroy the entire city, including every last inhabitant, man, woman and child. I will spare your dogs, however, since I am partial to them."

"Now my terms are simple. You surrender, open the gates, and we enter and take over. No one will be harmed unless they attempt to offer resistance. We are not interested in raping your women, pillaging, and stealing everything in sight. We are not the barbarians. See, I said it was simple. However, if you do not accept my terms, then you will feel my wrath. I have no desire to see everyone in the city dead, but if I have to storm the walls to take the city, you have my word that none will be spared. I will give you two days to think it over and open your gates. After that, then you may tell everyone in the city that their lives have been forfeited. In fact, I may just stay here all winter and summer and watch them all starve to death before my Centurions even attempt to enter the city. I like that even better, why should my men be hurt? Anyway, I give you two days to decide. That is all." He turned and left, though his men formed a human shield behind him so that archers could not shoot him in the back. The council members walked solemnly back within the walls, the gates were once more shut and barred.

Alicia knew at once that the High Council had a major problem. Hundreds of guards had overheard the Emperor's ultimatum. By nightfall, everyone in the city would know all about the proposed surrender deal. While she might conclude this was merely a bluff on Justinian's part, she suspected that the nearly hundred thousand folks in the city might think differently. After relaying a message to the Santi, she followed the others to the Sisterhood inn, where the High Council intended to meet. For the first time in her political career, Alicia desperately needed some advice from the Santi.

She sat quietly during the brief meeting, while the men belittled the Emperor, made light of his threats, and generally disbelieved he would go to such an extreme. No invader had yet been on a genocide trip. Convinced that they did not see the real danger, she finally spoke up, "Gentlemen, you are forgetting one major detail." Instantly the table talk ceased; these men respected her opinions, though not necessarily always following them.

"The proposal was overhead by nearly all the guards on the wall," she said quietly.

"So?" was the general instant response, except for the eldest of the council members. He spat and cursed; everyone turned to see why he was reacting thusly, as they didn't see any harm in the guards having heard the absurd proposal.

"She has a very important point. The ultimatum was overheard. By suppertime, everyone in the city will know about it. While we do not consider his threat seriously, I am sure that there will be large numbers of our ill-informed brethren who will believe that if we do not surrender, they will be killed. And that, my fellow members, bodes ill for us." Alicia sighed; at least one council member recognized the inherent danger in the situation. Perhaps this was precisely what the Emperor had in mind when he presented the ultimatum so close to the walls!

Alicia added, "We could have a rebellion on our hands by morning or worse still, a group of men could open the gates without our permission, allowing the Centurions into the city. Either way, we have a very serious problem on our hands." Although grumbling about it, the council agreed with her and discussed what to do about it. In the end, they merely doubled the guards on the gates. Alicia felt sure this was not the proper handling and spent the evening at the inn discussing the matter with her Communicator, Sally Whiteheath.

Bronze skinned, Spike slurped down another ale at the Dock Worker's Inn, the local tavern closest to the docks. Catering to the laborers who handled the heavy cargo of the ships, this inn was a rough and tumble one. Soot from the infrequently cleaned lanterns covered the ceiling as well as the glass globes; the lighting was dim. On normal nights before the siege, dockhands would stop in after work for some conversation and ale. This was their inn, as these opinionated men often declared. Outsiders not welcome here was the inn's motto. Of late, however, there was no work for the dockhands, only boring guard duty. Still, the men came, only now they came earlier and stayed far longer. Thus, business was good, at least until the stockpiles of ale ran out, but the innkeeper refused to think about that aspect of the siege.

Spike had been a dockhand for several years. Although his skin tone suggested that his ancestry was that of the Centurions, he acted as if he were born and raised here in Zargarb. Certainly, he had no telltale accent. Burly and unkempt, similar to all the dockhands, Spike had risen to foreman of his crew of ten. Along with that came a bit more respect from his peers. Most respected him because of his immense strength; few challengers to arm wrestling could beat him.

Tonight, however, Spike had a different agenda on his mind. Orders had come. The Dock Worker's Inn was crowded, every seat taken, standing room only and not much of that. Everyone was discussing the ultimatum that the Emperor had delivered this morning. Spike spoke up, "You know the Council is going to ignore it and not surrender the city. They don't give a rat's turd for the likes o'us! We're going to take the fall, not them. They've got all the money. I'm sure when the time comes, they will wave a bag o'gold before the Centurions and escape with their hides. But what about us? Eh? We ain't got no money to speak of, not since the dock shut down. Ain't going to have no money for a long time, I says."

He slurped some ale and continued, "Look at all them ships sunk beside the docks. Why it'll take months to clear them away. And what then? Whose ships are going to come here?" Spike had raised the ante on the conversation. He listened while others took up these same arguments, adding their own two-copper's worth to the mix.

Gradually, tempers rose; more and more men began condemning the High Council. When the mood was right, Spike threw more into the mix, "I wonder if we shouldn't just open the damn gates ourselves; let them in and put an end to this mess we are in. Leastwise, we won't all be killed." Folks took up the call and the general yelling increased. Only a very few voices attempted to say that would be treason. No one considered what life under the Centurion rule might entail, what hardships and sufferings might come of it. "What about your wives and kids? You all want them killed too?" He yelled out, spitting out ale in all directions; Spike was now rather drunk.

The consensus was that it would take more than the men here in the inn to subdue all the guards. Spike, intoxicated as he was, yelled out a suggestion, "Go get all the other dockhands. We're stronger than the measly guards!" Men staggered and swayed their way out of the inn to do just that.

Around midnight, over a hundred, half-drunk dockhands assembled outside of the inn. Most carried their city issued swords. At the suggestion of Spike, everyone carried a couple bottles of ale with them as well. His idea obviously was to offer the guards a break. If nothing else, suspicions would not be raised.

Although the hour was exceedingly late, Alicia was still up, chatting with Sally and several other Sisters. Her aides had all retired for the night, along with the approximately three hundred Sisters who still remained here within the walled city. "I'm sure glad that we were able to abandon North Point in time. Having this almost instantaneous communication skill sure has saved us."

"I know, we were able to mobilize the remaining fighters and get them, along with the other Sisters who were in the outlying towns safely to North Point. Going north onto the Paese di Dio was a brilliant idea of Ket's. Up there in God's Country, they travel with complete safety," Sally replied, sipping her fourth cup of tea.

"The Solamina Sisters joined them, I heard. I wonder where they are all now? Must have been hard on Rosalita to have to abandon the home she has kept at North Point for nearly a half century," Sister Angelica added.

"And on Antonio too, I'll wager," Alicia added. "But then this whole thing has been hard on all of us. I sure wish it were over. I'm confident that we've enough stored food to last us at least another six months. Perhaps by then, either they will give up their siege or help will come."

"You don't think they will at last begin assaulting the walls?" asked Angelica, who was the seamstress for the inn. She did all the fabulous embroidery on the towels and bedding. She knew little of warfare and always was keen to hear Alicia discuss matters of state. However, she was even more impressed with Sally, a real Guardian right here in the inn. Whenever Sally was about, Sister Angelica was nearby, listening.

"I just don't think that there are enough of them to make an attempt. So many will be killed or wounded when they close the distance. We've got thousands of archers, you know," Alicia replied. "No, what bothers me is the

High Council did not act this afternoon. Well, not effectively. Doubling the guards is like advertising that you expect trouble from inside the city, if you ask me. I think that they should have gone about letting the people in the city know the true situation."

Sally observed, "Well, that is what comes from having a group acting as the leader instead of a single person. Groups may be good for helping come up with ideas you might not have thought of on your own, but ultimately, one person has to be in charge. Have you ever noticed just what a group agrees upon? Well, I have; it is usually the dumbest things, just like today's double the guards. Of course, one should strengthen the guards, but you are entirely correct, in my opinion, Alicia, the people should have been informed. Perhaps tomorrow, you can do just that by informing the tradesmen and let them spread the word?"

"I believe I will," Alicia said, running her hands through her hair. "The council did not specifically say that we could not talk to our people about the ultimatum. The more that know the true situation, the better."

Just then, Sally became very uneasy. Sensitive to the minds of others, perhaps more so than many other Communicators, only at night could she let her guard down and relax. Of course, when doing so, she expanded and sensed a larger space than she normally did. Now, however, she began picking up violent emotions. "Something is very wrong somewhere!" she blurted out.

Startled, the other two women became silent, listening for the sounds of a fight or such outside the inn. The Sisterhood Inn complex was in the western side near the wall and close to the western gates. It was also just beyond the docks and warehouse district. The women could hear nothing, though, just crickets.

"I'm going to alert the Santi anyway," Sally declared. She was under orders to report to the Santi Communicator in the budding fortress just a mile east of the outer Zargarb wall. True, just now the fortress consisted only of a wall of stone barely four feet tall, but it clearly demarked the Santi grounds. Inside the perimeter were three hastily built, temporary housing units and one stable. When the stone buildings and towers were built, these would be removed. About three hundred Sisters who were now part of the Santi garrisoned it, along with ten Guardians. The tiny dock could only hold a single caravel at a time. The garrison force always flew the Santi flag, day and night, a red cross upon a black background. Thus far, the Centurions had given this crude fortress a wide berth; none had come within bow shot range of the low walls.

A minute later, she replied, "I contacted Tom. He's got the whole garrison awakened now and on high alert. He'll keep us posted if they see anything from their location," Sally relayed.

"What's it like? I mean this talent you have for reading minds?" asked Angelica, ever curious about a telepath. She had never heard of one before Sally came and was more than a little interested in just what it was all about.

Sally had often been asked similar questions. It was common nature for others to ask about a skill they did not have. "How do you know that I am sitting here?"

"I can see you," she replied, completely taken aback by the unexpected question.

"More like you can perceive me by using your sense of sight," Sally said a bit didactically. "I can sense the presence of other minds, just like you can sense my presence with your sense of sight. Oh heck, it is said that the object is worth a pile of words, so I'll just show you. I can tie your mind into my mind; we call it a Mind Link. Then, you will be sensing what I am sensing, and you can see or rather feel it for yourself."

"Me too," gushed Alicia, who had already had some experiences with other Communicator's Mind Links. "Angelica, this is so neat!"

Sally rapidly contacted both women's minds and made the link. "Oh!" exclaimed Angelica, completely startled by the strangeness of the sensations pouring through her mind. "This is so intimate!"

Sally laughed, "That's what everyone says."

"It's like rubbing a bit of silk from the Southlands across your face, the slightest of touches," Angelica continued to try to find words for this new, unparalleled experience.

"Okay, now I am going to relax my guard and let my awareness expand outward. Then you will be able to feel the uneasiness that I contacted a bit ago." Sally expanded her awareness outward as she had done a few minutes before. Only now, the emotions were far stronger, violent emotions.

"It feels kind of like some men are fighting, doesn't it?" Angelica attempted to put what she was feeling into tangible words.

"Yes, to be this strong, it must be a lot of men. Heaven help me if I ever get around two armies fighting each other! I'd probably go insane from all that uncontrolled violent emotion," Sally commented.

Sally, Tom here. There is action in the Centurion camp opposite the North Gates. The Santi Communicator relayed his message into Sally's mind, not knowing that she was also Mind Linked to her two friends. They, too, received his message, startling them enormously. Alicia jumped up from her chair, while Angelica dropped her teacup, which shattered on the floor.

Thanks Tom. I'm linked with a couple Sisters right now. What are the Centurions up to? Can you tell from where you are?

Pretty sexy, eh ladies? Tom sent. *They seem to be mustering, forming up ranks. I'll keep an eye on them. Have fun ladies.*

"Men often call this sexy. I call it intimate," Sally smiled.

"His voice appeared right in the middle of my head!" exclaimed Angelica.

"It is like he is right here talking with us," Sally explained.

"I have a very bad feeling about this," Alicia said, as fear slowly outlined her face. "Why would they muster in the dead of night? They are not going to attack what they cannot see."

"At least those violent emotions have gone away," Sally noted.

"Yes, but I am getting more and more concerned. Why would they muster at this time of night? Only if they had a great urgency to get to some place. You don't suppose that someone has actually opened the gates do you?" Alicia voiced her deepest fear, bordering on terror.

Legions are heading toward the North Gates. Sally, I think that the gates have been opened! Damn! Sally, alert all the Sisters. Get out of there now! That is an order. Plan A, execute it immediately! Tom's sense of urgency startled all three women. Sally dropped the Mind Link and her teacup, which joined Angelica's on the floor.

"Quick, rouse all the Sisters, but do not awaken the others staying here. Grab all that you want to take with you. We must all disappear before it is too late," ordered Sally.

"But I still have my position to handle," protested Alicia. "I'll help rouse the others, but I mean to stay as long as I can still do something to help." She determinedly bit her lip. The three women got up and raced out of the huge dining hall, into the lobby, and down the halls. All the Sisters were housed here on the first floor. All the other floors now held families from outlying towns who came to Zargarb seeking the protection of its walls.

Women opened their doors, sleep in their eyes, dressed only in their nightgowns. "Plan A. Now. Immediately. Gate's breached," was the message they delivered, short and to the point. Soon, other women, now partially dressed, joined them waking more Sisters, who then joined in sounding the alarm. In five minutes, all the Sisters had been awakened. Each went back into their rooms to finish dressing and gather up what they wanted to take with them.

By this time, they could hear the distant sounds of fighting, swords against shield and sword, along with some yelling. Hastily, the women headed down into the cavernous basement, which was their giant storage room, filled with food, linens, and bedding supplies. In the far western side of the last basement room was a huge tapestry. Behind it was a nearly invisible lever, now pulled down. A dark secret chamber lay before them. Into the tunnel chamber several fighters went, lighting the lanterns affixed to the side walls as they went, which revealed a long tunnel.

Alicia, on the other hand, had stepped outside into the street to see if she could see anything. All was confusion, men running in all directions, as though ants dislodged from their hole. One man ran up to her; she recognized Alberto, the handsome tinsmith that she had once been fond of, before she discovered that he had a drinking problem. Alberto called out, "Alicia, the north gates are opened; Centurions are flooding in. They are beheading all the noblemen. Five High Councilmen are already dead. Get inside and hide. Save yourself, for Jehosa's sake, save yourself. I still love you." With that, he ran off down the street heading for the mayor's house. Alicia, now terrified, did as he asked. She ran inside and down to the basement as fast as she could go. She was the last person to enter the now very crowed tunnel. A fighter lowered the tapestry and closed the secret door behind her. In a minute or two, all shaking of the tapestry would cease, giving no one a clue where the women had gone. Only the Sisterhood know of this secret exit.

The tunnel first led to a large, twenty-foot square weapons and valuables storeroom. For months now, most of the weapons had been handed out to the fighters. The twenty fighters grabbed the remaining few weapons. However, there also was a large crate of gold coins, a box of jewelry, and numerous sacks of gemstones. Additionally, bags of dried food had been stored here for just such an emergency, along with a number of water skins. Quickly, all the items were handed out to the women to carry, along with their sacks of personal possessions they planned to take with them.

Sister Lena was the fighter in charge. This had now become her responsibility. She barked out her first orders, "Okay everyone ready?" Many nods agreed. "Dose the tunnel lanterns please. Follow me. Fredrica, you bring up the rear and turn out the lights as you pass them. Quietly, ladies, follow me." Carrying a lantern, she descended the western tunnel that led from the room. This was their secret exit — a mile long tunnel that went under the western wall of the city, ending about a mile from the city, behind a hill. Its entrance out there was well concealed, again known only to the Sisterhood. However, now the Centurion army was encamped all around the city. There could even be an entire legion camped at the location where their exit was located.

Partway down the tunnel, an elderly cook began crying, "Who will make the morning tea and biscuits for all the inn guests?"

Another by her said, "Shh. They can make it themselves, if any of them want it. Besides, the place might be swarming with Centurions by morning anyway. Now hush."

A short while later, Lena reached the exit concealed door. Quickly, she insisted on complete quiet, opened the peephole a tiny crack, and peered outside. Her intake of breath told all. Indeed, a large group of Centurions had made their camp near their entrance, where they were safe from arrows from those manning the walls. They were trapped; they could not go back, nor could they leave the tunnel. Somewhere in the back of the long line, a woman whispered, "I got to go." Another replied, "Well do it right here then, but be quiet about it."

After a few minutes, Lena whispered, "Centurions outside, must wait," on down the line of women, who began sitting down on the stone floor. Sally decided to move on up to the front and see what she could do to help Lena. When Sally drew close, Lena whispered to her, "Centurions. Perhaps a whole legion, can't tell. Too many for us to fight."

"We need secrecy not a fight," cautioned Sally. "Let me see if the Santi can help us out a bit." She expanded her awareness to east of the city and immediately found Tom. *Bit of a mess here. Got three hundred or so women in the escape tunnel at the exit, but there seem to be a large number of Centurions camped near the concealed exit door. Ideas? Wait it out?*

Art is ready with some illusions to hide your passage this side of the city walls, but you are west of the city. Give us a couple minutes to figure something out, Tom sent back.

A long hour passed before Tom contacted her. *Art has snuck over to your side of the walls, but hang tight a little longer. Someone has opened the west gate and the legions are mobilizing. With luck, those around you are going to be marching to the gates shortly.* Sally relayed this bit of good news; Lena peeked to verify it. Indeed, the camp was now crawling with action.

"I hope they all go," Lena whispered to Sally. Ten minutes later, Lena gave the all clear signal. Stealthily, she opened the concealed door, her sword at the ready. Sally had her spells ready as well, just in case, but really a Judger's illusions would be far better in this situation, which called for invisibility. "Kill all lights. Grab hold of the person in front of you. Here we go. Remember, absolute quiet. We must not be discovered." Lena began moving out of the tunnel into the cold, clear nighttime.

Not too far away, the camp's bonfire still burned, casting flickering red illumination on the sprawling encampment. Lena glanced all around to make sure that there were not any guards present. Seeing none, she led the short way on down to the seacoast. Here, the land was lower than the hills, giving them some protective cover. Unless someone came to the edge of the bluff, the line of walking women on the shore would not be seen. The sound of waves breaking on the sandy shore seemed loud, but the noise of confusion within the city was clearly visible.

Single file, Lena moved the women slowly along the beach heading toward the wall. She found Art and several Sisterhood fighters already at the wall where it met the sea. Here, the women would have to step out into the water to get around the wall and thus be inside Zargarb. At this location lay the public beach, completely deserted in the middle of the night. Children flocked to the beach during the daytime, but not now, it was wintertime. While they could be seen by anyone looking out of the nearby windows, they carried no lights and rightly assumed that most people would be looking elsewhere just now. The long line of women snaked along the beach and then went under the docks. Here, Art held up a pale blue light, for it was pitch-black under the wharves. Several Sisters held special lanterns that emitted only a tiny ray of light.

Worse still, this place reeked of dead, decaying fish. The fishermen used under the docks as their garbage pit. Mountains of fish heads and other bits lay decomposing on the ground. No one ever walked around here under the docks. Pinching their noses from the stench, the women continued to move along, following Lena, who was following the lead of the Santi fighters.

By three in the morning, Lena had finally arrived at the eastern wall of the city. Once more, she had to wade out into the Med Sea to get around the edge of the wall. Here, Art had them walk along the seacoast the last mile to the Santi fortress.

At four in the morning, Lena, tired, exhausted, and stinking badly, finally entered the walls of the Santi fortress, where hundreds of others awaited them. Baths had been prepared as well as hot drinks. The routine was simple and efficient, into the bath where several other women helped her bathe quickly, then out and dry off, then into clean clothes, provided by the Santi residents. After eating quickly, she was ushered into a tent and to bed. As Lena lay there finally relaxing, the tent rapidly filled up. Space was at a premium at this point, but with so many in one tent, each helped the others stay warm. It was crude by Sisterhood inn standards, but more importantly, it was safe. Lena drifted off into a worried, fitful sleep. She kept having recurring dreams of Centurion fighters smashing down her bedroom door.

On December 1, 624, the walled city of Zargarb fell to the invading Centurions for the second time in a hundred years. One third of her fleet of ships was destroyed, most sunk in her own harbor. In spite of his promise, Justinian beheaded all the High Council members that could be found. No one knew what had happened to Alicia or the remaining Sisters; they had simply disappeared without a trace.

We learned later that Justinian asked the remaining members of the noble houses to pay him a steep ransom to keep their heads. Naturally, the wealthy quickly gave away their fortunes. However, without these funds, rebuilding the fleet of ships would be challenging. This action alone, destroying the city leaders and confiscating their wealth, did more to the destruction of the city than anything else did. Leaderless and lacking financing needed to restart their economy, Zargarb was at the mercy of their overlords.

As soon as the last scuffles ended a few days later, in came the Holy Paladins of Pope Yazi. Charged with keeping order and making sure that the taxation laws of Justinian were followed, these men rode roughshod over the city inhabitants. In fact, life under these paladins was far worse than it had been when the Centurions and a governor had controlled the city so long ago.

Four days after taking Zargarb, Emperor Justinian and most of his legions headed down the seacoast road for Solamina. He left only five legions behind, who took up a position blocking the road coming up from New Barq and who encamped only a mile from the Santi fortress. Their tasks were obvious: keep an eye on the Santi and block the road should the Santi forces in New Barq or the Crusaders attempt to retake the city.

Vastly overcrowded in the temporary fortress, Art decided to risk using the lone caravel. Once the Centurions had left and it was clear that we were not going to be attacked, he made the decision. Holding a general meeting, he explained, "Most of you are not fighters and living in these crowed conditions is not good. Thus, we are going to take those of you who are willing to Velona. However, Captain John has asked that we wait two more days before sailing. He wants to sail with the outgoing tide in the middle of the night. The only way they can catch a caravel is when it is going slowly into or out of a port. Hopefully, in the middle of the night, they will not see the ship leave until it is under full sail."

Someone asked, "But won't they just try to sink us out in the Med Sea somewhere?" Visions of all the sunken ships in the harbor were prominent in these women's minds.

"They have only tried that one time. The caravel took out six of their triremes with no damage at all to our caravel. Since then these many months, they have not tried to attack a Santi or Velona caravel, though they have been shadowed and followed for a time." More mundane questions followed next, such as how long would the voyage last, what could they take, what about all the Sisterhood's funds, and who could go. "Of course you can take your money with you, it is yours," he teased.

On December 8, the caravel sailed around two in the morning, carrying three hundred women crammed into every available space on board. Ten uneventful days later, they arrived in bustling Velona. Elona put them all up at one of the largest inns in the city, at much reduced rates. Now these remaining Sisters had to decide how they wanted to put their lives back together.

Back at the fortress, each day Art, dressed in a local fisherman's disguise, snuck into the city to find out what was happening. At once, he found himself along with everyone else being forced to go to church and listen to the priests of Yazi spout their version of religion. That women under the paladin's rule were going to be treated worse than dogs became obvious to him. Yet there was little we could do about this horrid regression.

On the positive side, because of the devastated economy and general lack of ruling authority, Art was able to hire ten times the number of laborers to work on the fortress. All throughout the winter construction continued, but at a vastly more rapid rate than before the invasion. By spring, the outer walls were now up to six feet tall, but more importantly, one stone building, a dormitory, was ready for occupancy.

The Santi fully briefed the Solamina Sisterhood representative on what had happened in Zargarb and how it had fallen. Through her, their High Council was fully informed, and they swore that they would not fall victim to the same internal treachery. On the first day of the new year, Emperor Justinian met with the Solamina High Council and gave them the very same speech he had given in Zargarb! Like before, hundreds of soldiers manning the walls overhead every word. At once, the High Council broadly explained the folly of the Emperor's words. It worked for a time. However, just as in Zargarb, someone got an angry mob fired up and they opened the gates to the enemy. Solamina fell on February 15.

The conclusion that the Santi as a whole came to was simply this: the Emperor must have long ago sent in spies to live among the population. They had been carefully trained so that when the "surrender or else" ultimatum from the Emperor came, they then went into action, working their treason from within, playing upon those that were the most downtrodden in the society. Once more, our findings and theories were passed on to all the remaining sectors, in hopes that they could avoid the treasonous situation. John Henry's comment was interesting: an idea can penetrate walls of stone, where mere force may not.

Chapter 34 The Spring's Mild Offensive

While there was lots to do, construction wise, in New Barq, I was bored. I missed my twins, my life, and even my music, which I had forsaken now for over a year. Although greatly saddened by the fall of Zargarb and then later of Solamina, I was also surprised that they had fallen victim to internal treason. Pieta was next on the Centurion hit list and, by the middle of March, the Centurion forces were at the city gates. Earlier, they had swarmed over the outlying countryside, eliminating any threats there, just as they had done during their initial invasions.

However, we now knew a great deal more about the overall strategy and tactics the Emperor was employing. The Santi leader in Pieta was Juan Diego and he took a different route. As soon as the enemy began infiltrating the countryside of their sector, he sent out a dozen scouts. Their task was to observe the enemy clandestinely, particularly their supply routes. Risky was such an assignment, for if one were discovered, he or she would be killed on the spot as a traitor to the Emperor. Nonetheless, he had more volunteers than he could use.

Slowly the key information was gleaned and widely communicated. All along the seacoast were small towns and villages, mostly dedicated to fishing, naturally. However, their docks could handle one or two at the most incoming ships. Using his merchant fleet, the Emperor was obtaining his supplies via shipment across the Med Sea from somewhere along the coast of the Red Desert. It made sense, because he certainly could not get them overland through New Barq. As well organized as this whole invasion was, I was convinced that using New Barq as a supply point was never in his plans. It had all been a ruse to tie up and eliminate as a force the Crusaders. However, I never mentioned this to those men or General Prada; they were jubilant over their victory in the Arad. Considering the price in lives and limbs they had to pay, I was more than willing to allow them their victory celebrations.

During the early days of the new year, my Circle, all the Protectors, and all the regimental commanders met daily. Our task was to figure out some way that we could stop the Emperor. To date, he had yet to suffer a casualty of war. Always, he positioned his army just out of bow range, letting treason do its dirty work. Thus, Justinian was still at his full strength, which had swelled to nearly seventy legions, including ten of cavalry. Even if we had wanted to face his army, we could not; we were outnumbered almost three to one. Had the Crusaders joined forces with us, the odds would drop to only two to one, against us. It was folly to think of directly attacking them. Yet, we had to do something and do it soon. What? That was the problem.

Finally, in early March, when we learned that Pieta was being besieged and heard the news about their lines of supply, Paul made a suggestion at our meeting. "What say we take our force and ride on down the entire coast line of the Red Sea. Let's find these supply locations and destroy them. That ought to put a damper on his attacks."

His idea was an instant hit, especially with all the regimental commanders, who longed for some positive action. However, Lilly Ann pointed out a sobering fact. "Look everyone, even if we do manage to eliminate all his supply points, he can still resupply by confiscating all the food and materials in the conquered sectors. That would make life even worse than it is for all those folks. Every action begets a reaction, you know. Are we willing to assume the responsibility for making life tougher for those in Solamina and Zargarb?"

In the end, we got John Henry to agree to use caravels to resupply the cities with grain, should they need it. I adopted Paul's plan and issued the marching orders, leaving the security of New Barq to General Prada and his valiant Crusaders. He was very pleased not to have to go into combat again; although he did not actually admit it to me, his face and voice told all.

On April 1, seven days after the fall of Pieta, the entire Santi Strike Force, including the regiments of archers, began the long trek along the coastline of the Red Desert. Mission: find the Centurion supply depots and eliminate them. Simple, as long as we could find them, that is. Fresh water would be our worst enemy, so we brought along numerous water wagons, equipped with fresh water gatherers, if it rained. We also hoped to find other sources of fresh water along the way, but no one had any idea of this terrain; none of us had ever traversed the long coastline before.

One day's ride south and east of New Barq and we arrived at the beginnings of the long coastline. The blue, clear Med Sea lay on our right, sparkling in the sunshine. Often at night, many went for a swim; some even went fishing. For days, I thought we were having one endless beach party. War should be this much fun. Ahead, the land had actual dirt soil with patches of grass, some hardy trees, and even low hills. To our left, the Red Desert always encroached. Usually, though, a steep hill or ridge rose steeply up to the level of the desert. The width of this narrow coastline varied enormously. Sometimes the ridge line began almost two miles inland; others, a mere quarter mile.

In some of the wider spots, small creeks did provide some fresh water, as did the frequent squalls that came in from the Med Sea, though these only lasted for brief minutes. Our wisdom in bringing along so much water proved invaluable. Water was a scarce commodity along our route.

As usual, I sent out our scouts. One group rode several miles ahead of us, while one stayed a good deal behind us making sure that no one attempted to come at our rear. I took no chances with my group. Further and most interestingly, I sent another squad on our left flank, up in the actual desert. This group was under orders not to go too deeply into the desert, because we just didn't know what to expect there. A half century ago, the sands were utterly deadly, but now the environment had sprung back to life. We had rescued all the Moon People from their underground bunkers in the desert years ago. Now others had moved into this hostile land. Hence, I wanted no surprises coming at our side.

For three days, nothing of interest appeared along the coastline. Inland, almost at once, the scouts began reporting eerie feelings, as if they did not belong out there in the sands. The Loremaster and Communicator of these squads were even more upset. The feelings were intense for them; it was all they could do to continue to ride along with the Sisters. Both swore that there were some supernatural powers or beings out there in the empty desert whose purpose was to drive them out.

Around noon on the third day, it got even weirder. The Scout Squad Communicator, Belinda Thistleton, alerted me. *Ket, a strange sandstorm is hitting us. It came up out of nowhere. Nothing in the weather patterns we've seen indicated any significant winds. Yet if we stand still, we are going to be buried alive! Squad is doing a hard right, heading for the edge. I sense the presence of other beings, though, most definitely. Could these be causing it? Gotta go, barely able to see the way.*

The squad was on our immediate left flank, just up over the steep dune edge, about a half mile to our left. The coastal plain here was nearly two miles wide. After alerting the others, I turned to see if I could see anything down here on the plain. The sight was incredible; I'd never seen anything like it. A strong wind was blowing giant mounds of sand with the tail end of it wisping tendrils of sand high over the steep edge, which then drifted downward like inverted smoke clouds. Sometimes the sand clouds arced high in the air before slowly descending down into the coastal plain. "What is that?" I heard repeated a dozen times by folks near me. I'd no answer for them.

Suddenly, a horse and rider appeared, struggling mightily against the wind and sand, heading now down the steep incline towards us. Then, another and another appeared. Within a few minutes, all the squad members lunged for the safety of the coastal plain. All were red, red faces, bodies, horses, and tack. Red sand literally covered them completely. I yelled, "Down to the sea, wash off." While I let the others continue our forward ride, I veered off to check up on the squad. My Circle followed me, naturally.

Horse and rider both splashed out into the sea, coughing up sand and dust. Since it was non-life threatening, I gave them time to wash off and recover. "I'll be barfing up sand for a week!" declared Belinda. "That was awful." Some near her seconded that and added additional explicatives. "Ket, something is out there in the desert!"

"I'm glad you all got back safely. Take the rest of the day off, you all deserve it. Have at the tea wagon, sassafras might help get the phlegm up," I suggested. To my Circle, I asked, "Well, you guys ready for a little adventure? I have to go find out what is out there. I hope it isn't one of those mantis creatures. I thought they had been destroyed years ago."

"Not those giant bug-like creatures?" whined Beth Ann, suddenly remembering all the stories passed along about them years ago. She did not want to tangle with some all-powerful creatures, nor did she desire to be covered in red dust and sand like the scouts.

"I don't know what's out there, but I aim to find out. You don't have to come with, that goes for all you. This is going to be a voluntary mission," I declared. "Andre, Lenkova, you two take command while I am gone, probably a boring command, but keep everyone moving along westward. We'll be back as soon as we find out what is threatening us on our flank."

"Take care," hollered Lenkova, smiling. Andre saluted. My Circle was off, peeling off to the left, we urged our horses up the very steep incline toward the desert basin proper. Thankfully, the freak dust storm had vanished. The day was crystal-clear, blue sky and red sand as we halted, horses panting from the exertion to reach the top and the beginning of the desert. As far as the eye could see, red sand dunes undulated up and then down. Not a soul was in sight, just a desolate desert.

"What's the plan?" asked Paul, eager to know the next step.

"Ride slowly directly out into the desert, well as straight as possible, considering all these dunes. I am going to expand my mind and see if I can sense the presence that the others have been saying they felt. Paulette, keep a Mind Link on me, and relay to the others as needed. If it is a mantis creature, then fire based attacks are our best bet. As I recall, that seemed to harry them in some way the last time we fought them." I was recalling all I could about our encounters with these fifty-foot long alien creatures, when we encountered them nearly a century ago as my Lightning Circle crossed the then poisonous Red Desert.

Leaving Paul to guide my horse, I relaxed and expanded my awareness outward into this quiet, still, yet strangely pretty desert land. As usual, I am a poor judge of distances when outside of my body and not using my physical eyes. Someone definitely was out here. I felt the presence of two very different minds! Two beings not within a fleshly body were occupying this vast space stretching out before us. One seemed rather small; one seemed huge. I put my attention on the smaller one first; perhaps I was just being cautious.

I sensed this being had a female body somewhere out here in the desert! That could only mean she was not a header! Akin to us druwids, she did not dwell within her body's head. Like me, she could back out of the area of the body and expand or cover a vast spatial distance. Now I was keenly interested! I sensed that she was about to create a wind once more, so I hastily made contact. *Hello. Why are you blasting my riders with sandstorms? We mean no one in the desert any harm.*

The back flash of energy I received was that of unexpected confusion, the growing winds instantly died off. *What does this mean? How can these people talk to us? Guardian, one has spoken to me!* The message was not addressed to me, but to the other huge spiritual being positioned beside the smaller female being. At least the sandstorm stopped before it could begin. I thought; it's a start. Since I had opened up a communication line, Paulette felt that the others ought to listen in, and I felt gentle tugs as my other Circle members joined the Mind Link.

The larger being spoke, much as a priest to his adept, *Spiritual beings can communicate just as we do, Juli, though such is unexpected from our enemies. The Infidels are not known for their spiritual awareness, even those who venture out here into the Anuir. I shall speak with this being.*

Suddenly, I felt the solid connection of this Guardian's communication line into me and my mind. *Behold, I am the Guardian of Anuir within the Red Desert. I am of Jehosa. I come from Jehosa. I protect this land for the Children of Anuir. Who art thou and why dost thou enter this sacred, protected land?*

Something was strangely familiar about this being; perhaps it was the wavelength of his radiations, the gentle touch of his mind upon mine. *I am Ket Bethany, leader of the Santi del Dio from Mont Blanc and the Sea Princes. We are here fighting against the Centurions of Megalos, the Infidels, who have once more invaded the Sea Princes. We mean no harm to anyone who lives in the desert, especially to those who follow Lord Jehosa.* I knew this being, something warm and fuzzy filled my heart, but I couldn't quite latch my mind upon who this was.

I know nothing of Ket Bethany nor of the Santi del Dio, but it is good that you fight against the Infidels. Why dost thou enter the sacred Anuir?

Suddenly, like a hammer, it hit me. I knew who this being was! *Jes, Jes Amir. Is that you? You knew me as Bethany, Bethany Madelyn Amir, your wife.*

A great hesitancy, an uncertainty came back over the communication line from him. I could see him looking at his mental pictures, vainly trying to remember. My last view of Jes was when he was sucked into the Grey Creature's machine, which scrambled all one's memories, one's pictures. Alabaster attempted to rescue him and was sucked in as well. I had spent much of this lifetime trying to find Alabaster, whose mind had also become scrambled. I found Jes in a similar plight. All his memories were a confused mess of detached sequences, such as kissing me followed by leading a goat out of a pen followed by healing an injured man, just a complete jumble.

Yes, I was perhaps once called Jes. He had latched onto an image of him and me playing out in the streets of Bethel, when we were teens. After an interminable period, he latched onto our farewell kiss when he left to battle the Grey Creatures. *Ah, I do recognize you, Bethany. My memories are dim and incoherent. I do know that somehow I failed my people.*

Not entirely, Jes. Alabaster and I got rid of both groups of alien creatures that were interfering with our power of choice and free will. No more Grey Creatures or mantises, I hope.

That is good. Oh, there is an image of a Grey Creature. Yes, sometime you must tell me all about them. After another long pause, he added, *I failed to enlighten my people. You wanted to be enlightened, I believe.*

Yes, we both want the same thing for the people of Tarra. You never did tell me how you did some of those "miracles," and you did promise me you would share that with me one day.

I'm truly sorry, but I don't have those memories available just now. I am now the Guardian of this land, the Anuir. I am working on freeing the faithful. Juli is my first pupil and has come a long way back towards her true self, that she may one day re-enter the Holy Realm of Jehosa. Pray, when you finish fighting the Infidels, return unto me that I may teach thee as I should have so long ago. I am just now working out just how to free my people and it is promising.

This was an invitation I could not refuse! *I certainly will, just as soon as I can. Pleased to meet you, Juli.*

Am I permitted to speak, Guardian? She asked, hesitatingly.

Of course, Juli. Bethany, Ket, has done much for spiritual enlightenment and freedom on Tarra. Speak freely.

I'm sorry about scaring your people. I thought that they might be more Infidels. Already, with much help from the Guardian, I have covered two groups of the Infidels in sand. They were coming into the Anuir from the New Barq area. The Infidels are also all along the coastline, so I thought you were them. I'm sorry.

Nothing to apologize about Juli; no harm done, not against the Santi anyway. When I can return to the Anuir, I'd like to meet you in person.

Juli, we shouldst allow Ket to return. I believest his Santi doth encounter the Infidels once more. Go with Jehosa, Ket, until one day you may return, the Guardian said. I said farewell and broke the link with Jes or rather the Guardian as he now called himself.

Paulette interjected, "Looks like Andre and Lenkova have come upon the first Centurion supply depot. We better hurry back or we will miss the action." We turned around and headed back down the steep incline, then galloped in pursuit of the Santi, who were miles ahead of us.

"So that was the Great Messiah, this Jes Amir," Paul commented, just a bit awed by the experience. "He sure seems to be able to operate without a body. Maybe he is a god."

"He seems a bit confused, though," Lilly Ann added.

"Just like Alabaster was when I found him. The Grey Creatures scrambled their memories. When I get the chance, I will try to help Jes using the techniques I figured out with Alabaster. Golly, this is keenly interesting. I would like to stay and talk with him for a long time. He finally promised to let me in on how he does things. We could learn tons from him, if we only get the chance. Instead, I have to deal with this darn war. Curse on it!" I exclaimed. Here I was about to be able to unlock keys to our spiritual powers and I had to deal with a ghastly war instead. No justice in this world.

Meanwhile, Paulette conferred with Andre's Communicator, Mary Bridgeport. She explained as we rode along, "Scouts discovered the depot about two miles ahead of the main force. Probably an entire legion is defending it; mostly they have a lot of wounded there from the Crusader battles. Andre and Lenkova led the initial charge through the depot. Thus far, ten waves have plowed through the camp. It's too small to hit with a large group at one time, she says. Some Centurions have taken a dozen dingys and paddled out to sea. Several merchant ships are moored just off shore. Lenkova is accepting their surrender now." Just then, we met up with the rear end of the many regiments of archers, who complained that they didn't get to see any action. I chuckled as we passed by.

In a few minutes, we came upon the depot and battle scene. All combat was over; Lenkova had her forces lining up the surrendering men, while Andre was working with his Healer, Ann, sorting out the wounded. "Ah, just in time to help patch everyone up," he called out cheerily, having just accomplished his first battle victory without my aid.

"What's the tally?" I asked, seeing once more the wounded men and women lying about waiting their turn.

"We lost only one, got two dozen lightly wounded. Lenkova is mustering up those that surrendered. Two dozen fled in the dingys out there." He pointed to the men rowing toward three merchant ships. Soon all the other Healers arrived, and in an hour, all were patched up.

Lenkova had lined up her forty-nine prisoners of war. Half were recovering wounded from Crusader battles. Only a half dozen had been wounded today. Evidently, those Centurions who chose to stand and fight were killed. Of course, now I had a new problem that I had not taken into consideration: what to do about prisoners we might take?

By now, the entire force had arrived and completely encircled this nice cove with a red sandy beach. I could see why this place was chosen for the depot; these Centurions were not dumb. Paul commented, "What are we going to do about those ships out there? If we ignore them, what's to keep them from landing a force of Centurions after we've gone and let them attack our rear?"

I didn't think that there was much chance of their launching a counter attack, however. Too few men, I wagered. Still, I didn't like having three ships with who knows who on board watching our every move. I had an idea. I called for the Longbow Regiments. "Give those three ships a few volleys of flaming arrows. Let's see if they take the hint and leave," I ordered. The archers were very happy to comply; they had something to do. In ten minutes, the first volley of flaming arrows arced out over the water and into the three ships. Given the range, only about seventy-five out of five hundred arrows actually hit the ships. Even from this distance, we could see crew dashing about trying to put out the small flames, especially those that hit in or near the canvas sails. After a few more volleys, the ships hastily set sail. While they had been out of normal bowshot range, they had not met the longbow. I had a satisfied look on my face when the three ships turned their sterns to us, sailing out to sea.

We made camp here for the night and held a council to try to figure out what to do with both the huge amount of supplies and the prisoners. Some thought they should be summarily executed, but I had the final word. "We'll send word to the Crusaders to send a bunch of wagons and troops to escort these prisoners back to New Barq. Make the able-bodied of them help load and unload the wagons. Then, let the Crusaders escort them to Al Mari and send them on their way back to Megalos. Without weapons and so few of them, they pose no real threat to us, even if by chance they have a weapons stockpile somewhere down the North-South road." The only real problem with this strategy is that we would have to wait here for the Crusaders to arrive in about a week's time.

In the end, we let a regiment of archers do the waiting, while the remainder of our force continued down the coastline the next day. Since the Centurions were methodical and I had discovered a marker flag at the supply depot that read XIII, I suspected that we had twelve more to go. Indeed, during the next two weeks, we encountered depots twelve through nine, eliminating each with little effort, because most were guarded by fewer than fifty men.

Depot VIII had recently been abandoned, perhaps just days before we arrived at the site. Litter lay all over the grounds; they did not even bother to cover their latrines! Now an eyesore, I ordered that the grounds be cleaned up and sent scouting parties out to ascertain if they fled on down the coast. No sign of coastal travel was discovered, so I concluded that they evacuated by sea. After spending a day here, we continued our westward journey.

Several days later, we discovered the next depot, which had also been abandoned. The Loremasters studied the site for clues and concluded that the location had been unoccupied for nearly a week. Speculations naturally began to fly among us. Chief among these, though not necessarily true, was that the Centurions were going to abandon all their supply locations along the coast, yielding this territory to us. Counter to this notion would be the very difficult task of using sea supply all the way from the Southlands or even Megalos. Such would be difficult at best and communications unbelievably slow. Now it dawned on me that one of our vitally important abilities, that of telepathy or near instantaneous communications across vast spaces, was a keen advantage. We needed to make more use of this, I concluded.

Thus, it went for another six weeks. Periodically, we encountered another abandoned supply depot, hastily departed. Nothing of value had been left behind. Yes, it was a very boring six weeks, broken only by the beauty of the coastline. Several places were particularly beautiful. One particular bay, though small, was ideal for our Velona style bay defenses. On a whim, I decided that we ought to build another Santi fortress here in this bay. Lilly Ann named our bay Nuova Vita. Naturally, our Planners liked the idea of yet another fortress, this time in a remote area, which could act as a springboard into the Red Desert. Velona lay almost due north of Nuova Vita.

Further scouting reports soon came in. In the past, the entire Centurion invasion army had been stationed about fifteen miles further west of Nuova Vita. Now we were convinced that we had forced the Emperor hastily to abandon all his supply depots along the northern coastline of the Red Desert. We did not find out until later that he had ordered them moved onto the mainland of the Sea Princes, near Pieta.

Strategically, the Santi was now in a very bad position. Overland, travel back to New Barq would require at least another two months. Considering how badly things were going in the Sea Prince sectors, John Henry and I decided on a risky move: transport the entire Santi force from Nuova Vita to Velona. Because of the war, very little commerce was currently being conducted, most of which was done by Velona with her fast caravels. The ships of many sectors were currently being safe-harbored in Velona, d'Grange, West Reach, and Calgary. On June 1, an impressive sight to behold appeared in our new little bay.

Fifty caravels accompanied by over a hundred older Sea Prince ships from many sectors anchored just off shore. This was the most impressive sailing fleet ever gathered in one location in the known history of Tarra. Because of the total size of the fleet and because so many caravels were with the older ships, the triremes did not dare interfere. The fleet required five trips to Velona to move us all. Sailing time between these two locations was three days, mostly due to the lengthy process of loading and unloading. Thus, the Santi was finally ready for mainland operations near July 1, an action that the Emperor had not anticipated. He had expected us to return to New Barq overland.

Chapter 35 The Bargains

Barcarole Occala, head nobleman of Pieta, argued with the other High Council members. "Look, Zargarb and Solamina have fallen. Now we are facing the entire strength of the invading army. They have left garrison duties to the Holy Paladins. And how is it that these walled cities, not unlike ourselves, fell? Need I remind you they fell because of traitors from within, likely Centurion spies sent long ago to infiltrate the cities. How do we know that we will not suffer the same fate, eh? Yes, yes, we could do as Emilio suggests, kill every bronzed skin person in Pieta. That means over half our population, I remind you, many are Arad immigrants. Folly, I say. Besides, at least half of our garrison forces are of Arad descent. Shall we throw away our honest defenders in hopes that we also get the one or two Centurion traitors?"

Much grumbling could be heard in the room. Of course, they could not outright kill so many in a vain attempt to kill the one who might spark the riot that would open the gates to the enemy. Barcarole was not finished, however. "May I point out the economics of the situation? For years, more than half of our shipping income comes from trading with Megalos, more than half. Grain, coal, iron ore, spices — the list is endless. We provide the shipping for them. Thus far, we have prudently avoided the disasters which have befallen Zargarb and Solamina; we've only lost a couple older ships."

"Yes, but what is your point?" angrily shouted another impatient council member. "Get to the point."

"Okay. I say we negotiate with the Emperor. Open our city gates to him and let him enter freely. Ignore the whole war thing. Make him welcome. Convince him that it is in his best interests not to harm one of his best trading partners. Thus far, Pieta has not done any aggressive actions toward his empire. No fighting, no bloodshed, just a pact between two trading partners. Negotiate I say is in our best interests."

Wild arguments followed for nearly an hour. Some wanted to call Barcarole a traitor to Pieta, but dared not, for he was still the single most powerful figure in Pieta. Used to getting his way, in the end, Barcarole succeeded once more. Thus, when the Emperor finally arrived on the outskirts of Pieta, he found the gates open and the walls not manned. An aide cried out, "My Lord, what devilish trick is Pieta playing on us? Their gates are opened, walls not manned. Have they surrendered already? I say it is a devilish trick."

"Trick or no trick, that is the question," Justinian pondered. "I know this Barcarole Occala, at least by name. He is the wealthiest man in Pieta, of that I am sure. Ships of his line do carry much of our iron ore from the mines in the Southlands. He is a business man, not a soldier, Lex, I say, let us hear what he has to say." Justinian had his aide read the short scroll message from Barcarole once more.

Lex, his aide, still feared treachery. "My Lord, you cannot enter this city

397

and dine with him. There would be so many ways that an assassin could kill you that we could not foresee them. No, you cannot accept his invitation."

Justinian sighed. While he longed to accept this businessman's hospitality, enjoy a public bath and fine dining, he realized that Lex was right. A drop of poison here, a well-aimed dagger there, the list would be endless, especially in an unsecured city as large as Pieta. "No, I agree. Let's invite him here, and then we can control the situation. Send word to him, please."

"Aye, my Lord." Lex hastily scratched out the Emperor's reply and sent it with the messenger who stood waiting outside the royal tent.

Around noon the next day, six of the High Council members, including Barcarole, rode up to his lavish tent. At least Barcarole had listened to the Sisterhood representative, who had insisted on keeping some of the council members safe inside of the city, just in case of treachery on the Emperor's side. "Greeting Emperor Justinian, very pleased to actually meet you," Barcarole exclaimed in his usual jubilant business manner. "All these many years we have been doing business together and yet we have not met." He offered his hand, but Justinian rebuked it. An aide whispered that no one was allowed to shake the Emperor's hand. If it bothered Barcarole, he made no outward sign.

"Come, let us dine," Justinian said in a grand manner, deflecting the awkward moment, gesturing toward the lavishly set table. A luncheon meeting was Barcarole's favorite time to conduct important business; he was in his prime setting. The other five council members totally deferred to Barcarole in most matters and did so again here, letting him handle the conversation.

After some small talk, he said, "And how may Pieta be of service to you? Long have we been perhaps your best shipping partner. I will freely admit to you that Megalos uses well over half of all our ships. For years now, it is Pieta ships, which bring spices to your land, moves coal and iron ore to your foundries, even grain from the Greenway. In all these years, Pieta has never been blessed with a royal visit of the Emperor of Megalos. Indeed, sire, we are extremely honored and proud to have you come to our fair city. As you no doubt have seen, the gates are wide open to you." Mentally, he ticked off all the key points that he had wanted to interject into his opening remarks, designed to convince the Emperor that they were allies, not warring enemies.

Justinian, taken completely by surprise, tried to look as nonchalant as possible while he hastily thought how to react to this unexpected turn of events. "It is true that a good deal of our shipping is handled by Pieta, although you realize that the precise details are left to those in charge of such affairs. Seldom am I directly involved in these matters." He could not outright say that this war was to elevate him into history by retaking the lands that were lost by his predecessors. He could not say I want all your money and ships.

"Oh, I understand perfectly. A leader leads and should not manage all the details, that is why we have our aides and managers. If we tried to manage everything, we'd have no time to lead. Surely, there is something that Pieta can help you with, shipping, finances, supplies. What can your shipping ally do for you today?" Cleverly, Barcarole shifted the focus to that of an ally and aide that could be given, hoping to deflect any latent animosity that may be behind the Emperor's war against the Sea Princes.

Poor Justinian, he could not just say I am here to conquer you or I want to take back Pieta, which was stolen from us by the barbarian invasion so many years ago. A shrewd politician, he was quick to size up a situation. "Ah, well you see I have a couple little problems in Megalos. My people, particularly the Senate, are demanding that the Sea Princes be returned to our control after the Galts forced us out. Between you and me, I think that they are feeling the lost revenues. Worse are the demands from the Church of Jehosanity. I must tell you that the church now has the backing of most of the citizens of Megalos, so I cannot just ignore their requests any longer, which are two. First, they want to be able to establish their churches here instead of the heathen Tur and the perverted Northern Orthodoxy churches. Secondly, they wish me to disband forcibly, if necessary, this association of women called the Sisterhood, which they believe totally perverts the role of women on Tarra. But we are businessmen first and foremost," Justinian added, knowing full well he had almost no interest in commerce, except counting his revenues, "I'm sure that we can come to some agreements on these without the use of force of arms." He added that last to make sure that Barcarole did not lose sight of the fact that he had his army camped on the doorstep of Pieta.

Barcarole stifled the urge to chuckle; Justinian had just given him his fondest desire on a silver platter! Long had he been opposed to the Sisterhood, as his father before him. He found it disgraceful if not utterly revolting and disgusting that women would band together in this Sisterhood and operate outside the boundaries of Pieta society. Money would not be a problem; he'd just raise the shipping fees to cover any taxation Megalos might place upon Pieta. Further, he cared little for religion, but all Pieta was tacitly followers of Tur, the God of the Sea, being primarily mariners. "Is that all that this is about? It's hardly worth all the bother. I'm sure that we can work out an equitable tithe to send to Megalos; after all, being shipping allies, what is good for you is also good for us. Your church can build all the churches it desires in Pieta, I don't think anyone would protest in the slightest. Mind you, most follow the sea god here. As far as the Sisterhood goes, why you will find many of us here in Pieta that believe the same as your church does. In fact, I will go so far as to say that you will find strong support here for abolishment of the Sisterhood."

Justinian smiled, he knew he had just conquered Pieta without lifting a finger. "Well, as far as the taxation issue goes, I am sure that I can convince the Senate to accept a gold ducat per year per person in the sector. That would be low enough so as not to place any hardships on your citizens, am I correct?" He was demanding the same amount from the other conquered cities, however.

Barcarole realized this was the same amount Megalos demanded years ago when they had control over the city. However, he had another compromise in mind. "I am sure that I can sell that amount," he coyly said, adding, "providing we don't have to have all those Holy Paladins riding rough-shod over the city and outlying towns. The High Council will monetarily guarantee you those funds each year, providing we are not threatened by those supposedly holy men. With that compromise, I am sure I can obtain their full agreement. Any deficit between the amount collected and the amount needed would be made up by the council."

"Oh, that is more than equitable, Barcarole, splendid indeed! You have my word that these Holy Paladins will be instructed to only provide church security here, nothing more. However, what can we do about this Sisterhood mess?"

"Leave that to the council, My Lord. It is only a just compromise on both sides. We will meet this afternoon and send you word later today." He looked at his silent fellow council members and added, "I'm sure that we can convince the others of this just and fair agreement." The two men shook hands to seal their pact. With that, the six High Council members left and headed back into the city.

At the quickly summoned meeting, Barcarole outlined his discussion and the terms that Justinian desired. He ended with a simple statement of the results, "Look, the taxation is not a problem; we just up our shipping costs slightly to cover it. There is no need even to make a big deal out of trying to collect something from every person. We already have a city gate entrance fee; we just increase it a tad as well. The people will be thoroughly behind us as long as they are not responsible for paying out a gold coin each year. We'll get it anyway from the fees and increased shipping costs. If we officially disband the Sisterhood, then that will keep those nasty Holy Paladins from terrorizing the city and towns as we've heard they are doing in Zargarb and Solamina. That alone is sufficient justification for the disbandment of the Sisterhood. Besides, we all know that they have already nearly completely disbanded, many joining with the Santi. What say you, Sister Mandi Zoria?" She was the Sisterhood's High Council representative.

Mandi already knew that in both Zargarb and Solamina, the Holy Paladins, in laying down the new laws, had outlawed the Sisterhood. Anyone caught belonging to that organization was to be slain on the spot. All remaining members either had been evacuated to Velona or had taken refuge within the Santi fortification there. On one level, she was loathed to have men even attempt to disband her organization; after all, it existed solely because of the atrocities men had committed upon women over the years. On the other hand, the Sisterhood worked for the welfare of the common man within Pieta. Clearly, it was in their best interests if these barbaric holy men were kept out of power in this sector. Thus, Mandi had no real choice, "For the good of our people here in Pieta, we will disband."

Without another word, she rose and left the meeting, never to return, heading for the Sisterhood Inn. She explained the situation to Rosita, who still led them, and the few remaining women. "So it has come to this," commented the elderly Rosita. "I've seen much in my day, but I never thought I would see us coming to an end. However, we all knew this was coming, one way or another. I thank Tur that Ket Bethany has given us another avenue to follow. Mandi, we are all packed. How soon should we leave?"

By dark, Justinian was relaxing in a public bath within Pieta, while the remnants of the Sisterhood there were being accommodated in the Santi fortress just outside the city. Juan Diego loaded the women onto the waiting caravel after dark, and the ship sailed in secret during the night. That the Holy Paladins might not honor the agreement never entered the mind of Barcarole or the other High Council members. On March 21, Pieta officially fell to the Centurions.

Although Justinian sent his foot soldiers on towards the next sector, Bonilla, he and his cavalry stayed a while in Pieta. He found it refreshing to stroll this strange city with all its shops. Instead of hostile inhabitants, he found the common folks only a bit confused about events. First, there was this push for a Crusade for Religious Freedom, then a push to defend the city, and now the city was an ally of the Centurions. Just as Barcarole had predicted, when the common citizen discovered that the city would be paying their taxes to Megalos for them, they backed the council's decision. Still, they were more than a little confused about the events, but most were not hostile, even glad to be relieved of the burdensome and threatening wall guard duty. Life could return to normal, most believed it would happen soon.

When Justinian was finally ready to depart for Bonilla, word came to him of the Santi destruction of Supply Depot XIII, followed within a few days of the next depot. Delaying his departure, he and his generals held councils to deal with this unexpected turn. "We must abandon all the supply depots," one general exclaimed. "How can a legion defend it against the thousands of invading Santi cavalry? Impossible. We will lose all our supplies that our ground forces need here."

Justinian saw that this was indeed true. Now he saw the wisdom of his recent compromise with Pieta. "Ah, but we no longer need a friendly supply base down there. Pieta is now our ally. Abandon all supply depots; send ships to bring the supplies and troops here to Pieta. We can store the goods in some of the warehouses. Send for Barcarole; let's press all available Pieta ships into service to help us move the depots before the Santi reach them." Aides jumped and headed to carry out his order.

"We might not be able to get to all the depots in time, My Lord," another general pointed out.

Justinian just waved his hand, "Of course, but what are a few men and supplies? They will slow down the advance of these Santi so that the other depots can be saved. Their sacrifice shall be noted. Scribe, take that down. Any Centurion lost at the depots is to have an imperial golden scroll given to his surviving family."

"What about eliminating the Santi that is already here. You know that their supposed 'fortress' is barely a wall that any man can step over, don't you.

We've got thousands of men; they've only got a handful that we have seen, many women too," a general proposed.

This struck a nerve in Justinian, akin to being called a coward, which he was. "No, we leave the Santi strictly alone. You have seen just how powerful they are. Some say that they have Evil Witches among them. How else can you explain these magical fires that nearly destroyed the triremes? How else can you explain the mighty waves that lifted the triremes out of the way of the caravels? No, General Brutus, attacking even their flimsy excuses for a fort would cost us lives. I have no doubt that we could take them out, but I am unwilling just now to lose that many men. Remember, we have a very limited number of legions and many more sectors to conquer."

He continued, "If our numbers get reduced here and there, we may end up failing to meet our objectives or even lose ground in counterattacks. Until we have conquered the Sea Prince sectors, the Santi are off-bounds. Once we have secured these lands, then, my dear Brutus, then we shall deal with the Santi. Besides, look where their main strike force is at and heading. They are going to spend months traveling across the northern coast of the Red Desert only to find nothing. Then, they have to back track all the way to New Barq and then up into the Zargarb sector. What a fortuitous strategic blunder they have made. We can now go ahead with our original plans and perhaps by winter return to Zargarb and deal with them."

"Excellent thinking," Brutus replied. "I see the larger picture now. Yes, their large strike force will be useless, sitting at Supply Depot I. They could not have made a dumber move." Everyone laughed loudly. "How soon do we move out?" he asked.

"I want to make sure that our supplies are on their way here first," Justinian reasoned aloud. Actually, he was thinking of his own stomach. If they ran out of food on the road, he hated to be forced to eat the disgusting local cuisine. Additionally, he discovered that much of the news of what was happening in Zargarb and Solamina had somehow mysteriously become known here in Pieta, sometimes long before he was informed of it. He had no idea how this could be; no ships were sailing between the cities yet. However, ignoring how this information was learned, he decided to make it work for him. Since his miraculous accomplishments here in Pieta, he wanted to give time for the news and details of the "compromise" to reach the other Sea Prince cities. In the back of his mind, he began to desire that these other cities would likewise sue for peace. Imagine his victory, retaking the Sea Princes without fighting a battle, without having to besiege walled cities!

Not until the middle of April did he lead his cavalry out of Pieta, onto the coastal road to Bonilla. Supplies secure in five warehouses and wagons lined up to begin overland transport, Justinian once more felt confident of a complete and total victory. He was also certain that had he not personally intervened and been here giving his generals their orders, the generals would have made a complete mess of the whole war, perhaps even losing the war!

Indeed, his strategy worked far better than he imagined. Emboldened by the surprise move made by Barcarole of Pieta, the High Council of Bonilla, also followers of Tur, quickly made the same arrangements the very minute that Justinian and his cavalry arrived outside Bonilla. It was as if they couldn't wait to surrender to him! On April 21, Bonilla opened its gates to the emperor from Megalos.

Seeing that neither city suffered any apparent harm with their bargains, the council members of Vito could not call it a surrender and to save face, they also made a similar pact on May 20. However, Barcella, whose High Council attempted to also sue for peace, became a significant problem both to the High Council and to Justinian. This sector worshiped Jehosa, and the common folks completely rebelled at the notion of having the Megalos version of Jehosanity replacing theirs. Thus, while the council surrendered the city, its population rebelled.

Centurion supply wagons were routinely attacked by bands of religious rebels. Buildings were sabotaged, and even lone legions were attacked openly. The streets were not safe for travel unless one was very well escorted with numerous fighters. In short, the High Council in surrendering to the same terms as Pieta found itself completely out of control of its population! The real power now fell into the hands of the Church of Jehosanity leaders, who continually preached open rebellion against the council and the invaders.

Now Justinian faced a major situation. He could not continue down the line to attack Velona in an orderly manner. Somehow, he had to subdue Barcella. He expected the enemy to form up a battle line and then both sides would close to do battle. Within a few hours or perhaps days, if the numbers were large, the war would be over. Here, the enemy never formed a battle line. Instead, large bands would suddenly appear, attack a supply column, kill as many Centurions as possible, inflict as much damage as possible, and then disappear as suddenly as they came. The tactic frustrated not only Justinian but also all his generals.

By the end of June, he had lost over two legions of men outright, dead, with many more on the casualty lists. Valuable supplies had been stolen as well. His entire campaign came to a screeching halt here in Barcella. "How in the name of heaven do we put down this rebellion?" bellowed Justinian for the tenth time. He was meeting with his generals once more. Blank stares told him he was wasting his time yelling at his generals. He fumed.

An aide interrupted his meeting, "My Lord, the Holy Paladins have arrived. General Sanchez wishes a word with you about this rebellion. Shall I send him in?"

"Hell yes! Maybe someone can tell me how to deal with this mess!" barked Justinian, highly frustrated. He was open to any suggestion that had remote merit.

In walked a tall man dressed in the familiar sky blue tunic with white cross emblazoned front and back. "General Ali Sanchez, at your service," the man said with a bit of an Arad accent. Justinian wondered about his ancestry, but motioned for him to take a seat.

"You are aware of the situation that we are facing here in Barcella, General Sanchez?" Justinian asked somewhat politely, pushing aside his anger for the moment. He should at least hear what this man had to say.

"I came just as soon as word of the rebellion of Barcella reached me. As you know, due to the chaotic situation in Zargarb and Solamina, I have been forced to leave five hundred Holy Paladins in each city to enforce your laws. However, while we may not agree on your not letting us control and enforce the laws in Vito, Pieta, and Bonilla, I have left only a hundred men in each city to guard the new churches springing up in those cities. The remaining seven hundred fighters I have brought with me. I believe that will be sufficient to put an end to the open rebellion here, My Lord."

"And just how do you propose to do that?" Justinian barked. He already hated this man after hearing these few sentences. The cockiness, the audacity, the air of superiority he exuded nearly forced the angry Justinian to smash in the man's face.

"Sire, we know how to deal with these rebels. Just give us a few days to implement the solution. We'll have the city and the sector under control in just a couple of weeks. These animals, these dogs, must be taught a lesson in a way that they can understand." He saw that Justinian was about to lose his temper, so he explained a bit further. "We will announce in each town and village that, if anyone there attacks or harms any of your men or us, we will immediately execute ten men, women, and children indiscriminately for every one of ours who is hurt in any way. Yes, we will be thoroughly brutal with public beheadings. After one or two of these public executions, you will find that the animals will behave. Give time for the word to spread. Now, if you will excuse me, I must get to work and bring your rebellion under control. May Jehosa be with you and guide you to victory."

He bowed and left quickly before Justinian could formulate a reply. He cared not whether the Emperor approved of his means or not, Justinian did not matter a donkey's ass, only the ultimate success of his church mattered to this man. The priests could not begin their work here until the rebellion ceased, General Sanchez intended it to end quickly!

Justinian was about to say something, when one of his generals beat him to it, "My Lord, that is heinous, brutal, savage, and barbaric." It was refreshing to hear another say aloud what he thought, and it gave him time to calm down.

"Well, let's give them their chance at it. If it does end this rebellion, then so be it. Obviously we have not been successful dealing with open rebellion," Justinian said rather calmly. Besides, he thought, if this obnoxious general failed, he could then ostracize him for his brutality. Yet, if it did end the fiasco, he could continue on to Velona, which he had calculated all along would be the most difficult to conquer, mostly because he had no spies in place in that sector, unlike those in Zargarb and Solamina. Then, there were the Axemen to consider. While no Centurion had yet faced them, word of their prowess as fighters was widespread. He needed his full strength to tackle

Velona.

During the next two weeks, word that the Butcher had come to Barcella spread everywhere. True to his word, he did precisely what he said he would do. Every time that the rebels struck, his men came into the town or village and slew outright ten for one. Over one thousand men, women, and children were beheaded during those two weeks! He carefully saved the actual city for last, allowing word of his ultimatum to reach the city's population. Thus, when he finally entered Barcella, everyone feared this man and the blue tunic men under his command. Still a few attacks were made on his men within the city walls. After he summarily executed fifty women and children, they too got the point. Finally, when he continued to slay citizens after even minor sabotages, all resistance quelled. Grandly, General Sanchez rode his horse around the city of Barcella, daring anyone to attempt any actions. None did and he pronounced the city ready for its occupation and implementation of the new laws.

Obliged to acknowledge the success of General Sanchez, Justinian was loathed to meet with him personally. Instead, he sent the general an imperial scroll, which merely said "Thank you for handling the situation." That night, Justinian slept poorly. "What have I unleashed upon these people?" he wondered. There was honor and glory standing upon a battlefield and defeating your enemy, but this outright slaughtering of completely innocents, even women and children, was revolting, and utterly barbaric. It was conduct far worse that the Galts had displayed, and they were the barbarians. Justinian felt sick at his stomach and barely slept at night.

In fact, nothing was the same for this Emperor after this point in time. No longer did sleep come naturally to him. Restless, he could only doze for a few hours each night, waking in a fearful sweat. No longer did he fully see his generals as they were. Had he been able to observe them, he would have seen that they too had lost their fighting spirit, their resolve, their will. A sullen, somber army began to maneuver toward the border with Velona in early July.

Chapter 36 The Battle for Velona

"It's not going to happen here. Yes, it is true that the weaker sectors have fallen to the enemy. You've heard what has happened as a result. It shall not happen here. We have no Centurion traitors in our midst nor am I going to sell out the city. Instead, we have drawn the line at the Mio River. No Centurion or Unholy Paladins will ever be allowed to cross; I give you my solemn word on that." Elona spoke sternly and with emphasis to yet another large crowd. For the last two weeks, she had been delivering nearly the same speech to all her subjects scattered throughout the sector. At this time, she was talking to the dockhands in Velona proper.

She continued, "As per the bargain I made with our new immigrants, the Axemen, in a time when Velona is threatened, shall come to our mutual defense. As you know, they have more than met their obligations. For nearly a year, they have manned their longboats, keeping the triremes at bay, ensuring the safety of our shipping. I am pleased to announce to you that they have now formed their own regiments and will be shortly marching out to the Mio River to form up battle lines. Ten regiments strong, our stalwart neighbors will join forces with the entire Santi Strike Force."

"My regular, well paid city guards, now some ten regiments strong, are also going off to the Mio River to help in our defense. I do not intend to allow the Centurions to flood all over the sector while we remain cooped up behind these walls. The walls shall be our very last defense, and I most definitely do not plan to need them. When our defenders move out to the Mio River, I will be joining them. While I am away, the High Council is responsible for running things in my absence. Please give them the support that you have always shown me."

"Finally, here is the latest bit of good news. Fortress d'Grange has just sent five regiments of their fighters to help in Velona's defense!" The crowd cheered her loudly; their clapping did not subside even after their highly popular monarch had given them three bows. She rejoined her Circle and asked, "Five hundred more. That surely will help. Jeesh, they are still applauding."

Alton nudged her, "Go take another bow, honey." She smiled and returned for yet another bow. Finally, the crowd began to disperse. "Well, that is the last of the speeches. We had better get packing." Ket had planned to leave in the morning and they did not want to delay him.

That night, Ket called all Guardians, all regimental commanders, and several others to a strategy council meeting. They filled the converted chapel area of the building that Elona had taken over as her headquarters. "On the eve of our departure, I've gathered you all here, my dear friends to discuss our strategy and tactics before we hit the trail and scatter. Based on all the information gathered on our enemy, when the Emperor moves into another sector, he fans his legions out and moves along the rim roads. We have six rim roads in Velona, plus the coast road. As each group moves down the trail, they conquer each town that they encounter, methodically."

"As you know this approach guarantees that by the time they all arrive at the gates of the namesake city, all the outlying towns and villages are subdued. We have two choices. One, we can used this against them. By attacking them in smaller numbers, we can so reduce their superiority in numbers, perhaps swaying the final confrontation into our favor. Two, we can form a widely visible battle line and attempt to get them to commit to a single battle at the onset. No matter which approach is used, they outnumber us still."

"Elona does not want to allow them to ransack any of the outlying towns and villages. Thus, we are not going to allow them to execute their usual pattern of attacks. If we attempt to follow the first choice, attack them in their smaller groups, we run the risk of having our forces scattered all over the eastern border with Barcella. Worse, if one of their groups breaks through, we then face the possibility of enemy attacks from the rear of our other groups. Hence, I have vetoed the first choice. Somehow we must get them to commit to a single, all-out battle."

"We know that Justinian has finally left with his cavalry, heading down the coastal road. I'm sure glad that we established a Santi base near each of the Sea Prince cities; the information we have been getting has been utterly crucial. Based on their estimated travel time, we have a week to get into position at the Mio River. The problem remains as to how to get them to commit to a single battle. This is where we use a little subterfuge and make excellent use of Elona's city guards. We know that the foot soldier leaders wait for orders from the Emperor, before launching their rim road attacks. What we are going to do is to destroy the few bridges over the river at those six locations and build a defensive barricade at that location, manned with the city guards. We have made a pair of straw dummy soldiers for each of the guards, so with a little trickery on our part, it will seem that we have triple the number of fighters manning those key locations than we actually do have."

"The five Scout Squads will also be in those five northerly locations and will make sure that the foot soldiers do not make an attempt to cross the river on foot. It is my belief that when these leaders suddenly see a relatively large defensive line at the crossing and see the bridges are gone, they will halt and send word to the Emperor. Here at the coastal road where the Emperor is expected, we must make it seem that we are more formidable than expected so that he will withdraw his more northerly foot soldiers to come down to his aid."

"Now for the battle plans. At the Mio River, on both sides of the river are many vineyards — the trees have long been cut down for shipbuilding, I'm told. Wherever the battlefield is located, that area is going to be trampled and crushed. Thus, we will do battle on Barcella's side. What will we be facing? The most dangerous item that the enemy has is the war chariot. Hence, the topmost priority for all Protectors is the destruction of those vehicles long before they can close to battle. If not, we will be cut to pieces. I know, I've seen that happen before."

"From everything we've learned from their previous attacks, the main thrust will be done by their foot soldiers, with the cavalry behind them. Whenever a group of soldiers needs support, the cavalry charges through them and eliminates the threat. Hence, we can expect their cavalry to be stationed somewhat behind the foot soldiers. We must take advantage of this."

"The foot soldiers all carry huge shields, which offset our archer's abilities to rain down a decisive death blow. We will not be able to fake them out as we did back in New Barq, where we were able to get them to all turn their backs to the archers. However, the cavalry do not have any shields. Further, they have never seen longbows in action. Thus, we wait and allow the foot soldiers to come within short bow range before our short bow regiments open fire. This they will be expecting. What they will not be expecting are the longbows! All longbows open fire at the cavalry *behind* the front line troops."

"Their cavalry outnumber our strike force over two to one. I am counting on your longbows to lower those odds for us before we charge them. We will give the archers plenty of time to do what they can before we charge the front lines. Once our charging forces are too close to continue firing arrows, that's when the Axemen charge. I need your Axemen to follow the path we cavalry take. We will smash a hole in their lines, you follow up and seal the breach and have at them to your heart's content."

"While we are thus engaged, all archers are to use opportunity fire. By that, I mean shoot whomever you desire as long as the shot does not endanger our own people on the battlefield. I am counting on the archery regiments to make sure that none of the enemy forces can get behind our front lines. I do not want the archery personnel involved in hand-to-hand combat if it can be avoided. Only go hand-to-hand in defense when the enemy is upon you, just as you women have been trained to do. You see, I aim to exercise all the skills that we have in the manner appropriate to those skills."

"Healing Squads, you already know your job. The d'Grange regiments, I am holding you back from the initial charge. Your task is to wait and see what develops. When you see an area of the battle that needs support, and then act as you have been trained. I'm told that many of your members have brought their bows with them, so have them start out with the other archers and lend a hand in lowering the odds. But as soon as we charge into their front line, regroup, and prepare to take whatever action you deem best. Only be careful of the Axemen; they tend to get a bit of a battle lust and might mistake you for the enemy. Just joking, Gar," I smiled at their general as though in a tease, although I really did mean it.

"Finally, what is the purpose of our main strike force? First, we must drive a hole in their foot soldier line so that the Axemen can take advantage of it. Next, we hit the remainder of their cavalry. However, our total objective once we hit their cavalry line is to bust through and kill the Emperor. The

Emperor Justinian must be killed, and the sooner that we can do it, the sooner the battle will end and the fewer lives on both sides will be lost."

"He will undoubtedly be riding in a war chariot, probably at the rear and most likely heavily guarded. I don't care how we do it; just kill that man. To make it more interesting, Elona has offered a five hundred gold piece reward for the person or persons who actually do the deed. I hope someone beats her to the task; I know she will be gunning for that man." This brought cheers and hollers from the entire group.

"Okay, now let's go over the details one more time. I have some bits of wood here so we can make a little mock layout of the battle. I want to make triply sure that each of you knows the entire plan. We cannot afford any mistakes, besides I am fond of you all and do not want anyone hurt, if it can possibly be avoided." With the help of my Circle, we laid out the battle, identifying what each item represented and went over the plans several more times, until I was convinced everyone here knew the totality of the tactics.

By July 15, all our forces were in position, the scouts out on patrols, the bridges gone, and the fake soldiers in place. Now we had nothing to do but wait. The next day, scouts began reporting the leading edge of the foot soldier legions approaching the key locations. As I expected, when they saw that the bridges were gone and a relatively large number of troops manning the makeshift wooden barricades just across the river, they halted and reported back. I had not underestimated their strength, thankfully. Perhaps three legions were at the five more northerly rim roads, fifteen legions all told. I estimated that we ought to be seeing at least another twenty-five legions here at the coastal road bridge. However, I did not know that he had lost effectively five of those to the rebel attacks within Barcella. Hence, only twenty legions of foot soldiers eventually faced our forces there.

Slowly during the next two days, we watched the buildup of enemy troops on the other side of the river. We had our dummy soldiers prominently on display, hoping to create confusing and misjudgments among the enemy leaders. On July 18, we saw the cavalry and war chariots moving into position, and I issued the order to cross the river. I must admit that we looked impressive. The nearly nine hundred strong Santi Strike Force rode in one long line across the river, while a thousand Axemen followed on foot. Over two thousand of our mounted archers trotted over behind us, followed by the five hundred from d'Grange. The remaining few hundred of Velona City Guards remained behind, helping out the Healing Squads, protecting them from harm, if possible. However, to the enemy, it appeared that an equal number of soldiers remained on the Velona side in defense.

Now we waited. Everything depended upon timing. The day was dark and grey, compliments of the druwids, who wanted access to as much lightning potential as they desired. Me, I knew that I would never again be able to bring down lightning. I could not trust myself. Fire, I could use that. I whispered to Lilly Ann, "Promise me that if anything happens to me that you will look after the twins. See that they are protected and raised well."

"Damn you, Ket. Don't talk like that. Nothing is going to happen to you. I won't let it," she said almost tearfully. Yet she added, "I promise." I felt relieved. I felt sick. In a few minutes or hours, some of these wonderful people were going to be mutilated and killed. I was their leader leading them into this mess, this war. Ultimately, I was the one responsible for all these people. They placed their faith in me, yet had I thought of everything? Had I neglected something that would become vital? Doubts crept into my mind the longer I sat motionless on my horse.

A telepathic message came from a northerly scout, saying that the soldiers there were moving south. I took that as a very good sign; only I hoped the Emperor would not wait for days until all those legions arrived. Then more messages came through that all the other legions were now on the move, heading south to join the battle. The nearest ones would join up within a day or two, but it would be a week at least before the most northerly ones got down here. Dutifully, the scouts kept track of the enemy's southerly progress, just in case they attempted a river crossing below our troops. Following orders, those at the bridges also moved southward along the river. I intended to take no chances.

Justinian met with his generals. "Well, how about this? Velona is attempting to stand and do battle outside their walls! Now we can have a real, textbook battle, gentlemen. Yes, I know that they have a large amount of troops guarding all the other rim roads. But look, that means we face a far weaker force here. We can mop up those up north later on after we take these out. Besides, this means that Velona must be nearly unguarded. Once we have eliminated this bunch, the sector will be ours for the taking."

"Standard battle formations, My Lord?" asked one general.

"Yes, I leave the details in your capable hands, generals. As usual, I will remain in the rear, watching. My small force here will come to your aide should you need it," he spoke the words that he knew the generals wanted to hear. However, he had no intention of going to their aid if trouble brewed. "Let's show this rabble how a real battle is fought!" He attempted to infuse his generals with a bit of enthusiasm, which had been lacking ever since they had left Barcella.

"But what about the Santi, My Lord. It appears that somehow magically they are not down in the Red Desert but have appeared here, or my eyes deceive me."

"Damn those Santi anyway! How on Tarra did they get here?" Justinian felt his knees become slightly weak. Suddenly he had an idea. "Generals, spread the word among your troops. I will offer a bounty of ten ducats per Santi head slain to every man who can do the deed!" The generals grinned; they knew that this would most definitely bolster the morale of their men.

Justinian watched as twenty legions fanned out to form up a long battle line. Five additional legions, his personal guards, took up a position a good distance behind the front line. Next, his ten legions of cavalry moved into position about evenly spaced behind and along the foot soldier line. Lastly, the fifty war chariots moved out in front of the armada. Their task was simple, drive into the enemy lines and let the scything blades cut everything to ribbons as the foot soldiers then followed up. At his signal, trumpeters began blowing the attack signals, and his mighty army began to move slowly toward the enemy's thin line just across the river.

The sound of the trumpets was slightly unnerving to all the waiting defenders. However, Fergus had a special trick up his sleeve that I knew nothing about. Many of the Highlanders in his force had brought their bagpipes. Suddenly, with the telltale attack sound that only a bagpipe can make, the nasally sounds of a lively Highlander war tune countered the trumpets. Our side began cheering wildly. Way to go, Fergus, I thought. It made an impressive sound, no doubt about that. Still we waited. I could sense the others growing a bit anxious, but we had to stick to the plan. The druwids needed time to eliminate those war chariots or we were doomed.

Paul was in charge of coordinating the attacks on the chariots, and dutifully, I also awaited his signal to attack them. The chariots halted, while the men extended the cutting blades on each of the wheels. This action was designed to show the enemy, us in this case, the scything blades, and just how dangerous these chariots were going to be, as they sliced a bloody path through our lines. Once they were set and moving toward us, trumpets sounded the charge, and the entire Centurion massive line began moving towards our long, extended lines.

Located on a slight rise, we looked down on the approaching Centurion army with their gleaming shields, spears at the ready, cavalry trotting behind them, and chariots charging towards us. It was impressive and a bit daunting. Blood was about to flow freely on this dark day in July. "Now!" yelled Paul, and Paulette telepathically relayed the signal to other Communicators up and down our lines, although it was not really needed. All the Guardians were simply watching for the first strike by Paul. As planned, he brought down a lightning strike on the chariot approaching his position, only he struck the horses, sending the chariot flying through the air as the horses crumpled to the ground. Yes, it was a complete destruction of the vehicle. I did not want to be the driver or the spearmen, who were cast flying through the air.

Almost simultaneously, other strikes hit the remaining chariots, while a few of us, myself included, chose to throw up a wall of flames before the oncoming horses, who either shied away suddenly, which also overturned and destroyed the chariot, or they ran into the flames and their hair burst into flames ending in a similar result. Within a couple minutes, the wreckage of the chariots of war littered the valley before us.

However, at this point the front lines of the foot soldiers had come within range of our short bows. I gave the archers the signal to fire at will. This they had expected. The well trained men, seeing the sudden flight of several thousand arrows arcing like rain drops through the air heading their way, simply dropped down on one knee and raised their shields to cover their bodies. Almost in unison the thousands of men moved, like a well-choreographed dance movement. Even from our distance, we heard the resounding thuds mixed with groans as the arrows hit shields and flesh. Admittedly, few hit their bodies.

The real target of the archers was the cavalry, who were positioned just behind these foot soldiers. While they stayed just out of short bow range, they were well within longbow range, just as I had planned. Five hundred plus arrows began to fall upon them. The shock and total surprise of these men as the metal tipped shafts sunk into their arms, heads, torsos, legs, and horses told all. As the first volley struck home and many fell off their horses wounded, their confusion rose. No bows ought to have been able to reach their position; their generals had placed them well out of short bow range. Unable to fathom what was happening, they remained more or less frozen to the spot and the next volley rained down upon them, wreaking more havoc in their lines.

With fully a third of their numbers fallen, the cavalry had no choice but to retreat, moving diagonally left and right towards the rear, reforming into two main groups. That was the time for us to move. "Strike Force, charge! Goal, kill the Emperor at the very rear!" I yelled and kicked my horse into an all-out canter. Nine hundred Santi, stretching out in a very long line, unhesitatingly followed my charge. Quickly, we all formed up in a straight line, chain mail gleaming in the dim light, our black tunics with red crosses fluttering in the wind, all galloping down the slight hill straight toward the ranks of the foot soldiers.

Behind me, I heard the bellowing voices of the charging Axemen and knew that as soon as we passed through the front lines, the Axemen would plow into the remnants. Butchery would soon follow. All these men and women had spent much of their lives practicing their combat moves. Hour by hour in the hot sun they would feint and parry and thrust, honing their skills. Here on this field this day, the amount of hours spent by everyone practicing their fighting skills would fill many men's entire lifetimes. Yet, when it came at last to the actual thing, a real combat, life was but seconds from death.

Our thundering horses hit the front line of the Centurions at a full gallop, time only for one well-chosen swing of the sword, time for only one well-placed spear and dodge. Time suddenly moved into slow motion as we hit. I saw a man plant his spear so that my horse would take it in its chest. The man on my right pivoted out of the reach of my anticipated sword swing. I leaned to my right, my horse followed my direction, narrowly missing the tip of the spear; my arm swung downward and connected with a neck nearly pulling my weapon from my hand.

The noise of our hit was like one enormous thump. Horse, men, and riders dropped out of the charge wave. Only about half of us continued the gallop. I watched in horror as Lilly Ann's horse disappeared from being immediately on my right. She went down, but there was nothing I could do about it. Instinctively, the remaining cavalry moved to close ranks into a single unit. Paul moved in on my left; he had survived the smash; that was something. On my right, Lenkova had moved into Lilly Ann's position; she held her sword pointing forward, aiming at the still distant Emperor.

Now the cavalry reacted. Both groups kicked into an all-out charge towards us. Heading straight down the center of the battlefield and straight towards the Emperor's rear position, the remnants of his cavalry rode diagonally from our left and right, intent upon intercepting us, three great masses of cavalry heading towards one final engagement. Paul ordered a "V" formation with him, Lenkova, and me at the point. I watched fascinated as our cavalry quickly moved into this new defensive position. In less than a minute, the three forces collided in one massive pile of galloping horses and men.

I kept my attention full on the Emperor, who now had turned his horses around, maneuvering his chariot to retreat from the battlefield. His guards moved to form a defensive line to stop any of us that somehow survived the onslaught. Here is where the "V" shape defense proved its worth. The enemy cavalry hit the slanted line, while we three pushed on ahead unopposed. Now it was three against the final defensive line of foot soldiers.

Paul called out, "Ket, drop in behind us." I did as he asked, while Lenkova and he moved out in front of me. "Try to jump the line," he called back to me. Then we smashed into this last line of defense. In a tumble the horses went down, spears had taken their toll. I hit the ground and did a rolling move continuing my forward momentum. Paul and Lenkova did likewise. The two took up a defensive position behind me. "Go get him," Paul cried out. "We'll watch your back."

The Emperor, looking back over his shoulder, slowed his retreat, as the threat appeared to have been stopped. Staring at him, I threw up a wall of flames before his horses. They bolted and veered, knocking the chariot over, spilling the Emperor onto the ground and trampling his two companions. He tried to run from the battlefield. Up went another wall of fire in the direction he was running. He stopped and tried to veer to the right to get around it. Wham, up came another of my flaming walls, at right angles to the other one. He wheeled and reversed direction in a panic, and I threw up yet another wall, boxing him in. The only direction he could now move was towards me. His terror-filled eyes met mine. I pointed and the fourth wall blocked him from view. He was inside a box of flames. Now I merely moved the walls close together until I felt the searing burning of the Emperor along with his utter terror and panic. The walls disappeared, leaving behind a flaming man vainly flailing about. He slumped to the ground and left his body while it still smoldered. I had now killed my second Emperor of Megalos.

"Little help back here," Paul called out. I whirled around to see Lenkova and Paul fighting off a wall of Centurions. She was providing cover for him, and he was casting spells as fast as he could. He had three walls of flames keeping many away, while Lenkova was keeping six from reaching him.

Since they could not help but witness what I had just done, I yelled to them in their own tongue, "Flee the battlefield immediately, and I will let you live. Stay and my flames will consume you." I immediately threw up another wall of flames, more like a sheet really, in their general direction. For an instant they hesitated, then turned and fled to either side of us.

"Don't know what you said to them, but I like it," panted Lenkova. She was bleeding from several wounds, as was Paul, though he had fared better because of her assistance. "If you don't mind, I've gotta sit for a spell." She collapsed onto the ground, but I was quicker and broke her fall, laying her gently on the grassy earth. "Thanks," she managed to mutter. She was exhausted and wounded. Together, we three looked back on the bloody battlefield, bodies lay everywhere in a mass confusion.

The enemy cavalry, what was left of it that was still mounted, was last seen galloping back toward Barcella. We saw isolated Centurions running for their lives in all directions away from Velona. However, the Axemen and the cavalry from d'Grange had boxed in two other legions. In self-defense, they had moved into their closed box formation, a last ditch stand against overwhelming odds. I had seen this before. Initially, twenty-five men formed each side of the square. As men fell, the closed ranks and shrunk their square. The Axemen showed no mercy and continued to splinter shields with mighty swings from their battleaxes. It was slow butchery; I was powerless to stop the berserk Axemen fighters. The d'Grange cavalry at last allowed their boxed group to flee by giving them purposely an opening toward Barcella. The offer, once made, was immediately taken by all those on that side; the others followed warily, but the cavalry did not hinder their retreat.

Andrea rode up bringing three horses. "Looks like you three need a ride," she jested. "We won the day. Ket gets the prize. How badly are you wounded? Lenkova, you look a mess! Let me help you up."

Having caught her breath somewhat, she struggled weakly to her feet. "Damn, this chain mail is something else! I ought to have been dead three times over. Thanks, I don't think I can walk just yet. Gee Ket, you look a mess too."

"Huh?" I said. Then, I noticed I was bleeding from a head wound and had several cuts on my arms, yet I had not even noticed receiving them!

"Let's get all three of you to the Healers immediately," declared Andrea. She led us back across the battlefield, moving in and around the fallen bodies. The archery regiments had now moved on down onto the field and were assisting the wounded as well as making sure the dead enemy was in fact dead. Sisterhood thoroughness was once more at work.

"Anyone seen Lilly Ann?" I kept calling out as we passed them. At last, one Sister yelled back that she was at the Healing Station. I relaxed somewhat, at least she was alive.

As we arrived at one of the Healing wagons, a friendly voice called out, "Aye, there you are laddie. Come to be patched up, I see. She's just about — ouch! Finished with me," Fergus called out. His arm was being sewn up, but otherwise my sister's husband looked all right. Again, I gave a huge sigh of relief.

After depositing us there, Andrea said, "I will see to the body count, Ket. Let you know as soon as I have it tallied." Sisterhood efficiency at work once more, I knew she would not rest until she had counted the entire field.

I insisted that Lenkova be looked after first and then Paul. Carefully, the Healer removed her chain mail and under garments, revealing the extent of her wounds. Huge black and blue welts covered her arms, legs, and chest. However, the blows had mostly been deflected by the chain mail; none were deep, none life threatening. I joined in with their praise for the chain mail.

I had just gotten three wounds sewn up and bandaged when Lilly Ann called out, "Ah there you are. Been looking for you. Nice job on the Emperor," she said. Her right arm was in a sling, broken. She had several facial cuts and bruises but she seemed unusually perky. We hugged as best we could, very gently, but only brushed lips, she had a very painful split lip.

"Got my horse," she explained, "did a roll and a wee bit of conjuring that made them think I was dead. Possum, works every time. The Axemen saved most all our lives, Ket. They hit them hard before they could kill those of us who fell during the charge. They really do go rather berserk with battle lust. I certainly never want to tangle with them!"

"Neither do I. Come on; let's get something to drink and then lend a hand, or rather your one hand, to the Healers. Many more will likely be coming in soon," I replied. While Lenkova went to find out about her regiments, we three reported to the Healer for active service.

Most of the nine hundred in the Strike Force had one or more wounds. However, those that were alive had relatively minor wounds. On Tarra, chain mail had never before been tested on such a large scale as this. The outcome was indeed incredibly impressive. In contrast, the Axemen were in the worst shape of all our fighters. Shunning most armor, their wounds often were deep and serious, and the Healers, and the rest of the Guardians that could, pitched in to save their lives and limbs. Yes, the rest of the day was spent patching up the wounded.

At supper, Andrea gave us the official body count. Ten in the Santi Strike Force had been killed. Of those, half were irreplaceable Guardians. Additionally, fifty of the Axemen and two from d'Grange had died. Of the approximately nine hundred in the Strike Force, only a handful had escaped with no wounds at all. Yet, our armor kept us from the serious wounds suffered by the Axemen, of which three hundred required substantial care after the battle. We lost three hundred horses, however, which would cripple our actions. Elona, on the other hand, discovering this, promised to supply us with new mounts.

One thousand three hundred forty-two Centurions were dead. Of their other casualties, none can say, as those fled the battlefield. The tally meant that we had eliminated at least half of their entire force here today. Since we knew that by evening the first of the northern legions would be arriving, the archery regiments, totally unwounded, took up defensive positions to protect the rest of us. Whenever a group came marching toward the battlefield, they fired a round of arrows in their general direction. Uniformly, each legion double-timed southeast toward Barcella.

Around a bonfire that evening, I summoned all the Guardians and the regimental commanders for a briefing. However, Elona beat me to it, saying, "I want to personally thank all you for having come to the aid of Velona and saving our country from the invaders. Thank you all from the bottom of my heart and from all our people." We all acknowledged her and then she said, "On a lighter note, Ket, you get the prize." She handed me a sack with the five hundred gold coins in it.

I passed it over to Lenkova, saying, "I must be honest, and share it with Paul and Lenkova, for without them keeping the fighters off me, the Emperor would have gotten away." Both appreciated the monetary gesture.

"Now to business," I said. Andrea presented the formal counts and everyone had the highest praise for the effectiveness of the chain mail, the valor of the Axemen, and the incredible efficiency of the archery regiments. Andrea broke the count down and over half had been slain by one or more arrow shots. The archers were most pleased with this detail. I had not seen them in action once we charged, but I found out that they had taken a large number of key opportunity shots to great advantage.

Near the end of the meeting, someone asked, "Tomorrow do we ride for Barcella and begin to take back the sectors from the Centurions?"

I stood up, "While there is nothing better that I would like to do, at this time that is only wishful thinking. We are few and they many and they will defend the walled city. We have no siege engines and insufficient forces to retake them. That's the plain truth. Heaven help us, I wish we could, but such an action would be folly on our part. We have at least saved Velona and have a foothold in the Arad. Now we must make sure that we can hold on to these and get the fortresses in the occupied lands strong enough that they cannot be taken. From those strong points, we can reach out to aid those in need."

How might history have been rewritten had we been able to press on with our attacks, freeing the Sea Princes none can say. Over time, a great deal of speculation has been made on this very idea. Some even say that the Dark Ages could have been avoided had we been able to pursue our victory here today.

Later that night my Circle insisted on an informal meeting. "You know we need to brace all the other fortress groups for reprisals," Lilly Ann advised. "And then there are the triremes in the Med Sea to consider. We don't dare leave them to continue to sink ships, can we?"

"The hunters could become the hunted," Paul suggested, "if we can get all Elona's caravels into a pack and take a lot of Protectors on board. We could do the job."

Paulette, who usually was silent, added, "If we don't stop them now, what's to prevent them from striking ships when we least expect or can handle it? This is the second time that Megalos has attacked these lands. What's to prevent them from rebuilding their army and trying again? Those nasty ships serve no other purpose than to sink other people's boats."

I had to agree with her assessment; it was precisely what I had already concluded. "Okay," I replied, "Paulette, you are in charge of contacting all the relevant Communicators and such. Your task is to find out how many are left and where they are located. Tomorrow I will speak with Elona about borrowing her fleet. Perhaps we can make some arrangements with her. However, gang, I am more concerned about how to protect all the forts we have started that are in the enemy sectors."

"Well, that is easy," Lilly Ann answered without any hesitation. "We get in touch with the different Santi leaders in each and have them deliver a message to the 'leader' of each sector. The message would be something like: we will not bother you, if you do not bother us. The Santi have no quarrel with you; our goal is to ensure the safety of shipments by sea and by land. You know, sort of a peace offering to ease any fears of continued attacks from us."

"Will those in charge buy this?" I asked, my mind trying to ascertain the many possible points of view that they may have and how they may react.

Lilly Ann launched into an explanation, "It eases the immediate situation, knowing that we are not intending to continue down the line, beginning with Barcella. If we do not move into that sector within say a month, they are likely to become convinced of the truth of it. Still, they may decide to take matters into their own hands and attempt to wipe out these beginnings of fortresses. If such happens, we must be prepared to launch a massive counterstrike to disabuse them and others from doing so. It is safe to say that these people only understand the use of physical force, because their reasoning has thus far been highly specious, designed only to justify their own actions."

"I wonder about their manpower," Allan said thoughtfully. "What was it about fifty years ago they took a devastating loss of men from the plague in Velona. Not long afterwards, they took another huge loss of men during the Galt invasions. They have had to wait a whole generation to rebuild up their manpower. This time, there just does not seem to be that many men fielded. Of course, that church is usurping some from the available pool of men, but overall there just didn't seem to be that many here this time. Besides, we've eliminated maybe a third of them already. As far as I can tell, they have not changed tactics since their original first invasion, despite all that has defeated them. Further, their skills did not seem as sharp as my memory has them from way back when the Lightning Circle first saw them. Maybe we will not have to face another invasion during our lifetimes." It sounded hopeful at least.

"You may have something there, Allan," I answered him. "But right now, we must do everything in our power to ensure that these new fortresses that we are building can withstand any siege. Once we have a base of power, we can work toward effective changes across the lands. Paulette, you'd better send our message to those in the fortresses. Let's give those in power in the occupied lands a chance to leave us alone." She did and we finally retired for the night.

News trickled in all the next day, while we made our rounds as Healers, changing bandages and such. Phenomenal luck was apparently on our side. All dozen of the remaining triremes were moored in the bay at Barcella, awaiting the Emperor's next orders, which now would never come. "Let's not be hasty with our ultimatum," Paul cautioned. "If we give the order to scuttle the triremes now, they may make an attempt to flee. We do not have sufficient caravels just now to stop or track them. We could lose this wonderful opportunity. Let's have our three monitor them and see if Elona is willing to take a bunch of us Protectors to sea on her ships. Once in place, then give them the ultimatum."

As usual, I followed the advice of my Protector. Elona was very willing to loan us much of her fleet, especially since their goal was to eliminate this trireme threat for good. Later that afternoon, all the remaining Protectors, including Alton and Elona, gathered on the dock and boarded twenty caravels. Each also had a Communicator; naturally, Paulette went with her brother. We waved goodbye to these brave men and women. The fate of the triremes was now in their hands.

The rest of us went back to join the Santi near the battlefield, continuing our Healing and repair operations. By now, many wagons from Velona had arrived and the confiscated armor and weapons were loaded and taken away. I suspected that the metal in the armor would be melted down and reused for other more useful purposes. The weapons would go into the armory of Velona for future use.

Bodies buried, battlefield cleaned up, weapons repaired, arrows recovered, horses mended, horses acquired, such actions occupied us for the next few days, to say nothing of the tending of the many wounded. Elona had all the armorers in Velona working on making chain mail repairs, but so many suits had been damaged that months would be required. We settled on having as many repaired as possible.

Four days after the caravel fleet sailed, the reports came back. The Centurions were notified in Barcella: scuttle the triremes in the bay or we would destroy them. Several attempted to sail out of the harbor, but quickly turned back when they spied the sheer number of caravels parked out at sea at various locations just off Barcella. Later that day, a compromise was reached. The port master did not want the ships scuttled in the bay because that would block shipping. Instead a skeleton crew was allowed to sail them out into the Med Sea and scuttle them there, sailing back in dingys. Thus, the reign of terror caused by these ramming ships of Megalos ended without our having to attack and destroy them. I believe every mariner in the Sea Princes cheered this minor success, whether occupied or not. The sinking of an ocean-going vessel was very significant to these people.

Next came shore leave. I let everyone return to Velona and covered their living expenses while they were there. The Sisters really enjoyed this opportunity to find their missing friends and companions. Lenkova spent time with her mother and father. For the non-combatant Sisters who had not joined the Santi officially, such as the leaders of the various Sisterhoods, this was a particularly difficult time. Forced to leave their homes and most possessions behind, they found themselves in a strange city. More importantly, their tightly knit group was gone, disbanded officially.

Elona and I stepped in with solutions. First, I made it clear that they could still join the Santi if they desired to do so. Elona suggested that those that did not want to join the Santi could start up a Velona Sisterhood, one that would merge all the other sector's groups into one single unit. This appealed to many of them, and they readily accepted. She even went so far as to give them a building for their headquarters, selling it below the cost of its construction. Knowing that once word spread that a new Sisterhood was being formed in Velona, many of the Sisters who had joined the Santi organization might wish they could drop out and join with their Sisters. Thus, I made it very clear that anyone who wanted out could do so immediately with no repercussions. Surprisingly, very few jumped ship.

Next, I had to deal with Elona's biggest concern, how to protect her borders after the Santi left. At any time, she expected that the Centurions might regroup or that the Holy Paladins might arrive on her doorstep en mass. Allan suggested a series of Santi Fortresses uniformly spaced along the border with Barcella would provide the kind of protection she desired. This went well with our group because then many of the women could be relatively near their old friends in the newly formed Sisterhood. To help, Elona offered to help defray the cost of the ten proposed stone fortifications along her border with Barcella. Thus, by the middle of August, the sites had been found and initial construction of the outer walls began.

The middle of August also ended our time of recovery and reorganization. We received an urgent message from John Henry on August 16. The Galts had finally invaded Southway, having conquered all the other kingdoms to the east of us. Percival was besieged with over two thousand Galts. John Henry's message was simple: come at once!

As soon as I relayed the information to the others, everyone wanted to leave immediately. However, we needed to arrange for the delivery of supplies and such. Fortress d'Grange not only offered their five hundred fighters once more, but also they volunteered to handle the acquisition and deliver of the supplies for us. This way, our entire group could ride hard up the coast to d'Grange, on to Mont Blanc, and then to Percival's aid. The entire Santi force left Velona on August 17, moving at a rapid pace for Fortress d'Grange.

Five days later, we galloped through the streets of d'Grange. Huge crowds cheered and waved banners and flags as we passed through, which could not help impress all of us, especially the Sisters, who were not used to having such good will from the common folks. Another two hard days riding and we approached Mont Blanc. Here we paused for the night. It was the first time that many of the Sisters with us had ever seen the Fortress at Mont Blanc.

Yes, they were very impressed with Fortress d'Grange, what little they could see of it as they rode through the city. Here at Mont Blanc, the number of buildings, the varied architecture, and the large size of the complex definitely made strong impressions. Most gaped at the two tall towers. Further, the walls were much more solid than those of the Sea Prince cities.

Now the Santi members could more readily visualize what the final products of all our new constructions abroad would look like when they were done. They were impressed.

While we spent some time with John Henry and his Moon Circle discussing the situation we were about to face, Lilly Ann and I took this opportunity to spend as much time as we could with the twins. Both of us longed for these conflicts to end so we could enjoy the simple pleasures of life, including raising the twins. We found them healthy and much larger in size than when we left them, almost a year ago. I really hated to part with them the next morning, however, but we had to rescue Percival in Middleton, Southway.

Chapter 37 Of Lenkova and Illanovich

The bright sun shone down on us as we rode along the well-traveled road, northward toward Middleton. The dog days of summer were upon us, hot and humid. Lenkova trotted up to me to have a word with me. "You know that I am going to have to kill my own brother, don't you? I want to be the one to do it, please, Ket. I know he is acting evil, but he is still my brother." She valiantly withheld tears. If her brother had to die, she did not want it done by some stranger's hand.

"If it comes to that, Lenkova, I promise that I will let you be the one to end it," I replied, hoping I could live up to my promise. However, something she said made me rethink our whole strategy. John Henry and Percival had decided that the best thing we could do would be to charge into their encirclement camps and attack. Meanwhile, Percival would bring his cavalry out of his fortification and charge as well. Visions of yet another bloodbath all around filled my mind, unbidden.

Could there possibly be another way out of this mess, I wondered. If there was, I only had hours to figure it out. Middleton was only a good thirty-six hour ride north of Mont Blanc, if you pushed the horses. I reflected all that George had told me; after all, he knew these people better than anyone else, having spent his entire life spying on them for the Guardians. Something he said stuck out in my mind, "These are a very superstitious people." Yet, there was something else he had said, something that Lenkova had nearly said a moment ago, but I just could not put my finger on what that connection might be.

I remembered the last time I had done major battle with the Galts. I had just lost my young body to an arrow in the forehead, and with Alabaster's aid and a renegade druwid, we three brought down a rain of lightning strikes that killed nearly a thousand in their war party. But that was a long time ago, three lifetimes, in fact. After that incursion, the Galts left the Greenway alone for a very long time, choosing instead to attack first the Arad and then the Sea Princes before attempting to conquer the Southlands and Megalos itself, which they very nearly did accomplish. Yet, during that war, Mikhailovich Strokova had purposely left the Greenway alone, intending to attack us only when he had all the rest of the inhabited world under his control.

However, why did he decide to leave his next door neighbor alone for so long? Surely, this was the key that I was seeking. Suddenly it flashed by in my mind: the Galts were convinced that there were Evil Witches residing in the Greenway. George told me about how they told such stories to their children. Convinced that there were Evil Witches in the Greenway was why Mikhailovich Strokova did not attack us back then. Could I make some use of this fear now?

These Evil Witches were in fact us Guardians with our spells. Now I began to understand what had been happening these past few years with the Galts. Somehow, Illanovich had convinced them that there were no Evil Witches in the Greenway. Indeed, they had now conquered all the Greenway except the last two kingdoms, Southway and Calgary. These petty kingdoms had driven out all us Guardians a number of years ago. Thus, the Galts encountered nothing remotely like an "Evil Witch" as they attacked these kingdoms.

I sent for Lenkova. When she came trotting up, I said, "Lenkova, I believe that there may be a way for us to drive the Galts and your brother out of here without killing him." Her eyes were slightly red. I suspected she had been crying, although she hid it well from her companions. Now, she perked up, her eyes brightened and she looked outward instead of inward.

"How?" was all she could manage to say.

"The problem I am facing is that Galt is one of the languages that I am not very fluent in. Do you perhaps speak it?" I asked.

"Well, yes, not very good, but for a time we traded with some Galt traders. I could speak enough to get by, why?"

"I need a good translator. The best one is way down in the Arad at the moment, George." I then outlined the basic idea that I had formulated. The details remained to be worked out. Lenkova promised to act as translator and I let her fall back to her regiment while I conferred with my Circle.

Halfway there, I called a complete halt to our hasty ride, allowing Paulette time to contact Percival and his defenders to alert them to the total change in strategy. Meanwhile, I called for a large conference meeting, pulling together all the Guardians and all the other leaders down to the individual squad level. We made a rather large gathering indeed. I looked over our valiant bunch. Bandages were still the most prevalent item among us, but the will to succeed ran strong in all of us.

"I am changing the strategy completely. If I am successful, the Galts will leave without a fight." I paused to let this sink in to their minds, which it slowly did.

Lenkova spoke for many when she exclaimed, "How can this be?"

"The Galts are a superstitious people. Long ago, a thousand invaded the Greenway when it was totally under the protection of the Guardians, when we were welcomed nearly everywhere. Alabaster, Erline, and I brought down such a wave of lightning bolts that we killed at least a thousand of them outright. Ever since that time, the Galts were convinced that Evil Witches lived within the Greenway. When the Barbarian Invasion came a number of years ago, when the Galts very nearly conquered all Tarra, Mikhailovich Strokova purposely left the Greenway alone, because he too feared the Evil Witches. Actually, I added to those fears because I had to use some spells on some of his men when my family and I were fleeing the Arad. Unfortunately, somehow Illanovich has convinced his people that there are no Evil Witches in the Greenway. This has been proven to them at least ten times, because no Guardian lives within the ten kingdoms that he has already conquered. By now, they must be convinced that all that was just superstition, tales parents tell their children to scare them into obeying."

"I plan to change all that. Let's give them back their Evil Witches. Here's what I want to try to do," and I outlined the basic idea that I had developed. No one could spot any real flaw in it, knowing that if it failed, we would just revert to the original plan of massive attack. This time, everything hinged upon not taking the enemy by surprise. In fact I sent our scouts out ahead to alert the Galts to our coming. If my plan was to work, I needed the Galts to know that a large army was about to descend upon them.

Two hours later, our scouts began reporting back, the enemy outlying sentries had been sighted. While the scouts hated to do it, they made themselves highly visible to these men, pretending not to see them, and continued toward the city. As expected the enemy guards quietly retreated, bringing word of our arrival. A few miles from Middleton, the scouts had to halt. Ahead lay the outskirts of the enemy's encirclement camps, rounded, dome-like, hide huts dotted the valleys, while guard posts stood on the higher ground. Horses seemed to be tethered everywhere. Over two thousand Galts had besieged the fortress at Middleton.

Our scouts watched from a safe distance as the normally quiet camp sprang to life, preparing to meet this unexpected new threat coming up from the south. So far, all was going according to my wishes.

"Wake up Illi, Mica, trouble is coming!" Mik Radstov yelled urgently into the Czar's hut. Sentries had just reported seeing the advance line of enemy scouts coming up from the south. For Illi, this whole campaign this summer had been utterly boring. Ride into an unprotected town, issue his demands, repeat it over and over until at least they would reach the local wooden fortress housing the king of this land. There, they would wreak some havoc, usually involving lighting some fires to convince the king that they were serious, and then presiding over the peace talks, presenting what the Czar demanded of this new conquered land. Boring, all of it boring. Yes, the first time with the kingdom just west of the Elbe River, Czar Illi had found it most interesting. After the tenth time of it, Illi was far beyond merely bored. He had even toyed with the idea of heading home, leaving all the conquering to Mik and the other clan leaders. However, Mica pointed out that the Czar and Czarina's place was with the army. "The conquered just have to see us, their new rulers, you see." Well, he didn't see, but went along with his lovely wife.

"Honey, don't forget your sword," she reminded him, as he started to leave the hut.

Sheepishly, he said, "Thanks. I wonder how serious this is. Maybe it is just an attempt to worry us." Outside, everyone scrambled to saddle horses, preparing for some unknown threat. Most of the tents were in the valley, while their sentries stood guard upon the nearby ridges or hills. They had camped about a quarter mile from the stone walled fortress city. The brown limestone walls entirely encircled the town and stood ten feet tall. On the inner side, walkways allowed the defenders to stand and peer between the periodic barbicans, firing arrows as needed. Mik was careful to keep everyone out of short bow range of the walls.

Within the city, several similar stone buildings rose to considerable heights, perhaps the most impressive structures that Illi had yet seen anywhere in the Greenway. One was supposed to house the king and his court, but the taller one appeared to be some kind of guard or observation tower. From the tower top, anyone could look down and see the entire encircling camp of the Czar's forces.

Someone had their two horses saddled; Illi helped Mica aboard and then mounted. His court guards immediately rode over to join him. Mik had insisted that twenty men always accompany the Czar and Czarina. They rode up the nearest ridge where the others were heading, on the southern edge of their camp amid a large stand of oak trees.

He found Mik and moved nearer to his army leader and friend. "What's up?"

Mik pointed to the next hilltop due south along the road. "There, on yonder hill about a mile off, see the riders. And over there and there. Our sentries have counted perhaps a hundred riders, all armed, and wearing those strange cloaks. We cannot tell for sure who or what they are from this distance."

"They do look like fighters," Mica commented. "Surely a hundred will not be a problem for us." After a pause she added, "They seem to be waiting for something."

"I'm playing it safe," Mik told Illi. "I'm issuing full battle formations, just in case there are a lot more of them. You two stay here for the time being, until the lines have formed, and you can then find your position." Illi and Mica always stayed in the very rear, Illi was not a fighter, rather a leader who allowed Mik, who had such skills, to lead his army. Unlike his father, Illi was not a good fighter nor at tactics, preferring to allow others who were to lead. Mik had more than proved himself capable not only to Illi, but to all the other clan leaders. Had they not thus far conquered ten kingdoms without losing very many men in the process?

Separating the two hills was a green valley, dotted with late summer crops waving in the gentle afternoon breeze. These were the local Middleton crops, usually tended by farmers who lived within the walled city. The standard battle formations of which Mik spoke consisted of groups of twenty-five men. Mik commanded eighty such battle groups, which took up positions three groups deep along the far edge of the hill. Illi and his guards at last moved in behind the center of the line. Mik's group was in the front with two other groups separating him and Mik. The line formation took nearly twenty minutes to form fully in attack readiness.

While all this movement and preparations for a battle were clearly visible to the distant riders, they took no action of their own. They seemed to be doing nothing but watching the Galts. Illi suddenly thought he saw a dust cloud even further in the distance. Mik turned to point it out to Illi. Both men knew those signs; a large number of mounted people were coming, most likely a small army, maybe even a cavalry army.

Mik fell back to Illi's position. "I don't like this. Looks like cavalry is coming and a lot of them."

"Looks like our dust clouds when we move," Mica noted. Illi didn't like the sound of this.

"Where are they coming from? Who could they be? From Calgary? Do you suppose that Calgary is trying to come to the rescue of this kingdom, what's it called again?" Illi asked.

"Southway," Mica answered him, a little peeved that Illi could not remember the kingdom's name. He would be lost without her, she thought.

"That must be who they are," Mik agreed, "though so far no other kingdom has ever come to the aid of the one we were attacking. Isn't this Calgary city supposed to be southwest of here? These are coming from the south not the west."

"Well it is an army all right! Look there!" Mica exclaimed, slightly worried. Riders by the dozens were arriving atop the distant hills and ridges in force! They streamed out in a long line, just as long as the Galt lines were. All were mounted; all wore similar cloaks or tunics, blackish with a bit of perhaps red. Now the late afternoon sun began reflecting off bits of metal here and there on the distant riders.

"They must be wearing some form of armor. Look at the reflecting light, particularly off their arms. Damn, their numbers must be close to ours, maybe larger!" cried Mik in surprise, although there was no way to get an actual count from this distance.

"How can this be?" cried Illi. "We were told that Calgary had at most a couple thousand city guards and almost no cavalry. Yet, these riders look akin to us; they must be cavalry. How can this be? Were we lied to on purpose?"

"Look there, maybe we are about to find out!" exclaimed Mik. Six riders had appeared on the road heading down the distant hill, moving slowly towards them. One carried a white flag. "Parley. Whoever they are, they want to talk first. That is a good sign. Perhaps we can glean who and what we are up against here so I can take a more effective approach in the coming battle," Mik commented. "Send for Rostov!" he barked his order. He knew that he needed his Greenway translator immediately.

"We will go with you to the parley. The Czar must be seen as being the one ultimately in charge here," Illi said. Mica would go to; nothing could squelch her curiosity, and she always went where he did. Protocol, she would always say. Mik picked two of his trusted guards to accompany them. Soon Rostov came galloping over to Mik. He did not need orders to know that his services were once again needed by his Czar. Someone handed Mik a white cloth on a pole, and he handed it to one of his guards to carry. The six then started out down their side of the hill, intending to hold the parley about half way between the two hills in the middle of an oat field.

Evidently, this was the same idea their opponents had, for they reached the midpoint and halted on the road, awaiting the arrival of the Czar of the Northern Steppes. A few minutes later, the two groups sat facing one another. Now all could see that these were indeed well armed cavalry, wearing chain mail armor making them very tough opponents indeed. But who were they and what did they want. Half of them were women, Mica noted, although one looked like a very tough fighter and another, though armored, stayed well back of the other five. All them wore a black tunic with a red cross on their front and back, prominently displayed. Conclusion: some kind of religious warriors, perhaps, Illi thought.

The one very young man with the very long flaming red hair spoke with a horrible Galt accent. Another man to his far left spoke fairly good Galt and was obviously translating for him. "Greetings. I am Ket Bethany, leader of the Santi del Dio. We wish to speak to the leader or leaders of the Galts from the Northern Steppes. I understand that he may be Illanovich Strokova."

They are certainly well informed, thought Illi. "I am Czar Illi Strokova, of whom you speak. This is the Czarina Mica, my Field Commander, Mik Radstov. What is this Santi and what is it that you wish to say to the Czar?" He tried to keep it simple and his translator echoed his words in a fair rendition of the Greenway dialect.

Ket bowed to Illi as though it would be an acceptable greeting for someone of his rank. "Thank you for meeting with us. This is my wife, Lilly Ann, my Protector Paul, and his sister Paulette behind us. She is relaying what we say back to the others on the hills behind us. And she you should know, your sister, Lenkova." I purposely hinted at unseen powers but ended with what might be a bit of a shock to Illanovich.

"Sister?" he said totally unnerved and surprised. He recovered quickly, "You are a very long way from home, Sister!" He said that last word in a very derogatory manner.

"Hello brother," Lenkova replied, biting her lip. She wanted to jump on top of him and beat some sense into him, but bit her lip instead.

I replied, "The Sisterhood is no more. The Centurions have conquered much of the Sea Princes and have disbanded that organization. It no longer exists, as you knew it. Many of their fighters have banded together with us Guardians of the Greenway; together we have formed the religious order known as the Santi del Dio. We have just returned from Velona where we ended the Centurion assault on Velona, killing half of their army outright. I personally killed their Emperor Justinian. They will be attacking no other lands for quite some time. You need have no fear that the Centurions will be invading the Northern Steppes from the Arad. We now control New Barq and the road into the Southlands."

"The Arad Raiders and Qa Fahdi are also our allies, and together we guarantee you that the Centurions will not be bothering your southern borders. We are the ones who guarantee peace in this section of Tarra." I thought that was a good start, knowing that the mention of the Arad Raiders now being allied with us would strike home with them, since they had already made a similar bargain with Qa Fahdi. I added, "Velona and d'Grange remain free and unoccupied by the Centurions of Megalos and will remain so."

"So the rumors we've heard that the Centurions were actually defeated is true, then. How is it that you know Qa Fahdi? I am curious," Illi replied. I detected a note of curiosity mingled with his covert hostility.

"The Crusader Army had killed or wounded nearly four thousand Centurions during a month long battle north of New Barq. The Santi attacked and eliminated another two thousand Centurions marching up the road from the Southway, thus denying them their expected re-enforcements. Then, we took New Barq, driving all remaining Centurions out into the Red Desert. Since their numbers were reduced, Qa attacked the remaining Centurions, killing them all. However, many of his men were severely wounded during that daylong battle. The Santi are known as the best Healers on Tarra. We healed all his wounded men, women, and horses. We have become good friends in the process."

My explanation seemed to satisfy him. "You must have a large army if you are able to defeat so many Centurions." Illi made a statement that was really a question. I took his intent.

"Yes, we currently number over three thousand, all mounted. Over two thousand are superb archers, some of which can send an arrow into my hand from yonder hill," I pointed to the line of archers on the distant hill. "We are well armored, which is one reason that we had so few dead in our recent battle with the Centurions. May I give you a demonstration of our archers?"

Part of my strategy was to convince him of our superiority. "No arrow can fly that distance!" Illi protested.

"I'd like to see it," Mica added, just in case her husband refused. She knew that no arrow could possibly go that far. While Illi might not call his bluff, she would.

"At this extreme distance, hitting a target is naturally more difficult. For your safety, I wish my people to act as a shield between the archer and you, if we may?" Lilly Ann, Paul, and Lenkova moved their horses between Illi and me. Paulette and the translator move aside some distance. "Okay Paulette, signal our archer." Illi and the others watched Paulette, but she made no movement or visible signal, only saying it is done.

A lone archer raised her longbow, making sure that we could see her, then released it. Her arrow arced high into the air, then leveled off and descended. We had agreed that she would aim for me, trying to hit me with the shot. Of course, at this extreme distance a slight miss would be magnified. Indeed, I needed to move my horse a couple feet to the left and then deftly caught the arrow mid-flight, before it could hit anyone or anything. Thus, our skill and prowess was entered into Illi's computations. We turned around, resuming our facing positions, and I handed the arrow to Illi, "Here, you may keep this as a souvenir."

They had just witnessed two impossible feats, from their perspective. None of their archers could fire over such a distance, not even close, let alone with that accuracy. Further, I had actually caught the arrow in my hand, another impossible feat. The startled and amazed looks on all their faces told me that I had succeeded. I added for emphasis, "We have thousands of such archers." I did not explain that not all were equipped with longbows, however.

Mica finally spoke, "That was just incredible. You can catch arrows?"

"Oh yes, many of the Santi can catch arrows mid-flight. I figured you folks can do that trick too." I added.

Mica caught herself from saying, "Hardly!" Instead, she said, "That is a very long distance to shoot an arrow," and left it at that.

Mik then spoke, "If we may ask, what is your purpose in coming here?" He was being very direct and to the point, as I would expect from the field commander of an army.

"Southern Arad, Velona, d'Grange, West Reach, Calgary, and the Southway are under the protection of the Santi. We heard that you were besieging Middleton and came to rescue them." I gave an equally blunt answer. "However, before you make any decisions, there is one other thing that you need to know." I paused before I said, "I believe your word for us is Evil Witches. The Santi have a large number of these Evil Witches. However, your term for us is not very accurate. You are looking at five right now. Only your sister is not one. We are not evil, but that depends upon your viewpoint doesn't it? If you are attacking us or someone we are protecting with our powers, then yes, I can see how your term applies. However, those that we are protecting may call us Good Witches, since we are saving their lives. Matter of viewpoint, really."

As I was talking, I watched their faces pale, especially Illanovich's. I knew I hit a very touchy spot, although I did not know the true depth of their hidden fears. "Will you allow me another harmless demonstration, Czar Illanovich?"

Mica replied even before Illi had the chance, "Oh, please do!" She wanted to see for herself just what these legendary Evil Witches might be able to do. She fell for my master plan wholeheartedly.

"Please do not be alarmed. We will not harm anyone with the demonstration," I added. "It is a sunny day, so do not expect lightning bolts, though perhaps we could summon a storm, if you insist. Instead, allow me to show you how we eliminated the Centurion war chariots. Paulette, if you will give the signal please." She smiled and made the contact with the waiting minds. Suddenly, fifty walls of vertical flames appeared in a long line across the valley floor, some distance from all of us. Unfortunately, they began scorching the green fields, and I halted the demonstration before anything caught fire. The loss of some crops would be a small price to pay for ending the siege.

Mica's face altered between utter terror and complete fascination, denoting both the awe and the fear our powers brought. "Yes, as you can tell from the burn patch on the ground, it is real fire. One more demonstration, I'll make a wall of ice appear here." I did so, placing it between us. "Go ahead and feel it, punch it. Like ice, it will shatter." One by one, they did touch it and were amazed.

"This would be handy on very hot days," Mica volunteered, seeing numerous uses for conjuring ice in the hot dog days of summer.

Finally, to drive my point home, I added, "Many years ago when we Guardians were protecting all the Greenway, over a thousand Galts invaded and began conquering our lands. There Guardians fought back using lightning bolts from the sky, killing many of them. If lightning is needed, we can summon a storm." I did not add that action would take the concentrated efforts of many and over several days to accomplish.

"My point, Czar Illanovich, is that your siege of Southway is now over, one way or another. Please note that we are only protecting Southway and Calgary. All the other kingdoms that you have conquered remain yours. We are not currently protecting them nor have any plans to do so in the near future. We are asking nothing of you except to leave Southway, preferably peacefully. Honestly, we do not really want to fight you and your army. Yet, if fight we must, we will use all that we command to succeed. We would rather settle for a truce, allowing you to retain the other kingdoms, just leave Southway and Calgary alone."

I had done what I had intended. Revealing that we had numerous Evil Witches and demonstrating the flame spells in such a manner that all two thousand of his men could witness it; I had laid our powers out on the table, so to speak. Every fighter there would know what they would have to fight and see how awful it would go for them. Even if by chance the Czar would not see reason, then every fighter would have an instinctive fear of any Santi, which would drastically lower their morale in a fight.

"What say you, Czar Illanovich, shall we have a mutual truce between us?" Lilly Ann had been secretly coaching me so that I made it seem as if two equals were making a bargain, allowing him to save face.

Illanovich swallowed; he had lost his voice utterly since the flames appeared. His voice was slightly squeaky, "Yes, a mutual truce would be in the best interests to all of us. I have your promise not to interfere in the other ten kingdoms?"

"Yes, you have my word we will not interfere there. If one of those kings should one day come to us and ask for our aid, then I will notify you in writing of our intent long before we take any action. I doubt that those kings will ever do so, because they have long ago forced us out of their lands, and we are not eager to go back there. It's rather like a man who continually kicks his horse. The horse may finally decide to have nothing to do with that man."

"Yes, the horse would be the wiser of the two," Illanovich replied with a grin. "Then, we have a truce." I extended my hand, and we shook on it.

"How long do we have to depart? It may take us a few days," Illanovich asked.

"We are in no real hurry. That is fine. In the meantime, perhaps Lenkova and you would like some private time together." It was a suggestion.

After all, they were brother and sister. Lenkova had resolved to kill him if need be; now I gave her another option. Many things in this world are in fact just a matter of viewpoint. Perhaps Illanovich was not the monster for which she took him.

"Sister, you are welcome to come to my hut and join my wife for dinner tonight," Illanovich replied, extending a peace offering. I suspected that he wanted to ply her with questions to gain more key information about the Santi. I would give that to him for her sake.

Lenkova softened a little, "Well only if I can bring my husband with me. He is an Evil Witch, you know." Mica's eyes brightened at this prospect of actually meeting one close up in her hut.

Mica replied, "Oh please do bring him! I'd love to meet him." Well that settled that detail; she now could not refuse. With Andre with her, I need not worry about them being poisoned; he could detect that easily. Even if they did harm the two, it was obvious that our retribution would be swift and exceedingly deadly as well as one sided. "Come about dark, please. Just ask anyone where the Czar's hut is located. We'll be expecting you two." Mica seemed very pleased with the arrangement, though Illanovich seemed much more reticent and reserved. I suspected these two had much to discuss.

"It's been a pleasure meeting you, Czar, Czarina, Mik," I said. "I guess I had best return to the others and let them know there will be no fighting today, just making camp instead." He grinned, and we parted, heading back the way we came. Paul, however, kept one eye out for trouble, but none came.

On the slow ride back up the hill, Lilly Ann commented, "Very well done, Ket. I'll make a Judger out of you yet!" She was rightly proud of our accomplishment today, a deadly war completely averted. Paulette relayed the news to John Henry and to Percival, who was waiting anxiously inside the fortified city. Once we got back to the others, everyone wanted to hear the news, which Lilly Ann retold in detail for me. Everyone gave me a round of applause and cheers. Andrea actually gave me a hug!

Lenkova was taking the transition rather difficultly. To Andre, she exclaimed, "I was ready to kill him. I don't get this viewpoint thing that Ket kept harping about. Now I have to go have supper with him! Maybe I'll have to kill him after we eat. Maybe he'll try to kill us so we can retaliate. Do you suppose he'll try something like that?"

"No dear, after Ket's performance, he knows his entire army would be utterly decimated if he did. He values his life and very likely that of his wife. She is rather pretty, don't you think?" Lenkova gave a huff and went to setup their campsite.

As dinnertime approached, Lenkova rechecked her weapons, made sure she had her daggers in her boots at the ready. She straightened her chain mail and tunic. Finally, she did brush her hair slightly. If anyone tried anything, she intended to be the one who finished it! Andre brought up their two horses, and together they rode the short distance into the heart of the Galt camp. Evidently, they were expected. As they approached, sentries directed them toward the Czar's hut. Others even took their horses and tied them to the draglines along with their horses.

The first thing Lenkova really noticed was the horses. Galt horses were shorter that those of the Sea Princes and the Greenway, also hairier, an adaption to the colder winter climates. "Good behavior dear," Andre whispered into her ear as they walked up to the hut. The aroma of fresh baked bread drifted from the hide hut. Another sentry at the entrance announced their arrival and opened the flap so they could enter.

Inside the domed hut, Illanovich, Mica, and Mik were waiting for them. "Come on in," Mica exclaimed cheerily. "I do hope we don't need a translator. We promise to speak clearly and slowly."

"That will do fine," Andre replied. "We do speak your language a little." The inside was actually larger than both had expected, a small cooking stove was opposite the door. The center held a low table and various furs and hides lay on the ground around it. Obviously, one had to sit on the furs to eat.

"Oh, just pile your swords by the door. We find it's terribly awkward to sit with a sword strapped to your side. Yes, there by ours is fine," Mica continued in her Czarina hostess manner. They took off their swords and laid them beside the others near the door. Lenkova was doubly glad that she had her trusty boot daggers at the ready.

"Hope you all like venison and hare. I made some of Illi's favorite bread and there is some local corn as well. Oh yes, and plenty of strong sassafras tea. Just sit anywhere. Lenkova watched Illi and purposely sat opposite him, Andre sat on her right, Mik placed himself between Andre and Illi, leaving room for Mica next to Illi and Lenkova. Obviously, Mik was also acting as a bodyguard as well as Illi's closest friend.

She served up the meal and took her place. Noticing the stiffness that both Illi and Lenkova displayed, she gaily opened up the conversation as they ate. "Have you noticed our horses? I am a breda, a breeder of some of the fastest and hardiest horses in all the steppes." She went on about her horses, and both Lenkova and Andre soon became fascinated hearing about them. Horses were a necessity of life for both, and this was a topic they could enjoy.

Illanovich, on the other hand, had been worrying all afternoon about what to say to his sister. He'd abandoned her when they were barely in their teens. Well, perhaps not abandoned, he just didn't take her with him, because she liked living with those interminable Sisters. In reality, he had no idea what had become of her, but now he saw that she was clearly a fighter of some renown. Certainly, she was as well built for combat as Mik, and she acted the role. Did she still think that he had abandoned her or did she hate him for leaving him or did she hate him because he had invaded lands that she obviously was protecting? For a fleeting moment, he wondered what had become of his mother. They said that the Sisterhood had been destroyed; did that mean she had been killed? Serve her right if she had, he thought.

Yet, all this talk of horses put everyone else in a communal mind; it was something on which both sides could agree. Agreeing increased their level of communication and their liking of each other, despite apparently being on opposite sides. Eventually, he did relax; the discussion had at least calmed his fears and apprehensions. Finally, during a slight lull after Mica had told about how her breed line had performed at the last troka, Illi spoke up.

"When I last saw you, you were twelve. Guess a lot has happened since then. As you know I hated living in those dank caves with all those women. I lit out for the steppes, our ancestral home." He emphasized that last, as if she should have done so as well, as Strokova's child. "I was appalled at what I found. Our people," once more he stressed the word our, "were slowly dying. They had mounds of gold and silver, so much so that they could no longer move their camps! We have always been nomads, seeking newer pastures for our horses and game for our tables. Forced to stay in one location as they were, the grass was gone and so was the game. Our people were slowly starving to death."

"I convinced Mik here to abandon the gold that you cannot eat and moved his clan to fresh lands. The clan's recovery was miraculous. Within a year, everyone was strong and alive once more, including our horses. We found green grass and plenty of game. Slowly, one by one, I convinced the other clans to do the same. With Mik's help, I reclaimed our birthright; I am their Czar. Since then, I have led all our people out of the arms of death back into live and vitality once more."

"With Mik's help, we drove the Axemen, who were plundering our villages, completely out of the steppes. They have not been back since. Still, we needed food to survive. Since no one was giving us food and the Greenway has an abundance, we came here in force to obtain the food of life. We have taken no gold, looted no homes, and raped no women, unlike our ill-informed father. I have avoided all the mistakes that he made. We now have ten kingdoms that regularly send us grain and dried foods so that our families may survive the long, cold steppes winter. No longer is the name Strokova associated with death, pain, loss, and destruction, but now it stands for life and vitality." He finally finished, thinking for a moment if he had left out any critical detail in his summary. He added, "You see, dad raped, robbed, and pillaged, leaving destruction in his wake. What good is a mountain of gold? When you are starving out on the steppes, it is a heavy weight that pulls you under the river's water to drown."

As she listened to his story, a change gradually came over Lenkova. Her intense hatred began dissolve, like the sugar in her tea. He had actually rescued the entire Galt nation from near death by starvation and done it without the use of force or coercion. In spite of her earlier feelings, she found that she could at least admire some of what he had accomplished. Driving the Axemen out interested her, since she knew just how powerful these men actually were. "How did you manage to force the Axemen to leave?" she asked, the fighter in her greatly desired to know this. Mik explained what they had done; grizzly as the details were, it had worked.

Andre then stated, "You know, you could have asked someone for assistance with your shortage of food."

"Who?" Illanovich replied tersely. "The Arads are in just as bad a shape as we are, maybe worse. The Greenway kingdom on our border could care less and probably wanted us dead anyway."

"You do have a point. It would have been nigh on impossible for you to travele all the way to Mont Blanc. However, I'm sure that if there had been some way for those there to know about the starvation, they would have likely found some way to help. I'm not so sure that the folks in Zargarb would have helped, however. I think many hold a long-standing grudge against the Galts. You can understand why."

"You see my point," Illanovich declared flatly, welcomed to see that others outside his land agreed with him, if only in part.

"Yet, times change, Illanovich," Andre continued. "At this point in time, do you realize that a small bag of gold will buy you a whole wagon load of grain from the dealers in the larger towns of the Greenway, especially at harvest time?"

Illi shot a shocked look at Andre. "What? Do these farmers have some way of eating gold?"

"No, no, not eat. It is merely a more convenient means of exchange. The grain dealers accept a bag of gold for a wagon load of grain. In turn, the dealers then pay a portion of the gold to the farmer who grew the grain. The farmer then trades some of the gold to town merchants to buy dried food that he had no time to make himself. He trades for new shovels and rakes. Often, they trade it for shoes and even for some new draft horses. They find it far more convenient to carry around a small sack of gold coins to trade rather than a basket of eggs or a pail of goat's milk." Andre explained, keeping it as simple as possible.

"Really?" Mik interjected. "Trade gold for food supplies? Who ever heard of that?" Clearly, the Galts had never considered this possibility. Gold was for decoration and ornamentation, though sometimes they had swapped gold for a particular horse or saddle.

"Yes, but something else you should consider, especially as Czar, Illi," Andre added, falling into the pattern of address the other Galts used. "Suppose you had two horses. Both are nearly identical, good, strong, fine horses, you know, no real difference between them. Now one horse you have personally raised from a colt, or perhaps like Mica, you have bred her as well. The other horse you simple took away from some other person. I ask you, Illi, which horse would you rather lose? The one you raised or the one you took?"

"What a silly question," Illi declared. "The one I took, of course. What's the point?"

"People value what they themselves create, not what they take from someone else. It is true with food and grain. If your people traded with these kingdoms for the grain and supplies that you want, your own people would value that grain and supplies far more than they do now. It's something to think about as leader of your people. We have found that taking things without giving something of comparable value in return sets people on the path toward eventually losing their own self-respect."

Mica, listening to all this complicated talk about gold and grain, grasped what Andre was saying. "I see the wisdom in that! When I was a girl, I once snatched a whole berry pie that mom had made for everyone's supper. I ate the whole thing. When I then saw that no one else in the family had any of it for supper, I felt awful. Even though while I was eating it, I felt wonderful, later I wished I had not done it, but I couldn't un-eat the pie."

"Exactly, Mica. Surely you now have gotten enough food and supplies so that your people are no longer wanting or starving. Perhaps now is the time to begin to exchange something in return for future supplies? Just a suggestion, mind you. Just an outsider's idea, that's all," Andre added quickly. He did not want to sound pushy or demanding or as if he was issuing any kind of order.

"Yes, that's all well and good," Illi declared, "but we have no experience in such dealings. We know not how to go about such matters. The dealers might ask for three bags not one and we would not know the difference."

"Excellent observation, Czar, well stated indeed!" Andre complimented him sincerely. "That's where it pays to have a good ally or friend to help handle such matters. The Santi at Mont Blanc have long helped many others with the trading; we ensure that they are not cheated in any way. If they are sold a wagon load of rotting grain, which was supposed to be in fine condition, we make the seller make it right with the buyer. Fairness in trades brings about a trust among people. Trust brings about peace between neighbors. Peace is what the Santi most desire, so it is in our own best interests to help others this way. If you decide you want to try it, why, all you need to do is ask the Santi for help. Unless I am completely wrong, they will be more than glad to lend you a hand, make the arrangements, and see that you are treated fairly, not cheated."

"What do you get in return?" asked Mik. "It's my experience that people don't do something for nothing."

"In return we get what we want most, peace and harmony among people," Andre answered quietly. "Honestly, Czar, Mik, we Santi absolutely hate wars and fighting. Yes, we may well be the most powerful fighters on Tarra, or nearly so, but all of us 'Evil Witches' just hate it. If there is any other way out of a conflict besides going to war, we try to find it."

"Like you did today?" Mica suddenly interrupted. She had just put two and two together. Andre noted that she did have a sharp mind indeed.

"Yes, Mica, like today. We could have come charging down upon you, tossing flaming sheets everywhere, launching a deadly rain of arrows from very long range, as we were forced to do against the Centurions, who gave us no other options. However, we didn't. Why fight when we can be friends? You had not harmed us, so why should we harm you, if there was any other way to stop your siege of this kingdom to which we were pledged to aid? Instead, you and we reached an amicable truce, one that benefits us both, doesn't it?" Mica smiled, but Illi, slightly ill at ease over this touchy detail, decided to change the subject.

"And what of your life, sister?" he asked Lenkova. "What have you done?"

Andre quickly placed into her mind, *The less you say about the Sisterhood the better. Remember he is very touchy about them.*

"I have been a fighter protecting the people and commerce of Zargarb for many years. I used to be a fighter group leader, before I joined the Santi organization. Now I am a top commander of several regiments." She tried to explain it in simple terms. Then, inspiration struck. He had good reality on the Axemen, and he undoubtedly wanted to know more about the Evil Witches. "Let me tell you about how I first met Ket Bethany and Andre. I was trying to protect a lot of women and children." She purposely did not mention North Point, where she and Illi had been raised. "This was when the Axemen first began appearing in large numbers. They would raid a village on the border with the Arad, raping and pillaging, and worse, taking away villagers to become their slaves. Well, one day, Ket and his small band, something like a dozen, came by. Just then, we got word from our scouts that a very large number of Axemen had invaded our land, captured a village, taking away slaves. Worse, their entire army was perhaps five hundred strong and was headed towards a village of women and children. I had to act. I only had fifty fighters with me, but I had to do something. Ket volunteered to help. At first, I had my doubts. When we met up with the Axemen, it was ten to one odds against us."

Andre noted that all three were completely spellbound, listening to her every word, a very good sign, he concluded. "My fighters were all women, good at defense, but not against ten Axemen to one of us!" She went on to describe how at Heartbreak Hill, they had made their final stand and how Ket and the others had used an intense volley of lightning bolts to help them eliminate the Axemen invasion. "Even though I had a terrible leg wound, I could still ride. Andre and I then headed after the Axemen, who had taken some fifty villagers away as slaves. We caught up to them just inside the steppes and rescued all them. Honestly, brother, the Santi avoid fighting if possible. But when it matters, they can be counted upon to do what is needed. That was the most incredible battle I have ever been in, though some of my later ones come close to it, like dealing with the Centurions a few months ago. I will never forget battling those men alongside of the Santi."

"Impressive!" declared Mik.

Lenkova found talking much easier now, "You know, Illanovich, I've even met our aunt. She has really changed for the better. She recognized what she and our father had done was horribly, terribly wrong and has devoted her life to helping all others who are in need in the Arad, no matter who they may be. If you can ever meet her, you would probably really like her too."

"Zdlenka? She's alive? After all these years?" blurted out Illanovich. "She was killed with our father; everyone knows that."

"No, she escaped and shortly afterwards realized just how terrible her actions had been. I think that she stayed in the Arad to help others there because they did the vilest actions there. That's probably why she never returned to the steppes. Between you and me, I don't think she ever could return to the steppes after what she has done to your people and to so many other people on Tarra. She is helping those in need, whether they are Centurions, Arads, or Galts. I found it pretty amazing."

Before he could stop himself, Illi found himself blurting out, "One day I should like to meet her." He bit his lip. How could he face Aunt Zdlenka? She and his father had nearly wiped out the entire population of the steppes!

"I don't know when I will ever get the chance to see her again, but I will let her know that you would like to meet her. I'll tell her all the good that you have done. Maybe a visit could be arranged," Lenkova sounded hopeful. She added, "You see, she has kept her identity a secret all these years, so that she could help others in dire need. If she had not, many would have sought her out to kill her, and then she would not have been able to devote the rest of her life to making amends for her terrible actions with our father."

Mik yawned, "Well that certainly makes sense. Any number of Galts today still holds those two responsible for our woes."

Andre took that as a sign that they should be leaving. "It's getting late. We are quite tired, you know, riding long and hard to get here. I thank you for the excellent dinner. Perhaps we can do this again one day." He rose. Believe it or not, Lenkova did give her brother a parting hug.

After they said their farewells and were riding back to the Santi encampment, Andre said quietly, "You did very well, my dear. Good job."

"He's not the ogre I thought he was. I know that invading and conquering these kingdoms was wrong. I cannot condone those actions. But the rest — he did save all his people and even got the Axemen to leave the steppes. He actually got people to throw away their gold and silver! You know, I am beginning to see what Ket meant by it sometimes is just a matter of viewpoint." Andre leaned over and gave her a hug and a quick kiss, saying nothing.

The next day, a messenger arrived at the Santi camp. Illanovich formally asked for the Santi's aid in establishing trading negotiations with his ten conquered kingdoms. I, more than a bit flabbergasted, immediately asked Andre and Lenkova what they had said that night. Andre filled me in on the details. I could only smile in reply. I sent an entire Scouting Squad accompanied by three Judgers to lend them a hand. The scouts knew the land and would protect my Judgers. Yes, I felt great all that day!

The Galts left the next day. I sent most of the Santi back to Mont Blanc, while my Circle and a few others visited a few days with Percival, my daughter Sarah, and their growing family. Then, we too returned home to our twins.

Chapter 38 Winding Down

We spent a good deal of time at Mont Blanc with our twins and just relaxing. However, word had come that many of the Crusaders in New Barq were eager to return home. Of course, the problems were two-fold: how to get there and what to expect when they got there. If they had lived in the now occupied sectors, life would be tough upon returning into lands your enemy now controlled, especially when so many of your fellow Crusaders had died fighting the very enemies who now controlled your homeland. Travel to anywhere out of the Arad necessitated moving through all the occupied sectors, if you lived in Velona or beyond.

"We owe these men safe passage; it is the least we can do," I argued before the Santi council leaders. "We should send enough ships to carry them all back before the winter comes. With the triremes gone, sailing should be uneventful." In the end, I had my way. Once more, Elona volunteered many of her caravels for the voyage. My Circle decided to go as well, and I brought along my twins, unwilling to be separated yet again from them. Theoretically, this should be a simple trip, go there, load up, and return, a vacation from fighting.

On September 1, forty-five caravels set sail from Velona, including our three ships. Ten days of smooth sailing later, we arrived at the docks of New Barq. I was amazed to see how the construction of the fortification had grown since I last saw it. The outer wall was nearly complete, and the foundations of several new stone buildings were clearly visible.

First action of business was to meet with all the crusaders and explain the reality of their situation. Over a thousand crammed into one large barracks hall to hear my words. "On behalf of everyone, please accept our thank you for a job very well done." They cheered and clapped for a minute. "All of you have received your pay; I hope you still have some of it left." Catcalls and chuckling told me that many had already spent every coin.

"Now it's time to go home. We have brought a fleet of ships to take you back swiftly. However, as you already know, some of you are facing the terrible situation of having to return home to an enemy occupied sector." Many boo's echoed through the packed room. "I'm afraid at this time, there is nothing we can do about it. Even if we combined all our forces, we would not have enough to oust the Centurions and the Holy Paladins. It's as simple as that, too few of us. Yet, we are strong enough to guarantee that they will conquer no other lands, but we cannot retake what they have taken." More boo's and jeers.

"I know that returning home to a conquered sector is fraught with perils for you. Hence, I have a proposal for those leery of returning to a conquered land. We need soldiers here to help guard New Barq. Any that wish to remain here will be paid at double your previous rate, compliments of the Santi. On the other hand, if any of you wish to immigrate to another free sector or land, we will deliver you there on our return voyage. However, some of you who live in the occupied lands have family there and may wish to return anyway. If you find that you need to evacuate your families, just bring them to the Santi fortress near each major city, and we will see that you are rescued in due time. Finally, some of you may wish to join the Santi organization, if so, please see Paul here before we sail. Once more, we all do thank you sincerely for all that you have done."

As we left the room, the buzz of conversation drowned out any attempt to chat among ourselves. Outside, General Antonio Prada caught me, "Sir, may I have a brief word with you?"

Although I was now once more holding my twins, I said, "Sure."

"Well, I was wondering if I stayed if I could remain the general in charge of the forces here? I really do not have much of anything to go back to, in Zargarb, that is. My life would not be worth a copper if I showed my face there. Here, I can be of use, seeing that we hold on to this hard won area."

I did not hesitate. "Absolutely you can stay, General, and at double your previous pay." He would have shaken my hand, but they were both filled with wiggling boys. "If you need anything, just let the Santi know, and we will try to obtain it for you. By the way, I am very impressed with the overall progress that has been made here on the fortifications."

"Thank you Sir! Yes, we have given the local economy a spurt with all the new construction. I think it is a better use of their skills, building, that is, instead of making weapons. Your children?" he asked.

We chatted a bit about the twins and then duties called for both of us. As we walked back to the docks, Paul added, "Good move. Now we have a general to take charge here. I wonder if there will be enough staying or if we will have to send back a number of Santi just to guard against a surprise attempt to retake the city."

During the next two days, the tallies were completed. Over two hundred decided to accept our offer of double pay to stay and protect New Barq. Another four hundred or so wanted to return home to Velona, the Greenway, and West Reach. Over three hundred decided to seek their fortunes in a another country, and Lilly Ann held numerous smaller meetings discussing their options, what the lands were like, and their overall potential there. However, ninety-four had family in the occupied sectors and wanted to return there, despite the potential backlash.

Thus, the ships were loaded according to their ultimate destinations. We put the ninety-four on our ship. In addition to the normal protection Santi on board, having a full Circle along was an added measure of safety needed to enter the enemy waters. We needed to drop off soldiers in all the occupied sectors. Our plan was simple, dock at the Santi fortress near each city, unload the men during the night, and help them get on their way to wherever they lived within that sector. It was simple, yet fraught with unknown perils for the men.

A nighttime docking is quite dangerous. Only one small directional lantern pointed out to sea was the captain's guide. Painstakingly slowly, the caravel moved towards land until finally it slipped alongside, bumping gently into the stationary timbers. Once mooring ropes were tied, the men were escorted safely onto the dock, and off into Santi huts, there to be briefed, equipped, and sent on their way. Meanwhile, the mooring lines were undone, and our captain even more slowly maneuvered out to sea once more. Twice we nearly bottomed out attempting to get back into the sea. Yet, we did make our six drops successfully without mishap.

Mid-October, we finally docked at our own bay, where the ship would spend the winter. While most of the Santi, especially the archers, spent the winter in the Velona sector, carving out a new life there, I opted to stay at Mont Blanc, which felt more like home to me. Besides, my Circle greatly appreciated being so close to their extended families.

During the winter, I spent many hours in the Planning Room, as the old Circle meeting room high atop the tallest tower was now called. John Henry's Circle and mine spent hours upon hours planning for the huge spring construction season. Besides trying to expand Mont Banc, we now had nine new fortresses to be constructed in the Sea Princes, New Barq, and on the Red Desert coast. Additionally, I had promised to build a string of fortresses along the Velona-Barcella borderline. I had also promised Fergus that we would build one on West Reach, but that has now become two. King Lachlan Laird, via the Guardians on the island, let me know that the Grande High Council had requested a Santi Fortification in the south near Bregia. Thus, we needed to find the funds to continue all these constructions, to say nothing of the skilled manpower and raw materials.

Our Langdoc region is mostly limestone, barely fit for grazing sheep. Hence, we decided that we would hire as many stone miners as we could and ship rough-cut stone blocks to these construction sites. This alleviated the local problems of where and how to obtain the mountains of stone that was going to be needed. We had to calculate the amount of stone required each year for each of these, then determine how much had to be cut here each month, allowing for transportation lags. Knowing the approximate rate of blocks cut per man-day, we could then estimate the total number of miners needed. Knowing that we needed approximately a thousand miners, the next step was to find or train them.

Of course, we would need to expand our own caravel fleet greatly to handle the shipping, to say nothing of the teamsters required to move the stone from the quarry to the port. Unwilling to renege on our planned fortifications, we diligently worked all winter on the ways and means of accomplishing this enormous construction task. In the end, we anticipated that the construction would consume at least twenty years in order to get each fortification to our anticipated final design, one that could withstand a lengthy, determined siege.

The problem of funds next raised its ugly head. In the end, based upon financial data provided by the new Sisterhood in Velona, we could estimate how much income we could generate, if we provided the type of guaranteed, secure transportation that they had done in the past. In fact, we really had no other viable options but to open up negotiations with the occupied sectors, offering our services on secure shipments.

Hence, I ordered the Santi leaders in each of the occupied sectors plus New Barq to open up a dialog with the "leaders," explaining what we could provide. On our side of the balance sheet were two salient facts. One, we had indeed provided the security shipments during the war. Two, many of our members were ex-Sisterhood fighters, already known for doing just this. Gradually during the winter, our secure shipments gained acceptance nearly everywhere. As the years flew by, our transportation services became the rule, but that is getting ahead of the narrative.

Finally, during the long winter, my services as a preacher only grew larger and larger. Everyone insisted and demanded that I conduct Sunday Services. Usually my four services spanned the morning and afternoon. Soon, we received word from Velona that many there greatly desired my preaching as well. I was literally forced to make three trips down to Velona during the winter, spending a week preaching during each stay. Yet, what I wanted to do most was spend quiet time with Lilly Ann and the twins. That and somehow figure out a way to get down to the Red Desert and spend time with Jes or the Guardian as his new personality proclaimed. Many questions I had for him may well be answered. My duties kept me here, however.

Two other minor events, as they seemed at the time, also occupied the back of my mind. Our illusion, which in the past kept our fortress at Mont Blanc hidden from the sight of others, had been dispelled. Designed to befuddle the minds of a few people at a time, when the thousands of Santi came and went, the illusion faded. We no longer had enough Judgers in residence to re-establish the illusion nor was it desirable any longer. Too many people needed to come and go especially the stone miners and transporters, to say nothing of the Santi personnel. A few times late at night, I pondered whether having become visible to outsiders was beneficial or destructive. I could reach no positive conclusion, one way, or the other.

The other event bothered me for a few days and then passed out of my mind. I received word that a bronzed skin stranger had been poking around in the Layamon region of West Reach. He asked subtle questions about the heritage of Jes. He had discovered that Cathleen still lived as well as the fact that she had married and was going to have children. Immediately, many anti-assassination steps were taken both by her Protectors there and by us here at Mont Blanc. For days, we were on edge, fearing the worse, but nothing whatsoever came from it.

Paranoid, I had Percival keep a close eye on all the bronzed skinned visitors to his kingdom, of which there were several dozen. Some were descended from the original Centurions who came here many years ago and had fathered children. Still, I feared for Sarah and her children. One of these may well be the same inquisitive man who had discovered Cathleen still lived. Although he reported no unusual activity, his kingdom was large and contained numerous towns and villages, all which knew all about their king and queen and their large family.

In mid-December while I was away to Velona on one of the three trips there, a report came to me that also disturbed me. A lone, strange rider rode up the spur road to within a mile of our fortress at Mont Blanc, paused for a minute, and then left. John Henry had him followed, but he simply rode on to Calgary and disappeared within the huge city, now counting over sixty thousand residents.

A side note, on the first day of the new year, Rea Niccolo married John Smith, a Judger about the same age as she. They had fallen in love. More importantly I thought, John totally appreciated her art and that of her father. He constantly encouraged her to do more and to begin to have major art shows in Calgary this coming spring.

Chapter 39 The Church of Jehosanity, Megalos

In early November, word finally reached Megalos that Emperor Justinian had been killed on the battlefield and that the Centurion plans to reconquer Tarra had been halted. Still, the war had been a partial success; Megalos now controlled six of the eight Sea Prince sectors, though many grumbled about the loss of their overland route and New Barq.

Pope Yazi I held two meetings that day. First, he gathered all his bishops together to discuss the ramifications of this unexpected news. The Rooster, of course, sat quietly in the back of the room, wondering about the health of his mentor, the Pope. Yazi had been coughing regularly for the last couple of weeks. If it was just a cold, why had it not gone away? Yazi spoke slowly and deliberately. "As you all know, our Ministers and the Holy Paladins have been doing an excellent job in our newly acquired lands. I admit that it is regrettable that Justinian was not able to complete the task and wipe out the last two remaining strongholds of heathenism. Two lands still cling to their perversions of Jehosanity, Velona and West Reach. Of the two, Velona is our major concern; Gnosticism there is rapidly growing. At this time, I have no plan to thwart it; I am truly sorry that I do not."

"On the positive side, I can report that our Holy Ministers have been very successful at founding six monasteries in each sector. Ultimately, these holy refuges will produce new priests to expand our churches. Also, each has an abbey for chaste women, nuns. As we get their unholy women slowly converted, many will be sent to the nunneries for proper religious training so that they may see the errors of their ways, repent, and seek the salvation of our Lord."

"Perhaps even more importantly in the long run are the two dozen Scholastic Universities we have established there. If the heathens are ever to understand the wisdom of Jehosa, they must learn to read. We are offering a free education to any who wishes it. Naturally, as planned, the students will be thoroughly indoctrinated into the ways of Jehosa. None of this artistic freethinking as some call it will be allowed. Years from now, when the universities have done their work, we will have countries in which the common man knows, respects, and honors the ways of our Lord." The Rooster picked up Yazi's unspoken addendum, that the Church here will be able to control the lives of the people a thousand miles or more distant from Megalos!

"So all appears to be going mostly as we have planned. Are there any questions before I discuss the death of Justinian?" he paused for a lengthy cough and to sip some wine. It seemed to help.

"What of the rumors that things are becoming so disorderly outside of the major cities, out in the countryside? Is banditry really growing?" asked one priest.

"We anticipated some; that is why the Holy Paladins are there, to maintain law and order. Given time, it will pass away, as all things do," Yazi sidestepped a direct answer.

"Now I have given a good deal of thought about the death of Justinian. Historically, the main church on Megalos, the Temple of Sol, would be asked by the Senate to elect a new emperor to rule. However, our church is now the dominate one. Many of you feel that this time, it should be we who choose the next Emperor of Megalos. I have considered this long and hard, praying to Jehosa for guidance many nights. It has come to me that, if we should insist upon our legal right to so do, to choose the next emperor, much trouble, upset, and strife will come from doing so. Many followers of Sol will be greatly offended. At this time, we need to focus all our attention on our expansion works in the Sea Princes, not on fending off philosophical battles here at home. In my prayers, it came to me that we should go to the Senate, present our case for being the ones to elect the next emperor, and then humbly propose instead that no emperor be elected by anyone. Rather, it is time that the Senate itself took over the reins of the government. After all, the senators are the duly elected representatives of their people, or often are."

"You see, the Senate, if left to run the government, will only be able to do so poorly. A group cannot run a country, only a single person must ultimately make the vital decisions, as the Pope does in our church. Already, our influence is strong within the Senate. Thus, with the Senate in power, we can more easily affect legislation and expand our control over the people here, to help them regain the Kingdom of Heaven."

"Father Aran, you are a most eloquent speaker. I am assigning the task to prepare and deliver such a speech to the Senate in my place. This lingering cold of mine is wearing me down. I will go with you and say a brief few words, but this is your hour to shine, my son. Go now and prepare. We must meet the Senators just as soon as it can be arranged, certainly within two days."

Aran bowed his head to Yazi. This was the greatest honor yet bestowed upon him, and he vowed that he would not let his Pope down. "Oh, yes, there is one other piece of business to relate. Now that we are growing so rapidly, we need a better ecclesiastical organization. I have decided that all you shall hence forth with be known as Cardinals. To distinguish you as being second only to the Pope himself, you may wear a scarlet skullcap. I am open to suggestions as to whether or not your robes should also be red. Your duties remain the same, to handle the religious and administrative duties of your zone. However, those immediately under you in those zones shall now be called bishops and wear a pale red skullcap. They will oversee one or more parishes with their local priests. The new pope ought to come from the pool of cardinals. Before I pass on into Jehosa's Realm, I will name my successor. However, I have decided that after that, a conclave of all you cardinals shall pick the popes after that." This pleased these men who had been doing much of the grunt work in setting up the vast spread of Jehosanity throughout Megalos and now the Sea Princes. From now on, wherever they went in public, they could not help but be highly visible. Since the meeting was over, one by one, the holy men filed out to carry on their many duties, chatting among themselves about all these new changes.

The Rooster remained quietly in his seat. A few minutes after all had left, Cax entered, his second in command of the security forces. He shut the door so that they could not be overheard.

After another bout of coughing had passed, Yazi spoke once more. "Any further messages from Thondakas?"

"Yes, I have unfortunate news to report. It seems that some survived the assassinations by Karlos. In West Reach, one Cathleen, daughter of Emil Amir, survived. She has now married and is expecting a child. She has assumed the throne of her father. All others there have been verified as eliminated. He is moving on to Greenway and is probably there now or even on his way back here. It takes months to get messages through, as you know."

"Speculation," the Rooster finally spoke up softly. "If one survived Karlos in West Reach, it is highly likely that some did as well in the Greenway. This Mont Blanc thing has always bothered me. I hope that he will be able to shed some light on that mystery, my Lord."

"Hum, I agree. However, we have so many other more pressing matters, as planned; we will deal with the survivors later. We dare not lose the Sea Princes now that we have finally gained a foothold there," Yazi replied.

"With the death of Justinian and the loss of so many fighters, whoever takes control of the government here certainly will set about raising another army. Let's make sure that we step up our recruitment of men. We need to quadruple the size of our Holy Paladins, at the very least." Both men nodded their agreement.

After a pause, Yazi asked, "How goes the recruitment of the Security Forces?" Secretly the Rooster had been slowly adding key personnel in his ever-growing force, whose purpose was to protect the Pope and the Church proper.

"I am pleased to report that we have just added the one thousandth man yesterday. All are superb fighters, men you can trust with your life. Out of these, Cax has fifty specially trained, as he and I are." This was a subtle hint that there were now fifty assassins trained and ready for clandestine operations.

"Excellent, excellent!" Yazi seemed very pleased to hear this special news. After another coughing spell passed, he added, "Both of you, my days here are numbered before I go to Jehosa's Realm. One day soon, you will have another Pope to protect with your lives. Do not forget your promise to me to protect my successor as you have me." Again, both men swore, although the Rooster was somewhat annoyed, this being the tenth time Yazi had spoken those words within the last month.

"You shall live a good many more years, Holy Pope!" the Rooster declared emphatically, although he began to have the idea that this may not be actuality, rather his personal wish.

"I am getting old, my dear friend. Come; walk with me. Let's see how the construction of the largest cathedral on Tarra is coming along." With

Rooster steadying his mentor, the two walked slowly out of the stone habitation complex to view the massive construction site just outside.

Already the outer walls around their entire city were beginning to take shape, according to Rooster's precise specifications. White marble walls now rose around five feet all around their city within a city. Actually, their city lay just at the edge of the port city. When the walls were complete, they would average ten feet thick at their base and rise a dozen from the surrounding ground. From a distance, the white marble would make the entire city appear as if the hand of Jehosa had touched it. Near the center, the vast cathedral foundations had been laid and wooden scaffolding rose everywhere around it. This as yet unnamed church would rise nearly a hundred feet high, its enormous dome was planned to be nearly five hundred feet in diameter at its outer edges. The entire surface of the dome would be gold in color, giving the illusion of being godlike. Its main altar room would hold a thousand worshipers at one time. Already numerous artworks were being commissioned, while some statues and ornate decorations destined to be used around the entrances and within the holy chapel were being stored in the housing building. True, the chapel would take many years to complete, but once done, this church would be the most spectacular religious building anywhere in the known world.

"Rooster, one thing still bothers me," Yazi whispered, noticing that they were completely alone. Dusk was falling. "We now have wiped off the face of Tarra the Northern Orthodoxy perversion. Yet, in six sectors, no sign of the Holy Crosses have been found. No trace. Worse still, we have not yet accounted for all the handwritten gospels written by the Holy Disciples. Indeed, no trace of them has been found either. Surely, the Northern Orthodoxy has had such in their possession, but where are they now?"

"Your Holiness, if I were their Archdeacon, facing an invasion from the south and possible subjugation, I would secretly transport anything of religious value out of my lands into some safe, secure location. I would bet anything that such lie somewhere in Velona. If not there, then perhaps this dubious Mont Blanc of which we continually receive conflicting tales. A last resort could be on the island of West Reach, but I would guess Velona as the most likely location, where the vile Gnostics reign," Rooster replied solemnly.

After pause, he added, "We really face three critical actions, anyone of which could undermine our Church, as I see it. Please correct me if I am wrong on this. First, we still have living kin from the Great Messiah living in West Reach and most likely the Greenway. However, lacking an army or great forces at this time, there is little they could do now. As you say, seek and locate, but keep on the back burner, so to speak." Yazi nodded.

"Secondly, the Holy Relics and gospels could cause immense problems for us, particularly if they were somehow made into books the learned could read. Once we locate them, we should, without fail, retrieve them before they can be used to damage the Church. As I understand the orders, the Holy Paladins are still searching high and low for them or for any word concerning them. Perhaps their next message will bear some news." Again, Yazi nodded. He avoided talking to keep from aggravating his coughing.

"Third, this Santi del Dio organization that has sprung up out of nowhere I view as a very significant threat to our Church."

Yazi raised his eyebrows. "You really think that they pose a significant threat to us?"

"I just do not know," Rooster replied sadly. He knew that he was in some small measure letting him down. "As I understand the messages, most all the Santi members are Sisterhood fighters from the now disbanded Sisterhoods. I do not understand these women. Why they would want to take on a man's role in life? However, I am hoping now that they consider the war to be over, these women will leave and take up a normal woman's role in their societies. If this happens, then the Santi would have perhaps a thousand members at the very most, many of whom are ex-Greenway Guardians. However, I simply do not know what a Guardian is supposed to be. Nevertheless, I would not expect any serious long-term trouble coming from such a small, relatively isolated group. However, all this may change, since I really know almost nothing about them."

"I agree with you. I think that these women are mostly battered women. I would not expect them to last long in any male dominated fighter organization. Probably within a few months, they will leave for who knows where. At least they are not going to be allowed to settle in our sectors. Let them make trouble elsewhere," Yazi declared. He was cut short by another coughing spell.

As the two strolled back inside, Yazi asked his Security General, "The triremes are all lost. Is this going to be a problem for us?"

"Not at all. It made no sense to sink all those Sea Prince ships. These people are mariners who make their living trading with others. With so many ships lost, their entire economy is liable to be disastrously ruined. The late Emperor certainly was not wise in ordering the destruction of so many ships."

"Ah, then Zargarb will be in particularly bad shape. I've heard that they have lost nearly half of their fleet. We will need to redirect their entire economy over to an agrarian one. Put all those people now out of work to work on something constructive. Bad timing though, I understand that it is now winter there and something called snow is falling. Plants won't grow in the cold. Time enough then for us to discuss the matter and send new orders to the Holy Paladins running Zargarb and the other sectors."

The next day, Pope Yazi I looked over the notes on the proposed speech that Father Aran, now Cardinal Aran, was to deliver this afternoon to the full Senate. The President of the Senate had already agreed to allow the Church, namely Pope Yazi, to address them in the late afternoon session. Yazi only made a few changes to the wording. Then, they climbed into the royal coaches to take the long ride up to Galantas. Naturally, the Mano del Dio provided the security; the Rooster personally accompanied his Pope in the carriage.

Escorted onto the platform in the center of the amphitheater, Pope Yazi and Cardinal Aran were dwarfed in size by the sheer number of senators and the physical size of the arena. With his hood entirely covering his head, the Rooster stood guard behind the two men. The pope began, "We come here humbly today to morn with you the loss of our esteemed Emperor, who died a valiant death. His legacy will not be forgotten. I ask you all whether or not you supported the Emperor in life, please let us all take a moment of silent prayer to pray for his soul." This went over very well, and for a minute, you could hear nearly complete silence, broken only by the sounds of breathing and the catch in Yazi's chest as he breathed in and out.

"Since I am under the weather, I have asked Cardinal Aran to say a few words for our Church." He took a slight step back while Aran took one step forward.

"Good day esteemed Senators, one and all. I thank you for honoring our request to address you today. Facing Megalos immediately is the choosing of a new Emperor. Historically, the Church of Sol, which used to represent the vast majority of the citizens of Megalos, would choose the new person to lead our country, the new Emperor. Yet, at this moment in time, the Church of Sol has dwindled and now has very few followers. In contrast, the Church of Jehosanity continues to grow. We estimate that nearly eight out of ten citizens on Megalos worship in our churches."

"With this transition in religious faith and power, many of you have been speculating and some even requesting that this time the Church of Jehosanity should be the ones to choose the next Emperor of Megalos. Not a day has gone by for months now that someone has not told us that they believe that our Church should be the ones choosing the next leader of Megalos. Yes, it would be a great disservice to the many to have so few choose the leader for all of us. I think that we can all agree on this point. So we have come before you today to notify you that if you ask us to choose the next leader of our magnificent country, we will honor your request and do so, fairly and equitably." This of course brought numerous whispers among the senators, as Aran had predicted.

After a slight pause, he continued, "However, before you request us or anyone else to choose our next leader, the Church of Jehosanity would like to make another suggestion. We of the Church believe that the Senate, being the duly elected representatives of the people of your areas, should be the ones running the government of Megalos, not some man who answers to no one. You are the elected people; you should be the ones making the decisions that affect our citizens. You have the expertise and skills and competence and know-how to run our country. Why yield this to a single man who is not answerable to anyone, save perhaps a direct Senate order, if that?"

Now the side talking crescendoed. Even from this distance, Cardinal Aran could hear the men commenting to each other. No one had ever offered the Senate such a thing; yet overall the offered hand of power would be very difficult for the senators to relinquish. He continued, "The benefits of this would be many. When you pass legislation, you will know that it will be carried out as stated. No more bantering back and forth about what was meant by the legislation. I ask you, who is better trained and equipped to run our country than you, the senators? We can think of no one, to be bluntly honest about it. In summary, senators, if you wish to honor the Church of Jehosanity by allowing us to choose the next emperor, we will obey your request. However, our first choice would be to allow the Senate to be the ruler. If you decide otherwise and wish us to pick someone, then we will obey your request. Just let us know in a timely fashion. We all agree that the vacuum in leadership must be filled at once. We have soldiers out there in the field awaiting orders. If the war is truly over, we owe them a great deal for their outstanding successes, and ought to bring our fighting men home to their families as soon as possible."

He had punched all the right reactive buttons of the group. "In closing, let me add that the Church of Jehosanity is commissioning a large marble statue of our late Emperor to honor his noble accomplishments. However, we ask the Senate for guidance; we do not know the most appropriate location in which to proudly display this marvelous new work of art honoring Justinian." He stepped back beside Yazi, who made barely discernable nod to Aran, indicating that Yazi felt that he had made an excellent presentation indeed.

The President hastily joined them on the central raised platform. "Thank you Pope Yazi I and Cardinal Aran for your most interesting, heartfelt words, and wisdom in this, the gravest of matters. Let me assure you both that the Senate will give your request its proper consideration and in a very timely manner. Personally, and perhaps I also speak for many here, I am very surprised that your church would yield such power to us, the Senate. For that, we are deeply and profoundly grateful. We will contact you as soon as we reach our decision. Thank you for coming here today. We look forward to your quick return to health." He bowed, signaling that their meeting was finished. The three quickly left the Senate floor, returning to the armed escort of Rooster's men just outside the Senate. Almost as quickly, they got back into the coaches and left, returning to Constanza City just after sunset.

Tired, Yazi slept most of the way home. However, before he nodded off, he said, "I do believe that we have them. Few will pass on an opportunity to gain real power." Aran smiled, as did the Rooster.

Two days later, word came to Yazi that the Senate had graciously accepted the will of the majority Church of Megalos. From now on, the Senate would run the government. The era of the emperors had ended. Senate activity rose immediately, dozens of new committees were hastily formed, tackling the many problems of ruling such a large enterprise.

Just as Yazi had predicted, during the ensuing months, the Church received numerous requests for their advice on matters of state from various committee members. The Rooster marveled over the latest miracle his mentor had created: the Holy Church now had a huge say in the running of the entire country, albeit quietly from the sidelines. Such was completely unheard of even a year ago.

Quietly and in secret, writing in ancient Arad, Pope Yazi I wrote in his personal diary. "On November 20, 624, I, Pope Yazi I, have finally brought down the unholy Infidel government of the largest, most powerful country on Tarra. The emperors are no more. The Senate now runs the country by committees, and they ask me for guidance in critical matters. I have done what Jes Amir could only dream of doing. May Jehosa now accept me into his Holy Realm." He locked his journal up in his special compartment here in the hidden tunnels beneath the Constanza City. Smiling, he walked slowly back out of the catacombs.

Early January, finished reading the latest message from Thondakas, who was wintering in Calgary, the Rooster spat into a corner of his sparsely furnished room. "I have greatly misjudged nearly everything up north. It comes from my not being there and looking myself! How on Tarra can I explain my failings to His Holiness? He has placed everything about our very survival into my hands, and I have completely let him down!" He paced the small room dozens of times before he got the courage to face Pope Yazi I with the terrible news.

"Thank you for seeing me," he began humbly. Yazi had agreed instantly to meet with him behind closed doors. They were in the official meeting room, door closed, so that it was impossible for anyone to overhear their conversation. "Please, please forgive me, Your Holiness, but I have failed you."

This was not what Yazi had expected and was somewhat surprised. He had infinite faith in the Rooster. "My son, what troubles you? I will think not less of you. Tell me how it is that you believe you have failed."

With a sigh, the Rooster knew that he had to tell all, placing himself at the mercy of his mentor. "This just came from Thondakas. I am afraid I was wrong on all matters up north. It is best that you read it for yourself." He handed him the message; he had decoded it for Yazi. When members of his order, Mano del Dio, sent messages to one another, they now used the secret code that the Rooster had invented. Thus, if intercepted, the message would be unreadable. He had carefully translated the words for Yazi.

Holy Supreme Prelate Thraxton,

It is with the utmost sorrow that I must report that Karlos has failed us rather significantly. While in the Greenway, I have learned much, although I must be exceedingly careful. They are on the lookout for anyone asking the questions we wish to ask, understandable after the Holy Assassinations performed by Karlos.

First, Karlos made a huge blunder when he eliminated Caitlyn Amir. She had just given birth to twins that very night! The twins are now safe and believed to be under the care of their father, who is none other than the leader of the Santi del Dio, Ket Bethany! The twins are now most likely within the heavily guarded fortress at Mont Blanc.

Karlos was fooled completely. Mont Blanc is not a graveyard but the strongest, most heavily fortified stone fortress that anyone has ever seen! I have seen it with my own eyes. It is huge, spectacular, and even has open-air marble temple structures as we do in Galantas. Two tall towers rise high behind walls of stone that I estimate are at least fifteen feet tall capped with barbicans. The complex has all stone buildings with slate roofs that are impervious to fire. I viewed it from the crossroads nearly a mile away, for I dared not get any closer; sentries are on continual lookout.

This means within those walls are twins, who are direct descendants and pose a terrible threat to us. They are to be kings when they become of age. Ket has a regent acting in their behalf in Nuadilan and Amathon, West Reach. Worse still, Sarah and her many children are not dead, as we have supposed. Some are within the walls of Mont Blanc, others are members of the Santi organization, and Sarah herself still is the Queen of Southway. She is surrounded by King Percival and many guards at all times.

It is far worse than this, I must report. I have discovered that these Guardians are extremely special people. Some call them Evil Witches, perhaps rightly so. I've heard from more than one source that these people can cast mighty spells. Lightning from the sky, burning fires out of thin air, even sheets of ice. Another rumor suggests they can even control the weather, but I seriously doubt that. Kicked out of most of the Greenway, these Guardians are now found only in the Southway and Calgary kingdoms. However, they have all banded together with the ex-Sisterhood members to form what we know as the Santi del Dio! Reputedly, there are nearly a thousand of these witches!

This now explains what happened to Justinian and his army. They were attacked by these very same Santi witches. Many burned to death, including Justinian, who, on the field of battle, tried to escape their conjured flames. The Santi have destroyed the Emperor's mighty fleet of triremes. They did it with their magical spells.

Worse still, I have heard many rumors that the Santi are building a large number of their stone fortresses and towers all over Tarra, including West Reach. However, the Gnostic sector of Velona is supposed to have an entire line of these forts along their border with Barcella, obviously to protect that sector from invasion.

As far as Karlos is concerned, I have heard some rumors that the sinking of his ship and his death might not have been an accident, but a well-orchestrated killing at the hands of these very same Guardians. No proof as yet.

The port of Calgary is locked in ice through the winter. It is very cold here. I am laying low, gathering what rumors I can and await your orders. I wish I had better news.

Your Servant,

Supreme Prelate Thondakas

Tears streaming down his cheeks, the Rooster found no words to atone for his horrible misjudgments. "There, there, Rooster. None of this is your fault. I would not let you go personally, because I needed you here. We both have made a terrible misjudgment. Neither of us could have known about this. These treacherous Guardian witches deceived even Karlos. We had no way of knowing about them. You have not failed me, Rooster. Look, your wisdom in sending Thondakas to verify what Karlos accomplished has finally yielded us the truth! You are to be praised, not condemned! Whatever would I do without you?" He hugged the Rooster for a time, while the Rooster regained his composure.

He stopped crying, finally seeing the wisdom of Pope Yazi I, once more illuminating what he had seen as the darkest moment of his life, turning it into an act of supreme wisdom and intelligence. Yazi explained, "I need your help now more than ever. Together, we must decide what to do about these Evil Witches and the remaining heirs of Jes Amir. On the bright side, Karlos did manage to exterminate at least half of the abominations. Now we must figure out how to remove the remaining ones. Come; let us share some Holy Wine and Bread."

While eating, the Rooster commented, "It is clear that we cannot assail these abominations with force. If Emperor Justinian and his mighty army with war chariots failed utterly, we cannot hope to defeat them on the battlefield. We must find other ways."

"I agree completely. A direct attack would be folly, even if we could muster such a force as needed. Now things are becoming clearer to me. Remember the reports from the Holy Paladins, which said that these very same Santi had approached them with offers to provide safe, secure transport of nearly anything, anywhere? At first, I thought that this was just an extension of what the Sisterhood had been providing. All reports have told us that before we conquered them, the Sisterhood was always the most trusted, safest means of delivery, though costly. Whenever someone had a valuable item to be transported, the Sisterhood was employed to guarantee its safe delivery. We assumed that was because they were superb fighters, as our history tells us."

"However, now that they have joined forces with the Evil Witches from the Greenway, all signs indicate that they wish to continue in their traditional action. As you know, with banditry on the rise in the conquered sectors, months ago, I authorized the Holy Paladins to utilize their services on critical shipments. At the time, it seemed the prudent thing to do. Possibly, it still does."

Rooster replied, "We use their services. Yet in our favor, they do not know that we know who and what they actually are. Perhaps we can use that to our advantage in the future. At least we can monitor their operations. From that, a clue may arise. In the meantime, I will instruct Thondakas to make an accurate count of the descendants who live, their names, where they are located, and even their occupations and habits. When stalking an enemy, it is wise to know all that you can about them. From their habits often comes what is needed to defeat them."

"Precisely, very good. There is yet one other datum that can be surmised about the Santi, Rooster. While they may have evil spells at their command, probably sent by the devil himself, they are not strong enough to attack us directly. After defeating Justinian, they did not march on Barcella, retaking that city or any other city for that matter. The only conclusion I can draw is that in spite of their supposed magics, they are not strong enough to conquer a walled city. So I do not think that we need to worry about a surprise attack from the Santi in an attempt to retake one or more of the Sea Prince cities." Yazi commented.

"Ah, perhaps we could slowly conscript an army of local fighters in these lands. Then use them against the Santi or to protect against any Santi incursion," the Rooster volunteered. "It still bothers me that these Santi are building their stone fortifications right beside the walled cities. Tis like the hawk watching its prey from a treetop. Still, its prey can watch the hawk."

"Aye, that is precisely what we shall do: watch them as the hawk does its prey. One day when the time is right, we strike," Yazi declared, but then broke into yet another coughing fit. Rooster poured his mentor some more wine, and it seemed to help.

When he could talk once more, Yazi asked, "Any word on the Holy Relics?"

"Not a thing. I will ask Thondakas to keep an ear out for any rumors about them. He has done his job superbly."

"Yes, give him my personal thanks will you Rooster? You know," he said after a pause, "I just had an idea. We should take a tip from these Santi. They have established an outpost in each of our new colonies. Why should we not do the same? How does this idea sound to you: suppose that we setup a Megalos consulate office in these other places not under our dominion? We build our own strategic foothold in places like West Reach, Velona, and Calgary. From there, our people can keep a close eye upon the goings on, spy for us, even take remedial actions from those headquarters."

"Perfect. You ought to put a small church there as well. Not only could our people still receive mass while they were off in these distant lands, but it can form the start of a local reformation."

"Yes, indeed," Yazi smiled. "Sometimes I think that you should be the pope, you have brilliant ideas, Rooster." He meant this as a supreme compliment. "Well, this will give my cardinals something more to discuss and plan tomorrow. I think that I ought to take a little nap now. Thank you, Rooster." He bowed and backed out of Yazi's meeting room. Whereas just a little while ago, life looked dark and bleak to the Rooster, now life appeared bright and hopeful once more.

The cardinals met for several days before they arrived at a consensus on just how to go about implementing their Pope's latest proposal for establishing consulates in the non-occupied lands. Since these consulates would also be representing the government, they decided to get Senate approval for the arrangements. By having the Church of Jehosanity handle all the necessary finances, naturally the Senate totally approved of the idea. They would have diplomatic relations with other countries with all the benefits of such, but without the expenses needed to establish such. A royal proclamation outlining the terms was drawn up by a committee and eventually delivered to the Church.

In early April 625, a lone Megalos merchant ship tacked slowly into the bay of Velona, flying a white flag. On board, Cardinal Maximus Thrall paced the quarterdeck nervously. "Relax Your Eminence, I'm sure we will not be attacked," the tall bronzed skin captain of the Felix Arauo. "Look, we are approaching the outer barrier chain. Impressive. Glad that the chain is lowered. It could cut our mast clean off, if not sinking us first. See, we are not yet challenged." He sounded hopeful, after all, why would a lone merchant ship from Megalos be attacked as it came unwarlike into dock?

The ship continued its slow tack towards the large docks. Ten of the new sleek caravels were already docked, either loading or unloading. From this distance, the vast flotilla of Axeman longboats could also be seen docked somewhat south of the main walled city of Velona. Additionally, a lone caravel was docked to the east, also beyond the walls of the city, presumably the Santi fortress dock and ship. As they neared, the captain saw a number of Axemen rushing to launch several of their longboats. Now small figures bearing arms could be seen rushing towards the docks from various locations within the city.

"Sure has changed since I was last here," muttered the captain. "Never saw it quite so large and, well, thriving, I guess is the word for it. Sure has changed." Maximus paid him little heed, staring at the well-armed, burly men climbing into the longboats. Soon they were floating all around the lone merchant ship, escorting it into the docks. Wary eyes were continually now upon them, especially the tall man in scarlet robes on the quarterdeck.

The harbor master signaled the captain to come in on the left side of pier five, centrally located. A caravel was docked on the opposite side of the pier and another on the pier next to them. The small ship would thus become sandwiched between the two much larger ships. The huge shipyards were now clearly visible on the eastern side of town. Many new caravels were in various stages of construction. An enormous pile of logs lay to one side of this large construction area. However, Cardinal Maximus put his full attention on the ever-growing crowd of soldiers now arrayed in full battle formation on the dock, blocking any attempt to get into the city from the pier. Slowly the ship slid into its berth; mooring lines flew out from its crew and were securely fastened by three dockhands.

As Cardinal Maximus walked to the side where the gangplank was being attached, he saw the guards part and several people walking past them towards the ship. Some looked like fighters, while some were women. One wore long robes of purple and green. Nervously, he fussed with his robes, making himself as presentable as possible. He knew just how important first impressions could be. Much was riding upon his performance here. Carefully he walked down the narrow path onto the docks. It did feel fabulous to have his feet on solid earth once more. On the second day out of Megalos, he had decided he did not like sea travel. His opinion had not altered during the long months to get here, even though the ship carried no cargo and was going far faster than normal, according to the captain.

He walked up to the foursome awaiting him; now he began to panic slightly. Was his Sea Prince dialect up to the occasion? The woman in robes spoke first, "Hail strangers from Megalos. I am High Priestess Elona Po, the Monarch of Velona. What brings you to Velona?"

Although unused to dealing with women in positions of power, such was almost unheard of back in Megalos, save for a few senators, he was elated. She was the person that he needed to see. "Very pleased to meet you at last. I am Cardinal Maximus Thrall of the Church of Jehosanity, Constanza City, Megalos. I have come on a mission of peace between our countries. I do hope my speech is not too terribly poor." Several of her male companions were grinning.

"Then welcome Cardinal Maximus. You do have an accent, but we understand you. This is my husband and Guardian Alton Woodgrove Po, my Protectors Ben Thrush and Thomas Algrove, and my Communicator Sally Longton. How may we help you? How long do you plan to stay?"

"Greetings one and all. I have come to meet with you, actually High Priestess. I have a matter that may be beneficial to both of our countries. Once we have discussed it, then I shall be on my way."

"I see. Are you alone or are there others that you wish to bring ashore?" she replied.

He smiled; she is sharp and coy, he thought to himself. "No, just me."

"Okay. Then if you will follow us, we will meet in my office. However, please inform your ship's captain that he and his men are not going to be allowed off the dock. They can stretch on the pier, however. This way then." She motioned for him to follow, and the small group headed toward the long line of guards, who parted to allow them to pass and then closed ranks to prevent anyone else from the ship to follow. Once beyond the line of guards, Maximus could see the wide dock loading area; warehouses dotted the vista. Hundreds of men and women stopped their activities to stare at him as he followed solemnly behind Elona. He could not help but notice that one Protector slipped between Elona's back and himself, while the other slipped in behind him.

Soon, they entered the city proper. He was amazed to find it so civilized, so organized, and so well kept. The Sea Princes were supposed to be barely above a barbarism, or so everyone back in Megalos was led to believe. Yet, this was definitely not so here. And so many people, even flower vendors, he thought, as he passed by noting the smell of fresh cut lilacs. Ahead, he saw what had to be a huge church. A little surprised, Elona walked into its doors. He followed. Inside was anything but barbaric! Carpets covered the stone floor; tapestries adorned many walls, and paintings and bronze sculptures lined walls and alcoves. She passed through a pair of highly decorated oaken doors into a huge meeting room. One wall was filled with paper scrolls. Many tables had parchments sprawled on them. She led the way to one corner and motioned for everyone to take a seat. Cardinal Maximus took a seat on a magnificently made oaken chair. Elona signaled for refreshments. Soon tea, biscuits, and cheese was brought in by Alton and the group snacked.

"I hope you find my office not too littered with stuff. I am overseeing a great many projects at the moment. So what brings you here?" she said.

"I've come to make a proposal that would benefit both of our countries, High Priestess," Cardinal Maximus began formally.

"Please, just Elona," she interjected.

He nodded, "We would like to establish what could be called a consulate somewhere here in Velona. We would pay for all our expenses of running the office. Your people would have direct access to an official of our country; visitors from our land would have a place to go for assistance. Such close contact can only help improve the relations between our two countries. Of course, we would also expect that you would also open up a consulate of your own on Megalos as well. Then, your ships and people who come to Megalos would have someone they can go to for assistance as well."

"I have the official document from our Senate authorizing such consulates. You see, Megalos is no longer being ruled by an emperor. Instead, the Senate, consisting of duly elected officials from the various sections of our land, passes needed legislation, and is now in full control of our government. Here, you may read it for yourself. I'm sorry, perhaps you cannot read our written words," he apologized.

"True, I cannot, but I have someone who can. Sally, will you contact Ket and allow him to read it for us, please?" She handed her the official scroll. "This will only take a minute."

Cardinal Maximus had no idea about what she was talking, and concluded that his mastery of their language was insufficient. He continued so as not to show his ignorance, "You see, we actually got the idea from your own Santi del Dio, if I have pronounced it right." All eyes suddenly looked straight at him.

For an instant, he faltered but hastily continued. "In the Sea Prince sectors under our watchful eye, your Santi del Dio have built essentially a fortified consulate, which acts totally autonomous to the sector's control. We think that this is a marvelously good idea. Everyone wins. The Santi have a guaranteed safe place to dock; our leaders there do not have to concern themselves with anything about the fortresses. Both sides can exchange important information when the need arises. What a perfect arrangement indeed. Our Senate hopes to expand this concept and establish a Megalos Consulate in Velona, West Reach, d'Grange, and even Calgary. We also hope and pray that each of these countries reciprocates and establishes a consulate of theirs down in Megalos. If all comes to pass, a new era in open communications between our countries shall begin."

"Sounds more like all sides spying upon the other," Alton grumbled aloud his reservations.

"Ah, but what is spying? It is just knowing what the other country is doing and planning. With open consulates, we all know the truth of what the other is doing and so avoid any possible misunderstandings and confusions. In addition, we each have a home away from home. For example, suppose one of your new caravels is damaged in a storm off of Megalos. It can put in at our docks, but having your consulate there, the crew can have lodging, supplies, and even assistance in repairs from your own people. As it now is, the crew would be at the mercy of any unscrupulous dealer. After all, how many of your caravel crew can speak or write our language? Same is true of our ships; I doubt any can read your language. Yes, perhaps our various captains can speak simple words in Sea Prince or Megalos dialects, but most likely only crudely, certainly not enough to handle a major crisis that a storm-damaged ship might have to face. A consulate could totally circumvent all such language barriers. Spying, certainly I understand that."

"After all, at this point in time, there is enough distrust on both our sides. Establishing consulates here and in Megalos can go a long way to establishing understanding of one another. I must admit that even I can benefit, before I came, I expected to find a rather primitive city, by our standards. Instead, I find that Velona is a thriving, well designed city indeed."

Elona smiled at the compliment. "Ket has just read your document to us. However, we do need some time to consider the matter."

Again, he did not understand what she had said; it made no sense. Ket, could she be referring to the Santi leader? He was not here. Maximus heard no one reading the scroll, but he did expect her reply. "Ah yes, that is as it should be. How long do you desire? I ask because if you wish to study the proposal for say a couple of weeks, then I will sail on to d'Grange and perhaps to Calgary and West Reach, and present our proposal to them. I can then return here for further discussion. My ship is at my beck and call for as long as we need to decide this important proposal."

"Oh certainly not that long, Cardinal. A day is all we need, I suspect. Why don't we have someone take you on a tour of Velona, while we meet? If I find that we may need another day, I can let you know. For sure, we should have our decision before this time tomorrow."

"Oh, so quickly! Yes, a tour would be an excellent idea. Such a grand city you have here. I would love to stroll and see for myself. Such flowers. So many flower vendors I saw just in the short distance to your office. We do not have many in our city, I'm afraid." She smiled and signaled for an aide. She gave him some instructions and said, "Guillermo here will take you on a tour. I hope you don't mind, but I will send along a small escort of guards to make sure of your safety. There may yet be some who house animosity toward you and your people — you know the recent war and all that."

"I understand fully. Thank you so much," he replied and followed the young man out of the room. Although he had a tour of the city, Elona did ask him to stop back after visiting the others. This decision was most troubling to everyone.

"He didn't even blink when I mentioned Ket had read it to us," Elona said when the door was shut once more. Sally had made a Mind Link with Ket, and Lilly Ann and he had read the document to them all here. Lilly Ann had given them a brief summary of its good and bad points.

"I wouldn't make too much of that," Sally replied. "I don't think that he actually grasped what you were saying. I don't think it made any sense to him. His command of our language is that of a young child."

"At least he was honest about the spying," Alton added. "I was certain that he would take offense with my stating it so bluntly. Yet, he seemed to expect my observation and take it in stride. So each side is fully aware that they would be letting the enemy, so to speak, into their country to observe what they will."

Via the Mind Link still in operation, Lilly Ann sent, *There are both advantages and disadvantages to opening consulates in our lands. We ought to consider this proposal carefully. One thing is certain, even if we open our land to Megalos spies, we still have one advantage that they do not: instant communications. It will take months for them to get a message from here to there.*

I like the idea of having a Santi fortress on Megalos, Ket sent. *I find it very hopeful that they no longer have an emperor running their country, but the Senate. However, from what little I know about their Senate, I suspect a bungled job of it. I need to talk to Rea about this. She may be able to shed some light on the proposal. You all discuss it, and we'll get back to you directly.*

"I want to be on record now as opposing it," Alton replied. "While it may give us the opportunity to meddle down at the source of everything, it opens wide the door to them. It is giving the enemy a foothold into our otherwise secure lands. I vote no."

The others acknowledged him, and the Mind Link was broken. Elona summoned the rest of her Circle. After filling the others in on the proposal, their discussion began in earnest. Pros and cons flew fast at first. Having official representatives of Velona and the Santi residing on Megalos with the freedom to visit nearly anywhere offered keen insights into their enemy, their mindset, and plans. On the other hand, having a Centurion here in Velona free to roam anywhere would give away any of their plans, forcing them to operate in secret. All too frequently, secrets have a way of becoming known, however.

As I sat back reflecting upon this sudden new development, I had a deeply felt intuition that the decision I had to make would have a far reaching, long term impact, good or ill. Sometimes one has these feelings like this decision, this issue, will come back to haunt you many, many years later. Momentous might be an adjective to describe this offer of opening up consulates. Yet, it seemed to me more like inviting the enemy into your lands. Were we about to open the door to trouble?

Lilly Ann pointed out that more communication between opposing fractions yields resolutions, not less. After all, were we not building all these autonomous fortresses within the occupied sectors for the very purpose of helping the oppressed within them? By having a consulate on Megalos, would we not be able to disseminate our points of view? Would we not be able to influence events there?

I countered with the datum I learned the hard way; you cannot rationally discuss matters with an insane man. Indeed, I considered this new church in Megalos to be just that, rather insane on the subject of man and religion. Yet, having total access to wander the streets of Megalos could yield such invaluable information. Certainly, they must also know this.

"You are dwelling on the spy aspects, Ket," Lilly Ann continued to argue. "Had someone talked straight to the late Emperor, perhaps the entire war could have been avoided. Better trading deals could be worked out. Strictly on a person to person basis, their people may come to see that everyone who lives beyond their island are not barbarians. Need I continue?" she said rather didactically.

My decision: let each country or kingdom determine their own fate. I refused to allow a Megalos consulate at Mont Blanc. King Percival likewise refused, as did Elona Po. However, Calgary thought such would good for their trading and welcomed the idea. On West Reach or Cymry, the Grande Council of Kings, never really having been bothered too much by the long arm of the Centurions, allowed an exchange of consulates as well, hoping to increase their stature in the world of countries. Fortress d'Grange, long a very independent group, saw no reason to break with their tradition and politely refused the offer.

Last to refuse, Elona commented to their ambassador, "We will see how things go with West Reach and Calgary. If we like what we see there, then perhaps the day will come when we can exchange diplomats. However, for now, there is too much hatred for what your people have done to our fellow sectors for me to accept this. I am afraid that we would not be able to provide you with significant protection from those who have recently lost so much."

Ever the diplomat, Maximus replied graciously, "I accept your decision. However, I do beseech you to observe how beneficial the exchange is for West Reach and Calgary. As you say, perhaps another day will come. It has been a pleasure meeting you."

Chapter 40 In the Aftermath, the Three Roses

By the summer of 625, some six months from the fall of Zargarb, the situation in the occupied sectors had become grim indeed. Daily, reports filtered in from the various Santi fortresses. With fiery rhetoric, the new priests assailed the enforced churchgoers with damnation to the Flaming Pits of Hell should they disobey the Laws of God, Jehosa, as made up by the Pope.

"Your soul shall burn eternally in the sulfur fires of Hell if you do not repent of your sins and accept the Word of God and obey," one priest yelled to his congregation. "Each one of us, you, and you, and you," he pointed to various members of his audience whom he recognized as the more prominent members of the town, "are born on this earth as sinners. Yea, we are all born as sinners, greed, lust, avarice — is there anyone among us who has never felt these sins? Nay, none, all are born sinners. Yet, I say unto you, women are ten times the sinners as men. It was woman who ate of the forbidden fruit and caused man along with her to be cast out of the Holy Realm, the Heaven of Jehosa, far above us. Women, not men, have brought us to our mighty downfall. The blame rests squarely upon them. Change not thy ways, and thy precious soul shalt be damned to eternal suffering in the Pits of Hell."

"Dost thou not know that Lord Jehosa sees all? He, the Creator of Tarra and these mortal bodies that house our precious souls, is omniscient, all-knowing, all watching. He sees you when you are in bed; he is watching as you work; he is everywhere. Furthermore, he keeps a ledger on each and every one of us mortals! Two columns hast this ledger: one marked good and one marked bad. One page for each and every one of us. What dost Lord Jehosa do with this ledger you ask? As he watches your every action, each and every day, he tallies your behavior. You generously donate a tithe to the Church and a checkmark is placed in the good column. You consume too much wine and a check goes into the bad column. You flirt with another woman or man who is not your spouse and another bad check is logged."

"And what you ask does the Lord Jehosa do with this Holy Ledger? When your frail, human body dies, your soul is met by a servant of Lord Jehosa and taken unto him. He looks at the ledger, tallying the marks. If the good outweigh the bad, your soul goes on into his Holy Realm of Heaven. Yet, if bad wins, your precious soul is given unto Lucifer to be taken to his land of eternal fires, there to burn and sweat and starve and toil ceaselessly unto the end of all time! There is no second chance; there is no mercy, only the ledger denoting what you have done here on Tarra. We, the Holy Priests of Jehosa, are here to help you and your soul gain the good marks. We want each and every one of your souls to enter the Holy Kingdom of Heaven, not burn forever in Hell."

"This is why we have been demanding that each and every one of you attend church at least once a week. Lord Jehosa then places at least one good mark beside your name in the Holy Ledger! Each week, you should be studying the Holy Gospels." He waived a copy of the newly printed holy book before his audience.

"Yet, few of you can read, to say nothing of writing. Hence, we have begun the Scholastic Universities, where we can teach you to read and write so that you may read the holy words for yourselves! Our teachers will also instruct you in many subjects so that you are no longer ignorant of the knowledge of the world. These gain you many good marks."

"Spreading the Holy Words of Jehosa to thy neighbors gains you a good mark. Reporting your neighbor's transgressions to our servants, the Holy Paladins, gains you a good mark. In this way, we can attempt to alter the bad behavior of your neighbor before it is too late and he faces eternal damnation in the Pits of Hell. Truly, we your holy priests of Jehosanity, have your very best interests in our hearts."

"Of course, because of their gender, women begin life on Tarra with a ledger filled with bad marks, unlike the ledger of a man. It is a hundred times easier to salvage the soul of a man than that of a woman, who was born from sin. We all must work together to help salvage women from their ledger of bad marks. It will not be easy. Women must be subservient to man in all things. Women must please men in all ways, each one gaining them another good mark. Women must never contradict the words of a man, either openly or in secret, for Lord Jehosa knows what is in every heart and mind. He is everywhere and sees all; nothing can be hidden from his eyes."

"Yet, we all know that some women cannot or will not even try to purify their souls, to gain enough good marks so that their souls can enter the Holy Heaven. I say unto you, we men must do all that we can to help our fairer sex overcome the evil that they were born with! Some may think that our methods are too harsh, but I say unto you, a woman who can no longer speak cannot easily gain more bad marks arguing with a man! A prostitute who can no longer see or perhaps walk can no longer continue their life of sin, which leads their souls only unto Hell! We only have their eternal souls upon our minds. We want their souls to go to Heaven, not to Lucifer."

"Still, many of you will encounter women who just refuse to obey, arguing, protesting, and perhaps even living a life of lasciviousness and greed. Despair not wholly. We have created a last line of hope for such women, the Nunneries. Yes, we have created special convents where troublesome women can be sent. There, under the expert care of other women, who have devoted their entire lives to the worship of Jehosa, forsaking marriage and all worldly ties, these troublesome women will be cared for and taught right from wrong, taught to tally up only good marks that one day they, too, shall have their eternal souls enter Heaven with those of us men."

"We men owe our women all the aid that we can provide them, for they begin life, even as a babe, flush with the ledger full of bad marks. After all, even their bodies are fighting for good marks, for do they not bleed out the evil every month? Men have no inherent evil to bleed out, do we? Nay, we must do all that we can to help our women gain good marks, not more bad ones. So report all transgressions you see or even suspect they might be doing to your local Holy Paladins or even bring them to us priests. We promise you that we will do all that is humanly possible to get them to change their evil ways, to begin gaining the good marks that will ultimately lead them as well unto the Holy Realm of Heaven."

Over the months, an unending diatribe of such dribble was relayed to our headquarters at Mont Blanc and in turn was relayed to all other Santi groups as well as the forming new Sisterhood in Velona. The older ex-Sisterhood leaders and even some older ex-members knew where this was heading, complete slavery of women, and casting women's rights back over a century, wiping out all the progress they had fought so long and hard to gain. Alicia, the ex-High Council representative of Zargarb, was sick over this news. Ranting and raving, she convinced all the other ex-Sisterhood members to cease their attempts to reform a new Sisterhood in Velona. Instead, all the remaining women joined the Santi del Dio en-mass, swelling our numbers considerably. During the summer, I was faced with how to incorporate all these mainly non-combatant personnel, often leaders and planners, into our growing organization. Concurrent events provided the answer.

Spring had come in Zargarb, Jenna Rose had just turned twenty-five. Her establishment, the Lady's Inn, had become quite profitable. Her long blonde hair, firm bosom, enchanting eyes, and shapely body had been put to good use. She had five other women working for her plus a bar tender and a bouncer, who expelled the unruly. Entertainment was what she and her employees provided. No man could resist her flirtations. The Lady's Inn was the place to be for tantalizing enjoyment. Her rules insisted upon no actual sexual acts on the premises, but she did not attempt to dictate what her women did when they left the inn later in the night. She did not consider herself a prostitute, for she had never sold her body. Still, she enjoyed the intimate company of a handsome man when the time was right.

On March 21 after closing, she once more counted her receipts, placing her worker's pay in a strongbox behind the counter for the others to pick up tomorrow. Her profits, she carefully hid in a secret compartment known only to her, which lay hidden beneath a floorboard, also behind the bar. Wrapping her shawl around her, she stepped out into the chilly spring night, locking the door behind her.

"Jenna Rose?" called out a cold voice; chills shot down her spine. She turned to face the speaker. Six of the hated Holy Paladins formed a semicircle around the door. Any idea of fleeing was eliminated. She nodded, and the taller man said, "Come with us. You are under arrest for unholy actions."

Although she tried to protest, strong arms bodily carried her off with them. Although struggling to get free, all that happened was that the shooting pains in her arms worsened as they tightened their grip. No use in screaming.

No one ever dared go against these abominable men. They entered one of the many churches within the city walls. Still struggling to free herself, she was thrust into a dimly lit room. One man wearing priestly robes with a hood that hid his face from view sat behind a desk.

The man's icy voice spoke, "Jenna Rose, you are hereby found guilty of vile prostitution and endangering the souls of men. You are duly sentenced to have your hands removed and sent to live in the Nun's Abbey in the old Sisterhood Inn. That is all."

Jenna screamed, "Pig! Who gives you the right to mutilate me? How dare you try me for crimes I have not committed? I. . ." She did not complete her protests, a heavy blow landed upon her head and everything went black and silent. Sometime later, she awoke with a massive headache. Although she felt that she was lying in a bed, her body was wracked with pain. Instinctively, she raised her hands to massage the back of her head. In absolute shock, she stared at a pair of heavily bandaged stumps where her hands had last been. Her shriek of horror echoed loudly in the dimly lit room.

Just outside the door, she heard a woman's voice say calmly, "She is awake now. Let Sister Anastasia know." Jenna continued to scream with the most violent yells she could make. Even when the door opened and a nun wearing the familiar blue habit entered making "shh shh" sounds, she continued her screams just as loudly as she could, as if that would somehow deal with the horrid situation. Finally, her head throbbing and arms tremendously aching, she passed out.

Sometime later, she awoke once more to find some of the intense pain had subsided. Three nuns were bathing her body and changing the dressings on her wounds. "You have undergone a great deal, my dear," one of the nuns, probably Sister Anastasia explained in a soft, quiet voice. "Thank Jehosa that you are still alive and can now work only for good marks on the Holy Ledger. You are fortunate that you still have the time to erase all the many bad marks so that your soul can go to Heaven."

Jenna found this talk utterly stupid. She'd never seen this thing called a soul anywhere, although she had looked for it a couple times out of curiosity. "Just relax; we will attend to your needs. Later on, after you have healed, we will move you into the domestic wing where other women who are working on their penance to Lord Jehosa stay." Jenna resisted the temptation to scream yet again. She did need a bath, and she found it comforting to have these women gently washing her naked body for her. When they finished, they helped her into a loose fitting slip, rather like a sack, explaining that others could help her more easily with such a simple dress.

While two cleaned up the mess, another woman helped her sip refreshing tea, which was laced with something that Jenna could not identify. Soon warmth spread from her stomach, and she felt drowsy and was asleep before they laid her down in the bed. No dreams came.

Days passed by in a blur; someone appeared to help her with bodily functions, eating, and drinking. Someone mentioned that everyone was given a bath each week. Although she tried to count the baths, she soon lost count. Whatever was in the tea befuddled her mind and made her feel extremely docile.

Finally, Sister Anastasia came one day and announced, "There, you no longer require any more bandages." Jenna stared at the scarred, pinkish stumps where her lovely hands had been. She nearly vomited. "Today, you may move in with others, who like yourself, are working on their penances. Come with me, please, Jenna." She had no options but to meekly follow this nun out of the room. She had not walked much during all this time and found her legs a bit weak and was glad when the nun finally stopped before another door, knocked, and then opened it. "Here we are, Jenna. This will be your new home. You are to share this room with two other women. We encourage each of you to help each other as much as you can. There simply are not enough of us caring women, nuns as you may call us, to attend to your needs continually. Perhaps more of the kindhearted women of Zargarb will join our order one day. Jehosa knows how much we need them. Here are your roommates."

"This is Christina Locamelli, she has no tongue and cannot speak." Jenna saw another young woman, who was probably around twenty years old with typical short blonde hair and slightly golden skin, suggesting she had some Arad blood in her. She was pretty, but her sad, downcast eyes told Jenna much. "And this is Lorissa Moeti; she is blind and will need much help from you. See, Christina, I told you that soon you would have some help with Lorissa. Now Lorissa, Jenna here has no hands, so you will have to help her do many things. I will leave you all to get acquainted. Remember to do good things; each good action you do offsets one of the many bad marks on your Holy Ledger." Lorissa was slightly older than Jenna was, with brown hair and thick lips. However, Jenna found it unnerving to stare at her empty eye sockets.

Even more unnerving to Jenna was Lorissa's voice; she spoke but did not look at her. She had no idea where in the room Jenna was! In spite of her awful predicament, Jenna felt compassion for her two roommates and rushed to the bedside of Lorissa.

"I'm right here, beside you." Immediately, brandishing a bright smile, Christina came over and sat on the other side of Christina, putting her arm around her, some strange noses emanating from her tongueless mouth.

"Can I feel you?" Lorissa said quietly. "I can't see anymore, so I have to feel about to get some idea of things. Chrissy can't speak, so we rather have to guess what she wants. When we get it right, she nods her head. I usually have to put my hands on her head to tell. But now that you are here, you can see her and that will help a lot."

Lorissa fumbled over Jenna's body, trying to get some idea of her shape and size. An awful intake of breath occurred when she felt the ends of Jenna's arms. "My god, they really did cut off your hands!" She began to cry, but tears only filled the empty sockets and dripped down her face. Chrissy knew what to do and dabbed her face gently with a cloth. "I can't believe they did this to you!

The filthy butchers."

"I can't believe what they have done to you two," Jenna replied, her compassion rising above her own misery. Here were two who had awful situations of their own. Soon the three began getting acquainted, beginning with their own stories.

Lorissa could only guess at Christina's tale. Speaking for Chrissy, she explained, "I think that Christina is married or was, not sure anymore, and has a son and daughter. They never let them visit, I asked once. The nun said that no one would ever be allowed to come and visit us. I guess she will never see her family again. Probably just as well. Her husband is a real bastard to have turned her in for speaking her mind about the family finances and such. At least that is what I have gleaned from her. Perhaps you can ask her more proper question and see her reactions where I cannot."

"Me, well I got in trouble because I kept the accounts for Ace Shipping and called a lot of irregularities to the attention of the owner. Now that I have had time to think about it, I think that I caught him stealing from the company funds, which is why I was blinded. How about you? Are you married?"

"No, I run, no, used to run, my own inn. Very profitable, I might add. They claimed that I am a prostitute, but I have never sold my body for money. My girls and I tease, excite, and entertain men, but that's all. God, I hope my other girls have not met the same fate as me! How can we tell if others have been brought here? How many of us are there in here?"

"Sorry, Jenna, I can't see, I've no idea at all. You have to ask yes-no questions so Chrissy can answer. She can see." Thus, the three women began to bond together. Mealtimes and bodily functions were the most trying for them, especially for the nearly helpless Jenna, who found that she could do nothing for herself and depended utterly on Chrissy for help. However, they quickly found some methods in the madness of the situation, and the three found that they could work together to accomplish all basic tasks of living. True, even the smallest normal action became a challenge for these three; they soon found that they could rely upon the skills of each other. Their tight bond to each other would soon be tested.

At least daily, one nun would come and read them the so-called Holy Gospels. Chrissy, who had been a worshiper of the Northern Orthodoxy before it had been wiped out, found so many alterations and outright lies, that she closed her mind to the nun's voice. She wished desperately that she could somehow tell the others that all this was mumbo jumbo, but she could not.

After what must have been a month of their routine, Jenna had finally had enough. While some in her predicament would have fallen into a deep, hopeless apathy or worse, Jenna, a self-taught business woman, became all the more defiant, until at last, Lorissa warned her, "Jenna, if you don't stop talking like this where the nuns can hear you, they will cut out your tongue like they did Chrissy. Please stop; I don't think I can stand the utter silence any more. Please, I beg you."

"That's it then. We have to get out of here somehow. I promise to behave, Lorissa. I think you have it worse than Chrissy or myself. Let's put our heads together, and see if we can find a way out of here. If I can only get to my secret stash, I have a lot of money saved up; we can all live nicely on it."

"Don't talk like that," Lorissa complained. "Where on Tarra can we go? I am nearly helpless. Chrissy cannot even tell us her problems, and we have to care for your every need."

"Look, we are a team. Together, we can survive all this. I swear to you both that I will never desert you two. I will always be with you; I promise never to be away from either of you," Jenna replied with a newfound enthusiasm, a new purpose for her life.

Lorissa began crying, and Chrissy dutifully wiped her cheeks. Between sobs and fumbling to find Jenna's arms to hold on to tightly, she said, "Thank you, Jenna. I promise too. Never shall we part." Chrissy nodded her head as well, and Jenna relayed that to Lorissa.

"Okay, then, it's going to be one for all and all for one from now on!" Jenna declared. "Let's call ourselves the Three Roses! After all, we are all very pretty women."

"Now you are going too far," protested Lorissa. Chrissy hung her head down nearly to her waist.

"Look you two, I have got eyes. I know men, I know women, and I have had lots of experience in my twenty-five years. So I don't have hands and cannot make myself look dolled up any more. In bed, no one will notice anyway. Just because you don't have any eyes, doesn't suddenly make you ugly, Lorissa. You are still stunning, if only we didn't have to wear these ugly sacks. You just need some coaching on how to flirt without eyes, that's all. And as for you, my pretty Chrissy, so you can't talk. Big deal, you still can look ravishing and who talks in bed anyway? Did your sleazy husband talk to you in bed much?" Chrissy reluctantly shook her head no. "See, we all just need to adjust our ways."

"Oh get real, Jenna!" retorted Lorissa. "What man in any country will want to take a blind woman, a dumb woman, or a hopeless cripple as a wife? Okay, well maybe some really dumb, ugly, drunk, street bum might, because he cannot get anything better."

Jenna did not have an immediate comeback for this one; Lorissa did have a valid point. "Well, the Three Roses will never, I promise you, never, join up with street bums! I'd rather have you two pleasure me than suffer such indignation as that! I never have been a prostitute and I never will, nor will I ever permit you two to do so. What I am telling you both is that we are still young and pretty. Don't despair; we have our whole lives before us still, and the very first thing we have to do is find a way out of here somehow."

"Where would we go?" Lorissa asked, coming around to Jenna's optimism. She realized right then that two paths were open to her: one of acceptance of being a hopeless, blind cripple waiting for death to take her out of her misery and one of making a solid attempt of a somehow rewarding life, although she had no idea what that might be.

Chrissy began animatedly gesturing, trying to communicate that she had an idea. "Chrissy is trying to tell us something," Jenna relayed to Lorissa. "Oh I get it; this is just like a charade guessing game, Lorissa. She just acts it out, and we have to guess. I'll relay what she is doing, and we both can guess. It's just like we are at a party, Chrissy!" This brought a huge smile to Chrissy. For the first time, her infirmity was being treated as no more than a party game. Eagerly she threw herself into the acting.

Before long, Lorissa guessed it. "The Santi!" Chrissy's exaggerated head nodding confirmed it. "Yes, she's right. The Santi has a lot of the old Sisterhood members in it. Some of them had been mistreated as we have been. I bet that if we could talk to them, they would help us out, somehow, though I don't know how."

"Terrific idea, Chrissy. Now all we have to do is figure out how to get out of here and get to the Santi Fortress just outside the city walls. Let's see, we are going to need some shoes, that's for sure and some cloaks to hide ourselves. We will have to go out the gates during the daytime, hide until dark, and then walk over to the Santi. If we go there in the daytime, someone will get suspicious and try to stop us."

"That won't work, someone will be sure to miss us at least at mealtimes and sound the alarm. The bastards will be hunting for us everywhere after that," Lorissa declared vehemently. "What if we are stopped by the guards at the gate?"

"Hum, okay. Suppose we sneak out in the wee hours of the morning and go out the gate with the hunters and farmers just as soon as the gates are opened. If we carry baskets, we can say we are going flower hunting for our store. It may take us an hour or so to circle around the city to the Santi Fort. It is too risky for the three of us to walk all the way across the city to the eastern gate. The western gate is only a couple blocks away." This idea they liked. Now they began making plans in earnest. Chrissy indicated she knew where they could swipe shoes and cloaks from the nun's storage closet at the end of the hall. However, none knew the layout of the abbey or where the exits were located compared to their room.

"Chrissy, you stand guard. If you hear someone coming, you snap your fingers once, and I'll rush back," Jenna proposed. After the nun came for their afternoon reading, if all went as it usually did, no one would check on them until supper was brought up to them. Quietly, Chrissy opened the door and peered cautiously up and down the long, dimly lit hallway. No one was in sight. She stepped out, holding it open for Jenna. They smiled at each other.

Jenna began walking quietly on the plush carpet toward the far end of the hall. A surge of adrenaline coursed through her body; she was finally doing something about her situation, and a sense of adventure and exhilaration flowed within her frame. At the end of the hall, she saw sunlight coming through the lone window and peered out. They were on the second floor. To her right was a door, which led to a stairs. Ordinarily, she would have just opened it and continued her stealthy explorations. However, when she involuntarily reached out her hand to open it, she realized this would be more difficult now. Determined not to let a door stop her, she fumbled around with her arms and managed to get it to open. Seeing a rock at the side of the wall, she realized that it was there for a purpose, a doorstop, used when guests were making frequent trips up to their rooms carrying baggage. Holding the door open and using her feet, she got the rock to prop the door open.

Having accomplished all this, she felt a renewed rush of life; she was not entirely helpless. Cautiously, she went down the stairs and found that there was an outside door. A huge metal rod securely locked the door shut from the inside. No one on the outside could open the door unless the cross rod was removed. Confident that she had their exit route discovered, she quickly retraced her steps, cautiously moving the rock back, and letting the door close quietly. Just as the door closed, she heard the finger snap from Chrissy and saw her worried, frantic expression. Jenna ran as fast as she could; together, they ducked into their room as the footsteps came perilously close to their hallway. "Mission accomplished," Jenna breathlessly whispered to her fellow conspirators. "It will be very easy to sneak out at night."

Chrissy shrugged her shoulders, as if asking a question. "Tonight, rather early tomorrow morning we make our break out!" Jenna declared. "We should snitch the shoes and clothes when everyone has retired for the night. I think we will need some time to get ready, as clumsy as the Roses are," she teased. Chrissy had a light in her eyes that Jenna had never seen. She knew that her friend was just as excited about gaining their freedom as she was. She spent an hour going over the details of just what Lorissa could expect. She realized that going down steps completely blind was going to be more than a bit of a challenge for Lorissa.

After the nun removed their supper trays, the Three Roses waited impatiently for the abbey to settle down for the night. When Jenna thought it was safe, she and Chrissy opened their door. A lone oil light provided dim illumination of their long hallway. The two reversed roles, Jenna held the door open while Chrissy went to the closet. In five minutes, the first step was accomplished. Indeed, it took them a little time to get ready. Just try putting on unfamiliar shoes with your eyes closed or without using your hands. Chrissy did much of the work. Next, they experimented with the cloaks and found that they would cover nearly all their bodies; they were intended for rainy days.

"We should practice walking with Lorissa. We don't want anyone to realize she cannot see. Make sure, Chrissy, that my stubs are not visible, that would give us away. Lorissa, you are going to have to depend utterly on us while walking. You cannot appear to be blind. Chrissy, you take her right arm and I'll take her left. Let's practice walking around our room." For several hours, the Three Roses practiced; slowly Lorissa relaxed and began to trust the gentle body pressure signals that the two gave her. She hoped that she would not give them away when the time came.

When Jenna guessed it was time to make their big move, she put her arms around both women and said, "Okay, time to escape. Remember, all for one and one for all; here we go!" Lorissa felt a knot in her stomach; she had never done anything like this before; a wee bit of fear crept into her mind, which she could not dispel. Chrissy opened the door, and Jenna helped Lorissa out. Once outside and the door closed, the two took up their positions, and the three began walking down the hall, as quietly as a mouse. By the time they reached the door to the stairs, Lorissa had become accustomed to walking, but feared the stairs ahead. She took a deep breath as Chrissy opened the door and put the rock in place.

Once the Three Roses were on the other side at the landing, she removed the rock and let the door close quietly. Now came the horrible stairs. It was pitch black. Both women now experienced what life was like for Lorissa, as the three ever so slowly descended the stairs. "The door's here, Chrissy," Jenna whispered. "See if you can feel it and find the iron bar. It should lift up." After a couple of worrisome minutes, Jenna heard the dull sound of the bar being raised. Chrissy opened the door, and all three felt the rush of fresh, cool summer air upon their bodies. Outside, the early dawn twilight had barely begun to announce the coming of the new day. Carefully making sure no one was in sight, the three stepped outside, and Chrissy shut the door. A sense of freedom rushed through all three.

The Three Roses stepped out into the street. Chrissy quickly adjusted their cloaks, making sure that Lorissa's face was entirely hidden, and that Jenna's arms did not show. Satisfied, Chrissy motioned ahead, and they began walking slowly down the street. Before long, they encountered the market square, which was close to the inn and the gate, the last market before the western gate. Jenna and Chrissy looked around for suitable baskets and found a couple near one farmer's stall. Chrissy quickly took two, giving one to Lorissa to hold in her hands and one for her. Satisfied, they walked slowly down the street toward the gate. "We should hide in the last alleyway," Jenna whispered.

"How long do we stand here? Is anyone around?" whispered a terribly nervous Lorissa, who had never done anything this secretive before.

"Men have already begun gathering at the gate," Jenna whispered. "Not much longer."

Shortly, a couple of city guards walked up to the gate and unlocked it. "I'll go get us some tea and biscuits," one said to the other. Jenna thought this was even better, only one guard potentially to have to handle. From the darken alley, she and Chrissy watched nearly fifty men march or ride out of the gates. Some carried hunting weapons, others farming tools. As the last of the men moved up to the gate following the long line, the Three Roses moved slowly out of hiding and began their walk to the gate as well.

"Morning ladies," the gate man said as they approached.

"Hi," Jenna cheerily replied. "Going flower hunting. Bid us good luck." The man smiled and so wished them. After passing through the gate, they had to make an awkward sideways movement to get out of the way of a wagon. Finally, they were some distance from the gate, and all three relaxed, walking down the paved Centurion made roadway.

"Chrissy, keep your eyes open for some flowers we can pick. If we have some in the baskets, it will help with our subterfuge." Once they had climbed the hill just beyond the gate, they were free from spying eyes. Now came the more difficult part of their trek, they had to go cross-country, circling around the entire city, leading Lorissa over the rough ground.

The ill-fitting shoes did not help. After what seemed an eternity, around ten in the morning, the Three Roses finally arrived at the gate to the Santi fortress. However, the gates were closed. Sensing that something was wrong, Lorissa asked, "What's the matter?"

"Gates are closed. Chrissy, please knock for us," Jenna took charge. A man slid a small wooden slab aside a tiny window in the door and peered out at them. "Just three women, sir, may we enter?" Jenna asked politely. The sound of the wooden slab being shut seemed very loud, but then they heard the latches being undone and the door creaked open.

"This way, ladies. Welcome to the Santi Fortress. How can we help you?" the man said with definitely a foreign accent.

"We would like to speak with whoever is in charge please," Jenna replied, for the first time unsure of exactly what she ought to say.

After securing the gate, he said, "Follow me, please." He led them at a brisk pace through the many men working on the various construction projects toward the only real building, a hastily constructed wooden square house, one side of which was a stable for horses.

"Please sir, not so fast. We cannot keep up," Jenna finally had to plead and reveal their situation. "She is blind; she cannot speak; and I have no hands. Just a bit slower." She hated to have to reveal their abnormalities to a stranger, but she had no other choice.

The gate man stopped abruptly and faced them, a look of horror on his face. "Excuse me ladies. I did not know. My god, what have they done to you? Yes, Tom will see you; I'm certain. Let me know if I go too fast. You have hidden it well from me," he complimented them. Jenna felt a surge of success in her mind, for it had worked nearly to perfection this time. They could do it again if they had to do so!

At the building, the man knocked on the door and announced, "Tom, three women are here to see you. Looks like the bastards have been at it again." A voice inside said to send them on in, and the man opened the door for the women. Awkwardly, the three maneuvered Lorissa inside.

"Here, have a seat at our table, take off your cloaks and make yourselves comfortable. Sorry about all the mess; we are going over the construction plans right now. I am Tom Whiteheath, the leader of this fortress, my wife, Sally, and our expert Judger Art Longton. How may we help you? Oh my god!" he exclaimed. They had removed their cloaks, and Chrissy maneuvered Lorissa to a chair, Tom could now see them fully and was appalled at what he saw.

"Oh dear God," Sally added. "I bet you are starving. Let me rustle up something to eat." Although she apparently meant well, Jenna did not see her leave the room or even signal some servant somewhere. Only these three seemed to be in the small, overly crowed room. "Let me get you three some descent clothes! What are you wearing, sacks? Golly!"

Jenna spoke for them, "Yes, we are hungry. Clothes, now that would be a most welcome addition! Our standard issue nun's sacks leave everything to be desired. We are the Three Roses. We are inseparable." She then gave the introductions and briefly told them what had happened to each of them. When she finished, a woman dressed in chain mail entered bringing a tray with hot tea, biscuits, honey, and cheese. This surprised Jenna, since she would have sworn that Sally had done nothing to let someone know to bring food.

"I must apologize for our unseemly eating methods. I have to be fed and Chrissy has a very hard time as you can see."

"No problem. I am just glad that you three are alive and in such good health and spirits. We've seen some pretty horrible things these past few months," Sally consoled them. "You go right ahead and eat any way you can. Some of the women that have passed through here have been beaten to an inch of their lives, horribly disfigured. We've treated so many broken bones that I've totally lost count. You three are indeed lucky, at least on that account."

Jenna continued her plea. "We have come here seeking sanctuary and our freedom. We ask only two things of you: never ever separate us and please have someone help me recover my money stash within the city. I will gladly pay for your services and for our keep, after my stash is recovered."

Grinning, Tom replied formally, "Sanctuary is hereby granted ladies. You are free at last. Gladly I accept your terms, Jenna. No pay initially is needed. However, as you can probably tell from all the construction going on outside, we are not yet equipped to take care of guests. Unless you object, we will take you to some place where you will be completely safe and can start new lives, perhaps Velona. Is that acceptable to the Three Roses?"

"Yes, sir," Jenna replied for the others, who nodded their agreement.

Art could contain his enthusiasm no longer, "Tom, do I detect yet another nefarious escapade within the city?" he chuckled.

Tom explained, "Art here just loves to sneak into the city and undermine anything. He has a real knack for it. You've certainly come to the right people to help you recover your stash!" She beamed.

"Might I ask what is the significance of your name, the Three Roses?" Tom asked.

Sally answered before Jenna could reply. Looking at Jenna, she suggested, "Men. Dear, these are three very pretty young women, three roses in full bloom. Very appropriate, I think," she winked at Jenna, who whispered to Lorissa that she had blinked at them, which brought a smile to Lorissa's face.

Red faced, Tom said, "Okay, okay I get it. Yes, I must agree with Sally, only I would say three gorgeous women. After you eat, Sally can help you find something to wear, the sooner we get you out of those rags, the better. Now then, Jenna, please tell Art about your stash and where it is located. I think that we best retrieve it yet tonight, Art. Let me know whom you wish to accompany you."

"Actually, my sir name is Rose," Jenna teased. "About my stash, I'll be going along," Jenna declared. Turning to her companions, "This may not take long, and I'll return with my stash or die trying. It's going to be far too dangerous to take you along with me, and really there is nothing you two could do to help on this one. I will only be gone a little while. If we are successful, the Three Roses will have all the money we need."

Turning to Art, she then carefully outlined where her inn was located and what needed to be done. Art asked about how large a sack to bring along in which to carry back her stash. "Gosh, I've never tried to move it before or had it all out. I just kept salting my profits away. Maybe three sacks?"

He grinned, "Okay, I will come prepared. Sally, make sure she gets dressed in a shirt and pants and some descent shoes. She will need her freedom of movement."

"How many of us do you want to go with you, Art?" asked Tom.

"Just one will be enough. Either you or Lena will be fine. I know you are busy, and Lena can both fight and look after Jenna. We should be in and out in just a few minutes. Allow an hour there and one to get back. Big question is when to leave. I'd say because it is in an inn, which may be in use, midnight might be wisest. The hardest part will be helping Jenna climb up the ladder to the docks; with no hands, it can be a bit tricky."

"Good. Sally will monitor you. Just let her know if you run into anything unexpected that you can't handle. We best let Sally find our new guests something to wear." On cue, she led them into a back room, took their measurements, and went in search of spare clothes.

As the midnight hour approached, Jenna, now wearing a leather outfit of Lena's sat at the same table. Lena, a woman of thirty, explained, "I used to be a Sisterhood fighter and leader of our group. I could have gone off to Velona with the rest of my dear friends, but I have always been a fighter and felt I'd be of more use here. Trust me, if anyone tries to lay a hand on you, it will be the last thing that they ever try!"

"How did you become a Sister? I mean did men do bad things to you?" Jenna asked. Before now, she had only heard rumors, never having met any actual Sisters.

"Yea gods, not like they did to you!" she exclaimed. "Why if someone tried to do that to me, I'd kill them!" Then she realized that even if Jenna had wanted to attack those who had mutilated her, she had no hands with which to do it, and she flushed at her own outburst. "No, my husband kept getting drunk and beating me. I kept telling myself that he really meant what he said the next day, 'I'm sorry, I'll change.' He never did, but when he tried to have his drunken friends rape me, I slit his throat with a butcher's knife. Joined the Sisterhood and learned to fight properly, got good at it, if I do say so myself. Say, if you want revenge on the man who did this to you, let me know. I can arrange for him to meet with an 'accident,'" she grinned.

Jenna sighed, "No, the coward had his face hidden when he pronounced judgment on me. I was knocked out and wound up like this in the abbey. I have no idea against whom to strike out at in retaliation. What's done is done now. I have to move on with my life. I should have known bad things would result when these beasts took over control of our city, should have packed up and left, though I don't know where I could have gone really. Honestly, meeting up with Lorissa and Christina have been one of the best things that's happened to me. They really need me, such as I am. It's good to feel needed and wanted, you know."

Their conversation was cut short by Art as he poked his head in the door and said, "Okay, ladies, let's get this adventure on the road." As the two walked outside into the darkness, Art handed Lena a second lantern. Like the one he held, this one allowed only a tiny beam of light to shine, which they pointed to the ground before them. Quietly, they left the main gate and walked down to the Med Sea shore. There, they marched along the beach up towards the looming great wall around the city. The wall extended only a short distance into the sea. Thus, they merely walked out into the cool waters, which came up to Jenna's waist, and circumvented the barrier easily. A short distance further, the dark shadows of the wooden docks rose over their heads. The stench of rotting fish was overpowering down here on the hidden shoreline. Steadily the trio maneuvered through the rotting pile of the city dumping grounds until they reached a ladder.

This vertical ladder led up to a trap door in the flooring of the dock, allowing folks access to the down below area for maintenance purposes or just to dump their garbage. Shining his thin beam upwards, he asked, "Think you can climb this?" Jenna said she could, although she had no idea if she was merely being optimistic or not. Lena went first, carefully opening the trap door making sure the dock area was deserted. Satisfied, she climbed on up and out onto the docks, drew her sword, and stood guard. Jenna went next, Art close behind her. If she should slip, he was prepared to catch her and break her fall. She found it more of a challenge than she had thought and had to invent new methods of holding on using her arms and elbows. A short while later, the strong arms of Lena helped her up the last step onto the docks. Both women were smiling. Art followed right behind them, shutting the door. He motioned for them to follow him, and they set off, lanterns shielded so that no light emitted.

Art knew the general location of her inn, but had never actually visited it. Yet, Jenna's directions were very precise, and in a half hour, the trio stood quietly outside her old establishment. Her sign had been torn down, replaced with one that read Ducky's Inn. Art tried the door; naturally, it was locked. Jenna whispered, "Look in the pot of that plant. I kept a spare key in there in case I forgot mine." Art allowed a small beam of light to guide him and found the key. It worked and the trio slipped quietly inside.

"Nothing appears to have been changed," Jenna whispered. "Behind the bar, this way." She led them to her secret, loose floorboard. "Push on that edge; it lifts up. I can't do it any more, no hands." Art followed her orders and soon had the board lifted up and out. He allowed the tiny beam to illuminate the stash.

"Going to need a number of sacks," he teased. "Lena, watch the door." Slowly, he pulled out small pouches and moneybags, placing them in the large sacks he had brought. Rather amazed, it took him fifteen minutes to retrieve them all. As Jenna stuffed new bags into her hole, the others had been pushed back, so it took some doing to get them all. He did a final search to make sure he left none behind. Then he replaced the board. He hoisted three very heavy sacks to his shoulders when Lena whispered that guards were coming. Art replied, disgustedly, "We've left the key in the key hole. No time to retrieve it!"

The guards moved closer to the inn. "I'll handle this," Art whispered and began chanting, while the women ducked down behind the bar out of sight. Jenna caught a tiny fragment of Art's final words, "All secure here. Let's move on." Just then the heavy boot steps of the tramped up towards the door with the telltale key still in the lock. To her amazement, she heard one guard say, "All secure here. Let's move on." The noisy trampling moved away, growing fainter and fainter, until all was silent once more.

"All clear, come on," Art called out. Once outside, Lena took up a guard position while Art relocked the door and placed the key back in its hiding place. "Here, take one, Lena, these are heavy!" She smiled and hoisted one sack on her left shoulder. Now they quietly retraced their path back to the docks. However, when they neared the location of the trap door, two guards were standing nearby, gazing out to sea, and smoking their pipes.

"Shall we take them?" Lena whispered, judging their chances of taking them by surprise.

"No, allow me." Art began another chant. Jenna tried to listen to what he was saying but only caught a few words, "Smell's awful here. Let's go down by the ships." To Jenna's utter amazement, one of the men said, "Smell's awful here. Let's go down by those ships there." Both men wandered away, heading off toward the piers, where a single ship was moored.

Quickly they moved to the trap door and opened it. "Lena, go down. I'll hand you the sacks. Then Jenna goes. I'll bring up the rear." Jenna kept her eyes on the backs of the distant men, while Art and Lena managed to get the sacks down to the ground, some twenty feet below. Fortunately, the men did not look back their way. When it was Jenna's turn to go down, she discovered that going down without hands was even trickier that climbing up! She had an awful time positioning herself to get safely to the first step. Art held on to her arms until she got the hang of it. Seeing her difficulties, Lena climbed up and acted as a clamp, holding her securely to the ladder. Once Jenna was partway down, Art followed, closing the door above him. He felt that he was pressing his luck staying visible for so long. Once the door closed over him, he relaxed; the worst was over.

A short while later the trio arrived at the Santi gate, which opened just as they came up to it. Someone knew their precise movements, Jenna concluded. They walked straight to the wooden office building and entered. Once inside, Sally and Tom were waiting for them. Dropping the three heavy sacks onto the table, Art said mildly, "Total success. No one saw us. In and out. Nothing to report, except these are mighty heavy sacks, my lady!" he teased Jenna, who really had no accurate count of her savings.

"Well, come on Jenna; let's get you out of those wet leathers and into something dry. Then, you can see if it is all there." Lena came with them to change herself, while Art went into a side room. A few minutes later, they all returned to the table to find that Tom had turned up several lanterns so that they could see well.

"May I do the honors of dumping it all out?" asked Art.

Grinning, Jenna said, "You had better do it. If you want me to do it, why, we will still be here at sunup! By the way, Art, whatever did you do back there with the city guards who came up to the door and also to those two men on the docks?"

"Oh that, you noticed? Observant woman thee be," Art teased, as he began dumping out the three large sacks onto the table, now cleared of the many papers that had covered them when Jenna arrived. "In simple terms, Jenna, men hear and see what they expect to see and hear. I merely made the right suggestion at the right time. Positive suggestion, you might call it."

"I call it mind tweaking," Lena countered. "He plants thoughts into their minds, he does. Be careful around Art; he can make you climb into bed with him thinking it is your own idea to do so!" She and Sally gave a chuckle; Jenna smiled coyly, for she also knew how to get a man into her bed just as easily.

Jenna replied, "I think I sort of understand. When I ran my inn, I would do certain gestures and such to get the men to buy another pitcher of ale. You give them what they think they expect or want, and they respond like dogs," Jenna said.

Art paused in his dumping to stare at her, "Jenna, you continually keep surprising me. Yes, you are very correct in your observations. You would make good Guardian material, what do you think, Tom?"

Tom now had to explain the druwids and their special training and skills to Jenna. Art had opened the door, and he could not let her remain ignorant of what Art had said. When he had mostly finished, Art interrupted, "Seldom have I seen a woman as cool in a tight situation as Jenna here was tonight. That ladder was almost the straw that broke the donkey's back. Yet, she didn't complain and worked out a way to climb, nary one comment about having no hands to do it. Jenna is one levelheaded person. We've seen many a person now minus limbs, especially those who fought in the Crusader army. Moaning, groaning, and wallowing in self-pity most of them are, but not Jenna here. Boss, I know what I am talking about."

"Okay, okay, Art. I'll have Sally relay the data up the line," Tom replied. To Jenna he explained, "When the caravel docks wherever it ends up docking in our lands, someone special will be there to meet you and help you three out.

While you are sailing there, I will have one of our special Santi, who guards the ship, fully brief you on who and what the Santi are. From there, it will be up to you three to decide what you want to do. Now let's see what your stash amounts to, shall we?"

All three began opening and dumping out the numerous small pouches and bags. Jenna was a bit surprised to see the ever-growing pile of coins; she had not realized the full extent of her accumulated savings. Sally and Lena sorted out the coins into types, gold, silver, and copper, and then into piles of ten each. Soon the entire table was filled with neat stacks of coins.

"Brother you were right, Jenna, you have one big stash here. May I suggest that we visit a moneychanger and convert these coins into gemstones? They are much more portable, far less weight. Then, you and your friends can carry your stash. Three large sacks were almost more than I could carry," Art suggested.

"Would you? That would be great. I can give you something for your troubles, Art," she offered.

"Thanks, Jenna. But you three will need this far, far more than we do. Besides, I have had more than enough rewards by enjoying your company and having met you. Your name, the Three Roses is very accurate indeed, in more ways than one, ma'am. Besides, I feel that as a man, I owe it to you to show you that all men are not evil and wicked." He would have used other words, had he not been in the company of three women. Instinctively, she gave him a hug. Then it was time for bed. Sally led her outside to the tent in which her two friends were sound asleep. She helped her get snuggled into the makeshift bed and then left Jenna alone with her thoughts.

During the next day, Art and several other men visited many different moneychangers within the city, converting the coins into gemstones of various values. This way, they did not draw attention, which would have occurred had such a large pile of coins been exchanged at one time. That afternoon, Art proudly presented Jenna with several small pouches of the precious stones. "Jenna, I am pleased to present you with your stash, now in gems. Do you realize that you have well over five thousand gold coins worth of gems here? What a stash indeed!"

"You are incredibly wealthy!" exclaimed Lorissa, quite taken aback by the huge sum. Chrissy made gurgling sounds indicating an equal surprise.

"Honestly, I did not know how much I had saved all these years. Business had been good, obviously," she gave him a flirting eye twitch and a sly grin. "I did said that I would be able to help us all," Jenna replied, more than a little awed by the total amount she had saved up.

Sally came in with her arms full of packages. "Roses, I have a little something for you." The twinkle in her eyes Jenna recognized as similar to what she felt after having splurged and gone shopping. She was right in her observation; Sally had purchased clothing and other essentials for the three women. She knew that they did not dare set foot in Zargarb. Besides, they would need proper clothing for the long voyage to Velona. Sally really did desire to show these brave women some kindness, thoughtfulness, and consideration.

For an hour, the Three Roses ooh'ed and ah'ed over their new wardrobe. Each had a durable set of supple leather tops and bottoms and two relatively fancy dresses, plus unmentionables. Jenna's dresses were designed to display her womanly aspects, Sally judged. Christina's were more subdued and dainty, as befitting her personality. Finding the right ones for Lorissa had been more challenging. Lacking sight, colors were irrelevant. Instead, textures were paramount. One dress was made from Southland silk and the other from the softest linen Sally could find. She hoped that Lorissa would feel more womanly wearing these and she was right. As Lorissa showed off her new silk dress, Sally saw the woman smile broadly for the first time and that made her long day of shopping more than worthwhile.

A week later, the Three Roses stood on the poop deck looking back at the Santi fortress as it drifted slowly away from the Freedom Fighter, a caravel out of Velona, who had stopped to pick them up. Jenna described the magnificent scene for Lorissa, while Christina watched with tears in her eyes. The hard reality that she would never again see her children or her home city again had finally swelled up from deep within her mind. Lorissa interrupted the poetic descriptions of Jenna to ask, "What's wrong with Chrissy? I sense something."

"She's crying." Jenna looked at her and added, "I think that she is thinking of her children."

"There, there, Chrissy," Lorissa fumbled to find her dear friend's hand. "We understand. We have all lost enormously, and perhaps you most of all."

Chrissy wiped her eyes and shook her head no, pointing to Jenna's arms. Lorissa knew what she meant. "Well, I must apologize to you both," Lorissa said determinedly. "I have been an old grouch. Ever since they took my eyes away, I have been feeling sorry for myself. I bet you all think I was groveling in self-pity." While Chrissy bravely shook her head to say no, Lorissa added, "And you were right. I was. It took Jenna and her incredible spirit to bring me to my senses. Chrissy, you and I can still function and even to a large extent can look after ourselves, as long as I know where things are at so I don't bump into them. She needs our help for so many small actions of life that you and I take for granted. And we have not heard her grumble, complain, or anything. She is so utterly upbeat that I would not know she has anything wrong with her."

"Oh brother," Jenna teased, half-heartedly. "Seriously, thanks for the compliment. It has been hard to keep such thoughts at bay. When I need to use the chamber pot, I sometimes have the most dreadful thoughts. But hey, this is the way things are now. None of us can do anything about it, unless you can brew up a potion that grows new hands, eyes, and tongues. Actually, if you could do that, why, we would all be millionaires." Everyone chuckled.

"You have such a way with words, Jenna. That is what I didn't know how to say. Accept what is and go on with life. By golly, Chrissy, that is just what the Three Roses must do! I used to be rather good making clothes. I bet with a little practice, I could do so once more. We just have to learn new and different ways to do things."

Jenna interrupted her, "Chrissy's waving her parchment pieces Sally gave her. I think she is trying to say 'Like now I can write what I want to say.' Right Chrissy. She is nodding yes." Lorissa smiled.

"Are you ladies comfortable?" the young captain of the caravel approached them, now that he had set their course. "Will you dine with me at my table tonight?"

"With pleasure," Jenna replied, although Chrissy cast her a doubtful look. She was still rather embarrassed eating in the presence of others.

"No, my pleasure. Seldom do I get to entertain three lovely women on the long voyages. Oh, yes, I almost forgot. Our Protector and his wife, Aaron and Leann, wish to speak with you when you are done watching Zargarb disappear. I told them that this was your first voyage and that folks often love to take it all in, new experience and all that. We mariners sometimes forget how new and strange it is on your first voyage."

Since land was now very distant on the horizon, the three allowed the captain to lead them below to the main cabins. Both Jenna and Lorissa found walking on a swaying ship a bit unnerving, but for different reasons. Chrissy merely held on to the railing to steady herself and the other two.

Normally the cabins were built to sleep two people. Since the beginning of the war last year, the Protector and his wife along with an Axeman and five Sisterhood fighters always accompanied the ship. Now, of course, all except the Axeman, were members of the Santi del Dio. For this meeting, Aaron had everyone meet in the dining hall, close to the cargo hold. He introduced everyone to the three women and was careful to provide descriptions for Lorissa's sake.

"My name is Aaron Wilkinson and the leader of this small band who are here to provide the ship's protection." He graciously shook Lorissa's hand and then Chrissy's. As he came to Jenna, she stuck out her arm, but he looked awkwardly at it.

"Well, go ahead and shake it; it won't bite," Jenna teased him. Rather self-consciously, he took her arm, but she gave it a good shake anyway. "Thanks, I don't want to be treated any differently that my dear friends here." He smiled and then described himself to Lorissa. He was in his sixties as was his wife, Leann. One by one, all the other members were introduced and shook hands.

One Sister timidly asked her if it hurt. Jenna replied, "Not anymore."

After the introductions were done, Aaron explained, "We are here to ensure your safety and comfort. If you ever need anything, just ask any one of us. Just don't ask the normal crew members because they have their hands full running the ship. Okay, you all can go about your duties now." Aaron and Leann remained at the table, sitting across from the three women.

"I've been requested to tell you quite a lot about the Santi. Sally said that you three were very special and that I was to brief you fully. Even more interesting, I've been ordered to have you three meet with the top leader of our organization, Ket Bethany. I'm beginning to see what Sally meant."

Jenna could stand it no longer, interrupting him. "Wait just a minute. How could you possibly know all this? You only arrived today, and Sally was with us clear up to the time we boarded this ship."

"Yes, it does seem a bit odd, Jenna," Lorissa added. "I've noticed Sally's remarks a couple times didn't seem to make sense."

"Observant are we," Aaron chuckled. "It's all Leann's doing. Let me explain a bit, will you. Some of us in the Santi can use telepathy to communicate over vast distances. Sally and Leann are both so trained. The day you arrived seeking sanctuary, Sally contacted a number of us, and I was, via Leann, ordered to make for Zargarb to pick you up."

Seeing the looks of disbelief or shock on the women's faces, Leann added, "Look, I spent ten long years studying from dawn until late at night to get the skill I now have. Sally got those dresses for you didn't she? And you, Jenna, you accompanied Art and Lena to retrieve your stash, and big one it was. Via Sally via Art, I know all about your adventure that night. Need I go on?"

She didn't. Jenna knew that there was no way she could have known all this by any other means. "Now please ladies, let me give you a full and complete understanding of us." They listened intently for several hours as Aaron explained about the Guardians, the Sisterhood, and the formation of the Santi, bringing them up to date on all significant events, as far as the Santi were concerned.

So enthralled were they with the discussion that Chrissy didn't even flinch when several Sisters brought in lunch. When he had finally finished, Jenna asked, "So why does this Ket Bethany want to see us? Just because we have been brutalized by evil men?"

"No, not that. We, well not us personally, but many other ships have ferried probably a hundred other women who have been similarly harmed in the occupied sectors. The Unholy Paladins have been doing similar things in all the sectors that they control. Know that you are not the only victims of their wicked ways. The really lucky women were just beaten to an inch of their lives, the truly unlucky ones perished from their ordeals."

"Okay, interesting and sad to know that, but that still doesn't answer my question. Why us?" Jenna prodded him. She was very used to getting what she wanted. "Is it because I have money? He wants my money?"

"Oh heavens no!" Aaron replied. "Sometimes I think that we have more money than we know what to do with. We are doing things because we feel it is the right thing to do. My wife and I were retired some three years when this war broke out. We saw that it was threatening everything that we hold dear, including our friends. We came out of retirement to lend a hand helping others. Now that the war is over, she and I, well, we find that we rather enjoy all this sailing around Tarra. Guess the sea has gotten into our blood."

She gave him a stern look; he got back to her point. "No, the reason is that Sally believes that there is something special about you three women. Personally, I will not say anything more, well, only this. You insisted on shaking hands, Jenna. That took me by total surprise."

Prod as she might, Jenna could not get anything further from him and had to settle for what little he had said. While the three chatted about the Santi and what they had learned during the rest of the voyage, none had any real idea about why it was so important to meet their leader. The days passed slowly and most enjoyably, all three found the salty, fresh air new and very different from anything that they had ever experienced.

Me, as the summer was neigh, I wanted to get away from all the planning. And I was overdue on making an appearance at Cymry's Grande High Council. Since they had decided to open relations with Megalos, I feared for the safety of Cathleen and wanted some private words with her Guardians. Hence, Lilly Ann, our twins, and I set sail for Cymry.

After spending a couple weeks there, we went to Velona to see firsthand how things were progressing there. Secondly, Elona wished to discuss what was rapidly becoming a problem for her: massive immigration from the occupied sectors. We decided that the best approach would be to determine if she needed the skills that any given immigrant had. If so, put them to work in that field. Otherwise, encourage them to become farmers, because Velona was going to need more than double the food supplies than it had produced last year, maybe more.

Finally, I wanted to see how the fortress at Nuova Vita was coming on the opposite shores, beside the Red Desert. What I really wanted was to take time off to go learn from Jes or whatever he now called himself. Too many obligations had to be met before I could do so with a free heart. At the present, based upon the reports that Lilly Ann had from Sally, I did indeed wish to see the Three Roses, and I arranged for their ship to dock here Nuova Vita so I could see for myself. If nothing else, I intended to see that they were relocated in an environment conducive to their optimum survival, probably in Velona.

"We are here; that's the new town that is rising on the shores of the Red Desert. We are just opposite of Velona," Aaron explained to the Three Roses. "Sally tells me that Ket is on his way here, probably arriving tomorrow. You ladies can spend the day on the beach, if you like."

A half hour later, the three walked carefully down the narrow gangway to the relatively crude dock. A number of workers were busy working on the limestone walls. What they found most striking was the beach, which had the reddest sand they had ever seen. In fact, they had never seen anything quite like it. While Jenna described the breathtaking vista, the three navigated around the construction to the long beach area. Once upon the sands, they removed their shoes and felt the warmth of the sands beneath their feet.

Now they were out of the sight of the workers, Chrissy made several gestures for Jenna to interpret. Smiling, she said, "Yes, I know. Many of the workers, Lorissa, watched us as we walked by. I think that they have been away from women far too long. Yes, a couple winked at you Chrissy. I saw it too. Come on, let's go wading." They waded for a while finding the waters warm and soothing.

After a while, Jenna deciphered another Chrissy set of gestures. "Chrissy wants to go swimming. I think that is a splendid idea. We all could use a bath!"

Lorissa began to protest, "But I can't see where I am going."

"Ah, we won't let you drift out to sea. Besides if you just relax, the tide is flowing in to the beach; it'll bring you ashore," Jenna replied.

"Okay. Honestly, I used to love to go for a swim. I swam at least once every week when I was in my teens. Oh, let's!" Lorissa's enthusiasm rose, and she began removing her clothes. Suddenly she stopped, "Jenna, how can you swim? I mean you have no hands."

"Who knows? I used to swim. I guess I'll just have to use my feet more. I am certainly not going to let that stop me from taking a dip in this magnificent beach!" she said stoically, although she began to wonder just how awkward this was going to be.

Both Lorissa and Chrissy helped her remove her clothes and then the three, holding arms walked out into the warm, refreshing waters together. The gentle waves broke upon their bodies, and at last, they began to swim. Sometime later, Jenna managed to say, "Hey, a back stroke works best for me!"

"Good for you! I think I can tell where the shore is, that way right?" Lorissa replied. She was correct. Chrissy thoroughly enjoyed herself, but kept a watchful eye on her friends.

An hour later, Jenna called out, "I see another ship is coming in, another caravel, probably this Ket fellow. We better head back and get dried off."

Sometime later, the three still working on their hair strolled back up the beach toward the construction site. Indeed the other ship had docked opposite theirs, and a number of people were milling around. "I hope we aren't keeping them waiting," Jenna commented slightly worried that this might offend the Santi leader.

"What do you see?" Lorissa implored her as they neared the area.

"I don't see anyone that looks like a king. Maybe we are in luck and haven't kept them waiting. I see a small crowd looking at the walls. Looks like a family. Two are holding infants, maybe a year or so old. One has the most stunningly beautiful long red hair, down to her waist even. Impressive. The other has shorter brownish hair. Some others are wearing the black Santi tunics with the red crosses on them. Ah, they are waving for us to join them." She yelled toward them, "Coming, just a bit slow here. Sorry for the delay. We went for a swim."

The large bunch turned to face the three, and the one with the long red hair holding one of the infants stepped out in front of the others. "Oh my,

Lorissa, she's a man — I mean the one with the red hair!"

"Hello and welcome, the Three Roses, I presume? I am Ket Bethany, my wife Lilly Ann, and our twins." As Chrissy came up, I extended one arm and gave her a handshake. "Let me guess, Chrissy?" She nodded and smiled. I moved to the right, took Lorissa's hand, and shook it. "Lorissa?"

"Yes, that's me," she said, slightly nervously.

"Ah, then you must be Jenna," I said, and extended my hand, took hold of her arm, and gave her a shake as well. She surprised me slightly by placing her other arm on top of my hand, looking me squarely in my eyes, adding to the greeting.

"Yes, that's me. Such impressive hair!"

"Tewdwr, I come from that part of West Reach noted for red heads, plus, I love long hair," I replied honestly, while shifting the weight of my son slightly.

"You have a man's voice," Lorissa said, "but is it really as long as Jenna is telling me?"

"Let me have him, Ket. You need time to spend with these three," Lilly Ann said, taking him from me in her other arm. "Arm full aren't they?" she jested.

"Here, feel for yourself," I said and took her hand and positioned it on my backside so she could feel its length. It was very critical that I make a good first impression on these women, demonstrating that I was not ill at ease around them and that I could adapt to their special needs easily.

I felt her hands gently running its length before she uttered, "Well I'll be! It is as long as she says. Very pleased to meet you Ket."

"Same here, Lorissa. I would like to have a private talk with you three, somewhere where we will not be interrupted nor overheard, so we can be honest and frank with one another. Come; let's go back down on the beach near where you were swimming." This time, I took one side of Lorissa, while Chrissy, the other. I offered my other arm to Jenna, as a gentleman ought. She did not hesitate and thrust her arm through mine. Together, we walked slowly back to a sheltered part of the beach. "This looks like a good place; shall we sit and relax on the sands?"

I positioned them in a semicircle around me so I could see all three of them at the same time, and they, me. "I understand that you are more or less confused about why I should want to meet you personally. I will explain why, but first let me discuss some related facts, which may help you more fully to understand me. To begin with, we are all immortal spiritual beings, which are for a time inhabiting these fleshly bodies. Everyone knows that they have a mortal body, that goes without saying, you three perhaps more so than many. You also have a mind; let me illustrate. Can you create an image of a nice alley cat?" I watched them closely as they did so. "Now let's be sure that it is your cat and not a picture of some cat you have seen. Let's turn the cat blue." They did so. "Now let's have the cat's hair grow exceedingly long." They chuckled over this one.

"You must have a fetish for long hair," Jenna commented wryly. I smiled and said that I did.

"Okay, that is your mind. Now there is a third part of man, the spiritual being. I ask you, who is looking at the image of the long haired cat?"

"Well, I am, what a silly question," Lorissa said rather impertinently.

"That is you, the spiritual being, that which is immortal, that which is the personality, it's you." I paused to let that sink in a bit.

"So where is this infernal soul that those invaders have been harping about and causing so much evil and destruction over, going to hell and all that?" asked Jenna, slight anger in her voice.

"I'm afraid that those men and so called priests have completely misunderstood everything. What they are calling a soul is really just you, the spiritual being. They have completely lost touch with their own identity as a spiritual being. Horrible but true, they now consider they are just fleshly bodies and have some intangible possession they call a soul. What they are talking about in fact doesn't exist. Only you, the spiritual being exist."

"Oh good god! All this pain, suffering, and mutilations are for nothing! Bastards!" Jenna cursed, while Lorissa and Chrissy had tears flowing.

"Oh, not for nothing, my observant Jenna," I countered. "Think about it for a minute and what results they are actually accomplishing."

"Well, they are sure dominating and controlling the entire city to their will that's for sure," she replied after a moment.

"Precisely, this is their covert way of taking over complete control of all the people in what we call the occupied sectors."

Chrissy tried to say something, but only unintelligible sounds came out. Jenna saw it and quickly said, "Chrissy, play the guessing game. Tell us what it is you want to say." She started to, but then stopped and pulled out her parchment scraps Sally had given her. She wrote it instead. Instinctively, Jenna read it aloud for the benefit of Lorissa.

"My husband fell for it. He turned me in and they did this to me. It is true, they only want to control us all and make us do what they want us to do, like dogs."

"Yes, indeed, Chrissy," I replied. "That's precisely it. What is worse and what makes me sick is that so darn many people are buying in to their perverted take on the pure religion, which used to be what Jehosanity was all about. They have taken a perfectly fine religion and totally corrupted and perverted it to their own ends, rather despicable, if you ask me."

We chatted a bit more on this before I then asked what I really wanted to ask. I began with Jenna, because I could see for myself where she was located. "Now Jenna, you were looking at the long haired cat. May I ask where you are at, relative to your body?"

"Where I always am, above and behind its head. Why? Isn't everyone?" she replied with a childish sheepishness of some unspoken, but presumed fact.

"Before I answer you, how about you Lorissa?"

"Well, since I lost my eyes, I am very close to my head now, like I am trying really hard to sense things now that I cannot see."

"Chrissy?" She pointed to just behind her head.

"Thank you for being honest with me. Now to answer your question, Jenna, no most people, especially those so called Holy Paladins are completely and thoroughly stuck inside their body's heads. I am something of an expert in these matters, and by my own observations, maybe one in a hundred are not stuck firmly and solidly within their body's head. Those of us who are still outside the head are very few; we are rare here on Tarra. I do not know why this is so, although I have some theories."

"This is all well and good, if not interesting, but what does it mean, that we are outside our heads?" Jenna inquired, her anger turning to one of curiosity.

"Has Aaron and his wife told you about we Guardians?" They nodded. "We are all as you are, residing outside of our heads. After ten long, arduous years of study, we have learned many ways of Nature, which others might call magic. We do not get lost on long journeys; we can bring down sheets of fire or ice; we can bring down bolts of lightning; we can even control the weather at times, although we usually have to work together for several days to make that happen."

"Ah, and can you make some men think what you want them to think?" asked Jenna. I knew where she was headed.

"Yes, that is what Art did with the city guards that night you went to retrieve your stash. A *very* few of us can even communicate via our minds; it's called telepathy."

"Now that one I am certain has happened. Sally must be one of those, because everyone we encounter seems to know all about us, and there hasn't been enough time for any kind of message to have gotten through," Jenna declared.

"Yes, she and Leann are telepaths; so am I for that matter. Lilly Ann, my wife, is similar in skills to Art. She can make others think what she wants them to think. You see our skills lie in seven major areas, or specialties." I described them in detail. "Please do not think that I am about to say that our Healers can make new eyes for Lorissa here, grow new hands for Jenna, or grow a new tongue for Chrissy. I'm terribly sorry that we cannot." I had to defuse any such notions that might be going through their minds about now.

"What is important is that in the past, we would find children who were as you are, residing outside their heads and offer them the chance to become educated and trained as a Guardian, but the specialty is of their own personal choosing. After all these many years, we have never been able to train someone who resides within their head to any great deal. Yes, they become wiser and more learned about Nature and the ways of man, but none has ever reached remotely the skill level required to work what you might call 'magic' or spells. So you see, from our point of view, you three are special beings indeed."

"Normally, we begin their training when they are six and finish up when they are sixteen. While not impossible, it is much harder to train someone fully who is as old as you three are, but it has been done. Nonetheless, even if you do not have the time or inclination to master everything that we can teach you, what you can learn you will find particularly valuable in your lives. That I can promise you. Jenna, a long time ago, the Guardians had a leader much like yourself; she too had no hands, yet had the knowledge and wisdom to lead us all. Her name was Isabel, by the way."

Jenna stared at me long and hard, absorbing this completely unexpected remark. "No, you do not need hands to bring down lightning bolts, I swear. Nor sheets of fire or ice. It is done by you with your knowledge of Nature and how she operates. However, these things are only mastered in the tenth year of study; they are not easily done."

"What happens to us when we die?" Jenna inserted. I could tell she was still having thoughts about these unholy paladins.

"You, Jenna, cannot die, that which is looking at your pictures, that which is you, is immortal. Only your physical body dies. Ah, what then happens to us when our bodies die? That is a very good question. I cannot tell you what happens or has happened to you, Jenna. You must find that out for yourself. As for me and many others that I know, we have been simply picking up a new baby body and starting over. This is my third body since I came to Tarra. Before that, I cannot remember. My last two bodies were female."

"Ah, then that may account for your strong liking of long hair," Lorissa astutely remarked. "Now it makes some sense why you would."

I laughed along with her, and the others finally grasped what Lorissa had already discovered about me. "Yes, and I freely admit that this lifetime, I have been very confused about my gender on more than one occasion."

"So you are saying that we have lived before?" Jenna continued to pressure me.

"That, my beautiful Jenna is something only you can answer, not I."

"You are not going to tell me, then," she teased, rather pleadingly.

"Nope," I changed the topic, "Lorissa, I have a dear friend of mine who was blinded by her first husband. She is now the most famous musician in Velona and currently resides in d'Grange with her new loving husband. She accompanied me when we traveled the length and breadth of the Sea Princes and the Arad several years ago as traveling musicians. I know you are not a musician, but our special training has enabled her to have very acute other senses. You would be flabbergasted to see just how alert and able Jolina has become. While we cannot give you new eyes, we can help you to enormously expand your other senses, in part making up for the lack of sight."

"And Chrissy, you are not alone in your special situation. Three of my dear friends in my Circle of Seven — their grandmother had the same problem as you. A Guardian found her barely surviving, selling flowers on a street corner in Velona; they fell in love, and were married and lived out their lives at Mont Blanc. Thus, many of us completely understand your situation. Her name was Thallia, and her loving, doting husband also had some telepathic ability, and in that way she and he could communicate everything. Actually, many people were rather envious of the two. They'd sit silent as lambs, but communicating together like mad. I don't know if you have any such latent telepathic abilities, but with our training, we certainly can make your life much more bearable. There is absolutely nothing ever to be embarrassed about how you are now forced to eat and drink. By the way, the writing pad of Sally's is a terrific idea, don't you think so?" She grinned and nodded.

"I know all three of you have the capability of being far more able than you might suppose at the moment. Already I have seen such with my own eyes. Lorissa, did you not know where the shore was at while you were swimming? I could go on, but I don't want to seem like a busybody prying on you."

"Whether you accept my offer or not, here's what I am going to do. It is completely your choice. If you would rather not accept our guidance and training, then I want to help you obtain a new home that is conducive to your easy survival and well-being, within Velona, if possible. If you want to try the training route, I have someone who will provide it for you, once again in a totally safe place where you can survive easily and without hassles and embarrassments."

"What will all this cost us? My entire savings?" Jenna asked, never having trusted men when it came to financial matters.

"Let me make one thing absolutely, completely clear, Jenna. Under no circumstances whatsoever, will I or anyone else connected with the Santi ever make any request for as much as a copper from your savings. That is your money to use as you desire. If you do not want our assistance, you will need it to help you three survive well. If you accept our help, then what is asked in return is that you help in ways that you are able. The exchange is your help and assistance, nothing more, and certainly not your money."

Lorissa smiled, "Then we accept you offer to be trained. How can we not at least try, Jenna, Chrissy. If it doesn't work out, we can try something else." Jenna looked at her with a smiling surprise. This was the first time that Lorissa spoke out first and for the Three Roses!

Christina also realized this as well and gave her vigorous assent as well. "Okay, then where do we have to go and who is going to train us in all this stuff?" Jenna asked, resuming her mother hen attitude.

"I think that you would be more comfortable being close enough to the big city of Velona; you could get there with a good walk or short horse ride. Out in the country in a cottage might be best, away from prying eyes, at least until you become comfortable in your new surroundings. I've located a small farm about three miles northeast of Velona that would work very well for you three. It even has a small pond on the estate."

"The person who has agreed to train you is Hank Weston. In fact, he is also in need of some healing as well. He is twenty-five and is a Loremaster, one who is attuned to Nature, plants, and animals. However, recently, he has lost his wife and two small children to the Galt invasion up in the Greenway. He was out in the fields and could not get to them in time. Can you imagine how horrible it must be to see your own loving wife and children butchered right before your own eyes and yet be helpless to get there in time to prevent it? Yes, I am afraid that Hank bears a deep emotional scar from it, one that he has not been able to shake off these past two years. I'm hoping that you three being around him will help bring him out of his grief and back into the land of the living once more. However, as a Guardian, he will protect you with his life, without question if need be, make no mistake about that. Is this agreeable with you?"

"Yes, it seems fair, but," Jenna added sternly, "what if he and we do not get along? What if it doesn't work out with him? Then what?"

"I'll find you someone else to train you or if you do not want to pursue your training any further, I'll help you find a more suitable living arrangement wherever you like. Is that fair enough?"

"That seems fair," Jenna admitted. "You realize that all my life I have been educated the hard way not to trust men farther than I can see them. No one has ever looked out after me, but me. Look where trusting men has gotten these two."

"I understand you fully, Jenna. One last thing, High Priestess Elona Po rules Velona , and she is one of us, a Protector, as well. If you ever need anything, and I do mean anything, just get word to her. I'll arrange to have her meet you when you dock at Velona. If I know Elona, she will want to come and visit you every so often." We stood up to return to our ships.

Jenna reached out with her arms to grab my hand, "Thank you for being so caring." She also gave me a hug. Arm in arm, as before, we strolled back to the docks and said farewell. Within the hour, their caravel sailed for Velona, but a half day away.

"Here, you take them both!" Lilly Ann carefully deposited both boys into my arms. "My arms are killing me. I swear they have both gained ten pounds in the last day!" She was teasing of course. Together, my Circle and I strolled around the construction site, Allan pointing out many details. It felt good knowing that now we had a fortress on either side of the entrance to the Med Sea. In the future, Megalos would have a far more difficult time bringing triremes into this sea.

For a time, I stared out into the rolling sand dunes of the desert. Lilly Ann commented, "Yes, I know you would give anything to wander out there and learn from Jes Amir. However, right now, we have far too many duties to spend the time required. We are the only force keeping this perverted religion and people from taking a complete and utter strangle hold over all Tarra. It will just have to wait a little longer, Ket."

"I know love, I know," I sighed.

At noon the next day, the caravel pulled into the bustling, thriving docks of Velona. Standing on the foredeck, the Three Roses stared at the splendor of this city. Jenna was rapidly relaying the sights to Lorissa, from the outer defensive cables to the huge number of ships docked, coming or going. The stark contrast between Zargarb and Velona stood out in their minds.

Once the ship had been moored and the walkway extended, the three women walked down onto the wooden docks. Workers were coming and going, some moving heavy loads onto and off the ships. When they finally reached the main landing, a middle aged woman wearing purple robes was waiting for them. Several others stood behind her. As they approached, she spoke, "Welcome to Velona. I am its ruler, High Priestess Elona Po, descendant of the original founder of Velona. On behalf of everyone, let me be the first to welcome you to your new home." While Jenna was rapidly describing Elona to Lorissa, the priestess shook hands with each woman, including Jenna, who was beginning to think no one really cared much about her missing hands. They would shake anyway, which pleased her. The last thing in the world Jenna wanted was to be considered a poor, helpless cripple.

Elona outlined her immigration policies and what it meant to be a citizen of her land. It could be summarized as do what you can to help make Velona the very best it can be. She suggest that they might come to her church on Sundays to increase their understanding of just what the people here believed in, as far as religion went. Finally, she introduced Hank Weston to his new apprentices. Her parting words were, "Remember, if you ever need anything at all, just get word to me by any means. I will see that the situation is resolved. Glad having you in our land."

Hank smiled as Elona left them alone, "She sounds awfully formal these days, but she has a really good heart and has turned this country totally around. Enough of her, I hope your voyage was not too trying." Jenna introduced each woman in turn, and Hank gently shook their hands. "I have a wagon waiting for us. However, if there is anything from here in town that you need before we go to the estate or if you are hungry, let me know and we can stop and grab something. Here, I have a little something for each of you that I picked up on my way here." He carefully inserted a red rose into each woman's hair. "Three roses for three roses." This pleased the women, who then followed him the short distance to his wagon.

"How long will it take to get there?" Jenna asked as they climbed on board.

"Only about forty-five minutes if we go slowly; half that if we go fast."

"Then I think it is best we go there first. We can see what's what and figure out what all we may need. Say, what is the cost to enter the gates here?" Jenna asked trying to make sure that she did not overlook any detail that could be important later on. She was surprised by his answer.

"Nothing, all may pass freely through the gates. They are not even locked at night, unless there is a war going on and Velona feels threatened." She smiled; this sector was completely different from Zargarb. The women sat back and enjoyed the short ride to their new home. Jenna also studied their mentor while he drove. Beneath his polite, social face, she could not help but see a great sadness, bordering upon apathy. Still, he was likeable, even thoughtful, she noted.

Now the events that took place over the next several months with these four people play a significant role in what was to happen to me later on, so bear with me as I present the necessary highlights and key background information.

The official name of their estate was Villa con Stagno, that is, an estate with a pond, which covered about five acres all told. Years ago, it had hosted a vineyard with olive grove, but years of neglect and invasions had destroyed the crops and trees. Still, it's home, though large, was stout and well built, with a typical red tile roof. Jenna described it as picturesque. "How did you come by this estate?" She asked as they rode up to the main door of the manor house. "I thought you used to live up north somewhere, pardon me if my geography is not so good."

All three women suddenly detected the heavy burden of sadness that overwhelmed this young man as he replied slowly, attempting to keep back his grief, "Years ago I had a farm up in the Greenway, but my wife and two children were killed in a Galt raid. I just could not stand living in that empty house, so I sold it. Ket helped me find a new place down here, but it hasn't helped me. I still have the nightmares from that day. Enough of me. Let's get you inside, and I'll show you around. I tried to fix it up so that you three would be most comfortable here."

As they took a guided tour of their large, new home, Hank explained, "I took the liberty of removing all the door locks. You can open any door just by pushing on it. However, in your bedroom, I put a sliding deadbolt that Jenna can easily operate so that you can be guaranteed of your privacy when you desire it." Now Jenna understood why all the doors looked a bit unusual, no doorknobs or latches.

"This is to be your room. With all the vast numbers of folks immigrating to Velona, I was unable to buy three beds for you. I had to settle for one very large one. I hope you will not be offended if you three have to sleep in the same bed. If you are, let me know and I will order new beds, but the waiting list is now over two months at least."

Lorissa replied for them, "Oh this will do very nicely indeed. We don't mind at all. Someone lead me to the bed so I can feel it, please." Chrissy did so. "Oh, this *is* nice," she commented. Jenna smiled, while Chrissy displayed a broad grin. The bed and bedding were very elegant, probably once owned by a nobleman. They would be sleeping like royalty on this bed.

"Oh yes, I'm sure you will want to unpack and freshen up and all that, so when you are ready, come on down to the kitchen. I'll make us some lunch, I'm starved." He turned toward the door, but then thought of another thing. "One more thing, Jenna, over on that chair you will find a specially made chamber pot, one that I think you will be able to use without help. And on the dresser, I made you a special hair brush that you will be able to use. Make yourselves at home." He left for the kitchen.

Jenna just had to look at the two items. Indeed the flared sides of the pot she could easily maneuver and even carry with her arms. Chrissy, however, headed for the dresser to see the hairbrush. Excitedly, she brought it over to Jenna, insisting that she try it right now. It had a leather strap attached to the handle so that all she needed to do was insert her arm in the hoop and push it snug. Viola, a brush she could somewhat use. She tried it out. It was awkward, but for the first time she could at least brush her own hair a little. Chrissy smiled and clapped, then Lorissa had to feel it for herself.

Over lunch, Hank explained their situation here at the villa. "I am charged with trying to find out what crops will grow well in Velona. You see, there are so many people arriving here nearly every day, that food is becoming a problem. Elona has asked me, as a Loremaster, to discover what crops can be effectively grown here. This is now also your charge. I will expect you three to lend me a hand in the farming for a couple hours each day. I will devote at least six hours during the day to your training, but in the other hours, you must lend me a hand with the farming. I will not disappoint Elona Po. Too much is at stake here to let her down. Is this agreeable with you?"

"But we know nothing about farming," Jenna answered. "I'm not sure what help we can really be; however, you have our word that we will help as we can."

During the next few weeks, their mornings were spent helping Hank with the gardening. Now he was plowing up another section of land to sew. While he did the plowing, the three women planted the seeds. Lorissa could easily follow the trough in which the seeds were placed, so she and Chrissy placed the seeds in the ground. Jenna came along behind them and covered up the trough. At least once a week, the group loaded the wagon with the fresh produce that was ready for market and rode into Velona to drop it off at the farmer's markets, where Hank received some coins in exchange for the goods.

After lunches and continuing until dark, Hank worked with each, beginning with the usual Observing the Obvious lessons. He found three eager pupils in these women. One day, Chrissy wrote on her paper, "Hank is really cute. I wish he was not always so sad though." Now that their powers of simple observations had been so greatly increased, they could tell that Hank found the early evenings somehow painful to endure, more so than any other time of day.

In mid-September, after supper, Hank was more morose than normal. Jenna just could not stand it any longer, whispering to her friends, "We just have to try something to help him." They agreed on this, but what? Later on when asked how she figured out what she did, she could only answer, "Dumb luck." Perhaps it was the penetrating discussion she had with Ket when they first met more than a month ago.

She asked Hank, "Hank, it looks to me like you are looking at some memories. Please, tell me about them, as sad as they are." Hank sighed, and reluctantly relived that horrible day some two years ago, describing the whole dismal attack. When he had finished, Jenna fought the temptation to show him sympathy, remembering how she hated others to give her sympathy over her hands. Instead, she said, "Can you tell us about it once more, leaving out no details, please. We are not quite sure that we understood everything." This was a small fib on her part, but she could think of nothing else to say.

Once more, Hank began to relive that awful event, this time describing what had happened in more detail. Jenna noticed two things: first, he was giving them more vivid details, and second, his grief and sadness had somehow changed slightly to that of a numbness bordering upon despair. At least this was better than an apathetic, pitiful grief. Encouraged by his change in emotion, she asked him to re-experience it again, leaving nothing out. Hank complied, actually, with the mood he was in, she could have asked him to go jump off a cliff and he would have obeyed, if only to end his misery. He repeated what had happened to him once more. By the time he finished this recounting, Hank was positively angry and antagonistic, swearing death upon every Galt in the world!

Chrissy wrote, "Don't stop now!" on her parchment; encouraged, Jenna had him go through it all once more. A few more little details appeared, and he became rather bored with it all by the time he'd finished going through it this time.

Jenna was contemplating what to say next, when all a sudden Hank burst out with, "Good god! I have another memory here that is somehow tied to this one!"

"Tell us about it," Jenna exclaimed, more than thankful that he had discovered something else.

"I see a woman. She's being restrained by some ugly men. Gods! That's me! I'm that woman! I'm watching some other fat, brutish men who are stabbing my husband. Now they are threatening to kill my sons if I don't cooperate with them. They throw me on the ground and have their way with me. I just lay there in total apathy; there was nothing I could do to stop them."

When he was partway through it a second time, which all three women found fabulously entertaining and fascinating, he began laughing, "It wasn't that there was nothing I could do. Twice I could have stabbed the fat pigs on me with their own knives. It was more like I felt so sorry for myself that I did nothing. I didn't even feel sorry for my husband or boys. What an idiot I was back then." Hank began laughing wholeheartedly. Gone was his grief, gone for good.

Later, Hank said to Jenna, "I don't know what you did for me, but it sure worked! The master has learned from his students." Both chuckled; Jenna felt truly happy that she had worked a minor miracle for him.

However, a week after this, everyone was rudely awakened in the middle of the night by Jenna's piercing screams of stark terror. The women in bed with her tried to console her and quiet her down, but Jenna was lost to them. Hank, barely dressed, sword in hand, came rushing into their room, afraid some horrible calamity had befallen the women in his care.

"She's having a nightmare, I believe," Lorissa only guessed. "She's never done it before."

He dropped his sword by the door, came over to the bed, and sat beside her. He only had limited telepathic abilities, but he could certainly sense what she was reliving. "Jenna, tell us what is going on, all the details." He had to

490

repeat his command several times to get it through to her. At last, the screams subsided, and she spoke instead, describing how she had been abducted that fateful night as she was closing her inn. After she had gone through it several times, calming down considerably, she suddenly realized something.

"I was knocked out and didn't remember anything until I woke up like this. However, I have a complete running set of images of what actually happened, what they did, and how they did it. How can this be?"

"Don't know, but please, go through it all once more, telling us every detail that happened," he requested. She did, but now she no longer repeated the hideous screams that she had made when she had awakened to find her missing hands. Hank had her go through it several more times, just as she had done with him, wondering all the while what he ought to be doing next, wondering if Ket ought to be here and might know what to do.

After going through it several more times, Chrissy wrote down for Hank, "See, she is now getting rather bored with it. I think you are getting somewhere with it. Don't stop." He smiled at her wisdom, and had Jenna go through it all one more time.

Partway through it, Jenna suddenly stopped, saying, "Wait a minute! I see some other memory, pretty vague and dim, but there is something else here." After a few yawns, she burst out, "It's happened to me before! Long time ago. They are cutting my whole arm off! Bastards!" Hank encouraged her to begin at the beginning and tell them all about the experience, the memory.

"I was a young woman, I think in Zargarb maybe even. They are accusing me of something I didn't do. Guilty. Right there in the street, they hacked off my right arm at the shoulder! I was screaming at the top of my lungs and then passed out. They seared it with my own red hot frying pan, the bastards. Wait, while I am lying there, some women dressed in leather with yellow headbands find me and carry me away. Well I'll be, I joined the Sisterhood and became a left-handed fighter. Ha, ha, ha, a couple years later, one by one, I found those vile men and ran them through their hearts with my sword. Heh, heh, I got even all right! Ha, ha, ha. Nobody messes with me! Ha, ha, ha."

Her laughter was infectious, and soon all four joined her amazing discovery. Ever since that night, Jenna no longer had ghost pains in her arms or any more nightmares about her ordeal, most fascinating indeed.

The next day, Jenna and Hank discussed what had happened and its ramifications. Jenna suggested, "Why don't we try this out on Lorissa and see if she can, well, feel better about everything?" In the end, they asked her if she wanted to try.

A bit reluctant at first, Lorissa agreed to try. After working with her for several hours, Lorissa was laughing wildly, the trauma had been wiped from her mind as well. However, Hank noted another vital detail; Lorissa was now uniformly several feet above and behind her body, no longer plastered to tightly up against its head. This he found exceedingly interesting indeed, so much so, that he contacted Elona who contacted me. I Mind Linked with him to get the details of Jenna and Hank's discovery firsthand.

Chrissy wrote on her paper, "I would really like to try it too, but I can't speak, so I can't do it." Indeed, she felt completely left out in the dark, for the first time since having met Lorissa, long ago. It was all she could do to stem the flow of tears; she bit her lip hard to keep from crying.

Hank replied, "Chrissy, you don't get off this easily," he made an attempt at brevity. "Ket is telepathically connected to me at this moment. He and I can communicate just by thinking what we want to say. If you want to try this for yourself, Ket will Mind Join with you and with the rest of us here. Then, as you go through your memories, we all will see them too and your thoughts as well. Are you willing to have Ket connected to you with the rest of us watching on the sidelines?"

She didn't hesitate an instant, nodding her head wildly yes. She uttered what was interpreted as an "Oh!" when Ket joined with her. Jenna and Lorissa had similar very vocal expressions as they too joined the Mind Link with Hank and me.

Okay, we are all here, Chrissy. You only need to think and we will receive your thought. Can you identify all of us?

Yes! This is so utterly intimate! What a feeling!

I think we all agree with you. Now what do we do, Jenna? Perhaps you should run the session while I watch.

Spooky. I just think? Are you getting this? Jenna timidly thought. She jumped when we all replied that we were. Quickly she settled down and told Chrissy, *I want you to return to when you had your tongue cut out, the very beginning of it. Then tell us all about it as you go through those memories until you get to the end. Okay?*

For several hours, we watched the images roll by in Cristina's mind, how her own husband had betrayed her, the butchery at the hands of the Holy Paladins, and of her great sorry and loss from being denied her own children. I noted that each time she went through it, more details appeared. Further, the emotional and physical impact it had on her lessened with each recounting. Then, suddenly I saw it, another set of memories were appended somehow to this one. Shortly Chrissy too discovered them.

I see a young boy. No, that's me! I've lived before. I wonder what happened? Oh does my ear ever hurt.

Go through it and tell us what happened, Jenna coached her to get her back on the right track.

Oh, I am an artist. I paint really good, portraits and stills. I am getting a lot of money. Oh no! My patron is betraying me to some men in robes, churchmen, looks like Tur priests. Damn, they are cutting off my ears! I scream. It hurts so. Feels a bit funny. Always wore my hair long after that to cover my no ears.

After a few times through this one, she sent, I'll show them. *I'll be the best damn artist in the land and never do a single painting for them! I did too.* However, even after recounting this one several more times, she was not laughing as had the others. I detected a slight worry in Jenna's thoughts. Thus, I looked more closely at Chrissy's mind. Sure enough, there were some other memories still somehow latched upon these two. After another recounting and just when I was about to butt in and tell her to see if she could see this other memory, Chrissy found it herself. I was thankful I had the patience not to intervene.

I see something else here. Long time ago I think. On a ship. Really old ship. We are searching for good places to make towns along the Med Sea, I think. I found a good one here. Oh no! Another captain, he is betraying me, claiming he found it first, when I had. Oh no! He's making me walk the plank. My hands are tied; he pushes me off into the sea. I sink, going to drown. No wait, I have a knife in my boot. Lungs are bursting; now I am free and come up. Gasping for air. Ships are sailing away now, leaving me. Got to swim to shore. Nice beach.

Once more, after several times through this one, she began laughing. *Sitting on the beach, I was determined to show them up. I remembered that they had to bring the arbitrator back and officially show him their claim. However, if there were already construction at the site, his claim to be there first would be null and void. So using my knife, I began to make a house, rather crude it was, right there on the beach. A few weeks later, several ships put in by the beach. Arbitrator awarded this place to me. I got even; the guy who betrayed me was livid!* She laughed with all her heart, adding, *See, I always get even in the end! That's me. I get even!*

Very well done indeed, Chrissy, Jenna sent. For some time, I kept the link in operation as we all discussed this new way of helping people deal with the trauma in their lives. For the very first time, I had something solid, something concrete with which to work.

Roses, I will be in Velona in three weeks, and I will host a formal dance with music and all in your honor! Thank you, thank you, thank you! With this, we may be able to help many, many more people! Hank, you see to it that they get some splendid new dresses; spare no expense; it's on me. See you in three weeks. I gotta go now, the twins need a diaper change most urgently!

Okay, the dance got delayed a week. I wanted a big celebration and decided to hold a reunion concert with the Cymry Minstrels, less of course Caitlyn. Partly, this concert would be in her honor, though only a select few knew this fact. I met my sister and Fergus at Bregia, having already picked up Edgar and Jolina in d'Grange. I put my Circle to good use having them help me carry around all my instruments.

Elona arranged for us to play at the largest dance hall in Velona. Nevertheless, the place was packed to overflowing. The Three Roses looked positively stunning wearing their new ball gowns. I'll keep this short. We all had an absolutely enjoyable night.

Chrissy had an even more interesting evening; she met another Guardian about her own age, who was also a Communicator, stationed now at one of the new fortresses along the border with Barcella. She fell for him, and he, her. All during the winter, he called upon her at the villa, taking her everywhere. More importantly, they shared their private thoughts via telepathy. Probably that meant the world to Chrissy. In the following spring, Christina and Frederick Waterton were married at the villa in a private ceremony. I helped by reassigning him closer to Velona, where he and Hank built a small cottage at the edge of the estate so that the Three Roses would not be parted. More importantly, he encouraged her artistry, and Christina Waterton became the most prolific and famous writer Velona has ever had. Her twenty books have never been outdone, and she is still read even today. It's said that she could pack more emotional wallop in a paragraph than many could in an entire chapter.

However, I had a third ulterior motive in holding this reunion gig. I wanted to bring Jolina and Lorissa together, not only so they could meet, but also so perform an experiment on Lorissa. I allowed Jolina to make the first move of my grand experiment, as I knew she would. While the two women were sipping tea after the concert, getting to know each other, Jolina asked me if I would cast my blue light upon Lorissa so that she could see what she looked like in her fancy ball gown. I did so, knowing that years ago, we had discovered that Jolina, the spiritual being, could actually see our magical pale blue light. Imagine the shock Lorissa experienced when she too discovered that she could see dimly Jolina and me and a small portion of the room!

Hank now had new orders: work with Lorissa until she can cast a blue light for herself. The enthusiasm with which Lorissa threw herself into learning how to do that was notable. After two long months, she had the spell down perfectly. Now she was no longer "blind" when she desired to see something. Of course, she knew that she could not go around casting a blue light everywhere she went, that would cause more problems with others than any of us would care to handle. Yet, being able to see when she really needed to made all the difference in her outlook on life.

About the same time, Hank also discovered that Lorissa had another hidden talent, one that turned out to be incredibly valuable to the Santi. She could sense whether a person was telling the truth or not. It was uncanny testing her to find her limits with this skill. We never did find any such limit. Near the summer, she decided to join the Santi, becoming our number one soothsayer. No one could tell a fib around her. She became vital in the Santi organization and one of the most respected members.

Jenna? Well, she and Hank also married; it was actually a double wedding, with Frederick and Chrissy. She continued her druwid training, but also began to use her therapy upon others in dire need. In the ensuing years, the people in Velona called her the Great Healer. Yet, she still has a role to play with me in later years.

Chapter 41 Into the Red Desert

Ten years passed by quickly for me. It was the spring of 635 now. Running the ever-expanding Santi organization demanded vast amounts of my time. With the situation deteriorating weekly in the occupied sectors, the future of Tarra lay in our hands; I could not afford a single mistake.

Our organization now had five thousand chain mail clad warriors with an equal number of guidance and support personnel, largely women. Our secure shipment business was thriving beyond all expectations. Indeed, because of the unruly and desperate situation in the occupied sectors, our services were now in demand nearly everywhere. During the course of a year, vast sums of money and merchandise passed through our hands safely to their destinations. With the incredible volume of requests, the support personnel were kept constantly busy. To keep up with the demand, via the shipwrights in Velona, we added another two dozen caravels to our personal fleet. Velona's fleet numbered over a hundred-fifty of these fast ships.

The immigration had finally subsided. I felt a bit sorry for those of Arad descent. Driven out of their homeland in Juda Arad by numerous barbaric invasions, they had immigrated to the Sea Princes, particularly in Zargarb Sector. Now however, under the iron fist and from my viewpoint, insane rule of the Holy Paladins of the Church of Jehosanity, Megalos, banditry was rampant within those sectors they attempted to micro-manage. Forced to adopt a foreign and perverted version of their own religion or face horrible consequences, they once more migrated westward, settling in the gnostic capital of Tarra or on to West Reach.

Velona now boasted over two hundred thousand citizens, more than double that of any other sector. Intense efforts had yielded a new agricultural industry borne out of necessity to feed this large a population. Elona wisely settled most of the new arrivals out within the sector, rather than swell the main city to overflowing. In these rural areas, farming sprang up in earnest, based upon the crops that Hank had determined would grow best in this land, mostly cereal grains.

My twins were now approaching their teens and I received an unexpected visitor at our ever growing fortress at Mont Blanc. One day in early march, a robe clad monk appeared at the gates, seeking me personally. He introduced himself when I got to the gate. Bowing honorably to me, he said, "I am Brother Jake. I have come to train your sons as promised." I had forgotten all about the monks and Alabaster's promise.

Thus, the twins had an incredible teacher in the fighting arts. When one coupled that specialized training with that of us druwids, I knew that my sons would be given the best possible chances for success. Yet, Lilly Ann and I now had children of our own. Leslie Ann was nine and had her mother's eyes and my precociousness. Sarah Amber was eight and followed me everywhere. Curt

Thomas was five and idolized the twins, following them everywhere, much to their annoyance.

Our many stone fortresses scattered all over the Med Sea basin and beyond were now livable. The impregnable walls were finished, and the main castles with their tall watchtowers were in use. All that remained was the construction of many churches and living quarters with stables and storage facilities. Still, another ten years would be required before we could completely finish our initial plans for these bastions of strength.

On a sadder note, eight years before, in 627, Cathleen and her small family met with a hunting accident. While we could not prove that it was not an accidental calamity, many of us suspected another assassination attempt from the Pope. On that very same day, Sarah was nearly hit by a stray quarrel while she was out riding. Although her guards searched high and low, the shooter was never found. Percival reported that the quarrel's tip was indeed poisoned. Fearing yet another assassination plot on the lives of all descendants of Jes Amir, the Great Messiah, we quadrupled the security on Sarah and her offspring, wherever they went or lived.

However, even with our stepped up security, we could not find the assassin, if there was one in the first place. The poison suggested there was, however. Nothing has happened since that supposed accident. To prevent any other such attempts, Percival issued a standing order that under no circumstances is anyone with bronzed skin ever to be allowed within his castle proper. His assumption was that the would be assassins come from Megalos. For six years now, the preventative measures have worked. Sarah lives and is now forty-eight.

Here on the 23rd of March, I got a message from Percival to come to Middleton at once. Sarah had died under unusual circumstances within the castle. Greatly upset, I gathered my Circle, including Beth Ann and Lilly Ann, since Sarah was their mother. We rode hard and fast to Middleton, arriving at sunset. The twins were crying most of the way. Percival met us at the gate, now under very heavy guard. Inside, the twins found their other siblings and their families, who had been brought here to be safe, just in case. Arthur and Justus went to Lilly Ann and Beth Ann at once, supporting each other. I followed Percival into the castle manor house.

Only inside, did he say, "Thanks for coming so quickly. I have not touched anything, in spite of everyone's wishes to cover her up and or move her to a place of mourning. I wanted you to examine it. I just cannot imagine how this can be anything other than an accident, Ket. But times are perilous. God, I miss her already!" Tears he had been fighting back finally flowed as he led me down the hall to the main stone stairs.

Sarah's body lay in a crumpled mass at the bottom of the three-story set of stairs. Suppressing my own tears, Paul and I began to investigate. "Neck was broken," Paul observed. "Several other bones are broken as well, right arm here, both legs, there and there. She hit the stone steps quite hard."

"I see. The only conclusion is that she fell a considerable distance, her momentum building up until it reached a critical amount sufficient to break bones," I noted.

"Her room is on the third floor," Percival added. "This is what I thought happened too."

"Well, let's not be hasty, Percival. Her death is from falling down the stairs. Of that, I don't think there can be any doubt. However, let's examine her body more closely, Paul. Suppose that she was poisoned or struck first and then fell." Carefully, we examined every inch of her body, but could find nothing out of the ordinary. She had not been struck nor had any tiny puncture marks, which would suggest a poisoned dart, for example. "I think that we can rule out everything but having been pushed, Percival. No signs of a struggle or being poisoned. Now, let's retrace her steps."

Slowly, Paul and I, holding lanterns close to the steps inched our way upwards. Here and there, we saw signs where her body had hit the stone. Reaching at last the top landing, nothing along the way suggested anything was abnormal. Paul hollered down, "Looks like she just had a really bad fall, Percival. Nothing amiss."

"I hope that was all," he called back up. "Can we attend to her body now?" I nodded, and Paul replied that he could now move her and let her children and grandchildren see her.

"Paul, look here, just back of her doorway. What do you make of this?" There on the stone landing behind where she would have stood when she came out of her room were three tiny drops of blood.

"Damn curious," he replied and bent low to study them. "Not much to go on."

"Here, you pretend that you are Sarah and come out of her door there and head downstairs." I had Paul re-enacting what might have happened. I stepped as far back on the landing as I could. The drops of blood were directly beneath my feet. Paul stepped out. From the angle that the door opened, he could not see me. As he moved to go down the steps, I had a clear shot at his back. One slight push and down he would go.

"She was murdered!" I yelled so that Percival could hear as well. "Come up here at once!"

"You are right! I didn't even see you there, a blind spot. But what has the blood got to do with it?" Percival came running up the steps, two at a time. I showed him the blood drops and had him stand there, while Paul demonstrated what we thought had happened.

"But what do these tiny blood drops mean?" asked Percival. "Was the assassin standing there wounded somehow?"

"Remember Paul, that one assassin the last time? He was wearing some kind of pain inflicting waistband that had barbs that cut into his flesh. Masochists, for darn sure. Let's assume that the assassin was similar to the Karlos, who was here years ago. If they stood in one spot for a long time, it is likely that a small amount of blood might reach the floor here. It is in the right spot, if I were he standing here against the wall."

"But my guards are under orders not to let any bronzed skin person within the gates. How could he have gotten in? Bribed a guard?" Percival became furious with his own idea.

"No, Percival, let's not jump to conclusions. Let's see if there are any other clues he might have left behind," I cautioned and advised. "Assume that he gave her the fatal push. Next, he would have to make a very fast get away or else it would not appear accidental. Where could he go from here? Certainly not into her room, he had probably not seen it yet because she was in there. Say, where does this landing lead?"

"To a back window," Percival replied. "He'd have to be a bird to get in that way." I walked to the end and began studying the window. It was an open space about three feet high and two wide, more than enough space for a man to squeeze through. I leaned out and looked out the window. The ground was way below me, a sheer wall all the way down. However, the fortress's outer wall lay only ten feet from the wall, its top was about fifteen feet below the window.

Next, I had the two hold the lanterns close to the bottom of the window, while I looked the stone ledge over very carefully. "Look, these are fresh scrape marks. Probably metal upon stone. He got in using a grappling hook, probably thrown up from the top of your outer wall down there. He tied it off somewhere below and climbed up and in, perfect for a fast getaway. Before she hit the bottom, he was likely out the window and down the rope. While everyone was running to her, no one would be noticing him undoing the grappling hook and departing outside the wall. Come on; let's go out there, and have a look see."

We ran down the steps. I was very thankful that someone had already taken Sarah's body away. As I passed my Circle members, I called out "Murder, come on." All of us along with a number of guards bearing lanterns ran outside of the gate and around to the backside of the fortress. I had to keep everyone back for fear that they would trample any signs the assassin might have left. Carefully, lanterns in hand, my Circle fanned out closely inspecting the ground for any clues. This location was isolated and rocky, a perfect place from which to launch a secret attack. Paul and I looked for signs on the wall. Sure enough, we found the point of contact of the grappling hook, where he had initially used it to climb the fifteen-foot tall sheer wall.

"I've got some footprints here," called out our Loremaster, Ben Wilkins. "You all stay back for a bit. They are leading that way. I wish it was daytime." We watched as Ben maneuvered this way and that bent over searching the ground. "Here's another one. Weird, behind this boulder are a few drops of blood." He kept on moving further away from the fort. Finally, he disappeared altogether from view over the ridge. I decided to follow him and see for myself. The rest of my Circle accompanied me.

At last, we caught up to Ben, "He tethered his horse here. From the dung, I'd say the horse was here for about six hours or so. He came and went the same way, there. Probably we can track him when it's light, but considering the direction, I'll bet he came up the road from Calgary and returned the same way. When we came here, we, ourselves, have probably wiped out any trail that he left. I'd say Calgary, however."

"Damn, they have a Megalos Consulate there," I spat on the ground, more than ever glad that we did not accept their offer to open diplomatic relations made some ten years ago.

Paul commented mostly to Percival, "One thing is certain, this was an assassination and the guy was very skilled and clever. Plus, he had to know where Sarah's room was located. He had to have known the layout of your fort and castle."

"You mean that I have a traitor in my midst?" Percival replied, growing very angry at the thought of such a person being in his pay.

Her eyes red from crying, Lilly Ann answered him; this was her area of expertise. "Not necessarily, dad. While someone could have been a traitor, it is more likely that someone overheard people talking in the inns in town. You have many people who come and go, servants, stewards, stable hands; many townsfolk know the basic layout. Everyone knows that the king and queen live on the top floor of the castle tower. There are numerous ways that the assassin could have found out what he needed to know, dad, without there being a real traitor in your employ. He could have even paid a villager to make the inquiries for him. If you want, I can launch a full investigation, but it will likely take a month to interview everyone with no guarantee that we will find out how. I think Ben is right, when it is daylight, let's see if we can pick up his trail and track this butcher down."

Suddenly, I realized that I had just been a complete idiot! Here I was running all over the place looking for clues and such, completely avoiding doing the rather obvious thing: find and ask Sarah what happened! "Come on; let's get inside. I feel very stupid. I should have first located and Mind Linked with Sarah and asked her! Come on."

Once inside, we went to the room where servants had already cleaned her up, ready for the many who would want to pay their last respects to this loving woman and queen. My Circle shooed everyone except Percival and his sons out of the room, while I sat cross-legged on the floor, closed my eyes, and began expanding my awareness. I was searching for my daughter, Sarah, from my last lifetime, a being whom I knew intimately. I found her in shock, sitting at the bottom of the stairs down which she had fallen.

Sarah, it's me, Ket Bethany. How are you holding up?

What, what happened? I remember falling and everything went black. I am still in shock, I think. I'm so glad you are here.

Can you remember what happened to you, why you fell?

Not really, it is a black blur. I was not about to give up. I remembered Jenna and her newfound therapy. I wondered if it would work even when the person had no physical body. I had to try.

Okay, I want you to go to the start of this accident, and as you look at those memories, tell me what you are seeing. I thought that was a good way to begin. She did so. Some forty-five minutes later and numerous recountings, she finally found the very beginning.

Oh, I was pushed! Someone pushed me down the stairs! Who was it? God, I hope it wasn't one of the children. All signs of the recent trauma seemed to be relieved, and she was now talking rapidly with me, so I decided to reply and told her what we had found out.

Thank goodness. I was worried that one of my grandchildren accidentally bumped me. That would have been horrible. But an assassin! Oh my. Are you all going to look for him? What about everyone else? Are they all safe?

I assured her that everyone else was safe and secure and that we would track down her assassin. Finally, now that she had recovered, I expanded the Mind Link to all her children and Percival, so that they could say their final farewells. Once more, I saw how important this final bit of communication was for those who were living with their loss. Percival asked her what she was going to do next.

Oh, I will just go get another baby body up in Mont Blanc. I don't trust anyone else except the Guardians.

Lilly Ann interjected, *Mom don't worry. I'm expecting again in December. Just hang around me and this one is for you.*

If she had a physical body, Sarah would have laughed long and hard. She thanked Lilly Ann and added, *Well, Ket, looks like you are going to be my parent once more. You can't seem to get rid of me.* That settled, I broke the link, and we adjourned to make the burial arrangements and such.

Lilly Ann and Beth Ann did their best to try to convince their brothers to move their families to the safety of Mont Blanc. However, neither would do so. That would mean separating their wives and children from all their other relatives, and they just could not do so. Arthur pointed out that they got to their mom inside the most heavily protected spot in the kingdom, so they decided to do nothing, except be more vigilant and careful around strangers.

Unfortunately, it rained during the night, and the next day, we were unable to follow the trail very far. We were convinced that the assassin came from Calgary, but that was as much as we ever found out. A sad, depressed Circle re-entered Mont Blanc the next day.

To my surprise, when we returned home, I found that a letter had come for me. I recognized Hank's handwriting; his was distinctive, with curled letters. I opened it and saw that he had not written it, but had addressed the cover so that it could get to me. The handwriting was barely legible, huge, ill formed letters, with no attempt at case nor even in a straight line, each letter of each word made at different angles and alignment. I glanced at the signature; it was Jenna's! Somehow, she had written me, though I could not imagine how she had managed it. I read.

Dear Ket,

Hope you can read this. I studied with Elona. Know about Jes. I need to meet him. Can you take me or arrange it? Please!!

Jenna

I later learned that she had taken nearly two days to write this letter, unwilling to let Hank write it for her. She felt that she had to write this personally. How could I refuse? Besides, this was an excellent opportunity for me to get Lilly Ann and Beth Ann safely out of town, where the assassin could not find us, just in case he had planned more killings. I announced my planned trip to the Red Desert at once. Of course, my Circle was thoroughly excited about getting away from here for a while, but it took us a week to make the necessary preparations. We would be commandeering one caravel for an extended period. I let Hank know that we were coming and would meet them in Velona at the docks.

Naturally, the kids were very excited about taking a long trip and seeing the desert. Brother Jake pronounced that he would come with us, not allowing the twins to miss training days. In the end, we all took our complete families, babies, and all. If nothing else, they could stay in the fortress in safety. As far as our families were concerned, this was going to be a lengthy vacation!

When we pulled in at the busy Velona docks, Hank, Jenna, and their three children were waiting for us. Jenna had a large sack sitting beside her. As soon as we docked, I went to meet them, but Jenna rushed up to me, throwing her arms enthusiastically around me, giving me a solid hug, and even a kiss on my forehead. "Thank you ever so much. This means everything to me, Ket!"

I held both her arms and looked at her; she still looked as radiant and pretty as I remembered her, a rose. Hank and her children had now joined us. "Where is all the rest of your gear?" I asked.

"They are not coming with me, Ket. Hank has such vital work to do here; so many lives depend upon him. That is, they are staying behind, if some of you will lend me a hand when I need it."

"Anytime, anywhere, just let us know. We brought our families, so you will have more hands than you know what to do with," I teased. Yet, I sensed that there was something more significant about this visit, something so important that she did not want the added responsibility of caring for her family. I agreed and we said farewell.

Hank teased, "You bring her back in one piece, with all the pieces and in the right places, please." She and I both laughed at that one. She waved and then kissed each child. I took her large sack, and arm in arm, we walked onto the caravel.

On board, after all the welcomes and introductions, in which Jenna did not fail to shake everyone's hands, which caused many of the children to ask her lots of questions about her missing hands, we watched the grand city recede into the distance. Had we not been sailing, I'm sure that the many children would have pestered Jenna for hours.

Although she too wanted to watch the city shrink, she said, "We need to talk privately soon, but I want to watch, if I can." I understood, and we watched the breathtaking beauty of the scene before us. Only after we were

501

officially at sea, land was no longer visible, and after everyone had their assigned locations below deck, did I meet with Jenna, who had one of the poop deck cabins for herself. Most of the rest of us were bunking out in the cargo hold.

She began by saying rather sheepishly, "I hope you could read it; my feeble attempt at writing did not turn out so well."

"Totally legible. I must say I was completely surprised and very impressed. You actually did it, incredible, Jenna."

"Yes, well, I really, really need to meet this Jes Amir being, and I had to do something that was sure to get your complete attention and agreement to take me there. I know how busy you must be and all that."

"My dear, you only need to ask. But yes, the letter absolutely guaranteed it and at once. Plus one for Jenna. You are a crafty woman."

"I know," she coyly grinned. "Did you know that I have been maintaining Hank's accounting records? Each time he comes back from the market, he piles all the coins onto the table. I sort, count, and bag them, and even keep his ledger for him. Of course, it takes me nearly a day to do that, very awkward, but that frees him to concentrate on farming. Only things I really cannot do are light the fires, saddle horses, and cook meals. Just no real way for me to do those things fast enough to warrant it. Takes me all day to make one meal; we'd all starve before I got dinner made." I knew that this woman never took no for an answer.

"Okay, so why Jes Amir?"

"Well, as I said, I have been going to church regularly and have had lots of long talks with Elona and Alton. I know that the being who used to be the Great Messiah, Jes Amir, is now out in the Red Desert and that you have met him. I know that he has performed great miracles in the past. I talked with some Sisters who told me about his miracle of growing a new hand for that Sister."

I had the uneasy feeling that she was going on this trip to ask Jes to give her new hands, a miracle. God, I hoped that this was not what this was all about. If so, I had no idea whether Jes could still do such things or whether he even would. The Sister whom he had healed had done a great service for his church; the miracle was her reward.

Jenna continued not noticing my hesitancy, "You see, I have been studying diligently with Hank. I can even cast a blue light now. However, Hank has said that I am rapidly approaching the time when I should be specializing, but I am not suited to being a Protector. I don't have any telepathic abilities as Lorissa has. I cannot heal, as the Healers do — no hands to sew or even bandage a wound. I am not like you; I don't want to know all about everything; I'm not cut out to be a Wid. I certainly am not a Planner; if nothing else I cannot draw out even the simplest sketch, even if I could design something in my head. I am not a Judger, although I do know men and how to flirt with them to get them to do anything I want. No, no Judger for me. Honestly, I just do not enjoy plants and animals the way that Hank does, so

Loremaster is out for me."

I began to see her situation. She had just run out of specialties from which to choose. Actually, if I were to admit the truth, when I originally set the Three Roses on their course of druwid training, I did not expect any of the three actually to make it to the tenth year and into a specialty area. Yet, Jenna had arrived at just this spot.

She continued to talk, thankfully, for I had no ideas to offer just yet. "Now you probably already know this, but I have been using this therapy we discovered on many people. Three hundred and five, to be exact. In every case, we made substantial progress, although the degree of recovery from the trauma varied from person to person. In well over half of the cases I treated, the person ended up recalling some trauma from a previous incarnation or lifetime, whatever we choose to call it." She looked at me to see if I was still following her.

"This does all tie together, Ket. I want to discuss all this with the Great Messiah himself, because he is the closest representative of a higher being that I know about. It is very important that I speak with him personally. There, does this make any sense?"

"Yes, it does. When I met him some ten years ago now, Jes seems to have been somewhat confused about his last life as Jes Amir. The Grey Creature encounter has scrambled his memories rather well. As far as I can tell, he is no longer performing miracles like growing the new hand for the Sister as a way to get others to have faith in Jehosa. Instead, he is working on a different approach, which I desperately want to know all about. I freely admit I am looking forward to spending time with him too."

"Oh," she flushed red faced, "I didn't mean that I want him to regrow me new hands!" She had suddenly observed what I was indirectly alluding to, "No, it is about spiritual matters that I so need to talk to him. So I don't have hands, big deal, inconvenient, and awkward, but in the grand scheme of things, it is not important." What a woman, I thought!

"Same here, spiritual abilities," I replied. "That's what is critical for me to know."

"Good, then we are thinking along the same lines," she said. "Any idea where we find him or how long we must sail?"

"Last time he was in the desert not too far from New Barq. However, that location is not safe to leave our families unguarded for any length of time. I am going to land us at Nuova Vita, on the opposite shore from Velona. Our Santi fortress there is totally secure, and we can ride down the coast of the desert in search of Jes, knowing that our families are safe and enjoying the splendid beach."

The next day, we arrived at Nuova Vita and spent a day meeting those that were there and getting our families all settled in. For safety and security, only Paul and Paulette would accompany Jenna and me on our quest. The others looked after the families, but could come to our rescue if need be. Along the coast of the Red Desert, we did not expect to find any one, and in fact did not, although it took us two weeks to ride the distance.

Paulette and Jenna became fast friends, bonding during the long ride. Both Paul and Paulette now saw just how independent Jenna actually was, despite her handicap. Jenna was a real trooper, only asking for help when she could not do something or it would take so long that the delay was not worth her being independent. However, Paulette being a telepath, could sense when Jenna needed assistance and was right there for her without Jenna having to ask for it. This of course made quite an impression on Jenna, in a very positive way, mind you.

The long ride allowed me to forget about the sudden death of Sarah and all the countless other minor worries that came with running the Santi. Besides, I rationalized, it would do the Santi well to get along without me at the helm for a time. With our families now at Nuova Vita, they were out of the reach of the assassins from Megalos.

Finally, I decided that we were fairly near where we had encountered Jes and Juli ten years ago. I found an easy slope up and out onto the desert proper. We paused to look at the spectacular beauty of the Red Desert. Rolling dunes stretched as far as the eye could see. Up close, the sands had peculiar patterns delicately shaped by the winds, a slate to be erased and redrawn each day. "I had no idea it was this beautiful, but so utterly barren!" Jenna said, her words breaking the absolute silence that had enveloped us once we left the breakers below. "How can anything live out here?"

"It is a hard life, Jenna. Water and salt are gold in the desert. There are some oases scattered about, only how to find them is the real problem. I have no knowledge of anything out here anymore, so we are not just going to ride off in some direction and hope for the best. Last time, after our riders rode out here, he found them. So we will try that. Let's ride inland a little further, wait, and see. I don't want to stray too far from that freshwater stream back there along the coast. No telling where the next watering hole is out here." We rode inland up and down dunes for another hour before I decided to stop and wait. I wondered if I should try to make telepathic contact with Jes or perhaps Juli.

We stayed mounted for a time, waiting and sipping water. Actually, we were more like baking in the hot sun, though this was still springtime. Soon sweat began pouring down our bodies, and I remembered that we ought to have brought more suitable desert clothing, but since I now had none, it was a moot point. Time began to play tricks on us. Time is measured by the change of something in space. Yet, here with the wind nearly still, only the slow movement of the hot sun overhead marked any time. Had an hour passed? Two? Three? Or was it only wishful thinking and only minutes?

Jenna broke the silence. "It's interesting. Nothing is moving. It's as if time is standing still, only I can tell it has not, because the sun has moved a little. My horse's shadow has moved over that way a bit. If there is nothing moving, has any time elapsed? Suppose not even the sun has moved. Would there still be time? Can you have time if there is no motion to observe?"

"You are beyond me," Paul commented. "Way beyond me, that's Ket's province." Paulette smiled, but he was right.

"If there is no motion of anything, then there is no time as we know time. However, I don't know of anything or anywhere on Tarra where there is no motion at all. It only has that illusion here. Our bodies are moving, I need to take a pit stop. If you'll excuse me." The others laughed and joined me, setting foot on the soft hot sand.

We all took another long drink, and Paul gave the horses a drink as well. I was about ready to pack it in for today and try again tomorrow when Paulette whispered, "Someone is watching us. I sense someone."

"Where?" Paul exclaimed, his hand went to his sword, but he wisely did not draw it.

"I feel it too," I whispered. "Oh, it's Juli, the woman that Jes was training!" I recognized her at once, even though it had been ten years. I closed my eyes and reached out for her.

You are slow to observe Ket Bethany. You have come here again. Welcome. Our oasis is some twenty miles from here. I see you have three others with you. I will let your hosts know that four are coming for supper. If you will follow me, I will lead you.

Thanks, Juli, and I am very glad to see you once more. Er how will I see you to follow you?

Silly man. I noticed that Paulette had subtly Mind Linked the others to me and thus everyone had heard Juli's words and her chiding. Jenna smiled at me, as did Paul.

To our surprise, shortly, a wind appeared from nowhere, swirling up the sand, forming what looked like a sandman! Its arm motioned for us to follow it. We mounted and began following this strange apparition. "It's not an apparition," Paulette scolded me, as she finally dropped the link. "She is making the sand form into that shape. I think that is a pretty neat spell."

Near dusk, we spied their oasis; stately date and palm trees outlined the only watering hole for miles in all directions. Crude adobe buildings had taken the place of their nomadic hide tents. The obvious conclusion is they decided to make this oasis their home. I suspected that replacing worn out hide coverings would be difficult out here in the open desert. Admittedly, I had no idea what game, if any, lived here. Much had changed since I had encountered the subterranean Moon People over a century ago.

As we drew closer, two more sandmen suddenly appeared, towering many feet over the one created by Juli. Their massive arms were raised as if to threaten or ward off intruders. At first, I didn't recognize either of the two beings who were causing these apparitions. Juli's sand form waved to them and just as quickly as they had appeared, they were gone, piles of sand upon the desert. Juli spoke to us all mentally, *Messiah Ali Martek and my husband, Karmanski Zolgoti, wish to you wait at the edge of our village until the evening prayers are finished, then you will be welcomed.*

We stopped, dismounted, stretched our legs, and waited patiently. The holy chanting of some three hundred voices seem to blend with the gentle evening breeze and the rolling dunes, giving one a great sense of peace and contentment with the world. While I understood Arad, my companions did not, so I softly translated as I could. They were nearly done when we arrived, so our wait was only a few minutes. Once the chant ended, everyone rose and went about their evening duties. The three walked over towards us, Ali, Karmanski, and Juli, with Juli motioning for us to come to them.

Messiah Ali spoke, "On behalf of the Anuir, I bid thee welcome once more, Ket Bethany. It has been a long time since we have seen you. I trust the sandmen that Karmanski and I created did not startle you. We are in charge of direct protection of our village here." Karmanski and Juli had their arms around each other, young lovers still in love, although both were now approaching forty years of age. "Ah, you have brought guests with you I see."

"Yes, I have. I hope you don't mind, but we have come to stay a while this time." I introduced my companions. He shook hands with each as I said their names, but when I came at last to Jenna, he looked startled.

"Oh my. I did not know that women of other lands do not have hands!" he was genuinely surprised. Hearing this, both Juli and Karmanski took a closer look at Jenna; from their reactions, I could tell that none had ever seen a handless person before.

Jenna, surprised that they could think such a thought, answered, "No, the Unholy Paladins who conquered Zargarb cut them off. But we still must shake; they don't hurt." She held out her arms and gently both men shook them.

Karmanski angrily cursed and spat on the sands, "Vile Infidels! There is no low that they will not sink too! I curse them. Curses to all Infidels!" Blood poured into his veins around his face, adding to his vehement look. "Just so you know," he added calming down slightly, "I am now ready to face the Infidels should they enter the Anuir!" Just then, none of us knew what he meant, but we would soon find out.

Juli Aldari-Zolgoti, far more sympathetic as she moved forward to shake Jenna's arms, said, "Oh you poor thing. That must have been truly awful. How can you get by without any hands? I don't know what I would do without mine?"

"Hey, what's done is done. I cannot grow new hands. Either you can become an apathetic, hopeless cripple dependent upon others to live or you can accept the situation and move on. I have long ago moved on. I do very well without them, except of course with some things I do need assistance. Personally, I was doing very well financially before this happened. However, after losing them, I have gained something that is far, far more important than hands. That is why I came here, to discuss this with Jes Amir, your Guardian being."

Juli replied, "All of us in the village will help you with anything you need, Jenna."

"Just let me ask first," Jenna chuckled. "It's annoying when I am trying to do something for myself and others impatient at my speed or feeling sorry for me intervene without asking. I don't do diapers at all well," she turned it into a jest. Indeed, she always let others handle this chore while raising her three children.

"Well, come let us get you some dinner and a place to sleep. Our people sleep very soon after evening prayers, rising in time to welcome the dawn of a new day," Juli explained.

"We've brought our own tents," I explained. "We do not want someone to give up their home for us. Where should be erect them?"

Ali smiled, "Ah ha. See Karmanski, I told you." Juli's husband stared at the ground. "When we began building our new homes, I made them build an extra house for any guests that might come calling. Everyone has made fun of me for doing that. You are the very first guests to come. Please, stay in our guesthouse. It is large enough for the four of you and is close to the water."

We agreed. As he led us to the adobe home, he explained to Jenna, "I am afraid that when the villagers see you tomorrow, they will be staring at you. None of us has ever seen someone such as yourself. Please let me apologize for their stares ahead of time."

"No problem. I get that everywhere I go. Normally, I like to think that they are staring at me because I am a beautiful woman," she teased, and he caught her jest. Indeed, Jenna was still a striking figure of a woman, although now middle aged, with lines appearing where there had been none.

"Also, if you cannot understand our Arad speech, just ask Juli, Karmanski, or me. We are the only three here who can speak your Sea Prince dialect," Ali added as we entered the virgin adobe home. The building was square in shape, the front half served as dining room, kitchen, panty, and living room, sporting a crude wicker table made from palm trees and for similar chairs. The back half was divided into two bedrooms, perfect for our needs. Juli brought over some blankets and other small items, explaining that although it had been built, since they had had no visitors as yet, it was not "supplied."

We awoke to the chanting of over three hundred voices, men, women, and children, singing praises to Lord Jehosa as the sun rose over the desert. Jenna watched as each person sat on a thin reed mat, bowed their heads, rose up, and chanted their responses to the callings of Messiah Ali. Again, it instilled us with a great tranquility.

After prayers, the women went about the task of making breakfast, while the men played with all the children. I did not remember there being this many youngsters here the last time I visited, ten years ago. Evidently, the village was prospering quite well. Many children pestered Jenna, asking her endless questions about her missing hands, all of which she took in stride. Once the meal was over, the men went about their tasks; some tended the small gardens that grew on the other side of the oasis, while others herded the flocks of sheep out in search of sparse grasses, though I wondered where they could possibly find any grass out here.

At last, Juli came over to us, "Now, those of you who wish to speak to

507

the Guardian of the Anuir, please follow me. We will sit on yonder dune as usual." All four of us followed her out of the village, climbing to the top. The view was inspiring, if nothing else. She brought a mat for each of us to sit upon, and we followed her lead.

"Ali and Karmanski will be joining us today. Close your eyes and behold the Guardian of the Anuir." I looked around but saw neither man, before I closed my eyes obediently.

Welcome Ket Bethany. It is good to see you once more. It was Jes; in our terms, he had just Mind Linked with all four of us and with the three of them, only I saw Juli was floating way above her body's head. Right beside her was Karmanski and Ali, yet their bodies were still nowhere in sight. I introduced my companions, one by one.

I thought, *You have accomplished much since I was last here, Jes, or should I call you Guardian?*

Ah, yes, yes we have. The bodies of Ali and Karmanski are out working on their tasks, while they appear here before us. Three I have now taught many skills. If Infidels enter the Anuir, either one of the three is completely capable of destroying them without my assistance. Never before have I had such progress. He paused, *After our last meeting, I looked at my scrambled memories, attempting to put them into some kind of order, as you suggested. Then, I discovered that I do not need memories, I can just know. I still have a great fondness for you, my Bethany. Have you come to learn at last? Oh, call me as you will.*

I know you as Jes, so Jes, it is. I can see that you now have three most able spiritual beings. I am envious. In all our married years, I never knew how you did even one of your actions, like moving someone outside of their head so that they could recognize just who and what they actually are. I think that would be an invaluable skill to have. But before we digress on what I am after or think I am after, I want to introduce you to a special friend of mine, Jenna Rose. It is because of her that I am here today.

How do I do this? Jenna fumbled about, *"Just think what I want to say?*

Yes, but you are not Arad, Sea Princes?

Yes, originally from Zargarb, but I now live just outside Velona. I need to explain what all has happened to me and what I have done, so that I can ask proper questions.

Do spiritual beings have expressions and emotions? You bet, it is you, your personality. We detected an immediate bit of mirth from our hosts, as if this was going to be one of the long story telling times. Jes, in better humor than I had seen him display since long before he and I began our preaching days so long ago, replied, *No need for that much work on your part Jenna. If you will allow me, it will go much faster. Some of my pupils have not learned yet their lessons of patience,* an obvious reference to Karmanski's sometimes temper against the Infidels.

What happened next had me completely at a loss for words. Like a motion picture only with full sound, vision, emotions, smells, all senses, the images that Jenna wanted to communicate about her life and experiences were projected into our minds, almost faster than we could absorb them! Still, Jenna was in control over what was revealed. She began that fateful night when she was closing up her inn. Thankfully, she skipped over the incredible trauma and shock that she endured for several months after that. Rapidly, she showed how she and the Three Roses banded together and began to survive as individuals once more. She showed how they met me and how they began their new lives with Hank.

Then she began to show the first of her many therapy sessions, beginning with Hank's. All of a sudden, Jes slowed everything down, even replaying critical portions of that first session several time. Obviously, Jes found this therapy that Jenna had stumbled upon or invented, very vital and important. Although Jenna had only intended to show a few of her sessions, Jes insisted on viewing every one of them, and in all their details! Even I was impressed with the volume of Jenna's work; although I knew she was there helping, I did not really grasp just how many people she had treated and with what success. By the time that Jes had finally seen the last of the sessions, we all realized that our bodies were starving; it was well past lunch time.

Jes picked this up at once and said, *Imagine the finest meal you could eat for lunch*. After a short pause, he stated, *It is now within your stomachs*. Suddenly, my stomach felt completely full, nearly gorged upon a pork roast. What a remarkable occurrence. *Yes, it is real*, he added, detecting the wonder from the others. Now we will not be bothered by hungry bodies and can continue. The other three had experienced this "miracle" before, but we four had certainly not!

Paulette thought, *Well, I do prefer to eat it more slowly*. We all laughed at her jest, including the other three.

May we continue? Jes insisted. We calmed down and he went on. *Jenna, now that I know of you, why is it that you have sought me out?*

I have listened to the preaching of all the gnostics of Velona: the druwid's Nature and Harmony, the original Arad teachings of Jehosa, the teachings of the Blessed Holy Mother, and even Elona Po's attempts to merge these into a whole. As you have just seen, I have seen that people of all cultures seem to be spiritual beings; many have recalled and erased the impact of traumas suffered in a previous incarnation or physical body. I apologize for not having the right words to say this. Question one is: are not all of us on Tarra immortal spiritual beings, not just those of Arad descent?

Yes, dear child. I am the son of Lord Jehosa, just as you and everyone else on Tarra is as well. It was my great mistake to have focused all my attempts long ago solely on those of Arad lineage. I have paid a terrible price for having made that error in judgment.

Question two: since receiving my therapy sessions and running out a trauma of a former lifetime, many of these people now are either located further from their heads if they tended to reside outside it to begin with or have at least moved out a little to experience themselves as a being. That is what I concluded. Is this a correct interpretation of what happened?

I deem your conclusion to be valid.

Thank you for the validation. I have been studying under the druwids for some time now. Only spiritual beings who reside outside of their body's heads are able to master the druwid's most powerful spells, such as bringing down bolts of lightning. Although I have made many discrete inquiries, I have found no person who resided within his or her head who could be taught these things. My conclusion is that a person must have a good knowledge of their own identity as a spiritual being before they can command such forces of Nature. Question three: is this also a correct interpretation?

I know little of Bethany's druwids, she can answer better than I. I defer to you, Bethany.

Yes, that is true. Never has a header, as we derogatorily used to call those people who are stuck solidly within their heads, never has one ever mastered the power spells of Nature. Let me show you all one event from my past, if I may. Jes, can you do what you did with Jenna?

Suddenly, in three dimensional, color vision, complete with emotions, my sessions with Alabaster were displayed for all to see, those in which he taught me to defend myself from lightning bolt attacks. When I began, I acted as if I was still being a young girl and of course failed completely. I jumped ahead to the first time I succeeded at it; there I was acting as myself, simply a spiritual being in touch with all that was going on in the world around me, independent of the fleshly body. *I know of only nine spiritual beings on Tarra who can defend against lightning strikes, fire sheets, and such. Well, maybe Jes can, and I don't know about you three,* I added being completely honest.

Jes replied at last. *This ties in with what I am accomplishing here. When I have a pupil exterior to their body, I can teach them to do many things. Yet, everything depends upon the person becoming free from the fetters of the mortal body, which I view as nothing more than an aesthetic trap. Does this fully answer you?*

Jenna replied, *Yes, it does. I can see that my analysis has thus far been perfect. I have then but one more question to ask. At this time in my training, the tenth year it is called, we are to choose an area in which to specialize. Having no hands is limiting my choices. Well, to be perfectly honest, not entirely. I really am not interested in sewing up wounds as Beth Ann does so well. I just use no hands as a convenient excuse. I have no desire for fighting skills; once more, no hands gives me a polite way to avoid that choice. I have no telepathic skills, though I have tried. I do not enjoy designing buildings and forts and such, again no hands gives me a friendly way out of that choice. I have no patience or desire to be the judger of facts, the arbitrator of disputes, although my lack of hands cannot be used here. Unlike Ket Bethany, I do not desire to know all about everything, so a Wid is out. Only a Loremaster choice remains. I have tried very hard to get into Nature with plants and animals, since my husband is a Loremaster. I have even helped him plant and harvest, though I am clumsy at it. Realistically, that one is out. I am left with no choices.*

I had not fully realized the impossible position I had really put this person into — training diligently only to fail at the very end. I felt rather sheepish. The others ignored me, and Jenna continued, *So I began to see just what hidden talents I might have that could possibly be improved upon. I am good with getting men to do what I want them to do, made a fortune at it before I lost my hands, but there must be something else I might be able to do. Then, I realized that there is something, something that I feel I am this close to being able to do, but cannot manage. Again, I have no word for it, so will have to describe it.*

I feel that I ought to be able to move things around without the use of my body. So my final question is thus: it must be possible for someone to learn how to do this because I heard that you and Juli have done this very thing to the Infidels. I saw it with my own eyes when we first arrived; all three of you seemed to be doing what it is that I think I ought to be able to do somehow. My question is this: can you teach me to move things about without my body?

Jes laughed, not at Jenna, but at what she had not asked for. He at last explained, *Jenna, when you first came, I would have predicted that you would ask me for a miracle to regrow new hands. What person in your situation would not have done so? In fact, both Juli and Karmanski asked me that very question this morning before she came to get you. I have a memory somewhere here where I did indeed once regrow a woman's hand. However, that action did not really result in any real improvement in her spirituality. You are wise beyond wise, Jenna Rose. Yes, if you could move anything around at will without your body, for what would you then need hands?*

You have already shared with me a great treasure, your therapy. I did not know this could be done, or how it may be worked. While the time may have seemed short to you, I have mastered your technique and will be applying it to those under our care here at the oasis. I know that I can give you what you ask for since that is precisely what my three pupils here have already mastered. The only remaining question is how long will it take you to learn. For me, time has little meaning, but for those of you with bodies, you have a somewhat different viewpoint. I will teach you, Jenna Rose, for as long as you desire to learn.

Thank you, Jes, Jenna replied. *Ket, I will now have a specialty: a mover of things. I leave it to you to name it.* Again, Jenna was teasing me, and I smiled back at her, being to being.

Chapter 42 The Training of Jenna Rose

Jenna scarcely could conceal her excitement as she sat down on the reed mat upon the dune overlooking the oasis, ready for her first lesson. *Are you ready to begin?* Jes asked, she most definitely was ready. *Tell me why you think you ought to be able to move objects.*

Well, ever since I was a little girl, I always had dreams that I was moving things about our home. In my most private thoughts, I kept thinking that this is something I should know how to do, but never could, though I tried. I stopped trying when my parents died, and I took over the inn.

Very good. Now you see that tiny little speck of sand there that I am highlighting? I want you give it a little push. Jenna tried, but nothing happened. *Okay, now imagine there is a huge storm raging around us and along comes a big gust of wind. Create a great big gust of wind and move that spec.* Jenna pictured a raging gale as if it was blowing full on at the tiny piece of sand.

It moved! It really did!

I saw it. Now let's get ten of those storms blowing ten times as hard. See if you can push that sand down the side of the dune. Jenna created the requisite images of ten big storms all bowing straight at that tiny spec of sand. This time the grain hopped, bobbed, and rolled quite a ways down the side of the dune.

I'm doing it! I really am doing it! Jenna exclaimed suddenly full of unbridled excitement at her accomplishment. However, at that instant, a large black mass engulfed her, crushing her enthusiasm, sending her into the deepest pits of apathy. She sat there nearly asleep, as if she had been heavily drugged.

Jes was quite startled by her reaction. He concluded that she must have endured some kind of heavy trauma in the past that somehow related to moving a grain of sand. Ali had also shown a similar manifestation when he began to move sand around. Jes had spent countless hours working with him to get him over that barrier. Now, Jes had discovered from Jenna herself a new tool that might just assist him. Patiently he asked her, *What do you see or hear?*

I promised never to do that ever again. I did. I must. I cannot, she cried. Her body below her reacted with an outpouring of tears, though she did not notice it. *I am a failure. I must not do it again. I mustn't.*

Jenna, I want you to go through the memories and tell me what is going on.

I see a black massy thing. I must not do it ever again. I mustn't, I mustn't.

Mustn't do what? Are you at the beginning of that memory or at the end of it?

Don't know what. Where does it begin? I don't want to see it. I mustn't do it again ever. I don't want to see it. Must never, ever do it again. Oh, I am at the end. Now I see it's raining, dark outside. I am in my house. It's late. I can't sleep. No, my daughter woke me up! She's screaming, terrified. I jumped out of bed and am running to her room. Can't see, stumble on something, hear a bone in my foot crack, pain, lots of pain. Stagger into her room, hopping on one foot. Lightning flashes, see her screaming, sitting in her bed. See a dark shape by her window. Rain and wind blowing in. Intruder there waving hands. Got to protect her. My body is shaking, can't stand up. Fall down. Protect her. Picked up her commode and hurled it across the room, smashing into the intruder. He doesn't move. Time stands still. No lightning keeps flashing. Can't get up. Light a lantern. We crawl over to the commode, I move it. She says Mommy you killed daddy! I just stared at him. I had crushed him. Strong odor of wine. He was drunk, probably lost his key and broke in her window. I killed him. I killed him. I must never do it again. Mustn't move things ever again. I cried for hours. I swore I'd never move things ever again.

Very good, Jenna. Now let's go over that once more and tell me all the details. Jes found this fascinating. She had once had the very ability she now desired, but had misused it. She herself was the cause of her inability to move things in the present. For Jes, this came as a revelation. She went through the dreadful incident several more times. He noted that her heavy grief slowly eased off and that she continued to discover more details about what had happened. Sometime later, Jenna began laughing about it all.

You know I really am not a bad person. It was just a stupid mix-up, a comedy of errors and judgment. If I had not broken my foot and been in so much pain, I would have handled the intruder differently. You know my decision not to move things really did stick. I've never been able to do that since then.

Excellent job, Jenna. Now how about seeing if you can move that grain of sand down there? Jes watched and hoped.

Once again, Jenna invented or imagined ten large, swirling storms blowing straight at the sand particle. To her amazement and that of Jes, a large chunk of sand was dislodged, cascading down the side of the dune! *Wow!* exclaimed Jenna, overcome with the joy of success.

After some additional experimentation, Jes ended the morning's session. He told her, *Your therapy methods have taught me quite a lot, given me an insight that I did not have before. Ali had similar difficulties at the beginning. I continued using my known methods with him until he too could move sand as you have just done. The only problem was that it took us nearly a month as opposed to mere hours. I now have much to ponder, Jenna Rose.*

Jenna bounded down the dune to report to me what had happened, ecstatic beyond words at her accomplishment. While we ate, she had to explain what had happened in detail. For her, this morning was one of those monumental turning points in life and she needed someone with which to share it. Then, it was my turn to visit with Jes.

First, he filled me in on how well the first session went with Jenna. *Her therapy method works perfectly. What I am finding true is that the person himself causes his or her own degradation of ability. I have seen this many, many times. Bethany, if one misuses an ability, the person then decides to never use it again because of the damage they cause by so using it. In short, the person no longer can trust himself. A person is their own worst enemy when it comes to abilities.*

I concurred, thinking of my own insanity situation with lightning bolts. He went on, *Bethany, since our last visit some time ago, I have examined pieces of our memories. Correct me if I am wrong in my observations, but in the intervening years since our intertwined lives, something has happened to you. You seem now to have some darkish, grey mass surrounding you that you did not have before.*

Damn, was it that obvious? I sighed, *Well, yes. It happened again only this time I killed four of my own men.* Jes asked me to tell him about it and so I told him about the attack on Nuadilan and how I had stopped the awful charge of the enemy that would have otherwise overrun the town. I had gone into that black, insane madness, pulling down lightning bolts, totally out of proportion to what was needed, and ended up killing four of the overly enthusiastic Axemen who had strayed too close to the front lines.

They say I struck every object on the battlefield something like ten times after each was already dead. My friends almost could not get me to stop. I just lost it completely once more. I lose it every time I get into such a life or death situation. I just go temporarily insane. In the past, I was incredibly lucky not to have harmed any on my side, but this time, I killed four valiant warriors. I swore that I would never use lightning bolts ever again. Now, I am afraid that I cannot even do it at all. I seem to have forgotten how. I've let others use their spells, while I used other means. So yes, Jes, I have only added to my own black mass, and there is nothing that can be done about it. But my long standing question for you is how do you get someone out of their head so that they can see and experience what they really are, a spiritual being separate from the body. You never told me when we were married, and I am still waiting to know. I would like to be able to do just that.

First things first, Bethany. Understanding of one leads to understanding of the other. Let's re-experience the attack, which killed four of your men. Begin at the beginning, please.

Jes, I dare not. If I truly re-live that day, I will be right back in that black insanity mass, which I seem helpless to get out of by myself. I'm terrified of it. There, I had finally admitted it to another person. I felt a little anxiety relief now that another person knew I was terrified of it.

I understand. You have me. I will not let any harm come to you, I promise. Now let's go to the beginning of that day, please. Remember, my love, truth will set you free.

He had not called me that since he left me to do battle with the Grey Creatures! Vanity, maybe, but I felt a new burst of confidence. *Okay, don't say I didn't warn you.* Slowly, I began re-visiting that day's images in detail. He had me go over it several times, but always I blanked completely out partway through it. Once the black madness came over me, I went unconscious to nearly everything, awakening near the end when my friends were desperately trying to pull me out of it and get me to stop the rain of lightning bolts.

He saw that I was getting nowhere with the blackness. Following the guidelines set forth by Jenna, he asked me if there was an earlier time that was somehow similar in nature to this one. Of course there was, when I was on Heartbreak Hill with Lenkova fighting the Axemen. Although we went over it numerous times, during the middle at the height of the madness, I completely blanked out, recalling nothing. The black mass took me over, and I was a mere puppet to the action.

Once more, he asked me if there was yet another earlier time. I began describing the very first time that I went mad, bringing down lightning bolts there in Uru, when I thought the cavalrymen had already killed Ellen, my mentor, and my family. Repeatedly, we went over this one. I could recall it in utter vivid detail, complete to water drops falling on my face, the anger and horror of seeing Ellen pierced by quarrels, my brother and sister likewise shot. Again, about halfway through it, I blacked out, totally overwhelmed by that black energy mass. Still I did remember hearing the singing voice trying to break its hold over me. Memories returned at the shelter cabin near the end of the incident.

Poor Jes, he too thought that this one had to be the first time this had ever happened to me, just as I did. Many times, we went over it with nothing much happening in the way of a result. Finally, he asked me if there was another incident similar to this that was earlier in time. At first, I was about to tell him flatly that I had no memories before this time, that it was my first lifetime on Tarra and that I had no memories before I was six there in Uru. However, just as I was about to tell him so, I saw something embedded in the black mass, the mass that has always occluded my more distant past. Something was there!

Go to the beginning of that one and go through it telling me what happens as you go along. I was suddenly into unknown territory! I had no idea what this memory was. It had been completely forgotten, totally occluded from my own knowledge!

Boy, this was hard, confronting my own unknown, forgotten memories from who knows when and where! *I see a bunch of men. I seem to be in a heated argument with them. No they are the bosses. Planetary bosses, I think. It's a tribunal. Damn, I am on trial. They want me to stop interfering with their experiments. I am refusing.*

Next time through it, I picked up some more details. *They are growing bodies on some planets and experimenting putting spiritual beings into them such that they cannot get out of those bodies. I think this is criminal on their*

515

part and tell them so. Oh, I have been secretly sabotaging their efforts and was caught doing it. I wonder who their victims are? I think that they are trying to en-prison as docile slaves those beings in their society whom they cannot control. Artists, some are artists I think, maybe philosophers. They don't listen to me and are sentencing me to exile some place that is very, very far away from their civilization. I get the feeling that the place would be terribly distant, with no way for me to find my way back. They are sending a special vehicle to transport me there.

Oh, they are marching me down to that strange ship. Looks like a potato or something. Just as we got there, I went into action. Ah, I could control energy then, much like lightning bolts. I began launching a tremendous volume of energy blasts, in all directions. I knew that they would eventually counter it and get me. So I rigged the whole thing on sort of total automatic. A tiny part of me would just blast away at random, using a flat out maximum continuous blasting, while I tried to make my escape. I just shut my eyes to the situation and let loose with everything I had, while I drifted slowly away in the utter confusion. I know that the entire place completely exploded, blew up in a gigantic ball of fire, but I had my perceptions cut off so that I didn't actually see it. Thus, everything was black, as I semi-unconsciously floated away. Oh, I had decided that I would come to one of their abandoned failed projects, Tarra, and set about the goal of rescuing all the entrapped beings there. The company had long ago written the whole planet off as a failed experiment and had completely abandoned it not even making the slightest effort to rescue the beings they had manipulated there.

Jes! This is incredible! I know why I came here! I am still trying to do what I set out to do back then. Wow! Unbelievable! Incredible. Amazing. I don't have words for this. Thank you for getting me through it. God, Jenna is the one who found out how to undo these trauma events! I have to thank her too. Wow. Oh wow!

For a time, Jes was silent, listening to me carry on in my wild enthusiasm. I am glad he did. I was so excited, so happy, so incredibly relieved. That grey mass that I could never seem to penetrate on my own now had a large hole right in the middle of it!

At last, he said, Incredibly well done, dearest Bethany! Well done indeed. You know, from the very first day I met you, I sensed that our purposes here on Tarra were very similar, although I could not articulate it then. I just felt it was so. If I am to be honest with you, my love, I am overjoyed to find a companion, a helper, to share our mission. To free these entrapped beings here on Tarra has always been my goal as well. We are very much akin, my Bethany. I have not yet thanked you for doing what I was unable to do, eliminate the two controlling, manipulating alien groups. So thank you. Without that having been done, we stood no chance at all. They were undoing what we were doing far faster than any progress we made. I am deeply indebted to you and Alabaster. Today, I am filled with such hope *for the future that I cannot describe it, but I think you know what I feel.*

The sun was low in the west, time for evening prayers and supper. I was famished, more than I would have expected from a long afternoon. When I found Jenna happily discretely moving sand piles around, I just had to stop her and give her one enormous hug. "It worked on me! Your techniques! They lifted the black veil! I am so happy. So much is now clear to me. Jenna, I owe you more than I can ever repay you. If you ever need anything, and I do mean anything, I'll see that you get it. I cannot ever repay you enough for what you've done."

Somewhat taken aback by my sudden outburst of genuine sincerity and enthusiasm, she just patted me with her arms. Recovering, she took my hand in her arms and said, "Look, you have already given me my life back, when I had nothing to give in return except money. I think that we are square, Ket. If you had not taken such good care of the Three Roses, I would never have really recovered. Really, we are even." I saw her point; we just hugged long instead of saying more words.

During my time with Jes the next day, we discussed the answer to my remaining, very long-standing question. *These are my preliminary observations, subject to further examination, Bethany, so take them as a study in progress. I have found several plausible reasons for why all these beings are trapped or stuck in their heads. Before I can answer your question of how do I manage to get some out of their heads, you must hear these observations, or it will not make much sense to you.*

One possibility is that they become forced into the head this way. The spiritual being must have a physical connection to the body through which to receive sensory perceptions. Suppose that an innocent being is going along nicely outside and behind a body's head and then that body is subjected to a sudden, intense pain of some kind. Since the sensory line is still connected at the moment that huge surge of pain hits, it snaps the being straight into the body. Try it sometime; get someone to hit you and see if your attention doesn't suddenly go straight into the body. Although I have yet no definitive proof, I suspect that this was the actions done to the beings here long before our arrival by our enemies.

A second possibility lends itself more to explaining why they remain in their heads and cannot get back out at will. It is a matter of directional flows. All speech is an outflow only from the mouth. Hearing is strictly an inflow into the ears at the side. Eyesight is inflow only. Touch is inflow only. However, the main ones are speech and hearing. Notice that we hear what we speak. Now you have already seen what happens when a flow goes only in one direction. Your caravels are an example. When you are moving forward rapidly, that represents speech going outwards. Now what happens behind the ship? Just as with the ship, as the words and sounds leave and go forward, they tend to create a vacuum behind it. Don't your caravels leave a swirling hole behind them, which fills up with other water? If a being gets too close to this particle flow, they are sucked right on into the head, like the water filling up in the ship's wake. If they try to move out, they immediately run right into these particles rushing in to fill the vacuum left by outgoing senses.

Now this might not be all that is there, but I have seen this in operation many times. There must be more to all this, because what would then prevent one from leaving if everything is very quiet and the person isn't speaking? Remember all those that I did it to, like Jackal and his wife, even Josh and Milla. I got them out for a brief time; yet within a short while, they all were back in their heads once more, sucked right back in by this vacuum and flow mechanism that the body has.

There is a third possibility: desire for sensation. These fleshly bodies are capable of furnishing one with lots of pre-made sensations, particularly sex, though by no means is that the only sensation available. It is one that I found commonly valued and exploited here on Tarra. It has a valid purpose, to ensure that there are future generations. Spiritual beings, who have forgotten how to make their own even more powerful sensations, have become dependent upon the fleshly bodies to provide sensations for them and are thus unwilling to abandon this source of pleasure.

Perhaps, it is a combination of all three. I am not completely certain yet. Do you follow all these? I did, but didn't see that they explained how he got them out of their heads.

What I used to do, Bethany, was temporarily nullify the energy flows around their heads. Remember that I would place my hands on either side of their heads? Well, I then absorbed all the energy around their heads and gave them a slight nudge up and out. That's all I did. I agree it was most effective on many, allowing them to perceive their true nature. Yet, in the end, my doing so had little overall effect, in so far as to keep them out. All went right back in within a short while, as you witnessed. Yes, it changed their perspective on life, but they did not become more able and powerful as a spiritual being as a result. Thus, I failed to achieve my goal of freeing them.

I replied, Well, they were certainly highly enlightened and that changed their lives for the better. You don't dispute that?

No, I don't. Compare those results to what I am now achieving with my three, make that four, pupils here? There is no comparison. However, it had been a very arduous and slow process to get their abilities back to where they are at today. Jenna's therapy promises to cut the time needed drastically. Still, we have three spiritual beings that are getting back into their native states and abilities once more.

Jes, we have hundreds of thousands, perhaps millions, of beings here on Tarra to rescue. Three more or less salvaged in ten plus years? You know how long this is going to take?

I detected a huge amount of sadness suddenly emanating from Jes. I had touched a very sensitive area with him, but I could not retract what I had said. I know, but now I have more help. Are you fully with me?

Of course, Jes. You know that. However, the rest of Tarra is slowly going in the wrong direction, toward even more slavery and deceit and inhumanity.

You have more connections to those who are more able yet here on Tarra. Can you and your friends help buy me more time so that I can continue my work here, undisturbed? That would help me immensely. Do what you can to help get Tarra more civilized and a better, calmer place to live. Get the individual trauma levels down. No more of these wars.

Yes, division of labors is what we need. I'll do all that I can to get a thriving, stable, peaceful Tarra, and you keep on freeing the beings. Together, we may just be able to pull this off. You are right. I have more connections to the world of men than you do currently. It makes sense then for me to work on that angle. However, do keep me informed of any breakthroughs and successes. In my spare time, I may want to work on some myself, if I have any spare time.

Jes laughed, *Spare time? What is that?* I laughed along with him.

Later that day, I decided that we should be heading back to the others at our fortress. Paulette wanted to stay behind with Jenna to help and assist her. None of us felt comfortable leaving her behind without one of us nearby. With our Communicator staying with Jenna, I would receive constant updates on her progress and such. Only Paul and I rode back to the fortress. He and I had much to discuss, as I bounced ideas off him as we rode hard for ten days.

Six months passed swiftly, before Paulette notified us that she and Jenna were ready to return home. I sent a caravel to pick them up and notified everyone. Meanwhile, I was rather tied up helping get the first printing press operational. Rea had shown us one of her father's inventions, a machine that allowed one to create or rather print books. Until now, each book had to be hand copied, a very labor-intensive project. Since I wanted to publish the true writings of Jes Amir and Jehosanity, I needed a way to mass-produce them. We had constructed a prototype and it worked beautifully. The first published book was Christina's first novel, *It Happened One Stormy Night*. As a footnote, this book became wildly popular in Velona, forcing numerous reprints. Now I was engaged upon getting a dozen presses constructed, most being sent to Velona.

Hank and the children were standing on the docks, watching the caravel slowly approach. "I see her! I see her," their youngest kept calling out. Yes, the children were very excited to see their mother again; she had been gone for what had seemed like an eternity, six months. Slowly the caravel docked and the gangplank secured. Finally, Paulette and Jenna walked down the narrow board and onto the docks. The kids bolted and ran to her, everyone hugging each other. Hank, having missed his wife more than he could ever vocalize, resisted the urge to run to her, walking briskly instead.

After hugs and kisses all around, Hank commented, "My, what a tan you have, Jenna. You look radiant. I've, we've all missed you so!"

She grinned, "Yes, the desert is very hot. Not sure I want to live there. It is very good to be home. I've missed you all very much too, but it was more than worth it. Thanks, Paulette." She gave her a farewell hug, just as Paul came running up to them.

Just then, loud gongs began to sound an alarm. Many dockhands first looked seaward, half expecting to see some unexpected sea invasion. However, from the continuing sounds, all realized that something was very wrong within the city. Many dropped everything and began running into the city.

"What's up?" asked Paulette, Hank, and Jenna, nearly simultaneously.

"Construction disaster at the new church. I was just coming to get you all. Come on, I'll explain on the way." Hank gathered up the women's sacks, and they joined the crowd heading inland.

He explained, "They were attempting to put on the last row of stone on the cathedral today when the scaffolding collapsed. Happened just a couple minutes ago. Half of the dome came crashing down. However, the wood has protected the workers, well sort of. Instead of being crushed under the tons of stone blocks, two dozen workers are now trapped in a hollow. Entombed might be a better description. They are alive, but buried under tons of stone blocks. Now the problem is how in the world do we get them out of there. Everyone's trying to lend a hand. What a disaster."

Within minutes, they arrived at the construction site. Elona herself was there directing the rescue operations. However, no one could agree on how best to rescue the men without causing the stones to collapse further, crushing them all. Considering the weight of just one stone block, many men were required just to lift it. However, the jumble of stones did not permit enough men to get to one spot to lift a stone.

"Good god!" exclaimed Jenna, as she tried to see around the throng of people gathering to watch and help as they could. "Hank, get me to some place high where I can see down on this, please." He didn't hesitate, but led them to a nearby building, a warehouse. Quickly, the small group climbed to the upper level and peered out a window. "This will do. Now I can see. What a mess. Hank, is there someone around who can tell me where each stone is supposed to go?"

"What on Tarra are you talking about?" Hank protested.

"What do you need?" asked Paulette, her druwid training kicking into high gear. "I can get in touch with whomever you need."

"Well, I can move the stones, but I don't know where it's safe to put them. I suppose the best thing is to put them where they are supposed to go, don't you think?" Jenna replied. Hank looked at her dumbfounded.

Paulette contacted Elona and relayed Jenna's message. As they watched, they saw Elona turn, look up at them, and wave. "She said that in a couple minutes, five Planners are going to be here to advise. Until then, she is going to keep everyone back. Apparently, there is too great a risk of the pile collapsing, killing the trapped men."

Allan and four others stood around the edges of the construction site, surveying the damage. Jenna asked, "Paulette, I hate ask you this, but can you

Mind Link me with Allan please?" Paulette gave her a funny look, but complied

Allan, Jenna here. I can move the stones, but I don't know where to put them. I suppose the best place for them is where they should go. Can you direct me, stone by stone?

Yes, I know where they were supposed to go, but whatever are you talking about, Jenna?

As Allan, and everyone else for that matter, was looking at the pile of collapsed dome stone, the top stone slowly moved up in the air, floating as if lifted by some unknown giant's hand. *Where's this one go?* asked Jenna.

The large crowd gasped almost in unison! Allan stared in utter disbelief, too dumbfounded to answer. *Come on; where does this one go?*

Ah, Allan fumbled for words. Instead, he sent her a picture of where that one belonged. Slowly the giant stone moved to the location pictured. Allan gave her a few more directions and the stone lowered into position.

It will not stay here. It wants to fall down, Jenna complained.

That's what the scaffolding was supposed to do, support these until the top capstone is in place. Rather like this. He sent a series of images of how it was supposed to all go together over many months of work, ending with the top, final stone, which would then hold the entire dome ceiling together.

Oh, I think I see. All right, how about this one? Where does it go?

Allan continued to direct her, stone by stone. Meanwhile down at the sight, people began whispering about the divine miracle happening before their very eyes. Shortly, Elona's Communicator joined with her, and the largest Mind Link in druwid history slowly began. Before long, every druwid was linked up, seeing what Elona and her Circle members were seeing. No one dared touch Paulette, and she dared not do anything by maintain Jenna and Allan's joining.

An hour later, workers cleared the wooden scaffolding mess and rescued the trapped workers, a few of which had some broken bones, but no life threatening injuries. Still Jenna did not stop. Had she, the stones would have fallen once more. Stone by stone, now coming from the storage pile, continued to rise to their places in the dome. Progress was swifter now that she did not have to be extra cautious to protect the workers. Another half hour and the final cap stone was in place.

Now test it slightly; see if it holds itself, Allan cautioned. *It should. At least it did in the scale models we built.* Jenna slowly released her hold; the dome didn't move. At last, she let go entirely. It still held. *Thank you! Thank you! Do you realize that you not only saved the lives of the workers, but also cut about six months off the construction time! Unbelievable, Jenna. Thank you!*

Hey, you two, I have to break the link. I'm exhausted! Paulette broke in on them and then dropped the mind link.

At this point in time over half of Velona had packed in and around the square, staring and gawking at the new dome sitting high atop their new church. By nightfall, everyone in Velona had seen the church at least once! That a Holy Construction Miracle had occurred was the topic of conversation for the next month.

Later, Elona, who had not yet named her new cathedral, decided to call it the Church of the Holy Rose, in honor of Jenna. However, only certain Santi members knew why she chose this name. Yes, Jenna had now officially introduced a new discipline to us druwids.

Chapter 43 The Death of Pope Yazi I

Winter of 635 arrived in Megalos, although unless you were a local, you'd never know it had come. Noon temperatures were substantially cooler. A lone ship docked at the new tiny port at Constanza City. One man, carrying a small bag, disembarked and headed for the main priest quarters. The Rooster had finally arrived home with both good and bad news for his mentor, who he sought out at once. He perfunctorily greeted the various guards and went straight to the bedroom where Pope Yazi now spent the largest portion of his days.

Pope Yazi was old and frail, approaching eighty years of age. His chronic cough had only worsened with each passing year. Still, he continued his advance planning. The Rooster knocked and entered, when he heard the faint, beloved voice call out. "Welcome back," whispered Yazi.

"I came straight here," the Rooster began. "We cannot be overheard?" The Pope nodded affirmative, so he continued. "I have verified that our previous mission was indeed totally successful. Cathleen Amir and her line have perished in a 'hunting accident.' Only Sarah Amir's line remains. I was able to arrange an accident for her. She has been eliminated. I've verified my own handiwork. However, these Santi are indeed powerful and observant. This Ket Bethany saw through the accidental fall right away and even found my entrance point into the castle."

"Ah, so at last Sarah has been eliminated. That is good news, my dear friend, good news to these old ears."

"The bad news, Your Holiness, is that her children and their children still live. Most are kept securely within the Santi fortress at Mont Blanc. I've studied that fortress, and I must admit that even I, the Rooster, would not be able to gain clandestine access to it, let alone find them and carry out what must be done. No chance at all, I hate to report. So many Santi there are Evil Witches, as the Galts call them. Rightly so. They possess powerful, conjured, magical spells that only Lucifer himself could have bestowed upon them. Ket Bethany represents the most powerful witch of them all, and he watches over the children and children's children like a hawk."

"I have made a verified list of the remaining offspring. From Sarah, there are Arthur Penton, Justus Penton, and the witch twins, Lilly Ann Bethany, wife of Ket, and Beth Ann. Both Beth Ann and Lilly Ann are constant companions of Ket, never leaving his side. Further, Caitlyn Amir had twin sons, Tegid and Taliesin, who are now twelve. Lilly Ann and Ket have had three more. I swear they are like mice. The more we eliminate, the more they propagate!"

"I fear there is more. I have verified that it was indeed this Ket Bethany who, by use of the wicked fire spells of Lucifer, killed most brutally our Emperor Justinian. Those reports are literally true. Ket Bethany does indeed control the entire Santi organization from his fortress at Mont Blanc. Hence, our next action must see to his demise. I don't see any other way to get closer to those children except to eliminate him from the picture first. On my long voyage back here, I have come up with a plan. I must draw him out of his fortress to a location and circumstance in which he is vulnerable. I believe I have a way."

"I concur. The disciple of Lucifer must be eliminated. Cut off the head of the snake and the long body dies," the Pope whispered, stifling another coughing spell before it wracked his body once again. He had to keep up his appearance for the Rooster and not cause his trusted friend to become distracted.

"This Ket is also the Master Wizard for the West Reach Grande Council of Kings, led by King Lachlan Laird. Several times a year, he briefly visits their meetings. Seldom does he attend with others of the Santi accompanying him. Only here is he vulnerable. I must say that having the Megalos Consulate in Bregia, West Reach, has proven to be invaluable in gaining information and access to that land. I must once more commend you, my Pope, on such a brilliant scheme!"

The Pope smiled and the Rooster continued. "I know when the next time that Ket is scheduled to make an appearance before the council. If I have your okay, I will make my strike at that time, eliminating this most powerful opponent. It should be done this spring, though I must admit that this will be the greatest challenge that I have ever faced."

"Can it be done? I do not want to lose you, Rooster, not at this most critical time."

"Bregia is locked in sheets of ice by now. No ships can dock there until the spring thaw anyway. If you okay the mission, then I have several months before I need to sail for Bregia, Your Holiness."

"Ah, that is good. I missed your ever-present company these past many months, my dear friend. Say, what of the progress in our new colonies in the Sea Princes? Did you get a firsthand look at them? Are the reports we are receiving accurate?"

"Aye, they are actually correct. I do admit that I was surprised to find that so. We have no choice but to hire the Santi to transport our more valuable cargos. Piracy in the Med Sea has indeed become a major problem. It's rumored that there are some ten pirate ships operating there, capturing the slower ships. I saw one of these ships on my voyages and noted that the ship was of the older designs, not one of the new fast caravels. Thus, the caravels of the Santi are untouchable by these sea brigands. On land, it is true that our Holy Paladins are unable to control the outer lands of the sectors. Bands of robbers operate freely, but never dare venture closer than about twenty-five miles from the heavily populated cities and surroundings. Overland cargo caravans are attacked almost at will, unless the Santi protect them. To date, no Santi escorted shipment has ever been lost to the bandits. Indeed, what robber could stand to these highly trained, skilled, chain mail clad warriors? I could find no connection at all between the robbers and the Santi, none."

"Thus, we must continue to use the Santi to get any shipment of value through. Conditions are extremely poor in the outlying areas of our new colonies. Perhaps they are even deteriorating there. I can't tell for sure just yet."

"How about our new towns?"

"Ah, there our Holy Paladins have worked miracles, Your Holiness. All is as they report. The population has been subdued and is following the laws that have been set down for them. Attendance at Church is quite high. Women know their place in society and accept it. The nunneries are flourishing with women who strive to regain their holiness. The universities are overflowing with young students eager to learn what we have to teach. What surprised me the most were the abbeys. So many men have become monks, casting aside their mortal lives in search of spiritual enlightenment, that the abbeys are uniformly being forced to acquire more buildings. I would not have believed it had I not seen it with my own eyes."

"Ah, that is perhaps the best news of all, excepting that of Sarah. You have done well, my son, better than I had hoped for. Now go and take care of your needs. It is such a long voyage, and I am sure you are in need of many things. We can talk more tomorrow. I owe you so much, dear friend, so much." Unfortunately, all the talk brought on another coughing spell, and the Rooster quietly left his venerated Pope, afraid that he had overly excited the aging man.

He slept fitfully, this first night on land in several months. Darkness still enveloped the world, when the large church bells began clanging their doleful sounds, stirring him alert. Bells should not be sounding at this hour, he muttered as he crawled out of bed. Just then, rough knocking resonated on his heavy wooden door. "Coming," he called out, hastily throwing his Supreme Prelate cloak over his semi-naked body.

Opening the door, one of his Mano del Dio men spoke hastily, "Your Holiness, I've come to inform you that His Holiness, Pope Yazi I, has just passed away. Your presence is requested at the Cardinal's Conclave as soon as possible."

He was shocked. Yes, the Rooster had known this day was coming for years now. Still the shock of losing his mentor, the one person in the world who appreciate him for what he was had now left him alone. He shuttered involuntarily. He remembered his vow to Yazi, "Provide Security to the Pope." He'd sworn to do just that, but now it would be to a new Pope. Filled with trepidation, he hurriedly dressed. At the last minute, he added a few of his special tools of trade, slipping them into their concealed locations within the voluminous fabric of his robes. Satisfied, he headed out into the hallway and set off for the meeting room.

Footsteps echoed up and down the stone tiled hallways; everyone was now out of bed; whispered rumors and fears added to the surreal scene before him. He blocked them out, concentrating upon his duties. He slipped quietly into the rear of the large meeting room, now filled with Cardinals, talking in hushed, solemn voices.

Within a few minutes, all the solemn cardinals had arrived and taken their usual seats around the huge table. Striking was the absence of the Pope, whose seat at the head of the table was empty. Many of these men could not restrain their grief; tears trickled, and noses sniffled. As the last holy man entered, the door was shut. Cardinal Silas rose and said a prayer for Pope Yazi I.

With great reverence, he opened the sealed envelope. The outside was labeled: "To be opened upon my death and entrance into the Holy Realm of Jehosa." It bore the Pope's signature. Silas began reading aloud.

Holy Cardinals, Supreme Prelate

This is my last blessing upon you all and my last orders for our church. You have all faithfully served our Lord during the most trying times and circumstances. For that, know that I am eternally grateful, and I know that our Lord on High has observed your service as well.

However, the death of my fleshly body will bring yet another crisis unto our Church. This I have foreseen and via divine guidance, have worked out its handling. Beyond this crisis, I can no longer advise you. Please follow these, my last orders to you all, my dearest friends and companions.

When the population of Megalos gets news of my death, many may likely vacillate in their faith and trust in our church. We cannot let this happen. If the succession of the Pope is not handled swiftly, all that we have worked for may be in dire jeopardy. Hence, at this time, I appoint Cardinal Silas to be the next Pope. Please give him your trust and support that you have shown me all these many years. Anoint him at once, so that he may wear the robes of office immediately. Let him conduct whatever services you deem our parishioners expect. Let all the world see that the death of the fleshly body of our Pope in no way harms or lessens the Church of Jehosanity. Failure to do so will cause vast repercussions and begin our downfall.

As I have said in the past, when Pope Silas has come to join me and our Lord, then you, the Cardinals, are free to elect whomever you desire to become the next Pope. You see, at that time, the faithful will have already seen that the church can survive the death of its leader without any problems developing.

Again, please accept my final blessing upon all you and my heartfelt thanks for having done such a wonderful job making our Church the church of all Tarra.

Pope Yazi I

Silas: Do not read the rest of this to the other Cardinals. It is for your eyes only.

Silas stopped where indicated, although he greatly wondered what other instructions Yazi had left for him. However, that would have to wait until he could be alone. Several of the Cardinals were plainly upset with the choice of their new Pope. However, none dared openly speak out against Silas now. They had to put their own personal feelings and desires below that of the survival of the Church. Dutifully, one Cardinal performed the Holy Ceremony, making it official. Silas was their newly anointed Pope.

The new Pope arose and spoke solemnly, "Hence forth with, I shall be called Pope Amir I, after our long spiritual heritage. As we have discussed before, the funeral for the Pope must be a very holy ceremony, very public as well. First, let's send forth the word of his death and that a Holy Viewing for the general public will be held tomorrow in Galantas at the Church where he performed so many Holy Miracles. Let everyone know that afterwards at the Holy Hour, the new Pope Amir I will conduct the Holy Burial Ceremony. For now, I know we are all feeling deep grief and shock, so let's hold the next planning meeting after supper tonight. Oh, excuse me, Supreme Prelate; will that give you enough time to handle any security arrangements for the viewing and ceremony?" He just remembered that he ought to check with the Rooster first before committing to a plan of action. The Rooster, valiantly withholding his tears, could only nod his head yes. With that, the meeting adjourned, and the Cardinals solemnly filed out, shaking and kissing the hand of their new Pope, as was their custom.

The Rooster, as was his practice, was the last one to leave. He found it difficult to kiss the offered hand, for it was not that of his beloved Pope Yazi. He forced himself to do it, however.

"One moment, Supreme Prelate. I need a private word with you." The magic words were spoken. Instantly, his training kicked into high gear. In one swift motion, he shut the door so that no prying ears could hear what his Pope had to say. "Pope Yazi has a special page of instructions for me to read, marked for my eyes only. Also, there is another envelope here, this one is addressed for your eyes only. I suggest that we read them at once in here at the same time. I have a feeling that this is what Yazi would have wanted." He handed the Rooster the sealed, small parcel.

Yazi could scarcely believe his eyes; his Holiness had left him special instructions, private instructions. With great care and solemnity, he opened his final communication from his beloved Pope, for which he had devoted his life.

Supreme Prelate and Most Dearest, Trusted Friend,

Here are my final words to you. I hold you to your promise to protect the Pope, which is now Silas. As you know or may not know fully, the business with the whore's children and her line was known only to you and me. The other Cardinals may have some ideas about it, for it is hard to keep everything secret from them. Some may have guessed at the truth of the matter, more than likely only bits and pieces. However, Silas is being informed of the situation in a special letter for his eyes only.

I am only telling him enough so that he will allow you to continue to remove this "obstacle" from our path. I am not telling him everything. However, if you deem it necessary or prudent, you have my permission to relate everything about it to him. I leave it to your discretion how much to tell him. Realize that I foresee the whore's children as being the most serious threat to the continued existence of our church. I entrust the future of the Church of Jehosanity into the hands of the Mano del Dio.

As your first official act, please escort him into the underground maze and show him the secret Pope's vault. You know where I keep the only key.

Bless you my son,

Your Eternally Holy Pope Yazi I

Rooster could not hold back his tears any longer. He let them flow, but was determined to follow his final orders to the letter. Silas was not finished reading his, for which he was grateful; Silas did not see the flow of tears from the Rooster's eyes.

Finally, Silas looked up, both worried and surprised. "Oh my. Supreme Prelate Thraxton, I had no idea of the purpose of your recent voyage to the Sea Princes. Later, you must brief me so I know how to advise you fully. Yes, you must handle the situation, no questions asked. He also mentions that you have a key for me and a special vault?"

"Your Holiness, yes. Only the Pope is allowed access to his special locked vault. It is well hidden, and there is only one key. Other than the Pope, I am the only one who knows where the key is kept. He always insisted on extremely tight security. If you will follow me, I will show you where the key is kept. My instructions are to take you to the vault. I have no idea what is in there nor do I want to know. It was always my master's most private thing. This way," the Rooster led the new Pope into the main study, showed him how to operate a hidden compartment in the writing desk. Inside the tiny cavity was the iron key.

"You take it, Pope Amir," the Rooster insisted. "My hands have never been worthy even to touch this most holy key." Silas grinned, but kept his thoughts to himself. A few minutes later, the pair arrived at the Pope's special chamber, hidden deep in the catacombs below the complex. The Rooster lit the two oil lamps for his new Pope, showed him the key hole, and made sure that the Pope could open it. Just as soon as the key turned the latch, he said, "Excuse me. I will leave you now." Quickly, the Rooster returned to his room.

"What is all this?" mused Silas, as he thumbed through the various documents, scrolls, and ledgers. One caught his eye, it was marked "Silas — Your Eyes Only." This one he opened and began reading in earnest. Only the damp, dark walls heard his numerous "Oh my!" comments.

Pope Amir I swore that half of Megalos turned out to pay their last respects to their beloved Pope Yazi I. So huge were the throngs of people lined up to walk through the Church past the body that the actual funeral ceremony had to be postponed for two days! Thousands upon thousands walked past the late Pope, lying in state, regally dressed, his ornamental, golden scepter at his side. Throughout that first day, Pope Amir I stood piously beside the High Altar, blessing each soul as they paid their last respects. He could not help but notice that nearly everyone took note that already their church had a new Pope, that everything would continue as it had in the past. Only now did he realize fully how much seeing a new Pope on the scene meant to the parishioners. Yet again, Pope Yazi I had been precisely correct, Silas felt humbled once more.

In fact, all the Cardinals were profoundly impressed by the outflowing of grief and sorrow over the death of their Pope. Seeing the sheer number of people filing past the body, they hastily revised their burial plans, making it even more an extravagant event. Never in the history of Megalos, well at least in the memory of anyone, had this many people turned out for a funeral. Not even the death of an emperor brought this many to pay their last respects.

The third day, Pope Amir I held the Holy Burial Ceremony outside the church so that far more could witness the proceedings. Once he'd conducted this massive final mass, the body was loaded onto a special wagon, pulled by a team of twenty horses. Slowly the procession moved through the streets of Galantas and then on down the road to Constanza City, where the Pope would be placed into the Holy Crypt beneath the Church.

However, the Rooster faced a security nightmare. All along the route, throngs of worshipers lined the side of the road, all twenty-five miles of it, hoping to get a last glimpse of this Holy Man. To the great relief of everyone in the Mano del Dio, there were no incidents whatsoever, just an outpouring of love and grief upon the passing of this man.

Two weeks later, having finally gotten comfortable in the Pope's chair, Pope Amir I had the reins of command firmly established. Yes, these had been a rough two weeks, what with the expanded funeral details, to say nothing of attempting to control the Church. Finally, Silas discovered how best to proceed: operate just as Yazi had. That is, pretend that he was the late Yazi and do and act just as he had, signing only what Yazi would have signed, approving only what Yazi would have. In short, do only what Yazi would have done. "Path of least resistance," he told himself when he was alone that the evening. "I've got big plans for the Church, but I can see that I need to bide my time. It's just too soon after Yazi's death; I need the Cardinals to become comfortable with me. Just now, when I put forth my own ideas, they resist me like a bunch of scared chickens. All right, I'll play along; I have all the time in the world. Give them a few weeks and then the Cardinals will get used to my rule, which is going to be very different from Yazi's. He didn't give any of us credit for our great ideas. Instead, he was always leaning on the Mano del Dio and Thraxton for everything. Well, that is going to change; they'll see. Now let's see what all this is."

Silas was finally spending the time to examine everything in the Pope's Private Vault. Until now, he had been too distracted actually to spend the needed time here in the catacombs reading all the scrolls and packets. A number of the books he simply could not read; they were written in some kind of foreign language. Many of the documents he had already seen at one time or another, the originals of the Papal Orders, for example. At last, his eyes rested upon one booklet entitled, "Mano del Dio." He began to read, more out of curiosity. Perhaps he would find out more about these men, this whole suborder in which Yazi had put such great faith.

The more he read, the more his eyes opened and mouth gaped. "Good god! These are assassins!" He continued reading; his surprise and disgust slowly changed to that of a sneering chuckle. "So that is how Yazi got that nasty situation handled! Interesting." An hour passed as Silas read carefully the entire booklet. "Do what you have to do to ensure the survival of the Church of Jehosanity. So many souls are at stake; do not allow it to fail." Those were the last words that Yazi had written in the booklet. It gave Silas something to ponder, but he knew that he now had the ultimate control over the actions of the Mano del Dio. He, Silas, was still in charge; this booklet ensured their full cooperation with him. He smiled at the shrewdness of old Yazi. "Brilliant man," he commented to a spider which was crawling on the wall.

On February 1, 636, the Rooster met privately with Pope Amir I. His ship was to sail for their consulate on West Reach that afternoon, and the Rooster felt obligated to relay more details of his trip to the Pope. Yes, he admitted to himself, there was a chance that he might not be returning. His was to be a deadly trip, one that would require every ounce of training, of skill, of cunning that the Rooster possessed. He must not fail. Yet, he just could not bring himself to trust completely this new Pope, although he had tried.

"I've asked for this meeting, Your Holiness, because I am leaving on a trip from which I might not come back. Perhaps, this is to be my ultimate sacrifice for our Church. Remember my sealed orders from Pope Yazi I?" Silas nodded that he did, he had often wondered what those orders were. Perhaps now he might find out.

"Pope Yazi told me that he purposely did not tell you the entirety of the matter up North. He has entrusted me to relay this news, but I must have your word that you will tell no one. If others knew about this, it could destroy the entire Church of Jehosanity. Promise me that you will speak of this to no one." The Rooster was stern and intense, as he watched carefully the reactions on the face of his new Pope.

"I so swear," Silas replied. A rush of adrenaline flowed through his veins; he was about to find out key, critical information that had been denied him thus far. He leaned over closer to this man.

Still, the Rooster did not trust him. "Our Savior, Jes Amir, once had, shall we say, a temptation of the flesh. He took a whore to bed, but then repented his sin and was forgiven. However, the whore had offspring from his seed. When he died upon the cross, this whore fled Juda Arad, taking the bastard children with her, fleeing all the way to West Reach. There, this abomination settled down, preaching her bastardized version of Jehosanity. To this day, many on that island still worship her, damming them into the Pits of Hell for all eternity."

"Through the years, her children became kings and begat more of this putrid line. Long it was before Pope Yazi discovered what this prostitute had done and begat. He sent the Mano del Dio north at last to uncover this lineage.

530

We were charged with seeing to it that this incredible threat to our very existence met with shall we say untimely accidents?"

"You do realize the powerful threat these people present to our Church, do you not?" Silas agreed wholeheartedly, envisioning Jes Amir's bastard sons arising, claiming to be the sons of God, and condemning the Megalos Church of Jehosanity.

"I can report that the whore and her children are no more. Last year, the last of them, Sarah, fell down three flights of stone steps to her death. I just needed to give her a slight push. However, the task is far from over. Children have had children who have had children in their own right. Still more remain, anyone of which could at any time rise up and destroy the very foundations of our Church. Here is a list of all known, still living, descendants of this whore prostitute. I give it to you in case I do not return."

"Most of these are now kept in the incredibly well guarded Fortress Mont Blanc. The Santi leader, this Ket Bethany, has them under such close watch, that at this time, it is impossible to get to any of them. Your Holiness, if I cannot reach them, no one can. Thus, Pope Yazi and I have agreed, that this Ket Bethany must have an untimely accident and soon. His death will also solve most all our problems with this Santi organization, since he is its leader, as you well know. Pope Yazi has already blessed my return voyage. I have devised a foolproof plan for his accident and will see to it personally. However, Ket is an Evil Witch, sent here by Lucifer himself. Thus, it may be that I shall not survive to return, but I will promise you that the Ket fellow will no longer be a problem, no matter what else happens. You have my solemn word on that."

"In the event that I do not return, this list is your guide. Brief fully my successor so that with Ket out of the way, these remaining bastard children may be returned to the Pits of Hell, joining their maker, Lucifer."

Pope Amir I hugged the Supreme Prelate, tears flowing down his cheeks. "My dearest Thraxton. Words cannot convey how deeply I and the entire Church of Jehosanity are in your debt! Go with my highest blessings, my child. Know that I will support you in any way possible. There is no way the Church can ever repay you for all that you and your staff have done for us. Bless you my son. Go with the vengeance of God behind you. You cannot fail."

Tears now streamed down the Rooster's face. Such an outpouring of love and support he had not expected from this new Pope. Perhaps he had been wrong in his estimation of Silas. Now he knew that he could not fail. It was with an uplifted spirit that the Rooster set sail that afternoon, bound for Bregia, West Reach. Nevertheless, his second in command found a parchment written in their secret code sitting on his dresser that evening. It was marked: "To be opened and read if I do not return, R. Thraxton."

Chapter 44 Untimely Ending

Spring of 636 had arrived, and Lilly Ann and I were about to become parents yet again, our fourth, not counting the twins. We both knew that Sarah Amir Penton was hanging around her, waiting for the blessed day so she could become my daughter once again. Picking a name had occupied many days, since we already had one Sarah, Sarah Amber, who was going on nine now. After much discussion, we finally decided to call her Sarah Ann or Emil Benjamin, depending on whether it was a girl or a boy.

It was going to be close — her due date and my departure for Cymry and the Grande Council of Kings meeting. I had to put in my yearly appearance as their magician, and I needed at least to check up on how the twin's towns were faring. As luck would have it, Sarah Ann was born on May Day, 636, a week before I sailed to West Reach. This trip to the island would take about two weeks. We planned to spend only a couple days in Nuadilan and Amathon, and one at the council meeting. Most of the time I wanted to spend with my sister, Fianna, and my friend Fergus. Since it was to be a quick trip, only Paul would accompany me, along with a dozen Santi cavalry.

The council meeting was to be on May 15, so on the 14th, I begrudgingly said farewell to Fianna and Fergus. I was having such a wonderful time visiting with them on this relaxed vacation that I found it hard to leave. Yet, leave we did, riding slowly up the road deeper into the Highlands. Our destination was Brea, home of King Lachlan Laird, host of the council this year. It was a quiet, warm spring day; highland flowers were in full bloom. The air, heady with their combined fragrances. I wish Lilly Ann could have been by my side, such was the beauty around us.

Late that afternoon, we passed into a small forested region, where trees grew thick on either side of the road. As we neared a bend in the road, we heard cries for help. It sounded as if several women were in trouble. Immediately, our group galloped on ahead to see what was happening, but Paul insisted that I bring up the rear, just in case of trouble. Even though I saw no sign of any other trouble, I did as he asked, staying about twenty feet behind him and a good ways behind the Santi, who had gone ahead to investigate.

I heard the twang of a crossbow firing from behind me. I attempted to turn my head to see, but something hit my neck, and I felt my body go limp. A great darkness flooded over me.

"Damm, Ket's been shot!" Paul screamed. I heard a good deal of activity coming towards me. My mind simply thought, "Who could have done this?"

At last, I could see once more. I was about ten feet above the ground. Below me I saw Paul standing over my body, inspecting the quarrel protruding from my neck. I heard him say, "He's dead! Someone's assassinated Ket! Poisoned dart!"

That was the key word, assassinated! Instantly, I began moving in the direction from which the quarrel had come, looking for my assailant. Below me, others were fanning out, looking for the assassin as well, but no one could see him. I found thinking to be a bit difficult, but I forced myself to mock up a mental image of the event, estimating from where the quarrel had been fired. Next, I moved slowly along my guessed path, looking for my attacker. The angle was curiously high; the further from my fallen body that I moved, the higher I rose.

Then, I spied him, nearly invisible, nicely camouflaged, sitting about twenty-five feet above the ground in a tree. I flew straight at him. Yes, I admit that I was now violently angry, viciously angry if the truth were known. I put out two hands around his neck and began to strangle the man. Now that I think back on it, I didn't have any hands with which to strangle him. Yet the man flailed his arms in a vain attempt to break free of my strangle hold. His head was highly distorted, as if someone had squashed the sides of his head inward. His hair grew unruly upwards, like a cock's comb. His face began turning colors; his flailing arms subsided. Below me, I heard others calling out, "There he is! What's happening to him?"

Paul's voice spoke, "I swear someone is strangling him. Ket, is that you?"

Now the body became limp in my hands. I watched a spiritual being, entirely encased in a blackish mass drift up out of the body's head. I shot after him, hanging the dead body by its neck in a 'v' crack in a branch. *Hey, come back here! I'm not through with you! How dare you kill me, you damn coward!*

Confusion flooded back to me over the communication line I had enforced upon the being. *What's happening? I should be going to Heaven now.*

Who are you anyway? I drilled into his mind so hard that he could not help but answer. *Who sent you?*

Supreme Prelate Rooster Thraxton. The Pope. He had no choice but to answer, so strong was my attention.

You damn fool. You have been deceived utterly. You are a spiritual being, you idiot. Yazi has fed you a pack of outright lies.

Then, I picked up his mental viewpoint of myself. I was appearing to him as a giant yellow-white energy mass. *Are you an angel?* He asked shaking and shivering all over, as if he still had a body to do so.

I am Ket Bethany, whose body you just killed! I blasted into his mind so vehemently that he could never forget it. *Look at me you damn, utter fool!* I forced him to confront me, which shattered his reality completely.

You, you, you are not Lucifer?

No, I am not. I am from Jehosa. Yazi is from Lucifer. I admit it; at this instant, I dabbled with the truth somewhat. This man had been insanely following the wrong path in life; he had assassinated or caused to be slain too many people. You cannot reason with the insane, that I already knew firsthand. So this time, I tried something different.

Suddenly he began blubbering, *Forgive me Lord Jehosa. I have sinned greatly. What must I do now? I must make amends.* Wallowing in immense self-pity, I just could not stomach this being any longer. A flurry of his memories past by me in rapid fire; in days to come, I replayed these and was more than a little enlightened.

Oh, go get a new baby body and learn the proper path this time, I replied and broke the connection with him, floating back down to see what was happening to my body far below. I saw him shoot off like a rocket, heading south and east towards Megalos. I half-wondered what would ultimately happen in the future to this assassin.

I made the mistake of putting a line back on my body, checking up on it. Immediately, I entered a dark greyish mass, which collapsed my awareness way down. I was in some kind of drugged stupor, that's the best way I can describe it. Vaguely, I heard voices from time to time.

Much later, I learned from others what happened after this point. I'll ignore the recriminations many expressed, however. Paul and several others examined my fallen body. He correctly diagnosed that the quarrel protruding from the base of my neck was indeed poisoned. Everyone concluded that my body was dead. It certainly was not breathing or moving. Carefully, they transported my body back to Fergus and Fianna's home. From there, the Santi at Mont Blanc was contacted and informed of the tragedy.

A great discussion was held on how to properly bury me. Many wanted to bring the body back to Mont Blanc. However, John Henry properly handled it. Since Fianna was my closest direct relative, it was to be her call; she and I were Tewdwr after all. Having been coached on how to become a queen, she decided that I should have the highest honors that our heritage bestowed upon its most famous heroes in the distant past.

My body was placed in a sailing dingy, covered with rich cloths and fine linens. Normally, the fallen hero's sword would be placed upon his chest. However, Fianna knew how I hated swords, so she had my staff take its place, but she did put the finest dagger that I had around my waist. Then at sunset and with a large group of them watching, the dingy was sailed out from the ghost town of Cuch Glen out beyond the barrier rocks and set adrift to float on out into the vast western ocean. As I understand the various descriptions that I've subsequently heard, it was quite a nice send off.

Back at Mont Blanc, I will bypass the massive grief that everyone felt and displayed, instead concentrating upon the key events that are vitally important. When news of my death reached Mont Blanc, John Henry retrieved the special, heavily wrapped package that I had marked "To be opened upon my death only." No, I was not psychic, no premonitions, just pragmatic.

> If you are reading this, then my body has died. For the survival of the Santi and the Amir line, these are my final orders. Please follow them precisely.

1. I want Jenna Rose Weston to be the leader of the Santi del Dio, taking my place at the top of the leadership pyramid and my place within my Circle. Do not ask why; just trust me as you always have.

2. My death means that the Mano del Dio's arm has become long indeed. None in the direct Amir line is now safe. If they can get to me, then they can get to anyone else. Thus, your number one priority is to devise some means of protecting the others, especially Lilly Ann, Beth Ann, and our children. I do not know what that solution is. The only advice I can think of at this writing is to protect them in several different ways. Do not rely on one single method for all. Subterfuge is called for from now on.

3. Do not despair over my body's death. I am still in the "game." I shall return full force. Jes, the Guardian, and I have a mission here on Tarra, one that will not stop because a fleshly body has passed away. Look for me once more in the not too distant future. Jenna will understand.

All I ask is that you keep the Santi going until I can get back into the game once more. John Henry, share this letter to everyone you deem appropriate.

I love you all. You are the greatest spiritual beings on Tarra.
Love,
Ket Bethany

It was late evening at the Weston Estate. Jenna and Hank had just gotten all the children to bed. Now they sat with their arms around each other, letting their grief flow. They'd heard the news of my death early this very morning. "I cannot believe he's gone," Jenna bawled.

"Damned assassins!" Hank cursed. "May they rot in their own hell."

Just then, they heard numerous horses riding up the cobblestone path to their front door. "Who can that be?" Fearing the worst, Hank fetched his sword.

The riders reined in close to their front door. "John Henry here. It's safe," he called out and then knocked on Hank's door. He inherently knew that his band would probably be giving those inside a bit of a scare, but the Communicators were all exhausted by this time, relaying messages nearly constantly since my death.

Hank opened the door allowing John Henry, his Circle, my Circle, and all our children inside. "Welcome, I think," Hank exclaimed, putting his sword back over the mantle where he normally kept it.

"Oh, do come in," Jenna exclaimed. "Hank, better put on a large pot of water." Then she saw the children. "Oh my, the children. I'm so sorry for you Lilly Ann. We should find a place for them to sleep. It's so late, and they look like they are falling asleep on their feet."

"I'm sorry to bother you two this late, but it is vital and important. However, Jenna, you are right. Perhaps we should put the kids to bed first," John Henry apologized. Lilly Ann's eyes were red and swollen; she said little, holding our baby tightly.

"Bring them this way, Lilly Ann," Jenna said, motioning for Hank to give her a hand. "We'll put them up in our room. I think they'll all fit."

Minutes later, everyone gathered around the living room table. There were not enough chairs for everyone. Some chose to sit on the floor. John Henry began, "We can worry about tea later, Hank. Come join us. We must speak now." Jenna sat on Hank's lap so at least another could have a seat. "Ket left me some instructions. Somehow, he knew that something like this might happen. Don't ask me how. Here, you both need to read this." He unwrapped my final letter and positioned it on the table so that they could both read it together.

"What?" exclaimed Jenna as she read the first point. "Me? But it should be you, John Henry. Me? He cannot be serious, can he?"

"I'm old, if you haven't noticed, but read on, Jenna," he explained. Both continued reading. When they finished, he asked, "Jenna, what does he mean exactly by getting back in the game?"

"Jes calls himself the Guardian of the Anuir. There are five of us now, five spiritual beings, who are dedicated to the same goal, to achieve spiritual freedom and ability for all beings on Tarra. You probably will not understand, but Ket and I are working on one aspect of this gargantuan project, while the other three are working on the other aspect. Fundamentally, our job is to keep Tarra free from wars and strife long enough for Jes and the others to accomplish their task. More, I am not at liberty to say, primarily because you all would not fully understand at this time. I promise to enlighten you, one by one, as time and your abilities permit. What he means is that Ket will be picking up a new body and within a few years be picking up where he left off with us. He is not gone, just delayed a while. Have you located where he is at, by chance?"

"Ah, it is mostly as I thought," John Henry replied, although he really did not know the details. He wanted to ply her with numerous questions, but decided it would be better to do that one on one, not with everyone else present. "Er, that is the problem, Jenna. We have not located him. You see, locating another spiritual being was really one of Ket's special abilities. Very few of us can do it as easily as he. I'm afraid that we have more or less lost track of him. That is, he does not seem to be where he ought to be, given the circumstances."

"What? I don't understand," Jenna pleaded for an explanation. How can you *lose* a being?

"We all expect that he would be somewhere around us, Lilly Ann perhaps, Mont Blanc, Velona, or possibly Cymry as a long shot. Our Communicators cannot detect his presence in any of these locations. Hence, we've mostly lost track of where he might be," John Henry replied honestly.

"Well, I shouldn't worry too much about that," Jenna said optimistically. "He'll turn up when he's ready. Perhaps he also finds it just too emotionally painful to be here with us at this moment. I was crying when you all came." Everyone accepted this as a reasonable explanation.

"So Jenna, are you willing to step into Ket's shoes and lead us?" asked John Henry.

"If we are to follow his orders, then I must, though I have no idea why he should have chosen me. I'll do it, but I am going to hate having to move to Mont Blanc, I, we love it here," Jenna replied.

"Thank you for accepting, Jenna. No, I don't think you ought to move just now. I assumed that you would accept, which is one of the reasons I brought along the other members of the Circle. They will stay here with you, if that is acceptable. Also, it's time for subterfuge, according to Ket. My idea is to pretend that I am the leader of the Santi. Only the druwids among us will know otherwise. That should give you considerable autonomy and protection."

Hank broke in, "Hey, I like your thinking. It sure will. I hate deceiving the Sisters among us, but it adds a layer of security that we need."

Paul interrupted, "Jenna, I failed Ket, but I will do everything in my power to protect you and your family." Tears streamed down his face.

"You didn't fail Ket," John Henry chastised him yet again. "Assassins are inherently deadly. That's the other reason I brought Lilly Ann and the kids here. Subterfuge. Our first order of business must be to work out new ways and means of protecting the Amir line. Frankly, Jenna, I have run out of clever ideas. Tomorrow, let's all put our heads together and find some new ways. Ket is very insistent that we do this at once."

"Our brothers are being rather obstinate about it," Beth Ann added. "I feel like I am walking around with a price tag on my head, like some brigand."

Lilly Ann began crying, "I don't want our children murdered!"

"There, there, Lilly Ann, neither do I," Jenna consoled her. "Can we discuss this further in the morning? I think everyone is overly tired and stressed just now. Hank, where can we put all our guests?"

"Not a problem, we've brought our bedrolls. Your living room floor will do for tonight," John Henry answered.

"Hank, get all the spare blankets. Let's put us women in the dining room, men in here. Lilly Ann, you come with me," and she put her arm around her, nudging her to come with her.

Within a few minutes, Lilly Ann was resting comfortably on the floor, covered with warm blankets; Sarah Ann cradled in her arms. Jenna lay down beside them. She whispered in her ear, "Lilly Ann, I want you to begin when you first heard that Ket was in trouble. Tell me all about it, what you are seeing, what you are hearing, smelling, feeling, everything."

"Well, I was feeding Sarah Ann, when I had this awful feeling in my stomach. . .
The End.

A Favor to Other Readers

How about helping other readers? Many readers rely on reviews to make the decision whether to buy a book. You can help them make their decision by leaving your opinions and viewpoint in a short review of the positive things of this book. Writing the review and expressing your opinion only takes a few minutes, and other readers will appreciate your efforts.

Click this link: Volume 4 Chaos in the Aftermath
scroll down to Customer Reviews; click on Write a Review, and enter your review. Thank you.

Author Information

Visit My Amazon.com Author Page
Vic Broquard Author Page

Follow My Blog
Vic Broquard's Blog

Follow Me on Social Media
Facebook
Google+
LinkedIn
YouTube

Other Books by Vic Broquard

Without Warning (fantasy)

The Trident Series: (fantasy)
     Volume 1 The Trident and the Book
     Volume 2 The Trident and the Scepter
     Volume 3 The Trident and the Resurrection

The Adventures of Elizabeth Stanton Series: (science fiction)
     Volume 1 The Evolution of the Path
     Volume 2 The Great Messiah
     Volume 3 Of Kings and Queens and Troubadours
     Volume 4 Chaos in the Aftermath
     Volume 5 Power Plays
     Volume 6 Age of Exploration
     Volume 7 Abducted
     Volume 8 The Emperor and Empress
     Volume 9 A Job Worth Doing
     Volume 10 Degradation
     Volume 11 The Second Crusade
     Volume 12 When Worlds Collide
     Volume 13 Dark Ages

The Lindsey Barron Series: (fantasy)
     Volume 1 The Rod of the Apocalypse
     Volume 2 The Board of Governors
     Volume 3 The Crown of Moses
     Volume 4 Dominus for President
     Volume 5 The National Health Care Program
     Volume 6 States Justice
     Volume 7 Cross and Double-cross

Zoran Chronicles Series: (fantasy)
     Volume 1 A Dragon in Our Town
     Volume 2 Dragons, Power, Courts, and War

Planet of the Orange-red Sun Series: (science fiction)
     Volume 1 When Kingdoms Fall
     Volume 2 Dark Ages
     Volume 3 Age of the Towers
     Volume 4 Difficillis Exitus
     Volume 5 Age of the Lords
     Volume 6 The Renegade Tower
     Volume 7 Rebellions

The Return of the Wizards: Twelve Companions – The Making of Wizards (fantasy)